The Starlight Chronicles

Integration:
Seventh-Level

JONATHAN WAGGONER

THE LIGHT GROUP

LIGHT Group books may be ordered by visiting their website at iamlumen.com or by emailing their International Liaison, Jonathan Waggoner at author@iamlumen.com.

The LIGHT Group
Isla Verde Division
A registered organization of the Lumen Council of South America
Operating under the sovereignty of The Sevenfold Assembly

ISBN-10: 0-9853940-2-1
ISBN-13: 978-0-9853940-2-8

Library of Congress Control Number: TX0007508287
Printed in the United States of America
First Edition rev. date: 2/29/2012

Cover photos shot by: Wes Hanson (quetzal plumes); Amy Frankel (emperor tamarins). All rights reserved by photographers, who will receive a percentage of all special edition cover proceeds.

Cover arrangement by Jonathan Waggoner via CreateSpace. 2012.

–For EmmaLee, Hillary, and Austin—my summer literature buddies–

Send forth your light and your truth,
that they may guide me to your holy mountain,
that they may lead me to the place where you dwell.

Psalm 43:3

Table of Contents

Failed Class Trip

This pretty much bites. A boy around the age of fourteen trudged along under the jade canopy formed by the dense trees that enclosed him. He and his party were following an ancient path formed over hundreds of years by the ancestors of the group's tour guide. Unfortunately, the boy found himself near the back of the procession, too far behind to hear the guide's endless stories and explanations regarding the forest. He sighed and turned the next corner to the left. The boy had failed to hear the guide say, "Watch your step—there's monkey droppings around the corner." He soon found himself on the ground with a dung-streaked left pant leg and an unnaturally brown shoe. *Ugh...*

"Smooth moves, Manny," said another boy passing by on the right.

"Literally," added a third, jeering at Manny from beside the second boy and laughing as the two continued down the path.

Why didn't I listen to Mamá and at least bring a couple tissues? Looking around, Manny discovered a plant with enormous leaves growing beside the path. He grabbed the stem of one such leaf, tugged deftly, flipped it, and began wiping the ape excretions from his clothes as a handful of students walked by, all holding their noses and most laughing. None stopped to help.

Now Manny, formally known as Manuel Luis López, was a unique boy. Yes, yes, some young individuals have outrageous physical talents or striking mental abilities, and though Manny was actually quite capable physically and adept in a number of academic areas, he was most commonly known for the color of his skin, which just happened to be bright white. Now this white was not to be mistaken with a pale white, commonly seen in albinos and those lacking in exposure to the sun. No, this boy's skin shone in the sun, as though he were infused with billions of tiny glass beads smaller than the tip of a needle. He often appeared as one does upon exiting a body of water while the sunlight cascades down, or as if he were always wearing a great deal of body oil. In the darkness, if the slightest light hit him, he seemed to glow. "You're my special boy," Manny's mother would always say. "A light scaring away the darkness in my life." *Yeah, well, shadows never hurt anyone. At least some shade once in a while would be nice.* Such were his thoughts as of late.

Susana María López, Manny's mother, never allowed any government official to run tests regarding her son's distinctive dermatological traits. "God makes us the way we are for a reason," she argued. "We may only discover why with time."

Fortunately for the boy, Carlos Manuel López, Manny's father, was proud of his son's many facets. Though many fathers experience shame when their children differ from others in appearance, Carlos cherished his son and had great hopes for the boy's life. "I will teach my son what my father taught me—to be a man of integrity, one that cares for his family and pursues his dreams, and quizás some baseball on the side," Carlos would say to his friends as he mixed his Spanish and English with a smile. "Dios sabe that I was an excellent player. Hopefully Manny will be, too."

Though the positive sentiments of his parents often encouraged Manny when he was sad, they could not, however, remove the monkey feces from the boy's pant leg nor erase the public embarrassment his slip had caused. *Besides, Mamá y Papá are what, maybe two thousand miles away? There's no way they can help me here, and being different only makes things worse.*

Manny, like many other Hispanic children, grew up in one of the southern states of the United States of America. Similar to many children of equal heritage, he spoke Spanish as well as English and was quite proficient in both languages. Yet, unlike so many Hispanic children, his skin was a radiant white, and he felt estranged, somehow foreign.

Just as Manny had plucked another leaf and begun removing the dung from his shoe, an older and shorter fellow, the assistant to the lead guide, stopped two feet in front of the boy and said, "Tienes que levanta'te pa'que no te'lejes del grupo. ¡Ándale!" He pointed down the path and shuffled in place.

"Too late," Manny mumbled. "I'm already alienated from the group." He folded the leaf and began wiping the outside of his shoe. Manny noticed the guide wave for him to come, the man looking over his shoulder and then back at the boy with concern.

"Ahora," said the guide.

"Sí, sí, ahorita vengo," replied the boy. "One more second."

"Hay que ir ahora," reaffirmed the guide. "Adelante hay una bifurcació y no sé por dónde vaya mi jefe hoy. ¡Vamos!"

"You just go on ahead and I'll be right behind you," said Manny. The guide simply stared at the boy in concern. "Déjeme, lo sigo ahorita."

As many people succumb to temptation under pressure, so did this particular man, turning, staring down the path, glancing back one more time at the boy, and finally plunging ahead with a quickened pace.

"At least now no one is here to pester me," Manny said to himself. "Maybe I can actually begin to enjoy this class trip." Tossing the soiled leaf alongside the path, the boy rose to his feet and stretched, arms reaching to the sky. Jade light glanced his fingertips, which glittered. *Here goes nothing.* Manny took five steps along the path when he realized that he had left his backpack behind by the monkey manure. *Can't forget that.* Turning around the boy met eyes with a small black monkey measuring roughly three feet in stature and boasting a snow white beard. In the monkey's left hand was the boy's camera. "Now this is the family camera, Manuel," María had said. "Take un montón de fotos but do not lose it." Manny narrowed his eyes at the bearded monkey. *So I slip in his poop and now he tries to steal my camera... He's going down.*

As Manny took a step forward, the primate hopped away from the backpack toward the western side of the path. Manny froze in place, staring at the monkey and the monkey at Manny. *What a little turd. No...* The monkey had ceased staring at the boy and seemed to have raised its eyebrows, gently turning the silver camera in his leather-padded hands and analyzing it with those silent jet eyes. *That rot isn't examining my camera, is he?* Now, as the monkey held the device up to the sun, Manny saw the jade light convert into a prism over the creature's face as the photons passed through the lens and out the window of the camera.

"Don't break it," said Manny. Still holding the camera in the air, the monkey turned its head to the left to face the boy, a quizzical expression on its face. *Maybe he only understands Spanish.* "No la rompas." Again the monkey simply stared at the boy quizzically; but then his expression softened, eyebrows falling and eyes scanning the boy. *No way; the thief's not smiling at me, is he?*

Manny lifted his foot to step forward. "What are you—" But at the boy's advance the monkey threw the camera into the air with his left hand and performed a speedy backward somersault, snapping the camera with his tail in mid-spin and sending the apparatus crashing down onto the worn path as he bolted into the foliage and disappeared. Manny's sole met ground and he stood agape, staring at the place where the monkey had melted into the scenery and hearing nothing. *Quick little snot.* Manny turned his head to the forest floor and found himself quite surprised.

The silver family camera, the one his mother had told him to protect and use with great care, was gone, or at least it appeared to be. Lying in the center of the trail was a wooden object of a deliciously rich brown, similar to that of mahogany wood, winking in the sun. Manny approached the object and knelt to pick it up.

"Weird." Manny turned the mahogany box in his hands, examining the wooden device with eyebrows raised. *It can't be...* On one side of the object he found a barrel but no lens. *No...* The center of the opposite side contained a small window; looking through, Manny saw his foot. *Get out!* The remainder of the device was completely smooth, seemingly polished, excluding the knob on the upper-right rim of the device. Holding the object up to the viridian rays piercing the foliage above, Manny peered through the window and smiled. Through this small vista the boy watched as the shafts of light broke into thousands of colorful beams, bathing the path in every hue imaginable. "I don't believe this."

Manny slid his finger along the rim of the camera-like device, and his stomach leapt. *What will happen if I push the button? Will it actually take a picture? I don't see any compartment*

9

for film and there's definitely no place to insert memory cards or connect it to a computer. His finger now lay over the button. He shrugged. *What the heck.* But the button refused to depress. "What's wrong?" he said, pulling his eye from the dancing prisms in frustration. He applied more pressure, even laying the device on the ground and pressing with all his weight, but the button never budged.

The boy sat and glowered at the device on the forest floor. "What a piece of junk!" *Mamá's gonna kill me. Me va a matar. This thing doesn't even work; it would be a poor substitute for the camera.* Despite his rising anger toward the apparatus, the device continued to intrigue him. *Hopefully I can at least sell it at a thrift store back home.* So, stowing the device in his pack, Manny turned away from the place where the monkey had vanished and continued down the path.

Sunlight grazed the boy's shoulders as he trudged along; interestingly, although his skin shone under the tiniest ray of light, Manny's hair seemed to act as a polar opposite. Essentially, the boy's hair seemed to absorb light, never shining, simply lying upon his head, blacker than coal, darker than the deepest night.

Oddly, or at least to Manny, many animals started to appear along the trail, apparently just to stare at him. Wild hares, turtles, otters, and countless other creatures simply sat and gazed at the boy. Most curious of all were the animals he saw in the trees as he passed—a pair of toucans—*Were they just talking?*—a snake as wide around as Manny's upper arm—*That isn't an anaconda, is it?*—three squirrels sitting together—*Was that one just pointing a finger?*—and finally, stretched out over a branch above the left side of the trail, was a velvet figure crowned with a pair of bright, amber colored eyes. *A panther! Why would they lead us down a trail where panthers could snatch us?!* But despite Manny's fears, the large cat merely lay there, her eyes following the child expressionlessly.

"I've gotta find the rest of the group. Ándale, Manny."

Quickening his pace, Manny passed the panther; but surprisingly, as he came along beside of her, his fear subsided. He then glanced over his shoulder and noticed that she had gone.

Strange. Approximately one hundred steps later and around a bend to the right, Manny slowed and came to a stop before a fork in the road, at the center of which rose a wooden post about the boy's height. The post boasted two weather-worn signs with arrows directing travelers along either route. Manny's eyes widened. *That's beautiful.* Perched atop the highest sign was the most dignified bird Manny had ever seen.

One could not confuse this bird with any other, seeing as its plumage shone emerald, its breast burned crimson, and the creature's tail, should it be male, as this specimen indeed was, often grew to the length of the average teenager's arm. *Wow. Is this some exotic peacock, or what's the deal?*

"Do you require guidance?" a voice asked. Utterly startled, Manny jumped and spun on the spot. His eyes open wide, he searched for the voice's origin, half expecting to find the panther staring at him again. All that met his eyes were the trail twisting back to the left and jade-foiled trees—no panther, no apparent threat.

"Are you generally this rude," chimed the high, rich voice, "or have I acted erroneously in assuming that you indeed are Manuel Luis López, a Seventh-Level Lumen?"

Manny stood rigid, mouth dry, mind racing. *What is happening? No one is here! Dear Jesus…*

"Why do you persist in ignoring me, child?!" The voice was now furious, but Manny had no time to contemplate this as he felt a sharp pain on the back of his head and a strange, soft feeling along his neck as something brushed close to his face. Sounds of ruffling filled his ears. Manny held his head down, covering the spot where the pain originated with his hands as he swung around just in time to catch sight of the beautiful bird alighting once again on the sign. As they stared at one another, Manny noticed a unique feature about the bird, and his jaw dropped. *He's frowning at me. Birds don't frown!*

The emerald bird opened its beak, and Manny heard the high, melodic voice, again laced with anger. "Insolent child! Speak!"

"Are you, like, m-mechanical?" stuttered the boy.

"Mechaniwhat?" replied the bird, head cocked but still wearing a frown.

"Mechanical. You know, b-because birds don't talk of their own accord unless they are a certain species of bird, l-like a cockatiel or parrot; but you don't look like any type of parrot that I've ever seen."

"A PARROT!" burst the bird in a stream of fury, soaring into the air and circling Manny. "I have never, in my LIFE, the duration of which is 47 years, been insulted to this degree, accused of being an ignorant yapper such as that, a creature that cannot even speak of its own free will!" At these words the bird trilled fiercely. *Perhaps that was a scream.* "And why do you smile at my rage, child?" With a seething screech, the bird again dove at the boy, but this time Manny rolled under his attacker, turning to face the flaming emerald and hiding a smile. *This thing's spastic!*

"I'm sorry, but I didn't mean to insult you, um, sir." The boy's face was quite ambiguous as regret mixed with hidden amusement, the result of which looked as though he were about to sneeze.

"Do you mock me?" the bird asked in a dangerously quiet voice.

Straightening his face, Manny replied, "No! It's just that—well, I'm really confused." He set his pack on the ground in front of the sign-post and sat down, cross-legged. "Animals aren't supposed to talk," he finished, closing his eyes and massaging his temples.

"That may well be," began the bird, his voice drawing closer, "but we do. At least a handful of us, anyway." By the sound of his voice, Manny could tell that the bird was just a couple of hops in front of him.

Manny breathed deeply and sighed. *A handful of animals can talk? I've seen more than a handful of animals in my life and none of them have ever spoken to me!*

"Did I scare you, child?" The bird turned his head slowly, his frown lifting.

Manny opened his eyes and looked up, asking, "But why?"

"Well," the bird ruffled his feathers and scratched the ground with his claws, "you see, it is actually quite dangerous to anger a quetzal…"

Shaking his head and focusing on the bird, Manny said, "No, I mean why can animals talk? And you're a what?"

"Child, we do not have the time for histories that take years to detail," replied the quetzal, its deep, black eyes gazing into Manny's hazel ones. The quetzal's head cocked further to the right as he continued. "And I am a quetzal, a bird that inhabits parts of Central America, particularly Costa Rica. But avoiding detailed demographics of my own, let me ask you a question." The quetzal blinked. "Why do your eyes burst like a broken star? And why does your skin glitter?" The bird stared intensely into Manny's eyes for several seconds before he began hopping around the boy, grazing Manny's skin with his wings and raising feathered brow in interest. Gazing at Manny's head he finished, "And how does your hair not reflect light?"

Manny glanced to his right and found the quetzal standing next to his pack. Leaning back on his arms, he replied, "I know even less about those things than I do about talking animals." *But I like this—talking to animals. At least he's not nasty about the way I look. He's actually interested, and not for personal gain, I can tell.*

"At times we are all a mystery to ourselves, I suppose," said the quetzal, hopping casually, eyes glinting. "We can only unravel such mysteries with time."

It's been almost 14 years, how much longer do I have to wait? Oh. "What's your name, Mr. Quetzal?"

"Mr. Quetzal?" replied the bird, chirping sweetly several times and then cooing. *That had to be a laugh.* "I daresay that none have ever called me Mr. Quetzal. Respectful though, I suppose." Ruffling his feathers, he continued, "In any case, child, my name is Julius, Julius Rumblefeather. I am pleased to make your acquaintance, Manuel Luis López." Julius snapped his beak happily and his black eyes shone.

"It's nice to meet you Julius Rumblefeather," said Manny appreciatively. "But you can just call me Manny." *What a kind stranger. What a kind bird for that matter…*

"I take it then, Manny," began Julius, lowering his tiny head slightly and giving the boy a knowing look, "given that you can understand me, that you are a Seventh-Level Lumen?"

There he goes again. "I honestly have no idea what you're talking about, Julius," Manny replied flatly. "As you said, I'm Manny López. I grew up in Arizona, in the United States, and I'm an only child." As he continued, Manny raised his hand to accentuate his speech. "I'm on some useless eighth-grade class trip with a bunch of losers that hate me, and now I'll probably get into a ton of trouble for being so far behind."

Julius hopped half-a-feather closer to Manny, tilted his head ever so slightly and said, "But this trip is indeed not useless, Manny! Have you not received your wand? Is it not now revealed that you are a Lumen?"

"About that," began Manny, turning to face Julius and frowning. "What in God's green Earth is a Lumen? And what are you talking about a wand for?"

Ruffling his feathers and frowning slightly, Julius said, "I have brought up the issue of wands because Lumens use wands!"

"For what?" Manny was becoming more than slightly exasperated. "I've only ever heard of two types of wands—a bubble wand and a magic wand."

"A bubble wand?" said Julius, his head twisted nearly halfway around in the opposite direction now. "What is this you speak of?"

"You know—" *Or maybe you don't.* "—Those plastic wands with rings on the end that you dip in a soapy solution, pull them out, and blow through them to make bubbles."

"I have never heard of such technology," replied Julius, beak open slightly. "You must show me, pull out your wand."

Manny sighed and said calmly, "But I don't have a wand."

"Of course you do child, or else you could not be speaking with me," chirped Julius chidingly. "Now empty your rucksack and show me that wand!"

A bit abashed, Manny obeyed, reaching for the pack on his left, setting it in his lap, emptying its contents onto the ground one by one, and providing a narrative for the quetzal in order to demonstrate that no wand could be found inside.

"These are the crackers that Nacho smashed on the plane," he began. "They're basically disintegrated; but I've gotten used to eating my snacks that way." Manny smiled and Julius cocked his head, eyeing the boy attentively. "Now here are some fruit-flavored antacids," he grimaced slightly. Julius pecked the bottle. "They actually do taste good." *At least some of them; not the red ones.* "Okay, we've got a flashlight, sweat rags, bottles of warm drinking water—" *Yuck!* "—A few dollars and colones, playing cards—you ought to try those." Pulling out a few cards as an example, Manny watched as Julius hopped up to the box of cards, crooked his head sharply, and suddenly nipped the corner off the Ace of Clubs. The boy rolled his eyes and the quetzal dropped the torn paper from his beak, frowning. *They're not for eating.* Manny took a short breath. "Anyway, all that's left are my sketchpad and the remnant of my family's camera."

As Manny pulled out the sketchpad, a pencil, and the apparent camera, Julius chirped melodiously. "That's it!" The quetzal flew into the air to the height of the boy's chest and then landed again softly, his plumage somewhat disheveled.

Glancing again at the articles in his arms to reassure himself that indeed no wand could be found in his grasp, Manny had a realization. *The pencil!* "Okay, listen, Julius," began the boy, laying down the sketchpad and camera-like device and raising the pencil to the level of the quetzal's eyes. "This is not a wand. It's called a pencil. You see, I can draw and write…"

The quetzal, furious once more, flapped into the air and dove at the boy. "I know what a pencil is, you silly child!" he screeched, swooping down in front of Manny. "Open your eyes and see!"

Uncovering his face, Manny saw the remnant of the family camera floating before his eyes—Julius's claws were clasping the device's strap tightly. *This bird has issues.* The boy took a deep breath and began, "It's just…"

"This is indeed not just anything!" chirped the quetzal, swinging the strap, dropping the device onto the ground before Manny, and landing again to face him. "Watch!"

Leaning forward, Julius appeared to be straining to reach the device, his beak slightly open and tiny eyes glinting. *What is he trying to do, lick it?* For all his efforts, all the chirps, squawks, and frustrated whistles, the quetzal could come no closer than a finger's breadth to the device.

"For goodness' sake, if you want to touch it, then here," said Manny, grabbing the device and sliding it along the ground toward Julius. *It won't matter if it gets scratched now anyway, since it's just a block of wood.* The boy was startled to see the quetzal's fearful expression as the device knocked the bird off-balance as if hitting him forcefully. The quetzal gave a shrill chirp as he flipped backward and hit the ground. For a few seconds Julius simply lay there before the camera, claws stretched toward the canopy, head shaking slowly.

What is he doing? After almost a minute the quetzal spoke. "Do you attempt to kill me?" Julius glanced up over his claws and feathers to meet Manny's eye.

The boy's expression was one of confusion. Manny shook his head and sighed. "What are you talking about?"

Struggling to his feet with a great measure of flapping and hopping, Julius faced Manny and sighed as well. "You must know that one Lumen cannot touch the wand of another Lumen, do you not? You must have known that by pushing your wand toward me its protective field would knock me over, as I cannot touch it?"

"That camera is not a wand, Julius," Manny stated flatly.

"Then why could I not touch it?" asked Julius simply.

Slightly taken aback, Manny replied, "I don't know." *But really, why couldn't he touch it?*

Julius sighed again. "Child, pick it up."

Fine. Manny obeyed, reaching out and grasping the device. As he brought it toward himself, a warm, wave-like sensation passed from his fingertips and throughout his whole hand. *That's odd.* Looking where the camera had been lying, the boy noted that it had not been in the sun. *Why is it warm?*

"Think, child, about a wand," said Julius calmly. Manny thought he saw the quetzal's feathers ruffle very slightly.

Lowering the device, Manny stared patiently into Julius's eyes. "Listen, Julius. Wands are not blocks of wood, they are long and round and—" Manny gasped. Heat ran up his arm and to his heart as the block of wood became light, as though it were floating from his hand. Instinctively the boy clasped the device and let out a small yelp—the item in his hand was now thin and smooth, not at all like a camera but instead thick, like a straw.

A happy chirp issued from in front of Manny as the boy looked down, mouth agape. "Impossible." A cylindrical object, slightly shorter than the length of his forearm and a deep, rich brown in color, lay in Manny's hand. "It is a wand..."

"It is my pleasure, Manny, to finally acknowledge that we are of one accord," chirped the quetzal happily. "But it is not just a wand—it is your wand. No other Lumen may ever manipulate it for good or bad. But you, child, how will you utilize it?"

Wow. "I have no idea, honestly," said Manny blankly. *What are wands used for?* "Aren't wands used for magic?"

"In a sense."

"So I can use this wand," began Manny, lifting his hand and nodding at the object in it, "to perform magic?"

"Figuratively speaking, yes," the bird chirped.

Waitaminute. "Does that make me a wizard, Julius?" asked Manny.

"Most certainly not!" squawked the bird haughtily. "Wizards, and witches for that matter, generally have no idea of the powers that they are tampering with, though a number of them do. To be truthful, 'magic' is a poor term for the powers that Lumens may access, or manipulate. Lumens manipulate light."

"So I'm not a wizard," said Manny slowly while staring into the quetzal's jet eyes. Julius shook his head in reply.

I get it, I think. "I am a 'Lumen,' as you've been calling it?" said Manny with more certainty in his voice.

"Most assuredly," said Julius.

"And I can use this, 'wand,' to 'manipulate' light?"

"Essentially, child, we Lumens bend the light. At the most elemental level, we fold the light we find around us to create and manipulate items in our environment and accomplish innumerable tasks," explained the quetzal, now glowing, his chest feathers puffed out.

"That's pretty heavy," stated Manny with a sigh. He smiled. "Wow."

"Yes, well," began Julius in a roundabout way, "now that you have finally acknowledged your wand, why not show me this 'bubble wand' that you speak of?"

Bubble wand, what is he...? Oh. "How can I show you a bubble wand?" began Manny, perplexed. "Now that the camera's a wand, and seeing as I have no idea how to bend light, how can I get a bubble wand? I don't think they sell them here in the surrounding towns."

"Do not be foolish, Manny," said Julius, shaking his head slightly and smiling. "Your wand may take the form of any object you desire—within reason, of course."

"What do you mean, 'within reason'?" asked the boy, eyebrows raised and holding the wand up to a light ray. He grew excited. "I can't make a car, can I?"

"Of course not!" chirped Julius sharply. "A car! You teenagers and your cars! I will never understand how you enjoy traveling while sitting when flight is the prime, and coincidentally most pleasurable option. In all cases, a Lumen generally cannot mold his or her wand into a form any larger than a hawk's nest."

A hawk's nest? How large is that? "I guess I wasn't listening or reading closely enough in biology class to recall the average size of a hawk's nest," said Manny simply. "Is it bigger than a swallow's nest?"

"Most definitely!" exclaimed the quetzal with surprise. "Just as a swallow's nest is to a hummingbird's!"

That really doesn't help me any. I don't even think I've ever seen a hummingbird nest. I bet they're small, though. "Julius, I suppose that I am sadly unaware of typical nest sizes," said Manny plainly. "Is a hawk's nest bigger than a bread box?"

"Actually," began Julius, lightening up, "I have heard many Lumens of your species describe the wand transformation limit as such. You do consume a great deal more bread than we birds, I suppose. Excluding those feverish North American ducks…"

Now that we've lined that out… "So how do I get my wand to take the form of a bubble wand? Do I just think about a bubble wand and 'Poof!', it changes?"

"That description sounds accurate," replied Julius, hopping once.

A bubble wand, right. Long, flimsy, with a figure eight at the tip. Manny witnessed as the baton shrank slightly and molded to the shape his thoughts described. "It worked!" exclaimed the boy. "Amazing."

"Empty those lungs, boy!" the quetzal cried, exploding from the ground and whirling about Manny like a green flame. "Blow! I wish to see the bubbles you described!"

Crap. "We don't have any solution," said Manny morosely. Julius landed before the boy and looked at him curiously.

"Oh, yes, to dip the wand into," the quetzal said quietly. "What can be done?" The bird raised a feathered brow and stared at the boy with a half-smile. "Think!"

Okay, so we need bubble solution. That only comes in a container. Mamá always used to buy the big bottles… Suddenly weighted down, Manny's hand dropped abruptly to the forest floor and he yelled in pain. The boy pulled his fist up and began rubbing his bruised knuckles. Glancing to his left he noted a tall, wooden bottle the length of his forearm lying on its side. *Is that what smashed my hand? That sucker is heavier than it looks… I've got to be careful what object I think of or I might end up with broken joints in the near future.*

"My knuckles are crushed, but at least we have the solution."

"Are you quite sure of that?" asked Julius deprecatingly. "Check the bottle."

Lifting the bottle and unscrewing the cap, Manny observed that the container was empty, though he could hear the thin bubble wand clanking around from within as he shook the bottle.

What a bother. "How come it's empty? Shouldn't it have solution?"

"Simply because Seventh-Level Lumens have not yet acquired the capacity to create liquids," Julius offered constructively. "Therefore, no. But allow me to aid you. Hold up the bottle."

Opening his radiant, emerald wings, the quetzal flicked his head and Manny saw a cherry red pendant dance on the bird's breast. Numerous, tiny streams of light immediately filtered down from the canopy and siphoned into the bottle. Manny grasped the container with both hands to support its new weight.

"What did you do?" Manny set the bottle on the path and peered inside. The container was full of clear liquid.

"Principally, I bent the light to form the 'soapy solution' that you mentioned before," explained Julius naturally.

Simply awesome. "So is that cherry pendant your wand?"

"Indeed," Julius replied knowingly. "We quetzals generally opt to wear our wands as an adornment rather than hassle with the burden of a stick in our claws. I mean no disrespect, of course."

The boy smiled. "None taken."

"If you will, then, Manny." Julius nodded toward the bottle.

Oh, yeah! "No hay problema," the boy said affably as he withdrew the wand, dripping with solution, and blew a stream of spheres into the limelight of the glade. With an exhilarated screech the quetzal shot up, arcing through the air as he began popping the torrent of newly formed bubbles. Manny drew another breath and released a second wave, chuckling at the bird's elation and unable to recall having experienced such a singularly odd moment in all his life.

20

Mending Misdeeds

Manny lay on the ground, head propped up on his rucksack, gazing at the auburn rays piercing the darkening forest canopy, a bag of disintegrated crackers in his right hand. The boy wore a smile on his face. *I have never had a day like this one. Zane will never believe that I have a wand and that I can change it into whatever I want. Unfortunately I can't do much else than that, though. At least for now. What am I gonna tell Papá y Mamá cuando regrese? They'll probably kill me, force me to sleep outside with the cacti and scorpions until I can earn enough money to pay them back for the camera. $300. I'm dead.*

Atop the signpost sat the quetzal, now a sticky green bundle, his feathers protruding in countless directions and covered in congealed liquid soap. Julius dozed in the afternoon light, his tail rising in an arc as he dipped forward lazily, looking as a water pump operated by invisible hands.

A concerned expression gripped Manny's face as he withdrew a lukewarm bottle of water from his rucksack, returned his head to the pouch, and unscrewed the cap to take a much-needed drink. He grimaced. *Perhaps I could learn to make money from light before I return home. Quizás...* Sipping again, Manny shuddered and recapped the bottle. *Yeah, Julius could teach me! He seems to be pretty proficient with this Lumen stuff. Maybe before I return home I could move up to be a Sixth-Level Lumen, or if I'm lucky, a Level Five! I could be a First-Level Lumen in a matter of weeks!*

Manny glanced up at the rocking quetzal, noting the glint of the cherry pendant on the bird's breast as Julius teetered in the sunlight. *Yeah, it looked pretty easy. All Julius did to make up some bubble solution was shake his pendant and 'Poof,' there was liquid in the bottle. I'll be a pro in no time.* Lowering his eyes to his own chest, Manny analyzed the thin, mahogany wand lying there. He grasped the wand with his right hand, holding it up to a ray of light that fell by his side. The wand sparkled, as though embedded with several miniature diamonds here and there. Rolling the wand up and down his palm, Manny considered his favorite sport. For an instant the wood shone brighter then suddenly coalesced to form a baseball, the heaviest Manny had ever held. *If I could only get this thing to break the breadbox limit, I could have the sweetest bat on next spring's team! I could out-hit Nacho then for sure! Oh, well...*

A rustling in the leaves above startled Manny, causing him to drop the baseball. His heart began to pound rapidly as his mind wandered through the branches to his right, considering the panther that he had encountered just two hours before. *Please don't be the panther. Oh, please don't be the panther...* Suddenly a tiny object flew from the foliage in the direction of the quetzal. Manny heard a dull clunk followed by an extremely shrill shriek from Julius. The branches jolted. For a millisecond the boy wondered whether the tree itself had hurled the stone-like object at the bird. Manny's mind instantly registered, however, that a wave seemed to be swiftly progressing through the canopy above the path to the right, its undulations disappearing around a bend. His eyes dropping back on Julius, Manny now found the quetzal lying with wings sprawled open on the forest floor. The boy swung round on his knees and began to crawl toward the bird. *He can't be dead...*

Just as Manny reached Julius, the bird squawked. "Ow..."

At least he isn't dead... "Can I help you up?" whispered Manny, an arm's length from the dirty, gooey green bundle that was the quetzal.

A puff of air embodying half a whistle was the boy's only reply.

Is he coughing? "Do you need a drink? I've got some water handy." *I don't know whether it will make you feel any better, though.*

Julius simply puffed again in reply, jerking slightly. *Is he sneezing?*

"If you need a tissue, I might have a handkerchief in my rucksack somewhere," the boy interjected consolingly.

"Huh!" the quetzal puffed again, rocking his head from one side to the other, clearly upset. He raised his head from the ground

22

slightly and shook it weakly. Manny glanced up as he noted several strings of golden light wrap around Julius's wing joints, lifting him and setting him on his tiny claws. Now facing the boy, Julius opened his eyes and pierced Manny with his gaze.

"Huh!" he repeated haughtily. As Julius continued, his voice was considerably lower and cracked sporadically. "First, you call me a—p-parrot, yet I forgave your i-ignorance. Now you attempt my—l-life by launching a nut at my skull. Simply l-l-ludicrous, child!"

Not this again… "It wasn't me, Julius! Let me explain." The bird swayed forward and Manny reached out to catch him, retracting his hand quickly as the quetzal snapped at him with his tiny beak.

"Do not touch me," Julius snipped severely, still swaying. "I think you have done enough damage for the moment." As Julius continued to sway, Manny noted that a red blotch had covered the left side of his crown. The bird abruptly crumpled, swooning forward, and Manny caught him just before he hit the ground, taking care to avoid the bird's beak.

Don't die. Don't die… "Julius, pay attention to me," Manny began, worried. "Your head is bleeding. What can I do to help you?"

Julius's head merely lolled from left to right.

I can't let him die. God help me, please! Looking up, Manny searched the clearing for any sign of help, any guidance as to what step he should take next; no inspiration came. Faced with three deserted paths and two weatherworn signs, Manny began to consider his options. *Well, nothing's behind me, and I don't want to take the right path, because then I would be following the thing that attacked Julius. Let's go to the left.*

With the limp bird in his arms, the boy bolted toward the left path when Julius whispered, "Not to the left. There is no help there."

Manny became frustrated. "But the attacker—"

Julius interjected, his eyes closed. "To the right there is a healer, a friend. You must part from the path where you see a stream."

Manny's feet were frozen in place. *I can't follow the attacker!* The boy paused, inhaling deeply. *Julius would know this area though, I suppose, since he does live in the rainforest.* "Ugh..." groaned the boy, taking a most reluctant step toward the other path.

"Do not forget your wand," added Julius, his faced furrowed in pain.

I nearly forgot! Manny bolted to the center of the clearing and grabbed the baseball with his right hand. *Wand.* As the baseball transformed into the shape of a wand, the boy turned, passed the post on his left, and proceeded along the path on the right.

Julius had groaned once or twice but had now grown quiet over the past twenty minutes, causing Manny's worry to increase ten-fold and his pace to double. As twilight engulfed the boy, he was forced to again walk more slowly, scanning the perimeter of the path for any signs of water, for the stream. Darkness soon enveloped the pair, the only remaining lights the stars that peeked down through the foliage above. The boy stopped to think.

Okay, the healer person probably doesn't live on the left, because he would be less concealed in the heart of two trails. Right. So I need to scan the right side. But now that it's so dark, I'll have to crawl. Manny smiled as he knelt along the west side of the path, thankful for the first time in ages for the unique brilliance of his skin. *At least I've got my own built-in night light.* Manny cradled the quetzal in his left arm and held out his radiant right hand to illuminate the undergrowth. He abruptly noticed that the wand was still in his hand. *What am I going to do with this thing?* His brow furrowed. *It's not like it will fit in any of my pockets.* The boy stared at the miniature mahogany shaft for a moment, until his expression gradually softened. *Yeah.* Holding his hand palm up, Manny rolled the wand down to his wrist and witnessed as the tool shone faintly and wrapped itself around his lower arm. Turning his wrist over, he scanned the face of his newly-formed watch, beaming. His smile sank slightly, however, as he noted that the minute hand was frozen at seventeen past. *I guess I can't have it all...* Manny opened his palm to illumine the undergrowth then resumed the hunt for the stream.

There's that same type of plant that I used to extract that monkey's feces from my shoes. The warm light reflected by Manny's hand revealed not only the massive leaves that he had employed earlier, but countless other species of plants and animals, from reaching ferns and exploding flowers to night-laboring insects and glowing reptiles with beady eyes. *These are the kind of plants that most people see in books; I get to scope them out up close and personal.* Manny grinned, his legs propelling him forward steadily. *Too bad it couldn't have been under better circumstances though…* His joy faded as the gleaming flora and fauna soon paled to the creeping ache in his lower back and tightening knees. *Just more evidence that I wasn't born to be a catcher. If only I knew how to make a flashlight or lantern or something with my wand, I could stand up and walk along.*

Another ten minutes later, Manny's back had nearly molded itself into a permanent arch. Stopping to sit on his knees and straighten his back, he lifted his left arm, nearly numb, to inspect Julius. Manny raised his free hand to illuminate the bird's profile, his stomach lurching nervously at the sight of the quetzal's bloodstained brow. Then rising from its downward swoop, Manny's stomach ripped up through his throat in a burst of anger that launched the boy to his feet.

"This is ridiculous!" he yelled, his voice tearing through his throat. "I don't understand how the pathway to a healer could be so difficult to find if someone really needed it!" Manny's golden eyes tore through the darkness before him, seeking out even the tiniest glimmer of water. The intensity of his glow grew suddenly brighter as he made a fist with his hand. "Where is the path!" he roared, his heart shuddering and tears rising in his eyes for the friend he had known for only a matter of hours, a seemingly true friend that might be ripped from his arms at any moment, leaving him alone again. "Where!" he repeated, voice cracking, fist shaking. Then a most peculiar phenomenon occurred to the boy's glistening eyes.

25

Miniscule tresses of the faintest light began to weave down through the canopy to a point ahead that Manny could not see. The boy sniffed, staring at the scene as veins of light continued to curl down. Manny's fist melted and his muscles relaxed as he began to walk along the path, drawn toward the descending light. Somehow, the light calmed him. After a minute he turned a corner to the right, noting the focal point of the light's migration—a snaking strand traversing the path over two hundred steps ahead. His pace quickened as he began to run toward the strand, his heart lifting and hope returning, however slightly. The boy's feet were soon planted before a small stream, a thread the breadth of two fingers that scarcely scored a path across the trail.

As Manny's eyes scanned the vegetation to the right of the path he whispered, "I don't know how this happened, but thank you, God." Stepping nearer to the edge, Manny noted that the light seemed to be funneling down and hovering over the water, floating upstream and deeper into the forest. The boy set his jaw and stepped into the undergrowth. A shallow rustling met his ears. *Oh my gosh, I hope there's not some huge lizard under those leaves.* Taking care not to step on the stream and to watch for strange creatures, he proceeded forward, catching glimpses of the lit stream through a break in the ferns here and beside a large rock there.

After roughly fifteen steps, Manny tripped on a gnarled root hidden by the foliage, landing hard on his right side. Despite his aching ribs and a throbbing right shin, Manny was glad he had managed to land cradling the quetzal safely to his chest. *Gracias a Dios I didn't crush him. But now I'm all wet.* Though the stream appeared thin, it had not failed to soak the boy's shirt and pants. *Gross.*

Struggling to get up, Manny glanced to his right and lurched back suddenly. An enormous lizard lay a foot from his head, staring at him. *That sucker's mouth is huge. What if he's a Komodo dragon? Do those things eat people?* The lizard blinked. *I've got to hurry; I don't have time to mess with this.* Manny felt with his hand for something with which he could scare the lizard, quickly finding a stick and smacking the tree beside him. The lizard hissed, turned nearly instantly, and scurried away. *Saved.* As he rose again from the ravenous undergrowth, Manny discarded the stick, planted his feet firmly, and lowered his hand to inspect his right leg. *Just great.* He too was bleeding, yet not profusely. *Yeah, perfect.* Rising again, Manny set his face, and as he forged on, he took care to feel out the way before him to prevent any additional falls.

About five minutes later Manny noticed a light piercing the crowded trees. Within a minute he found himself at the edge of a clearing bathed in blue light, a circle of trees encompassing a small hill and a cream-toned cabana boasting a roof thatched with palm leaves. Manny observed that the stream had been dammed along the west side of the grove, forming a mirror-like reservoir from which a magnificent, chestnut-hued horse was drinking. The boy wasted no time in approaching the animal.

"Listen, I need your help. My friend Julius here was attacked by something along the path and he's been bleeding for nearly an hour. He told me that I could find a healer here and I need you to heal him. Hurry, please," ended the boy, holding the quetzal out imploringly to the horse. Raising its handsome head from the waters, the animal stared at the boy, snorting through its nostrils and dripping water all over the bird.

"Oh, so your breath and this water will heal him," Manny said, staring into the horse's eyes with a subtle stab of doubt. Taking no note of the blood-soaked bird, the horse continued to stare at the boy, snorting again a moment later.

Maybe he doesn't understand English. "¿Son tu aliento y el agua los que sanen a mi amigo?" The horse merely blinked, tossed its mane, and lowered his head back down to the water, slurping loudly.

"Did I insult you somehow?" asked the boy, friend in hand and mind torn.

"M'ijo, none of your beseeching words could offend a simple animal such as this horse," called a warm voice from the left. Jumping and nearly dropping Julius, Manny recovered and glanced toward the hill to find the most majestic sight he had ever beheld.

Now many tales and stories speak of the stateliest of beasts, the most regal yet somehow fearsome and wise animal of legend, which Manny found himself facing at that moment. Though this creature is depicted in countless histories, some of which beguile the reader into viewing him as flighty and feminine, few have uncovered the honor and strength of the true unicorn.

Manny, average for his thirteen years of age at well over five feet, now found himself below eye level to the unicorn that gazed down upon him. As the beast strode across the blue lawn, the boy wondered at the flexion of the enormous muscles rippling from the unicorn's shoulders, the graceful yet powerful steps, the sunglow mane falling to one side and the spiraling, pearl and gold woven horn protruding from the base of the skull. The cerulean moonlight cast a soft hue on the unicorn's massive torso and head. The boy was speechless, and, similarly, at a loss for thought as well.

"I may deduce, then, that you were not raised in the Lumen world," stated the unicorn calmly, blinking its knowing, cobalt eyes at the boy. "It has been long since I spoke to a Seventh-Level Lumen of the outside world." The unicorn stopped five steps from the horse and Manny. "Paz, Laurelio, retírate." At this the horse raised its head from the pond, shook its mane, and retired to the other side of the cabana.

The unicorn blinked at the boy. The beast's eyes were not so much piercing as comforting. "Let me inspect Julius," said the unicorn. Manny jumped slightly, having momentarily forgotten about the quetzal. He glanced down at the bird and approached the unicorn, all wonder lost at the thought of his wounded friend.

"He was struck by something around an hour ago," said the boy just above a whisper. "He told me about you and how to get here." Finally lifting his eyes from the quetzal, Manny noted that the unicorn was staring at the bird, head turned yet eyes steady.

Raising an eye to the boy the unicorn spoke in its deep, warm voice. "Follow me." The beast then turned around, leading Manny up the hill and to the door of the cabana. The unicorn's head shook slightly and the door melted away, allowing the two to enter. *I don't suppose a unicorn could turn a doorknob… Nor a horse for that matter.*

Manny found himself within the coziest site he had ever been. To the left he spied two soft-looking beds, a fireplace in the center at the far end, and an enormous bed of straw in the far right corner. Bottles and flasks of all shapes and colors glinted from the walls, while a rich sage, gold, and coffee-hued rug filled the floor. Shaking his head again, the unicorn approached the center of the room where a wooden table suddenly rose to the height of Manny's chest. The boy's pupils dilated. *I'm still not used to this.* Manny, too, approached the table and laid his friend upon it, stepping back and eyeing the unicorn with continued amazement. *This is all just crazy. Talking birds that I haven't even heard of before…. Unicorns… Gosh, I used to think of unicorns as stuff for girls, but boy, this unicorn is about as girly as a lion.*

Gazing upon the unicorn intently, Manny marveled at the strength and certainty in the animal's eyes as it inspected Julius further, looking this way and that. Manny noticed that with the faintest tilt of the unicorn's head, the unconscious bird would follow suit—one wing lifting from the table and falling, then another, and even lifting from the wood entirely to rotate slowly. The unicorn spent a moment analyzing the wound on Julius's head, blinking for the first time and lowering the bird to the table once again. Cocking his head toward the hearth, the unicorn caused streaks of light to jet toward the fresh logs and ignite them. Entrancing Manny yet further, the flames turned blue and the tiny kettle hanging over the fire filled with water that was promptly boiling. *I bet Mamá wishes she could boil agua that fast.* Curving his neck in elegant strokes, the healer brought several glowing flasks and bottles from the walls to the table. The items came to rest upon the platform and ceased to glow.

Unable to contain himself, Manny asked, "How do you do that?"

"We unicorns are illuminated," replied the healer, blinking once. "As you are now, also."

Illuminated? What's that supposed to mean? Manny opened his mouth to pose another question when he found himself again at a loss for words. As the unicorn shook its head, multiple curls of snaking light wound in through the windows, converging over the table to form a small, white towel. The boy watched in amazement as the newly-formed towel, as though of its own accord, plunged into the pot of boiling water, sprung out and wrung itself of all excess moisture, and then hastily returned to the injured quetzal. A purple gash gradually appeared as the towel gently wiped away the dried and crusted blood upon the bird's brow. Manny's stomach sank, crushing on his toes. *How could a small animal like that have survived with a wound that bad?*

With a toss of his stunning mane, the unicorn unassimilated the hovering cloth, which quickly dissolved in a flash of light. The beast now turned his attention to the containers resting on the table. Guiding his head in swift, succinct motions, the healer unstopped a flask containing a crimson liquid, pulled a thread of the liquid through the air to partially fill a smaller bottle, and then topped the solution off with a stream of boiling water from the kettle. *Illuminated… So this thing's a Lumen, too? I don't know if I could ever do stuff like that. I can barely pour water into a cup without splashing the counter.* After re-stopping both the flask and the bottle, the unicorn raised its head and made a short, twirling motion. At this the boiling solution shot into the air and began to spin so rapidly that Manny was sure it would either explode or burst through a window and out into the night. Yet, in spite of his trepidation, the bottle soon slowed and came to a gradual, mid-air stop, whereupon it sank through the air before coming to rest upon the table, wholly intact.

"Wow," Manny whispered.

The unicorn blinked at the boy and unstopped the bottle once again with a flick of the head, now craning his neck and using delicate movements to open the bird's beak and feed the quetzal the solution bit by bit. A realization hit Manny. *He's swallowing! That mean's he's not dead! But how?*

"M'ijo," said the unicorn as he continued the delicate process of administering the now pinkish liquid to Julius, "I do find it ever so strange how a Lumen of the outside world could be so stunned by the work of a healer." Manny swallowed and shut his gaping mouth, staring blankly at the unicorn's mane. He never turned to look at Manny while he spoke. "What I am trying to say is that—are there not healers in the outside world? Do not such healers tend to your sick with age-old techniques such as this?"

Manny swallowed again; his mouth was quite dry. He actually had not felt this nervous and singled out since his last presentation in World History class. Shaking his head and straining a third swallow, he answered, "Well, you see, I guess you could say that we have 'healers' in a sense, but they're called something else."

The flask was nearly empty now as the unicorn replied, "Differences of names and terms are not enough to distinguish between a healer such as myself and one of the outside world. If I am a healer, and so are those of the outside world, why do you act so surprised?"

"Um…" Manny began. "To begin with, our healers are called 'doctors,' and they can't do what you just did."

"What do you mean?" replied the unicorn, just giving the quetzal the last of the liquid and guiding the broken bird gently through the air to the nearest straw bed on Manny's left. The unicorn's blue eyes burned inquisitively as he turned his ivory head to face the boy. "What I mean to say is, can your 'doctors' not tend to the wounds of the injured and blend medicines for their healing?"

Manny recalled a program that he had seen on television just a month earlier in which an ER doctor performed emergency surgery on a wreck victim. Unlike the unicorn that stood before him, the surgeon's gown and gloves were covered in blood. The boy threaded his fingers together and wrung his hands as he said, "Well, yes, they cut people open and stitch them up, they clean wounds and give out medicine, but they can't just make stuff fly. They have to use their hands."

"Of course they do," said the unicorn, stomping his back hoof on the wooden floor and neighing a chuckle. "They are humans. But I am a unicorn, and I have no hands, so I must guide my tools with light. Even Lumen healers of your species use their hands during the curing process. Essentially, your doctors and we healers are one and the same."

31

Manny felt as though he were trapped in a box, locked within an idea that he could not escape. Yet somehow he could see through the wall, peer through the narrow tunnel of his mind to the open space where the unicorn was, beaming after having resolved any and all doubts regarding the likeness of Lumen and non-Lumen healers.

The boy shook his head and smiled, discarding his misgivings and exiting the tunnel. "I suppose you're right."

Several hours later Manny awoke, jolting in bed and searching his surroundings breathlessly. *Where in the world am I?* Above him he found shelves lined with bottles. A table was several steps away. *Oh my gosh, where am I?* Manny's heart thundered in his chest as he stared out the window to his left, out into an opening with trees that shined oddly with a crumpled light. His heart slowed slightly as he soon recalled that he had gone on a school trip to Costa Rica with his eighth-grade class. After splitting their first two days in Monteverde and Alajuela, the early hours of the third day had involved a trek through the streets of San José. *What a joy. Those jerks left me in a store and I was lost for like an hour looking for the group. Necios... In the afternoon they swam at the beach. That was fun. I hung out with that cute muchacha, Maricarmen, for a good twenty minutes until Nacho and his cronies came along and told her that I had a flesh-eating disease named La Chagra and that's why no one hangs out with me.*

Manny clenched his fist and punched the bed; the impact made a crunching noise. He abruptly realized that he was not lying on a regular mattress but on an odd, fiber-like padding. Manny turned and the padding crunched again, rustling slightly. The boy frowned. *What is this?* Reaching over the side of the bed Manny stuck his hand below the covers and retracted it quickly, not in pain, as one might have expected, but out of shock. *It feels like thick, sharp bristles.* He reached back over the side of the bed and touched the padding a second time, grazing the bristles for a moment until he grabbed one and pulled it close to his face. In the light his skin reflected from the smoldering fire Manny could see that the material was approximately the length of his hand. The object was burnt yellow in color and bent reluctantly under the pressure of his forefingers. He smelled it—the material gave off the odor of a field in the fall. *Is this straw? Who sleeps on straw? Am I in some run down hotel close to the coast? Where did we go after the beach?*

It hit him. The fourth day he and his classmates had followed a pair of rural tour guides into the rainforest early in the afternoon to observe the wildlife and the various plant species. About two hours into the trek Manny had slipped on... *That stupid monkey! If I ever see that little monster again, I will grab him by his tail and launch him into the trees, but not until I first drag him through a field of Costa Rican cow dung!* "Ugh!" he growled angrily. A whimper issued from just beyond the foot of his bed, and ice pierced his heart.

"Oh my gosh..." breathed Manny. *I'm in that cottage in the middle of the rainforest, and that was Julius.* The boy swallowed, expecting fear to knot his gut; but he was taken off guard as a sensation of rapture shot through his chest and straight to his brain, rendering his limbs light and making him feel that he could run for miles or even just take off into the sky. *This is awesome! Everything that happened yesterday was true!* For a moment he smiled at the wooden table, framed in the firelight. He then remembered the flying bottles and his friend's wound. *Well, it's all awesome except for the fact that Julius almost died.* He sat up quickly, remembering his friend's healer. Manny's eyes dashed from the door to the enormous bed of straw just beyond the fireplace. "No way..." he breathed. "It is true." Lying in the opposite corner of the cabana, Manny distinguished the massive outline of the Lumen unicorn that he had met beside the lake yesterday. The embers cast a soft, auburn light on the beast's haunches. Manny's eyes rose from the unicorn to the moonlit windowpane above as he again noted the strangely lit trees, almost dancing in the crinkled light. *¡Sí! ¡Eso es el lago! That's the moonlight reflecting off the lake! Gotta check it out...*

33

Trying to make as little noise as possible, Manny made his way cautiously into the open air. The boy was certain that every sound he made would wake his companions: the horrendous sigh of the bed as he rose from it; the creaking board not two steps from Julius's bed; the nerve-twisting, squeaking hinges; the click of the door as it came shut. Yet Manny soon found himself standing alone in the cool, night air with a breeze soothing his skin. He turned to the left and crept down the hill to sit beside the lake.

All breath left Manny as he sprawled out on the shore, his eyes perusing space as he compared this unfamiliar sky to the Arizona stars he knew so well. *Abuelito…* Lying outside as a boy on summer nights with his grandfather, Manny had discovered a handful of constellations that decorated the northern reaches of the Milky Way, including Cassiopeia, Orion, and both the Big and Little Dippers. His grandfather had taught him to espy several planets as well, Venus and Jupiter for example. Yet never, not during a single evening either with his grandfather or simply observing the cosmos alone, had Manny felt so enveloped by the arm of the galaxy's glittering stream of stars. On that hill, with his bare feet resting just a fingertip from the waters, the heavens appeared brighter and more alive than ever in his life. Not billions, but trillions of glowing spots seemed to shine down on Manny from the night sky. His heart tugged and he gazed up and to his left. A star shot across the sky. He wondered if it fell to the Earth. *Do stars even really fall to the Earth?* Manny's heart pulled again. *What?* He felt a yearning for something, but he could not discern what called to him. After gazing for another few moments and drinking in the light, Manny raised his arm to point to where he saw the star fall. He jumped instantly to his feet.

"What is going on with my skin?" he said, startled. Staring at his left hand, Manny gawked as he noted that he could no longer distinguish the pores in his skin. His hand and arm were not merely glowing as they usually did, but they appeared to be virtually pure light. The boy clenched his fist. *At least I can still see my fingernails.* Lowering his hand, Manny stood mesmerized by the reflection of his face in the lake. His complexion had never been so bright, nor his hair so dark. *My head looks like a radioactive light bulb.* He smiled, but could barely see his lips. *Weird.* A stone crashed through Manny's stomach as he glanced at his right arm. "Oh, no, I did not..." He jerked his hand up to his face, verifying his fears. "No—I couldn't have been so stupid..."

Manny spun around on the spot, bolted toward the cabana door, and grabbed the handle, opening the door quickly, yet quietly. He glanced from the quetzal to the unicorn and sighed with relief. *They're both still asleep.* Striding across the room with a faint hope in his chest, Manny reached his bed. *It's weird how when you try to be quiet, you seem to make so much noise, but when you don't care so much anymore, you don't seem to make any at all.* The boy's hands searched succinctly throughout the covers and bed sheets, under the pillow, beneath the bed, but though the minimal firelight reflected by his skin illuminated the sleeping area, he could not find his quarry. *¡Caray! ¡No lo puedo creer! How could I misplace something so important?!*

He paused for a second to scan the table before leaving the cabana again, shutting the door carefully. Despite turning and walking slowly down the hill, Manny was extremely aggravated. "I am probably the first Lumen ever to lose his wand on the first day of getting it!" he exclaimed to himself, fists clenched. Manny searched the entire rim of the lake, a slightly awkward feat when it came to maneuvering around the trees that thirstily reached into the depths along the far end—though he managed—scanning the waters all the while to ensure that the wand was not floating in some obscure corner of the lake. His search ended fruitlessly at the point where he met Laurelio the horse. As his mind raced through his memories in a mad hunt for the wand, Manny recounted his steps, hardly noticing that he was staring at himself in the surface of the water again.

"Okay, I had it when I left the fork in the path because Julius reminded me to get it." *Check.* "When I knelt down to crawl along the path, I turned the wand into a watch." *Well then, why isn't it on my wrist?!* He raised his fist to his face and growled at his naked arm. He added lowly, "Adelante, pues. When I reached the stream I still had it, so then we took off into the forest and I tripped and saw that lizard. But I'm sure I still had my wand on my wrist!" *What happened next?* "So then I grabbed a stick and smacked a tree to…." His voice trailed away. "No…" Manny turned to face the point where he had entered the clearing several hours earlier, the spot where the stream began to etch a path into the forest. He chuckled to himself, his hands on his hips. "I reached for a stick and found one—my wand! And then I just threw it away."

Without looking back Manny plunged into the forest. Though he failed to notice, the nocturnal sounds of the jungle quelled themselves almost instantly, the grasshopper tune halting, the frog song dying, the bird coo ceasing. The whole forest listened in wait to the thundering and rustling passage of the glittering, two-legged being over the infant stream. At one point Manny thought he saw a shadow move in the treetops to his left, but he halted no more than a second before pressing onward. He never fell once, and within three minutes Manny distinguished moonlight on the path some thirty steps ahead. After five more steps, the boy stopped abruptly and, to tell the truth, found himself rather scared.

A small shadow had just descended from the canopy, diving into the undergrowth less than two meters ahead. Manny's heart pounded in his throat as he concealed himself behind a nearby tree. *What do I do? That's right where my wand is!* Peering around the tree and staring for a moment to see what might take place, Manny observed the shadow hop up beside the trunk and then drop again, hissing. *That's no snake. Is it hissing because it's angry?* A breath later the shadow leapt higher into the tree before it dropped once again and began to apparently flail the ground. *This is insane! What is it doing?* A weighty suspicion struck him. *Oh no, he's not breaking my wand!* Manny leapt from behind the tree, blazing beneath the starlight, and met a horrible face.

A set of four fangs flashed in the darkness. Manny stopped suddenly and cried, "You!" Just two steps in front of the boy was the waist-high, white-bearded monkey that had transformed Manny's family camera the day before. But the monkey's face was now neither quizzical nor amused, but twisted in hatred at the boy as it screamed fiercely. Several birds squawked and took off into the sky above the scene. Manny could not help looking up, and when he had again lowered his view to the monkey, he saw that the animal was attempting to snatch the wand with a tong-like apparatus. A flame burst in the boy's heart, a searing fire boiling in his stomach. "¡Bestia tú! Get away from it!" Manny shouted, lunging at the monkey and reaching for its arm. "¡Déjalo, you little monster!" But the monkey evaded Manny's grab and shot back toward the path, the wand slipping from the steel tongs and spinning through the air. Manny took his chance and snatched the wand, forming it into a small club and bolting toward the edge of the wood from where the monkey was again hissing.

"No!" cried a deep voice from behind Manny, and the boy watched as several blades of light struck the monkey in the stomach and forced it across the path. Instantaneously numerous fingers of light assembled to form a barrier blocking the pathway. "Follow me, m'ijo, it's not safe in the forest at night!" Manny turned to find the unicorn standing ten paces away, scanning the boy with its unwavering eyes. "Quickly! Return with me to sanctuary before that creature doubles back!"

Without waiting for a response, the unicorn shook its mane and began to turn, the light barrier dragging Manny further from the foe that he so desired to reach, on whom he wished to exact his revenge. *I am not letting that filthy runt escape me this time.* Manny pressed against the advancing wall with all the strength he could muster, beating the barrier with his now club-wand, but to no avail. He then turned and glared at the unicorn's back.

"Wait," said the boy sharply.

The unicorn halted, glancing back over his shoulder. "We must hurry. Those primates often travel in groups, and I would rather heal wounds than create them."

Manny's jaw was set, fire still burning in his core. "Let me pass," he said in a low voice.

"I will not," replied the unicorn calmly, turning again to face Manny and confronting him with those cool, blue eyes. "You will follow me to sanctuary," he finished, stomping his back-right hoof.

Manny balled his fists. *I would break through this wall if I were a more experienced Lumen.* He had not the least idea of how to bend light and pass through the barrier, so he begged instead.

"If I don't stop that little runt now——" began Manny.

"To sanctuary, this instant," the unicorn cut in icily, a blue flame blazing in his deep eyes. He turned and trotted with swift precision over the undergrowth and hidden roots. Shaking his golden mane a second time, the unicorn propelled the wall immediately forward, compelling Manny along somewhat forcefully now. The boy nearly fell, but he had no choice but to follow. He had no time to even look back to see if the monkey had recovered. *That little wretch*... Within two minutes the unicorn and the reluctant boy had reached the sanctuary grove. Upon crossing the tree line, Manny spun around only to discover that the wall remained in place, spreading to bar his return passage.

"Why did you do that?!" Manny cried, nearly screaming and holding his hands out in frustration.

The unicorn turned slowly to face Manny, the beast's eyes still solid, yet fire gone. He faced Manny and considered him for a moment, noting the dissatisfaction in the boy's flashing eyes. Blinking once, the beast answered, "Por favor, sit by the lake. Hay que hablar."

"I don't want to talk!" Manny replied loudly. "That beast tried to steal my wand, and earlier he made me slip in his dung so he could try to steal my stuff!"

"And what do you presume to do to the poor creature?" asked the unicorn simply, turning to the left and approaching the lake. "It is not as if you have been trained to wield your wand and command light." The unicorn stopped before the water, gazing upon the heavens reflected in the surface.

Manny clamped his right fist, scrutinizing his wand. The truth had lanced him, and he had no reply. As he stared, a subversive thought formed in his mind. "Well if it weren't for that wall you made, I could have beaten some sense into the beast." Manny threw the unicorn an oblique glance in hopes of gauging his response.

"No, you could not," the creature coolly countered.

"And why couldn't I?" began Manny, puffing up again. "I transformed my wand into a club and—"

"Whether you were aware of this or not, a Lumen wand cannot come in contact with anyone but its owner," replied the unicorn soberly. "The best you could have done with your 'club' would be to push the monkey away from you, and that would have served little purpose if the beast leapt over your hands to lunge at your face with its fangs."

This dart inarguably burst the boy's pride, carrying with it a stinging wave of fear and shock, which then ebbed away to reveal gratitude for the unicorn's efforts. *That little turd did have some nasty fangs—gosh, he could have torn me up bad.* Realizing that he had lowered his wand and was now staring at the ground, Manny looked up to find the unicorn bending over the lake for a drink. *Thank God he came.* The boy turned and approached the unicorn, transforming his wand into a wristwatch again and kneeling beside the beast. Manny cupped his hands to acquire a drink for himself.

After the second gulp Manny said, "Thanks for what you did out there; I was a little out of my mind, I think."

Not looking up, the unicorn replied, "You are welcome." As Manny bent down to scoop up more water from the rippling surface, a jet of water burst from the boy's hands and into his face. Manny jumped violently in surprise. A moment later he could hear a high, odd sound, like a strange and continuous cascade of whinnying coming from over his shoulder. Rubbing the water from his eyes, Manny turned gapingly to see the unicorn rolling in the grass beside the lake. The boy was startled. *He isn't choking, is he?*

"Are you alright?" Manny asked quickly.

"Just, yee-hee, f-fine," choked out the unicorn. "I just thought you ought to, yee-hee-hee, ought to learn to cool off, once in a while." The beast shook some more, as if he were scratching his back on the bank.

Instantly several streams of water arched up from the lake and shot Manny in the chest and face. The incessant, whinnying noise broke out even more loudly as Manny stumbled in utter shock, wiping water from his brow and shaking it from his hands. It hit him. "You sly old excuse for a horse," said Manny with a smile. The unicorn froze. *That got him, but wait 'til he sees this.* Manny brought his right hand behind his back and transformed his wand into a short, broad-headed oar.

The unicorn craned his head around to see the boy. "Perchance did you call me a 'horse'?" After waiting for a reply that never came, the unicorn blinked once and added, "Being a novice as you are, let me enlighten you to the differences—"

Manny struck the water at the word 'novice,' showering the unicorn, who jolted in shock, his explanation unexpectedly abbreviated. The beast rolled quickly and tried to return to a standing position, but Manny jumped into the lake and began splashing wave after wave of water on him. After nearly slipping once, the unicorn rose up on its legs and turned, dripping pitifully from horn to tail.

"I do regret this," the unicorn began with a smile in his eyes. Shaking his massive body, the creature rid himself of the excess moisture heaped upon him by the boy; but curiously, the water droplets froze in mid-air, glowing like thousands of miniatures moons.

At this Manny swallowed his grin. *I'm dead.*

The unicorn then nodded toward Manny as the countless beads bolted through the space between beast and boy, soaking every inch of the latter. Manny rose to his feet, water streaming from his clothes, but smiling.

"You see," finished the unicorn, "as I have no hands, I must even the odds."

"I suppose you're right," Manny replied happily. "I haven't had such a great water fight since my tenth birthday party."

"And now you are fourteen," interjected the unicorn knowingly.

Not quite, but close enough. I still have twenty days to go. Or is it nineteen now? Slightly confused, Manny asked, "But how do you know my age?"

"All Seventh-Level Lumens receive their wands at the age of fourteen. It is common knowledge in the Lumen world," the unicorn explained simply.

"Oh." Manny ran his left hand through his hair to shake out the moisture. "Wait a sec. So you're a First-Level Lumen, correct?"

"Correct," the unicorn replied, nodding.

Manny removed a wet finger from his left ear. He could still feel water trapped in his head. "So how old are you?"

"Before I tell you my age, let us first be formally introduced. As you fell asleep so abruptly after I healed Julius last night, I have not had the delight of acquiring your name, nor you mine," the unicorn stated positively. "My name is Octavio Gilderbrand, but you may call me Tavo for short. I come from a tribe of unicorns originating in central Amazonia, where the river curves back to the southeast. ¿Y tú?"

"Pues, my name is Manuel López, but my pals call me Manny—not that I have an overabundance of friends or anything…" replied the boy as he removed his t-shirt and wrung out the water. "I grew up in Siete Arenas. It's northeast of Phoenix. You know my age," he added, smiling, "so, ¿cuántos años tiene?"

"I am forty-six," Tavo replied brightly. "After practicing as a healer in Amazonia for several years, I migrated north, here to Central America, to provide aid in this region after the healer died five years ago."

Manny swallowed hard. *Abuelito died five years ago.* He shook his head vaguely then finished putting his shirt back on. Just to change the subject, Manny asked, "So, Tavo, since you're from Amazonia, does that make you a Brazilian unicorn?"

"Actually, no. Despite the fact that I grew up as a colt in Brazilian territory, I have had difficulty coercing the Brazilian government to recognize my existence at all, let alone grant me citizenship," Tavo finished wryly.

"Oh, well, that makes sense." Manny felt sheepish at how ignorant his question now sounded to him. *Does that make you a Brazilian unicorn? Geez…* "Um, so, I guess I should say it's nice to meet you, Tavo. I would shake your hand, but, you know…" Manny smiled and shrugged.

"In point of fact, when a human desires to greet a unicorn, it is customary for the human to pat the unicorn twice on the left shoulder for friendship," Tavo elucidated.

Interesting. "Okay, then." Eschewing all feelings of awkwardness Manny stepped forward and patted the unicorn on the shoulder. The boy's hand shimmered over the unicorn's lucent hair, which he found to be extremely smooth. Stepping back, Manny added, "I am pleased to meet you, Tavo, and thank you for saving me back there." Manny met Tavo's bright blue eyes but then looked hastily to the ground. A sliver of shame still ate at him for how he had yelled at Tavo earlier.

"Indeed, this is a most rare pleasure, Manny," said Tavo congenially. "Truth be told, I have not spoken to a Seventh-Level since leaving the Amazon five years ago."

Pang. Five years ago. Memories of his grandfather's death thrust against Manny's mind. Manny forced them away. "So why did you become a healer?"

Tavo turned his head to the stars and gazed at them for a moment. Though the moon was now gone, the myriad of lights continued to coat the sky like falling snow. He set a moist eye on Manny then answered quietly, "I wanted to help."

That was slightly vague. "What do you mean?"

The unicorn blinked, his eyes shining as he shook his mane powerfully. "Enough of me and my history," he exclaimed dismissively, his firm gaze telling the boy that the discussion of Tavo's past had ended.

Maybe I can get more out of him later. But I wonder why he doesn't want to talk about it?

"Now that you have cooled off," the unicorn continued, tilting his head at the lake with the hint of a smile, "and we have been formally introduced," he nodded, "Hay que hablar."

Though Manny had been unwilling to talk with Tavo earlier, the boy now assented readily. "Sure. How 'bout we sit down?"

"That would be excellent." Tavo led the boy to a dry patch along the bank. "But you sit; I shall stand."

Manny crossed his legs and gazed out at the star strewn water. "So what's on your mind?" He looked up at Tavo to his left. The unicorn's brow was creased.

"What caused you to leave your bed and enter the forest?" asked Tavo, his voice deep.

The boy swallowed as his eyes drifted back to the lake. *I can't believe I lost my wand. Should I tell him the truth? What will he say? Will he take it from me and keep it because I wasn't being responsible? Mamá would do that.* "Um—I lost something." He did not look back up at Tavo.

Manny heard the unicorn snort through his nostrils and stamp the ground in reply. With an edge to his voice Tavo pressed on, "What object could be so important as to throw your life into the paws of disease-ridden animals?"

An egg—no, a small boulder—rose in the boy's throat. *That was so stupid. I can't believe I ran into the forest expecting to make it out alright. But if I hadn't gone, that ape would now have my wand.* Manny raised his eyes from the mahogany watch resting coolly on his wrist to confront Tavo's unyielding eye, which flamed again, however slightly. "I will make wiser choices from here on out," Manny answered resolutely. "And I will take greater care of my possessions." *Particularly my wand.*

"I should hope so," said Tavo, his cadence somewhat perilous.

Was he just looking at my wand when he said that?

"Be aware that a Lumen, no matter his age or species, has many objects for which to care—" Here the unicorn's eyes blazed, "be they wand or loved ones." Frigid flames diminishing, Tavo turned his gaze to the lake, and his expression softened.

"I will be more careful," Manny whispered, scanning the unicorn's magnificent yet simultaneously threatening profile. *I will care for my wand.* He rested his right hand on the watch. *And for my family, too.* Manny considered his mother nearly one thousand miles away. He imagined her kissing his father goodbye as he left for work in the early hours of the morning. Both Carlos and María López had emigrated from El Salvador as young children during a turbulent time in their country's history, growing up and building their lives in a foreign country. *De verdad. You'll be proud of me. And I will protect you both, just as you have me.*

Transforming his wristwatch back into a wand, Manny returned to the present and contemplated the unicorn once again. *Tavo es tan chévere. He healed Julius in a matter of minutes, shooting liquid through the air and mixing medicines—he didn't lose a drop. He even protected me with that wall of light when I about threw my life into that idiot monkey's hands...* Another thought crept into the boy's mind. *But how did he...?* Manny scanned the unicorn's frame, searching. *Where is it?* Manny found himself perplexed. "But how did you do all that without a wand?"

"Are the stars not beautiful, m'ijo?" Tavo asked, engrossed by the heavens.

Didn't he hear me? What's the deal? "Yeah, they're great," Manny said offhandedly, "but what I'm really concerned about is—"

Tavo interrupted him. "During what you would consider the winter months a constellation by the name of Monoceros crosses the sky. He soars along the Milky Way between Canis Major and Minor and just behind Orion. Have you heard of him?"

Manny shook his head, his thoughts suddenly in a tangle. "Uh—yeah," he stuttered, "mi abuelito taught my cousin Zane and me that constellation when he was visiting one Christmas—seven years ago, I think."

"Really?" Tavo asked, glancing back in amazement. "Isn't it rare for those of your former culture to know such faint constellations?"

Former culture? That's a strange way of putting it... Manny blinked. "But Orion isn't faint—it's easy to spot during the holi—"

"Oh, I'm not referring to Orion, m'ijo," Tavo interrupted, "I speak of Monoceros, the constellation of my clan."

"Monoceros? Mi abuelito never mentioned a constellation by that name..."

Tavo nodded sympathetically. "That's quite understandable, considering its subtle luminance."

Manny frowned. *But what if he didn't even know Monoceros existed?* His grandfather suddenly seemed smaller, somehow less strong and wise than before.

"But no matter," Tavo continued. "As I was saying, Monoceros pierces the night canopy with his glowing horn just as we earthly unicorns scatter the darkness with ours." Tavo transfixed Manny with a bright eye. "I believe that should answer your question."

¿Mi pregunta? Manny pinched his eyes together tightly. "Okay, so hold on," he said, abandoning his disillusionment as he rifled through memories of the past night and early morning. "So when you want to bend light, you just have to move your horn—like by shaking or tilting your head, for example?"

"In more or less words, yes."

"But all other Lumens have a wand, like Julius and me," Manny concluded as he glanced at the wand in his right hand and considered Julius's cherry necklace that he had shaken to create the bubble solution. *I think I get it.*

"No, Manny, that is actually incorrect," Tavo replied. "Throughout the world one may find a number of Lumens whose wands function as a facet of their anatomy; three such species live on this very continent."

Manny sat up, wiping his eyes. "This is all so fascinating," he said as he stretched his arms to the sky. "I can't wait to learn more about this stuff."

"You will," nodded Tavo. "But first, all Lumens, young and old, need their rest. Hay que dormir. We've both lost enough sleep already."

"But I have a ton more questions." Manny yawned, realizing that he indeed was very tired.

"As do I," replied Tavo, "but they must wait." The unicorn turned about and led the boy back to the cabana, their discussion ended. Tavo shook his mane, the door dissolved, and he proceeded forward. Just as he passed the hearth, he bowed his head and the flames glittered blue, renewing their dance and providing a burst of light that revealed Julius's frame resting on the first bed.

The quetzal looked peaceful. *At least he's alive.* After transforming his wand back into a watch and silently pulling off his shoes, Manny slid into the second bed and sighed, his thoughts ebbing steadily away into unconsciousness. *I'm glad he... survived. Now I have... two friends... Julius... and... Tavo.*

"Muchacho," called a voice from Manny's chest.

Though the boy was still more than half asleep, he could feel a minute, prickling sensation proceeding up his sternum from the direction of his stomach.

"What...?" muttered Manny, rubbing his eyes. He opened them slightly, only able to distinguish a green blur. *¿Qué?* The boy was quite groggy.

"Muchacho, quiero hablarte," clipped the voice in reply, the prickly sensation settling around Manny's collar bone.

The boy felt something light and soft brush along his left hand. *What is that?* He shook his head and opened his eyes widely. Slightly surprised, Manny found Julius resting on his chest, the bird's emerald tail feathers arcing along and resting on the boy's hand. *Oh...* "Um, what did you say, Julius?" asked Manny, his voice low and gravelly.

With the hint of a glare, the quetzal ruffled his feathers. "I would like to talk to you about how you brought me to the sanctuary," he stated slowly and clearly. "I would have died if it were not for you," Julius added, looking quickly away and dancing on his claws.

Oh, yeah... As he focused more clearly on the bird's head, Manny noted that the purple gash yet remained. *It looks a little better though.* "You know, Tavo really knows his stuff. You should be thanking him." The fear from the quetzal's near-fatal experience lingered in the boy's mind, somehow twisting itself into a pervasive

46

sense of guilt. *He almost died... If I had arrived even a moment later...*

"Most assuredly," clipped the quetzal, hopping imperceptibly. "I already have. We took a stroll earlier, before you awoke..." Julius's voice trailed off as he gazed out one of the southerly windows. After a few moments he continued edgily. "We discussed a number of things. He will be returning soon with breakfast."

Manny eyed the quetzal. *Is he frowning?* His stomach grumbled before he could ponder the point further. "Actually, I'm really hungry. I haven't eaten since lunch yesterday." A pause. "But I guess I was busy with other things." He thought of the bird, the unicorn, the monkey. *Stupid monkey.*

"Um, Julius," Manny began doubtfully, "you remember earlier, when—" He stopped, pointing at his own forehead. The quetzal cocked his head quizzically. *He's not getting me.* "Do you—" He paused again, swallowing hard. "Do you remember what happened back at the fork in the road?"

Julius ruffled his feathers, his frown deepening.

Is that a yes? "Are—are you still mad at me about how you got hurt?" Manny stuttered finally.

Julius flapped his wings, teetering awkwardly on the boy's chest until he rose into the air and flew slowly backward to land haphazardly on the headboard of the other bed. Balancing himself, he folded his wings and stared at the boy, who gingerly had sat up and crossed his legs.

Manny braced himself. *Is he about to explode?*

Quietly, Julius began. "As I told you, I have spoken with Tavo." He paused, blinking several times and breathing deeply.

Oh boy...

"Though I had believed that you had attacked me, Tavo does not."

Manny sighed in relief. *Thank you, God.*

"He believes that you are of greater moral character than to commit such a deed."

"I most certainly do," called a voice from beyond the now empty doorframe. Tavo entered, steady eyes set on Julius's comparably minute frame. The quetzal merely ruffled his feathers in reply, once again inhaling deeply, yet exhaling somewhat begrudgingly. Stopping before the table, Tavo looked to Manny and added, "Buenos días, m'ijo."

"Good morning," replied Manny brightly; yet before he could continue, Julius interjected.

"I would still like to know what truly happened."

"As you know, mi amigo, we have not the time," Tavo retorted, shaking his mane and widening the table's breadth. With another flick of the head several light rays converged before the fireplace to form a tall, wooden chair. "We have a pressing issue to discuss." Tavo glanced from Julius to Manny. "And a fast to break."

Manny's stomach tore at his insides again. *I could eat a horse.* He looked away from Tavo's benevolent eyes quickly. *Oh my gosh, I better not say anything like that.* Swallowing guiltily, he returned his gaze to the unicorn and said, "I'm so hungry I could…" The boy blinked. "Well, I'm just hungry."

Tavo nodded understandingly and said, "Siéntate."

As Manny rose from the bed and approached the table to sit down, he noticed the horse from the day before standing calmly just outside the door, laden with two baskets that framed his upper back. *What was his name?*

Shaking his mane once more, Tavo glanced over his shoulder just as the glowing baskets floated over his head toward the barren table. "Gracias, Laurelio. Go and eat."

Oh yeah—Laurelio!

Looking back over the table Tavo asked, "You enjoy fruit, I presume?"

"Definitely!" Manny responded eagerly. Growing up in a Salvadoran-American home with a mother faithful to her home country's cuisine had presented Manny with countless opportunities to appreciate the vast varieties of tropical fruit. "I don't think there's a fruta que no me guste. They're all my favorite!" Looking into the baskets the boy found a number of fruits, from pineapple and mango to papaya and bananas. *We need to peel these.* "Do you have a knife I can borrow?"

"That is not necessary," replied Tavo benignly, nodding at the baskets. As the fruit rose into the air and began peeling itself, Tavo added, "Let us dine quickly," and looking to Julius he finished, "We must discuss a matter of utmost salience. Correct?"

Glaring severely in reply, Julius ruffled his feathers and asserted, "And what matter could be of greater importance than the question of my attacker?" With his final word Julius nearly fell from the headboard, recovering none-too-gracefully and flitting pitifully to the edge of the table in his rage. Just before landing, the quetzal made an awkward half-swoop, causing his cherry pendant to dance slightly and a miniature pedestal to flash into existence immediately below his claws. Turning his open-mouthed gaze from the self-peeling fruit, Manny eyed the interaction between the haughty quetzal and the unwavering unicorn.

I wonder who would win in a duel…

Icing Julius's rage with his cool stare, Tavo said, "As I stated earlier, though we cannot allow such an attack to pass by unnoticed, we must first make arrangements for the boy's return to the outside world."

Julius lifted his wings to protest, but Manny interrupted. "What?" he cried, tearing Julius and Tavo's gaze from one another, the quetzal almost toppling over. "What do you mean my 'return to the outside world'? I have to go back?"

"Pues, sí, m'ijo," replied Tavo candidly, "You cannot stay here, especially when—"

"But why not?" asked Manny, voice rising. "I could stay here, you know, and live in the forest with you two." Manny looked at them both, desperately searching for a yes. The unicorn and the quetzal looked at one another with softened expressions, though Julius was still notably agitated. Just as Tavo turned with pity-filled eyes and open mouth to reply, Manny continued. "Come on, just think about it. You two could teach me to be an expert Lumen in no time. I mean, Tavo, you could show me healing techniques, and Julius, you could, well, you could…" At this the bird raised his

49

plumed brow in expectancy, leaning slightly toward Manny. "You could, um…" *Oh, what is he? Tavo's a healer, but all I've seen Julius do is make bubble solution and a perch.* "I'm sure you could teach me a great deal of useful techniques yourself."

"I indeed should say so," clipped the quetzal, dissatisfied with the abstraction of Manny's last comment. "But as this hut is not a school," added Julius, waving a wing about the small homestead, "you cannot expect to stay here and be properly educated."

"But you don't understand!" Manny cried, his voice cracking. *Nobody understands.* "You two—" began the boy, looking at Tavo's reassuring blue eyes and Julius's steely black ones, "—you two are the only people outside my family that have treated me like I'm actually worth something." He unclenched his fists from the table edge and raised open hands. "You're my friends."

Tavo smiled in reply, his eyes shining; Julius, however, was visibly shaken. The bird blinked several times at the boy, his plumage settling and the encaged anger melting away. Manny noted that the quetzal sat more erect on the perch, his dignity and joyful wit from the previous day returning to him. Opening his wings and expanding his crimson chest with a renewed breath of satisfaction, Julius stated, "Boy, I thank you sincerely for saving my life. Had you not faithfully carried me to our dear friend Tavo, here," he continued, signaling with a wing tip to the unicorn on his right, "I would now be food for who knows what wild beast."

Manny swallowed nervously, recalling the panther with its electric eyes from the previous day. Before his thoughts could wander any farther, a shrill, yet surprisingly melodic call drug Manny back to the present. *What in the world? Was that Julius?*

The bird hopped on his perch and snapped his beak exuberantly. "Manny, though you may dearly wish to remain here, you cannot." The boy opened his mouth to argue, but Julius pressed on before Manny could argue. "First and foremost, the closest Lumen academy is over a two day trip to the south, as the quetzal flies."

That doesn't sound all that far. I mean, how fast could he fly? I bet someone could drive me there everyday, if I ever met another human Lumen that is... Boy that sounds weird.

"Such a trip would be several hundred miles in your terms, you see," Julius clarified.

Nope. That's too far.

"Consequently, you could not lodge here and receive an adequate education," the quetzal said. Tavo nodded in agreement. "But more importantly, you cannot remain in the Lumen world without your parents' permission," Julius ended congenially.

Well, I'll never get to come back, then. It took months to convince Mamá to allow me to travel to Costa Rica for just five days. "She'll never let me come back," said Manny, crestfallen, his hopes sinking through the cracks in the table.

"Of whom do you speak?" Tavo asked.

"When she finds out about me getting separated from the rest of the tour group, I'll probably never be allowed to leave again," Manny muttered to himself, ignoring the unicorn's question.

Tavo tilted his head. "Are you referring to your mother?"

"Tour group?" squawked Julius, thunderstruck. He turned to face Tavo. "How do we approach this?"

The unicorn blinked at the quetzal once before saying, "Amigo, as I am not as enlightened as you in the ways of the outside world, I am unaware of what a tour group is." Tavo looked to the boy. "Manny, could you shed some light on the situation for me?"

"What? What situation?" asked Manny, lost in his thoughts.

"The tour group," replied Tavo patiently. "What does it involve?"

The tour group? Manny frowned. "Oh, you mean Sr. Soriano's class?"

"Class?" muttered Tavo, confused. "Then a 'tour group,' as you call it, is another word for a 'class' in the outside world?" Tavo appeared uncertain, his head angled to the side.

Julius shifted on his perch, and Manny thought that he again caught the hint of a frown on the quetzal's brow as the boy replied, "Um, no. Most classes don't fit the tour group mold. My class is

51

visiting several popular sights in Costa Rica—that's called 'touring'."

Tavo blinked twice, muttering to himself, "Touring, hmmm… a new concept. I suppose it is good to learn a new thing or two everyday." Raising his eyebrows with a perplexed expression, he asked, "But why would you tour Costa Rica if you live here, within the country itself?"

Julius rolled his eyes and looked at the table, shaking his head in disbelief. "One would think he were a horse," breathed the quetzal quietly.

Manny's eyes widened in fear of Tavo's retort. But whether the unicorn did not hear Julius or simply chose to ignore him, Tavo asked, "You are Costa Rican, are you not?"

"Well, no, Tavo. I'm from the United States—from Arizona, actually," explained Manny lightly, trying not to make the unicorn appear stupid and eyeing Julius all the while. *At least he's not scowling.* "I came here with some other students and my teacher for our eighth-grade class trip. We flew in on Sunday night on a five-day tour of the country, and we're flying back on Friday morning from San José to Phoenix."

Julius coughed to draw Tavo's attention, but the unicorn plunged ahead in conversation.

"So, has your 'tour,' as you call it, been an enjoyable one?" asked Tavo, blinking confidently. The quetzal glared sharply.

"Pues, the trip was honestly pretty lame until I met you guys," the boy answered with a smile. *At least I haven't had to see Nacho and those other jerks for a while. Ha! They'd die if they knew what I've been doing.*

Julius opened his beak to interject, but Tavo was too quick for the quetzal.

"Why had you not enjoyed your time here before yesterday?" asked the unicorn, confused again. "Is this not a beautiful country with kind people?"

Julius huffed.

"Well, it's not that. I love the countryside, the forest, the beach and all, and I guess the people are alright." *They still stared a lot, though.* "But like I said, not everyone's as nice as you two. Honestly, the rest of my class is a bunch of jerks." *Especially Nacho.*

"Why do you say—" began Tavo.

"¡Basta ya!" screeched Julius, once again enraged. "We do not have time to chat, as you so deftly stated when you entered with the breakfast that has not yet been eaten for the flapping of your enormous lips!"

Wow. Though Manny noted that Tavo was visibly hurt, the boy could not decide which beast seemed to be in a worst state of affairs—the stricken unicorn with the light of innocent shock in his eyes, or the perturbed quetzal, several feathers askew and purple knot bulging. *Definitely Julius.*

Julius's rigid glare fractured and crumbled as he saw the unicorn mutter breathlessly, "Enormous lips?"

His lips are big, but that's normal for an animal of his type... I guess.

"Perdóname, amigo. I am very sorry," Julius said apologetically, shame assuaging the bird's rage. "It's not that I—I mean, I know that in school the other students, they—can you find it in your heart to—"

This is taking a bad turn. "Now, I'm not an expert on this stuff, but I'm willing to bet that since Tavo's your bud, he'd be willing to let a senseless comment or two slide, " said Manny encouragingly to the stuttering quetzal.

The bird glanced at the boy and considered this for a moment, then lowered his jade head and stared at the table as he eyed the unicorn furtively. But Tavo was now contemplating Manny with candid interest.

When Manny turned his eyes to Tavo, the unicorn looked down quickly, noticing the bowl filled copiously with the freshly peeled fruit. Shaking his mane gently, Tavo wove three miniature bowls from several strands of morning light, filling the first recipient with glittering passion fruit and sliding it to the quetzal. Manny received a bowl heaped with pineapple, bananas, and kiwi, while Tavo anticipated the papaya. Manny had inhaled half the bowl when

53

he heard Tavo say, "Buen provecho," nodding coolly first to Manny, then to Julius. The unicorn lowered his head and began to eat.

"Uh, yeah," spoke Manny through a mouthful of fruit, "eat up!" Manny swallowed and smiled at Tavo, whose lips were now stained orange. "And gracias for the fruta!"

"Verdad," chirped Julius positively. "I agree," he added, diving ravenously into the crimson fruit.

A moment later Manny reached for the bowl at the center of the table to acquire more fruit. "That's won't be necessary," stated the quetzal kindly, "I can get that." Shaking his cherry pendant, Julius transferred a generous helping of papaya and melon into Manny's bowl. "But before you continue," said Julius, catching Manny with a handful of papaya just a breath from the boy's mouth, "I must ask you a question."

Ugh. I'm so hungry. Manny's mouth was watering as he replied, "Shoot." *I can't believe I just spit on the table.* The boy's face glittered brightly with embarrassment.

"At what time were you to leave the village?" Julius asked interestedly.

What time was that? Ten or eleven... "Ten-thirty," said Manny quickly, taking his chance to devour the juicy papaya.

"Why do you ask, Ju—" Tavo paused. "Oh..." he added heavily. The next second the unicorn turned his head to the left, gauging the sunlight through the door.

"Caramba," muttered Julius to himself, distressed.

"What's the big deal?" asked Manny between bites of honeydew.

As Tavo turned his head to reply, Manny noted that the unicorn's features were pallid and dull, rather than bright white. "It's Friday, Manny," said the unicorn sickly. "And it's eleven o'clock."

Ripped to Shreds

Kevin Soriano was generally a patient man, or so he thought, until he volunteered to lead a twenty-student trip to Central America in order to broaden his pupils' horizons. 'This was supposed to be the perfect opportunity for them to practice their Spanish,' he thought to himself. 'A safe environment, under the supervision of a faculty chaperone and a pair of adept local tour guides,' he recalled.

"Adept my a—," he started, finding himself aching in the very part of his body that he attempted to postulate, having slipped in a slick, mud-like substance. "Dang," he muttered to himself. "What was that?" He searched the the forest path until he located the source of his fall, which clung to the new pair of hiking boots that he had purchased prior to his departure five days earlier. The man grimaced as he ran his finger through the substance, drawing the sludge close to his nose and sniffing hastily. He nearly gagged as the ripe scent ripped through his nostrils.

Recovering a moment later he said, "What is this, monkey sh —" But before he could finish his question, a tiny, bullet-like object tore through the air and cracked the man on the skull. "Geez!" he cried, shielding his face with his hands for fear of what might come next. "Is this punishment for being a bad teacher?" he yelped.

Standing up cautiously, he took several wary steps forward, dragging his left foot along the ground to discard the animal feces, half-expecting a subsequent attack. Stopping, he knelt to pick up the tiny missile that had met his cranium a moment before. "A nut? Nuts don't fall from trees at that kind of velocity..." Soriano said, rolling the sphere in his palm. As he dared to face the canopy, the sunlight illuminated the man's sharp features and black hair, though his light brown eyes hid below his left hand.

'Is that an eye?' he asked himself. Blinking, he lost sight of the jet orb in the myriad of leaves. He shivered. "Weird," he muttered, continuing on at a cautious pace, then speeding up to a jog and an outright run when he recalled why he had reentered the forest in the first place. The avid runner that he was, he found his track to be rather easy. 'If only I were back home, I wouldn't be in a problem like this,' he thought.

Little more than five minutes later, Soriano reached a small clearing and nearly toppled to the ground over his now leaden feet. "Oh, no," he groaned, despair inundating him. His mind raced. 'I am going to lose my job. No—wait! Maybe I can somehow cover this up. What can I do?' Soriano's eyes rolled over the scene before him, over the set of blue playing cards scattered and thrown from one end of the glade to the other; over the disassembled flashlight whose batteries lay below the signpost on his left; over the torn, multi-colored sweat rags and defaced drawings; all buried below an ocean of disintegrated crackers and antacids.

Dragging his feet through the debris, Soriano approached the center of the clearing and grabbed a blue strap that protruded from beneath countless shreds of paper to reveal a mutilated backpack, torn severely and missing the sister strap. Within the pack lay half a pencil and two colones. Running his fingers along the slashed fabric, Soriano wondered aloud. "It's not frayed. If an animal had done this, like a jaguar or something, the fabric would be frayed. Why's it smooth? It looks like it's been—" His finger stopped over a bubbled section of fibers. "Has it been burnt?" Another thought occurred to him. "There's not any blood," he stated, surprised. "But that means —Manny could still be alive."

Lowering the pack in his right hand, Soriano searched the clearing again, this time noticing another path branching off to the right that mirrored the path from which he had entered. Facing north he considered a third path that proceeded straight ahead several paces and then turned abruptly east.

'He could be anywhere,' Soriano thought. "Anywhere except the village," he said dully. Another thought penetrated his worried mind. "But what if he's been kidnapped?" he asked himself. 'I'm going to lose my job,' he reasoned. 'If only those guides had been doing theirs, Manny wouldn't have been lost in the first place.' Soriano stared at the backpack for a moment, his brow creased.

"There's no way I can cover this up," he concluded finally. "I have to find him. And those oh-so-adept guides are going to help me," he added nastily, dropping the backpack and running back down the path from which he came.

Coasting into the village and breathing heavily, Soriano checked his watch. 'It's eleven-fifteen,' he thought. "We'll probably miss our flight," he mumbled, clenching his fist. 'But if I can find Manny, I won't have lost my job,' he reflected.

As his feet met a dirt road Soriano headed east, trudging along past several brightly colored houses and through a small plaza displaying a handful of scantily frequented shops selling such items as baskets and traditional clothing to handcrafted jewelry and instruments.

Just as Soriano had turned south and was about to exit the plaza, a shopkeeper called, "¡Americano! You want see my clothes?" The shopkeeper, a short man boasting dark copper skin and a wide, kind face, was of indigenous descent, specifically known as El Bibrí. He was clutching a tunic woven of fabrics of various tropical colors that glinted in the warm morning sun. Soriano, however, met the man's offer with a callous glare, leaving both the plaza and the grinning Bibrí behind in his wake.

"No tengo tiempo para necedades," Soriano muttered to himself. 'I've got to find Manny,' he thought, jogging the last hundred steps to reach a large building that looked much like a compound, being surrounded by brick walls on three sides and a black iron fence along the front. The man stopped before the gate and rattled the locked door.

"¡Abre paso!" bellowed Soriano forcefully. He waited several seconds before losing his patience and shaking the barred door violently. "Hey, let me in!" he repeated, his voice rising and tearing through the high-windowed, blue building.

Less than two seconds later a pair of children came running out onto the flower-covered terrace looking out over the lush patio bounded by the iron fence.

"¿Qué tiene, Sr. Soriano?" called the girl, her face framed by scores of tropical orchids as she leaned over the balcony.

"What's up?" yelled the boy, hopping up and sitting on the stone banister beside a substantial flower pot.

"Nothing's wrong," grunted Soriano to the girl. "And get down, Esteban, before you fall and break your neck." Glaring at the boy, he thought, 'I don't need any more parents mad at me than are already going to be.'

As Esteban slid down, smiling, the girl leaned further over the balcony, her long, dark brown hair floating among the orchids. "Are you sure you're okay, Señor? Esteban and I are pretty good at solving problems you know," she chimed encouragingly. Esteban nodded. Standing beside one another they looked very much alike, both having the same soft features arranged in an expression of utmost helpfulness.

Soriano loosened his grip on the gate. "Gracias, Estela, pero I need you and Esteban to go and tell Miguel and Luis to come and let me in." A pause. "We need to talk," he growled through his teeth.

"Well, actually—" Estela began.

"They fell asleep on the patio out back," blurted Esteban.

"Are you serious?" yelled Soriano incredulously, drawing the heads of two additional students to the window nearest the balcony.

"Oh, hey, Señor!" cried one of the girls, waving.

"Where have you been?" the other called.

Submerged in seething thought, Soriano ignored his pupils. 'I left them to supervise the kids, and they're asleep! What kind of guides are they? But what should I expect if they couldn't even do a proper head count when we left the forest yesterday? I don't deserve this.' Soriano grabbed his throbbing skull.

"¡Eh, Señor!" called Esteban, now remounted upon the banister. "Weren't we supposed to leave for San José, like at ten?"

"No!" cried Estela, glaring at her brother, "We were supposed to leave at ten-thirty!"

"But it's nearly twelve, Señor! ¿Qué pasa?" called Esteban again.

"Yeah, what's the deal," yelled the first girl from the window.

"And when's lunch, Señor?" called the other. "¡Me muero de hambre!"

"No kidding, I'm starving!" cried Esteban.

This unforeseen barrage of interrogation punctured what patience Soriano had left. As he let go, his stability hung in the stagnant air for a moment, until a subtle breeze carried away all restraint, dispersing it among the towering trees. "Just get down here and let me in!" barked the teacher.

Estela raised her eyebrows in surprise, leaning back and glancing at her brother. With her left hand she motioned for him to go downstairs and let Soriano in. He shook his head, dumbfounded by Soriano's rage.

"Have you ever seen him that angry?" whispered one of the girls in the window to the other.

"Fine!" Estela said loudly, spinning around and whipping the swaying orchids with her hair. A moment later she stomped onto the patio and turned, crossing a brick path to reach a pillar at the southeast foundation of the building. After flipping a switch, she walked out onto the grass and crossed her arms, throwing a fiery glare up at her brother through the palm leaves. When she looked back down she noticed that Soriano had already crossed the patio and entered the building. Jumping, Estela realized that she had left the gate open, so she quickly ran back to the column and flipped the switch again, for 'you never know what a foreigner might do if he gets in here,' she thought. Now afraid, she bolted to the door, threw herself inside, and locked it—all in under five seconds.

"Señor?" she called, concern lining her voice. No one answered as she scanned the first floor, looking straight ahead into the bright dining area, left through the kitchen door, and finally right toward the curving staircase, which she swiftly climbed to reach the hallway that stretched north and south along the second floor. To her right Estela saw two girls walking hurriedly toward her, both apparently quite offended and chatting rapidly.

"Can you believe what he said?" asked one, glancing at the other in anticipation.

"No," replied the other, stunned. "Why's he being such a jerk all of a sudden?"

By now the pair was immediately in front of Estela. "Who's being a jerk?" she asked. They halted, facing her.

"Sr. Soriano!" said the first, angrily pointing back down the hallway. "He told me to buzz off and go to my room! Can you believe that?"

"No…" said Estela, surprised, following the girl's finger with wide eyes. "I can't."

"Well, believe it!" snapped the other girl. "Or just go find out for yourself. Let's go, Anita!" she added, grabbing Anita by the arm and dragging her up the hall.

"Qué extraño," muttered Estela to herself, perplexed. Walking down the hall, she slowly approached the open doorway on the right. Just before she reached the door a shoe came flying through the air and hit the opposing wall, causing the girl to jump with fright.

"Señor?" she squeaked, her voice stretched taut in worry. "What's wrong?" She peeked carefully around the doorframe in fear of a subsequent projectile meeting her in the face. "Can I help?" Estela was startled to find her teacher's room littered with shirts, pants, and hiking tools. 'He's not like this at school; everything is all nice and organized in our classroom,' she thought, frowning deeply.

"Where are my two-way radios?" he growled fiercely as he dumped his rucksack onto his bed. 'If only I had taken them out of my pack before we set off into the forest, none of this mess would ever have happened,' he thought. "They should be in here… Ugh!" he yelled, throwing down the pack and turning around voraciously. Estela jumped again, Soriano's unnaturally feverish eyes piercing her own.

"What?" he barked.

"I—I saw my brother playing with one last night," she said shrilly.

"Those aren't toys!" he bellowed, tearing past her increasingly wet face and up the hall toward the balcony. "Esteban!" he yelled, reaching the balcony not a second later. "¿Dónde están mis radios?"

"Whoa!" cried Esteban, his mind locking in shock as he toppled backward over the banister. Fortunately for Esteban, however, Soriano lunged forward just in time to snag the boy by the ankle. Soriano's free hand, now locked on the banister, provided sufficient leverage for him to hoist Esteban back up over the stone railing just as Estela reached the balcony and screamed.

"What happened?" she shrieked, her voice cleaving the air. "What did you do to mi hermano?" As Soriano laid Esteban on the ground, Estela ran up to the man and thrust him away. "You are acting completely loco, Señor!" she cried, pulling her brother further and further away from their teacher.

Estela's reaction wrenched Soriano's mind back into reality, his conscience smashing his heart to the ground for his belligerent behavior. He stared at the great stone-tiled floor in utter shame.

"Well?" cut Estela searingly. "What do you have to say about all this?"

"I—" stuttered Soriano, eyes frozen to the floor. A moment later he tore his gaze from the tiles and said, "I'm truly sorry for losing myself, kids." His dark complexion was splotched crimson. "I'm sorry, Esteban, for yelling at you and scaring you and causing you to fall." For a moment he looked down again, but he quickly looked back up into Estela's eyes and said, "But I didn't push your brother over the balcony, if that's what you were thinking!"

"Good!" she replied sharply. "But mi mamá still won't be happy about this. And just wait 'til Papá finds out!"

"I don't see why we have to—" began Esteban.

"¡Cállate!" she said, glaring at him. "How do we even know we can trust him anymore?"

At this point a crowd of ten or more students had huddled around the entrance to the balcony. When Estela made this last comment nearly all had gasped, staring at one another open-mouthed. Facing her peers on the left, Estela said, "What are you all gaping for? Haven't you heard Sr. Soriano ranting and raving for the past ten minutes?"

Several of the girls whispered to one another through the corners of their mouths. Most of the boys just shrugged.

"Como sea…" muttered Estela, turning back to Soriano. "Señor, you never act like this in class. What's the deal?"

Most of the girls nodded in agreement and one whispered, "Sí," eyeing Soriano closely.

Soriano felt the pressure of their earnest stares boring down upon him. "Well, uh—" he stammered. 'I can't tell them why I really got upset; they might blab to their parents and I'll lose my job for sure.' Estela's brow was becoming increasingly furrowed, coinciding with the tightening death grip she had around her brother's ribcage. "You see, I—" Soriano's mind raced, jumping from the torn backpack up the trail to the village square to the iron gate and up the stairs to his room…

"My two-way radios!" he screamed, causing all the children to jump. One of the girls nearly fell over for surprise. Thankfully, her friend caught her. Soriano's eyes leapt back to Esteban, but the man repressed a frown. The boy gulped. "Tu hermana told me that you might know where they are, Esteban," said Soriano evenly, careful not to betray any hint of displeasure or accusation. The boy swallowed again.

After glancing from her nearly petrified brother to her now seemingly benign teacher, Estela snapped, "Why do you care? It's not like you need them now, anyway. It's time to go! Our flight has probably already left!"

"Yeah!" agreed three of the boys, speaking for the first time.

"And when's lunch," called a taller boy with soft features and lighter skin than his classmates. "I'm starving."

"Sí," agreed the girls again, louder this time.

"Escúchenme," Soriano said, stretching out one hand toward the children in the entryway and rising to his full height. "I, well, lost something in the forest, and we can't leave until I find it." He scanned their earnest faces. Turning to Esteban he added, "I need the radios to get it back."

"Why do you need them?" called a girl.

"So Miguel, Luis, and I can go out and search for it," Soriano replied.

"And what about all of us, here?" asked Estela sharply. "You can't just leave us." Several of the boys' eyes lit up at this prospect, particularly the taller one.

Soriano balled his left fist. "No, I can't. I hadn't thought of that," he said, slightly aggravated. At this Estela seemed more satisfied, consequently loosening her grip around her brother's waist. "I guess Luis will just have to stay here with you guys." The tall boy's eyes grew enormous.

"But he doesn't speak English, Señor," commented one girl.

"I know, Anita, but—" began Soriano.

"And he's weird," added the girl next to her.

"And what about almuerzo?" asked a boy, unknowingly cradling his stomach.

"Escuchen, all of you," said Soriano with a slight edge. "You will just have to deal with it. I know you all still have some snacks from yesterday when we were in the plaza. Eat those. And listen to Luis," Soriano said as he turned to Esteban, missing the tall boy's increasingly hungry scowl. The man's eyes were set as he asked, "¿Dónde están?"

Ribs aching, Esteban coughed, pushing his sister away from him. "Pues, you see, I did play with one last night," he said, his eyes running along the grooves between the tiles, "but I wasn't the last one to have all three." The tall boy's eyes flashed. Another boy to his left shuffled uncomfortably.

"Who was?" asked Soriano sternly.

Esteban looked quickly to the tall boy, whose eyes were blazing, then back at the floor. "I forgot," he muttered.

Soriano turned and scrutinized the children's faces, noting the tall boy's innocent brown eyes among similar stares. "Who knows where they are?" Soriano asked the group. A hot breeze blew in reply. He turned back to Esteban and said objectively, "You know we can't leave until I get the radios and find what I lost." The boy shuffled his feet, silently counting the tiles. "Esteban, look at me."

Esteban tore his eyes from the tiles and stared at Soriano for a moment, the boy's resolve steadily crumbling. With his left hand he motioned for the teacher to follow him to the edge of the balcony. Soriano caught Estela's watchful eye as he approached the center of the terrace, next to Esteban. The boy pointed down through the orchids and whispered, "Act like I'm showing you something."

Soriano shook his head imperceptibly then caught on, nodding significantly. "Oh, that?" he blurted loudly, pointing to the ground below.

The tall boy was now on tiptoes, straining to see over the edge but failing.

"So, I'll get killed if I tell you who had them in front of everyone," continued Esteban in a whisper. "But I figure we'll never get out of here if I don't." He looked at Soriano out of the corner of his eye. "And I'm hungry," he added, looking back down at the patio and pointing exaggeratedly. "It was Nacho."

Nodding for a second, Soriano waited. He then exclaimed, quite loudly, "I see. Well if you don't want to tell me who had them, then, that's fine. I'll just have to find out on my own." Soriano turned around and faced the remaining students, which now included everyone on the trip. Stepping forward, Soriano noted the tall boy's satisfied smile.

"Where are the radios, Nacho?" Soriano asked gruffly.

Nacho's smile melted, nearly instantly transforming from confusion to distaste. Just as quickly the boy assumed a blank expression and said, "Whatever you may think, I didn't have the radios last." Turning and pointing at the closed door behind him, Nacho added, "Manny did."

"Wh-what do you mean by that?" stammered Soriano, caught off-guard.

"Just like I said, Manny had the radios last," stated Nacho flatly.

"But, I don't understand—" Soriano ejected. "H-how could he?"

"How could he? Because he's a little jerk, that's how!" Nacho exclaimed. "For your information, I saw Esteban, Tom, and Antonio playing with the radios last night when I thought to myself, 'Now Sr. Soriano wouldn't like that—those aren't toys.' So you know what? I took the radios and was on my way to your room to put them back when Manny knocked me down, snatched them from me, and locked himself in his room with them."

"That's impossible," muttered Soriano, his mind racing. 'If Manny was here last night, then when did he go missing?' he thought.

"That's because Nacho's a liar!" yelled Esteban, eyes flaming. "He's the one who grabbed your radios in the first place! It was his idea to play with them!" Nacho stared back with triumphantly cold eyes.

Thoroughly confused, Soriano's inhibition left him and he raised his hands. "Wait a minute!" he yelled. "When was the last time any of you saw Manny?"

Looking from side to side, several students shrugged. Anita and her ginger-haired friend whispered something to one another, but the majority stared vacantly back at Soriano.

"Who cares?" asked Nacho loudly.

"I care," replied Soriano sharply. "And didn't you just say that he had my two-way radios? So you had to have seen him last night."

"Uh, yeah, of course I did," replied Nacho, his voice stumbling momentarily but recovering quickly. "I wouldn't be surprised if he stuffed them in his backpack, or better yet, his luggage—that's where he puts everything else he steals, I bet," he said convincingly.

Soriano laughed, saying, "Oh, they're not in his backpack." A number of the students gazed back at him with confused faces; Estela glared.

"And how would you know that they're not in his backpack?" she retorted.

"Well…" Soriano began, his thoughts leaping to the mutilated backpack and the littered clearing. No two-way radios came to his mind. "Let's just say that I trust Manny on this one," he finished, smile fading.

"Well, you better check his luggage, then!" called Nacho pointedly. "I'm telling you, you can't trust him!"

"Fine," conceded Soriano, stepping forward as the children parted to reveal a poorly-painted, wooden door. Grasping the doorknob and opening the door, Soriano continued, "But I really doubt that—" He froze, choking on his words. "How did you—? But when—?" Soriano subsequently slipped inside, closing the door tightly on Nacho's incredulous stare.

Before the man, on a small, wood-framed bed, sat Manny. Light poured in through the window behind the boy, striking his skin and illuminating the small room. A shadow approached the door as Soriano at last vocalized his bewilderment. "But you were gone. How did you get back?"

Despite his outwardly calm appearance, Manny's mind was squirming. *Just great, what am I gonna tell him? There's more to getting back safely than simply reaching your room unnoticed. Why couldn't Julius have given me any ideas for an alibi?* "Uh, what do you mean, 'gone'?" he asked.

"I mean 'disappeared,' 'missing,' 'possibly attacked' or 'kidnapped,'" said Soriano frantically, hands in the air.

What can I tell him? What can I tell him? Ugh... "Well, I did just use the bathroom—is that what you mean?" Manny asked hesitantly. *He's never gonna buy that.*

"The bathroom?" answered Soriano, stunned. "You mean you've been here?"

"Pues, sí," replied Manny. *At least for a few minutes.*

"Hold on," Soriano said, snatching a chair and sitting down across from the boy. The man's brain was throbbing as he gazed at the floor, head in hands. Gathering up his scattered thoughts from the pockmarked floor Soriano peered at Manny and asked, "What about your backpack?"

"My backpack?" Manny wondered aloud. He suddenly jumped. *My backpack! I left it in the clearing when Julius was attacked. That's when I almost left my wand.* Manny's hand lay on the mahogany watch on his wrist as he replied, "What about it?"

"What about it?!" exclaimed Soriano in disbelief. "Why was it nearly torn to shreds? Weren't you attacked?"

What the—? Torn to shreds! Manny frowned. "Well, I wasn't attacked..." he muttered mysteriously, emphasis on self.

"What do you mean by that?" Soriano stipulated.

Manny shook himself. "Oh! I, well, uh—no, Sr. Soriano. I wasn't attacked," he stated, backpedaling.

"Well, I was," mumbled Soriano, once again running his sore eyes along the floor.

"It wasn't a nut, was it?" snorted the boy.

"Yes, actually, it was," began Soriano slowly. "How did you know?" he asked suspiciously, head raised and gazing into the boy's inexcusably perplexed face.

"Lucky guess?" postulated Manny evasively. "I'm glad to see you're alright and that you didn't need any bandages," he added quickly. "Projectiles like that can be dangerous, you know." *What's the deal, anyway? Who's taking pot shots at everyone in the forest?*

"Thanks, I suppose," replied Soriano blankly. Frowning, he sat up. "But how did your backpack end up in that clearing, then, if you weren't attacked? The contents were thrown every which way and the backpack actually appeared to have been singed."

Singed? What in the world? "I guess I must've left it behind on accident," resolved Manny, though he thought Soriano still eyed him skeptically. Before the man could continue, however, the boy asked, "What do you mean by 'singed?'"

Opening his hands before him Soriano explained, "You know, as if the fabric were melted where the backpack had been cut. It was very strange. If it were an animal, I would have expected the fabric to be frayed..."

Singed... I'll have to store that in my memory banks and think on it later. "So, Sr. Soriano, hadn't we ought to leave pretty soon?" asked Manny, feigning passivity. "We really don't want to miss our flight."

Soriano blinked twice before the message registered. "Oh, yeah," he acknowledged, rising to his feet somewhat doggedly. "But just to make sure your story cross-checks with Nacho's, I better have a look in here." The man stumbled awkwardly toward Manny's luggage case, which he lay lengthwise across the floor and swiftly unzipped.

"What are you doing?" asked Manny, startled.

"I'm looking for something," replied Soriano furtively.

"Well, what?" asked the boy, his voice rising. "All that's in there are my clothes and some souvenirs." *Oh, don't touch my underwear, Sr. Soriano. That's just weird.*

"Not in here, I guess," mumbled the man, zipping the main compartment back up and turning the case to scavenge through the front pockets.

What's not in there? Manny began, "You know, Sr. Soriano, I really feel like you're invading my—"

"Ah, here they are!" interjected Soriano, reaching down into the deepest pocket.

"There what is?" asked Manny, at a loss and rather aggravated.

Standing up and facing the boy, Soriano raised his right hand to display three black radios, antennas clasped tightly in the man's fingers. He smiled knowingly and said, "Sometimes people tell the truth and the only way to know is to catch them in a lie."

Okay, that made no sense at all. I think he's even more lost than I am. "Where did those come from?" asked Manny in surprise.

"Don't play dumb with me, Manuel López," replied Soriano cleverly. "I know that you took these from Nacho last night and planned to keep them. You're just fortunate that I didn't find any other stolen goods in your luggage."

Stolen goods? "What are you talking about?" snapped Manny. "I haven't stolen anything, and I don't know how those got in my luggage. Are they Nacho's? I've never seen them in my life."

Soriano furrowed his brow and glared at the boy, as if to kindle within Manny any amount of guilt that he might be repressing or denying regarding the radios.

I never get that look, well, except from Mamá.

Nevertheless, the man's glare softened, creasing into one last look of confusion. "But if you were here last night, why did I find pillows stuffed under your sheets this morning when I couldn't find you?"

Good question. I don't know the answer to that one myself. Who did do that? Recalling breakfast in Tavo's cabana, Manny responded placidly, "That's probably about the time when I was just sitting and enjoying the sunshine."

"Oh," muttered Soriano. "But why the pillows if—"

Three loud knocks came at the door and caused both man and boy to jump with fright. "Ya es hora de salir," called a voice. The door opened and a short man with solid, caramel eyes peered around the frame until he met Soriano's gaze. "Miguel dice que necesitamo' salir ahora. Ya estamo' atrasado'."

"Espere, Luis," said Soriano to the man, left hand raised. Turning back to face the boy he continued, "Manny—"

"Miguel dice ahora," Luis cut in sternly. "Ya 'stán atrasa'os y si no nos partimos pa'l aeropuerto, perderán su vuelo."

Glaring at the boy for a moment, Soriano finally said, "You're lucky we're late. And you'll be even more lucky if I don't punish you for stealing my two-way radios," he finished, turning quickly and following Luis into the hall, the pair rattling away in Spanish. A moment later Manny heard Soriano yell, "Everyone, get your stuff on the bus, now! And pray that we reach the airport in time to catch our flight!"

"Wow, that was close." Manny sighed. *And what's he getting at saying that I stole his stuff?* Glancing to the right, he scanned his luggage bag, which was now surrounded by a heaping moat of clothes and underwear. "Geez." Manny leaned forward, intending to get up and collect his belongings, when without warning a pair of hands slammed into his chest and forced him back down onto the bed.

"¿Qué te pasa?" cried Manny, kicking instinctively to defend himself and clipping his attacker's jaw. Recovering in a flash,

Manny pushed himself back up to find Nacho rubbing the side of his mouth. "What was that for, you jerk?" snapped Manny.

Pointing at Manny with his right hand, Nacho said, "I don't know how you got back in here, but next time, you're going down for sure. If I had my way, you would have gotten expelled."

"¿Qué es tu problema?" Manny cut back, trying to rise to his feet.

"My problem? You're my problem," growled Nacho, pushing Manny back down onto the bed. "You're lame, you're annoying, and I'm sick of looking at you!"

"Oh, get over yourself and go harass Antonio!" exclaimed Manny, eyes bursting aflame. "I've never done anything to you!"

"You're a fool," replied Nacho. "But I will get you expelled," he added, pointing again.

"Oh, and how do you expect to do that?" Manny mocked. *Hold it.* "Soriano said something about me taking his radios from you. Did you put those with my stuff?"

Nacho clapped. "Simply amazing, Sherlock. But Luis helped you weasel out of that," he said, glaring. "I can't believe he bought it that you were here! Soriano's even dumber than you are!"

"Who's to say I wasn't here?" asked Manny, surreptitiously scooting to the edge of the bed.

"Of course you weren't here!" cried Nacho. "But I'm the only person on this trip with enough sense to notice when someone's gone missing. Too bad you weren't mauled by a wild animal or something," he jeered wryly.

Manny considered the monkey's vicious fangs. *You don't know the half of it.*

Sobering slightly, Nacho continued, "Actually, I helped you in a way."

"What the heck do you mean?" Manny asked, his face screwed up in disbelief.

"The pillows, nitwit," bit Nacho.

Now stationed at the corner of the bed, Manny promptly realized that his left hand lay on top of one of the concealed pillows.

Oh. "You planted these?" he asked, signaling the remaining pillows with his hand.

"Uh, yeah," scoffed Nacho. "But if I hadn't, Soriano would have caught you last night and it would have been adiós Manny."

"If I'm lucky I won't have to put up with you next year, anyway," Manny stated severely. Before Nacho could form a retort Manny shot to his feet, shoving his opponent hard in the chest and causing him to stumble out the door and onto the balcony. "So stay away from me."

"Manuel, Ignacio, get your carcasses out of that house and onto this bus in under a minute or you both will have to apply for Costa Rican citizenship!" roared Soriano from beyond the terrace.

Manny jolted, instantly turning and cramming his clothing back into his luggage as he heard Nacho say, "You're dead."

"Como sea," muttered Manny, rolling his eyes and his luggage out into the hallway, from which point he clattered down the stairs, dashed through the wooden doors, past the gate and up to the beige bus, leaving his luggage just outside the door for Luis to stuff into the back. "Gracias, Luis," he called, soaring up into the cab and nodding at Miguel, now performing the role of driver. Smiling awkwardly as he passed Soriano on his right, Manny walked along the aisle until he found an open seat halfway along the left side of the vehicle, stifling laughter as he watched Nacho nearly trip over his own luggage on the way across the patio.

"Finally," uttered Soriano sarcastically as Nacho tromped up the aisle to the very back of the bus.

"Muévete," he commanded a shorter boy with a round face and darker skin, who at once scooted over to allow Nacho the comfortable aisle seat.

After Luis had finished loading the luggage and boarded the bus, Miguel executed a speedy U-turn and tore off to the north along the rutted dirt road, narrowly dodging potholes and children at play.

Manny sighed as he peered across the bus and into the jade trees. *What a great trip.*

Friction

"What do you mean you almost missed the plane?" came a sharp voice, its words mincing the air.

Manny shifted uncomfortably in the back seat of the silver car, glancing to his right into the blue desert and feeling the slight prick of the dark cacti racing along the outside of the window. "Mamá, don't worry about it," he replied calmly, hoping his mother would drop the issue and ask him about a less dangerous topic, such as the beach at Puerto Limón or the streets of San José.

"¿No te preocupes?" María repeated in disbelief. "How can I not worry? If you had missed the plane, there's a chance that you all would have been forced to take separate flights back home. That means some of you would have been traveling without a chaperone!" she added, twisting around in the passenger side seat to pincer Manny with her gaze. His chest ached under the pressure-clench of her eyes. *How does she do that?* After turning and straightening up in her seat, María asked in a lighter tone, "Exactly why did you almost miss the flight in the first place?"

Swallowing hard, Manny felt needles pierce his throat. *I can't tell her what really happened... She'd ground me for eternity and then I'd never get to be a Lumen.*

"I asked you a question, Manuel," María clipped dangerously.

Throat so tight he could hardly speak, Manny replied, "Well, honestly, something got lost and Sr. Soriano spent some time trying to find it."

"Oh he did, did he?" she asked sharply. "And what item could have been so important as to delay your return to the airport?"

"Maybe he misplaced the students' identification," commented a helpful voice from the driver's seat.

"Oh, Carlos, how could he misplace those?" argued María. "Surely he kept your identification in a safe place, didn't he, Manuel? He probably carried it on him wherever you all went."

"Yeah, he did," Manny answered dully, gazing into the desert with his head propped up on his right arm. *I don't want to talk about Sr. Soriano anymore.*

"Maybe he lost his car keys. Was that it, Manny?" asked an animated boy sitting on Manny's left.

"You're right, Zane, that would be a problem," stated Carlos objectively. "A man needs his keys to drive."

"Oh, he didn't drive in Costa Rica, you two! And Carlos, you should've known that! Don't you remember the last orientation meeting we had before the kids left? Kevin said that the tour guides would be driving them around in a bus. Kevin wouldn't've had the keys anyway!" María concluded.

Kevin... Manny almost shivered as he considered Soriano's first name. *That just sounds weird.*

"I suppose I forgot, dear," replied Carlos mellowly.

"Good guess, anyway," said Manny to Zane with a light punch to his younger cousin's arm.

Pushing back with a half smile, Zane asked, "So what was he looking for?"

Can't we just drop this?

"Yes, Manny, what was it?" asked María expectantly as she glanced back over her seat.

Manny's mind raced, eyes combing the still-warm sand stretching out under the stars. *Oh!* He quickly turned to face his mother and cousin. "Well, actually, we left right after he found his two-way radios," he said.

"Two-way radios?" muttered Zane.

"You would need those," Carlos observed. "Especially if you were leading as many kids as he was."

"¡Qué ridículo!" cried María, causing the other three to jump.

Carlos pulled the car back into the right lane, narrowly missing a truck, its horn thundering. "Whoa," he muttered. "Cálmate, María."

"You mean to tell us that you almost missed your plane over a set of walkie-talkies?" she roared, ignoring her husband. "If I had gone, as I thought I should have, not only would the radios not have been lost, but we would have arrived at the airport three hours early!"

"Mamá, I told you, it would have been so embarrassing if you'd gone with us," Manny groaned.

"They're bad enough as it is," muttered Zane, adding in a whisper, "Could you imagine how horrible your trip would have been if your mom went with you?"

"I don't even want to think about that," replied Manny with a sickened look.

"I agree with Manny," Carlos added. "A boy needs some time to stretch his legs and run on his own."

With a steel glare to her husband, María said, "Well, since I wasn't there, Sr. Soriano should have been more responsible. I'll be talking to him tomorrow about his negligent behavior as the faculty chaperone."

Manny's eyes nearly fell from his face as his parents kept talking. *No!*

"¿Qué pasó, Manny?" asked Zane, suddenly concerned.

Glancing at the back of his mother's seat, Manny whispered, "I've got a major problem."

"What?" Zane asked covertly, eyes jumping from cousin to aunt and back again.

"I'll have to tell you about it later," Manny breathed, nodding toward María with eyebrows raised.

"Está bien," Zane replied with a nod of his own.

"...so I'll just drive out to his house and line this whole thing out," said María resolutely.

"You are a woman with no bounds. Just don't embarrass Manny when you go out there," Carlos insisted.

"Embarrass him?" said María irately. "I'm more concerned about our son's well-being in that man's classroom if he can't even keep track of two walkie-talkies!"

It was three, actually.

"That's what I was afraid of," groaned Carlos.

"What is that supposed to mean?" she snapped.

"Ugh…" Carlos groaned, rolling his eyes.

Maybe I can get out of the house before she leaves for Sr. Soriano's house. "Hey, Zane, how long are you staying at our house tomorrow?" Manny whispered.

"I dunno," Zane replied. "Mamá said that she's taking Berta and me out to lunch and then shopping for summer clothes, though." He too rolled his eyes.

Sounds boring. Manny thought of Soriano and his mother both grilling him at once. "Can I come?" he asked.

"I was hoping I could get out of it and just stay at your house," Zane replied, half pleading.

That could work, too. "Let's go for that. We can surely convince your mom to let you stay since I've been trapped with twenty people that hate me for a week," Manny said brightly.

"Awesome," sighed Zane in relief. "I hate shopping."

"…no, just listen to me. There is only one day left of school. What could happen to Manny if he's in Sr. Soriano's room for just forty-five minutes?" contended Carlos.

"Forty-five minutes later and the kids would have missed their flight!" stormed María.

"That makes no sense at all…" Carlos countered.

A question picked at Manny's mind as the car drew further and further north, the lights from Phoenix progressively diminishing and countless stars emerging in the velvet sky above the evergreen trees on the hills ahead. *If Mamá barely let me go for a week to Costa Rica, how am I gonna get her to let me leave for what—like, months—to wherever the Lumen Academy is?* Manny sighed, gazing past the clouds and into the stars. *Maybe one of you can take me there.*

***

"Wait, wait wait. Are you kidding me?" asked Zane from the padded desk chair in the corner of Manny's room. "Birds don't talk for real, let alone that kaytza thingey that you're talking about. What are you getting at?"

75

"Just listen, man," pleaded Manny from his bed, staring hard into his cousin's annoyed eyes.

Zane sat back and crossed his arms, glaring skeptically through lucent eyes of cobalt steel. Second only to Manny, Zane had the lightest skin tone in the family, though he still maintained the López trait of having rich brown hair. "Do you think I'm an idiot?"

"Zane, geez, no, I don't think you're an idiot!" Manny tore back. "Just listen for a sec, will ya? Now the quetzal told me his name was Julius, and that I was a Lumen and that my camera was a wand."

"Your camera was a wand," repeated Zane, rolling his eyes.

"Yeah, it got changed into a block of wood and now I can mold it into any shape I want," Manny continued quickly. "Just watch!"

"You can't mold wood, Man—" But Zane stopped short as his cousin slipped the wooden watch from his left wrist as the timepiece began to glow, nearly instantly fusing together into a ball that lengthened and narrowed to form a cylindrical object.

As the light faded, Zane's voice constricted. "It's-It's a—"

"A wand. I told you," asserted Manny, slightly irritated that his cousin would not believe him on his word alone. *I guess I didn't believe Julius at first, though, either...* "Here, check it out," he added in a brighter tone, scooting to the edge of the bed and laying the wand in front of Zane.

"It's so dark," wondered Zane aloud, scanning the wand closely. "Do you know what type of wood it is?"

"No," Manny replied. "I never thought to ask.

"Oh," muttered Zane, looking back at the wand as he reached out his hand. "So how do I mold it?"

"Um, you can't," said Manny candidly.

"Hey, what's the deal?" exclaimed Zane, becoming aggravated as the wand kept rolling further and further from his hand. "Is it magnetic or something?"

"My bad," Manny laughed. "I forgot to mention that nobody can touch another person's wand."

"C'mon, I'm getting short-changed twice over here," Zane grumbled.

Manny was suddenly confused. "What are you talking about?"

"Well, first of all—why can't I have one of those?" Zane asked, pointing to the wand. "And second, nobody's ever come and told me that I was a Loominathing, or whatever you called it."

"That would be a Lumen," corrected Manny, pronouncing the term slowly. "And I don't know how it all works exactly, but hopefully when you turn fourteen next March you'll get a wand and find out you're a Lumen, too."

Zane stared out the window on his right, lost in thought as his mind treaded the ancient paths of the Costa Rican rainforests. "So who gave you your wand?" he asked.

"Who gave me my...?" uttered Manny, his voice trailing off into silence. He shivered as a scowl scourged his face. "I haven't thought about that! It was that sick monkey!"

His eyes not leaving Manny's for a second, Zane listened as his cousin recounted the incredible tale, from the foul slip along the deserted path to the heated argument with Nacho in the room across from the balcony.

Once finished, Manny nervously eyed a motionless Zane. *He doesn't believe me...*

"This is simply amazing!" shouted Zane, exploding from his chair with hands raised. "You are the coolest person I know! I can't wait for my birthday to get here! I bet Lumen blood runs in our family or something!"

"Then why aren't any of our parents Lumens?" asked Manny doubtfully.

"Oh, yeah, you're right," Zane admitted dully, though a moment later his expression changed again. "But maybe Abuelito was a Lumen!"

Abuelito—a Lumen... "I could see that," Manny said progressively. "He did love gazing at the stars; a lot like Tavo. I miss him a lot."

"Well, you'll see him soon enough," replied Zane quickly, eyes fluorescent.

"What do you mean by that?" exclaimed Manny with an odd look.

"I mean you're going to go to one of those Lumen Academies Julius told you about!" cried Zane. "You'll get to see Tavo there since you miss him so much!"

"I was talking about Granddad," Manny explained. "But there's just one problem—"

Heavy steps thundered in the hallway outside before the door flew open and María appeared, dressed in a lavender nightgown and her hair draped over her shoulders. Eyes aflame, she hissed, "Zane Loften López, you will not yell in this house, particularly considering how late it is! It's past eleven o'clock!"

"Lo siento, Tía," splurted Zane as he crashed back into the desk chair.

"If it happens again your mother and I will be having a chat," she snapped. "Understood?"

"Yes, Tía," said Zane, avoiding her fiery eyes.

"Bien. Now what were you yelling about, anyway?" she asked.

His stomach twisting, Manny looked at Zane desperately. *Don't tell her anything about the Lumen stuff!* He coughed, attempting to get Zane's attention, but the gesture went unnoticed.

"Well," began Zane, trepidatious eyes focused on his aunt's feet, "Manny was just telling me about—"

"How I had such a great time on the trip, Mamá!" Manny interjected hastily. "Thanks for letting me go!" He forced a nervous smile. *Zane, don't say any more!*

María scanned the two boys suspiciously. "You are welcome, Manny," she finally said. "But that's the last trip you will be going on unless I am with you." Manny's stomach crashed through the floor and into the living room below. *Oh no...* Walking across the room, María gazed into her son's eyes and kissed him on the forehead. "I am so glad you're back home safe, m'ijo. Tomorrow you can tell your father and me about your trip, too. But for now, get

78

to bed soon—the both of you. Buenas noches," she said, walking back across the room and closing the door softly.

"That was close," muttered Manny.

"Not really," countered Zane lightly. "I wouldn't have really told her about you being a Lumen and all. Even if I did, I doubt she would've believed me anyway."

"Either way, I'm condemned," said Manny hopelessly.

"What do you mean you're condemned?"

"Mamá can't come with me to the Lumen Academy," Manny continued. "She's not a Lumen. And in any case, I don't want her to come. That would be as bad as her coming to high school with me everyday."

"Ooh—real bad," consented Zane, nodding his head ominously. "So do you think Tío Carlos would let you go?"

"Yeah, I do. Dad's a lot more laid back than Mom is—you know that."

"So do you think he could convince her to let you go?"

"That's a long shot; I really doubt it, Zane," Manny sighed. *It's hopeless.*

"But there's gotta be a way to talk her into it," insisted Zane vaguely.

"Only by an act of God," Manny replied.

"Abuelito, can you hear me?" asked Manny, staring into the velvet sky littered with glowing lights, wishing that a constellation of his grandfather would form to comfort and guide him. At this elevation, far from the Phoenix lights, the stars shone quietly in reply. There Manny sat, hoping, gazing out over the shadowed mesas and reaching valleys of the now pale Painted Desert. "What can I say to Mamá to make her listen to me?" he whispered, his eyes sweeping across the white blanket of the Milky Way, waiting for a shooting star, if nothing else; but none came. The boy breathed deeply and sighed, half smiling. "I remember how you used to sit

79

right here next to me, just talking to me about my dreams and how I could do anything." He paused. "Well Granddad, I really want to do this." Manny closed his eyes. "Help me, God."

A scraping noise came from behind as the patio door slid open and closed, followed by quiet footsteps across the tepid bricks. "Enjoying the warm evening, son?" called the voice of his father from over Manny's shoulder.

"Yeah," Manny replied, opening his eyes slowly. "I just like looking at the stars."

"Your grandfather did, too," Carlos remarked, sitting in the chair next to his son. "He always did; at least as long as I can remember."

Though his mind was clear, Manny could not think of an easy way to approach his father about the subject of Lumens. *I don't want him to think I'm crazy like Zane did.*

"So where's Zane?"

"Asleep."

"Oh. He does seem to shut down quickly at night, doesn't he?"

"Yep."

Carlos scanned the sky before turning to Manny and asking, "So I suppose you found the North Star already, right?"

"Up there," answered Manny, pointing high into the northeastern sky. "And there's the Big Dipper," he added, his hand moving slightly to the left.

"Don't forget the Little Dipper just above it," Carlos added, pointing at the North Star again.

A thought suddenly came to Manny. "Hey, Dad—did Abuelo ever teach you where the Monoceros constellation was, maybe when you were visiting El Salvador one time or something?"

"Monoceros?" repeated Carlos uncertainly. "No, I don't think so. Why?"

"'Cause someone down in Costa Rica mentioned it to me; his name was Tavo, and he said that it can only be seen during winter," Manny said simply.

"Oh, well that's too bad," replied Carlos. "Tu abuelo only ever came once to visit over Christmas, and I don't recall him mentioning it."

"Are you sure he didn't show it to you when you were little?" Manny asked hopefully.

"No, I wasn't even one when we moved to Arizona," Carlos answered. "And honestly, the first time I returned was when you were born there. Once you came, nobody had time to stop and look at the sky, much less discuss out of season constellations."

The boy's heart sagged. *But if Abuelito loved stars all that much and lived in Central America, he had to know about Monoceros, especially if he were a Lumen.* "Would Tío José know?" Manny asked desperately.

"Manny, your uncle's never even been to El Salvador. He was born here, in Phoenix," Carlos replied frankly.

"Oh, yeah." Manny felt flattened. "But Grandma might know!" he added excitedly, turning and sitting sideways on the lounge chair.

"Es verdad, but why don't you just wait until tomorrow to ask her?" said Carlos. "She's asleep by now."

"Alright," Manny conceded, but as he leaned back in the chair optimism gripped his chest tightly. *I'm sure Abuelita will know about Monoceros! I mean, she was married to Abuelito, after all. He had to have told her about it. Heck, on top of that, she would know if he was a Lumen!*

"Well, I think I'm gonna head off to bed, bud," yawned Carlos, leaning forward in his chair.

Manny nearly jumped from his own, exclaiming, "No, Papá, wait! I—I wanted to talk to you about something else."

"Oh yeah? What?" asked Carlos through tired eyes, lying back in his chair slowly.

How do I put this? "Um, you remember how I mentioned Tavo, Papá?" Manny began cautiously. His father nodded. "So, there was this other guy, named Julius, and he told me a little about some schools down around South America somewhere." Manny paused to see what his father might say, but whether Carlos was thinking or merely tired, he remained silent. *Is he mad?* "Okay, so, what would you say to me attending school in South America?" Manny ended expectantly.

"Sounds like a great idea, m'ijo," replied his father quickly.

"Really?" said Manny, surprised at how swiftly his father had come to that decision.

"Pues, sí," Carlos rejoined positively. "There are a lot of great colleges and universities, particularly in Chile and Argentina."

An arrow pierced Manny's stomach, his hope deflating rapidly. "C-college?" Manny stammered.

"Isn't that what you meant?"

"Not exactly."

"You don't mean high school?" Carlos asked, his voice lined with disbelief. Manny merely stared back in reply. "You mean like an exchange student?"

"Sort of, I guess," Manny said, his hopes bruising.

Carlos took a deep breath and ran his fingers through his short, wavy hair. "Your mother will never allow it," he stated flatly.

"I know, Dad, but maybe you can talk her into it!" Manny asserted.

"And how am I going to persuade her to let you leave the country again if I can't even talk her out of driving to your teacher's house tomorrow?" exclaimed Carlos emphatically. "When her mind is set, you can't budge her. You know that!"

"Yes, I know, but—"

"No," Carlos interrupted sternly. "Even I would have to consider allowing you to go to high school in a foreign country. A week with a teacher is one thing, but a year or longer surrounded by total strangers—that's a completely different story."

"But Julius and Tavo aren't strang—" Manny tried to say.

"Te dije que no, Manuel," his father cut sharply. "As I told you, I will have to think on this one. In the meantime, if you are serious about this, then you had better be planning a strategy for convincing your mother, because I'm not even going to try."

"Fine," Manny groaned, head hanging low.

A moment later Manny felt his father's reassuring hand on his shoulder. "Listen, m'ijo," Carlos began. "Whether you go to high school in Arizona or in Colombia, you're an amazing son. And you'll see—a lot of good things are in store for you. I'm sure of it."

Manny looked up into his father's steady eyes that shone softly in the light from the boy's skin. "Thanks, Dad," he said.

"De nada," Carlos replied, slapping Manny on the shoulder and rising to his feet. "I want to hear more about your trip tomorrow," he added as he turned and walked back toward the glass door. "Until then, sleep well, m'ijo."

"So did you meet any beautiful girls while you were down there, Manny?" asked a lively voice in Spanish as it hovered over the stove.

Zane, seated across from Manny at the white, circular kitchen table, gave him a curious look with one eyebrow raised. "Yeah, one, I guess, Abuelita," Manny called back.

"¿Sólo una?" asked his grandmother, walking toward the table with a platter of steaming tortillas in one hand and a scrambled eggs mixture in the other. "Aren't all of us Central American women beautiful, Manny?" She halted, turning her head slightly in anticipation of Manny's response and looking altogether exotic in her bright blue and green apron stamped with enormous pink lilies. The short, bright-eyed woman blinked twice, smiling roguishly.

"Sí, Abuela, I suppose so," Manny conceded as he eyed the food in her hands. *I'm so hungry. I haven't had anything since that airplane lasagna yesterday afternoon.*

"Oh…" marveled his grandmother as she sat the platters down at the center of the table, both Zane and Manny instantly filling their plates with tortilla, egg, and salsa. "You suppose so…" Sitting down next to the boys, she watched them devour the breakfast with an expression of mirthful contentment. "So where did you meet her? In San José?"

Manny swallowed and gulped down some cold milk before quickly saying, "No, Puerto Limón."

"On the beach, eh?" his grandmother replied playfully. "What did she look like?"

Under Zane's interested eye Manny answered, "Well, she had long, dark hair and brown skin, and her laugh was really pretty." While his right hand reached across the table to grab another tortilla to make a second burrito, Manny's left hand managed to pop several melon chunks into his mouth.

"¿Una morena, eh? You know, I was morena once," she said, brushing a lock of her snow-white hair from her dark face. "But that was before either of you were born."

"¿De veras, Abuelita?" Zane asked through a mouthful of egg.

"Yes, really, cariño," replied his grandmother. Turning back to Manny she continued her banter. "What was her name?"

"Maricarmen," mumbled Manny through the honeydew.

"Maricarmen," she repeated blissfully. "What a sweet name. Not as sweet as Minta, though," she added with another roguish smile. "So did you kiss her, eh?"

Manny nearly choked on the honeydew, his eyes watering as the piece slid down his throat unwillingly. "Abuelita, don't ask me questions like that!" he strained after sucking down more milk.

"So did you?" Zane asked with a curiosity bordering desperation, his eyes fixed on his cousin's.

Glancing from Zane to Minta and back again, Manny reluctantly answered, "No." Manny's face flashed brightly in embarrassment as the two of them continued to eye him in anticipation. "She, uh—well, I mean, we were getting along fine until, you know, it was just—"

"Did you say something stupid, Manny?" Zane asked sharply, egg falling from the end of his burrito.

"Now don't be so negative," Minta chided. "Manny here is a handsome and well-spoken young man, just like his abuelo Gabriel."

I'll take handsome, but I don't know how good I am with words.

"What about me, Abuelita?" Zane asked, slightly affronted. "Don't I look a lot like Abuelito, too?"

"Sí, sí, m'ijo, now just eat your eggs," she quickly replied, turning back to her other grandson. "Adelante, Manny, so what happened?"

How do people always manage to trap me in these uncomfortable situations? "Well, truthfully, Nacho came along and told her that I had some disease called La Chagra that made my skin white," he groaned. "She left pretty soon after that."

"Jerk!" exclaimed Zane, splashing another tortilla and the table with salsa.

"Tch, tch, tch," clicked Minta as she rose from the table. "If your mother really wanted to protect you, she'd go speak with the parents of that foolish boy rather than bothering your teacher," she remarked, submerging the frying pan in the sink filled with soapy water and beginning to wash.

The thought of his mother chatting with Soriano robbed Manny of what remained of his appetite. *If he tells her that he thought I was lost, even for just five minutes, not only is he dead, but so am I.* He swallowed hard before asking in a higher tone, "So, Abuelita, how do you know that Mamá was going to talk to Sr. Soriano?"

"She told me before she left," Minta replied simply. Manny's food splashed in his stomach in sequence with the water in the sink.

Seeing Manny's eyes, Zane stopped eating and asked, "When did Tía María leave, Abuelita?"

As she rinsed the pan, Minta answered, "Oh, half an hour before the two of you came downstairs."

Manny considered walking down the hall to his left, where the bathroom was located. He wondered if he would be sick. Instead he looked across the table at Zane and whispered nauseously, "She could be back any minute, Zane. And when she gets here, I just know she'll be furious at me."

Just as Zane opened his mouth to suggest that the two of them escape through the sliding door behind Manny, the front door slammed shut on the other side of the house and a seething voice cried, "Manuel! Where are you?"

Manny nearly fainted as Minta walked behind Zane into the hall, drying her hands with a towel and calling back, "Now María, there's no need to yell. We're in the kitchen and—"

"Minta, ¡ya!" snapped María, whipping past her mother-in-law and into the kitchen to find both boys on their feet and nearing the sliding door. "Sit! Both of you!" she roared. They obeyed, neither saying a word.

The eggs in Manny's stomach braced themselves for impact. *The apocalypse...* María stood rooted in place on Manny's left; in the corner of his eye she appeared broader and taller than the enormous refrigerator resting just behind Zane. *It's over.*

"Manuel," she began coldly. "Where is your teacher?"

So thoroughly thrown that he almost fell from his chair, Manny's eyes leapt to hers as he asked, "What?"

Glaring back suspiciously María growled, "Kevin Soriano—your teacher. Did he say where he would be today?"

"You mean you didn't talk to him!" interrupted Zane excitedly, though soon cowering under her livid glare.

"No," Manny answered, his soul flying up into his throat and releasing his constrained vocal chords. "I figured he'd be at his house resting; he seemed pretty stressed out when we got back." *This is fantastic!*

"His neighbors said they hadn't seen him leave," she remarked, her tone less severe now. "If I discover that he was ignoring me..."

Then I wouldn't want to be him.

As though waiting for a silent moment to return to the kitchen, Minta passed María and approached the table to collect the plates and the leftover food.

"Thank you, Minta, for preparing breakfast for the boys," María said with a hint of guilt in her voice. "I appreciate it."

"De nada," quipped Minta from the counter between the sink and the stove as she forcefully scraped the plates. Though Minta had lived in her son's house since her husband had died five years

86

earlier, at times it was still a struggle for her to tolerate her daughter-in-law's undulating temperament. "I'll let you finish the dishes," she added quietly, wiping her hands with a dishrag and walking back down the hall from whence María had entered. A door clicked shut in the foyer, signaling that Minta had entered her bedroom as María approached the sink with a blank expression.

Unearthly Discovery

Two figures heading northeast traversed the rugged landscape of the Painted Desert, great mountains and mesas baked by thousands of years under the sun looming to the left, while sporadic valleys littered with sagebrush and increasingly more petrified wood stretched out straight ahead. Lizards basked in the mid-morning light atop the limitless boulders and sienna stones that seemed to emerge from the ground itself. Valleys and ravines alike once carved by raging waters shown pale in the sun, scarcely revealing the countless layers of painted quartz that so readily glinted in the pale light at dusk and dawn. Surmounting another valley, the pair stopped to take a drink and survey their surroundings.

"We've passed several caves, Manny," said one to the other. "If we keep going too much further we'll just end up in the Petrified Forest."

"Zane, we're not going to end up in the Petrified Forest," Manny replied. "I'm just waiting to find the perfect cave."

"Well, it better come soon, because I'm gonna melt out here if not," Zane lamented. "Let's go."

Though Zane was a year younger, the two boys were nearly the same height and both were well-built, with soft features and identical facial expressions. The latter was true because the boys spent most of their free time together, playing their favorite sports and exploring local caves where Manny could turn off the flashlight and become a normal child for a time, engulfed in the darkness with no source of light for his skin to reflect. Despite their frequent exploits in spelunking, neither of them had yet ventured this far on foot in search of a potential cave.

"Do you remember the time I almost stepped on that rattler?" asked Zane in his boredom.

"Yeah, I was behind you. It lunged at your ankle, but thankfully you moved out of reach just in time. That's why it's not smart to just run along mindlessly," Manny replied pointedly.

"I wasn't running along mindlessly."

"Whatever," Manny said. "It still wasn't as close as when that lizard almost bit my hand."

"Talk about mindless," Zane said mockingly. "When does anybody just stretch out their hand for a Gila to eat it?"

"I didn't just stretch out my hand!" Manny retorted. "I was sitting on a rock and leaning with my hand on another."

"Same difference," Zane contended wryly. "You're just lucky I whacked him with my backpack!" After a series of vague chuckles, he became suddenly quiet. "So what do you think mauled your backpack down in Costa Rica?"

"I dunno," muttered Manny, sliding down the side of another small ravine.

"Could it have been that monkey?" Zane inquired.

Reaching the bottom of the ravine, Manny paused to consider this hypothesis. "Although I can't stand him, I don't think it could have been the monkey," he concluded.

"Well, why not?" Zane asked as he, too, slid to the bottom of the gorge.

Walking across to the opposite side, Manny reasoned, "Because monkeys don't have claws. Sr. Soriano said that my pack was torn up—you know—shredded. Monkeys can't shred things."

"Oh," mumbled Zane.

"What I do think, though, is that maybe it was that panther I saw before I reached Julius in the clearing."

"Wow. You're just lucky you weren't there when the panther showed up," Zane marveled. "I bet it came after your jerky, huh?"

"Nope," Manny quickly answered from halfway up the slope. "Nacho stole that, t—"

"You know, I hope one day somebody just up and steals him," Zane said, now scaling the slope. "What do you think about —" He stopped. "Manny, where'd you go?" Zane shifted his weight to prevent himself from sliding back down the rocky incline.

Standing as straight as he could, he peered up the slope and strained to see over the edge. "Are you up there, Manny?" No reply came. "This better not be some joke," he grumbled, a bit irritated as he continued up the slope, "or the next Gila Monster I see I'll hit at you!"

Just as Zane reached a creosote bush he heard someone call his name. "Manny?"

"Zane, can you... me?" the voice echoed hollowly to his right.

Staring oddly at the creosote bush, Zane shouted, "Manny, where are you?"

"...fell," called Manny indistinctly. "Just... creosote... hole."

"What?" Zane exclaimed, sliding a couple feet down the slope. This time he approached the bush from the right.

"I fell, Zane! There's a hole just behind the creosote bush!" Manny yelled. "Can you hear me?"

Though he would not have noticed it if he were merely climbing past, Zane distinguished a dark space stretching out behind the unusually thick creosote. Pushing the spindly, green bush to the side, he discovered a gaping hole measuring approximately three feet in diameter. "Manny, are you in there?" he called uneasily.

"Yeah! Zane, yes, I'm here!" cried Manny enthusiastically from the darkness. "When I fell I landed on my backpack and broke my flashlight. My back's a little sore but otherwise I'm fine. I can't see anything in here!"

Not particularly fond of drops, Zane wavered back and forth, unsure of how he could help his cousin. "Uh, Manny, how 'bout I just toss my flashlight down to you and run back to get your dad? I don't see how I can get you out of there!" he called.

"No!" bellowed Manny desperately. "If you do that my mamá will find out and she'll never let us go exploring again." He paused. "Did we bring any rope?"

"We never do," responded Zane anxiously. "We've never needed it."

"Oh, yeah," muttered Manny.

"What?" shouted Zane.

"Oh, uh, nothing," Manny called back. "Why don't you just slide through the hole and I'll try to catch you?" he proposed.

"You'll try?! Are you crazy?" Zane screamed. "There's no way!"

"It'll be fine! I'm standing immediately below the hole now! Just slide through and I'll break your fall! But you better toss me your backpack first!" Manny instructed.

His heart pounding with a mixture of fear and anger, Zane rolled over and lay on his back. He stared into the scorched sky, which was void of clouds. Sure—he wanted to get out of the sun, to find a nice, cool cave to delve into and relax for a few hours, but Manny was asking too much this time. What if he twisted his ankle or ended up breaking his leg? There was too much risk on his part, but then again his cousin—

"Zane!" strained Manny, desperation lining his voice heavily. "Where'd you go? You didn't leave me, did you?"

Taking a deep breath Zane rolled back over to the right and relented to Manny's pleas. After all, he only had one cousin, right? "No, I'm still here! Now be careful to catch my backpack—I don't want my flashlight to end up broken, too! We'll need it!" Zane gazed into the blackness as he unwillingly slid the straps from his shoulders, twisting the backpack around in front of him and dangling it by one hand over the hole. "Are you ready?" he called down.

"Yeah! I'm right below the backpack! You can drop it!" Manny yelled.

Releasing the strap with a prayer, Zane waited a moment before he called down, "Did you catch it?"

"Yep!" Manny called.

"And the flashlight's fine?" Zane added.

"Yes!" groaned Manny impatiently. "It's your turn now!" Zane held his breath as he edged toward the loose rocks and slid his legs over the lip of that gaping mouth. "I can see your feet and legs!" Manny called. "Ready?"

"You'd better catch me!" Zane gasped. A split second later he slid into the hole. Darkness quickly enveloped him as he fell for what seemed less than a second. Suddenly he felt his body collide with something; Zane heard a soft thud as he went rolling off to the left. Nimbly hopping to his feet he yelled, "Manny, are you alright?"

"Um, yeah," grunted Manny from the darkness off to Zane's right. "My back's killing me, though."

"Where's my backpack?" Zane asked feverishly as he stepped forward, stretching out his foot to feel what may lie in front of him. "Do you have it?"

"Nope," Manny moaned. "I put mine back on in case I fell backwards when I caught you. It worked," he groaned. "I think yours is somewhere to the left."

Turning in that direction, Zane kicked something with his foot. He quickly bent down to grab it. "I think I fou—" he began.

"What did you grab my foot for, dummy?!" yelled Manny, agitated. "I said your backpack was on the left."

"I went left!" argued Zane, releasing his cousin's shoe.

"I meant my left!" Manny growled.

"So how was I supposed to know that?" snapped Zane, veering to his right and searching the floor on hands and knees now. "I swear, every so often you act like Tía Mar—"

"Don't even think about saying that!" Manny interrupted ardently. "She's just crazy sometimes!"

"You're not far from it," muttered Zane to himself as his hand came to rest over the bulk of his backpack.

"What?" barked Manny.

"I think I found it!" Zane shouted as he shot to his feet. "Ah, crap!"

"What happened now?" asked Manny, slightly concerned but still agitated.

"I cracked my head against the wall," Zane whispered through his teeth, fire searing from his crown down through his forehead and into his nose. He felt like he needed to sneeze as he edged his way backward and away from the wall.

"Y'alright?"

Zane glared back in the darkness. "No!" he clipped, touching his head just above his hairline and inhaling sharply. Nearly instantly he located the zipper to the front pocket of his backpack, hoping that somehow when he flipped on the light that the pain would go away. He was partially right, for as he pulled out the flashlight and slid the button into the "on" position the ray of light hit Manny's arm, illuminating the walls of the cavern with faint, white light. Zane gasped as he stared at the glossy walls.

"Whoa," wondered Manny, scanning the subterranean room with wide eyes that reflected dozens of colors. Neither of them had expected the walls to be anything but a dull brown; but both boys found themselves in awe, encompassed by level upon level of tinted rock boasting such flaming colors as red, orange, and yellow to the cooler tones of blue, green, and even a deep, bruised purple.

Zane ran his fingers along the coarse wall, glad to finally be within a cave, and a beautiful one at that. "This is awesome," he whispered. He suddenly distinguished the flow of moist air pouring from a tunnel somewhere off to his left. As the breeze washed over him, it seemed to ease the pain in his burning brow.

"It is great," commented Manny, the air unable to soothe his throbbing back as easily as Zane's brow. "But I need to stand up; I'm gonna die if I'm down here much longer."

"Oops, I forgot." Zane turned and walked toward his cousin. Reaching down to grab his hand, Zane noted that Manny's face was twisted in pain as he pulled him up from the hard ground. "I guess you can stand alright, can't you?"

"Sort of," Manny gasped, his mid-back twitching violently. He cringed as he slid his backpack off, letting it fall to the ground. "Maybe I'll feel better if I walk around for a minute." Trying to stand as straight as he could, Manny walked counterclockwise around the cavern several times, his frown dissipating somewhat. While Manny walked, Zane stood in the center, faithful to keep the light shining on his cousin so that he could see his way around the color-washed cavern. Zane unconsciously measured the dimensions of the cavern, eyeing the tunnel leading off into darkness with earnest interest.

"I bet this cavern's about fifteen feet wide," Zane reflected as Manny continued walking. Looking up he added, "It's probably fifteen or twenty feet up to that hole." When Manny stopped to take a few deep breaths at the mouth of the tunnel, Zane proposed, "So, d'ya wanna see what's down there?"

Wincing a little as he turned his head to the right, Manny stared down the tunnel into the damp darkness. "That's what we came here for, isn't it?" he said, trying to strike a positive tone.

"As I remember, you got here by accident; and I slid down to help you," replied Zane jokingly.

"Sí, sí, I know," groaned Manny while he rubbed his back with a stiff hand.

"Thanks for catching me, anyway," Zane said, eyeing Manny's back.

"De nada," Manny replied quickly. "But let's get exploring so that I can get my mind on something else."

"Sure thing," Zane said enthusiastically as he stepped forward, donning both backpacks. Fortunately the tunnel was spacious enough for the two of them to walk along side by side, with Zane on the left. They had hardly taken twenty steps when another passage appeared on Zane's side. Zane shined the light down the adjacent tunnel, but it met a rock wall as it curved back yet again. "Which way d'you think we should go?"

"I don't wanna go left," Manny answered. "That way'll probably just lead back out into the desert. Shine your light ahead again—I thought I noticed the tunnel sloping downward."

As Zane angled the orange beam along the path ahead, the light revealed that the tunnel indeed proceeded at a shallow decline deeper into the earth. "This is so chévere!" exclaimed Zane, smiling broadly. "We might find some awesome rock formations down there, or maybe even an underground river!"

"You know, you're pretty excited for someone who was so reluctant to come in here in the first place," Manny replied teasingly as the pair trekked on into the fleeing darkness.

"Sometimes you don't know what's good until it hits you square in the head," Zane joked.

"Or in the back," Manny laughed. *Boy I'm glad to be back.*

After another hundred steps the tunnel flattened out again, opening into another cavern. Zane pointed the light around the broad room, discerning numerous mineral formations on either side; but the beam failed to illuminate the cavern as a whole. "Tch," Zane clicked in frustration.

"Here, I've got an idea," Manny said, extending his hand toward Zane. "Pass me the flashlight." Zane obeyed as Manny swiftly transferred the flashlight from his left to right hand, then grasped the glowing head in his palm. Instantly Manny's arms and face began to shine, but the light was still too pale to reveal the obscure corners of the cavern. "Just a sec," he added, flinching as he grabbed the front of his shirt in a painstaking attempt to pull it off.

"What are you doing?" asked Zane dumbfoundedly.

"As soon as I get this shirt off, my skin should produce enough light so we can see the rest of the cavern," Manny replied in agony. *Trying to pull this off one handed is killing me.*

"Oh, well, here, let me help you," Zane said as he grabbed the back of his cousin's shirt and pulled it off him. Zane then knelt down and deposited the shirt in one of the backpacks, rising to his feet to meet an amazing sight.

To be sure, Manny reasoned rightly when he told Zane that the luminescence produced by his skin would be sufficient to illuminate the cavern. Both boys stood agape, wondering at the countless stalactites reaching down from the shimmering ceiling and the eager stalagmites jutting up from the rugged floor; not to mention the glistening, crystal pools shining on either side; all of which was framed by the same rainbow walls as the first cavern. Neither of the two had ever witnessed a scene so subtly beautiful yet striking.

"Spectacular," whispered Zane.

"This is the cave we've been searching for all our lives," elucidated Manny.

Zane's euphoria carried him over to a pool just fifteen steps to his left. The boy quickly knelt down and said, "Ven aquí, Manny! Check this out!"

As Manny approached the pool he noticed numerous tiny figures sliding around in the shallow water. "What are those?" he whispered.

"I dunno," Zane replied in awe. "They look like tadpoles; but they're black and yellow. Aren't tadpoles green?"

Shrugging in reply, Manny continued to eye the small, speckled creatures. *They're so weird. Hey, what are those?* Pointing at the center of the pool, Manny asked, "Zane, do you see those?"

Squinting his eyes, Zane spied hundreds of miniature orbs that seemed to be filled with black dots. "Yeah. Are they eggs or something?"

"I guess," Manny speculated. "Maybe they hatch and turn into these tadpole thingies."

"I bet you're right." Without warning Zane jumped, pointing across the eight-foot wide pool with a shaky hand. "Manny, look over there—by those rocks. I saw something move." He shuddered. "It slithered like a snake, and it was black."

Manny's eyes inspected the smooth, crimson stones on the far side of the pool as he waited motionlessly to see if the creature would show itself. Zane opened his mouth to speak, but Manny raised a finger to signal his cousin to stay silent. After several moments a tiny, glistening black foot appeared over the rim of one of the rocks. *Snakes don't have feet…* In a flash a black and yellow spotted creature slid up onto the rock, glistening in the white light. Its body was winding and slender, featuring four short legs and a long, winding tail. Manny could just distinguish the creature's tiny heart beating in its chest. He smiled as he stared into the animal's beady-black eyes. "I think it's a lizard," he whispered through his teeth, careful not to scare the creature away. "Or maybe it's a salamander."

"Whatever it is, at least it's not a snake," Zane breathed.

Unsure whether he should move or not, Manny remained still, gazing into the salamander's onyx eyes. Suddenly, completely unexpectedly, a faint, golden light erupted from the creature's pupils; a split-second later it leapt into the pool and glided across the shimmering water, flexing left and right to propel itself forward.

Zane edged back a bit in fear, but the salamander took no notice; it was headed straight for Manny. The older boy kept calm, however, anticipating what the creature might do. Sliding from the water, the salamander cocked its head to one side and watched Manny with its now honey eyes, seemingly waiting. *What does it want me to do?*

"Don't touch it!" Zane hissed. "It might bite you!"

Most peculiarly, Manny found himself completely unruffled. "It's not going to hurt me," he reassured Zane. The salamander blinked in uninterrupted interest. Lowering his hand slowly, Manny reached down and pet the creature's head with his glowing forefinger. The salamander closed its eyes in sheer delight, and Manny laughed. "Look, Zane! He's happy!"

Peeking through his fingers, Zane said, "I can't believe you touched it!"

"C'mere and look at the little guy. He likes it when you pet him on the head," Manny encouraged.

Zane glared back, his cobalt eyes flashing. "Do you seriously want me to come over there? It's a cave animal!" he insisted.

"It's fine, Zane," Manny sighed. "Ven aquí."

With a heavy frown Zane scooted himself along the smooth floor, halting at arm's length from the yellow-spotted salamander. "He looks like he has a weird version of the chicken pox," Zane complained.

"Shut up and pet him. It's just the way his skin is. And besides, you're a cave explorer, so get used to cave animals!" *Why's he being such a wimp, anyway?*

As Zane stretched out his reluctant hand toward the salamander, Manny pulled his own away. The creature opened its eyes and blinked at Zane curiously. Zane slid his finger under the salamander's wet, cool chin and chuckled in surprise. "He does like it, Manny. Look!"

Sure enough the salamander had closed its eyes again happily. "I told you he's not that bad," Manny affirmed as Zane retracted his hand with a smile. "Well, let's keep exploring; I want to check out the rest of the cavern and what may lie beyond." Just as Manny set his hands on his knees to propel himself upwards, the salamander squeaked passionately. Looking down again, Manny met the creature's two tiny, pleading eyes. "What do you want, little guy?" This time it squeaked twice and took a step toward the boy. *What's it doing?*

"Maybe he wants to come with us," Zane guessed.

"Do you?" Manny asked the salamander with one eyebrow raised. It squeaked in reply. "Alright, then," he conceded, offering his open palm to the salamander. In less than a second the creature had scaled halfway up Manny's right arm, pausing for a brief moment to glance into the boy's eyes and to take a quick breath through his small mouth. Another second later the salamander had mounted Manny's shoulders where it wound its way around the boy's neck and gazed around the cavern with open eyes.

"Woo, that tickled," Manny said, a shiver running down his spine.

"So what are ya gonna call him?" Zane asked as both boys rose to their feet.

"What d'you mean?" Manny replied.

"I mean he's your pet now, so you need to give him a name. What about Spot?"

"That's lame," Manny countered. "Let me think." *What about Black Tail? No, that's too impersonal. Nightcrawler? No, too weird. Well, since he's a salamander I could call him Sal, or Sally... No, that's a girl's name...* "How about Mander?"

"How creative," replied Zane sarcastically.

"It's better than Spot," Manny contended. "And hey, you know what? It sounds a little bit like Manny!"

"There you go!" Zane asserted. "Manny! Let's call him Lil' Manny!"

"Lil' Manny," the other boy repeated. "Sounds good to me! Just don't get us confused."

"Other than identical brain size, I don't think I'll have any trouble," sniggered Zane.

Lil' Manny squeaked. "I don't think he liked that comment," Manny laughed. The salamander squeaked again. "Be careful, Zane. He might just bite you the next time he gets a chance."

Both boys laughed as they continued along the left side of the cave, counting the pools and collecting stones of various colors. After about fifty steps they came to a pillar where a stalactite and a stalagmite had fused into a glittering white limestone column laced in rusty tones. Hundreds of luminescent, sapphire beetles endlessly ascended and descended the column; until then neither Manny nor Zane had noticed the shining insects adorning the ceiling. As they approached the end of the cavern the boys observed a gaping tunnel nearly three times as wide and high as the one through which they had entered. Preferring to investigate the opposite side of the cavern before proceeding any further, the boys crossed the spacious floor to discover several more pools, stones, and columns. In one pool they marveled at the translucent crayfish that scoured the diluted basin dining on worms and miniature larvae. Lil' Manny held on tightly to Manny's neck as the boy leaned over the pool. *I hope none of those cross over and munch on any of Lil' Manny's brothers and sisters.* Close to the entrance to the cavern Zane happened upon a geode, a short rock that had been cracked open one way or another to reveal an inner lining of glittering pink amethyst and clear quartz.

"Well, I think we've pretty much done all the exploring we can in here," commented Manny, standing up after inspecting the geode. "What d'ya say we find out what's down that far tunnel?" he asked, pointing across the cavern.

"Espera un minuto," Zane asserted as he, too, rose to his full height. "First we've got to come up with a name for this place." Both boys scanned the entire breadth of the magnificent cavern, considering all they had seen. "I counted thirteen pools," Zane stated. "How about we call it Cavern 13?"

"Sounds like something out of a sci-fi movie," Manny said dismissively. "We've got to think of a name that captures the essence of the place." He gazed fixedly at each of the cavern's aspects. "It's really colorful," he observed. "And we are under the Painted Desert…"

"What about the Painted Cave?" Zane asked.

"No, that makes me think that the whole cave system is painted; we've only explored part of it. Let's call it the Painted Cavern," Manny concluded.

Zane nodded. "I agree. Are we ready now?"

"Sí," Manny affirmed as the two of them traversed the expansive distance of the Painted Cavern to reach the mouth of the tunnel at the far end. Moist, cool air washed over them as they gazed into the steeply falling passage. "Let's be careful," Manny cautioned. "We don't wanna fall down any holes or anything."

Both boys proceeded slowly, side by side, eyeing the path ahead for signs of abrupt fissures or drop offs leading into darkness. None came, and following a tense five minutes the ground leveled out and proceeded virtually straight ahead. From the distant blackness a subtle rumbling met their ears.

"¿Oyes eso?" Zane breathed.

"Sí, I can hear it," Manny answered quietly.

"You think it's water?"

"Maybe."

Stepping slowly at first, Manny and Zane pressed onward, the rumbling noise growing progressively stronger. After another three hundred steps the tunnel converted into a thin path the width of a mere five feet stretching across an abyss that seemed to expand infinitely to either side. Here the rumbling reverberated against the vast cavern walls, a thick mist rising far to the left. Peering over the edge of the natural bridge, the boys discerned the distant glint of running water.

"It's a river," marveled Zane.

"And there, behind the mist—I bet that's a waterfall," wondered Manny.

Indeed it was. In ages past the subterranean river had once carved this vast chasm, gradually cutting deeper and deeper into the Earth until all that remained of the original riverbed was the narrow path stretching across the expanse. Manny looked to his right and considered the floating bridge.

"I bet this thing's sturdy enough for us to cross."

"Oh, no," Zane contested swiftly. "I'm not going across that thing! It might crumble! And even if it doesn't, what if we slip? We'll die if we fall!"

"We're not going to fall. If this bridge has been here for thousands of years, I highly doubt that we're going to cause it to collapse now." Manny nodded across the chasm. "C'mon, let's go."

"No," Zane cut back. "There's too much risk."

"Fine," stated Manny decisively. "I'll see you when I get back." *He'll come.*

"Manny, your mamá will kill you!" Zane yelled.

"Mi mamá isn't here!" Manny called back. "And yours isn't either, so let's keep going!"

"Estás loco," Zane growled, watching as his cousin walked leisurely along the stone bridge.

Dropping the backpacks and dragging his feet away from the safety of the tunnel, Zane took two reluctant steps onto the bridge before Manny called, "You'll be fine as long as you don't look down! Just set your eyes on me and keep walking forward!"

Zane had taken ten more steps before he felt his chest quake and his head spin slightly. He quickly knelt to the ground, laying his hands on the firm rock. "Manny, I can't do this!"

"Sí, lo puedes," Manny encouraged.

"No, I can't!" Zane shouted desperately.

Manny stopped halfway along the bridge. "Okay, Zane, just listen to me! Lift your eyes up! Can you see my back?"

"Yes," Zane replied a moment later, his body trembling slightly.

"Stay focused on my back and just follow me across the bridge! I promise you'll make it alright!" Rising shakily, Zane kept his eyes locked on his cousin's back and started to walk forward. "How's it going?" Manny asked.

"B-better," Zane stammered.

"Like I said, just follow me!" Manny yelled as he, too, continued his journey across the bridge.

"Okay!" Zane assented, gaining confidence and speed with Manny's sure pace.

A minute later, just seconds after Manny's feet had left the bridge, Zane came trotting up from behind him. "Were you running?" Manny asked incredulously as he turned around.

"Not really," Zane replied with a smile and a sigh of relief. "Thanks for helping me across. That's two for today."

"No problem," Manny shrugged. "I'm sure you'll pay me back someday. Now let's find out what's down here!" he added excitedly as he pointed over his shoulder.

Both boys could see water shining in the distance as they passed through the widest and tallest tunnel yet. Thirty steps later the passage yielded to the most magnificent sight either had ever beheld. Not only were the walls tinted in the same antipodal mixture of fiery and cool hues, but hundreds of iridescent logs lay scattered across the cavern and were leaning against the walls, some shattered and others whole.

"Are those tree trunks?" Manny asked, open-mouthed.

"Yeah, they look just like the trees in the Petrified Forest!" Zane exclaimed.

"But they're so much brighter," Manny said, pausing for a second. "And the colors are amazing!"

Neither of the boys could have anticipated the splendor concealed over the millennia in this silent cache. Sweeping the cavern with their eyes, the boys inhaled the millions of hues that burst out at them from the once living trees now turned to stone. It was as if a rainbow had burrowed beneath the earth and exploded, leaving behind glistening fragments in all directions. No two logs looked exactly alike. Here shards sparkled like thousands of forgotten sapphires and emeralds, while there a wine-imbued trunk fused with fire and blood displayed a sight reminiscent of the setting sun.

"Can you believe this?" asked Manny, bending down and picking up a crimson shard of petrified wood. "It's amazing."

"Tell me about it," Zane said as he gingerly approached the crystal basin of water at his feet. Kneeling down at the edge he whispered, "Increíble."

Tearing his eyes from the stone in his hand, Manny glanced up at the silent lake. *Are those tropical fish? Underground?* Coming closer he discovered that the glistening blue, yellow, and green that emanated from beneath the surface were actually sunken stones like the one in his hand.

"Those are the strangest fish I've ever seen," Zane observed as he pointed toward the submerged stones.

"They're not fish, Zane—they're rocks, like this one." He stretched out his hand toward his cousin.

"Those are some pretty buoyant rocks, then," Zane replied wryly, ignoring Manny's outstretched hand. "Look—they're swimming, but you can hardly see some of them."

Sitting along the lake edge beside Zane, Manny analyzed the waters more closely. Three seconds later, he gasped. "There are fish! But they're clear!"

"And they don't have any eyes."

"So how do they keep from crashing into each other, I wonder?"

"Well, I've heard that some blind people develop a heightened sense of hearing; maybe it's the same case for these fish."

"I bet you're right," Manny agreed as he watched several of the translucent fish dart back and forth, maneuvering perfectly between one another. "And since they're in the water all the time, wouldn't you think their sense of touch would be sharpened, too?"

"Probably, but let's check. Hand me that rock in your hand."

"Why?" asked Manny defensively.

"I need it," Zane answered vaguely.

"But I wanted to keep it," Manny argued. *I like it.*

"There are like a million others in this room. Just get another one later," Zane said brusquely.

With a groan and a frown, Manny relented. "Fine." He handed Zane the shard. *But I better find a good one. No, a better one…*

"Mira," whispered Zane, leaning over the water and holding the stone just above the surface. The moment he lowered the shard

103

and tapped the water, the fish shot away almost faster than the boys' eyes could follow. One fish, however, rocketed toward the surface and attempted to swallow the tip of the shard. Discovering that the stone was not a potential meal, however, the fish descended and continued its vigil for food.

"Hypothesis verified," Zane said contently. "Good thinkin', Manny."

"Thanks," Manny replied. "Now can I ha—" But before he could finish his question, Zane had launched the stone across the cavern and into the center of the wide lake.

"Sí," muttered Zane happily.

"What did you do that for?!" exclaimed Manny angrily. "You already proved your point!"

"Oh, I just felt like it," shrugged Zane, eyeing the tiny ripples straining to reach the water's edge.

"You just felt like tossing my one of a kind rock into the center of a lake?!" cried Manny.

"Yeah," Zane answered calmly as he stood up. "But I guess I also wanted to make sure there wasn't some giant squid or any other monsters lurking in the heart of the lake."

"Giant squid...?" mumbled Manny. "Why would there be?"

"Oh, you know, I've read books..." Zane answered mysteriously. "So, you want some lunch?"

"I guess," Manny grumbled. *But what'd I really like is my rock.*

"Let's find a log and sit down to eat," Zane suggested. A moment later the boys were seated on a silver-white trunk slightly further up the shore. "Crap!"

"What?" Manny asked.

"The sandwiches are in our backpacks..." Zane answered.

"So take them out already."

"If you hadn't noticed, I'm not wearing the backpacks."

"Well, go get them!"

"No!" rebounded Zane.

"Why not?" Manny bellowed. *You're being such a jerk!* "Where are they?"

Turning and looking over his shoulder and into the now shadowy tunnel, Zane replied, "On the other side of the bridge."

Great. "So what're we gonna eat?"

"Have any snacks?"

"No," Manny said. "Do you?"

"Nope. I guess we could go back across the bridge and eat there…" Zane proposed doubtfully.

"But I'm not ready to leave yet," Manny said quickly.

"Eso es bueno, because I was gonna say that once we get across that bridge, I'm not coming back again," explained Zane in relief.

Suddenly something brushed Manny's neck, startling him and causing him to drop the flashlight. Both boys heard splashes as the light evaporated, sending them into inexorable darkness. "What touched me?" Manny yelped, his hand flying to his neck.

"Oh, no…" groaned Zane. "No puede ser…"

"Something touched my neck!" repeated Manny.

"It was just Lil' Manny, dummy," said Zane dismissively. "What I'm worried about is the linterna!

The flashlight? A boulder sunk in Manny's stomach. *Oh…* "It fell into the water…" he muttered despairingly.

Zane began to rant. "What're we gonna do? If the flashlight and batteries are wet, then we can't see. And if we can't see, how can we get out of here?"

"Calm down, Zane," Manny said, trying to concentrate.

"Manny, we're—"

"Zane, calm down!" Manny reiterated.

"We're gonna d—"

"Zane!" Manny shouted, his voice rebounding off the invisible walls of the cavern. "We're not going to die! Now just shut up for a sec and let me think!" Zane became silent, but the quaking trunk told Manny that his cousin was still terrified. *Maybe it's not too late to save the flashlight.* "Zane, I need your help," Manny directed coolly. "It may not be too late to retrieve the flashlight, so we've got to get it out of the water as soon as possible.

The log stopped shaking as Zane said weakly, "But we can't see anything."

"I know that, but we can still feel," Manny reminded him. "So come down to the water's edge and help me find the linterna." Planting his knees on the smooth rock, Manny plunged his face and torso into the cool water, blindly running his fingers over the petrified wood shards. After a moment a small wave washed over his ears, telling him that Zane, too, had taken up the blind hunt. *It all feels so weird.* Each stone presented a unique shape, some similar to rectangles, a few in the form of awkward triangles, and still others round and lumpy – but despite their irregularities, all were smooth. *I feel like a three-year-old trying to find the right block to fit in the hole.*

A violent splash to his left startled Manny, causing him to instantly pull himself from the thrashing water. "What's the ma—?"

"Something's got my hand!" shrieked Zane frantically, scattering stones in all directions as he wrestled with his beguiled attacker.

What if it's the squid?! Manny tried to stand but was quickly thrown to the floor by a severe blow to his left jaw. His right elbow burned fiercely, cut by a rock shard. *Oh my gosh! It slammed me with one of its tentacles!*

"Help me, Manny!" pleaded Zane hysterically as he tripped over a nearby log and crashed to the ground.

Manny had heard enough. If he did not act quickly, his cousin would soon be an unusually large, juicy meal for a subterranean water beast. Reaching for his left wrist, Manny removed his watch, which glowed momentarily before instantly assuming the shape of a wand. The indignation surging through Manny's veins fired him to his feet as a blindingly bright light burst from the boy's skin, dissolving all shadow in the cavern instantaneously. Manny leapt over the log and planted himself in front of Zane, brandishing his wand for the ensuing encounter. "Where is it?" he roared, searching the area around Zane feverishly. "Where's the squid?" Manny heard Zane make a choking noise and

106

saw him shake his hand violently. A second later a splash came from a tentacle's reach within the lake. "Stay behind me, Zane!"

"Uh, Manny, it's okay…" came Zane's voice awkwardly.

"What's okay?" Manny bellowed, not daring to turn his back from the deceptively pristine waters.

"I think I took care of it," Zane continued in the same sheepish tone.

Took care of it? "What about the squid?" Manny interrogated. "You didn't take care of him! You couldn't have!"

Zane coughed dodgily. "Th-there is no squid, Manny."

"Yes, there is!" *He must be out of his mind in fear.* "I heard you wrestling with it on the floor there! It had your hand! On top of that, it knocked me to the ground with its tentacle," Manny maintained. Zane chuckled suddenly. "What's so funny?"

"That tentacle was my foot," Zane said, still chuckling.

Was your…? "What are you talking about?" Manny asked, lowering his wand slightly.

"I mean that before you turned on your A1 Manny light, it was so dark in here that I couldn't see a thing, so I was kicking in all directions to keep my supposed attacker away. Instead of nailing the squid, like I thought, I must've hit you. That's when I tripped over the log," Zane explained.

"Okay, you kicked me, so what? The squid's still in there, waiting to nab us!" Manny redoubled, aiming the wand at the lake and flashing brightly.

"I told you, there's no squid." Zane was obviously smiling.

I'm gonna kill 'im. "Zane, this isn't funny. It's serious! There's some ginormous monster in the water and we've got to kill it before it eats us!"

"Manny, the only monstruo in that water is the crayfish that latched onto my hand," Zane said flatly.

"But the sq—"

"There's no squid," Zane asserted.

"You were wrestling with—"

"A crayfish," Zane finished.

All the energy ebbed out of Manny as he turned around, his wand dangling in his hand. In the fading light he could see that Zane was still lying flat on his back, his legs resting over the petrified trunk.

"Aren't you gonna help me up?" Zane asked impatiently, leaning forward and reaching out his hand.

Blinking dazedly, Manny molded the wand into a watch, returned it to his wrist, then bent forward and stretched out his rubbery right arm to awkwardly pull Zane to his feet.

Zane smiled broadly. "You're getting' pretty good at that Lumen stuff," he observed encouragingly, hoping to lighten Manny's foul mood.

"What?" Manny asked distractedly; the blood rushing from his head had suddenly left Manny's mind clouded and confused, and the fact that the cavern was progressively darkening did not help.

Patting his cousin on the shoulder, Zane said, "I mean, total darkness, no flashlight, when 'Wham!,' without warning you're blazing like a fireball with your wand ready! Julius and Tavo must've taught you a ton while you were down in Costa Rica!"

Huh? "Zane, the only thing they taught me was how to transform my wand; they didn't teach me to bend light at all," Manny corrected wearily. "Much less make myself shine at will." *Waitaminute.* "How did I do that?"

"Are you telling me that you can't turn your light on again whenever you want, like you did just now?" Zane sounded worried again.

"If I could do that, why would I waste my time carrying around a flashlight in my hand? That's just stupid."

"So you've never just glowed brighter all of a sudden before?" Zane prodded.

All the light had gone now as Manny closed his eyes to think. *What about when I was little? No. In the past few years? Can't think of an instance. In Costa Rica? I wasn't exactly plunged into a dark hole, there.* "I—"

"What about when you were exploring another cave some time? Did you glow then?" Zane interrupted.

"I've never gone exploring without you, Zane," Manny answered flatly. "Do you remember any time when I did?"

"Oh. I guess not."

"You know, I honestly don't remember ever just glowing of my own accord. There's always been some light for me to reflect," Manny concluded.

"Hey! I know!" Zane shouted, making Manny jump. "What about when Abuelita was talking to you about that girl on the beach in Costa Rica?"

"You mean Maricarmen? What about her?" asked Manny, his heart beating a little faster.

"I remember your cheeks started to glow a little when we asked you if you'd kissed her," Zane said, smiling.

"Oh, they did not," Manny defended, but suddenly he wondered how he could see Zane's face.

"Look! You're doing it again!" cried Zane.

"No I'm not!" Manny countered, covering his increasingly luminous cheeks.

"Ha! ¡Te lo dije! ¡Te lo dije!" Zane chanted.

"Okay, so what?" Manny snapped, pulling his hands away from his face and glaring at Zane. But without warning, the light had gone.

"What'd you do?" Zane yelled. "Why'd you shut it off?"

"I didn't shut it off!" roared Manny. "I told you that I can't control it!"

"Manny, we need light to get out of here," stated Zane seriously.

"Well, I can't just walk around embarrassed for twenty minutes until we find our way out of here! Feelings don't work that way, Zane!" Manny shouted. "And besides, even if I could, the light from my face isn't bright enough to show us where to walk so we can get across the bridge!"

"Oh, yeah, that's true," Zane admitted. "So how did you glow so brightly a minute ago?"

A minute ago... Hmm... "I guess I was upset cause I thought a non-existent squid was about to kill you."

"So all you have to do is get upset again!"

"Check your glasses, Zane! I've been upset with you for the past five minutes, and I'm not glowing now, am I?" Manny threw back. *Geez...*

"Verdad," Zane said. "And that means we're back in the same boat. The flashlight's somewhere in the lake and we have no light. We either starve or fall to our doom. How about you crawl across the bridge and come back for me later?"

"Well, sure, buddy," Manny replied sarcastically. "Are you crazy?"

A splash came from the water's edge just beside Manny's foot, but he did not care—he was seething.

"What was that?"

Maybe I'm lucky and it's an octopus. If it eats me I won't have to put up with you. "No me importa," Manny grumbled. Something moved along his pant leg, stopping at his knee. *Hey now! There're no oct—* A familiar squeak cleaved Manny's thoughts. "Lil' Manny?" he asked happily. Two squeaks came in answer as Manny lowered his hand to the invisible salamander. He felt the creature's tiny, soft paws rush over his palm as he lifted Lil' Manny up to his face. "Where've you been, lil' buddy?" Lil' Manny issued another purposeful squeak and then snapped his jaws contently. "Did you find a snack in the water? Lucky for you you weren't around when Zane kicked me in the head and started rolling around like a rabid Gila. You might've gotten crushed."

"Tch," Zane clicked disapprovingly. Manny smiled.

"Did you see our flashlight while you were swimming in the water," Manny asked the salamander; but no reply came. *I guess that means no.* With a cautious hand Manny began to pet the creature's head. "You wouldn't know where we can find a source of light, would you?" Manny's gaze faltered as he stared at the salamander before him—the creature's eyes had begun to glow a vivid honey color. A second later a spot on Lil' Manny's dangling tail flashed yellow and continued to glow. Manny stopped petting the salamander, watching in awe as each one of the amphibian's tiny

110

spots burst to life, glowing brightly. The light was so strong that Manny could easily distinguish Zane's stunned face on his left.

"What kind of salamander is that?" Zane stated in amazement.

"A pretty special one, I guess," replied Manny with a smile. Lil' Manny squeaked approvingly, snapping his luminescent tail and sending a streak of light across the water. Hope shot a lightning bolt into Manny's chest. *Awesome! I bet no one has a pet like this!*

"So do you ever remember them doing radioactive testing in the Grand Canyon or in the Petrified Forest?" Zane asked doubtfully. "Maybe that's what petrified the trees."

"Nope," Manny answered.

"I didn't think so. But hey! Thank God for Lil' Manny! He can lead us out of here!"

The salamander squeaked happily as Manny said, "Sin duda." Turning his eyes to Lil' Manny he asked, "So, how 'bout it? Will you be our guide?" Lil' Manny squeaked and tottered back and forth on his light paws, feigning to crawl. "Alright!" cried Manny as he set the salamander down in front of the faintly iridescent, yellow log. *Hey, they match!* Glancing at the lake Manny said, "Just a moment. I'm gonna get a drink."

Zane watched Manny step over the salamander and kneel down to the shining water. "Are you sure that's safe to drink?"

"I'm so thirsty I don't care," answered Manny frankly. Gulp upon gulp slid down his throat and into his empty stomach. After a minute he hopped to his feet and stood tall; he could hear the water beating the walls of his stomach. "Ah… Perfect."

"That's good for you, but I think I'll wait." Zane raised an eyebrow. "Ready?"

"Yep." Manny glanced down at the salamander and said, "Lead on, lil' buddy."

With a squeak Lil' Manny wound his way between the log and several multi-colored stones, his tail flitting back and forth behind him. Manny snatched Zane's hand and pulled him to his feet as the two of them swiftly followed the salamander, their eyes fixed on his spotted body as it passed over shards and around trunks.

Within a minute the trio had reached the tunnel, walking along carefully for fear of unexpectedly teetering over the edge of the chasm. Halfway along the tunnel, just as the distant sound of thundering water met their ears, Zane shouted, "Hold it! We forgot something!"

"¿Qué?" yelped Manny, nearly falling onto his amphibian counterpart. "We didn't bring anything else. The flashlight's gone for good."

"Ya lo sé, but we forgot something else—we didn't name the cavern!" Zane explained.

Manny rolled his eyes, but as his back was to the salamander, Zane could not see. "Fine."

"So what d'ya wanna call it?" Zane chimed.

"Oh, how about the Squid Emporium…" Manny replied sarcastically. "It'll always bring back memories."

"Yeah—or not," Zane riposted. "I say we call it the Petrified Cavern, since it's under the Petrified Forest and all," he said proudly.

"Hmm, sounds good to me. Now let's go! ¡Tengo hambre!" Manny asserted.

"Yeah, yeah. You just better hope that no cave creature has snatched our backpacks, or you won't get to eat until we reach the house!" Zane said humorously. Lil' Manny, who was waiting almost ten steps ahead, squeaked to herd the boys on. They quickly followed.

They better be there. Manny's stomach growled ravenously as they reached the stone bridge. "So how're we gonna do this?" he asked, glancing at Zane on his left.

"Lil' Manny leads, obviously."

Well, duh!

"Um, I think I'll just follow you again. There's no need to push my limits too far in one day," Zane decided.

"Está bien, but I think we should crawl across," Manny said. "We'll get dizzy if we stare at Lil' Manny while we walk, since he's down on the ground and all." The salamander squeaked defensively. "No insult intended."

Ten minutes later, with sore knees and sighs of relief, Manny and Zane reached their blue and orange backpacks. Deciding that it would be safer to eat in the Painted Cavern, the boys donned their packs and followed Lil' Manny along the passage and up the steep slope that eventually yielded their destination. "Hey, Lil' Manny," Zane called as they entered the cavern. The salamander stopped and turned to face the boy. "Let's eat by your pool. Sound good to you?" Lil' Manny squeaked as he bolted for the pool at a diagonal across the room, to the boys' right. Zane and Manny trotted along, driven by hunger and the need for light. The boys were still twenty steps from the pool when the salamander leapt through the air and into the water, scattering refracted light in all directions. Sitting beside the pool, they devoured their sandwiches while observing Lil' Manny slide through the water as he played tag with his tadpole-like siblings.

"So I guess your back feels better," Zane said after several moments.

"Huh?" Manny answered distractedly.

"Your back—it must feel better for you to have carried your pack all the way here," Zane explained.

"Oh, yeah, I'd almost forgotten about it completely," Manny said, tearing his gaze from the vibrant salamander. "The fight with the squid must have knocked something back in place," he laughed. "Or maybe it was just the water. Subterranean springs and all, you know. They're supposed to have healing properties."

Zane took a thoughtful bite of his sandwich. "I'm sure the squid urine didn't hurt any, either."

Damaged Trust

"Excuse me, muchachos, but would the two of you like to explain where in cielos you have been?" A tall woman, one hand on her left hip and blue eyes ablaze, stood facing Manny and Zane as they walked up to the back patio from the northeast. "Ahem," she prompted, tilting her head slightly with her long, blond ponytail floating in the burning breeze. The Arizona sun had tinted her normally fair skin a light almond.

"Mamá, Manny and I were just hoping that—"

"Zane, I don't want any excuses, do you hear me?" his mother called back. "You knew we were leaving at eleven to go to Flagstaff for lunch and to go shopping for summer clothes. Why weren't you back by then?"

Manny swallowed hard. *I'll take the rap. After all, I'm the one who fell down the hole.* "Tía Jane, it was my fault—"

"¡Mamá!" tore a voice from the sliding door. "He's back, so let's go already! We don't need to stop for lunch—Tía María already made some! All I need is clothes!" The girl's burnt chestnut ponytail dangled in the air as she leaned outside the door, her coffee eyes fixed on her mother. "¡Ándale!"

"Un momento, Berta," Jane responded. "I need to talk to your brother."

"He doesn't need clothes as bad as I do!" Berta argued. "He's not even going to be in high school next year!"

"Berta," Jane said pleadingly.

"Hmph!" the girl called, jerking back inside and slamming the door.

"I'm sorry, Mamá," Zane said honestly. "We went exploring, and I wasn't here when you told me to be."

"Gracias," Jane replied. "I appreciate that."

"It's just that Manny and I haven't seen each other for a whole week and we hoped that you'd let me stay instead of going shopping!"

Jane shook her head. "I'm sorry, honey, but I can't buy summer clothes for you if you're not with me."

"Why not?"

A firm glare met his eyes in reply.

"Okay, but can Manny at least come with us?" Zane begged. Both boys gazed at her with beseeching eyes.

Oh, please, please…

"María said that she needs to talk to Manny about something, and that since he's been gone for a week, he has to stay," Jane answered quietly.

"Ah, man…" Zane groused.

"Great…" Manny added sarcastically.

"You'll have plenty of time to see each other tomorrow, so just cool your jets," Jane said. "Manny, I'm glad you're back. Tell me more about your trip tomorrow, after lunch," she added, hugging her nephew. "Now Zane, let's go before your sister has a nervous breakdown.

"Adiós, Tía," Manny said glumly. "Nos vemos, Zane."

"Hasta mañana," Zane called back as he slid the door shut.

Alone again. Great. Manny glanced up at the blue sky, shielding his eyes. *The sun's a killer.* "Well, I either die out here from heat exhaustion, or inside by familial homicide. Which sounds worse?" he wondered aloud. Not altogether fond of high temperatures, Manny stepped inside the house, relieved to find the kitchen miraculously empty but the table set and laden with food. *It must be a trap.* His mouth watered slightly as he eyed the platter of rice mixed with sausage and colorful vegetables. *No, I've got to reach my room before she finds me.*

Turning left and walking around the table, Manny crept through the kitchen, passed the pantry, and entered the hallway, which in turn yielded to the foyer. An archway opened to the living room straight ahead. Just as he passed the laundry room and turned right to enter the foyer, a voice behind him called, "Manuel, that's not the backpack you took with you to Costa Rica, is it?"

He cringed. *She knows! She must have found Soriano!* "Sure isn't, Mamá," Manny replied, steadily nearing the protection of the stairs ahead of him. "That one was blue."

"Well, where is it, querido?" María called back softly as Manny turned about and set his foot on the first step. "I want to see the pictures you took while you were there."

He froze, his eyes bolting to the watch on his left wrist. *Soriano didn't know about the camera. He couldn't have told her that the monk—*

"After emptying your suitcase and washing all your dirty clothes from the trip, I realized that I hadn't seen your blue backpack anywhere, dear," she continued. "Your father and I would really like to see your photos."

Manny blinked a few times, second-guessing himself. "You mean Sr. Soriano didn't say anything to you about my backpack?" His hand flew to his mouth, but it was too late. *Dang it! I can't believe I said that!*

"Sr. Soriano? I told you that I couldn't find him this morning." María stopped folding, then stepped out of the narrow laundry room and into the foyer. She looked up at Manny, who by now had halfway ascended the stairs. "Why would he know anything about your backpack, Manuel?" she asked suspiciously.

"Don't ask me!" he said loudly, quickly climbing the remaining steps and bolting across the hall, to the right, and into the safety of his room. "What am I gonna do? I can't tell them that the monkey changed the camera into a wand! They'd think I was lying!" Manny's eyes searched the room for answers, bounding from his desk to his bed and then onto his dresser, which was littered with baseball cards, his mitt, and some loose change. "That's it! I'll just buy a new one!" He quickly mounted his bed and turned to face the west wall where three shelves displayed a variety of trophies, awards, and souvenirs. On the middle shelf sat the palm-sized, blue stone that his mother had given him when he was born. Dual clouds of blazing red and seething white violently cut the cylindrical rock down the center. Reaching behind the stone, Manny set his hands on the metal lunch box from his early elementary years, displaying the logo of his favorite baseball team—the Arizona Diamondbacks. Manny sat down on his bed as he opened the metal clasp and flipped the lid back. He counted the bills he had saved through his allowance and by completing chores over the past two years. He was disappointed to find only fifty dollars in his stash. "I would've had a hundred if I hadn't spent so much money on souvenirs in San José!" he exclaimed, turning and glaring at the wooden figures on his desk that he had purchased for his family. *Oh, well...* "I've gotta start somewhere."

"Manuel," called his mother's voice from the bottom of the stairs. "I don't know what you did with your backpack, but find it and bring down the camera so your papá and I can see your pictures!"

Stuffing the bills back inside the box, Manny haphazardly replaced his cache behind the tri-colored stone, which he accidentally knocked from its perch. "Whoo," he said, catching the stone before it hit his bed. "We really ought to move these shelves. If we had an earthquake while I was sleeping, this stuff would crush my head." He began to strategize as his feet hit the floor. *Now, I don't have the backpack, and I don't have the camera—well, actually, I do have the camera, but it's not really a camera anymore. At any rate, that can't help me right now. I'll just have to tell them the truth—or what I can of it, at least.* Taking a deep breath, Manny opened the door and descended the stairs, surprised to find just one butterfly flitting against the walls of his stomach. *I'm calmer than I thought.*

"Your papá's setting up the television in the living room," María called from the kitchen, "but I really think you should have some lunch before you show us the pictures, Manuel. Ven aquí y come."

He shrugged, crossing the foyer and turning left down the hall into the kitchen. *No harm postponing the inevitable.* Fortunately Manny's mother did not grill him any more about the backpack as he ate his second lunch; instead she sang to herself in Spanish as she did the dishes, splashing the water with her hands, happy that her family was together again under one roof.

"Gracias, Mamá," said Manny as he carried his plate to the counter beside the sink.

"De nada, m'ijo," chirped María happily. "Go ahead into the living room; I'll be there in a few minutes."

Moments later Manny found himself sitting in a chair facing both his parents on the couch. María, slightly heavyset and dark bronze in skin tone, was at least a head shorter than her husband. Conversely, Carlos was tall and thin, his skin a light cream. But despite their differences in height, complexion, and build, Manny's parents both gazed expectantly upon him with the same soft brown eyes.

"So, it hasn't taken me long to notice that you don't have the camera," Carlos observed. "¿Dónde está?"

"I told you to bring down—"

"Sí. I know, Mamá, but I need to tell you two something," Manny began bravely. "I know you really wanted to see the pictures I took in Costa Rica, like the carts in Alajuela, the streets of San José, the beach at Puerto Limón…" He paused as his parents nodded. "But… I left my backpack in the middle of the rainforest."

María clenched her husband's hand with an iron grip; but before she could speak, Carlos said, "That's not good, but at least it was just a backpack and the camera that were lost. We're glad you had a safe trip. Aren't we?" he added, turning his head to María, who glared back.

"Mamá, I'm sorry I was so irresponsible, but I tried my best to be careful in Costa Rica. I know that being sorry doesn't get you your camera back, so this summer I'll do whatever chores and odd jobs I can to earn the money to buy you and Papá another one," Manny continued.

A silent moment passed. "Well, I'm very disappointed in you, Manuel," she finally replied, her words stiff. "I expected you to be more mature than that."

Manny stared back expressionlessly. *If you only knew the truth, you'd be proud of me for saving my friend.*

"You have a good proposition there, son," Carlos said after a moment; but the rigid silence quickly returned.

Hoping to lighten the atmosphere, Manny looked to his mother and said, "If you want I can tell you about the trip now. I really—"

"No, Manuel. You can tell your father and me later," María interjected as she released her husband's hand. "For now, just go to your room and think about this. I am very disappointed in you," she repeated, her voice faltering, and she stood up and walked hastily from the room.

Manny spent a great deal of the afternoon pondering all that had happened to him over the past three days, wondering if there might have been any way that he could have prevented the monkey from changing the camera into a wand. *Why couldn't he have snapped a pencil or my sketchpad with his tail, instead?* Manny battered this question against the walls of his brain countless times. *But what could I do? I turned and he already had it… It wasn't my fault.* The boy also wondered if Julius had yet left Tavo's, or whether the two of them were beside the sanctuary lake, perhaps laughing as they recalled humorous stories from their days in school. Maybe Julius was still unable to fly and he needed a few more days to recuperate…

Nacho. *Why is he always such a jerk? I'm glad I finally got the opportunity to put him in his place.* At school Soriano never allowed Manny to say a cross word toward Nacho. It had always been that way—each teacher, each year incessantly poured out his or her praise and trust into Manny's enemy. *Are they all blind?* A thought came to Manny, a memory of his grandfather's words. *People who constantly hunt down others will in the end be hunted down themselves.* Manny blinked a few times. *Too bad that monkey didn't snatch Nacho before we left…*

Sitting in his computer chair, Manny stared out the broad window on the east side of his room, watching as the sunlight faded, bruising the desert with its last warm rays. His eyes roamed over the

119

valleys that serrated the dry land, searching for that one creosote behind which he had fallen into darkness to discover the cave system with its pools, its bridge, its la—*Its pools?* The boy's hand flew to the left side of his neck. Nothing. He hopped up, spinning around and hurriedly scanning the room. Unsatisfied, he threw himself to the floor and checked beneath the bed. *Still not here, either.* Manny then opened the door, quietly leaping across the hall and into his bathroom. "Lil' Manny, are you in here?" he whispered as he pulled aside the shower curtain. *Ugh...* He checked every niche and corner in both the bathroom and his bedroom, but to no avail. "Great," Manny exclaimed, staring out the north window in the progressing twilight. "If Mamá finds him, she'll probably freak and kill him like that rattler she decapitated a year ago." Defeated, he lay down and closed his eyes.

A few seconds later a knock came at the door. Manny's eyes jumped to the red and white Diamondbacks clock sitting atop his desk—it was seven o'clock. The door cracked. "M'ijo, it's time for supper," came his mother's constrained voice. Looking into the room she added, "You can come down."

"Mamá?" Manny replied, but apparently she had already gone.

Supper was an unusually quiet affair as Manny, his parents, and his grandmother sat around the kitchen table eating pupusas— round, palm-sized tortillas stuffed with variations of fried pork or cheese. True to her word, María, now on Manny's left, allowed her son to describe his trip to Costa Rica; but she never asked a single question throughout the entire meal. Carlos, across from the boy, enjoyed hearing about the volcanoes that the group had seen, but otherwise his attention seemed to wane; he, like his wife, often nodded or smiled distractedly. *What's their deal? It was just a camera.* Minta, on the other hand, was thrilled to pick up the conversation.

"Now, Manny, did you know that I met your Abuelito Gabriel in Alajuela, where you saw those beautifully painted carts?" Minta asked happily, her white curls shaking. "I was just a teenager, and it was my first time leaving Panamá, but my father allowed me

120

to come with him on business to purchase some of those carts for our farm. Gabriel had come to Alajuela from El Salvador to purchase carts as well—not for his family's farm, of course, but for their tortilla business. ¡Ay, corazón mío! You would not believe how handsome he was when I first saw him…"

Other than Minta's occasional anecdote, Manny felt as though he were talking to himself. He made sure to omit any details about the monkey, quetzal, and unicorn. *I still don't know how I'm gonna tell them about all that…* As Manny finished, he briefly described the group's trek through the rainforest and the scenery from the compound, trying to leave out Soriano as much as possible. An empty silence followed.

"Pues, María," chimed Minta brightly, "you and Carlos go take a rest; I believe Manny and I will do the dishes tonight."

But it's not my job to do them on weekends…

"Gracias, Minta," replied María after a moment. As she stood up she glanced at Manny with those same guarded eyes. Carlos followed her out of the kitchen and down the hall.

"M'ijo, recoge los platos de la mesa," Minta said as she approached the sink and began filling the basin with water. Manny quickly obeyed, carrying the plates to the counter beside his grandmother while simultaneously throwing furtive looks about the room in search of the salamander. A moment later all the plates were next to the sink and the water was ready. "You wash, I'll rinse."

"Está bien," Manny replied, sliding the first saucer into the warm, soapy water. *At least pupusas aren't very messy—I really don't have to scrub at all.*

"Tell me, Manny," began Minta slowly, "what did you do to your mother? I haven't seen her like that since she and Jane had that fight nearly three years ago."

Handing his grandmother the soapy plate, Manny answered, "I think she's mad about her camera."

"Oh, sí, I forgot all about las fotos. Why didn't you show them to us tonight?"

"Because I can't," he replied, passing her another plate and grabbing two cups. "I left my backpack in the rainforest."

"That would be a problem," Minta acknowledged. "But honestly, tu madre acts more hurt than mad."

Hurt? "What do you mean by that?"

"You know how tu madre acts when she's angry, Manny. At the table she wasn't ranting and raving; she was quiet and subdued. You can see it in her eyes," Minta added.

Hmmm... "She did say that she was disappointed in me," Manny recalled. "But I don't understand. People make mistakes all the time. I even said I'd save the money to replace the camera. Why can't she just forgive me and get over it?"

"Ask yourself why she's disappointed," Minta told him as she rinsed a pair of forks.

What else did she say? Something about— "She said that I should've been more responsible and mature. But it was just an accident," Manny asserted again as he dunked the frying pan in the water.

"Un accidente, ¿eh?" Minta said slyly. "Ask yourself this: do accidents exist, or do our misdeeds merely stem from carelessness?"

But I couldn't have prevented that stupid monkey from snatching the camera! I turned around and he had it in his hand before I could stop him! "Abuelita, we can't stop all bad things from happening to us!" Manny retorted.

"Of course not, Manny, but that's why God expects us to guard what we have," Minta explained.

Guard what I...? Oh. Guilt punted against the walls of Manny's stomach just as the frying pan clunked in the adjacent sink. *If I hadn't left my backpack when I got up after cleaning my shoe, then the monkey wouldn't've have had a chance to grab the camera in the first place.* He stood with his hands in the water for a brief moment, then pulled the stopper, listening as the drain eagerly sucked down the water. *Then again, if he hadn't grabbed the camera, would I still be a Lumen?* Manny nervously adjusted the watch on his wrist before he shook the suds from his hands, rinsing them as his grandmother set the dripping pan in the drain rack. "I think I get what you're saying, Abuelita," Manny finally replied, grabbing the dishtowel and drying his hands. "Mamá trusted me to

122

keep the camera and all my other possessions safe—she believed I would be careful, and that's why she let me go on the trip."

"You're growing into a sensible young hombre, nieto," Minta said, hugging Manny and leaving two moist handprints on his back. Letting go and taking the towel from his hands to dry her own, she gave him a knowing nod. "Wisdom, that's exactly what young people need today."

And maybe some luck, too, Abuelita. On top of convincing Mamá to let me go back to Latin America, now I've got to figure out a way to apologize. Stumped, the boy looked at the floor, remembering that he had still not spotted Lil' Manny. "Abuelita," Manny said, bending down and checking beneath the cabinets, "you haven't seen any sort of, uh, animal in the house, have you?"

"Animal?" she repeated, kneeling to the floor and whispering jokingly. "You mean other than your mother's parrot?"

"Why would I be looking for Lorillo under the kitchen counter?" Manny replied dryly. "And I'm not talking about a bird, anyway…"

"So what are we talking about?" she whispered, throwing him a playful smile, her snowy curls bobbing.

"Well, it's a—okay, um, you could say he's black, and he has a long tail—"

"No me digas que es una víbora, Manuel," Minta answered ominously, rising to her full height and considering whether she could mount the kitchen table in one leap.

"Shhh! No, Abuelita! I'm not talking about a snake, either!" he replied sharply. "Keep quiet so Mamá won't find out—I don't need her getting upset over anything else!"

"What is it then?" she whispered, still eyeing the table. "It's not a spider, is it? I hate spiders…"

"No, Abuelita, he's a salamander, and he's—"

"A salamander!" exclaimed Minta ecstatically. "Are you saying that there's a true salamander loose in our house? Do you know what this means?"

"What I do know is that if Mamá finds out about this, I'm dead," Manny answered, holding his palms out and motioning for his grandmother to be quiet. The boy's heart pounded as he looked down the hall, praying that his mother would not come thundering into the kitchen in a state of hysteria over a rabid amphibian roaming through her house.

"No, tonto, she wouldn't kill you! She would thank you!" corrected Minta, still excited but whispering again now. "You are the one who let him in, aren't you?"

Is this a trap? What should I say? I can't blame Zane, that wouldn't be—

"Good," continued Minta, deducing the truth by her grandson's guilty expression. "Your mother will be thrilled!"

"What are you talking about?" burst Manny impatiently. *Stupid! Why did you just yell?* "Oh, no," he groaned, hearing footsteps coming up the hall. *Prepare the guillotine…*

"You know when I was growing up in Panamá, it was considered extremely lucky to have a reptile or amphib—Carlos!" spat Minta happily as she floated across the kitchen and greeted her son, sliding one arm around his back; she looked extremely short beside him. "M'ijo, you won't believe what your son has brought into the house!"

"Mamá, frankly, as long as it's not a rattler, I don't care," Carlos replied tiredly. "I'm just glad the two of you haven't woken María up—she fell asleep on the couch."

Oh, thank God, I'm safe for a few more hours.

"Well she needs to be here to hear this!" said Minta passionately as she slipped out of her half-hug, intending to proceed down the hall and retrieve her daughter-in-law. Much to Minta's disliking, Carlos barred the way.

"No, Mamá," he said wearily. "Let her be."

"Are you trying to tell me what I can and cannot do?" Minta replied, her curls swaying and eyes flashing.

Manny smiled covertly. *So this is what it looks like when Mamá and I fight.*

"In this case, sí, Mamá," he replied somewhat forcefully. "If you couldn't tell, María's had a stressful day."

At these words a stone seemed to materialize in Manny's throat. *That would be my fault...*

"Why don't you and Manny sit down and play a game or something?" Carlos added, putting his hands on his mother's shoulders and guiding her to the table. Surprisingly, she offered little resistance. "I think I'll head back to the living room."

"Are you sure you don't want to hear about your son's new pet?" Minta asked enticingly. With a smile and a wink to Manny she added, "I wouldn't want it to startle you."

"I'll survive," groaned Carlos from the hallway.

Satisfied that her son was gone, Minta glanced at Manny with bright eyes. "¿Listo?" she asked.

"Ready? For what?"

"Siéntate por un momento," she said, disappearing into the pantry that ran perpendicular to the hallway.

Manny obeyed, sitting on the west side of the kitchen table. *What in the heck's she doing? That's not where the games are.* A moment later his grandmother reappeared carrying two jars—peanut butter in her left hand and honey in the right. "What are those for?" he asked, utterly perplexed. "I'm full from the pupusas."

"To lure your friend out, of course," she answered as she dropped the jars on the table and whisked by. Manny heard pieces of silverware chinking against one another.

"My friend?" he mused slowly. *Who are you—* "You mean Lil' Manny?"

Not a second later Minta slapped a butter knife and a spoon down on the table. Her eyes were playful as she said, "So you're his namesake, huh? How did that happen?" she asked, quickly diving in and out of the pantry to return with several paper plates in hand. "Can he glow in the dark, too?"

How'd she guess that? "Well, that's not how he got his name, but, yeah, actually, he can," answered Manny, a bit abashed.

Unscrewing the jars with one eyebrow raised, Minta said, "Now, Manny, don't make up stories. You may glow, but salamanders don't."

125

*This one does. And if he hadn't shown up today then both
your grandsons would probably still be trapped inside a cave.*
"We'll see," Manny said quietly. With a change of tone he asked,
"So how do you expect to attract a salamander with peanut butter
and honey?"

Spooning two medallions of the thick honey onto individual
saucers, Minta said, "Oh, you'll see."

"I can't believe that worked," said Manny incredulously.
"You've got to be the craziest abuelita in the world."

"You betcha," whispered Minta feistily. "Was there ever any
doubt?"

Their three-hour stakeout had been a surprise success, at
least as far as Manny was concerned. After daubing four plates with
peanut butter and honey, Minta snatched two sets of playing cards
from under the staircase and led Manny outside to the pleasantly-
warm patio. Placing the paper saucers several steps out on the rocky,
sand-covered terrain, Minta allowed an hour for the local ant
colonies to dispense their most capable collectors, only to lose them
to the sticky traps. She then set the saucers in strategic yet visible
locations in the kitchen—one under the table, another in the corner
formed by the refrigerator and the dining room wall, a third along
the outer wall of the pantry, and the last in front of the carved,
wooden stand along the north wall. Following Gabriel's death five
years earlier, Minta brought this ornamental oak table from El
Salvador as a gift to María for allowing her to stay in her home.
Receiving the gift happily, María earnestly began to adorn it with
decorations according to the season; currently, a hand-sized sun with
a painted red smile rested just next to an angled calendar displaying
a wide circle around the twenty-first of the month.

In order to maintain a watchful eye on the plates, Manny and
his grandmother placed the patio table just outside the sliding door.
Two hours into their vigil, Manny began to lose faith in Minta's

plan, growing impatient of fruitlessly glancing into the salamander-free kitchen. Yet fifteen games of Speed and an hour later, a tiny body with a winding tail darted under the kitchen table.

"So how do you plan on opening the door without scaring him?" asked Manny, still in awe.

"Let's go around front," Minta replied.

Rounding the house and entering the foyer as quietly as possible, the boy and his grandmother passed her bedroom door on the left, then stopped. They cautiously peered around the corner, down the hallway, and into the kitchen. The salamander was still under the table, his tail flicking happily as he devoured the immobile ant squadrons.

"¿Y ahora qué?" whispered Manny.

"Just follow me," Minta said, stepping soundlessly along the hall and into the kitchen. Luckily for her, the salamander was facing the other direction.

In spite of this fact, Manny clenched his teeth. *What are you doing? If you scare him he'll just take off and we'll have to start all over!* Nevertheless, Manny followed. *What else can I do?* Just as he stepped into the kitchen he heard a familiar squeak and saw the black figure zip in the direction of the dining room. "What did you do to Lil' Manny?" asked the boy through his teeth.

Rising from her knees, Minta replied, "The second I touched his tail, he shot straight into the dining room. At least we've got him cornered."

"How 'bout I go first this time," Manny stated, stepping in front of his grandmother as he walked past the refrigerator and turned left, coming to a halt in the dark doorway. *I know!* Running his left hand along the wall, Manny found the switch and quickly snuffed all the lights in the kitchen.

"Why'd you do that?" whispered Minta roughly. "Now he'll probably just run past our feet!"

"Shhh! Keep watching!" Manny breathed. Within seconds their eyes had adjusted to the darkness, allowing them to make out the frame of the long, oval table and the high-backed chairs. From under the table's base Manny distinguished a muffled light. *It worked.* "It's okay, Lil' Manny. It's just me. You can come out now—we're not going to hurt you," he said, kneeling down. A pair of golden orbs appeared from under the table base, blinking briefly. Not three seconds later the salamander had wound its way up Manny's leg and torso to come to rest on the side of the boy's neck. Manny turned, the speckled light emanating from his tiny counterpart revealing an open-mouthed Minta.

"He—he really does glow," she marveled.

"I told you so," Manny replied, smiling.

In order to provide adequate accommodations for his new pet, Manny and Minta searched through the mountain of forgotten keepsakes at the back of the garage until they found an old, grimy terrarium that Carlos had used to house an iguana when Manny was five years old. It was well after midnight when Manny and his grandmother set the reconditioned, shining glass casing down upon the floor of the boy's room. Resting upon a solid foundation of desert sand and moist pebbles sat a basin of water for Lil' Manny to dive into at his leisure. As an added bonus, Manny carried up the three remaining plates topped with the gooey ant mixture. Lil' Manny was elated, squeaking as he darted between his insect buffet and rock side pool.

As usual, the following Sunday morning was an early one as the entire López clan carpooled to a Hispanic church in Flagstaff, over two hours to the west of Siete Arenas, the town of nearly ten thousand inhabitants in which Manny and his family lived. In spite of the virtually silent car ride to Flagstaff, Manny and Zane found plenty of time on the return trip to discuss the events from the previous day as well as formulate barely audible plans for returning to the Painted Cave, intermittently discussing summer baseball along the way. Returning to Carlos and María's house at one o'clock, the ladies of the family—Minta, María, Jane, and Berta—set forth preparing the weekly Sunday dinner consisting of a flawless marriage of Salvadoran and Panamanian cooking. Carlos and his younger brother, José, perched on the couch in the living room to begin watching baseball, while the boys sprinted upstairs and into Manny's room to see how the salamander was faring.

Walking through the door, Zane whooped as he observed the terrarium covered in peanut butter. "Dirty little stinker, isn't he?"

Water splashed inside the basin a split second before Lil' Manny appeared over the rim of the smudged terrarium, squeaking defensively. "Well, you're the one that made the mess," Manny told the salamander frankly. Stepping across the hall and wetting a rag, he returned to his room to find Zane laughing hysterically with the salamander on his head.

"How do I look?" Zane cackled.

"No different then normal," Manny answered, hiding a smile as he wiped the terrarium clean. The salamander squeaked in protest.

Zane smirked back in reply. "So have you told tu mamá, yet?"

"Didn't have to," mumbled Manny vaguely.

"Well, why not?" asked Zane as the salamander darted down his neck and arm, stopping at his wrist and staring at the other boy.

"She came into my room to wake me up this morning," Manny began as he collected the ant-free plates, "and the second she saw Lil' Manny I think she leapt across the room and over the terrarium—I'm not joking! I woke up and she was squeezing the life out of me and kissing me all over my face!" He wiped his left cheek with the back of his hand.

"But I don't get it. I thought she'd be upset…"

"Nope—Abuelita was right, 'cause all Mamá kept going on about was what a blessing and how lucky it is to have a salamander in the house. She seemed to completely forget about ever being mad at me, and on top of that, she said I could take Lil' Manny with me anywhere in the house!" Zane frowned quizzically. "He'll eat any bugs we've got in the house," Manny clarified.

"Oh, well that makes sense," Zane said sardonically.

After an extensive lunch in which Manny spent over half an hour recounting his experiences in Costa Rica to Jane and José

(Berta did not really seem to care), the boys bolted to the living room to catch the last half of the Diamondbacks game. Five minutes later, José, Zane's father, walked into the living room and took a seat in a recliner on the boys' left. Slightly taller than his older brother, José had forest green eyes and the same dark skin tone of their mother, Minta. "Glad to hear you had such a good trip, Manny," José said in his typically energetic tone. "Now that you're back, are you gettin' excited about summer ball?"

"Can't wait!" exclaimed Manny excitedly.

"Papá, are we having practice tomorrow morning when school gets out?" Zane asked, tearing his eyes from the television.

"You and Manny may get out early tomorrow, but Carlos and I don't," José replied smoothly. "The team won't practice until seven o'clock, so if you want to get in some extra play time maybe either María or your Abuelita could take you both to the park before it gets too hot."

"Sounds good to me," said Manny.

"Yeah," added Zane, once again absorbed in the game.

***

"Sweet freedom," Manny whispered as he stepped from the long, yellow school bus and glided up the driveway in his euphoria. Breathing deeply he added, "No more school." *And if I'm lucky, I'll never have to see any of them again!*

Taking another deep breath as he walked along the red brick patio that skirted the dining room window, Manny reflected on the positive outcome of all the day's potential threats. To his dismay, at seven o'clock that morning his mother had informed him that she would be driving him to school to have an immediate conference with Kevin Soriano regarding the teacher's questionable leadership during the class trip. "I want you in there when I confront him, Manny," María had affirmed as she gripped the steering wheel tightly, her knuckles flashing white. "I expect you and the rest of the kids to attest as to what really happened that last day." At that moment the car shuddered violently, leaving Manny with the

130

sensation that the back tire had just run over his now missing stomach rather than the gaping pothole that María had swerved unsuccessfully to avoid.

Fortunately for Manny, however, Soriano had apparently vanished. While the boy remained in the classroom with his peers waiting for the substitute teacher to disperse their final grade cards, María stormed to the office to discover that Soriano had left a message with the principal. Pinned under her heavy stare, the principal relented to María's requests, allowing her to listen to Soriano's message. Several minutes later Manny heard a familiar voice raging along the sidewalk outside his classroom window; the only phrases that he could distinguish, however, were "overstressed" and "extensive time off." As he turned his head he saw his mother nearly rip the car door from its hinges before sliding in and storming away. Manny was elated.

But how am I gonna bring the issue of Lumen schooling up to Mamá? Maybe I should just ask her now... Manny stopped, his hand resting on the ornate brass doorknob. *No, wait. Okay maybe, but only if she's in a good mood. Otherwise I'll wait until she's cooled off. But that might take a couple days...* He then turned the knob and swung the door open, entering the foyer. As the door clicked, he froze. *Who's talking?* He turned his head slightly, straining to listen but hearing nothing. *Weird.* Passing the living room door on the right, he began to bound up the stairs, intent on checking on Lil' Manny before showing his report card to his mother.

"Manuel!" called María from the living room on the other side of the wall, catching Manny on the fourth step. He nearly fell. "Querido, can I speak with you?" she chimed brightly.

She doesn't sound mad... Manny looked longingly up toward his room. "Oh, well," he sighed, turning and dismounting the stairs to step into the living room. *At least she's in a good—* Manny's heart jolted as his eyes absorbed the unexpected sight before him. On the couch sat a man in a white suit and a iridescent blue tie that matched his shining eyes. On his left hand he wore a wooden ring. The man's sharp features and spiked blonde hair gave him a sleek and professional appearance. On the man's right, perched along the rim of the couch, was a brilliant, emerald-plumed bird with a crimson breast and a pair of dazzling tails. *J-Julius?*

"It's rude to stare, Manuel," María chided from an arched wooden chair near the sleeping television. "Close your mouth!" she whispered brusquely.

"Oh!" Manny blurted, shaking himself. *What do I say? How much does she know?*

Before Manny could formulate any words the man stood up and walked across the room, extending his hand. "It is an extreme pleasure to meet you, Manuel Luis López," the man said as he shook the boy's hand firmly. "My name is Lee Lightblade, and I'm a representative from the Lumen Centres of North America. I believe you already know Julius, am I correct?" Lightblade asked, stepping aside and gesturing smoothly to the quiet quetzal. Manny nodded. Julius flicked a tail; he seemed aggravated. "Good. Then why don't we all sit down and discuss your forthcoming integration into the Lumen community?"

Fully dumbfounded, Manny obeyed, taking the chair opposite his mother and facing the couch at an angle. He chanced a look at her, but María's eyes were focused on Lightblade.

"H-how long did you say you've been here?" stuttered Manny.

"Only five minutes," replied the young man coolly.

Thank God! A weight flew from Manny's chest. *They haven't had time to tell her anything!*

"Don't ask rude questions, Manuel!" snapped María. "Now, Mr. Lightblade, who did you say you're with again?"

"I'm a representative for the Lumen Centres of North America, ma'am," Lightblade replied patiently. "I'm here to interpret for Julius, who represents the Southern Hemisphere, and to explain your son's options regarding his future education."

"Future education?" she said, confused. "What do you mean?"

"Why would Julius need an interpreter?" interrupted Manny suddenly. His eyes leapt to the quetzal's head. *He looks better to me. I wouldn't think he'd have any trouble talking.* "What's up, Julius?"

The quetzal merely glared in reply.

"Although you can understand our friend, here," Lightblade began, "your mother cannot, as she's not a Lumen."

"What's a Lumen?" María asked, slightly perturbed at being ignored.

Lightblade opened his mouth to speak, but Manny cut in again. "That makes no sense at all. Julius can talk, so everyone should be able to understand him. He can even speak Spanish! Can't you, Julius?" The bird remained silent. "Say something!"

"What in blue feathers do you want me to say?" snapped Julius.

"I don't know…" Manny replied innocently. "Why are you so aggrava—"

"Oh, I do love to hear a quetzal sing," María interrupted, clapping her hands. "It reminds me of when I was a little girl."

"Sing?" Manny repeated. "He wasn't singing! He was talking!"

"Oh, don't be silly, Manuel," María reprimanded. "After all, he's not a parrot, like our Lorillo. Quetzals can't talk."

"Not a parrot?! Well, of course I'm not a parrot!" squawked Julius, spreading his wings in rage.

"My, my. Your bird's a feisty one, isn't he?" said María to Lightblade. "Maybe a nice chat with Lorillo would calm him down," she added, beginning to stand.

"No!" exclaimed Lightblade quickly. "I mean, no, that won't be necessary. Julius isn't all that fond of what you might call 'talking birds'."

"But he is a talking bird!" argued Manny.

"Stop your nonsense, Manuel!" María rebounded.

Julius screeched, hovering over the couch.

"Now all of you please stop!" Lightblade said loudly. "Julius, settle down! We're getting nowhere! Manuel, please try to understand! Mrs. López, let me explain. Julius and I are known as

133

Lumens—we have the capacity to communicate with one another and manipulate light. While Manuel was in Costa Rica, he discovered that he, too, is a Lumen. Julius and I have come here to answer any questions that you may have related to your son's abilities, his future, and the Lumen community as a whole."

María remained quiet, analyzing Lightblade's bright eyes and solemn expression for a moment.

Oh, no…

She blinked. "Correct me if I'm wrong, but you're telling me that you can talk to and understand that bird," she said, pointing at Julius.

"Yes," answered Lightblade.

"Okay," María replied evenly. "And what do you mean when you say that the two of you can 'manipulate light'?"

"We can bend it and use it to influence the environment," Lightblade said.

She's not gonna believe any of this.

"Show me," she replied with a slight note of curiosity.

What?

Lightblade waved his left hand smoothly before him. Tiny streams of light slid through the air from the windows on the north, east, and south walls, enveloping the glass coffee table in the center of the room. María gasped as the table rose from the floor and began to float, spinning slowly. As a final touch, Lightblade directed one of the artificial lilies to leap from the vase on the center of the table and gently glide over to her, coming to rest in her open hand just as the table legs met the floor. "Any questions?" the man asked with a smile.

"Amazing," whispered María, glowing. "I mean, no." Turning to Manny she asked, "So you can do all this, too, m'ijo?"

"Not exactly," Manny replied awkwardly.

"I'll speak now," clipped Julius.

"Mrs. López, Julius would like me to interpret for him now," Lightblade said. María looked eagerly at the quetzal.

I can't believe she's buying it! This is fantastic!

As Julius spoke in his rich, melodic voice, Lightblade interpreted. "Señora, it is a pleasure to make your acquaintance," the quetzal stated, now calm.

"Likewise," María smiled. "I'm sorry to have insulted you, Mr.?"

"Rumblefeather, but that's quite alright. You inquired whether or not your son could bend light. To answer your question—in theory, he can. But he lacks the knowledge and practice to do so. Manny is currently a Seventh-Level Lumen; in order for him to reach the accomplished First-Level as my colleague, Lightblade, and I have, your son must pursue seven years of formal Lumen training," Julius explained.

"Seven years? Can he do that here, in Siete Arenas?" María asked.

"Unfortunately, no," the quetzal replied. "He has two options—to study in either North or South America."

"Pues, he'll definitely be studying in North America, then," María said decisively.

"No!" cried Manny, exiting his state of silence. "I mean, no, Mamá, please. It was so awesome in the rainforest! Up here it's just so boring! And besides, I already know two Lumens from down there! Julius here is the first, and then there's Ta—"

"I'm sure you'll make friends quickly enough," María broke in. "Besides, wouldn't you prefer to be closer to your family?"

"Mamá—"

"Sra. López, before you come to a decision, you may want to consider the extent of your son's abilities," suggested Julius.

"My son's abilities? But I thought you just said that he isn't able to bend light yet. And why would it matter if he could? That shouldn't affect where he attends school," María argued.

"Señora, I'm not referring to his Lumen skills. Rather, I was pointing out his linguistic abilities—Manny is bilingual," explained the quetzal.

"Sí, I'm aware of that," said María tonelessly.

"You see, most Lumens who speak Spanish elect to study in the Southern Continent, surrounded by other Spanish speakers," Julius added.

"That may be, but as you said, Manuel is bilingual, so he could attend school in the United States just as easily as God's knows where in South America." María made no attempt to mask her impatience. "And since when has my Manuel been like most children, anyway?"

"So I have to be different from all the other Lumens now, too?" Manny snapped, leaping to his feet. "I've been different from all the other kids my entire life, and I've just had to put up with it! You always tell me I'm special, that I'm going to do something great with my life. Now I have the opportunity to do that and actually fit in, and you're trying to take it away from me! Why can't it just be my decision?"

Lightblade shifted in his seat uncomfortably. Julius blinked, stunned.

"Because I'm your mother, and I just couldn't live if you were that far away from me!" María cried, her voice faltering. "Anything might happen! And while we're on the subject, I should never have allowed you to go to Costa Rica without me! You could have been injured!"

"But I wasn't!" rebounded Manny. "I was careful, Mamá! And I'll be careful in South America!"

"Oh, if you're so careful, then how could you have left your backpack in the rainforest with the family's camera in it?" tore María. "I trusted you, Manuel! And what you've shown me is that you're not mature enough to be that far away from me!"

"The camera?" mused Julius. "Manny didn't leave the camera in the rainforest. Why, he has it with him this very moment!"

Julius! Why'd you have to go and—I wanted to avoid this and just buy a new one...

"What are you talking about?" shot María.

"He's wearing it on his wrist!" squawked Julius.

Glancing first at her son's arm, María turned to the quetzal and said dangerously, "I don't find you at all humorous."

136

"Manny, show her," Julius said.

Ugh! How'd we get on this subject anyway! I could just lie...
But then Julius would look like a fool and Mamá probably wouldn't
trust him anymore. "Fine," Manny groaned unwillingly. Under his
mother's scrutinizing eye, Manny slipped the dark mahogany watch
from his wrist and placed it in his right hand. He blinked, and the
watch transformed into a wooden block, strikingly similar to the
shape and type of the López family camera. "This is it, Mamá."

"You just—"

"I know, transformed my watch," Manny said offhandedly.
"All Lumens can transform their wands at will."

Overwhelmed, María leaned forward for a moment, cradling
her head in her hands. Manny glanced at Lightblade, who seemed
lost. *He looks pretty young. I wonder if he's new at this. If he is, I bet*
he's never encountered a woman like mi mamá.

Julius, however, looked positively delighted, his beaded eyes
shining.

I guess he thinks this is going well. I hope so.

"If that's the camera, Manuel, then what happened to it?"
María asked slowly, overcoming her disbelief and sitting straight
again. "The camera's made of metal."

"If I may, Señora, I believe I can answer that question,"
Julius offered benevolently. After listening to Lightblade's
interpretation, María nodded. "The first step to becoming a Lumen
is receiving a wand. Quite simply, another Lumen animal appeared
just before I met Manny and transformed one of his possessions,
which happened to be the camera, into a wand. This is a basic rule of
Lumen society."

"Oh…" said María wearily. She blinked twice before turning
to Manny and asking, "So why didn't you just tell me about all
this?"

"I didn't know how. And anyway, would you have believed
me?" Manny asked frankly.

"If you had shown me the camera—I mean the wand—oh,
whatever it is!" she replied in frustration. Manny simply glared
back. "Okay, I probably wouldn't have."

"Then we actually agree on something," said Manny humorlessly.

"Excellent," interjected Julius happily. "Then let us press on with our meeting and designate exactly where Manny is to pursue his Lumen training!"

"No, not now," María replied, exhausted. "I need to talk to his father first.

"A superb point," chirped Julius. "In that case, I will leave you a means to communicate with me when you come to your decision. Lightblade, if you will."

After he finished interpreting, Lightblade opened his suit jacket and pulled out an iridescent blue pen mounted with a silver dove, its wings spread. He then slipped the wooden ring from his left hand, transforming the band into a briefcase, which he flipped open to extract a small stack of gleaming paper. Lightblade set the paper and pen on the coffee table.

"So you want us to write you? But that takes so long," María began. "Couldn't we just call?"

"Heavens no!" the quetzal chirped. "Let me explain—this is paloma paper. Once you decide on where Manny will attend school, use this pen to write me. To send the letter, simply fold the paper and inscribe my name on the back."

"But I still don't understand," replied María. "Our postman can't reach you without an address."

"Postman?" chirped Julius, highly amused. "There's no need for a postman."

"Then how does the letter get to you?" asked Manny, intrigued.

"You will see," answered the quetzal mysteriously. "Just remember to write my full name, Julius Arden Rumblefeather, on the back."

A calm silence filled the room for a moment, similar to sunlight piercing the clouds after an exceptionally eventful storm. "I suppose we should be going," said Lightblade. "Thank you for your hospitality, ma'am."

"You're welcome," sighed María.

As Lightblade rose from the coach, Julius added, "I look forward to hearing from you. Take care, Señora." He gracefully rose from the furniture and maneuvered through the air to land on the man's right shoulder.

"Manuel, please walk our guests to the door," María prompted.

"Sí, Mamá," the boy replied, standing and leading the other Lumens to the oak door and out onto the brick patio. By now the heat from the sun was growing intense; in fact, Manny could feel the warmth of the baking bricks through his sneakers. As he reached the driveway, Manny turned around to face the man and the quetzal.

"Thanks a ton for coming today, guys. I didn't know how I was going to bring the subject up to Mom. I just hope she and Dad will let me attend school down there."

"As do I, m'ijo," chirped Julius. "And don't forget—you still haven't told me what really happened four days ago in the glade."

"I know, but hopefully I'll be seeing you soon enough," replied Manny. "I'll tell you then."

"That would be August, at the earliest," clipped Julius.

"August? Why so long?" exclaimed Manny.

"That's when students are allowed to move in with their host families," the quetzal answered simply.

"Oh…" Manny mumbled. *That bites. I'm ready to go now!* Manny shuffled in place, staring at the ground and kicking a nearby pebble.

"Cheer up, Manuel! Time passes faster than you may think," Lightblade said encouragingly. "But before we go, I'd like you to consider one thing—we have great Lumen schools in North America, too."

In a flash Julius spun and pecked Lightblade on the forehead. "You little—"

"What was that for?" yelled the man, shaking Julius from his shoulder and shielding his face from the raging bird.

"You should know not to attempt to steal a student of mine!" squawked Julius fiercely, nipping at one of the man's fingers. "If I weren't known for my restraint…" Manny laughed loudly. "Excuse

139

me?" cut the quetzal dangerously, whirling in the air to confront Manny.

"Oh—uh, nothing," said Manny quickly, chuckling.

"Just get in the car, Julius," snapped Lightblade as he transformed his briefcase into a wand and tapped the apparently empty air in front of the garage.

"What ca—" But Manny swallowed his question as an invisible cloth seemed to melt away from a stunningly white, four-door sedan. *Wow.*

The passenger side window dissolved as the quetzal glided through the air, shaking the cherry pendant on his breast. "Hope to hear from you soon, Manny," he clipped before diving into the vehicle.

Manny smiled. "Thank you, Mr. Lightblade," he said, trying to convey a positive tone yet feeling shame for the man. Lightblade nodded curtly as he started the silent, fume-less car, backed down the driveway, and disappeared along the road west to town.

***

That night, and for two weeks until his parents reached a decision regarding his education the following school year, Manny was extremely distracted. During baseball practice, he repeatedly dropped pop flies that under normal circumstances he would have caught with ease. On the field, as well as everywhere else, Manny found himself filled with constant worry and pervasive doubts that crippled his concentration. Not only were Carlos and José becoming frustrated with Manny's particularly poor performance, but Zane, too, began to show his displeasure toward his cousin's frequent drops, strikeouts, and failed steals. Nacho took great satisfaction the night his father's team, The Gilas, came out victorious over the Soaring Eagles, coached by the López brothers. For Nacho, the vengeance for his humiliation suffered on the last day in Costa Rica had only begun. "I fully expect to thrash you and your pathetic teammates this season," Nacho goaded as he passed Manny during the post-game shake.

140

Several days had passed following Julius and Lightblade's departure before Carlos approached his son regarding the boy's supposed Lumen skills. Manny was not sure whether to owe this delay to his mother's reluctance to discuss the issue with his father, or whether his father simply feared the idea of raising the topic to his son. Whatever the case, that Thursday, following an especially grueling practice, Carlos indirectly inquired about Manny's magical abilities. Recalling Julius's quick retort to this same subject, Manny corrected his father, affirming that Lumens were not wizards or magicians but people with the ability to move light. Despite the boy's vivid descriptions of all the light bending that he had seen, Carlos was still unnerved when he saw his son convert the mahogany watch into the remnant of the family camera. But in spite of Manny's impassioned questions as to where he might attend school in the fall, Carlos maintained a resilient silence.

Agony ate at Manny until the second Tuesday after Julius and Lightblade's visit. At dinner that evening, Carlos said, "So Manny, tu madre and I have been discussing your, uh, Lumen abilities."

Manny choked on a piece of plantain, feverishly reaching for his milk. "And?" he managed to gasp as the fruit painfully slid down his throat.

"Manuel, what happened in Costa Rica—"

"Mamá, I know you're disappointed because you trusted me to guard my possessions more carefully," Manny began understandingly. "But I just want you to know that I've learned my lesson and I'll be more responsible from here on out."

"But m'ijo—"

"Mamá, really," the boy continued genuinely. "I'm sorry I forgot about my backpack, but you can trust me now! I won't leave anything behind anymore!"

"Now just wait before you say anything else!" María said strongly, sliding her chair out and walking into the twilit dining room. When she returned, she carried a viciously mauled blue rucksack in her left hand.

141

"Th-that's my backpack!" Manny stuttered. "How did you get it?"

"Mr. Lightblade gave it to me before you arrived that day," she answered quietly. "Manuel, if this is what can happen to your backpack, what might happen if we let you—" But she choked, unable to finish.

"That won't happen to me!" Manny rebounded, searching for the words to strengthen his argument. "I—I know the other Lumens will protect me! They can do incredible things—in fact, Tavo made a wall of light that nobody could pass through! I'm sure they'll use those same techniques to stop any dangerous animals or threats!" The boy's mind raced. *After all, Tavo launched that monkey across the path like a rag doll... If I tell them about that, they'll never let me go. Should I tell them, though?* Manny's eyes snapped from his mother to his father. *No—I'm certain the other Lumens will protect me, so Mamá and Papá don't have anything to worry about. And besides, the rainforest is so big that I doubt I'll ever see that monkey again, anyway.*

María lowered the backpack, her eyes on the shredded fabric and the severed base of the missing strap. "I still don't know, Manuel. I think you would be safer in North America..."

"But you want to study in South America, right?" Carlos asked.

"Yes!" the boy replied breathlessly.

"Explain to me why," his father said, facing Manny attentively.

Why? Manny took a deep breath and considered his brief time in the rainforest of Costa Rica. "Papá, it was more amazing than any place I'd ever seen before—the trees and plants were all so green and alive, and the flowers were enormous! But even more important than all of that is the fact that Julius and Tavo, the two Lumens I met there, liked me for who I am rather than making fun of me for what I look like. I—I guess I'd have to say that they're the real reason why I want to go to school in South America."

At this Carlos turned and gave María a significant look. She swiftly returned her eyes to Manny. "But how do we truly know they'll protect you?" she persisted, her words wavering in the air.

"Sometimes you've just got to trust people, Mamá!" Manny answered firmly.

"I know, Manuel! I know! But look at Kevin Soriano—I entrusted my heart's most prized possession to him, and he almost left you stranded in a foreign country!" she countered desperately.

"But I'm fine, Mamá! I'm safe! And if you and Papá allow me to go to school there, I promise to be careful and responsible everywhere I go!" said Manny passionately.

"Enough!" she said, storming past Manny, down the hall and into the living room. The boy glanced at his father for an explanation, but Carlos merely shrugged, equally lost. Seconds later María returned to the kitchen, the stack of gleaming paloma paper in one hand and the iridescent blue pen in the other. Drawing her chair up closely to the table, she scribbled a brief note, folded the paper into thirds as if she were about to mail a letter, and wrote three words on the top. The instant María lifted the pen from the paper the letter shot into the air, hovering above the kitchen table and taking the form of a glowing, sky blue dove, which streaked through the translucent glass panel next to the sliding door and disappeared into the night, performing a 180 degree swoop and firing off over the rooftop to the south.

Manny and his parents gazed out the glass panels, overwhelmed. Silence flooded the kitchen, drowning their thoughts. "What are we getting ourselves into?" Carlos asked finally as he turned to face the other two.

"Nothing short of incredible," breathed María.

Before Manny could express any sort of opinion at all, an identical ray of blue light tore through the dining room and into the kitchen, halted suddenly above the table as a dove, and cooed loudly before floating gently down and landing in front of Manny's mother in the form of a letter, this time addressed to "Susana María López."

"Julius was right," Manny whispered. "That was fast."

"Why, he remembered my full name," María observed, blushing as she recovered the lettered and opened it.

"Who did? Are you talking about that Lightblade guy?" asked Carlos, gripped by jealousy.

"No, tonto!" she said, slapping her husband on the back of the hand. "I'm talking about that feisty little quetzal."

Manny rolled his eyes. *She's odd.* He scooted his chair to the left in order to read the letter over his mother's shoulder. "So, Mamá, did you write Julius telling him that I could attend school in South America?" the boy asked hopefully.

"I most certainly did not!" María rounded swiftly, turning the letter away from Manny so that he could not read it. After scanning the message a second time, María nodded contentedly and passed the paper to Carlos. "Tell me what you think."

Claws tore at Manny's stomach as he watched his father reading the letter. *What's it say?!*

"Wow, impenetrable light fields," Carlos said to María, ignoring Manny. She nodded with a smile as he continued to read. *This is torture.* Carlos raised his eyebrows and added, "Housed with an instructor! Fantastic!"

"Sí, I know," María agreed happily.

How can you both do this to me?

"Excellent," Carlos finished, setting the letter down beside his plate. Manny leaned this way and that, attempting to read the note from across the table.

Dang folds! I can't see a word!

"María, why don't we step outside and talk for a second."

"Perfecto," she replied as both stood up and walked to the sliding door.

"Manny, you can read the letter while we're outside," his father said as the boy snatched the luminescent paper up in his hands.

Finally! The door slid shut as Manny began to scan the paper, his life dangling from every one of Julius's flowing letters.

Dearest Sñra. López,

Allow me to sincerely thank you for expressing your concerns to me, a humble quetzal. Please be reassured that though the Amazon River Academy may be located in the center of the rainforest, the campus and surrounding Lumen city of Isla Verde actually comprise one of our safest communities in the world. Not only is crime significantly lower in the Lumen world than in your own, but no external threat may enter either the city or the academy owing to the impenetrable light fields created by the Stars centuries ago. Furthermore, should Manny leave the protective sphere of the island, he would be escorted by a First-Level Lumen with the highest defensive training to ensure that no harm befall your son. Provided that you allow Manny to attend the academy, I personally guarantee that he will be housed under the wise and vigilant protection of one of our prestigious instructors. Let me assure you that in the case that your son became injured in any way, even if he just scraped himself, our resident healers can repair him instantly.

Moreover, now that you have witnessed the effective mode of communication that is paloma paper, be confident that you may correspond with your son virtually instantaneously, wherever he may acquire his formal Lumen training. Should you begin to run low on paloma paper, simply notify me, and I will send as much as you need.

Best wishes,

J. Rumblefeather

The boy had just started to read the letter a third time when the familiar *Schwop!* told Manny that the sliding door had opened. His heart raced, threatening to combust in his chest as he analyzed his parents' expressionless faces as they passed through the door. *I'm going to die of a cardiac arrest at thirteen!* Carlos and María stopped in front of the kitchen sink and simply watched Manny, who suddenly noticed that his parents were holding hands.

"You will make wise choices, wherever you go, correct?" asked María, breaking the strained silence.

"Sí, Mamá," answered Manny, the letter slipping in his sweaty hands.

"And you'll write us at least once a day, two or three times if necessary?" Carlos asked solemnly.

"I can do that," Manny whispered anxiously.

"Then Manuel, your father and I have decided to allow you to attend school at the Amazon River Academy, in South America," María said happily.

"This is incredible!" Manny shouted as he exploded from his seat and across the kitchen to hug his parents. "I love you two! I've never been this happy in my life! Now I don't have to go to school with those jerks here anymore, and I can actually make friends! I—I" But he was lost for words. "Thank you," he said finally, squeezing them both tightly.

"But you must keep your promise to make wise choices and stay in contact daily," said María, embracing her son and husband with all her strength.

"Oh, I will!" Manny replied. "I promise!"

"Good," said Carlos as he and María stood back and looked upon their son proudly. "And I guess we should say, Happy Birthday!"

"Happy Birthday?" repeated Manny, extremely confused. "But today's not my—oh my gosh! I can't believe I forgot all about it! Tomorrow's my birthday! But you two don't need to get me anything—just being able to go to school in the rainforest is enough for me!"

146

Carlos and María laughed. "Are you sure you don't want to at least invite Zane to come stay the night?" María asked.

"We could have a cookout on the patio to celebrate," Carlos suggested.

"Sounds great!" Manny answered, ecstatic. "Fourteen's looking like it'll be my best year yet."

***

It is debatable which of the López boys was happier about Manny's upcoming journey into the Lumen world that fall. Although Manny's heart seemed to lift him from the floor and carry him wherever he went the next day, when Zane discovered the news he performed a cartwheel, shouting crazily toward the painted canyons north of Manny's house. Zane's unexpected reaction made Manny laugh hysterically. That evening Carlos and José cancelled baseball practice in honor of Manny's birthday, and the entire family came over to the boy's home for exploding bratwursts, charred hamburgers, and the infamous carne asada. Despite the fact that Manny had told his parents not to buy him anything, Carlos and María surprised their son with a new set of black luggage and a leather backpack for rough traveling in the rainforest. Zane and his family gave Manny a pool specifically designed for pet salamanders, and Minta stunned her oldest grandson with a pair of light yet durable hiking boots. To Manny and Zane's dismay, Carlos would not allow the boys to stay up all night, reminding them that they had a ball game the following evening. In any case, it was well past midnight before the boys stopped whispering their ideas to one another about what Isla Verde might look like as well as what classes Manny would be taking. Zane even formulated a detailed list of imaginary light bending techniques that he would use to fight off any threats in the rainforest. "I can't wait 'til next March, when I turn fourteen!" Zane had whispered, a little too loudly. "Then I'll become a Lumen, and in a year we'll be leaving for South America together!"

Upon receiving the confirmation letter that Manny would be attending the Amazon River Academy in the fall, Julius burst into a raucous series of squawks and chirps that very nearly unnerved the poor, young Lumen child with whom the quetzal had been talking just seconds before the letter arrived. 'It's been years since I've been this excited about a student,' the bird thought later. 'I suppose he did save my life, after all.' Throughout the summer Julius faithfully corresponded with the López family by means of paloma paper, sending and receiving glittering doves regarding the logistics of Manny's integration into the Lumen community. As the school term was to begin in early September, it was decided that Manny would fly to Iquitos, Perú in late August where a First-Level Lumen would transport him alongside any other students along the Amazon via boat until the group reached the city of Isla Verde, hidden within the western rainforests of Brazil. Manny would receive his class schedule upon arriving at Chiron's Hutch, where he would be staying under the care of Chiron, the esteemed astronomy instructor. There was no need for Manny to purchase his books before the trip, as students of the academy simply rent their textbooks from the school itself. Concerning monetary issues, Carlos and María opted to send a monthly allowance to Manny, which he could then easily exchange for Lumen currency in Isla Verde. In spite of his elaborate plans to sneak Lil' Manny to the island along with him, the boy was pleased to find that the school actually encouraged pets. By the beginning of August he and his parents had successfully gathered the clothing and supplies set forth in the packing list, and had fully prepared for the boy's approaching journey.

Of extreme interest is the fact that, following his birthday and during the entire summer season, the Soaring Eagles achieved a 32-1 record, taking second place in state. Needless to say, Nacho was utterly flummoxed and thoroughly irritated by Manny's renewed enthusiasm and virtually flawless technique on the field. In fact, a few of Manny's teammates began to treat him as a normal kid—even coming to his house after practice near the end of the season—laughing, playing games, and inhaling gallons of ice cream.

Midway through August, just a week before Manny was to leave, Zane's euphoric attitude began to change. "What's your problem?" Manny asked one afternoon when Zane staunchly refused to go spelunking. "I want to see the Painted Cave one last time before I leave." But Zane ignored him, electing to watch television instead.

The next day the boys found themselves interlocked in a violent wrestling match on the foyer floor, Zane screaming with rage as he pinned Manny. "You wanna know why I'm mad? Because my best friend's leaving me behind and I have no way to contact him!" Zane growled, punching the floor in his anger just before he leapt up and ran for the kitchen.

Shaking himself and wiping the blood from his burning lip, Manny got up and entered the empty kitchen. A minute later he found Zane sitting on the back patio under the blazing sun and staring at the mesas rising in the distance. A tear ran down the younger boy's cheek. "Here, take this," Manny said, shoving a stack of paper in Zane's face.

"A lot of good that's gonna do me!" Zane replied tersely, discounting the paper and continuing to stare forward.

"Oh, quit being a jerk!" Manny spat back as he slapped the paper onto Zane's lap. "You can use it to reach me anytime you want."

"Yeah, right," Zane countered coldly.

"How do you think we've stayed in contact with Julius all summer, you nitwit!" Manny said, and he briefly explained how paloma paper worked.

"Seriously?"

"Sí. And Julius said that you don't even have to use the pen that Lightblade gave Mamá. That's just a keepsake."

From that point on Zane returned to his generally jovial self. "So how 'bout we head for the Cave, then?"

The next evening was unseasonably cool as Manny sat out on the back patio to watch the characteristically painted sunset one last time before leaving on his flight from Phoenix the following morning. He sighed. Though most of his heart was full of great anticipation to enter the sister world to which he now belonged, there seemed to be a kink, a bleeding slit, a yawning hole in his core that threatened to devour the joy the boy had felt the entire summer. *I'll be gone for—for months. I-I may not even get to come home for Christmas.* Manny's heart pounded tightly as he gazed upon a sandstone gorge, its belly growing progressively pink. Sliding the mahogany watch from his wrist, Manny transformed the silent timepiece into a small briefcase, the clasps of which he gently flipped open. Around a month earlier Manny had been utterly perplexed as to how Lee Lightblade had successfully opened his wand-case to remove the paloma paper. After three days of painstaking transformations Manny finally realized that in order to mold his wand into a device with authentic mechanisms, he must first understand and envision the distinct components themselves. Less than five minutes after studying his father's briefcase, Manny triumphantly morphed his wand into a briefcase with functioning clasps and hinges as well as a storage compartment. His transformational hypothesis verified, Manny began to take advantage of this highly portable and space-efficient feature of his wand to store a number of his most prized possessions—his letters from Julius. In the dying light of his final Arizona sunset, Manny plunged his hands into the dark briefcase, rifling through the letters until he found one in particular:

I cannot express how vital it is that you exercise caution with whom you share the details of your newfound identity. (Though I doubt most people of the outside world would believe you, they cannot easily deny what they see.) For that reason,

I strongly discourage you from transforming your wand or using paloma paper around others, as the Lumen community is in no way interested in confronting formal investigations regarding its existence. Despite the fact that all educated Lumens know that we were granted our powers to protect the world as a whole, it is strict Lumen code that we hold the general population in its present state of ignorance to our world.

Heed my words, m'ijo,

Julius

Just as his eyes scanned the quetzal's ominous farewell, Manny heard the swoosh of the patio door opening. His heart nearly leapt from his chest as he quickly stowed the letter in the briefcase, slid the contraption under his legs, then transformed it back into the inconspicuous watch he had worn daily since his trip to Costa Rica. *I hope they didn't see that, whoever it was.*

"So this is where you've been hiding, Manny!" rang Jane's voice. "José and I just wanted to say goodbye and good luck before you leave tomorrow."

Excelente. Manny sighed in relief. *I don't think they saw anything.*

"You nervous?" José asked as the two of them sat next to one another on the lounge chair on Manny's left, their frames traced by the fleeing sun.

"Sí, I guess so," the boy confessed.

"I bet you're thinking it's just so far away," his uncle observed.

"Yeah," Manny sighed, staring up at the increasingly velvet sky.

151

"But what an adventure!" Jane exclaimed excitedly. "Not everyone gets to attend school in South America!"

"I know," said Manny sadly.

"If you're worried about being homesick, just remember that we're all only a call away," José encouraged. Manny merely stared blankly back in response. *I don't think they use phones in the Lumen world.*

"Now what is your school's name again?" asked Jane.

"Amazon River Academy," breathed Manny.

"Hmm," mumbled José. "I'd never heard of it before Carlos mentioned it."

I'm not surprised.

"And what exactly are you studying?" asked Jane, cocking her head inquisitively, her ponytail sliding across her back.

"Oh, it's this special program with a heavy concentration on physical sciences," Manny answered automatically. *But when I say 'physical,' I really mean 'light.'*

"Qué interesante," José said slowly.

"Since when have you been so fascinated with science?" his aunt asked, a slight hint of suspicion in her voice.

"Actually, I guess it was my trip to Costa Rica," Manny answered, a little happier now.

Despite his positive reply, Jane continued to measure Manny with searching eyes and a subtle frown. "I just don't understand why you need to go all the way to the Amazon to study science," she finally said.

"Jane, don't be a wet blanket," José said dryly. "Manny, I think this is a fantastic opportunity for you to learn more about the world and our roots. I'm sure it will be a life-changing experience that you'll never forget."

"Now wait un momento," interrupted Jane, annoyed. "There's still something off about all this, Manny. What are you all keeping from us? Is there another reason you're going down there?"

"Jane, leave it alone," José said in a low voice.

"No, José! María's keeping something from me and I want to know what it is!" she snapped. Turning to her nephew with suddenly delicate eyes, she said, "Manny, you can trust us."

"I know," Manny admitted. "But…" *But I'm not supposed to tell people about the Lumen world. Especially two people who own a newspaper, even if you are my aunt and uncle.*

"But what?" Jane persisted, impatience infiltrating her voice.

"Jane—"

"José!" she fired back, glaring at her husband. "There shouldn't be secrets in the family!"

"Whoever said there were secrets?" José countered, an argument beginning.

His mind racing, Manny tried to determine something truthful to say to assuage his aunt's burning curiosity and stop her from prying any further into the details of his education.

"…best that we leave now, I think," José ended, leaning forward to stand up.

"¡Esperen un momento!" Manny said, raising his hand to keep them from leaving. "I-I want to tell you what's so different about my school."

Jane's boiling cobalt gaze cooled slightly as José sat back down on the lounge chair. "Go ahead, then," relinquished José.

"Okay, well, this may sound really far out to the both of you, but," Manny gulped and inhaled dramatically, "I can't call home." Jane gazed expectantly at Manny in hopes that more details would come, but Manny simply looked back with his sincere, exploding hazel eyes.

"That's irregular," José said, breaking the silence.

"Why can't you?" Jane asked, here voice less severe now.

"I'll be in the middle of the Amazon," Manny replied. "The only way to stay in contact is by sending letters."

"Imagine that," wondered José. *At least he's convinced.*

A moment later Jane's fire seemed to smolder. "I-I can understand why María's acting so strangely, then," she said slowly. "Not being able to hear Berta or Zane's voice for over nine months would nearly kill me." She breathed deeply, her hard features melting as she lunged forward and embraced Manny tightly, an act that he had not anticipated. "Manny, we'll all miss you, especially Zane," she whispered, her voice faltering. "And don't be surprised if your mother shows up to visit you sometime during the school year. I might even come too!" she laughed, releasing the boy and staring at him with wet eyes, a bittersweet smile on her face.

Suddenly the door slid open. "¡Mamá! ¡Papá! ¡Vámonos, ya!" cried Berta, peering out from the kitchen. "I'm so bored!"

"Come out here and tell your cousin goodbye, then," José answered quickly. "You won't be seeing him for almost a year!"

"Está bien," Berta conceded as she slipped through the door and walked lightly across the now dark patio, stopping three steps in front of Manny's chair. "See ya, squirt," she said with a wave of her right hand. "Don't let any funky monkeys snuff your light out!"

"I won't, don't worry," Manny chuckled.

"And careful with those South American girls!" Berta added as she flipped her hair over her left shoulder. "I hear they're wild."

Wild?

"Thank you then, Miss Love Advice," Jane said sarcastically. "Manny, you know we all love you. Have a safe trip."

"Enjoy yourself," said José, rubbing Manny's short, black hair with his hand as he and his wife rose from the chair to follow their daughter to the door.

"Oh, and Manny, one more thing," called Jane, one foot in the kitchen and one on the patio.

"¿Sí, Tía?" he answered attentively.

"Make smart choices," Jane said, and she disappeared into the bright kitchen.

***

"Run that by me again, Manuel," María repeated, her voice constricted.

Careful not to roll his eyes, Manny took a shaky breath. Even more than annoyed from his mother's incessant queries regarding his traveling schedule, the boy was nervous. *It feels like all the butterflies in my stomach unexpectedly died and fused into a two-ton rock that's crushing my lungs.* Manny winced as the early morning light tore through the airport windows and pierced his pupils.

"Manuel," his mother prodded.

"Okay," he relented, finding his voice. "First I board flight 412 to Lima, Perú. Once I land in Lima I switch flights, taking a thirty-passenger jet called Catalina del Bosque. After arriving in Iquitos, a Lumen will meet me in the airport. From there, we will travel to the port, ride along the Amazon, and finally reach Isla Verde around ten or eleven at night," he ended, his heart jolting as they reached the entrance to the terminal.

"Ahem," coughed María.

Now I have to leave them. Manny's lungs tightened. *I-I don't think I want to go anymore.*

"Ahem! Aren't you forgetting something?!"

Manny's confused eyes met his mother's stern ones. He gave an apologetic half-shrug; she crossed her arms indignantly. "What is the first thing you'll do when you reach the Lumen boat?" she snapped.

"Oops! Sorry," Manny answered candidly. "I'll write you a letter on paloma paper."

"And when you reach Isla Verde?" María continued.

"I'll send you a letter," Manny replied, semi-dully.

"And when you step foot in Chiron's Hutch?" she asked, eyeing him carefully.

"I'll go to sleep," Manny replied jokingly. A fell glance quelled his laughter. "Mamá, of course. I'll send you a letter."

"Bien," she said, smiling serenely.

"But before you actually do go to bed, remember you've gotta send me a letter," Zane reminded Manny with a light punch to the shoulder.

"Don't worry, sir, I will," Manny replied with a smile, returning the gesture.

"Manny, your flight will probably start boarding in the next ten minutes, so you really oughta head that way soon," Carlos said, his voice steady.

"Before you do that, come here and give your abuela a fierce hug," said Minta, her arms open. Manny approached her and embraced her tightly. *Her hair always smells like roses.* "Manny," whispered Minta into the boy's right ear, "Gabriel would be proud of you." Stepping away, she gave him a knowing wink.

A firm hand grasped Manny's left shoulder. "Son, I'm amazed at your courage. At your age I would've been terrified to do what you're doing. I hope this is an incredible year for you, but remember," said Carlos, his grip tightening slightly, "remember your values, everything that your mother and I have taught you over the years." He paused, then hugged Manny firmly. "Think of God in all you do. I love you." Carlos coughed as he rose to his full height, turning and reading a nearby sign awkwardly.

I'm not brave, Dad.

"Manuel," said María, her voice scarcely audible. Looking left, Manny met his mother's firm gaze. "Ven." He obeyed, leaning into his mother's reassuring arms and nearly breaking. "M'ijo, wherever you go, be it South America or Asia, you'll always be my baby boy," she said, gently rubbing his head and neck.

"Mamá—" the boy choked, "I d-don't think I c-can do this."

"Manuel, you look at me," María whispered determinedly, leaning back and capturing his quaking eyes with her fierce, brown gaze. "You are a strong boy! Manuel, since the moment you were born and I first held you in my arms, I knew you were special, that you could do anything!"

"I'm just different on the outside," mumbled Manny sadly, his eyes falling.

"No! It's more than that!" María persisted, lifting his chin so that he met her eyes once again. "You're special here," she said, pressing the space on Manny's chest over his heart. "You're special here, and your skin, your wand, your Lumen abilities—they pale in comparison to your bravery here. Manuel, you stand tall in Isla Verde, and don't ever doubt the extent of your talent. You can do anything."

Manny stared into his mother's unbending brown eyes. "Te amo, Mamá," he said, hugging her one last time.

156

"I know, I love you, too. Never forget that my love goes with you, and that our God will protect you." Patting his cheek, she added, "I'm only a letter away."

"Sí," he laughed, tearing his heart from his mother's hands and forcing it to follow him backward toward the terminal entrance. Those four smiling faces were etched in his mind forever as he turned away and entered the terminal, despite the nervous chasm in his stomach. Before disappearing from sight, Manny looked over his shoulder and waved. "Bye!" he yelled.

"Bye!" they called in reply as the boy pushed forward into the unknown, his heart pounding steadily.

River Running

Air rushed past Manny's face as he sped along a busy street, holding tightly onto the suspension bar in front of him as the three-wheeled moto-kar in which he rode wove between and around dozens of scooters, cycles, and the occasional truck or car. Between his feet lay pincered the plastic carrier in which Lil' Manny fought against the forces of gravity and motion, squeaking in panic as he slid from one end to the other. *I won't be surprised if I find regurgitated ant guts all over the carrier by the time we reach the port. I'm sorry, little buddy.*

"So, is this your first time in Iquitos?" yelled the young woman on his left, her voice nearly drowned out by the rushing air, incessant honking, and laughter from the people along the streets.

Manny nodded in reply, catching a sidewise glimpse at the woman with her copper skin and dancing black tresses before the vehicle veered suddenly to the right. His hand accidentally slid along the bar and landed on hers. As the moto-kar straightened, Manny pulled his hand away, breathing, "Sorry," and blushing brightly.

"S'okay," she replied loudly. "Make sure you look left after we make our next turn, 'cause you'll see La Plaza de Armas. It's pretty cool."

This time Manny was prepared as the little driver tore to the left and sped along to the north. A moment later Manny sighted a pinnacled, beige building, the late afternoon light illuminating the red trim and golden bells of the steeple. Another breath and the church was swallowed by an explosion of vibrant green lawns and bustling people meandering around a blue fountain and respectfully eyeing the monument of a solemn stone soldier. Through the buzzing line of moto-kars and scooters heading in the opposite direction, Manny distinguished tourists and iquiteños alike eagerly flocking to roadside stands. The woman smiled at him and winked just as the driver maneuvered the vehicle along another lightning turn. Manny's stomach squirmed, not from the turn, but from her gorgeous features.

"So, did you like it?" she yelled, her hair flying.

"¡Sí!" Manny answered, his voice cracking; fortunately for him, though, the noise of the surrounding traffic effectively camouflaged the nervous flection in his reply.

"¡Fantástico!" she cried happily as the moto-kar hooked left for the last time, rocketing along the riverside as the sun drew progressively toward the horizon, scattering light across the dark waters of the Amazon. Seconds later Manny's eyes fell on white-sanded beaches abounding with hundreds of watercraft, from barges laden with mountains of fruit to motor boats and canoes. Manny watched as entire families of iquiteños as well as vividly-painted tribal natives crisscrossed the waters in the fleeing evening light. The moto-kar came to an abrupt halt in front of an elegantly carved, wooden cruise ship.

Manny's pupils pulsated, engulfing his irises. *Wow!*

"We're here!" the woman exclaimed as she leapt from the side of the moto-kar, adeptly snagging Manny's luggage from the small bay at the back of the cherry red vehicle. By the time Manny had paid the driver and slid from the back seat, the dizzied salamander's case in his hand, the woman was waiting several steps away, her back to the port. There she stood, one hand in her jean pocket and the other hanging free at her side, the orange light accenting her ornately woven, pink and green blouse. Her dark hair flowed over her shoulders, and along one side of her face several strands hung threaded through a series of pearl-colored, wooden beads.

"G-gracias, Keilani," stuttered Manny, trying not to blush.

"For what, Manny?" Keilani asked, her eyes twinkling.

"You know, for getting my luggage," he breathed, his heart barely allowing his lungs to function.

"No problem," she replied, casually flipping her long hair over her shoulder. "We ready?" Manny nodded as he stepped forward and reached for his luggage. "No, I've got it," she said, grabbing the plastic handle firmly. "You just protect your pet there."

She nodded toward Lil' Manny before turning and proceeding along the sturdy planks of the pier.

This is gonna be awesome! I've never ridden on a cruise ship, much less a wooden one! Yet Keilani veered to the left, leaving the cruiser behind in her wake.

"Where're you going? The boat's here!"

Keilani stopped, turning to find the boy with the glowing skin and the honey eyes naively rooted in front of the beautiful cruiser. "That's not our boat," she stated bluntly, spinning round and continuing along the pier.

"Not our boat…?" Manny whispered, perplexed, but Keilani had already disappeared along the next dock. Lil' Manny squeaked unhappily as the boy began to jog along the pier after Keilani. "Sorry," Manny apologized as he shifted to a brisk walk. Reaching the far side of the cruiser, the boy's hopes deflated. *You must be kidding me.* Manny drug his feet along as he scanned the boat tethered to the posts of the dock, first noticing the craft's paling size in comparison to the high-railed cruiser on the right. He groaned as he measured the low-riding barge on which he was to traverse the Amazon. *It's like, what, the size of my living room?* His eyes flitted from one end of the boat to the other. *There's not even a motor!*

As he approached the wooden ramp connecting the dock to the boat, Manny suddenly realized that a crowd of approximately twenty children his own age had already boarded the barge, some seated on benches, a few walking, and two standing along the opposite edge of the vessel and pointing at the forest spreading endlessly along the river as far as the eye could see. Despite their differences in skin tone, ranging from rich copper to a white nearly as bright as Manny's, all the children spoke in an exhilarated and impassioned Spanish. *I wonder if any of them speak English… I should've realized—*

"Aren't ya gonna get in?" Keilani tore loudly, staring up at Manny from the craft.

"S-sí," he faltered.

"Well, get down here then!" she continued. "They've been waiting on us! We leave as soon as you board!"

160

How embarrassing. But to Manny's surprise, no one was staring; no one even seemed to be listening. *Huh.* Stepping carefully along the ramp, Manny descended into the boat.

In a flash Keilani had hoisted the ramp into the boat, proceeding along the length of the bobbing vessel to untie the ropes connecting it to the dock. Once finished with these tasks, she made for the front of the boat, brushing the hair back from the side of her face as she leaned over the edge of the prow. Not a second later the boat began to gently ease away from the dock, and within a minute the vessel was steadily maneuvering along the center of the river.

Manny frowned. *But how…?*

Keilani sauntered along the boat toward Manny, a captivating half-smile stretching across her copper face. "You look confused, Manny," she told him, humor in her voice.

"I-I'm just—I mean, did you—? How is—"

"The boat moving?" she stated, finishing his question. "That would be the dolphins."

"Dolphins?" repeated Manny skeptically.

"Of course," Keilani replied with her roguish smile. "No better way to travel on the River!"

"I'm fourteen years old and I've never heard of dolphins in the Amazon," Manny answered wisely.

"Well I'm twenty and I grew up in Isla Verde, and I'm telling you that the Amazon is teeming with them."

"No te creo."

"You may not believe me, but you can't deceive your eyes— not Lumen eyes, anyway," Keilani shot back, grabbing Manny by the collar and dragging him to the front of the boat. "¡Mira!" she told him, nearly pulling him over the edge of the craft.

Manny obeyed, reluctant though he may have been, and peered into the rippling water. *What the heck?* "Those aren't dolphins!" he laughed, glancing back at Keilani in amusement.

"What d'you mean by that?" she retaliated, seizing his chin and forcing his head around. She pointed to the water. "What do you call those?"

"They're fins!"

161

"Exactly!" Keilani retorted matter-of-factly.

"But they're pink!" he exclaimed, pointing now as well.

"And...?"

Manny scoffed. "Dolphins aren't pink."

For a moment Keilani simply glared in response. "Rosefin! Riverrunner! Come up for a moment!" she abruptly shouted, her fiery eyes not leaving Manny's for a second.

A splash and a pair of high-pitched cackles met Manny's ears as an uncomfortable knot of shame took form in his chest. Keilani cocked her head, her face void of humor. Begrudgingly turning his gaze, Manny found two extremely large dolphins staring up at him, their dark eyes glinting earnestly in the diminishing light. *They are pink.* His eyes fell to the water.

"This is Manny López," Keilani told the dolphins. "He's from the United States."

Rosefin and Riverrunner blinked at the boy. "Nice to meet you," he said, waving a hand weakly. The dolphins cackled and nodded happily.

"We'd better get going," Keilani suggested, eyeing the aquatic pair benevolently.

The dolphin on the right chattered in agreement as both animals eagerly flipped and dove back into the shadowy waters. Manny noticed that each dolphin appeared to be wearing a golden harness linked to the boat by a pair of luminescent chords. *So that's how they pull the boat. Who'd've thought?*

"I guess I was wrong," Manny admitted guiltily.

"Yes, you were," she agreed, "But it takes a strong man to admit to when he's wrong." This statement hit Manny unexpectedly, leaving him with nothing to say. A moment passed as the two of them stood on the boat, simply staring at one another as the vessel glided deftly along a bend in the river to the east. Stars began to materialize as dusk descended, the deep violet blanket falling over the forest trees still-brimming with life. To the north and south Manny could hear birds babbling as they settled into their roosts; two short cat calls reached his ears from the southwest, while a band

162

of monkeys suddenly shrieked, tearing through the foliage on the far side and scattering birds in all directions.

Keilani took a deep breath. "It's getting dark. We need some light—other than you, I mean." She threw Manny a playful smile. Turning to face the length of the craft, she carelessly tossed her midnight tress with the wooden beads over her left shoulder. Instantly dozens of strands of light wound down from the sky, gracefully whisking across the vessel and tinting the outer hull a brilliant green. Manny blinked as the light rounded back, converging to form a luminous blue canopy spanning the entire boat.

"¡Perfecto!" rang a melodious voice from a nearby bench. "Truly exemplary of the superb student that you are!" Clapping met Manny's ears as he scanned the benches in search of the origin of that female voice. "I am anxious to see you graduate!"

"Gracias," Keilani replied humbly.

Who is she talking to?

"You are most welcome," the voice answered, followed by a high-pitched cough that sounded a good deal like a bark. Manny could see movement on the edge of the bench directly in front of Keilani, but he was unable to make out the shape of the speaker. "The only improvement that I would suggest would be to illuminate the benches, but that is simply an option."

Threading her beaded lock behind her ear, Keilani drew additional light from the distant stars to accent the wooden benches with a vibrant red. Manny frowned as a cat-like animal appeared before him, its long, dark claws clasping securely to the edge of the bench. *If that's a cat, then it's the weirdest one I've ever seen.* Though the animal's head was shaped like a feline's, its nose was black and its ears were a great deal smaller and rounded. The creature hopped agilely from the bench, approaching the boy. *That thing's tail is as long as its body!* Stopping just a step from Manny, the creature lifted its head and measured the boy with a pair of shining violet eyes. "Who is this young fellow, Keilani?" inquired the animal interestedly.

"This is Manny López," stated Keilani, as if he had been a topic of previous conversation.

163

"Oh, so you're Rumblefeather's student, are you? Well, it's a shame I had not met you first," the creature said with a smile, her tiny teeth glinting eerily. "Yes, 'tis an absolute shame." *This is awkward.* "And my, my, child! How the light shines through you."

Manny shifted uneasily. "Yeah, I've noticed," he mumbled.

"I mean you no harm, child!" the animal quickly exclaimed, opening her arms wide. "It is just that Rumblefeather failed to mention your distinct gift!"

"Gift? What gift?" the boy asked.

"Your skin, child! Any Lumen of your species, not to mention my own, would trade a fortune to produce light as you do!" the creature proclaimed in wonder. "And your eyes! The magnif—"

"But I can't produce light," Manny interrupted. "I only reflect it."

"Oh," the creature replied flatly. "What a shame. But my, my, I would be willing to wager that the females of your species find your glowing trait attractive! What would you say, Keilani?"

Coughing suddenly, Keilani turned. "I-I hadn't really considered that," she stuttered in reply. Manny wondered if she might be blushing.

Hoping to change the subject, at least for Keilani's sake, Manny said, "So you know Julius?"

"Know Julius? Julius Rumblefeather? Well, of course I do, child! We're colleagues!" exclaimed the creature.

Manny racked his brain in an attempt to recall the quetzal's formal title. *That's it.* "Then you're a representative for the Lumen Academies of South America?" he asked.

"In more or less words, yes," agreed the creature. "Within the Lumen community you may simply call us counselors, fulfilling a variety of roles from recruiting to advising. In fact, I was the wand-giver and light-bringer to Keilani, here!"

"What are those?" Manny asked quickly.

"Keilani," prompted the creature, turning and watching the young woman avidly.

"You see, Manny," began Keilani, her tone rather official, "a wand-giver is the term for the person who transforms one of your

164

personal items into your wand. A light-bringer, on the other hand, appears later to explain your options as a newly-called Lumen. Generally, the roles of wand-giver and light-bringer are performed by two distinct Lumens of species other than that of the Seventh-Level.

"A precise explanation!" said the creature happily. "Very precise!" Turning back to Manny she added, "Keilani is studying to be a counselor, just as Rumblefeather and I. This is her final year."

"So, Manny, we know that Julius is your light-bringer, but who was your wand-giver?" asked Keilani brightly, confident once again.

My wand-giver? Manny's stomach suddenly contorted. "A nasty little monkey!" he spat. Both the creature and Keilani burst into hysterical laughter. "What's so funny?" he asked, slightly annoyed.

"A monkey?" repeated Keilani, covering her mouth as she chuckled.

"¡Sí!" affirmed Manny indignantly.

The raucous laughter continued, drawing the attention of a group of nearby students from a heated game of cards. "You, child, definitely rival Rumblefeather for genuine humor!" laughed the creature as she wiped her wet eyes with her snake-like tail. "Although Rumblefeather is typically at his finest when raging mad," she muttered.

"I don't see any humor in my statement whatsoever," cut Manny dryly.

As the laugher subsided, the students resumed their card game. "Are you serious?" Keilani asked, stifling a final chuckle.

An icy glare told her that he was.

"You must be mistaken," affirmed the cat-like creature, striving for sobriety.

"I promise you," growled the boy, his light intensifying, "that the animal that created my wand was a monkey."

"That's simply impossible," the creature continued.

"And why's that?" snapped Manny, his patience fully lost.

"Child, only Lumens can transform wands," the creature said plainly.

"I don't see what you're getting at," Manny countered.

"Listen to me," the animal began, her arms open wide and violet eyes calm. "Monkeys are not Lumens."

"Well, this one was."

"No, it wasn't," Keilani told him understandingly. "I think I know what's going on here," she added as she turned to face the cat-like creature at their feet. "I believe Manny's wand-giver was a kinkajou." The creature's face lit up with comprehension.

"A kinkawhat?" exclaimed the boy.

"That would be a kink-a-jou," the creature answered, enunciating the separate syllables of the species' name with ultimate clarity. "Keilani is saying that your wand-giver must have been a creature of my species."

Hold it. Manny took a moment to analyze the kinkajou's profile, scanning her from ear to tail. "No way," he said confidently. "It was definitely a monkey."

Shaking her head, Keilani said, "It couldn't have been."

"Oh yes, it could!" Manny argued. "Yeah, sure, this kinkajou here and that monkey's tail match, and maybe their ears, but other than that, there's no similarity at all."

"This kinkajou has a name," said the creature crossly, "and it would be Melody Nightvine. Be grateful that my patience exceeds that of Rumblefeather, who I'm sure by now would have proffered you an extended tongue lashing."

With the look of death I really can't tell much difference. And anyway, you're the one that failed to introduce yourself.

Determined to stymie Manny's argument, Keilani said, "And exactly how are Melody and that supposed monkey so different, if I may ask?"

"To begin with, Melody is, what, two feet tall? The monkey was at least three, and its body was broader. And when you looked at its face you saw two pink nostrils instead of a little black nose. It's fur was a lot longer than Melody's, and it had a set of wicked fangs

166

framed by a beard, the whitest I've ever seen," Manny said, his eyebrows raised.

Looking down at Melody, Manny noticed that she had her left paw on her ear and her right paw feeling her teeth. "What color were its eyes?" she asked, captivated by the boy's description.

Its eyes? Manny thought back to when the light had filtered through his camera and had hit the monkey's face. "Jet black," he answered unwaveringly.

"This is absolutely ridiculous!" Keilani bellowed. "Ten minutes ago he didn't even know that there were dolphins in the River, much less that they were pink! He's from the outside world, Melody! How can we expect him to know the difference between a kinkajou and a monkey if he didn't even grow up here?"

"That's not a very hard one to figure out, Keilani," said Manny off-handedly.

"Obviously it is for you!" the young woman tore back, one hand on her hip.

"¡Basta!" interrupted Melody. "Lumens are to be people of peace, and this argument has gone far enough! Keilani, I agree with you that it must have been a kinkajou, though a rather wild-looking one at that—whoever heard of a kinkajou with a beard?" she added, her knowing eye's meeting Manny's. "And Manny—No! Listen! There is no harm in there being a mutual disagreement on this issue, for in spite of the questionable appearance of your wand-giver, he, or she, bestowed your wand upon you nonetheless."

Yeah, but I bet most wand-givers don't try to take it back later.

With a reluctant breath, Keilani stepped forward and offered her right hand to Manny, saying, "Let's leave this behind us, then."

"Alright," Manny conceded, taking Keilani's soft hand and shaking it. *I'm the one who's right, though.*

"Manny?" Melody said.

"Yes?" replied the boy, releasing Keilani's hand.

"In the heat of the moment I forgot to forward a message to you," the kinkajou said. "Rumblefeather wanted me to remind you to write your mother."

"Oh my gosh!" he exclaimed, setting the plastic carrier down on the floor of the boat and sliding off his watch. Sitting down in front of Melody, Manny transformed his wand into a briefcase, then removed the paloma paper and a pen, writing wildly.

Mamá,

We're on the Amazon right now. My trip went fine, and Iquitos was a beautiful yet busy city. I've already met some new friends—their names are Keilani and Melody. Keilani's a human—she picked me up at the airport. Melody's a kinkajou, which is nothing like a monkey; she's a counselor, like Julius.

I'll write you again as soon as we arrive in Isla Verde.

Love ya — Manny

Creasing the paper into thirds, Manny jotted down his mother's full name at lightning speed and witnessed as the message shot into the air as a dove, then fired off to the north. Before rising to his feet, the boy quickly scribbled another letter, which he immediately folded and pocketed. He had not been standing more than twenty seconds when a jet of blue light rocketed down from the north, imploding on itself with a sad warble and floating down into Manny's hands in the form of a letter addressed to him in his mother's handwriting.

Manuel,

I'm glad to hear you're safe and sound. Your papá and I were just drinking some café con leche at the kitchen table, wondering when you might write. Your abuela is out bowling again with her amigas. Gracias for writing me.

¡Te amo!

Tu mamá

"You're pretty good with your wand there," Keilani observed, a bit amazed.

"What d'you mean?" Manny asked, filing the letter into his briefcase, which he promptly molded back into a watch. "Everybody can transform their wand."

"Yes, but most Seventh-Levels have difficulties in creating wand mechanisms—your briefcase, for example," Melody elucidated.

"I was nearly a Sixth-Level by the time I learned to use my wand for storage purposes," Keilani said, flipping her beaded tress with her thumb.

It really isn't all that hard—you just need to have a good imagination.

"Which means you are slightly ahead of the game," Melody concluded. "Although I may not be your formal counselor, I am particularly anxious to see how you progress with your light bending in the coming months." The kinkajou's violet eyes sparkled as she flipped her tail to and fro in interest.

Silence fell as the three of them stood in contemplation. A chorus of laughter and an exclamation of, "I can't believe it!" came from the students intensely involved in the card game on the floor of the boat. In the distance frogs croaked and grasshoppers played their wiry tune, contributing a subtle note of nostalgia to the humid air. Melody took a deep breath, the sound of which drew Manny and Keilani back into reality. The kinkajou coughed purposefully as she turned toward Keilani, who stared back attentively, eyes wide. Melody raised her left fore-claw, her furry brow raised as she traced a horizontal circle in the air and gazed at the young woman.

"Oh!" Keilani exclaimed, pulling her hands from her pockets and rushing to the edge of the boat. "I'll get on it right away."

Slowly and serenely, the kinkajou turned to Manny. "Keilani needs to complete her rounds to ensure that the vessel, passengers, and dolphins are all making the voyage safely, so I would encourage you to mingle with your peers and make some friends.

Friends? Manny swallowed uncomfortably as Melody nimbly trotted toward a pole, scaled it in a breath, and mounted the canopy, disappearing from sight. Reluctantly peeling his eyes from the underside of the awning, Manny scanned the craft, estimating the risk of potential rejection and consequent humiliation that he would surely suffer when he tried to interact with the other students on the boat. *Those two asleep on the bench wouldn't hate me too much; they'd be boring, though. Okay, so, that guy with his friends over there by the luggage looks a little snotty; I'll avoid him. The kids playing cards seem to be having a lot of fun; maybe I should go check that out. If they don't like me, however, that would be majorly embarrassing. But still, it's easier to mold into a crowd than to walk up to individual strangers, so I'll just head for the card game.*

Just as Manny started to walk away, a terrified squeak came from behind him. *Oops!* "I'm sorry, Lil' Manny," he said as he whirled around and knelt down to the plastic carrier on the floor of the boat. The spotted salamander looked back at him with thankful eyes. "You want out?" Manny asked. A confirmation squeak was all the boy needed to prompt him to detach the clear lid of the carrier and gently peel the nervous salamander from the inside. Staring into the boy's eyes, Lil' Manny released a puff of relief; the next second the salamander had slid up the boy's arm and come to rest in the warm curve of Manny's neck. "Let's go meet some new people, then," the boy said, setting the carrier on the bench where Melody had originally perched and approaching the center of the boat bravely.

"¡Hola!" said a boy with light olive skin and brown hair as Manny stepped up to the excited crowd. "You waiting for a turn to play, too?"

"I dunno," shrugged Manny, looking over the heads of the players and observing the process of the game. "Depends on what everyone's playing." Manny immediately noted that each of the players held five cards in his or her hand and that there was a separate discard pile for each person as well. *They're all drawing from a pile in the middle.* "Is it poker?" Manny asked, suddenly interested.

"Nope," answered the girl seated at his feet, her back to Manny. "That's a good game, though."

"You must be an outsider if you don't know what we're playing," commented a boy two seats to the left of the girl.

Just perfect. Manny's heart sank.

The boy directly across from Manny discarded. "Where're you from?" the boy asked, looking swiftly up at Manny.

"The United States," Manny said, discouraged. *Here it comes.*

"Cool! Me, too!" said the girl at Manny's feet, hiding her cards from the others as she turned and smiled at Manny. "I'm from Texas. How 'bout you?"

Several eyes peered at Manny, the crowd's interest piqued. "Arizona," he said.

"I guess you don't play Piranha Sweep in Arizona, then," observed the boy on the left.

"Well, obviously he hasn't," retorted the boy across from Manny.

"Are you the first Lumen in your family?" asked a girl on Manny's right as she drew a card. He nodded in reply. *At least I think I am.* "That would explain why you've never heard of Piranha Sweep."

Before Manny could make any inquiries regarding the rules of the game, another boy across the circle and on Manny's right asked, "So why do you glow?"

Manny flexed his right hand nervously; all eyes had left the game with the transparent, glowing cards and were set on Manny's increasingly bright complexion. "Nobody knows. Ever since I was born I've just reflected light, even if you shine the tiniest bit on me."

Silence gripped the group, not a single eye turning from Manny. The boy on Manny's left blinked twice. *Here goes. I'm a goner.* "Sweet," the boy said simply.

"Yeah," agreed the boy across from Manny. "I wish I could glow," he added keenly. Two girls sitting on the bench to Manny's left giggled, eyeing him shyly. *Are they seriously looking at me?*

"Well, too bad you can't," the girl at Manny's feet said sarcastically. "Hurry it up already, y'all, 'cause I'm gonna thrash you!"

You mean they don't think I'm a weirdo?

"You think so, huh?" asked a girl on the right. "Wait 'til you see this hand," she added defiantly as she discarded her third card.

"I bet you don't even have a Piranha!" the boy on Manny's left challenged.

Manny exhaled in amazement. *They actually don't care that I look different!*

"Whoohoo!" exclaimed the girl at Manny's feet as she drew a card. From over her shoulder Manny observed that she now had a pair of nines featuring a blazing red fish with sharp teeth. *Are those Piranhas?* She discarded her sixth card, hardly able to suppress her joy.

Once play had returned to the boy across the circle, each player began to lay his or her hand down for all to see. "I stomped y'all!" cried the girl in front of Manny as the last boy laid down his hand. "Whoohoo! Two Piranhas!"

"Yeah, well, I did have two Aces," grumbled the girl on the right. *How can Nines beat Aces?*

172

"But one of 'em's mine, now!" drawled the girl at Manny's feet as she reached over to claim an Ace from her competitor's pile, leaving the second girl rather perturbed.

After recording everyone's points, the boy across from Manny said, "The game's not over—nobody's hit 500 yet."

"You just wait 'til next round," shot the girl in front of Manny.

"You're goin' down," threatened the boy on the left.

"Yeah, but by my hand, not yours," said the girl on the right as she confidently shuffled and dealt five cards to each player. *I like their competitive attitudes.*

Over the next hour Manny observed round after round of Piranha Sweep with ardent interest, taking careful note as to which card combinations seemed to excel over the rest. Although several players offered to allow Manny to take their place after the game was completed, he opted to wait and continue observing. Just when he felt brave enough to step in following yet another heated game, Keilani walked up to the group. Her tone was apologetic as she said, "Sorry, guys and gals, but you'll have to wrap up the card games, 'cause we'll be reaching the island in less than five minutes."

Geez! Manny's sentiments were shared by his peers, particularly those who had only gotten the chance to play one round since their departure from Iquitos. Stifled grumbles rose from the floor of the boat.

"Be ready with your luggage as soon as we land on the island," Keilani added, eyeing the group charily. "Those cards are mine if they're still out when we dock, got it?" Everyone stared back blankly. "Follow me, Manny," she whispered as she turned from the group, heading for the prow. *Might as well; I can't play now.*

"Hey, I'll see you all later, okay?" said Manny, waving at the group.

"¡Adiós!" several of them replied.

"We'll be playing in the Gardens tomorrow around ten or eleven if you wanna meet us there!" added a boy enthusiastically. Looking over his shoulder, Manny noticed that it was the boy that had been sitting across the circle from him.

"Alright! Thanks!" Manny answered, offering one last wave as he turned and followed Keilani to the prow.

"Since this is your first time in the Amazon and all, I figured you might enjoy taking in the sights from the front of the boat," she said as Manny came up and stood on her left.

"Sounds good," he replied. Seconds later the vessel veered sharply to the right, heading south along a subsidiary of the Amazon that was nearly half as broad as the main river.

"Now we're on the Lucero," Keilani said as the ship pitched forward sharply, then began charging fiercely down a wild side river, the thick foliage overhead swallowing the boat and its passengers. "Keep looking straight ahead and you can just make out the edge of the Falls."

Well that's interesting. "The Falls?" Manny asked, abruptly stricken by the idea of hurtling brutally over cascades of crushing water.

"Just watch or you'll miss it," Keilani replied smoothly.

Lil' Manny hooked his tail tightly around the back of the boy's neck as the boat continued to plunge deeper and deeper into the belly of the rainforest. Without warning a gap appeared in the tree line straight ahead, moonlight pouring down into the open space beyond. Fearing certain death, Manny clutched the edge of the boat as the vessel forked to the right. Manny caught a brief glimpse of reflective blue stone beyond the top of the Falls just before the dense vegetation obscured his vision once again.

"You need to chill out," Keilani said, staring at his death-locked hands. "We just passed the Falls on the left; we'll be on the Lake in no time." *The Lake?*

"Whoohoo!" cried an excited voice from behind Manny as the craft soared over a series of rapids, the dolphins leaping into the air to avoid the rocks.

"Why can't you be more like her?" Keilani asked, nodding behind them and smiling wryly.

"She's from Texas," Manny answered simply.

Keilani chuckled as the craft shuddered over yet another set of rapids. Manny's grip loosened slightly. *How deep are we going, anyway?* Beyond the awning all Manny could see was a green blur; he refrained from looking in any direction but forward, however, as his stomach swooped violently otherwise. Following several more rapids, countless bends, and one hairpin turn, the river's angle of descent suddenly decreased. The ship progressively slowed as the tree-lined tunnel yielded to more placid waters ahead.

"Is that it?" Manny asked. Keilani smiled and nodded as the boat eased out onto the Lake.

Manny was utterly speechless as his eyes absorbed the magnificent scene before him. Out of the vast Lake rose an expansive island bordered by brilliant white beaches. On the northeast side of the island a strangely luminescent, blue stone platform towered over the rest of the landscape. *I wonder what that's for?* As the vessel drew nearer to the western shore, Manny noted the narrow curtain of water coursing down from the northern lip of the valley. *Huh. The Falls are smaller than I thought.* To the south the boy saw a seemingly endless expanse of dense vegetation stretching out beyond the edge of the Lake. *Increíble. Zane's gonna be so jealous!*

***

"Can we really walk on those?" Manny asked worriedly.

"Yes," Keilani replied astutely as she skillfully hopped from the lush bank onto a circular, sage green platform floating on the water.

Manny frowned, still unconvinced. "Are you sure they're steady?"

Keilani rocked the disk to the left and right, splashing water onto the surrounding platforms. "They're perfectly safe—in fact, the only way to tip a moon lily pad is to stab it with a sharp object," she said practically. "Watch." Flicking her beaded braid gingerly, Keilani drew down two curls of moonlight to assimilate a knife, which floated oddly over an adjacent lily pad. With another flick of her thumb the tip of the blade pierced the base of the pad and then suddenly dissolved. Without warning the lily pad flipped violently, slamming the water and sending shock waves that disturbed the neighboring pads. None of the other pads capsized, however.

"As long as you don't try to cross with a sharp rock in your shoe, you should be fine," Keilani said, lightly skipping from pad to pad to cross the stream.

I guess it's a good thing I'm not wearing my cleats, then. "Here we go," Manny whispered as he stepped nervously down onto the round pad before him. Though the pad rocked slightly, he was pleasantly surprised with its sturdiness. *She's right yet again.* "So, Keilani, I didn't know there were giant water lilies in the Amazon," he shouted as he hopped onto the subsequent pad.

"Who'd have guessed that?" she said sarcastically as she leapt onto the far bank.

"Aren't you funny."

Keilani smiled back playfully. "Actually, there have always been lilies this size in the Basin. Those pads are from a special breed of Victoria Lily known as the Moon Lily, which can sustain a great deal of weight and has sharp reflexes, unlike the Victoria."

"Remember to mention their increased level of mobility," Melody chimed as she somersaulted onto a pad to Manny's left, the boy's luggage hovering in the air next to her just above the flowing water. "Did you happen to forget something?" she added, her eyes twinkling.

"Thanks, Melody," he said as he jumped from pad to pad in order to keep up with her. "I owe you one."

"No, you don't," she replied abruptly. "It's just part of my job."

A moment later the trio disappeared along a path into the dense island vegetation, leaving the stream behind them. Unlike in the rainforest of Costa Rica, Manny felt at ease on Isla Verde. Something was different—he could feel a unique vibe or buzz in the air that told him that exciting and unexpected things waited for him around every corner and that, one way or another, he would be safe. *It's like some sort of invisible electricity in the air is—*

"So your mother's pretty protective of you, huh?" Keilani asked, interrupting his train of thought.

"Are the letters really that much of a giveaway?" Manny asked.

"If you haven't noticed, I haven't sent any letters to mi mamá," Keilani replied jokingly.

"If you're out of paloma paper I can lend you some," he said, smiling.

"S'okay," Keilani declined. "She'll survive."

"Well, my mamá wouldn't. So, yeah, she's actually very protective. Honestly, it's a miracle she even let me come to school here."

"What does she fear?" Melody asked from overhead, pausing as she leapt from tree to tree.

"I guess she's afraid I'll die or something," Manny said as they continued along. "I'm an only child."

"How unusual," observed Melody.

"Why's that?" Manny asked.

"Most Lumen families are blessed with multiple children," the kinkajou replied.

"Well, my family really isn't a Lumen family," the boy said.

"How come?" asked Keilani, her interest kindled.

"'Cause I'm the first López that's ever been a Lumen," Manny said.

"I highly doubt that," Melody replied quickly. Manny looked up at her quizzically. *How would you know?* "You see, in the rare occasion that a Seventh-Level Lumen appears in a family from the outside, it is most commonly assumed that one of the young Lumen's ancestors was a Light Bender as well. Can you think of any relatives that might have been a Lumen?"

"Maybe my abuelito," answered Manny quietly.

"What makes you think your grandfather is a Lumen?" Keilani asked.

"He liked the stars," said Manny lucidly.

"Oh," replied Keilani, suddenly quiet. "Did you ever see him bend light?"

"Nope. Never."

"That's strange," Keilani replied.

"Perhaps not," Melody said. "Not all Lumens choose to remain in our world, and some even choose to abandon their powers. Remember that, both of you." Manny nodded, but Keilani watched the kinkajou with sharp eyes.

"I've never heard of anyone giving up their powers," Keilani said skeptically. "They never mentioned that in school or on any of our missions."

"That's because such circumstances are extremely rare," replied Melody as she performed a pair of mid-air somersaults and landed gracefully on the path before the young Lumens. "But I shall not criticize, for such people have their reasons," she added, eyeing Manny knowingly.

Let's change the subject—I don't wanna talk about this anymore.

"What was your grandfather's name?" asked Keilani.

"Gabriel," said Manny. His rising discomfort prompted him to quickly change the subject. "So when—"

"Did you know him, Melody?" Keilani inquired, cutting Manny's attempt short.

"Gabriel López…" mused Melody. "I'm not sure. What was his area of origin?"

"El Salvador," Manny said, his words sagging. Melody eyed the boy perceptively.

"I don't believe so," answered the kinkajou, flipping around on one of her front paws to face the path ahead and breach a new topic. "This shortcut meets the East Road just around the next bend, Manny. From there we cross the bridge and we'll be in Chiron's Hutch in no time."

Thank God. Manny sighed, happy to leave the path and the conversation behind.

The Mirror Has Two Faces

"This is Chiron's Hutch?" Manny asked, an air of more than slight distaste in his voice as he, Keilani, and Melody emerged from a heavily trodden path. "He lives there?"

"Quiet, Manny!" Keilani whispered tersely from his right. "He might hear you!"

"Remember, Manny, it is by his hospitality that you have come to stay with us in Isla Verde. You must be appreciative for what he is giving you. I trust you will not insult him," Melody lectured, flicking the back of Manny's left calf with her limber tail.

It's just not what I expected. All the rest of the Lumen houses have huge gardens and seemed to be made of brick or wood. This is made of— "Is that straw?" whispered Manny from the corner of his mouth.

"The roof is, but the rest is bamboo," replied Keilani quietly.

"You can't be ser—"

"Don't be rude!" the woman snapped, nailing Manny with a vicious elbow to the ribs. "He'll hear you!"

Manny gasped. *I'm dying...*

"No, he won't," stated Melody calmly as they approached the modest bamboo shack. "I've no doubt that he's stargazing this very moment."

Stargazing?

"He is the astronomy teacher, you recall?" the kinkajou added with a pointed look at Manny.

"That's right," he wheezed.

"Let us circumnavigate the hutch and meet Chiron on the hill," Melody directed with poise. "We will leave your belongings at the back of the building." The kinkajou lead her companions around the shack, her tail dancing playfully as she hopped across the soft jade lawn.

"Now that is a huge tree," observed Manny in wonder as he and Keilani set his luggage, backpack, and plastic carrier down just outside the rear door of the hutch.

"Finally! Something we can both agree on," exclaimed Keilani wryly as she stood beside Manny and gazed at the tree that seemed to explode from the ground some one hundred steps beyond the hutch.

"What kind is it?" he asked as the three of them steadily approached the tree's mountainous roots, which opened to form a gap both wide and tall enough for a small elephant to pass. *Its roots are wider than I am! And the trunk is—what—almost thirty feet around!*

"This is a kapok tree. Chiron's grandfather, Nahir, planted it when Chiron and his brother, Rigel, were very young. Hence the name Nahir's Hill," Melody revealed.

"Are kapok trees generally this tall?" the boy asked, stumbling backward as his eyes ran up the trunk to the canopy that opened high among the stars, or at least he thought.

"No, this is the tallest of its kind in the world," answered Keilani sagaciously. "You'll see why." Her words curled mysteriously up the trunk as she stepped forward and passed beneath the roots.

As Manny followed the woman and the kinkajou through the intricately twisted kapok gate, he noticed thousands of thorns protruding from the roots. *Don't think I wanna trip and bump into any of those.* For some odd reason, the stars appeared to shine brighter and closer once Manny had reached the other side of the tree. *That's neat.* "Hey, is that Chiron's horse?" asked Manny as he looked past Melody and Keilani to the top of the hill. *Maybe he's got a pet horse like Tavo does.*

Melody spun on the spot. "Manny! Don't even dare think such a thing!" she whispered desperately.

"Why?" he asked innocently. "It's okay if he has a horse. Lots of Lumens have pet horses, I would imagine. For example, while I was in Costa Rica, I met this healer named Tavo with a horse nam—"

"Shhh!" Keilani interrupted. Manny stared from one to the other, one eyebrow raised. *They're acting so weird.*

"Manny!" whispered Melody again. "¡Ven!" she said, beckoning him down to her height with her paw. The boy knelt down on his knees as the kinkajou hopped up next to him. "Chiron is a centaur," she breathed.

"What's a centaur?" he asked in a whisper, staring genuinely into Melody's vibrant eyes.

"Are you kidding me?" tore Keilani. "I know for a fact that people in the outside world know what centaurs are!"

"Well, this person doesn't," Manny mumbled dryly.

Grabbing him by the ears, Melody drew Manny up close to her again. "Listen carefully! A centaur is half man and half horse. In other words, from the waist down Chiron has the body of a horse— shoulders, legs, and all! But from the waist up he has the body of a man. Don't breathe a word about a pet horse! Are we understood?"

"Sí," Manny said, satisfied with his thirty-second anatomy lesson. *I wonder if centaurs wear shirts? It would get pretty cold if not.*

"Bien," said Melody, releasing the boy's ears and breathing a little more calmly. After dusting off her dark fur coat and adjusting the wooden band on her left ankle, she asked, "Are you ready to meet him, then?"

"Sure," said Manny positively.

"Be respectful," Keilani reminded him one last time as she and the boy followed the kinkajou up the perfectly smooth, emerald hill.

"Chiron?" said Melody tentatively, stopping several steps from the centaur, who stood facing the west, arms crossed and all four hooves planted firmly on the hilltop, his unyielding gaze piercing the complexities of the galaxies.

"Yes, Melody?" he responded, blinking out of his trance and turning slightly to face the toy-like kinkajou. *Nope. No shirt. Now I'd freeze at night if I were him.*

"Manny López has arrived," she continued, hopping to the left and gesturing toward the boy behind her.

Chiron's jet black eyes fell upon Manny. "I am most honored to meet you, Manuel," said the centaur in an eloquent voice, his deep words showering his guests in an undulating aura. Crossing his chest with his right arm and bowing slightly, he added, "I am Chiron Veridai."

"Nice to meet you, Sr. Veridai," said Manny courteously. "Gracias for letting me stay here with you for the year."

"It is my greatest pleasure," replied the centaur, his eyes sparkling curiously. "But please, call me Chiron. We centaur prefer to be addressed by our first names."

"I can do that," conceded Manny congenially.

"Are you well, Keilani?" asked the centaur, turning to look at the young woman.

"Yes, Chiron, very well, thank you," Keilani replied.

"And anxious to assume First-Level status, I would imagine," Chiron added with a shadow of a smile.

"Most definitely," Keilani said, her enthusiasm scintillating slightly.

"Chiron, I do not wish to be rude, but Keilani and I really should be heading back," Melody said.

"I understand," the centaur replied. "You have your cubs to care for, and I am sure that Keilani would like to visit her friends." He turned his knowing gaze to the young woman. "I will see you here next week for Astronomy class, will I not?"

"For sure. We can't leave on our final mission without sharpening our stargazing skills." As Keilani began to back down the hill her eyes shone, revealing the deep respect she held for the centaur.

"We have many important matters to discuss before your departure," said Chiron.

"I can't wait! ¡Nos vemos!" Keilani called as she turned to descend the hill after Melody.

"¡Hasta entonces, Chiron!" Melody exclaimed with a flick of her tail as she disappeared below the brow of the hill.

"Yes, and take care until then," the centaur replied kindly.

So this guy's called a centaur, huh? Manny scanned the creature's formidable frame under the starlight, noticing the striking contrast between the velvety-black of Chiron's lower half with the rosy hue of his upper half. *Tavo's got more muscle.* The hair atop the creature's head matched that of his horse body, and on his face he carried an expression of unshakable calm. *His eyes are strange. It's like they're all pupil and no color—like they could just suck you right in.*

"Are you cold?" asked Chiron after he saw the boy shiver.

"No," replied Manny quickly. "I mean, I'm fine, thanks."

"Because if you were, I could increase the temperature of the air to meet your preference," the centaur said. "It is understandable for you to discern a slight chill at this height."

A slight chill? We're barely a hundred feet above the hutch. But looking to the left, beyond the hill, Manny discovered that he was very wrong. He teetered dizzily for a moment, nearly falling over.

"Steady yourself, m'ijo," Chiron said firmly as he trotted toward the boy and laid his enormous hands on Manny's shoulders.

"How did we get so high up?" Manny asked, blinking several times, his vision focusing as he gazed at the grass at his feet.

"By passing through the tree you gained access to the true height of this hill," Chiron said patiently. "It would be foolish of me to teach astronomy from any point lower than this."

"So how high are we?" the boy asked, straightening up as he fully regained his balance.

"I will let you see for yourself," Chiron replied, gesturing for Manny to follow him to the western edge of the hill. "Come."

Ignoring all fears that he might topple to his doom, Manny walked to the edge of the hill's crown. "No way," he whispered, his breath nearly leaving him. Below him the Amazon River wound like a tiny line through a forest of miniature trees. Though patches of cloud obscured his vision in some places, Manny saw a distant glimmer on the horizon. *Is that the Pacific Ocean?*

"It is true that the land and water are amazing sights to behold, but I would suggest that you look up."

"This is fantastic!" erupted the boy, the light of trillions of stars reflecting off his eyes. "Where do all the colorful clouds come from? I've never seen them before."

"Those are collections of stellar dust—pieces of shattered planets, broken asteroids, and dead stars. You may call them nebulae."

"Nebulae," Manny repeated, his tongue tingling as he pronounced the word. "It sounds a lot like the word for 'cloud' in Spanish."

"Yes, 'nube' and 'nebula' both stem from the Latin word for 'cloud.' In essence, nebulae are space clouds," Chiron said slowly.

"Cool," said the boy as he continued to rake the sky with his eager eyes.

"Manuel," said the centaur purposefully after several moments. "You are from the outside world, am I correct?"

"Sí," said the boy as he turned and walked to the center of the hill to view the stars and nebulae to the north and east.

"But as you speak Spanish, I may assume that your family has roots in Hispanic America?" Chiron continued.

"Yes. Although my parents grew up in Arizona, they were both born in El Salvador," Manny explained. *Whoa! Look at that!* "I was born in El Salvador, too, but my parents brought me back to the United States a few days later."

"Most interesting," commented Chiron. "And do your parents glow as well?"

This question effectively wrenched Manny's gaze from the sky. "No. Why?" he asked, suspicion picking at his brain.

"Not many people have your ability," the centaur replied simply.

"I don't know anyone else who does," Manny answered, a bit pointedly.

"I do," said Chiron significantly, "and he is coming up the hill."

Manny ran to the southern edge of the ridge just in time to see the frame of a boy pass through the roots of the kapok tree. "He's not glowing!" argued Manny, turning to face the centaur.

"I would suggest that you look closer," the centaur advised.

This better not be a joke. Manny turned back to face the boy, who by that time was almost halfway up the hill. Unable to see his

184

face, Manny stared hard at the boy's arms, which on all accounts appeared to be the deepest bronze that he had ever seen. *How stupid.* "Chiron, if that boy could glow, his skin wouldn't be brown!" Manny insisted, facing the centaur once again.

"Chiron," called the other boy as he approached the top of the hill. "Would it be possible for me to talk to y—" But just as Manny turned around the boy looked up, unable to finish his question. Both of them gasped in shock as they met one another's identical, exploding hazel eyes.

But he's—

"You're—"

"Mirror images of one another," Chiron said shrewdly.

***

"Who are you?" threw Manny.

"Who am I? Who are you?" the other boy tore back. "And why do you look just like me?" he added with a tone of accusation.

"Brun, Manny, calm down," Chiron directed smoothly.

Brun?

Put bluntly, Chiron had substantial reason to say that Brun and Manny were mirror images of one another. Both boys measured the same height, were of matching build and facial features, and exhibited an unquenchable fire in their eyes. They even had identical hair texture. However, in spite of these similarities, the boys managed to maintain a pair of distinct differences—their skin and hair color. While Manny's skin shone intensely beneath the starlight, Brun's grew a dark shade of copper peppered with millions of tiny specks that gave off a faint hint of light. And although Manny's charcoal hair refused to reflect any light whatsoever, Brun's flashed a bright white, particularly when exposed to light.

"Manny was born in El Salvador," Chiron told Brun. "Could the two of you share common relation?"

"I was born in northeastern Brazil," answered Brun quickly, his eyes not leaving Manny for a second. "My family has been Brazilian for generations—we have no relatives in El Salvador."

"Well, I don't have any in Brazil," Manny retorted.

"That is very odd," observed Chiron. "Perhaps one or the other of you was adopted. Maybe you are even br—"

"Not possible!" cut Brun in a voice that, to Manny, sounded surprisingly similar to his own. "My name is Brun Kieran Dimirtis and I am an only child! My mother died while I was being born. My father, Renato, and my Aunt Liliana raised me. You can ask either of them if you like!"

"Yeah, well, I'm an only child, too; I wasn't adopted either," said Manny flatly. "I've got my birth certificate in my luggage to prove it."

"In light of this, let us answer one final question, then," said Chiron. "What are your birthdays?"

"December 21," said Brun instantly.

"June 21," Manny said. "That's as far apart as we could get," he added with a slight chuckle.

"I guess you're right," Brun admitted, also smiling.

"This situation is quite striking," said the centaur, his tone odd. "At second glance I must concede that the two of you appear to be perfect opposites."

That's what I said in the first place.

"Yet your similarities are uncanny. I find it very unusual that you are both children of the solstice."

"What's a solstice?" asked Brun, his tone and manner collected now.

He beat me to the punch.

"A solstice occurs twice a year when the sun is at its greatest distance from the equator," said Chiron.

"What does that have to do with us?" asked Manny.

"You, Manuel, were born during the summer solstice, on June 21, the longest day of the year for the northern hemisphere. Brun, on the other hand," continued Chiron, turning to the other boy, "your birthday is December 21, the winter solstice—the day when the sun shines the highest in the southern hemisphere."

"Complete opposites," Brun stated with a nod of certainty.

"But why do we look alike, then?" asked Manny, intrigued.

186

"That is the key question," Chiron began. "Despite your differences, the two of you are connected—yet I know not how. Manuel, you may not be aware of this as we are flooded with starlight at the present moment, but in the absence of light, Brun's skin begins to glow. I would guess that with lack of light your skin dims or perhaps ceases to shine altogether."

Manny considered the episode in the Painted Cavern when he dropped his flashlight in the lake. "You're right about that," he confessed. "That's why I like to go cave exploring, actually—it's the only place where I'm normal."

"Not me," Brun said morosely. "My light blares like a floodlight in caves."

"Crazy," muttered Manny.

"I know," blurted Brun, rolling his eyes.

"For roommates you two seem to be getting off to a positive start, at least after that initial clash," observed Chiron.

"We're roommates?" the boys asked in unison.

"Yes," laughed the centaur. "You are my guests for the next two years. I should say that I hope neither of you minds sleeping with a light on, because no matter what, you will be forced to do so."

"I'm used to it," the boys said together once again. Chiron laughed as Manny and Brun looked at each other with expressions of surprise.

"You are very much alike indeed."

***

"So why are you carrying a mudpuppy on your neck?" asked Brun as he and Manny passed through the kapok gate side by side. "Is it sick? I've never seen one with yellow spots."

What is he talking about? "Do you mean Lil' Manny?" the other boy asked, raising his right hand to his neck and allowing the salamander to crawl onto it. "He's not a muddog, or whatever you called it. Lil' Manny's my pet spotted salamander," he added, petting the creature's tiny head. The salamander closed its eyes happily.

187

"Not a muddog—a mudpuppy," Brun corrected. "They're salamanders, too. It's just that mudpuppies are a little bigger, and people don't generally carry them around their necks."

"So they're spotted, too?"

"No. Mudpuppies have bumpy brown skin—honestly, some of them look like little dinosaurs. They live in ponds or puddles in front of Lumen houses. People keep them as a pet because they're very loyal. They bark and they'll even toss balls of mud with their tails if a stranger gets too close."

"Bizarre," said Manny, raising his hand so the salamander could return to the warmth of the boy's neck.

"Not really," Brun replied coolly. "Just wait, I'm sure you'll see something weirder soon enough." Both boys stopped outside the back door of Chiron's Hutch. "You want me to get any of this for you?" asked Brun, motioning to Manny's belongings.

"Sure, if you'll take the carrier then I can get the rest," said Manny as he slipped on the backpack and grabbed the luggage handle. Brun opened the bamboo door with the wicker knob, allowing Manny to step inside first. "Where's the light? It's really dark in here."

"Not for long," replied Brun. A second later a flaming light filled the room.

What's the deal? Does he have a lantern or something? Manny turned around to discover that the source of the light was Brun's skin, which was now glowing a fiery red similar to that of metal being heated in a furnace. "Pretty tricky," commented Manny.

"Nothing you haven't seen before, I'm sure," Brun replied cleverly.

"You're right about that—but I don't glow in the dark," said Manny. *At least not under normal circumstances.* "It's funny, though. Your light doesn't set my skin off."

"That is weird," Brun admitted.

"Oh, well, whatever," Manny said as he turned around to scope out the room. On either side he found a hammock of masterfully braided, white chords and an elegantly carved, stained wood dresser with three small drawers and tiny, almond handles.

Noticing that Brun's belongings appeared to be on the left, Manny set his things on the right side, kneeling down in front of the dresser and hastily filling it with his clothing.

"So since you didn't know what a mudpuppy was, I guess it's not too far a shot for me to assume that you're from the outside world?" asked Brun, resting comfortably in his hammock.

"Nobody has much difficulty figuring that one out," answered Manny as he stuffed his underwear in the top drawer.

"What's it like?" Brun asked quietly.

"It bites," said Manny as he tried to cram his shirts into the middle drawer.

"There's also a closet for each of us in the hallway," said Brun helpfully.

Why didn't you tell me that before? Pulling several shirts from the drawer, Manny stepped into the hallway that led deeper into the deceptively spacious shack and opened the closet. "This thing's huge!" he exclaimed as he hung up his clothes.

"Lucky for us," Brun said. "So, anyway, why don't you like the outside world?"

"Basically, because everyone except my family treats me like a piece of trash," Manny replied as he placed his favorite shirt—his Arizona Diamondbacks jersey—on a hanger. "I hated school for that exact reason."

"I'm nervous about school for that exact reason."

"Why would anybody treat you bad?"

"I've never really actually spent much time with kids my age," Brun answered awkwardly.

"What do you mean?" Manny asked as he began to decorate his dresser top with his most prized possessions. "So what if you've never played a sport with other kids—it's not like you don't have any friends." Brun stared back silently in reply. "Are you serious?" asked Manny, nearly dropping his tin Diamondbacks lunchbox on the dirt floor. "How can you not have any friends? I mean—look at you! You're normal compared to me."

"Since when have you seen anyone else our age with a full head of white hair?" asked Brun dryly. "I'm sure they're all gonna laugh at me."

Manny rebounded in a flash. "Have they ever before?"

"No," replied Brun vaguely.

"Then why would they start now?"

Brun took a long breath, his eyes fixed on the straw-thatched ceiling.

Manny began to roll his eyes. *He doesn't have the slightest idea what it's like for other kids to—*

"I'd never seen another person my age until I came here," Brun confessed. "While my counselor led me across the island yesterday I saw tons of them, but you're the first I've ever talked to."

"That's impossible," Manny countered quickly. "Your school must've been full of kids our age."

"I've never gone to school," Brun answered, his voice a decibel shy of a whisper .

"Nuh uh."

"It's true. My Aunt Liliana raised me and taught me everything I know. The only other humans that I've ever seen are my father and his occasional guests," explained Brun. "Of course I know some Lumen animals, but still, none of them are my age."

And I thought I was isolated from the crowd. At least I've had Zane all these years. Out of the corner of his eye Manny looked at the snowy haired boy swinging nervously in the hammock. "Well, I think you're pretty cool," Manny said, zipping up his luggage and rolling it into the closet. "And I don't think you're strange at all. In fact," he continued as he positioned the plastic carrier under the west window, "You're a pretty sharp lookin' guy if I do say so myself."

A laugh erupted from Brun's tight chest. "You're not conceited at all, are you?"

"Admit it, Brun, the Lumen girls are gonna love us," Manny said as he sank into his hammock.

"And you know this from experience?" asked Brun with a wry smile.

"Just a hunch," replied Manny. "And, hey, maybe we'll see some tomorrow."

"Tomorrow? Why's that?"

"Oh, I figured you and I could explore the island tomorrow," Manny said, bouncing slightly in his hammock. "How 'bout it?"

Brun chewed on this proposition for a moment. "So you're telling me that the other kids won't care that my hair is white?"

"No way," Manny answered surely. "I mean, look at me! I'm the whitest thing they've ever seen, and they thought I was cool! I bet they'll love your hair!"

"What about my skin?" Brun added, masking the steadily increasing hope in his chest.

"Unless we find ourselves in some caves I don't think anyone'll know the difference. Especially if you're next to me."

Brun took a long moment to measure the truth in Manny's eyes. "Alright, then," he said finally. "I'll go."

"Great! I can't wait to see what's out there!" Manny exclaimed.

***

Pajamas? Check. Dirty clothes put away? Uh huh. Lil' Manny safe in his carrier? Yep. But I'm still forgetting something... From the comfort of his hammock Manny peered at the shadowy foliage surrounding his new home, his eyes losing focus as he replayed the day's events in his mind. *Duh!* In under thirty seconds the boy had transformed his wand into a briefcase, pulled out his glowing stationary, and hurriedly scribbled a letter:

Mamá,

Made it to Chiron's Hutch. It's an interesting shack made of bamboo. Guess what? I get to sleep in a hammock! Chiron seems really smart. He's nice, too. Oh! I have a roommate! Julius didn't tell us about that! His name is Brun and he's a blast—we have a lot in common! Well, write to you tomorrow.

G'night,

Manny

Alrighty then—that's done. But just as he secured the dual clasps of the briefcase, another shapeless thought began to pick at his mind. Manny stared at the case on his lap for a moment. *Zane! He's probably thinking I drowned in the Amazon or something!* Quickly removing a second sheet of paloma paper, Manny began yet another letter. He had written only a pair of sentences, however, when his mother's reply came:

Manuel,

Thank God you arrived safely! I'm glad you're happy and comfortable, but be careful and don't fall out of the hammock, querido. And remember to tell Chiron gracias for me for his hospitality—he's a very generous man to allow two students to board with him. Tell Brun hello!

¡Te amo!

Mamá

P.S. Write me back before dinner tomorrow.

That went over really well. I figured she'd have a fit over the fact that I'm staying in a house made of bamboo. Manny swiftly resumed his letter to Zane. Half an hour passed as he retold his trip from Iquitos to Chiron's Hutch in great detail, dedicating nearly an entire page to Brun. At the end of his letter Manny wrote the following:

> Since your parents don't know that I'm a Lumen, I think it's best that I only send you letters at night, probably midnight or later just to make sure you're in your room. If not they'll find out about paloma paper and then we'll all be in a mess. Remember what Julius said—we've got to keep my Lumen identity a secret.

Zane replied within minutes, showing little reluctance to agreeing to follow Manny's plan and promising to always be in his room after midnight. "Too bad I can't be there with you and Brun tomorrow," Zane wrote, among other things. "Guess I'll have to wait 'til next year."

***

"What the heck? I'm being attacked!" screamed Manny as he leapt forward, toppling haphazardly from his hammock and hurtling onto the dirt floor. Pain seared in his backside as he flipped around to see his attacker—an altogether menacing creature with an oval-shaped head, two rows of pointed fangs, and a leafy mane. It had a pod-like body, rather short, rooty legs, and vines for arms. "What is that thing?" he screamed, his voice surprisingly high as he scooted away from the chomping creature. *It looks like a lion turned plant!*

"Oh, that's Nipper," said Brun casually. "She's my pet Venus flytrap—she can be a little feisty when she meets someone she doesn't like."

"Well, what if I don't like her?!" Manny exclaimed as he edged further away from the apparently eyeless creature.

"What's not to like?"

"Are you kidding me? She bit me in the butt!"

"Don't worry, it won't hurt for long. You'll just have to make sure not to scare her for a while—at least until she gets used to you," Brun reassured him.

"Scare her?! She's the one that scared me!" defended Manny.

"She's just a plant, Manny."

Before Manny could continue his argument a violent hiss came from under Manny's hammock, instantly drawing Nipper's attention. *Lil' Manny?*

"Is that your salamander?"

"I guess so," replied Manny. "I've never heard him hiss before, though."

No sooner had the salamander hissed a second time than the Venus flytrap tore across the floor in a flash, wrenching the lid of the carrier away and chomping at the spotted amphibian. Water splashed in all directions as Nipper threw the bottom half of the carrier aside and lunged at the wall. Fortunately for Lil' Manny, his quick reflexes allowed him to scale the bamboo before the flytrap's pincers could snag him.

"Your plant is crazy!" cried Manny, witnessing in horror as Nipper's vine-like arms crept up the wall toward the tiny salamander.

"Nipper! No!" Brun ordered firmly. "He is not food!" The flytrap's tentacles stopped less than a foot from Lil' Manny. Retracting them, she turned around to face her master. "Good girl," Brun praised her.

Manny snorted, but Brun ignored him. *Good girl my butt.* He paused. *Okay—that's not funny.* Standing, Manny walked to the corner and offered his hand to the salamander, which continued to hiss hatefully at the flytrap even after Manny had placed him on his shoulder. As Manny knelt down to pick up the pieces of the carrier, Nipper started to lunge toward him.

"No!" exclaimed Brun. "Nipper, go outside!" The flytrap turned her great football head toward her master for a brief moment, hoping that he would change his mind; but he did not. Manny

194

watched as Nipper sulked toward the door and cracked it open, her head low and mane bobbing as she disappeared from view. *I've gotta lock that tonight.*

"Sorry about that," apologized Brun as he slid from his hammock. "She did go a little overboard."

I'd say she did.

***

"I wonder what that thing is," said Manny, nodding to his right at the glistening blue structure that towered over the island. "It looks really plain," he continued as he and Brun crossed the kilometer long wooden bridge connecting the eastern forest to the island. Far below the boys' feet distant breakers rolled across the waters of the Lake. "I mean, I can't see anything at the top. You'd think there'd be a building or something, but it's just bare. What do you think it is?"

"That's the loading dock for the Argo," replied Brun as he, too, gazed up at the structure with its strange way of reflecting the light.

"The Argo? What's that?"

"It's a Lumen ship," Brun answered evenly.

"A ship?" repeated Manny artlessly; he quickly narrowed his eyes. "Ships can't fly, Brun."

"The Argo can."

"Why didn't I see it last night when I arrived, then? And how 'bout now?" asked Manny suspiciously. "If that's the loading dock, where's the ship?"

"First off, the Argo only flies at night, so that's why you can't see it now. Second, there's only one flying ship—one Argo—so it doesn't arrive here every night. And third, even if it were docked, all you would be able to see would be a shimmer in the air—it's camouflaged from sight to prevent outsiders from seeing it," Brun explained.

Manny gawked at Brun uncertainly. "Did you just make that all up?"

195

"No. Why would I?" replied Brun, staring back at the other.

"I dunno. You said you'd never left your home in Brazil. If that's true, how come you know so much about Isla Verde and the Argo?"

"Just because I'd never left my home doesn't mean I've never learned anything about the Lumen world," said Brun bluntly. "Mi tía Liliana taught me everything she knows about Isla Verde and Lumen society. In fact," Brun paused, looking sideways at Manny, "I know this island so well that I can find shortcuts that some First-Levels may not even know about."

Manny set his eyes on the enormous island opening up before them like a small continent. "How can you know stuff like that if you've never been here?" he asked. *It just doesn't make sense.*

"I told you," Brun began with a slight edge in his voice, "that my aunt taught me everything she knew about the island. Before I left she even made me sketch and label a detailed map of the whole city! And when I say whole, I mean the surrounding forest, too."

"Whoa. Sr. Soriano seems like a wimp compared to her," Manny corresponded as they left the bridge and stepped onto the wide, dirt path running along before them.

"Who's Sr. Soriano?"

"Oh, just my eighth grade teacher," Manny said off-handedly. "I didn't like him very much—and he didn't really like me, either. He always took the side of my classmates when they blamed me for stuff I never did."

Brun blinked as he listened intently. "Well, that Soriano man may have been a bad teacher, but Tía Liliana sure wasn't. She told awesome stories about everywhere she'd traveled and been, and she tried to expose me to as much wildlife as she could—she wanted me to be ready when I came here."

"She seems cool." Manny paused. "So what's your papá like?"

"Hold on a sec," Brun said as he stopped suddenly to analyze the north side of the road. "It should be around here somewhere," he mumbled.

"What should?"

196

"Oh, there's this bromeliad that signals the way to a shortcut," muttered Brun.

"What's a bromeliad? A tree? Or is it just a weird Lumen word for a sign?"

"No, it's neither. It's this green type of plant with thick, pointed leaves and a bright yellow—there it is!" he exclaimed, pointing further ahead. Brun swiftly passed Manny and dove into the seemingly impenetrable undergrowth and tight trees.

Manny trotted along behind, coming to the place where Brun disappeared and pausing for a moment to inspect a plant that appeared to be growing out of a tree alongside the path. The plant was slightly bigger than the boy's head; and from the center grew three glowing yellow flowers. "You must have a sharp pair of eyes," he mumbled as he plunged into the green wall after Brun. Manny's feet slid over numerous roots as he pushed through the bushes and twisted to squeeze between trees. *This reminds me of when I was carrying Julius along the stream back in Costa Rica.* In this case, however, Manny emerged from the underbrush to discover a thin and winding path illuminated by scattered jade light filtering down through the foliage above.

"Took you long enough," said Brun at least twenty steps away. "¡Ándale!"

"Yeah, yeah, I'm coming, Mr. Know-it-all," Manny breathed as he hurried along to catch Brun, who had turned a corner to disappear from sight yet again. Jogging along, Manny reached him in no time at all.

"So where does this shortcut take us anyway?"

"Where do you think?" Brun replied baldly. "We're headed north-northeast."

"You're the one with the map skills."

"Just think about it." Brun pressed onward at a steady pace. In the shade of the pathway his chocolate skin glittered faintly.

North-northeast? Let me see… "The Argo dock," said Manny quickly.

"Sure thing. From there we'll be able to scope out the entire island—I wanted to go there yesterday, but, you know…"

197

Yeah. I know that feeling—all too well. Manny sighed. "Anyway, what were we talking about?"

"You tell me," Brun answered, looking up to catch a glimpse of the progressively nearing tower.

This is getting annoying. Okay—we talked about Sr. Soriano and then about his aunt. So… "Your papá," Manny pinpointed. "What's he like?"

"Honestly, I don't really know." Brun's tone was ironically light.

"How can you not know? He's your dad, isn't he?"

"Sí, of course he is. It's just that he never really spends all that much time with me. He's usually off on a trip to the other continents on Lumen business, so mi tía takes care of me. Even when he's home he's busy with work, having meetings in his office or just studying alone. In other words, we're not really all that close."

"Sounds to me like you don't know each other at all," Manny observed. "I can't imagine not spending time with my papá."

"Is he a nice guy?" asked Brun keenly.

"Oh, yeah, he's great. He and my tío José are my baseball coaches. Zane and I love practicing with our dads," Manny replied positively.

"Would Zane be your cousin, then?"

"Yep. He's thirteen, but he hopes to come to school here next year."

"If he's anything like you, then I can't wait to meet him," Brun said sincerely. "It's really fun being with a friend—my first friend."

A friend. "Yeah, you're right," agreed Manny. "It's great."

"Can you answer some questions about the outside world for me?"

"Sure."

"So what's 'eighth grade?' And 'baseball?' Is it a game? How do you play it? Maybe you could teach me," Brun said enthusiastically.

Manny laughed. "Well, a grade is…

***

"Too cool," Brun said, his hair flashing brightly under the morning sun and the warm wind hitting his face as he and Manny gazed at the expansive island stretching out below their feet. Both boys stood along the southwest parapet of the Argo Dock, their eyes drinking in the sea of trees that fell like a wave as the island moved west. Beaches and docks ran along all sides of the island, excluding the mountainous coasts of the east, of course. To their right, at the far northwest corner of the island, the boys spied a massive outcropping of rock, below which a wide, flat area similar to a garden opened, filled with tiny figures moving about viridian lawns dappled with flowering trees and bushes that seemed to pulsate with color. Through the hedge maze at the center of the park ran a crystal stream that crossed the entire island, eventually emptying into the Lake at the southeast corner. "Those are the Island Gardens," said Brun, pointing at the park, "and the river is called Carina, after the keel of the Argo."

"You mean the Argo is as long as that river?" asked Manny, his eyes open wide.

"No," Brun replied patiently. "It's called Carina because it shines brightly, like the keel of the Argo.

"Oh," muttered Manny. "So what's that big rock-face rising over the Gardens?"

"That would be Lookout Point, where everyone goes to watch lightboarding—a form of surfing," said Brun. "I've been waiting to watch some pros go at it."

Manny shielded his eyes with his right hand, squinting as he scanned the waters north of the island. Frowning, he said, "I don't see any surfers."

"You wouldn't," replied Brun obviously. "They don't start to surf 'til dusk."

"Of course! Who would surf in broad daylight, anyway?" stated Manny sarcastically.

199

"Yeah, well, you'll see why when we go to the Point later this evening," said Brun. "So, anyhow, does anything surprise you about the island?"

"You mean besides the fact that it even exists?"

"Obviously."

"Well, it's just seems so—huge. I expected it to be smaller somehow," Manny confessed.

"That's exactly what I was thinking!" exclaimed Brun. "I mean, look at all the tree houses popping out of the forest along the Five Roads—there are thousands! And with all the houses along the outer rim of the Lake and deeper into the Amazon, there have to be millions of people that live here!"

"I guess it's like Los Ángeles, but not so dirty," thought Manny aloud.

"The Angels? What are you talking about?" Brun turned to face Manny with a perplexed look.

"No—not the Angels! Los Ángeles! It's the name of one of the biggest cities in the United States."

"Was it built really high up in the sky?" asked Brun. Manny frowned. "You know, for it to be named after angels—"

"It has nothing to do with angels at all," interrupted Manny, striving to be patient but failing. "I honestly don't know how the city got its name, but it's not high up at all—it's actually right along the coast."

"Huh," grunted Brun. "So—back to why we came up here in the first place—did you notice the Plaza?"

"¡Sí! It's incredible!" Manny turned his eyes toward the heart of the isle to the point where the Five Roads—the North, South, East, West, and Dock Roads—coincided to form a circular clearing overflowing with people and buildings. "It's enormous! And check out that fountain in the center—you can see it from here!" Manny pointed at the glistening spray in the distance.

"There's a huge pool underneath it," said Brun brightly. "I can't wait to see it."

"Let's head there next, then," said Manny. "Now that we know where everything is, we can explore it all up close.

Taking one last fulfilling look at the island, Brun turned and lead the way as he and Manny crossed the Argo Dock and began their descent back down the tower stairs.

***

"It blows my mind how these shortcuts can take you completely out of the way and still get you where you want to go in under ten minutes," Manny declared as he and Brun stepped out from an invisible fold in the forest wall onto the Dock Road. "I mean, look! The Argo Dock has to be miles away from here!"

"They're not all this short," replied Brun, eyeing the Dock fleetingly as his excited feet drew nearer to the Plaza. "The West-South path takes almost twenty minutes, fifteen if you're quick about it."

Manny had to jog to catch up. "You must have slept really well last night to be this energetic."

"Yep. You'd be surprised what freedom can do for you."

"Freedom? It's not like you were a prisoner in your own home, Brun."

"You could've fooled me," Brun countered dryly.

Before Manny could pry any deeper, however, the two boys stepped into the Plaza, their minds instantly wiped blank by the singular site before them. People and animals from species that Manny could not even recognize intermingled throughout the passionately palpitating heart of the city—countless feet, paws, and hooves meandered in all directions, some leaving the myriad of shops on the boys' right to cross the Plaza and disappear into the open-air market that bordered the entire northwest side, where bright-colored tents flashed under the morning sun. Along the southeast rim of the Plaza the boys spied a set of three massive, white stone buildings towering over the crowd. *I wonder what those are...* On the adjacent end of the Plaza, Manny and Brun could just make out the extraordinary edifice of an unprecedented mansion, its polished wood reflecting the light. Yet what seemed to steal the boys' breath above all else was the magnificent kiosk with its marble pillars that enclosed the towering spray of the fountain in the very center of the Plaza. Weaving their way between humans and various beasts—from centaurs, unicorns, and kinkajou to river otters and red-eyed tree frogs riding large, rodent-like creatures—Manny and Brun reached the kiosk, passing beneath the structure's ivy-covered rim and mounting several steps, their stomachs clenched in anticipation.

Manny's jaw dropped. *How can water fire that high?* "Who made those sculptures? They look so—real."

"Lumen artists," whispered Brun, half in awe. "Let's check 'em out."

Rising out of the marble pool was a ring of stone figures, their backs forming a circle around the jet of water, which rose into the air and fell back down to form a shimmering aquatic dome. As the boys walked around the fountain, they noticed that plaques had been placed around the edge of the pool, each plate engraved with a name, Lumen animal, and short description.

"Who are these people?" Manny asked as he came to a sudden halt at the north end of the pool. He shuddered as he gazed at the figure of the stone woman with her right hand resting on the back of an enormous spider that stood as tall as she did.

"That has to be Oriana," said Brun as he turned around to look at the short-haired woman with happy eyes and a contented smile. "She illuminated the arachnids, if you couldn't tell. Let's see what the plaque says."

Both boys stepped closer to the golden plate in front of Oriana, reading:

Oriana Prochorus

&

The Crystal Spider

Oriana is the seventh-eldest child among the Light Brethren. Upon coming to Earth she became quite taken with arachnids, quickly deciding to illuminate several members of the genus to create the crystal spider. Throughout her many years in South America she strove to unite the crystal spider with the Lumen community as a whole, yet few ever came to share her affinity for this eight-legged creature.

"It's not really hard to figure out why…"

"What? You don't like spiders?" asked Brun.

Manny looked back and shrugged his shoulders. "Not really."

"All the same, crystal spiders are Lumens, and people have to learn to accept them despite their differences from the rest of us," Brun said, a faint glint in his eyes. "You know what I mean?"

"Yeah, I guess so," replied Manny reluctantly. "It's just that they're so—creepy…"

"Creepy or not, they're still Lumens—they're not gonna hurt you."

Well, I still don't ever want to meet one. Manny took a deep breath. "How 'bout we just continue around the fountain?"

Blinking coolly in reply, Brun turned and led the way around the rest of the fountain pool, occasionally pausing to read a plaque or simply to admire the beauty and complexity of the statues.

Halfway around the pool Manny stopped again. "I still don't get it. Who are the Light Brethren?"

"Who are the Light Brethren? They are!" exclaimed Brun, pointing at the ring of statues in the pool.

"I know that," said Manny obviously. "But why are they so important?"

"Manny, listen," began Brun calmly. "If it weren't for the Light Brethren, there wouldn't be any Lumens at all."

"Why not?" asked Manny, eyeing the figure of a man kneeling down and laughing at three otters playing at his feet. "So what if some guy named Rei Prochorus illuminated some river otters? Julius Rumblefeather's my light-bringer and he illuminated me. Why doesn't he have a statue of his own?"

"First of all, Julius did not illuminate you," stated Brun. "Illumination refers to when the Stars first came to Earth and transformed humans and animals into Lumens."

Tavo flitted into the back of Manny's mind. "Okay, I remember my friend Tavo telling me something like that. But still, what's that have to do with the Light Breth—" Manny stopped. "Oh. The Light Brethren are the Stars," he added quietly.

"Bingo."

I can be such a dummy sometimes. "Basically, these statues represent—what—the twelve Stars that came to Earth? And they each transformed one species of animal into a Lumen?" asked Manny tentatively.

"Right on," answered Brun with a nod.

"So are they still alive?" asked Manny excitedly. "Where do they live? We should go meet them!"

Brun turned around and scanned the southern end of the Plaza. "Okay. D'you see that big wooden mansion over there?" he asked, pointing to the building running along the rim of the Plaza between the West to the South Roads. "I'm pretty sure that's called the House of the Brethren. That's where they used to live."

That sucker's huge! "Used to?"

"Sí, they died hundreds of years ago, I think," said Brun with disappointment.

"Aren't stars supposed to live thousands of years? How could they be dead already?"

"I dunno. I never really thought about it…" said Brun quietly.

"Well, I'm gonna ask Chiron later when we see him at dinner," Manny said decidedly. *Dinner?* "Oh, geez! I need some money for lunch! Where's the bank?"

"It's gotta be one of those three buildings over there," said Brun, looking to the southeast end of the Plaza. "I still can't tell which from here—why don't we go find out?"

A moment later Brun and Manny had dived back into the intricate flow of creatures pulsating around the Plaza. Within a minute the boys were walking along the Río Carina in its progressive surge toward the middle of the three buildings, which stood less than one hundred steps away when a frightening cry like that of a terrified woman came from the edge of the river. Manny's heart froze as he turned to find a panther leaning over the opposite bank.

"I told you both not to play near the water!" roared the mother panther, her electric yellow eyes flashing angrily as she shook her head, the thin wooden necklace around her neck swaying as numerous streams of light converged upon a panther kitten struggling to swim in the rushing water. Not three seconds later the dripping kitten sat pitifully on the stone pavement next to his mother. "You just wait until your father gets home." To Manny's horror, the mother panther lifted her powerful head and gazed directly into the boy's eyes. "It's rude to stare, you know," said the panther, her tenor rumbling faintly. "Now come along," she said dangerously to the pair of kittens at her feet. "You'll be lucky if you even get the goat tail tonight for supper the way the both of you have been acting this morning—like a pair of silly cheetahs…"

"Manny," Brun called, several steps away. "Hey, Manny." But the boy did not answer, locked in a trance as he was. "Manny!" Brun said forcefully with a snap of his fingers.

Shaking himself back into reality, Manny said, "Whoa! Did you just see that?"

"See what?" asked Brun. "Nothing's happened."

"Oh, yes it has," Manny answered quickly. "There was this panther over there, and it could talk! It looked right into my eyes! I thought I was a goner…"

"Whatever," Brun said, rolling his own. "You're not gonna be attacked by a panther."

"And how do you know?" Manny shot back defensively.

"Any panther that you saw was a Lumen, Manny," Brun stated clearly and slowly. "Just like the crystal spiders, panthers aren't going to hurt you."

Manny blinked several times, attempting to process this information. "All this is gonna take a little while for me to digest."

"Maybe so," replied Brun. "But anyway, look. I found the bank. It's on the other side of the Carina—you can just make out the lettering on the arch over the entrance."

"Amazon River Bank," read Manny to himself as he followed Brun to a nearby bridge to cross the Carina. "Sounds funny."

Schism

"Lumen change is the coolest!" exclaimed Manny as he and Brun exited the bank. Manny pulled out a coin bordered with eight fiery ripples. "It really does look like a little sun!"

"Hence the name—one Sol," said Brun, a hint of dullness in his voice.

"Don't you think they're cool?" asked Manny animatedly.

"I've seen them all my life, Manny, so I really can't be impressed by them."

"Well, I am," Manny affirmed. "Our coins back home are boring compared to these. They're all just silver or bronze colored. They have started to make a few with some pretty cool designs, though…"

"Really? I've never seen foreign money up close. Maybe you could show me later," Brun said, suddenly interested.

"Not 'til my parents send me more," Manny replied. "I just traded it all for Sols, remember?"

"Duh," said Brun, mentally kicking himself. "So where're we goin' next?"

"I dunno." Manny stopped to read the names of the buildings next to the bank. "Lumen Resource Center," he breathed as he scanned the pillared structure through which the Carina ran. "I've never seen a building that has a river running through it."

"Lumen Resource Center? That must be the library," observed Brun. Indeed, through the wide arch he could distinguish several bookcases. "My tía Liliana always called it the LRC. Wanna check it out?"

Not really. "What about that building?" proposed Manny, walking past the library and pointing toward a three-tiered structure with expertly carved balconies. *I hope it's not an extension of the library.*

"Office of Lumen Studies," read Brun aloud. "That's where we go to get our class schedules! We're goin' there!"

"I thought our schedules were supposed to be at Chiron's Hutch. Why aren't they there already?"

"Chiron told me that they mail them right before the semester begins," Brun replied. "But we can get them early if we want. Hey! Then we could go to the LRC and get our books!"

"But there's still so much more of the island to see," said Manny persuasively. "I don't want to head back to Chiron's Hutch already carrying a load of books…"

"You won't have to carry—"

"Brun—look!" Manny interjected, his finger aimed toward the southern end of the Plaza. "Did you see her?"

"Her? Who are you talking about?" Brun felt a little aggravated at being cut short.

"It was Keilani." Manny quickly grabbed Brun by the arm and began to pull him through the crowd.

"Who's she?" asked Brun, stopping abruptly and forcing Manny to stumble.

"She brought me to Chiron's last night. She's twenty and very pretty. Didn't you see her there?" Manny asked, his heart racing as he imagined her disappearing along the South Road.

"No," Brun replied. "Like I told you, you were the first person even close to our age that I talked to."

"Well, I want you to meet her. C'mon." Manny gave Brun a significant look and turned around to resume his chase, his feet propelling him expeditiously forward as he traded the stone pavement for the well-trodden dirt of the South Road. His paced slowed a little as he scanned the heads of the crowd all around him. *¿Dónde está? I can't see her!* A moment later his heart jolted as he caught sight of a longhaired girl melting into the trees on the right side of the road. "There she is!" Manny exclaimed as he hastily jogged to the subtle break in the trees where she had disappeared. A second later Manny found himself under another green-canopied tunnel that ran straight ahead for several hundred steps before bending to the left. There was no sign of Keilani. "Gosh—she's fast. We need to hurry, Brun, if we're going to catch her." But no reply came. "Brun?" Manny turned around just in time to see Brun passing through the entrance to the shortcut.

"This girl better be beautiful for me to be running after her," said Brun, his breath slightly quicker than normal.

"Oh, she is," Manny promised. "Let's go."

After running side-by-side for a minute or two, Brun asked, "Isn't this Keilani girl a little old for you?"

"What makes you think that?" Manny puffed.

"You said she was twenty—we're fourteen, if you hadn't noticed."

"Nothin' can stop love," said Manny, laughing as he pushed forward and took the lead ahead of Brun.

"You're a dork," Brun shouted, catching up to Manny in an instant.

"How would you know?" Manny shot back with a smile. "You've lived in isolation all your life."

"It's a universal trait," Brun said wryly.

Less than a minute later the boys came to a break in the path. Stepping forward, Manny looked down along the trail as it continued to the left and right, hoping for a sign of Keilani but finding none. *Ugh!* "Which way do you think she went?"

"Probably to the right," Brun replied. The left just leads to the southern pier, and unless she's headed to the Flooded Forest, I doubt she went that way."

"Where does the right path lead, then?"

"Well, you can follow it all the way to the western pier, or you can turn to the north just a bit ahead to make for the Gardens. If I were to guess, I'd say she's headed that way," Brun said wisely.

"Alright, then." Manny's resolute words raced along the path just as fast as his eyes could gaze down it. "Vámonos."

Approximately one hundred steps later the path forked to the right yet again. "This is it," whispered Brun. "If we take this path, we'll come out in front of the Gardens."

Manny looked at Brun strangely. "That's fine and all, but why are you whispering?"

"There are snickering fruit snakes that live in the trees along this path," Brun replied quietly.

Manny chuckled. "Snickering fruit snakes? That's the dumbest thing I ever heard."

"Yeah, well, they may sound dumb, but if one of them hits you in the head with a rotten melon you'll think twice about even breathing loudly when you come along this path again," Brun said, maintaining his whisper.

"How's a snake gonna pelt me in the face with a melon? They don't even have hands!" Manny countered, amused.

"They don't need hands! They use their tails to launch fruit or whatever they can get their scales on to nail passersby in the head! Then they start to snicker at you…"

"Okay, so let's just pretend that I believe you—"

"Have I been wrong yet?" Brun interposed, an eyebrow raised.

Let's see… "No, I guess not," Manny replied after a moment. "Okay, so I believe you." *I really don't know what's weirder, though—pink dolphins or throwing snakes…*

"Gracias," whispered Brun appreciatively.

Manny nodded. "So by what you were saying, we can keep safe from these snakes if we're quiet?"

This time it was Brun's turn to nod. "Sí. And don't even say hi to anyone if you see them along the way—the snakes will hear it."

"Got it," Manny replied, assuming Brun's hushed tone. *I just hope I don't sneeze.*

The two boys walked quietly along the cool path, holding their breath for fear that their footsteps might disturb the fruit snakes. Fortunately, however, their feet produced little sound at all as they walked carefully along under the seemingly innocent tree boughs rising high above their heads. A couple of minutes into their stealthy journey a tiny figure, barely a foot tall, appeared ahead of them, hopping gingerly along the path with its head down. The creature's fur was the dark shade of coffee and it seemed to have no ears—at least none that Manny or Brun could see. Around the creature's ankle was a deep purple band of wood. *I've never seen wood that color before.* A breath later several things happened at once.

First, the tiny animal looked up, catching sight of Brun and Manny and smiling shyly—he had eyes like two small, dark cherries. From beyond a slight bend just ahead, four young men appeared, much taller than Manny or Brun. One of them snapped his wand in the creature's direction, causing a flash of light to explode over the animal's head and filling the path with a deafening crack.

Brun pulled Manny down to the ground just as a shower of fruit and nuts filled the air. Hissing laughter could be heard from the foliage above, the leaves and branches swaying oddly, as if the trees themselves were mocking the pitiful creature now covered in fruit juice and pulp.

"What's the matter?" mocked one of the young men, while two others waved their hands at the trees above, launching the snickering reptiles away into the air. "Is Firefoot's wil' baby bunny upset?"

As they looked up, Manny and Brun discovered that the animal before them was actually a hare, and that its ears, which were nearly as long as the creature was tall, stuck straight up into the air. A pile of broken bananas and squashed oranges lay around the tiny hare. Manny could not help but laugh.

"And what do you think's so funny?" asked the young man at the head of the pack.

Manny's face flushed. "I—" He laughed nervously. "I mean, check out those ears! I'm surprised he hasn't fallen over already as big as they are! It's a miracle he can even stand up!"

At that moment all Manny's hope fell from his chest, crumbling around him like the smashed fruit at the hare's feet. From behind the group of young men Manny could see a girl standing, hands on her hips as she seethed with anger, staring straight into Manny's eyes.

"I don't know who you are, you little jerk, but why don't you look in the mirror to see just how funny you look!" snapped the girl as she stomped along the path, passing by the young men and kneeling down behind the hare. A fire flashed in her chocolate eyes just before she turned her face from Manny. As she swept the mashed fruit away from around the hare, Manny noticed the all too familiar beaded braid along the left side of the girl's face. "I don't know what your name is, but will you come with me?" the girl asked the hare, her eyes suddenly soft and full of compassion. The hare's lip quivered slightly as he nodded, his ears bobbing awkwardly. "Good," she said, picking the creature up and setting him on her shoulder. "Let's get away from these idiots."

"Where do you think you're going, Kaya?" asked the young man at the front. "No one told you that you could take him anywhere."

"Shut up, Archer," snapped Kaya viciously. "You and your whole band of stupid friends." As she disappeared around the far bend in the path she added, "Don't you ever tell me what to do again, got it?"

This last statement left Archer, the tall young man with broad shoulders and a wide jaw, absolutely furious. "Can you believe that little brat just talked to me like that?"

"No way!" answered two of his friends from behind.

"Want me to get another snickering fruit snake after her?" asked the fourth.

Archer seemed to ponder this point for a moment, but in the end he said, "No. I'll think of something else…" Looking up and refocusing his eyes, Archer scowled at Manny and Brun. "What are you two freaks staring at, anyway?"

"Nothing," said Brun icily as he stepped in front of Manny to walk between the pathetic heap of fruit and the four young men, his eyes locked straight ahead. Manny followed without a second thought, his heart beating tensely until they rounded the bend. They walked along silently, leaving the others far behind.

"I'm so glad they didn't say anything else," Manny confessed, quite relieved.

"Well, you sure said enough," Brun said severely. "I never expected you—of all people— to do such a thing."

212

"Me? What did I do?" asked Manny, thoroughly thrown as he and Brun emerged from the shortcut to step onto the West Road.

Brun turned around slowly, his movements flowing and calm. "As I recall, you may have said something like, 'Hey, check out his ears,' and, 'It's a miracle he can even stand up.' Am I right?"

"Oh, well I didn't mean anything by it—"

"Didn't mean anything by it? That has nothing to do with it! Did you notice what impact your words had on that poor creature? You were worse than those guys were!" Brun said, his tone ardent.

"Now wait a minute," Manny began. "I'm not the one who startled the snakes. I'm not the one who caused the hare to get pummeled with fruit."

"No, but you're the one that made his lip quiver," Brun said quietly. "You told me last night that no one would make fun of me, that everyone would admire me for my differences. Well, that little hare was different, and you made fun of him! That's much worse than throwing fruit in his face, if you ask me."

The truth tasted bitter in Manny's mouth as he struggled with Brun's words. *How could I have said something like that? After all those years of putting up with Nacho and being poked fun at by the other kids, how could I turn around and do the same to someone else?* Manny swallowed guiltily, his eyes melting into the dirt at his feet. After a moment he looked up and saw that Brun had turned around and was scanning the road, which fell steadily from the Plaza to the western pier. On either side of the path countless brick, stone, and wooden homes rested below the shadow of soaring foliage and innumerable tree houses.

"Hey, Brun," Manny said quietly.

"I still find it just incredible that this many people could live in one place," mused Brun from the center of the road.

Maybe he didn't hear me. Dragging himself reluctantly along, Manny walked up to Brun. "Hey, Brun, listen, I've gotta tell you somethin'."

"Amazing," Brun whispered as he gazed up at a particularly complex tree house with expansive decks and bridges connecting the multiple living quarters. "I've gotta get me one of those someday."

213

Turning around, he began to yell, "Hey, Manny—oh, you're right here. Check out that tree house! Isn't it awesome?"

"Yeah, it is," said Manny as he glanced up, his voice deflated. "Brun, listen. I'm sorry I let you down like that. I guess I just got nervous 'cause of those guys, and that's why I said those things—so that they'd leave me alone and make fun of him instead. But I know that's no excuse, so I just want you to know I'm sorry and I get your point. Believe me, it won't happen again."

"Good," Brun answered, smiling slightly. "But I think the person who you really need to apologize to is that hare—he's the one who has to live with what you said."

Ouch. "Sí, I know. Next time I see him around I'll make sure to catch up with him and tell him," Manny assured.

"Let's just leave this behind us then," said Brun, extending his right hand. "Shake on it?"

"Yeah." The guilt on Manny's chest subsided as he took Brun's hand and shook it firmly.

"So, amigo," Brun continued as he released Manny's hand and turned to face the arched entrance to the Island Gardens. "It's still pretty early in the morning—I'm guessing we have maybe a couple of hours 'til noon. Wanna check out the Gardens?"

"Oh yeah! And the first thing I wanna do is get to the center of the maze!" Manny asserted, the enthusiasm returning in his voice.

"Huh," Brun scoffed lightly. "Fat chance of that."

***

"Manny, this is the thirtieth time we've ended up right back where we started," Brun stated monotonously. "I don't want to spend the whole day doing this."

A half hour had passed from the point when the boys first entered the Gardens, Manny dashing straight from the southern entrance to the circular hedge maze. Each dead end that the boys met mysteriously seemed to lead back to the entrance when they turned around to retrace their steps, puzzling Manny and boring Brun. There were no distinctive factors about the hedge wall

214

whatsoever—the tiny leaves formed an impervious barrier of forest green that towered nearly twice as tall as any grown man.

"Look at it this way, Brun—the further we advance into the maze, the better we'll get to know it. You just have to remember which turn you took that lead to a dead end and not take it the next time. We may not have time to reach the center today, but when we return later, we'll have a head start."

"No, we won't," Brun said frankly.

"¿Por qué no?" asked Manny, slightly put off.

"Because the maze shifts every night, so the paths are different from one day to the next. And the labyrinth design never repeats itself, either. The hedge seals itself off and thinks up a new puzzle from midnight to sunrise," Brun said.

"The hedge 'thinks,' Brun?" repeated Manny skeptically.

Before Brun could answer, the hedge wall shuddered, nearly hitting Manny and causing him to jump away in surprise.

"I don't think it liked the way you said that." Brun's cheek twisted in an amused smile.

"I'd say not." Manny eyed the hedge warily. "Now that you mention it, I'd rather not spend the whole day in the maze, either. No offense," he added as a side to the hedge. The holly-hued wall stood blankly in reply.

Brun heaved a sigh. "Good."

"So what do people do in the Gardens for fun?" Manny asked. "Besides walking, of course."

"Well, there's the challenge of the maze, obviously," Brun began, nodding toward the hedge, "but many Lumens like to sit along the north end and play games—checkers, chess, and Piranha Sweep for example. For little kids there's playground equipment. I know! We could always ph—"

"I forgot! The other kids on the boat invited me to play Piranha Sweep today around ten o'clock!" Manny interrupted. "Why don't we do that?"

"Sounds good to me," Brun answered swiftly.

Minutes later the boys had crossed the Gardens and entered the spacious park area facing the Lake and the waterfall to the north.

Thousands of people of all ages were seated at stone tables, laughing and telling exciting stories as they played game after game in the morning sun. After walking to the east end and turning around, Manny and Brun eventually found some familiar faces near the lofty wall of Lookout Point on the west side of the park.

"Hey, hombre!" called a boy from a circular table under the shade of an enormous tree with flaming orange flowers. "It's that kid with the bright skin from last night!" the boy exclaimed to his friends seated around the table, all of whom instantly set their cards face down to turn and look at Manny.

"¡Hola!" Manny replied, waving his right hand once through the air to greet the four card players.

"I see you brought your brother with you!" continued the brown-haired boy as he walked up to Manny and patted him on the shoulder. "But he wasn't on the boat, was he?"

"No, he wasn't," Manny said. "And he's not my brother—he's my roommate."

"You must be related, then," the boy replied, his blue eyes jumping from Manny to Brun and back again.

"Nope. It's just coincidence," Manny said simply.

"You two sure are a fine pair for being perfect strangers," called a girl with a southern drawl. Manny shrugged in reply.

"So what're your names?" the boy asked.

"I'm Manny López, and this is Brun D-D-" Manny paused. "What's your last name again?" he asked, turning to Brun.

"Dimirtis," Brun answered clearly.

"Well, it's nice to meet you, Manny and Brun," the boy replied happily. "My name's Nataniel Perón, but you can just call me Nate for short. I'm from Argentina.

"Manny an' Brun, huh?" said the girl with the heavy drawl and long blonde curls. "Nice names." She stood up and shook each of their hands. "I'm Millie Carroway, and as Manny already knows, I'm from Texas," she said, her gray eyes shining.

"Don't leave us out!" cried another boy from the table as he and a dark-skinned girl stood up and approached the group. "Manny,

I'm Serge Tres Soles," he said with a wave. "And Brun, if you're a friend of Manny's, you're a friend of ours."

"Thanks," Brun said, slightly surprised. "Where are you from?"

"Guatemala," Serge replied.

"Excuse me," said the girl as she stepped gracefully between Manny and Nate. She had straight black hair that fell over he shoulders and glinted in the sun. Her eyes were a light brown, that of café con leche. "My name's Araceli González," she said, catching Manny's eyes briefly before staring into Brun's. "It's a pleasure to meet you both," she added, winking playfully.

"Thanks," Brun replied, his stomach suddenly squirming.

"I'm from Mexico. Where are you from?" Araceli asked.

"Brazil," Brun answered, trying not to let his voice betray him.

"And you're from Arizona," Araceli said, turning to Manny. "You're the first Lumen in your family."

"Good memory there," Manny replied with a smile.

"Gracias," Araceli answered. "Why don't we play some cards? With you two we'll have six—it's always more fun to play Piranha Sweep with six people."

"How come?" Manny asked.

"It adds a greater level of suspense," Brun replied as the six teenagers took their seats around the table. "At least that's what I've heard."

"Whatcha mean 'you've heard'?" asked Millie from across the table. "You're from a Lumen family, aren't ya?"

"Sí, but I've never played with more than just two people," Brun answered openly.

"That's the weirdest thing I've ever heard," said Serge, who sat on Brun's left, just on the other side of Araceli.

"Then you haven't heard much," retorted Araceli, flipping her hair in Serge's face as she turned and said, "I'm sure you've got a good reason, don't you, Brun?"

"I guess so," Brun replied awkwardly.

"Well, what is it?" Nate asked, seated on Brun's right between Manny and Millie. "We won't laugh at you, whatever it is."

"Bueno, I, uh, I'd never left my house until two days ago," Brun confessed, a little embarrassed.

"Now that is weird!" exclaimed Serge, his green eyes flashing.

"So what!" Araceli shot back with a slap to Serge's shoulder that nearly knocked him from the bench.

"Why'd you never leave your house, Brun?" Millie asked, genuinely interested.

"Mi papá wouldn't let me," Brun stated.

Manny voiced the question that had been rolling around in the back of his mind since the previous night. "Why not?"

"I honestly don't know. My whole life he didn't want me interacting with other Lumens until now—he just said it was time and had my tía Liliana set up everything for me to come here," Brun explained.

"What about your mamá?" asked Nate.

"She died when I was born," Brun said quietly.

"Oh, Brun, I'm sorry," said Araceli, her warm eyes instantly soft and sympathetic. "That's terrible."

Sensing the approach of the infamous awkward silence, Millie turned to Nate and said, "How 'bout you deal the cards and we'll start the game already?"

"No problem," Nate replied, deftly dealing five cards to each player and setting the remaining 22 cards face down in a pile at the center of the table. "You draw first, Manny."

"Alright," Manny replied, confident that he understood the rules of the game as he drew a card and compared it to his other five. *A Seven—that's not gonna do me much good. Okay, I have a Nine, which is a Piranha and the highest card. So really, I don't need to worry about anything as long as no one gets more piranhas than me. I might as well keep the Seven and discard this Deuce.* "You're up, Brun buddy," Manny said as he laid the Deuce face down in front of himself.

"Thanks," Brun replied, smiling as he reached forward to draw his sixth card, which he quickly disposed.

Play continued in this fashion, each person in the circle drawing and discarding until three full turns had been completed. "You've gotta show us your cards first, Manny," Nate said as he laid down his third card to end the round. "Let's see if you can beat what I've got."

"More like what I've got," Millie said playfully.

"Two Piranhas," Manny said, displaying his cards for all to see.

"Me, too," said Brun as he placed his cards on the table next to Manny's.

Well, whatta we do now?

"That's just weird," Serge commented for the third time, though he quickly shut up following a hostile glance from Araceli.

"Well I can't beat either of you," Araceli said, turning from Serge. "The best I had was a Wand."

What's a Wand? Oh—an Ace.

"Yeah, well, with that card I would've had a Royal Straight," Serge said. "I almost had you two," he added with a nod to Brun and Manny. *But Piranhas are the highest cards!*

"I whupped you both!" exclaimed Millie as she revealed a trio of Aces. "Three Wands, and it's over!"

"I did have Four of a Kind in Eights," Nate muttered as he showed his cards to the group. "I would've won if it weren't for the mistress of luck over here!" he added, pointing at Millie. "She throttled us last night, too!"

"Your time will come," Serge told Millie, his voice ominous. "Unless you're a cheater…"

"I don't cheat!" Millie snapped. "You just don't get any good cards."

"Hold on a sec!" Manny interrupted, his fist clenched in frustration. "How can Aces, or Wands, or whatever they are beat Piranhas? I thought Piranhas were the highest card!"

"They are," said Brun abruptly.

"And there are card combinations that can beat a Piranha," Serge added helpfully.

"But Brun and I both had two! How can you beat that?" Manny continued.

"It's just the rules," Millie said. "Three Wands beat two Piranhas—there's no arguin' that."

Manny groaned, stifling his aggravation. *This doesn't make any sense.*

"It's just a game, Manny," Brun whispered through the corner of his mouth.

"Okay, Manny, listen," Millie began, leaning forward to address him as directly as she could. "Last night you asked us if we were playing poker, right? You thought that because you saw all the card combinations that we were laying down. Well, Piranha Sweep is like that—there are nine card combinations in the game, all of which are greater than one Piranha on its own. Give him a sheet of paper, Araceli."

"Alright," Araceli replied, pulling an extra page out from under the score sheet. "Just give me the pencil back when you're done so I can take down the score."

"Gracias," Manny said as he reached across Brun to take the pencil and paper.

"Ready?" Millie asked, her gray eyes solid and focused.

"Sí," Manny answered.

"Okay then, these are the card combinations in order from highest to lowest," Millie began. "First you've got Four Piranhas, which is a Piranha Sweep…

Following is the Piranha Sweep card combination list that Manny transcribed that afternoon:

Four Piranhas – Piranha Sweep (you steal everyone's cards – wow!)

Four Wands – remember that Wands are Aces

Three Piranhas (you steal one card from each player – cool!)

Three Wands

Four of a Kind – any card except Aces and Piranhas, of course

Royal Straight – an Ace, King, Queen, Jack, and Ten of any suit

Two Piranhas (steal one card from any player, provided you win)

Two Wands

Three of a Kind

From here on out the sequence goes Piranha (Nine, of course), Ten, Eight, etc.

Value of Each Card (in points when you tally them up)

$$P = 25$$

$$W = 20$$

$$KQJ = 15$$

$$6, 7, 8, 10 = 10$$

$$2, 3, 4, 5 = 5$$

*The winner of each round gets 25 extra points

Remember – the winner is the first person to 500 points

Oh – in case of a tie, whoever has the next highest card wins

"Thanks, guys—I think that just about answers all my questions," Manny said as he set the pencil down on the table. "Now I shouldn't get lost so easily." *And hopefully I won't discard anything important, like a Wand.*

"Let's count up the points, then," Nate directed.

"I need my pencil, Manny," Araceli hinted.

"Oh, yeah, sorry!" Manny replied, passing the utensil back to her as he tallied his score in his head. A moment later he said, "I've got 75 points."

"Mark me down for 65," Serge said.

"And 115 for me," said Millie.

"I'm at 55," said Nate.

"I had 95," Brun added.

"How'd you get higher than me?" Manny asked quickly. "We both had double Piranhas."

"Yeah, but you had a Two, Seven, and Ten, which is only 25 points. I had a King, Queen, and a Jack, which add up to 45 points. You've got to be careful what cards you discard and what ones you keep," Brun advised.

True. "I'll get you next time around, though," Manny replied with a smile.

"Good luck, then," Brun said, staring back coolly.

"So what'd you have, Araceli?" asked Nate.

"Smack dab in the middle with 70," Araceli answered.

"Time to start the next round—and it's your turn to deal, Manny," Nate said, pushing his cards to the left. "Think you got it down? Remember—five to each player."

"I know," Manny said as he slid all the cards into a single pile and began to shuffle.

Three rounds later the air was tense—with her uncanny ability to attract only the highest card combinations, Millie sat just five points below the 500 mark. Each of the remaining players, however, silently hoped that he or she might somehow collect the one and only combination that would enable victory this late in the game—the elusive Piranha Sweep.

Maybe, just maybe—ugh. Another Ten. That's pathetic; I didn't even draw one Piranha. Four Tens is better than nothing, though. Manny disposed of his final card, his hopes for the game irrevocably deflated. *Even if I win the round, Millie's still gonna get enough points to take the game.* Breathing deeply he watched as Brun slid a card in and out of his hand, discarding with seamless composure. *Geez, he always seems too calm. How's he do that?*

Drawing her final card, Millie let loose a cheerful whistle, never one to conceal her assurance of victory. "How 'bout that," she muttered to herself as she discarded.

Nate rolled his eyes and sighed as he set his cards out on the table. "I didn't have a thing."

"I had four Tens, but that won't help me overtake Millie," Manny said as he revealed his cards.

Millie was beaming with bliss as Brun set his cards down. "I had a Queen," he said. "And a Piranha Sweep."

"Get out," said Araceli incredulously, rising slowly from her seat to stare at Brun's cards. "He really does…"

"I haven't seen one of those in months," Serge reflected in wonder.

"That's the only hand that could've beaten this," Millie said, laying down a quartet of Wands. "Did you draw those throughout the round?"

"No, you dealt them to me," Brun answered calmly.

"Ha, ha!" laughed Nate loudly. "She dealt her own demise!"

"Wow," said Araceli. "I've never heard of that."

"I can't believe it," Millie confessed, shaking her head.

"So, how many points will that be, anyway?" Manny asked Araceli.

"Oh, geez, I don't know. Everybody tally your points," Araceli told them. A minute later she had the final count. "Brun, with all our cards you racked in 520 points that round for a grand total of 880 points."

"Way to go, man!" exclaimed Manny, patting Brun on the back.

"I'd say!" bolstered Nate, standing and leaning over the table to shake Brun's hand.

"Awesome!" said Serge excitedly.

"Congratulations," Millie said from the other side of the table.

"It was just luck," Brun replied quietly. "No skill was involved at all."

"Yeah, but isn't it a blast just to win?" erupted Millie in a laugh. "I think it's a riot just to see how the game ends! The tide can turn at any moment—that's what I love about it!"

Brun sat for a moment, then smiled. "You're right. So, guys, you wanna play again?"

"Yeah! Of course!" they all shouted, Manny's voice by no means the quietest.

* * *

"I am so hungry!" Manny's stomach contorted violently in a garrulous call for food.

"We'll be at the Café in under ten minutes," Brun replied, seated across from Manny in a small boat pulled forward across the northern stretch of the Lake by an otter astride a pink river dolphin. "You're gonna have to get used to eating around two o'clock, because from what I hear there are classes at both noon and one." Manny groaned in anguish. "I suppose we could always grab a snack on the way to our next class, if we have to," Brun added supportively.

"I'm sure I'll have to—six hours without food is killing me…" groaned Manny, his eyes fixed firmly on the thin curtain of water streaming down into the basin from the Lucero River above, the Falls altogether failing to conceal the lakeside restaurant with its hundreds of tables extending along the alcove that stretched east and west beneath the rocky lip of the valley. Manny let his fingers graze the cool water, the tiny ripples melting into the larger wake carved by the wooden ferry in which he traveled. Scanning the waters about him, Manny noted the high level of activity at this hour as the otters

224

with their rosy steeds shuttled humans and animals alike to a multitude of destinations. The reflection of the dark waters revealed wave after wave of airborne creatures soaring through the skies above. Manny's eyes leapt to and fro, tracing the path of the many falcons, quetzals, and butterflies engrossed in their lofty island commute.

"Is it always this busy at two in the afternoon?" Manny asked, his words wafting away gently in an easterly breeze.

"I'm sure it is; at least as long as everyone's as hungry as you are."

Manny grinned. "That's understandable, then."

Moments later the ferry slowed and swung to the side, allowing Brun and Manny to step from the shallow floor of the boat to dry rock.

"Take care, now," the otter called in a ruddy voice. "Don't slip and fall, lest Waterblade and I should 'ave to shuttle y'both straight to a healer."

"Don't worry, sir," Manny replied as he drew up next to Brun on the rocky shore. "We'll be careful."

"Thanks a lot," Brun said, tossing the creature a glittering Sol.

"What's a ferryotter for, lads?" called the otter good-heartedly as he caught the coin and slapped the dolphin's back with his tail. The two creatures promptly proceeded along the bank in search of additional customers in need of transport.

Manny gazed out over the heads of hundreds of people chatting and eating happily. "Where do we go from here?"

"Look, there's a counter near the rock wall." Brun nodded to the back. "Let's go," he added, leading the way in zigzag fashion between tables and around chairs. Within moments the boys reached a long stone counter, seemingly carved from the rock itself. From an arch in the wall behind poured server after server laden with circular trays packed with steaming food. Above the arch the boys observed a carved sign, its wood stained blue and etched letters painted white that read, "Café de la Catarata."

Manny's stomach contorted hungrily as he reached the counter. "Now what?"

"How many?" a bright voice asked from over Manny's shoulder. Spinning around, he found a young woman in a blue and white uniform with her hair in a ponytail."

"Dos," Brun answered.

"Follow me," the waitress replied, waving her hand and lifting a set of plates and silverware into the air from behind the stone counter. Manny nearly tripped as he attempted to follow the other two while keeping one eye on the floating utensils above.

"Excuse you!" bellowed a woman, utterly offended as Manny walked straight into her chair. "Watch where you're going, young man!"

"I'm sorry." Manny's cheeks radiated his embarrassment as he lowered his eyes to meet the woman's frowning face. "H-have a nice meal," he called as he swiftly fled.

"Well, I never…" he heard the woman begin.

"What would you like to drink?" the waitress asked just as Manny reached the table.

Oh, gosh. "Um, do you have horchata?"

"Definitely," the waitress replied.

"I'll have that then," said Manny.

"What flavors of agua fresca do you have?" Brun inquired.

"You name it, I can get it."

"Hmm… I'll have agua de melón, then."

"No problem! I'll be right back with your drinks and to take your order." The waitress stopped suddenly as she turned around. "I forgot your menus. Sorry." With a flick of her hand a pair of menus buzzed through the air, narrowly dodging several sets of flying silverware. "There you go, then," she said as the menus came to rest in the boys' hands. "Back in a second."

"Wow—they have everything here," Manny observed as he flipped through the book-like menu. "Even pizza."

"What's pizza?" Brun asked genuinely.

"You don't know what pizza is!" Manny exclaimed. "That's it! We're getting it. You can't live your life without trying pizza." He shut the menu decidedly.

"I'm kidding, Manny," Brun laughed. "Tía Liliana loves pizza—she makes it for me all the time."

"Aren't you just the funniest…" Manny grumbled as he reopened the menu.

Seconds later the waitress reappeared, handing a tall glass of white liquid to Manny, and another glass with a transparent green liquid to Brun. "Ready to order?" she asked, taking out a pad of paper.

"Sí," Brun answered. "I'd like paella, but with shrimp only, please."

"Okay then. And for you?"

"Could I have tamales wrapped in banana leaves?" Manny asked.

"Sure," the waitress replied. "Anything else?"

The boys looked at each other. "No. Thanks though," Brun said.

"It's my pleasure," she answered as she turned and disappeared once again among the maze of tables.

"I think we got the best seat in the house, Brun," Manny remarked as he gazed at the glistening curtain of water just beyond the rocky shelf on which they were seated. The verdant outline of the island swayed mysteriously through the powerful veil. "I have to admit, this is the first time I've ever looked at a waterfall from the inside."

Brun nodded. "Same goes for me."

Stretching out his arms, Manny commented, a bit loudly, "Yeah, Brun, this is great! We get to live with a centaur, play Piranha Sweep with our new friends, and eat whatever we want! On top of all that, we get to go to school and learn how to use light for all kinds of things, and those jerks that teased me back home are nowhere to be found!"

For a moment Brun simply stared at Manny with a blank expression. "Yeah, I like it more than I thought I would."

"Hmph!" called an irritated voice from behind Manny. "Let's get out of here, Iris. There's not enough room here with that kid's fat head taking up the whole waterfall."

What? Who's she talking about? Puzzled, Manny turned around to find the same girl from the fruit snake path earlier that morning, her long black hair and subtle pink beads flashing in the light reflected from the waterfall as she bent down to pick up the hare, setting him on her left shoulder. With an icy glare to Manny, she turned around and walked away.

"Keilani doesn't seem all that nice if you ask me," Brun pointed out. "But I guess she does have a good reason to be mad at you."

"That's not Keilani," he said gruffly, hopping up from his seat and weaving between the tables as he followed the girl and the hare to the counter. Manny tapped her on the shoulder and said, "Is that rabbit's name Iris?"

"He's not a rabbit," the girl said curtly as she spun around. "He's a hare."

"Oh, well—where'd he go?" Manny asked abruptly. "Didn't he just hop down onto the counter?"

"I don't see why that matters to you," the girl cut back. Scanning up and down the countertop, Manny noticed that the hare was seated on the far left corner. He attempted to turn in that direction, but the girl blocked his way.

"His name is Iris, isn't it?" Manny pressed. She stared back, her eyes like black ice. "I need to tell him something.

"He doesn't want to talk to you," the girl said severely. "And even if he did, you made your feelings clear about him this morning."

Manny swallowed, anxious to reach the hare. *I've got to apologize.* "But—"

"Just leave us both alone!" she said forcefully as she whirled on the spot, her hair whipping Manny in the face and stinging his eyes. For a moment everything was a blur as he blinked and rubbed his eyelids; when he next looked up, however, the girl and the hare were gone.

"How'd that go?" Brun asked as Manny approached the table and retook his seat.

"Just as well as it did this morning," Manny said dryly. "She even gave me a kiss goodbye."

"You two might need to slow down just a little," Brun joked, though his face did not show it. "So did you even get to talk to the hare?"

"No," Manny replied, slightly aggravated. "She blocked my way. And how did you know he was a hare, anyway?"

"The long ears," Brun answered simply.

How ironic. Manny closed his eyes, his chest tight as he inhaled deeply, then slowly breathed out a bit of his frustration.

"So, Manny, just before you took off after that girl you said she wasn't Keilani—who was she, then?"

Manny opened his eyes. "I didn't catch her name. But I do remember that one of those guys on the fruit snake path called her something that begins with a K. It definitely wasn't Keilani, though."

"In that case, how could you get them confused?"

"Brun, I'm telling you, it's weird, but she and Keilani look exactly alike. It's just that this other girl is a bit shorter—they both have the same eyes and identical beads in their hair," Manny explained. "No—I take that back. Keilani's beads are white. That other girl's are pink."

"I bet they're sisters," Brun said, his eyes keen. "Did you remember Keilani telling you anything about her family?"

Manny searched his thoughts for a moment, frowning a bit. "No, we really only talked about the island." *And how little I knew about it.*

"Do you know where she lives?"

"Why?"

"Because we could go there and ask her if she has a sister."

"Oh. That's a good idea—but no, I don't know where she lives," said Manny defeatedly.

"Well, next time you see her, ask if she has a sister," Brun suggested. "Keilani's gotta be beautiful if that was her little sister."

229

"Are you serious?" Manny punctuated. "That girl was meaner than a snake!"

Brun shrugged. "Mean or not, she was still cute."

"Your orders are ready!" rang a soft voice to Brun's left. The boys turned to find the blue clad waitress carrying a silver platter in her right hand. "Your paella, sir," she said as she set a dish of rice, vegetables, and shrimp down in front of Brun. "And your tamales," she continued, setting a wooden bowl piled high with plump green parcels on the table before Manny, "wrapped in banana leaves, of course."

"Gracias," they both replied, their mouths suddenly watering.

She smiled. "You're very welcome. Enjoy your meal."

Brun pulled his plate up close. "We will!"

***

"So what's yours say?" Manny asked.

"Here—have a look," Brun replied, passing a sheet of paper to Manny, who quickly compared it to his own:

		Amazon River Academy		
		Fall & Spring Schedule		
Brun Kieran Dimirtis				Level: 7
Class	**Instructor**	**Location**	**Time**	**Book**
Healing	M. Bluebolt	Harmony Falls	8 a.m. MWF	*The Science of Light*
Art	C. Flores	Southeast Garden	10 a.m. MWF	*Bring It to Life*
The Lumen World	S. Shadowflame	TBA	11 a.m. TR	*The Blue World*
Light Bending	A. Nochesol	Lucero Falls (Crown)	12 p.m. MWF	*Photokinesis*
Sentinels	F. Firefoot	Fire Flats	4 p.m. TR	*Guardians, Sentinels, & Light Keepers*
Astronomy	C. Veridai	Nahir's Hill	11 p.m. MWF	*Light at Night*

	Amazon River Academy			
	Fall & Spring Schedule			
Manny Luis López				Level: 7
Class	**Instructor**	**Location**	**Time**	**Book**
The Lumen World	S. Shadowflame	TBA	8 a.m. MWF	*The Blue World*
Healing	M. Bluebolt	Harmony Falls	10 a.m. MWF	*The Science of Light*
Art	C. Flores	Southeast Garden	11 a.m. TR	*Bring It to Life*
Light Bending	A. Nochesol	Lucero Falls (Crown)	12 p.m. MWF	*Photokinesis*
Sentinels	F. Firefoot	Fire Flats	4 p.m. TR	*Guardians, Sentinels, & Light Keepers*
Astronomy	C. Veridai	Nahir's Hill	11 p.m. MWF	*Light at Night*

"Just great," Manny grumbled.

"What?" Brun asked as he and Manny turned right and dove into a crowd of people.

"We've only got three classes together," Manny replied darkly, sidestepping a pair of kinkajous bolting off in the other direction. "I was hoping we'd have them all together."

"Yeah, that would've been nice," agreed Brun. "We do have the same classes, though, don't we?"

"Sí."

"Well, we can at least practice and do our homework together," Brun said positively.

"That's true," said Manny as the two boys reached the Carina, turning at a horizontal and following the river's southeast flow straight through the arched entrance of a towering, white marble building. A sudden thought hit Manny. "Hey! Maybe Nate and the gang will have some classes with us!"

"Hopefully," Brun said as he and Manny crossed an expansive hall, at the center of which a circular dais rose over the Carina, briefly concealing the river's flow that virtually cleaved the building into two massive halves before exiting through the far arch and plunging unflappably into a forested dell. The roof, a distant and translucent dome of glass supported by lofty pillars greater in width than the most pronounced redwoods, allowed the sun's warm rays to pierce the air and illuminate the millions of books covering the high walls of the building. Spiral staircases granted access to the numerous platforms and walkways suspended along the walls, enabling those hungry for knowledge to scour the library of literature resting there.

"Welcome to the Lumen Resource Center," chimed a cheerful voice from the circulation desk. "Can I help you in any way?"

"Sí," Brun replied as he and Manny reached the desk and set their arms upon it. "We need to check out our textbooks."

"That will be no problem at all," the voice replied. "I just need to see your schedules."

"Manny," Brun said, kicking his foot.

233

"Oh, sorry!" Manny replied, lowering the papers in his hands and staring curiously at a lucent butterfly roughly the size of his head perched on the counter before him. "Are you...?"

"A librarian?" the butterfly answered pleasantly. "Yes."

Manny blinked. "But how do you...?"

"Transport books? Just pass me those schedules and watch," she replied. Manny laid the schedules out flat upon the counter as the butterfly flitted a wing or two. After briefly scanning the papers with her black, pen tip eyes, she subtly snapped an antenna before bursting into the air in a flash of blue and silver, the schedules tailing along behind her as she elegantly wove around the pillars, shooting from one side of the library to the next as she collected a string of books that soared submissively in her wake. Just over a minute later she returned to the circulation desk, landing softly in front of the two boys as their textbooks and schedules floated gracefully and silently down into piles on either side of her. Brun's eyes shined; Manny's mouth hung open. "Would you like me to help you with anything else today?"

"Actually, yes," Brun began. "Could you—"

"What type of butterfly are you?" Manny interrupted.

"A blue morpho," she replied kindly.

"Oh. I've never heard of those," he confessed. The butterfly blinked mildly in reply.

"Anyway," Brun said. "Would it be possible—"

"What's your name?" Manny asked.

"Melinda," the insect answered. "Melinda Brightwing. It's a pleasure to meet you, Manny. And you, Brun."

How did she know my...? Oh, duh—she had my schedule. "You, too."

"Let me try this again," Brun resumed, a slight edge to his voice. "Melinda, do you have any paloma paper so we can send our books to our house?"

"Of course," the butterfly replied, flitting her antennae and producing two sheets of glistening paper from beneath the counter. "One moment and I'll have your books wrapped for you," she continued as she lifted into the air and snapped her antennae in the direction of the separate piles, which levitated above the counter as the seemingly small sheets of paper stretched to completely envelop both stacks of books. "To where should I address these?"

"Chiron's Hutch, Back Room," Brun answered.

In a breath the books were gone, firing up and through the glass roof in a bolt of blue light that disappeared into the skies above.

***

"What adventures did the two of you have today?" Chiron asked as Manny and Brun walked to the back of the bamboo hut.

"Too many to count!" Manny replied enthusiastically. Chiron raised an inquisitive brow.

"Nothing dangerous, Chiron, don't worry," Brun said quickly. "After looking at the island from the Argo Dock, we visited the Plaza and the park before eating lunch and getting our books."

"Yes, I know—I saw your books arrive less than half an hour ago," Chiron said. "Are you both eager to begin your studies?"

"Definitely! I can't wait for Art class!" Manny exclaimed.

"Indeed?" Chiron replied.

"Nothing against Astronomy, though," Manny said swiftly. "It's just that I really like to draw."

"You will be doing little of that in Art, I am afraid," Chiron said. Manny shot the centaur a quizzical look. "You see, Manuel, Lumen art focuses on creating, rather than just simply reflecting, what exists around us. And you, Brun? What class do you anticipate the most?"

Brun replied without a second's hesitation. "The Lumen World."

"With reason," Chiron said wisely. "After living your entire life in isolation from Lumen society, it is no wonder that you wish to study it greatly." Brun smiled and nodded. "If neither of you has plans for this evening, would you like to stargaze with me? I am expecting a meteor shower around nine o'clock—it will be most exhilarating."

"I love to stargaze," Manny said. "I'm in."

"Actually, Chiron, I was hoping Manny and I could go to Lookout Point to watch the lightboarders for a while," Brun said. "It's something that I've always wanted to see."

"Then you shall," Chiron replied. "And with any luck, you may return just in time to see the shower!"

***

"Can everybody do that?" Manny asked as he gazed out from his rocky seat high above the now turbulent lake as waves the size of houses relentlessly pelted the white sanded beaches.

"Only Lumens that can stand on two feet—you know—humans, kinkajous, frogs, green basilisks, and otters," Brun replied.

Manny frowned. *No, actually I didn't know.*

"But to do some of the tricks they're doing out there, you need tons of practice," Brun finished.

In the growing twilight Manny counted roughly a hundred surfers tearing across the waves on glowing lightboards. With every renewed surge of water the surfers shot along the breaker's belly, coasting in wait for the optimal moment to veer suddenly and mount the crest of the wave to soar into the air and perform a variety of flips, turns, and tricks. *They look like little surfing lightning bugs.* Manny squinted his eyes as he watched a surfer launch into the air, leaving the wave far below her as she executed several 360° turns before kneeling and grabbing one end of the lightboard an instant before she slid down the back of the wave. *It reminds me of something...*

"I wish I could do that..." Brun said in awe.

"Skateboarding!" Manny blurted.

"No, lightboarding," Brun corrected quickly. "What's a skate, anyway?"

"Of course this isn't skateboarding!" Manny retorted. "But the techniques these surfers are using remind me a lot of skateboarding back home."

236

Brun blinked, confused, as he reluctantly turned from the luminous surfers. "Like I asked—what's a skate?"

"Geez—sorry. It's not a skate, but a skateboard," Manny stated clearly. "It's a lot like a lightboard, I guess. You know—oval, made of wood—but skateboards have four wheels and they don't usually glow. At least none I've seen, anyway."

"How can wheels get you across water?" Brun asked.

"Obviously you don't ride a skateboard on water!" said Manny. "You ride it on concrete—the street, sidewalks, in parks. Professionals even skateboard in tubes called half pipes, firing into the air and doing the same tricks that these lightboarders are doing."

Brun pondered this for a moment as the sound of the excited voices of fellow spectators filled the air, framed by the ceaseless crashing of the waves below. "I bet skateboards don't fly, though," he said finally.

"What does that have to do with anything?"

"Because lightboards can."

"Can what?" Manny asked.

"Fly!" said Brun.

"Are you telling me that I could get on one of those lightboards and just take off into the air?"

"With some practice, yes," Brun replied evenly. "You've got two legs and apparently good balance."

Hmm… This sounds like it could be interesting… "So why aren't they flying into the air now, then?" Manny nodded toward the lightboarders.

"Because they're surfing," Brun said slowly and obviously. "They won't start air competitions for nearly a month."

"Wow—now that's what I want to see," Manny reflected.

As the light of dusk faded, casting the valley into growing darkness, the force of the waves diminished until they were little more than faint breakers teasing the now tranquil beaches. Manny watched attentively as the lightboarders in the distance all seemed to zip away into the air like tiny fireflies scattered by an invisible hand. *Cool.* To his surprise he noticed that one such lightboarder appeared to be moving straight toward his seat atop the cliff. In less than three seconds the surfer had reached the rock face, hopping from the lightboard, grabbing it and standing it on end.

"What's up, little lightning bug?" the surfer asked. "I noticed that you were here—and with your friend the firefly, at that."

"Keilani?" Manny asked, standing up and taking several steps toward the surfer.

"Sí, soy yo," Keilani replied, flipping her hair over her shoulders and eyeing Manny keenly. "At least you can recognize my voice. So who's your friend?"

"Oh, this is Brun—my roommate."

Keilani laughed. "Your roommate? How funny! So you glow white in the dark, and Brun glows red! Did your light-bringers know about this when they set you up to live with Chiron?"

"I don't know," they both replied in unison.

"What a trip!" she cackled loudly. "I know your light-bringer is Julius, but what about you, Brun?"

"His name is Rush," Brun answered.

"Rush Stickgrip, eh? Well I'll have to ask him or Julius, whichever I see first, whether they planned this out! How funny!" Keilani continued.

"It is pretty ironic," Brun conceded.

"Oh! You two are Seventh-Levels, right? Wait here just one minute! I want to introduce you to someone. I'll be right back!" Keilani mounted her lightboard and disappeared swiftly over the edge of the cliff.

"Boy, Brun, I don't know about jumping off the side of small mountains," Manny said. "I may not try lightboarding after all."

"Don't be a wuss, Manny," Brun said reproachfully.

A breath later Keilani had reappeared over the lip of the precipice, carrying another person with her, who actually seemed to be holding a small bundle in her arms. As Keilani and her guest descended from the lightboard, a fleeing shadow and the sound of scattering rocks on Manny's left made him jump.

"What was that?" Manny blurted.

"I dunno," said Brun hesitantly.

"Manny, Brun, I would like to introduce you to my little sister, Kaya," Keilani said, stepping aside and waving a hand to her guest, who stared stone-faced at Manny. In the faint orange light produced by the combined illumination of the boys' skin, Manny and Brun saw that Kaya, with her black hair and beaded braid, happened to be the same girl from the snake path and the Café. In fact, the only difference that either boy could notice between the sisters was that Kaya appeared to be a head shorter than Keilani.

"Sister?" repeated Manny, slightly disappointed.

"So I was right," asserted Brun.

"Right about what?" Keilani asked, smiling vaguely.

"Manny and I saw Kaya earlier today, and he told me that she looked a lot like you. So I said that you two were probably sisters, and you are," Brun explained.

"You didn't tell me you'd met Manny already, Kaya," said Keilani.

"That's because I haven't," Kaya replied shortly, not removing her fierce eyes from Manny for a second.

"Then you've never talked to him?" Keilani asked suspiciously. "You sure act like you recognize him now."

"I didn't say I'd never talked to him. I just said we hadn't met," Kaya retorted.

"Well, now you have!" said Keilani happily. "Since the three of you are all Seventh-Levels, maybe you can be friends! After all, Kaya, you don't know any outsiders, and I would imagine that they don't know very many people here, yet."

"Fat chance of that," snapped Kaya.

"What did you say?" Keilani asked, surprised.

"Why would I want to be friends with him?" Kaya cut back, her eyes stoning Manny.

"What did he ever do to you? You just told me that you'd never met—how could he already be on your bad side? Usually that takes a couple days," Keilani joked.

"Oh, he didn't do anything to me," Kaya said quietly. "But as for Iris—that's another story."

"Iris?" Keilani repeated. "Where is he, anyway? Weren't you carrying him on the way up here?"

"He took one look at Manny, here, and bolted away down the hill," Kaya illuminated.

"Now hold on one minute," Keilani began, her voice assuming a dangerous tone as she locked her hands on her hips. "You tell me what's going on here, and you tell me now. There's no reason that you and Iris should both be mad at Manny. He just arrived at Isla Verde yesterday! I know, because I brought him here!"

"A lot can happen in a day," Kaya replied laconically.

"Spit it out, Kaya!" Keilani demanded, her patience lost.

"Hey, if you want to be friends with a snobby jerk like him, then go ahead!" screamed Kaya as she turned to face her sister. "But as for me, I'm out of here! I'm not gonna hang with a trash talker!" And with that Kaya turned, kicked Keilani's lightboard over the edge of the cliff, and ran along the path leading away down the hill.

"You just wait 'til I get home!" Keilani yelled as she turned and flipped her beads to call her lightboard back. "Ugh!"

"Yowzers, Manny," Brun whispered. "You've got an odd taste in women."

"Tell me about it," Manny replied, his eyes wide.

"So what did you do to my sister to tick her off so bad?" Keilani queried heatedly.

"Um, uh, I—"

"Stuck his big foot in his mouth," Brun said. "We were all on the fruit snake path when some macho guy came stomping along with his friends and started making fun of Iris. When they turned to us, Manny said some things he shouldn't have, and Kaya heard him. The rest is history."

"Really..." Keilani mused. "Did you catch the guy's name?"

"I forget," Brun replied.

"It was Archer," Manny said quietly.

"Archer? Are you sure?" asked Keilani, a bit taken aback.

"Oh, yeah. I'll never forget that stupid scowl on his giant jaw," Manny replied. *He's like a big version of Nacho—they both make me sick.*

Keilani suddenly appeared upset. "I've gotta go," she said, mounting her lightboard. "Sorry," she added as she turned and shot away to the southeast across the island.

Brun shook his head. "Now if that wasn't the most awkward experience of my life, I don't know what was."

"She acted like she knows him. Didn't you think so?" Manny asked.

"For sure," said Brun. "Hey—maybe she's gonna go kick his butt right now!"

"Maybe… But she acted more disappointed then angry."

It grew silent as Manny and Brun peered out in different directions from the top of the cliff, the first casting his thoughtful eyes on the tiny waves below, while the other considered the forested terrain of the island stretching out beyond the Gardens ahead. After several minutes, Brun spoke. "Manny?"

"Yeah?" the other replied, his mind lost in the undulating waters.

"I have a question." Brun had his hands in his pockets as he gazed at the stars.

"Shoot," said Manny, taking a breath and sighing deeply as he sat down on a large rock.

"Why do you think people fight?"

"They're just mad at each other, I guess," Manny answered quickly.

"But why? What's the point? I mean, people get mad at each other so easily, over complete misunderstandings or slip-ups. Why do they have to get angry at all?" said Brun, his eyes searching the stars.

Manny took a moment to ponder this. "Maybe we're all just too impatient to see beyond ourselves; I mean, when I get upset, or say things I shouldn't, I guess I'm really only thinking about myself."

"But why?" Brun said, turning and facing Manny. "We're all just lucky to have each other! Imagine life without other people, living alone, no one to talk to... I would hate it."

"So what are you saying?"

"I guess just that, if we value being with others, then we shouldn't treat them so badly, even if they get on our nerves—'cause they could be gone in an instant, leaving us completely alone."

"I never thought of it that way..." Manny said. *I do get angry pretty easily...*

Crossing his arms, Brun turned to the east to gaze up at the polished blue Dock, gleaming in the starlight. Manny stared at his feet, considering his family over a thousand miles away, his parents, grandmother, cousins...

"Whoa—now that's cool!" Brun exclaimed.

Manny jerked his head up and looked into the eastern sky—an enormous object shimmered briefly, sliding down from the north and flickering like water disturbed by a stone, casting waves of colorful light in various directions. As Manny stood up, the object took shape—a silver-white keel materializing in the dark skies above mounted with a glowing mast and sails that changed colors depending upon where the observer stood.

"Is that the Argo?" Manny asked in wonder.

"It has to be," Brun whispered. "It's incredible."

Both boys stood with their mouths open in awe as the great Lumen ship, spanning the length of multiple football fields, slid into the lofty harbor and silently docked, not swaying in the least, but perfectly even.

"So, basically, the Argo is like a Lumen airplane," Manny observed.

"What's an airplane?"

Oh-my-gosh. Manny took a patient breath. "What I meant to say is that you can travel in it from place to place, right?"

"Only from certain places," Brun replied. "And only at night."

"That's all I wanted to know," Manny said as he gazed at the moonstone tower, its spiral stairs now filling with Lumens quickly descending to reach the Dock Road and then home. Here and there a lightboard bolted out over the parapet of the Dock, winding down into the forests below. Just as Manny was about to suggest leaving, a green dot appeared, floating down from the tower and heading straight for the cliff where the boys stood.

"What's that?" Brun asked. "It looks like a bird."

A flash of crimson on the bird's chest confirmed Manny's hopes. "Julius!"

Seconds later the jade quetzal with its streaming tail plumes landed majestically on the rock upon which Manny had been sitting moments earlier. "¡Buenas noches, muchachos!" Julius cried.

"You, too!" Manny said, his countenance glowing brightly. "Where have you been?"

"Oh, here and there—you know, visiting other schools, conferences, recruiting and the like," clipped the quetzal positively.

"Your head looks great, Julius," Manny noted.

"I think so," the bird replied happily. "All thanks to Tavo, you know."

"Yep!" Manny agreed.

"Who are you?" Brun asked bluntly. "And how did you find us here?"

Manny held up his palm to the bird, prompting him to allow Manny to perform the introductions. "Brun, this is my light-bringer, Julius Rumblefeather. I met him in Costa Rica and we had a really weird adventure there. And Julius, this is my roommate, Brun Dimirtis."

"It is a pleasure to meet you, young sir," said Julius, nodding slightly.

"Likewise," corresponded Brun.

"Allow me to answer your second question," the quetzal said, his beady eyes sparkling in the light radiating on the cliff top. "Upon exiting the Argo, I took one look over the parapet and saw a pair of glowing figures—one white, one red—standing atop Lookout Point. So I thought to myself, 'Julius, who do you know that can glow in the dark? Manny López! But who could that other fellow be, I wonder?' Consequently, I dove from the tower and now here I am, brimming with questions and stunned at what I've found! First of all, are you two brothers? If so, Manny, why did you not tell me you had a twin?"

"Because I don't," Manny answered quickly.

"We just look alike," Brun added. "At least where it comes to physical features. Chiron actually stated that we seem to be complete opposites."

"Verdad—I can see his reasoning," Julius replied as he lifted from the rock and soared around the boys. "Very strange—sí, muy extraño."

"So Manny, you said that you and Julius had a weird adventure in Costa Rica. What happened?" Brun fished, intent on drawing the attention away from himself.

"That's precisely what I would like to know!" chirped the quetzal as he lit upon the boulder once more.

"If you were involved, then how don't you know?" Brun said with a faint edge.

"In this I will allow Manny to speak." The quetzal nodded curtly to the other boy. "My memory fails me during part of our 'adventure,' as you both called it."

"Before I start, Julius, you've got to promise not to interrupt me until I'm finished," Manny stipulated. "Alright?"

"Of course," the quetzal acquiesced.

"I'm serious! Promise me!" Manny said fervently.

"Why are you so concerned all of a sudden, m'ijo?" Julius asked, cocking his head a tad to the left.

"I tried to tell some other people, but they didn't believe what I had to say. But never mind that—just promise me," Manny pleaded.

"Está bien, m'ijo," the quetzal conceded. "You have my word—not one chirp."

And so Manny described how he had been trekking through the rainforest with his class the past June when he met the bearded monkey, who had unexpectedly transformed his family camera into his now mahogany wand and disappeared abruptly. He related the truth of Julius's attack, explaining his suspicion that the monkey had

244

deliberately thrown the nut at the quetzal's head for whatever reason. Manny then went on to tell how he had dropped his wand along the stream on the way to the forest sanctuary, and how when he returned later that night, the same monkey seemed to be attempting to steal the wand. "He almost attacked me—the little creep! If it weren't for Tavo, we'd probably both be dead!" He then briefly recounted how the unicorn had forestalled the monkey and forced Manny to return to the sanctuary.

"That's crazy…" Brun muttered.

"You are finished, then?" Julius asked.

"Sí," Manny replied, his eyes bright as he was happy that the quetzal had kept his word.

"Then listen carefully, m'ijo," Julius began. "I understand that you believe that the monkey transformed your wand—but that is simply impossible."

"Why's that?" Brun cut in. "If Manny said it happened, then it did."

"No, it didn't, Brun," the bird answered. "Neither of you may know this, but monkeys are not Lumens—not in either of the American continents, nor in the rest of the illuminated world. It is effectively irrational to believe that a monkey could have done this."

Brun gazed intently at the quetzal, but remained quiet, his skin glowing a bright red.

"That's what Melody said, too; but Julius, you must be wrong! I didn't see a kinkajou, like she said! I saw a monkey—a real, live monkey!" Manny affirmed. "Maybe somehow another Lumen transformed him into a Lumen, too!"

"That is also unfeasible," Julius pushed on. "No Lumen holds the power to illuminate a new species. That power lies with the stars, all of which have long passed into the grave."

"But if they're stars then how can they be dead?" Brun asked pointedly. "Don't stars live for thousands of years?"

"Indeed," the quetzal granted. "But when the Light Brethren came to Earth, they became mortals—who eventually aged and died."

"I didn't know that…" said Brun quietly.

"In that case, there's a star running around somewhere who made that monkey a Lumen," Manny asserted. "There's no doubt in my mind."

"I am certain there is not," Julius countered.

"How come?" Manny asked swiftly. "How can you be sure another star hasn't come secretly?"

"We—Lumens, I mean—could sense his light," Julius replied.

"What if he was hiding it?" Brun proposed.

Julius appeared confused. "Hiding what?"

"His light—couldn't a star hide its light if it wanted?" said Brun.

Julius eyed Brun oddly, his feathered brow furrowed. "I suppose he could—but why would he?"

"Who knows? Maybe he doesn't want to be bothered," Manny suggested.

"I do not believe that," Julius said finally. "The Light Brethren were the benevolent founders of the Lumen order—I am certain any further stars would contact us instantly and teach us their ways."

"But—" both boys began.

"Neither of you will convince me to think otherwise, so do not try," the quetzal clipped. "Manny, though you may believe that your wand-giver was a monkey, I do not. Yet we will argue no further. Let us move on to the issue of the attack." Julius stopped to ruffle his feathers and flap his wings a time or two. "I would first like to say that I confide in you completely, and trust that you did not throw that nut at me."

"Thank you," Manny replied, though somewhat curtly.

"You are welcome. In which case, it is plausible that an animal threw the nut at me. As to why, I do not know," Julius concluded.

"If it was the same monkey, like Manny thinks, then maybe he wanted to eat you! Or better yet, maybe he was trying to take you out so he could snatch your wand, like when he went for Manny's along the stream!" Brun said zealously.

246

"Don't be ridiculous!" the bird snipped. "A monkey wouldn't want my wand, much less Manny's!"

"Then why was he using those tong-thingies to try and grab mine?" Manny asked ardently. "Wouldn't some regular, dumb old monkey just leave it alone once he discovered that he couldn't touch it?"

"Yes, a monkey would leave a Lumen's wand alone in that case—and therefore, in all cases," said Julius firmly. "Then the issue is resolved—he was not trying to thieve your wand, Manny."

"It's not resolved at all!" Manny riposted. "I think you've got to find out why that monkey was trying to steal my wand!"

"You should tell the instructors, Julius!" Brun insisted. "They could help you find that monkey!"

"He does not exist!" the quetzal snapped, fluttering heatedly in the air for a moment. "And even if he did, the instructors would not take such a proposition seriously—remember that monkeys are not Lumens."

Brun and Manny both threw a burning hazel glare at the quetzal.

"If you're right, then, I guess you'd better watch out," Brun said after a moment.

"Why do you say that?" Julius asked.

"Because that means that some hungry monkey out there is looking for quetzal meat," Manny explained. "I'd rather know a monkey's after my wand than my thigh."

"I wouldn't," Julius said distastefully. "Hungry monkeys we can handle, but wand thieves—that would be a point of concern."

"Then you should do something about it," Manny asserted for the last time.

A steel glare from the quetzal was his only reply.

Manny relented. "Fine then. But don't say I didn't warn you if peoples' wands begin to turn up missing." *I'm keeping a watch on mine.*

Party like a Rock Star

"Can you believe that Chiron can cook that well?" Brun asked Manny as the two of them lay in their hammocks, swaying in the cool night air and talking.

"Those burritos were awesome!" Manny agreed, raising his hands into the air and stretching his arms as he considered his unexpectedly delicious dinner beneath the burning rays of thousands of falling stars. Without warning, a blue light burst into the red-lit room, causing Manny to jump and Lil' Manny to squeak in alarm.

"It's just a letter, Manny," Brun said obviously.

"Oh," Manny muttered, raising his hand and catching the glittering paper that floated down from above him. Lil' Manny, however, eyed the sheet with concern, his long tail wrapped around his master's neck as their eyes scanned the message.

Manuel,

Again, gracias for writing me as you promised. I am so glad you've gotten to see Julius! How is he? Oh, never mind, I'll just write him myself—he's such a cute little bird...

Oh, ¡qué fascinante! It would be amazing to live with a centaur! I remember mi mamá telling us bedtime stories about centaurs in the forest when we were growing up! I'll have to come and visit you sometime so I can meet him! Oh, and not to mention Brun, too!

Well, take care and have fun this week! Everyone says hi! And remember to write us before dinner! ¡Todos los días!

Te quiero.   —Mamá

P.S. Write your next letter to your abuelita—she really misses you.

"Brun, I just don't think I know mi mamá anymore," Manny said as he laid the letter on his chest. "She's been completely weird since she let me come down here for school. What do you think?"

"I think you're lucky just to have a mom."

"Oh, I'm sorry, I didn't mean—"

"It's okay," Brun said lightly. "I have my tía Liliana who's been there for me since I was born—to tell you the truth, I don't think a mother could've done any more for me than she's done."

Tía Jane's a nice woman and all, but I prefer to keep my own mamá. Growing up with Jane taking care of me and no one else around just sounds—bizarre. Manny folded up the letter, but kept it tight in hand. "Brun, what's Liliana like? I mean, she must be really smart, since she home-schooled you and all, but what about her personality?"

"Her personality?" Brun repeated, sitting up slightly. "Hmm… Well, first of all, she's really funny—she loves to play games and to tell me hilarious stories about when she was a student. She's the one who taught me how to play Piranha Sweep." He paused to think. "I guess I'd also have to say she's adventurous— she always tells me that she was a pretty good lightboarder, although I've never actually gotten to see her on one."

"¿Por qué no?" Manny asked.

"Because Papá says lightboarding's dangerous—he doesn't want Liliana to have an accident or anything," Brun explained.

"Huh." *But if she were such a good lightboarder, wouldn't she be careful enough not to get hurt?*

"So, yeah, basically she's fun to be with, and she's a rockin' cook," Brun finished.

"What about your papá? Is he fun, too?"

"No," Brun replied frankly. "He's not. Like I said, most of the time he's off on business, and when he's home he either locks himself in his office or goes off alone to stay sharp on his light bending. I hope that when I come back next summer, I'll be able to practice with him."

"That would be great," Manny said. "Too bad I won't be able to practice light bending with my papá…"

"Why's that?"

"I'm the only Lumen in my family," Manny stated dully.

"But didn't you say you had a younger cousin? Maybe he'll become a Lumen soon."

"Yeah, Zane," said Manny, suddenly hopeful again. "He'll turn fourteen in March. We're both hopin' he becomes a Lumen then, 'cause we do everything together." Manny paused. "At least we used to, until I came here."

"We'll see him in a year, then," Brun encouraged.

Yet for some reason a faint hook of doubt seemed to prick and restrain Manny's hope. "I wonder how he's doing…"

As Manny pulled out another sheet of paloma paper, Brun asked, "Are you gonna write to Zane?"

"Sí." Manny elevated his knees to support the mahogany briefcase and begin his letter.

"Tell him 'Hola' for me, will ya?"

"No problem," Manny said, his pen scratching away.

***

Manny,

Mamá would kill me if she caught me writing this late, but—no way! I can't believe that Lumens can fly around on lightboards! I'm into that. And that restaurant—totally cool. I hope you can talk to Iris soon, as long as that Kaya girl doesn't get in your way—which seems likely. Maybe she's hating on you 'cause she really likes you. Did you think of that? Hold up — someone's in the hall! False alarm; it was just the cat. Anyhow, you and I are gonna reach the center of that maze when I get there (Brun can come, too).

I've got some bad news—Papá took me to school to register for my classes, and Sr Soriano is my teacher—bleh! We probably won't get to go on a class trip this spring, because I bet he's still all whacked out.

I'm going to bed now. Hasta mañana,

Zane

P.S. Tell Brun, "¿Qué pasa, compa?"

"Zane says, 'What's up, man?'" Manny forwarded as he lowered the letter.

"Really?" Brun replied. "When you write him again, tell him, 'No mucho. ¿Y tú?'"

"Sure thing." Manny yawned widely. "I'm goin' to sleep now. 'Night."

"Buenas noches." Brun turned over and considered the day's events. **This place is incredible!** Looking out through the east window he caught the tail of a stray meteor fleeing across the sky. **I thought people would hate me, but they don't!** He blinked and stared deep into the dark trees. **I miss Liliana, but it's good to have a real friend for once. Friends, if I count Nate and the rest of the gang.** With a great yawn he stretched out his arms and legs. **I'm actually looking forward to tomorrow...** His eyelids steadily falling, Brun sighed and drifted off into peaceful sleep, leaving Saturday far behind him.

***

"¡Muchachos! ¡Despiértense!" called a deep voice from the back door of the hutch. "I have exciting news!"

Oh-my-gosh... "Ugh..." groaned Manny as he rolled over in his hammock.

251

"It's way too early for good news, Chiron," Brun said hoarsely from his side of the room. "It has to be like six o'clock in the morning."

"I would venture to guess that's it's nine forty-five, actually," said the centaur genially. "Be aware that in only four days you must both wake up at seven o'clock in order to arrive to your first class on time."

"I don't even want to think about that," Manny said, covering his eyes and wishing for sleep to return.

"But you must!" Chiron went on. "Especially today! Remember that the three of us will be attending the orientation tonight at ten in the Plaza!"

"Key word being tonight," Brun replied dryly.

"What cheek," Chiron mused, the shadow of a smile breaking his lips.

"So you woke us up this early just to remind us about something that you had already told us about?" asked Manny, hiding his face from the light invading through the window. "How can that be good news?"

"Oh, yes! The good news! I had almost forgotten," the centaur said. "Andrés Dosfilos will be our keynote speaker tonight! That is a rare blessing indeed!"

"Who exactly is this Dosfilos guy?" muttered Brun as he turned over and eyed Chiron, his vision still blurry.

"Is he like some Lumen rock star?" Manny queried, chuckling.

"No, he is not a star," answered Chiron quite seriously. "He is the Chairman of the Lumen Council of South America—the leader of all Lumens on our continent. I am certain that his message will be both enlightening and engaging."

"He's the Lumen President, then?" Manny asked with a quick look toward the centaur.

"In essence, sí," Chiron answered.

"Is a president just another word for a leader in the outside world?" Brun asked.

"Sí," Manny and Chiron answered together.

As they had done the four days prior, Manny and Brun spent the day memorizing the locations for each of their classes, kicking up dust on the island's numerous shortcuts, and playing cards through the afternoon with their new friends in the park. Brun had grown impatient with Manny's insistence to delve into the garden maze, swiftly offering alternatives with elaborate excuses as to why the two should pursue other avenues, which generally ended in exploration or card playing. Despite Manny's determination to catch Iris alone, neither he nor Brun ever saw the tiny hare anywhere they went. The boys filled their evenings with long discussions seated atop Lookout Point as the surfers carved across and above the waves in their evening freestyle sessions highlighting daunting spins and unique wave grinding.

An hour before the orientation the boys met Chiron at the hutch to walk to the Plaza together, the centaur recounting the various feats of marvel during the span of Andrés Dosfilos forty short years. Apparently Dosfilos had once been an instructor for the Lumen Academies of South America, plunging forward in the field of Luminology and designing a number of innovative light bending techniques such as the photosphere, an impenetrable sphere of light effective for trapping opponents and rendering them powerless. "In fact, he even uncovered a new sentinel," Chiron added as he lead the boys out from a shortcut on the south side of the East Road—but you must ask Professor Firefoot about that—I am by no means an expert with sentinels."

Manny and Brun also discovered that following a brief absence after the disappearance of his sister years ago, Dosfilos reappeared, integrating himself once again into the Lumen community with a renewed flare and passion for justice, this time using his superior talents as a tribal leader, defending his fellow Lumens as a trusted protector. Throughout the years he helped capture and subdue hundreds of rogue Lumens and became so well known for his wisdom and strategy that he was nominated to the

Lumen Council. In under five years the Council elected Dosfilos as Chairperson, a position in which he oversees the Council's activities and fulfills the role of international ambassador to the Sevenfold Assembly.

"So what you're saying is that this guy is huge," Brun observed as the three of them entered the steadily filling Plaza.

"He's way bigger than a rock star," Manny said in awe.

"We Lumens hold Dosfilos in our hearts with great renown and admiration—he inspires both the young and the old—a rare trait in a leader," Chiron pointed out.

"Maybe he understands people better than the rest of us," Brun proposed.

Chiron glanced at the boy keenly. "I would say he does, Brun." The centaur stopped abruptly. "Boys, forgive me, but I must leave you now. As an instructor I am required to stand alongside the other professors during the orientation. My only suggestion would be to find a location commanding an excellent view of the House of the Brethren, as that is the point from which we will be presenting. I look forward to hearing your thoughts when we return home."

With that the centaur trotted off into the massing crowd, which seemed to be building and spreading from the southwest rim of the Plaza. By the time Manny and Brun crossed the kiosk they could go no further. There, standing on the final step, the boys gazed in all directions at the thousands of young Lumens, from shy and fuzzy chinchillas to falcons perched on the kiosk, all waiting with their families and friends under the starlight. Manny marveled at the manner in which the three buildings along the southeast corner of the Plaza seemed to glow like a trio of moonlit pearls. Even the ivy draped over the border of the kiosk radiated a cool green tone in the dark. Brun noticed that countless eyes seemed to turn and stare at his glowing skin, but to his relief he did not see one single scowl or frown.

"I could spot the pair o' you from halfway down the West Road!" called a twangy voice from the boys' right. A moment later a girl with bobbing blonde curls materialized from the crowd, followed close behind by another girl and two boys.

"Buenas noches, Millie!" Brun replied affably. "Glad you could find us!"

"Me, too!" said Serge, mounting the steps above Brun and Manny. "We didn't know where we were gonna stand!"

"Well, I do," said Araceli wryly as she slid up beside Brun, who suddenly shined a brighter red.

"Are you blushin'?" Millie asked.

"Leave him alone," Nate said. "It's embarrassing enough just to be seen in public with the two of you," he added with a nod to the girls.

"You're so funny," Araceli said sarcastically. Nate smiled.

"So are all of you psyched to hear what tonight's speaker has to say?" Manny asked the group.

"I imagine it'll just be one of the teachers giving us a boring old lecture on diligence or something," Serge said insipidly.

"Nope—Chiron told us Andrés Dosfilos was gonna be here to speak to us," Brun replied.

"The Andrés Dosfilos?" Nate asked, astonished.

"Who's he?" asked Millie.

"He's only the head of the Lumen Council of the Southern Continent!" Nate countered obviously. "How can you not know who he is?"

"Let's revisit that statement, shall we?" Araceli said with a sharp look to Nate. "As the rest of us know, Dosfilos is the leader of the South America—Millie's from Texas!"

Serge laughed. "She got you there, Nate."

The other boy, however, simply turned and stared at the roof of the dark oak mansion. "So Dosfilos is really gonna speak tonight?" Nate said after a moment.

"Sí—Brun and I aren't joking," said Manny.

"Why didn't you mention it earlier while I was throttling you all at Piranha Sweep?" Araceli asked.

"Probably because they were so amazed you actually had some good cards," Serge said jokingly.

"You watch out or you'll end up in the fountain before the night's over," Araceli threatened, her eyes narrow.

"¡Atención! ¡Estudiantes y familias, atención, por favor!" a squeaky voice called from above the crowd, a faint wave of light pulsating over the area with each spoken word. All grew quiet as they turned to face the mansion, their eyes rising to the balcony reaching out from the roof of the building. There, perched along the railing, sat a miniature figure, its green back and yellow and blue splashed stomach shining brightly in the light of several glowing orbs hovering over the corners of the terrace. "As roughly a third of you already know, I am Rush Stickgrip, one of three counselors for the Lumen Academies of South America. It is my honor to welcome everyone who has come, and to say that we have a most excellent program waiting for you this evening. Now, allow me to introduce my friend and colleague, Melody Nightvine."

To the right of the tree frog Manny noted the familiar form of the kinkajou that he had met on his journey along the Amazon. *I still think she looks like a cat with an extra long tail—not a monkey.* "My fellow Lumens," the kinkajou began, "We are most fortunate this year at the Amazon River Academy to have our very own Julius Rumblefeather step up to the position of Director. Yet not only will Professor Rumblefeather be leading us into a new academic year of much anticipated success and progress, but he will also continue fulfilling his duties as Head Counselor. Please, let us all give a much deserved round of applause to Director Rumblefeather!"

"I didn't know Julius was gonna be the Director!" Manny exclaimed as he clapped excitedly.

"Yeah! That's cool! I wonder why he didn't mention it the other night?" Brun replied. **Maybe he's just a really humble guy— bird, I mean.**

As the clapping, clicking, and stomping all died away, Manny watched the quetzal with the flowing tails glide down to land between the tree frog and the kinkajou. Shaking his scarlet breast, Julius began to speak. "¡Gracias! It is my greatest honor to serve as Director this coming year! I look forward to meeting you all and to collaborating with each of our most capable instructors to ensure that your experience here at the Amazon River Academy is a most advantageous and memorable one. You should all be aware that we are currently planning to hold the Seventh-Level Training Mission just east of Isla Verde. This mission will integrate the most intense challenges ever to face Seventh-Level students since the Brethren established the school centuries ago. Yet our greatest goal for the Mission is to unify the entire Lumen community—but I will step aside to allow our keynote speaker to discuss the issue in more detail. Now please welcome none other than Andrés Dosfilos, our highly admired Ambassador to the Sevenfold Assembly!"

"Dosfilos?" cried the crowd incredulously, followed by an instant surge of murmuring. "I can't believe it… I thought he was in Asia right now… Is this a joke…?"

"There he is!" shouted a tiny chinchilla from the center of the crowd, pointing her little pink paw toward the sky above the kiosk. All turned, bursting suddenly into a deafening cheer as a man expertly maneuvered an ice blue lightboard above the heads of the crowd, carving wide arcs and laughing as he caught sight of the thousands of faces lit with joy just to see him. Seconds later he had reached the terrace where he descended from his lightboard and stepped forward to face the crowd. From his spot on the kiosk steps Manny distinguished the man's flyaway brown hair and light skin. He seemed to be wearing a blue tunic or vest with a pair of white pants. Taller than average, Dosfilos gazed out at the energized crowd as he unclasped his cape, sliding his right hand to a loop along his belt and drawing out his wand, which he flicked at the crowd. Instantly a comet blasted from the center of the masses, rising high into the air until it exploded in a shower of light.

"That's insane," Manny said, his eyes wider than they had ever been before.

"¡Mira!" Brun said, pointing to the position where the comet exploded. "It's a star!" And without any doubt Manny discerned the shape of a seven-pointed star, its glistening body flickering brightly for a few moments before eventually dissolving in the cool wind.

"This hombre's good," Millie stated.

"My gentle Lumens and Ladies," called a voice rich with understanding, "may I state that it is my ultimate pleasure to be with you here tonight!" A cheer tore up from the crowd, their hands, paws, and heads waving in absolute excitement. Dosfilos smiled and raised his left hand for quiet; but just as the cheering finally dropped to a low buzzing, the little chinchilla toward the center of the crowd cried, "Sr. Dosfilos, I love you!" This caused the man to laugh, and several other young female Lumens to cry the same. "Gracias, m'ija," Dosfilos replied over the shouting and the laughter. "Be assured that I share the same sentiments for you and for everyone here." At this the chinchilla nearly toppled over.

"My people," Dosfilos began again, spreading his arms wide; all voices hushed. "We are gathered together here this warm evening to welcome the future guardians of our world into the very Lumen community that they have wished to join since their memories can bear witness. Since the 16th century of our Lord, when the founders of our society first came to Earth, the Amazon River Academy has faithfully instructed new Lumens, instilling in our young people the values and abilities that we hold dear in order to protect the Earth's many inhabitants. I would like to personally thank each Seventh-Level Lumen for stepping forward this day to care for the future of not only our civilization, but those of the entire planet." Lead by Dosfilos, a thundering applause rose into the air from the parents and older Lumens in the crowd, mother panthers slapping their velvety paws together and growling happily while father butterflies tore through the air yelling in a blaze of color.

"Man, Brun, this is all so weird, don't you think?" Manny asked.

"Yeah, whoever thought that a river otter could do cartwheels, anyway?" Brun said with a chuckle.

"As you all may know, the heart and focus of Lumen education is to provide our students with the most authentic and engaging instruction that we can offer, while still maintaining our children's safety, of course," Dosfilos continued with a nod to a concerned-looking kinkajou, her arm and tail wrapped tightly around her child. "It is for this reason that Director Rumblefeather and I have combined our efforts to begin designing a true-to-life mission for our Seventh-Levels this coming May, a mission that will dare these brave young Lumens to integrate each and every

258

technique that they will acquire this fall and spring, from the swiftest evasion to the quickest attack."

"However, my friends, before continuing, I must regress to a principal theme that Director Rumblefeather mentioned earlier—unity. Since I was a young boy, a particular aspect of our society has troubled me, as I hope it has for some or even many of you. Take a look around you, everyone," Dosfilos said, waving his hand over the crowd. "Do you not notice that we are missing a number of our comrades here this evening?"

"Missing someone?" wondered a green basilisk aloud as he balanced on his tail to rise into the air and scan the crowd. "Who in heavens could be missing?"

"I don't know about you, Brun, but I think it looks pretty packed in the Plaza tonight," Manny observed, the sea of people swallowing the kiosk from all directions. "If you ask me, just about every Seventh-Level in South America has to be here."

Brun blinked back coolly. "Actually, they're not. Think back to when we first walked around the Unity Fount—you are forgetting someone," Brun added knowingly.

I am?

"Have any of you realized who is missing?" Dosfilos asked, his vibrant blue eyes cutting across the crowds below. Suddenly he noticed a delicate pink paw raised in the air. "¿Sí, m'ija?"

"Sr. Dosfilos, I can tell you who's not here tonight," replied the tiny chinchilla bravely.

"Who, then?" Dosfilos asked, his eyes bright, yet benevolent.

The chinchilla glanced around her nervously and danced in place for a moment. She breathed an answer faintly.

"I'm sorry, child, but no one heard you," Dosfilos replied. "Could I invite you to come to the balcony with me?"

"Excuse me, señor," Julius began. "But do you really feel that is necessary?" Dosfilos glanced sideways in response, his eyes set. "Never mind, señor."

"Can I really?" the chinchilla squeaked. Dosfilos nodded in reply, snapping his wand in the direction of the creature and creating a glowing platform that she swiftly crawled upon. Her mother's little black eyes shined proudly as she watched her daughter glide through the air.

"Are you brave, little one?" whispered Dosfilos to the chinchilla now resting on the balcony rail. Though shivering from head to toe, she nodded determinedly. "Then tell them who is missing," he said, waving his wand as a tiny stream of light wove down the creature's throat to make her voice box tingle. "Turn around—they'll be able to hear you," Dosfilos directed.

Gazing out over her peers, the chinchilla took a deep breath, her incomparably soft gray fur glittering in the balcony lights. "What Sr. Dosfilos is trying to say," she began, her squeaky voice surprisingly steady, "is that we're all here except for one Lumen species—the crystal spider."

Oh—them.

"The crystal spider?!" rose a chorus of thousands of seemingly defrauded voices, followed by angry murmuring. "Now this is a joke! They're dangerous! I swear I've seen one eat a kinkajou before!" In point of fact, the young chinchilla's mother teetered and fainted.

"¡Paz, hermanos!" Dosfilos said, slightly raising his normally even-keeled voice. "Peace!" Nearly half a minute passed before the assembly grew quiet once again. "Indulge me, all you parents. Turn to your children and gaze into their eyes. Do you remember the day your child was born? What is his favorite food? Her favorite activity for you to do with her? Now, imagine that your child has just been stolen from you and placed on the other side of a wall that you can never climb. How do you feel? Saddened? Depressed? Hopeless? Yes, without a shred of doubt!"

Dosfilos drew a deep breath and lowered his arms. "This is how I feel when I consider the deep chasm separating us from our brothers, the crystal spiders. What hope is there for us in mending this world's problems if we cannot even mend ourselves? We cast blame on the crystal spiders and shun them merely for their appearance, allowing petty and misguided fears to drive a nail into our greatest strength—unity! This is shameful; if you search your

260

hearts, you will know it to be true." Not a single eye dared to rise and meet Dosfilos' gaze at this moment; even Manny felt shame for his original prejudice against the crystal spider.

"But let us not be disheartened," Dosfilos said consolingly, "for we still have time to bridge the chasm. Who will stand with me?" Paws, claws, and hands slowly rose into the air alongside wings, horns, and antennae. Manny and Brun nodded at one another, their hands reaching high. "Fantastic!" exclaimed Dosfilos.

"Yet I am sure that many of you are now asking yourselves, 'How can a training mission bring unity?' Allow me to explain. Director Rumblefeather and I have met with Crion Irradius, the chieftain of the spider tribe, several times over this past summer. Irradius and his people have volunteered to work alongside our most competent instructors to coordinate a search and recovery mission for our Seventh-Level students. As plans for the Mission progress, certain crystal spiders will be invited to visit with the students during their classes. We also hope that a number of Seventh-Level spiders may begin to attend the Academy sometime this spring."

Manny swallowed hard. *I don't know if I can do this...* Suddenly a hand fell upon the boy's shoulder; turning around, he found Serge, swaying, his skin slightly green. Manny helped him sit down on the steps. *Don't puke, don't puke, don't puke!* "You gonna be okay?" Manny asked. Serge nodded, still afraid to open his mouth. *At least I'm taking all this about the spiders better than him...*

"Amigos, I implore each and every one of you to carry an open heart and mind as the Brethren taught us. Now, my time here has ended, but Director Rumblefeather and the remaining professors will be providing students and families with additional information throughout the school year. I wish you all the best of luck, and I hope that your first year of Lumen education is as exciting as my own! But before I forget," Dosfilos said, sliding a free hand into the inside of his tunic, "I have a gift for one lucky Lumen—a sun beetle!"

As Dosfilos opened his hand, a large, shining gold beetle shot out into the air, zipping from one way to another as it buzzed over the ecstatic crowd. "Come here, little guy!" screamed a young unicorn. "I want it!" called a red-eyed tree frog as it hopped on the heads of its peers. "It's mine!" snapped a falcon in its arced dive. Yet somehow, the gilded beetle evaded all pursuit.

"Yes!" exclaimed Brun, who leapt nearly two feet into the air.

"Why'd it just hover over him like that?" Millie asked.

"I don't think that was fair," said a perturbed Nate. "I almost had it..."

"Too bad you can't glow like Brun," replied Araceli. "Nobody's like him," she added in awe.

Now wait just one moment. "Brun's not the only one here who can glow," argued Manny as he rose from beside Serge. *What are they talking about, anyway?*

"Yeah, but white's boring," Araceli retorted. "Red's the color for me!"

Whatever... "Why does it matter anyway whether he can glow or not?" Manny asked. "We've both been glowing since we got here, so why's everyone cheering for Brun now?"

"Because I got the sun beetle!" Brun shouted as he shot into the air again.

"Only because they're attracted to light," said Nate jealously.

"That answers my question, then," Millie observed.

Hold it. "What's a sun beetle?" Manny stared at Brun's right hand, which was balled into a fist.

"It's a photocache!" Brun answered.

"A photocash? You mean like money?" Manny asked.

"No! Not c-a-s-h! It's c-a-c-h-e, like a treasure!" snapped Araceli, her brown eyes flashing. "You can trade it in for a prize!"

"Normally you have to go hunting to find one," Brun explained in a high, energized voice. "But Dosfilos released this one and I caught it!"

"He did?" asked Manny, lost. "When?"

"Where have you been?" Nate said in disbelief. "Everyone was screaming and jumping for it!"

262

Without warning a retching sound rose from the kiosk steps at Manny's feet. "Serge! You puked on my shoes!" Manny yelled. "That stinks worse than a horse turd!" Millie cried. "At least I feel better," groaned Serge in relief.

Literary Confusion

"Brun, you've spent four days admiring that thing—are you gonna trade it in or not?" asked Manny as he and Brun slipped on their school uniforms, which included a pair of hiking boots, durable jeans, and a t-shirt embossed with the circular emblem of the Amazon River Academy. As the school had no fixed building in which the students met, the emblem reflected an authentic and brightly colored image of Isla Verde, serving the dual-purpose of both logo and map; a faint star sparkled northeast of the lake on the boys' shirts, telling them their exact location.

"I really doubt that any prize I could exchange it for would be as cool as the sun beetle itself," Brun answered as he tugged his shirt down.

"It's just a bug," Manny said as he began to tie his boots.

"Sí, pero it's my bug, and I intend to keep it," said Brun as he leaned over and began placing his books in his backpack.

"Yeah, well, if I were you I'd trade it."

"Good thing you're not," muttered Brun as he pulled *The Blue World* from his dresser.

"Do you really think we need to lug those around? Maybe the instructors won't require us to bring our books to class—ours don't always," Manny said, thinking back to his primary school years.

"I'm not taking any chances." Brun zipped up his backpack and heaved the straps over his shoulders. "Besides—all that carrying will build some muscle."

Or a sore back. Manny groaned as he filled his own backpack with his required texts for the day—*The Blue World*, *The Science of Light*, and *Photokinesis*. "Huh." *I wonder what photokinesis is, anyway.*

"See ya later, little buddy," Manny said to the salamander resting in its reassembled carrier beneath the boy's hammock. Lil' Manny squeaked pleadingly. "I can't let you out now—but I will when I get back after lunch." A violent squeak rose in reply. "What?" Manny asked, nearly falling backward under the heavy load of his books. He gazed at the salamander with a frown. "Are you afraid Nipper's gonna get you?" Lil' Manny whipped his tail affirmatively. *I dunno...* "If I let you out, will you promise to stay safe and not run away?" In an instant the salamander had bolted forward, placing his black paws on the clear plastic and licking it eagerly. "Alright, then." Shedding his two-ton book bag, Manny knelt down and opened the hatch to release Lil' Manny, who squeaked gratefully as he darted from the carrier, up the wall, and out the window.

Following a quick breakfast of fresh fruit, cow's milk, and toast, Manny and Brun hoisted their backpacks and prepared to leave.

"Un momento, muchachos," Chiron preempted. "Allow me to lighten your burdens." With a stamp of his back leg, Chiron formed two tiny orbs of light that momentarily flickered a pale yellow before cutting through the air and striking the boys' backpacks. Two seconds later both Manny and Brun were lying flat on the wet grass.

"What d'you knock us down for?" snapped Manny as he looked up at the centaur's towering frame.

"That was a little harsh," Brun mumbled.

"You caused yourselves to fall," Chiron corrected them.

"What are you talking about?" Manny asked as he and Brun easily lifted themselves from the ground.

"I am saying that you both failed to shift balance in response to the sudden change in weight of your backpacks; as the result, you fell forward," stated Chiron obviously.

"Whoa! Mine is lighter!" shouted Brun, realizing that the crushing weight upon his shoulders had seemingly disappeared.

"Check that out!" said Manny, lifting the straps and bouncing his pack in the air. "You've gotta teach us that one, Chiron!"

"Status changing orbs are not taught until the Fifth-Level," replied the centaur. "In any case, your backpacks will remain light unless another Lumen strikes them with a Heavyweight orb."

265

"Well, of course!" exclaimed Manny with a laugh.

"¡Gracias, Chiron!" Brun added as he and Manny raced each other to the other side of the hutch.

"At least they will not be late for their first class," the centaur said, amused, as he dissolved the table, chairs, and leftover food with the stamp of a hoof.

***

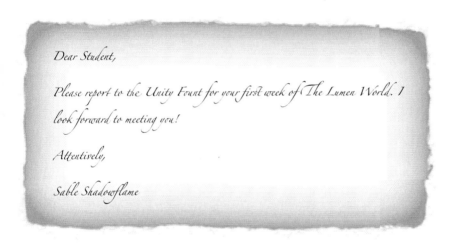

Dear Student,

Please report to the Unity Fount for your first week of The Lumen World. I look forward to meeting you!

Attentively,

Sable Shadowflame

"It's nearly eight o'clock, and there's the kiosk," Manny said to himself as he entered the already crowded Plaza from the East Road. Manny tucked away his letter as he mounted the kiosk steps, noticing an assembly of seventy to one hundred young Lumens of various species ambling around the base of the fountain. To his left Manny recognized a boy with brown hair and blue eyes, who quickly rushed over to talk.

"¡Buenos días, Manny!" the boy said.

"Good morning, Nate!" Manny replied.

"I didn't know we had The Lumen World together!" Nate exclaimed.

"Me either, but I'm glad we do, 'cause I wouldn't know anyone here if we didn't," Manny confessed with relief.

At that moment a clock mounted upon the House of the Brethren began to play an ominous tune, followed by eight heavy strokes. "Welcome, young ones, to your very first class at the Amazon River Academy!" called a transcendently rich feminine voice from the base of the fountain. "My name is Professor Shadowflame, and over the next nine months I will lead you in a journey to acquaint yourselves with the Lumen world of the Southern Continent. Are there any questions before we begin?"

Oh, boy... Manny's stomach wriggled as he set his gaze on the elegant black panther seated on the edge of the fountain, her ocean blue eyes scanning the students large and small.

"Are you alright, young man?" Shadowflame asked, her eyes glinting at Manny. "You look—startled—not to mention pale."

All eyes turned to Manny. *Don't do what Serge did, Manny. Anything but that.*

"It's okay, Señora, he's probably just nervous about the first day of classes, you know?" Nate said, patting Manny on the shoulder.

"Oh..." replied Shadowflame. "Then why is he so pale?"

"He always is," Nate answered wisely. "It's just the way he is."

Thank God for Nate.

Shadowflame flicked her tail in response, careful not to submerge it in the water. "Well, then, let us continue," she said, her heavy eyes looking toward a very short otter. "Can any of you tell me the origin of our Lumen powers?" Twenty hands, paws, and similar appendages shot into the air. "Tell us, young otter. Oh, but first, your name."

"Tobias Greenriver, Señora! And the answer to your question is the Stars!" shouted the otter happily as he teetered back and forth.

"Very good, young Tobias!" replied Shadowflame. "Can you also tell me the formal name that we give them?"

The otter nodded. "The Light Brethren, Señora! And there were seven sisters and five brothers!"

"Superb!" said Shadowflame. "But now allow me to challenge your knowledge. Which of the Brethren was the eldest?"

Tobias stopped teetering and scratched his head. "Is it Sophronia?"

"No, but close," replied Shadowflame. "She is the eldest sister and second only to... Oh, what was his name?" the panther asked, feigning ignorance as her tail gently slapped the plaque beside her.

"Could it perhaps be Aldis?" asked a sharp-eyed falcon perched atop the kiosk.

"Perhaps it would," answered Shadowflame with a pleasant smile. "Name?"

"Lakia Valwing, Señora," the tawny breasted falcon replied.

"You seem to have both keen eyes and wits, Lakia," Shadowflame said. Addressing the rest of the class she continued, "Note that behind me, in the fountain, is a statue of Aldis engaged in conversation with the centaur, whom he illuminated. As you can see, particularly you falcons and quetzals perched atop the kiosk, the Unity Fount features twelve sets of sculptures, each set representing one of the Brethren and the creature that he or she illuminated. Our objective today is to memorize these twelve sets in order to establish a firm base that we may build upon from this day forward."

Shadowflame began to walk east around the rim of the fountain. "Observe that our second subject is Sophronia, who transformed our lizard friend, the green basilisk. Proceeding in a counterclockwise fashion around the Fount you will find that each subsequent sculpture set pertains to a younger member of the Brethren. In other words, once we reach Tryphena, the youngest of the Twelve, we will have come full circle and will find ourselves standing before Aldis once again. Now, the third eldest is Eudocia, who happened to..."

"Thanks for speaking for me earlier," whispered Manny to Nate as they followed the class in its journey around the fountain.

"No problem," Nate replied. "You looked an awful lot like Serge after he—"

"Muchachos, what are your names?" Shadowflame called abruptly.

Embarrassment flooded Manny's face—he could feel it growing brighter. "M-Manny," he breathed.

"Excuse me?" Shadowflame asked.

"He's Manny," Nate stepped in loudly. "And I'm Nate, Señora."

"Well, then. Manny, Nate—pay attention. You will have plenty of time to chat when class is dismissed," Shadowflame stated with finality. "Now, estudiantes, we come to Bri, the fourth eldest of the twelve and the second male…"

"I still can't believe she's giving us a quiz on the second day of class!" Manny said as he and Nate reached the Lake's exterior beach via otter ferry. "Do you think we ticked her off 'cause we were talking?"

"Maybe—but somehow I think Professor Shadowflame is just like that. You know, like she's gonna be a tough teacher," Nate discerned. "After all, she did lecture for around an hour."

"I hope she doesn't do that everyday," Manny confessed. "That's worse than some of my teachers back home."

Maneuvering along a heavily trodden path in the forest, the two boys headed southwest, the ground falling steadily. To their right they could hear the roar of the Lucero River as it curved sharply toward the Lake. Lumens of all kinds passed the boys along the path, until suddenly Manny stopped. "Brun! I didn't think I'd see you until eleven!"

"We lucked out, I guess," Brun rejoined. "So how was The Lumen World?"

"Long," Manny answered dully. "And we have a quiz Wednesday, so pay attention to what Shadowflame's got to say."

"Did you just have Healing, then?" Nate asked, adjusting his hefty backpack.

Brun nodded. "Yep."

Manny looked hopeful. "How was it?"

"Let's just say you should be glad Chiron used that Lightweight orb on our backpacks," Brun replied. "We're gonna need it." Manny groaned.

"A Lightweight orb?" Nate repeated. "I could use one of those. Do you guys think Chiron would use one on my backpack tonight after Astronomy class?"

"Probably," said Brun. "I better get going, though. I'll see you guys later."

"Adiós," Manny and Nate replied.

The boys had barely taken five steps when around a bend came Kaya, bright eyed and holding *The Science of Light* close to her chest. Manny's heart jolted. *What do I do?* As Kaya's eyes focused upon him, she too came to an awkward halt, stumbling abruptly and nearly dropping her book. For a brief moment Manny and Kaya caught each other's gaze, which Kaya quickly broke as she stomped heatedly up the path. "Jerk!" she snipped, just before she disappeared.

"What was all that about?" Nate asked Manny, who stood transfixed.

"All what?" Manny retorted, shaking his head and turning to charge along the path.

"She seemed really ticked. Didn't you hear what she called you?" Nate continued. Manny nodded, but proceeded forward resolutely. "So what's her name?"

"Kaya," Manny mumbled, becoming abruptly fascinated with a azure bromeliad growing from a tree on his right.

"Why's she mad at you?" Nate prodded.

"Long story," said Manny vaguely. "But, hey! Look! We're here!" *What a relief.* The path leveled out and gave way to a wide, crescent-shaped bank bordering a circular pool fed steadily by a curtain of water streaming down from a tributary of the Lucero above. A pair of unicorns bowed their heads to drink from the crystal blue pool, their short horns reflecting brightly on the waters.

"¡Oye! Nate! Manny! Have either of you seen Brun?" Araceli asked, running toward the boys as she scanned the river of faces about her. "I wanted to walk with him to our next class!"

Nate nodded. "Sí. We met him up the path at least five minutes ago."

"Are you kidding me?" Araceli shot back. "What was he thinking?"

"I don't know, Araceli, but it's almost ten o'clock and if you're headed to Art, you've gotta be in the Gardens real quick. I wouldn't wanna be late to class on the first day," Manny said.

"He better have a good excuse for leaving me," Araceli smoldered as she fired along the path. *Probably didn't wanna be late...*

Over the next several minutes a shower of animal Lumens came pouring into the glade, from kinkajous sliding along vines to centaurs carrying tree frogs and fuzzy chinchillas. Three otters even appeared over the rim of the falls, leaping into the air to perform numerous somersaults before cleaving the water below. "That was sweet!" cried one as his head emerged from the pool. Seconds later the trio reached the water's edge and began wrestling over who touched land first.

Without warning, the curtain of water parted and a short lizard dashed out and across the basin, stopping a tail's length (which happened to be roughly two feet) from the wrestling otters. The lizard's body and tail reflected a brilliant green, except for a sapphire streak running along his back from the pair of tiny fans on his crown to the tip of his winding tail.

"I should hope that this playful tussling will not lead to any incidents requiring my assistance," said the lizard slowly. The wrestlers froze.

Manny screwed up his face. *How can he just stand there on the water without sinking?* The middle otter expressed Manny's sentiments.

"All green basilisks, otter pup, have the ability to run on water. Lumen basilisks, however, can walk—not to mention stand—on liquids. Hence the name Jesus Christ Lizard," the reptile replied, his aquamarine eyes flashing humorously.

"I didn't know that," Manny whispered.

"Me, either," Nate breathed.

A slap resounded in the glade, cutting all remaining conversation and rustling short. "Madison Bluebolt," stated the basilisk in his clear, resounding voice. "But you may call me Professor Bluebolt." A short creature yelped in surprise as Bluebolt whipped the pool with his tail a second time. Manny's eyes leapt forward to the water's edge. *Is that Iris?*

"Hey, Nate," Manny whispered. "Can you tell if that animal up there is a ha—"

"Anatomy," Bluebolt exclaimed powerfully. "In order to become effective and capable healers, you must first understand the many bodies and appendages that comprise Lumen society—from the unicorn's horn to human toes. For this essential reason," the lizard continued, strolling calmly along the pool, "the majority of your Seventh-Level studies will be dedicated to this purpose. However," he added, turning to face the class, "with the coming of spring you will acquire a number of minor healing techniques. Now, if you will, please turn to page ten in your copy of *The Science of Light*."

Manny sat down on the grass and pulled out his textbook. *Oh, now that's hilarious...* A wry smile crossed the boy's face as he noticed the Lumens about him opening textbooks proportional to their size. "Nate, check that out," Manny whispered with a nod to the right. "The pages in that frog's book are the size of my thumbnail."

Nate's blue eyes fell on the amphibian's tiny yellow fingers as they flipped through the pages filled with microscopic print. "Just the right size for his eyes, I guess," Nate mumbled.

A snapping sound drug Manny back into the present. "Eyes," said Bluebolt determinedly, just as Manny arrived at the designated page. *Oh, geez.* The boy's stomach throttled his gut as the hollow gaze of thirteen pairs of eyes stared back up at him; Manny had to turn away from the freezing glare of the crystal spider's threefold pair of eye clusters. Yet the second the boy looked up he saw the studious basilisk snap his tail in the direction of the falls to project an image of the very same page, causing a shiver to rock Manny's spine. "The optical organ is debatably the most intricate device housed within the Lumen body—second only to the brain, of course. Not only functioning as the medium through which our minds construct the environment around us, the eye enables us to perceive light—the essence of our powers. As such, it is only fitting to begin our analysis of Lumen anatomy with this most crucial organ," Bluebolt predicated thoughtfully.

After a series of detailed explanations and three-dimensional images followed by the dissection of actual Lumen eyes, Manny knew more than he ever anticipated (or wanted) about the organ of sight. "I hope I never have to think about, not to mention touch, another eyeball again," he confessed to Nate as Bluebolt dematerialized the tables, surgical instruments, and specimens with a crack of his tail.

"Pages ten through twenty-four," Bluebolt announced audibly. "Read them meticulously and be prepared to demonstrate a proper dissection and labeling of a random Lumen eye by Wednesday."

Manny nearly fainted. "Wednesday! That would take me all fall to do," he said despairingly.

"Maybe we could get together and practice tomorrow after Sentinels," Nate suggested. "Provided that Professor Firefoot doesn't keep us all evening."

Firefoot? Now where have I heard that...? "Iris!" Manny said abruptly, sliding on his feather-light backpack and facing the edge of the pool. "I've gotta apologize."

"What are you talking about?" Nate asked as he struggled under the weight of his own pack.

Manny was careful not to tread on any of the smaller Lumens as he made his way to the water's edge. There he found the tiny hare, his long ears folded over his back and burgundy fur glistening. "Your name's Iris, right?" Manny asked, his words bright as he hoped to set a positive tone for the conversation to follow. Visibly startled, the hare fell over, landing hard on his seat. The creature's violet eyes grew in fear as he looked up at the light-skinned, black-haired boy towering above him. Quicker than Manny could take a breath, the hare snatched his blue satchel and shot away into the sea of ferns.

"I just wanted to tell you something!" Manny yelled as he, too, reached the tree line. But due to the closeness of the trees the boy could proceed no further.

"Pity," called Bluebolt loudly from behind. "A student left his book. But who, I should wonder?" Manny turned to find the lizard holding a pinky-sized copy of *The Science of Light*. Nate stood nearby. "Iris Firefoot—well that's Fidelio's boy!"

"Isn't that the rabbit you were just talking to?" Nate asked.

Manny nodded. "Sí, but he's not a rabbit. He's a ha—"

"You know him, then?" Bluebolt swiftly interrupted.

"Sort of," the boy replied with a half-shrug.

"That's more than I can say," admitted Bluebolt bluntly. "And as you know, he needs his text to prepare for Wednesday's dissection. You must take it to him," the lizard said. With a snap of his tail Bluebolt directed the book up through the air and into Manny's hand. "I appreciate your kindness—and so will Iris." And with that the healer turned on his claw and bolted across the pool, straight through the waterfall.

"How am I supposed to get this back to Iris?" Manny asked, his words drowning helplessly in the water. *He won't even look at me.*

"We'll probably have another class with him before the day's out. You can give it to him then," Nate said constructively.

Yet as he and Nate left the clearing and trod up the path to the lakeshore, Manny wondered exactly how he could pin Iris down long enough to return the book, much less apologize.

"Hey, guys! You didn't just leave Healing, did you?" called Serge from a canoe just as Manny and Nate reached the shore.

"Yeah! Why?" Nate yelled across the swiftly widening gap between them.

"Because I just came from the same class and I didn't even see you there! Where did you sit?" Serge replied, his hands cupped around his mouth.

"In the back!" Nate bellowed. "How 'bout you?"

"Up in front with Tobias and the other otters. Maybe Wednesday we can sit together!" Serge screamed.

274

"¡Está bien!" Nate agreed as Serge and his canoe began to shrink from sight. Nate took a deep breath and turned to Manny. "So how should we make for the crown of the Falls? Is there a path along the outside of the Lake, or do we need to catch an otter ferry, too?"

"No, Brun and I reached the crown the other day from this side—we've just gotta cross the bridge over the mouth of the Lucero and climb up a windy path in the rock. It should only take about twenty minutes," Manny said casually.

Nate chuckled. "You know, for an outsider you know an awful lot about Isla Verde."

"What can I say—I like to explore. But honestly, Brun's the one who really knows this place inside and out."

Fifteen minutes later the boys had surmounted the rocky path, their feet now slapping over thousands of wooden planks as they traveled along a boardwalk above the northern rim of the valley bowl. Within minutes they came to a vast deck equipped with benches and a panoramic view of the entire island to the south. A faint mist rose from the southern balcony as the Lucero emptied a token of its strength into the Lake below.

"You two admiring the view, or are you wishing you were down below to catch some grub?" a voice asked from behind.

"You know I'm dyin' here, Brun," Manny said as he turned around to find his roommate standing next to Araceli, who was now smiling with a hint of smugness.

"Me, too," replied Brun significantly, rolling his eyes and nodding ever so faintly to Araceli on his right.

Manny smiled broadly. "I said you'd be a hit, now didn't I?"

"Shut up," Brun quipped with a chuckle.

"So, Araceli, I see you found Brun," Nate observed.

"Yes, I did," she replied contentedly.

Brun coughed. "Anyway… Have you guys heard anything about Professor Nochesol?"

"No, why?" Manny asked.

"I was just wondering if he was a human or a chinchilla or something. So far most of my teachers aren't human," answered Brun.

"Our teachers, you mean," Araceli said strongly. "And is there anything wrong with having non-human instructors?"

"No," replied Brun quietly. **There is something wrong with your mouth, however—it's too big.** "I was just curious."

"I'm guessing he's human," Araceli said as a gust of air rushed over Manny and Nate's necks. Mounted atop a lightboard stood a rather tall man dressed comparably to Andrés Dosfilos, though the present subject wore a scarlet cloak and a jade tunic in addition to his white pants and high-legged leather boots. Hopping from his board along the northern section of the deck, the man threw back his cloak and began to walk about the area, greeting each student one by one and bowing with a humble nod as introductions were exchanged.

"Amaris Nochesol," said the man as he took Araceli's hand. *Is she blushing?* "Whom do I have the pleasure of meeting?" To the boys' amazement, Araceli found herself at a loss for words before the dark-skinned man before her.

"Her name's Araceli, Professor," Brun piped up happily. "Araceli González, if you want to get specific."

"Well, then, Señorita González." Nochesol offered a slight bow. "It is a true pleasure." Utterly captivated, Araceli gazed at the man in awe.

"Who might you be, young man?" asked the instructor as he turned to face Brun. As Nochesol took a step closer, Brun noticed that his eyes seemed to shift from a golden hazel to a shady purple with each stride. **Weird.**

"My name's Brun Dimirtis, Señor," the boy replied as he shook the man's firm hand. **Huh—the emblem on his badge is the same as our t-shirts. That's cool.**

"Amaris Nochesol," the man replied. "Mucho gusto." Turning aside, Nochesol raised an eyebrow. "And I assume that you are Brun's brother?"

276

"No," Brun and Manny answered together. Nochesol blinked oddly.

"In that case," Nochesol began, inhaling deeply, "Whom do I have the pleasure of meeting?"

"Manny López, Professor," Manny said as he extended his hand to shake Nochesol's.

"A pleasure," said the man with a smile, one eye flashing purple and the other gold. *Now that's really weird.*

Several minutes later Nochesol directed all the students to sit on the benches along the southern end of the deck. With a wave of his hand Nochesol disintegrated the remaining benches and plants, which transformed into billions of light beads that seemed to hang in the air above the platform throughout the duration of the class.

Nochesol removed his cloak with a single sweeping motion, tossing it into the air to disintegrate it alongside the furniture. "Now that we have been introduced, let us all draw our wands." Nochesol slid a wooden ring from one hand, molding it into a crimson rod streaked with gold in the other.

Brun followed suit, transforming his pale birch ring into wand form, while Manny converted his dark mahogany watch into the traditional cylindrical shape. Within seconds the entire assembly sat brandishing their wands, eyeing Nochesol expectantly.

"The Lumen wand, my brethren, is your key to accessing the light around you," Nochesol proceeded. "Without your wand you are powerless, separated from the light and incapable of bending it whatsoever. Therefore, I beseech you, in all seriousness, to protect your wand. No means exists to replace a Lumen wand once it is lost; therefore, it is of utmost importance that you guard it, lest you discard the very gift through which you were set apart. Yet be aware that the Lumen wand is of indestructible design, meaning that it can always be found, though often after a great deal of trial and hardship, particularly if the wand is misplaced with utter carelessness."

"As you have most certainly discovered, the wand is infinitely malleable, capable of being molded into any shape that you desire, provided that the form does not exceed the mass of a customary bread box—or hawk's nest." Nochesol nodded to a falcon perched upon the banister. In a blink the man had transformed his wand into a breadbox, which the next second became a hawk's nest, then instantly returned to a rod. "These transformations are quite simple. But I wonder if you are aware that you can split your wand?" Nochesol queried intriguingly. Grasping both sides of the wand with his hands, Nochesol severed the rod, holding two separate halves.

"Wow! I didn't know you could do that! Neat!" exclaimed several students.

"Yet when the wand is split, it is still subject to the Second Law of Photodynamics, in that no one part can be displaced a distance greater than the smallest unit, as you can see." Nochesol dropped the left half of the rod, which swung in the air below the right half as though attached by an invisible chord. "In effect," he said, swinging the lower piece up like a nunchuk and catching it, "you may convert your wand into any number of units, as long as your wand's total weight does not exceed that of a breadbox." Suddenly Nochesol's hand filled with hundreds of red and white beads, which he tossed at the students, causing an assortment of squawks, croaks, and hisses as the students shielded their faces. Realizing that nothing had hit them, the students lowered their wings and arms to discover a string of beads stretching across the deck and up into their instructor's hand.

"So that's how Keilani does it," Manny whispered to Brun.

"Does what?" Brun asked.

"Wears her wand in her hair," Manny elucidated.

"Oh. But doesn't Kaya wear hers like that, too?" Brun asked. Manny merely glared in reply.

"But enough about wands," Nochesol stated as the beads shot back into his hand to once again form a rod. "It is time to commence our studies of photokinesis." A hush gripped the crowd, their entire mind focused upon the instructor's words. Before Nochesol could continue, however, a hand shot up into the air.

"P-Professor Nochesol," the voice began shakily. "What is ph-photokinesis?"

"An excellent question, my dear Araceli," Nochesol corresponded. "But before I answer it I need everyone to sit around me in a circle." The students' concentration was so complete that they had followed Nochesol's command in a mere ten seconds. Nochesol blinked, impressed. "What a desire to learn," he mused. "Now, close your eyes, and relax."

Not a student dared disobey. In the silence that followed, each pupil slowly began to distinguish the myriad of sounds enveloping him or her—the cool wind rushing down into the valley and tossing the leaves about; the birds and insects singing in the forest; the soft crashing of the Falls below. "As Lumens, you possess sharper instincts than the remaining members of your individual species." Nochesol's voice was steady, his tone peaceful. "An additional sense has been granted to you, one which you are about to tap into. Do you not feel a warmth on your skin? A tingling sensation emanating from above? Breathe deeply, and discern the light flowing above you, around you." Nochesol paused for several moments, allowing the students to search the air about them. "Who can sense the call of the light, pouring down from the sky, from the heavens above?"

"I can," whispered several students in unison. At this they smiled, but none opened their eyes, eager for further instruction.

"Excellent," said Nochesol happily. "Now raise your wands, point them at the light above you—the light that you can now feel—and connect to it."

Lifting his wand, Manny pointed it at the ocean of particles that he could feel floating just above him. Imagining an invisible link between his wand and the particles, Manny discerned a sudden tug.

"Have you connected to it? It to you?" Nochesol asked, excitement building in his voice.

"Sí," the students answered.

"Now, pull your wands down toward you while spinning them, and open your eyes," Nochesol directed.

A gasp issued from the mouth of nearly every student as they all opened their eyes and witnessed a curling spiral of light twisting down from the air above. "This is sweet! I finally did it! Papá's gonna be so proud! Check that out!"

An instantaneous wave of contentment and peace filled Manny's heart, overwhelming him as his breath caught in his chest. *I have waited my whole life to do this, and I never knew it.* On his left Brun shared identical sentiments. **Papá, I can't wait to show you.**

"Stay focused!" Nochesol bolstered as he turned about in the center of the circle. "Maintain your connection to the light with your mind!" With a deep intake of air, the students stared at the light now attached to their wands, many hardly daring to blink, and some forgetting to breathe. "Don't concentrate too hard!" laughed Nochesol. "The light is your friend—you don't have to stare it down to bend it. Instead, lead it through the air with your thoughts and by pointing your wand."

Waving his hand to the right, Manny traced a glowing arc through the air. *It's a lot like playing with a sparkler. I wonder ...* Manny raised his hand as he continued to draw letters and symbols in the air.

"Sí, Manny?" Nochesol called.

"Professor," Manny began, "I was wondering if the light will burn you if you touch it?"

"No, the frequency of your light stream needs to be much higher to damage objects. In fact, you won't practice fusion until the Fourth-Level," the instructor replied genially.

"In that case…" Manny shot his free arm forward in an attempt to grab the glowing stream trailing from his wand. To his dismay, however, his hand simply passed through.

"I tried that already, too," Brun stated disappointedly.

"Another question, Sr. López?" Nochesol asked brightly.

"Yes—why can't I grab the light stream? My hand just went through it."

"The stream that you are bending has zero mass—you cannot touch, much less grab, a beam of light in that state," Nochesol illuminated.

Brun's hand bolted up. "Then how can we make light have mass?"

280

"What passion!" declared Nochesol in wonder. "It's invigorating to encounter such a pair of eager pupils! And intuitive," he added with a smile. "To answer your question, you must cluster light to such a degree that the individual particles combine to form an object of mass, or weight."

"When do we get to do that?" asked a centaur to the boys' right who had been snapping his stream similar to a whip.

"Pronto," Nochesol replied. "Probably next month."

"I can't wait!" Manny said to Brun.

"¡Atención, clase!" Nochesol said firmly, raising a hand into the air. "Relax for a moment and allow the light to diffuse." All around the circle the streams of light seemed to melt away, evaporating into the air. "You have now learned the two most basic photokinetic techniques— 'sense' and 'call.' Remember that in order to interact with light, you must first sense and acknowledge its presence. Once you feel the light around you, call it with your wand and connect to it. Now, let us sharpen our bending skills. Allow me to demonstrate. First, sense the light and call it." Glancing up, Nochesol took a deep breath and hooked his wand, pulling down a stream of light with a slow, sweeping motion. "This time around, do not allow the light to touch your wand—you are connected nonetheless. Instead, direct the light through the air about you—both up high and down low—and remember to avoid all obstacles and people, lest you diffuse your stream and are forced to call down a new one."

Much laughter rose up between Manny, Brun, and Nate as they competed to see whose beam of light could race around the deck first, their streams ribboning around the banister, weaving around certain students, and finally splashing into the floor at their feet. When Nochesol called once again for silence, Manny felt quite pleased with his progress over the past hour.

"This has been an excellent first meeting," Nochesol admitted positively. "To ready yourselves for our next class, read pages one through twenty in *Photokinesis* and practice the techniques you find there. ¡Buena suerte!" As the students dispersed in their rush for lunch, Nochesol snapped his wand to perfectly reconstruct the deck furniture and plants, meticulously ensuring that each piece and pot rested in its respective place.

"¡Nos vemos, Professor!" yelled Manny as he, Brun, and Nate descended the stairs on the eastern edge of the deck. Nochesol nodded as he clasped his cloak about him, leaping upon his glowing green board and jetting off toward the island.

"I bet there's not a cooler teacher at this school!" Nate exclaimed.

"You're probably right, but let's hurry before Araceli wakes up from her trance and realizes that we're gone—she's been bugging me all day," Brun said wearily.

Manny laughed. "I told you so."

***

Meeting Serge at the Café de la Catarata, the four boys spent the afternoon eating and chatting nonstop about their classes. Eventually they headed for the Island Gardens where they developed an intricate obstacle course to challenge their light bending skills. Following a brief stint atop Lookout Point to watch the lightboarders at sunset, Manny and Brun said farewell to Nate and Serge.

When they had reached Chiron's Hutch and emptied their backpacks, Manny and Brun lay down on their hammocks to read their assignments. Manny abruptly realized that he had a rectangular bulge in his back pocket, which he quickly discovered was Iris's textbook.

"Dang," said the boy in frustration.

"What?" asked Brun, lowering his own copy of *The Science of Light*.

"I've got Iris's Healing book and I never saw him to give it to him today," Manny complained.

"Why do you have Iris's book?" Brun asked suspiciously.

"After Healing I noticed him up by the pool, so I went up there and tried to apologize. He got scared and tore off like a bullet through the forest, dropping this." Manny held up the miniature book. "Professor Bluebolt is making me find him to return it."

"That's weird," Brun said slowly. "You know, you could send it to him with paloma paper. Did you ever think of that?"

"No." Manny paused to mull over this proposition. "If I do that then how can I apologize to him?"

"You've got a point, there," Brun admitted. "The book's a good excuse to talk to him. I hope he doesn't think you stole it, somehow."

"Me, either," Manny muttered.

"Well, hey! Maybe he'll have Astronomy with us in a couple hours. You could give it to him then!" Brun commented helpfully.

"If he sees me, he'll just shoot away through the crowd. And since it'll be nighttime, it will be impossible not to see me under the stars," Manny groaned.

***

"Have you been here before?" asked a high, innocent voice as it bobbed up and down.

"Keilani brought me here once when I was seven," a soft voice replied. "She wanted to introduce me to Chiron and show me the constellations she'd been learning about."

"Oh, so you probably don't know Chiron very well, do you, Kaya?" the first person asked.

"No, not really," the girl replied off-handedly. "Why—do you, Iris?"

"Yep," the hare said as he hopped along. "Dad and I come to Chiron's Hutch every Friday during the school year for lunch. Chiron's a good cook, you know."

"Really?" asked Kaya, surprised. "I guess I never thought of a centaur as a cook."

"A centaur's the head chef at the Café, you know," said Iris, glancing up with his violet eyes at Kaya, her hair swaying and beads clacking.

"No way!" she replied in disbelief.

"Yeah—Dad loves his banana leaf salad," Iris explained as he and Kaya passed the back room of the bamboo hut. Kaya came to

283

a sudden halt. "¿Qué pasa?" Iris asked, flipping around swiftly. "Is something wrong?"

"No," Kaya answered oddly. "I just wonder who's staying here with Chiron. I see a pair of hammocks, some textbooks, and something like a glowing jar—but no one's there…" Taking a step closer, Kaya leaned in toward the window when a violent squeak erupted from the sill, causing her to stumble back and nearly fall over.

"What was that?" Iris yelled, bolting around the girl's leg and peering up at the window. A black salamander with glowing yellow spots appeared over the sill, hissing at the unwelcome visitors. "Is that a mudpuppy, Kaya?"

"If it is it must have fallen in a tar pit and gotten the chicken pox." She eyed the creature carefully. "No—mudpuppies live in puddles and ponds, not in houses. It must be another type of salamander." Kaya lean forward slightly. The salamander hissed, his spots shining more brightly.

"He doesn't seem to like you very much, and I don't want to be late for class, so let's just go," Iris said, tugging on her pant leg. With one last keen glance at the spotted creature, Kaya turned and walked alongside the hare toward the towering kapok tree with its root gate opening up the hill.

"So was anybody living here last year?" Kaya asked as they passed through the gate.

"No," Iris quickly replied. "I don't remember students ever staying with Chiron since Pop and I moved here from Europe. And I was five then."

"Huh. I wonder why he'd take in students now?" Kaya mused as they climbed the hill. A moment later she hastily swerved to the right, nudging Iris with her foot as she passed. "Go this way!" she whispered, her tone desperate.

"What? Why?" called Iris loudly. "I like sitting up at the top of the hill so I can see Chiron better. Everyone will be in my way if —"

"Iris—just look up the hill and to the left!" Kaya snapped as she continued along the hill's eastern flank.

Iris's long paws were rooted to the ground, his eyes skeptical as he scanned the slopes in the indicated direction. Then, without another blink the hare fired off around the base of the hill, overtaking Kaya and throwing furtive looks toward the glowing boy and his friends just over the crown. The hare did not turn around until he reached the northeastern edge of the hill, far from the eyes of that cruel boy. "Why'd he have to be here?" asked Iris edgily as Kaya trotted up beside him, bent slightly to conceal herself as well. "Of all my classes today I was looking forward to this one the most, and I can't even sit up there by Chiron, 'cause he might try and chase me down like he did this morning!"

"Yeah, you'd think they'd have a separate class section for jerks and idiots," Kaya said sardonically. "I'm sorry, Iris."

"Geez," Iris growled as a group of panthers prowled forward, sitting immediately in front of the hare and blocking his line of vision. "I can't believe this!"

"I can just barely see, Iris, so hop up here and sit on my shoulder—you'll be able to see Chiron alright. The Jerk shouldn't see you—as long as you keep your ears down," she said understandingly.

"What's that supposed to mean?" Iris threw her a dart-like glance.

"Iris, don't get cocky with me—I'm just trying to help," Kaya said dryly.

The hare took a deep breath. "Sorry. I'm just so ticked off…" Shaking off his agitation, he nimbly leapt onto her shoulder.

Seconds later Chiron, who stood at the top of the hill gazing with admiration at his scores of pupils, stamped his back hoof. The slopes fell instantly silent. "Bienvenidos," he said in his strong, velvet voice. "Though I know many of you, there are others that I do not. In light of this it is only fitting that I introduce myself—I am Chiron Veridai. But please refrain from calling me Professor Veridai. In the Lumen world it is proper to call centaurs by their first name only. Therefore, Chiron will be sufficient."

"I would like to make an additional introduction, that you all may come to know the pair of good-natured students who have

285

sought lodging with me the next two years. Their names are Brun Dimirtis and Manny López," Chiron stated with a gesture to his right. "Muchachos, please stand."

"The Jerk lives here?" whispered Kaya in livid incredulity. "No wonder that salamander was hissing at me!"

Iris yanked on Kaya's hair. "There's no way I'm coming here for lunch on Friday's—you've gotta invite me to your house so I've got an excuse," the hare said gravely.

"It's done," Kaya replied, her chocolate eyes boiling.

"Welcome, I say again, to your first Astronomy session of the Seventh-Level," Chiron resumed as the boys sat back down. "I am delighted to have each and every one of you here, for the astute Lumen knows the stars and the stories they tell. Astronomy is more than a simple matter of reading the stars—it is philosophy. Over the next two years your studies of the southern heavens will lead you to question and refine your actions, your beliefs, your very way of life. But before we continue," he said, pausing and gazing at the students with those piercing black eyes, "I must warn you that to succeed under my instruction you must listen closely, read the text, and reflect much."

Kaya pulled her copy of *Light at Night* out of her backpack, setting the book upon the grass and opening it. Its pages and images shined in the dark, allowing her eyes to easily scan its contents under the starlight.

"Thanks, Kaya," whispered Iris. "I was afraid if I opened mine it'd drag me down off your shoulder like an anchor."

Turning in a clockwise motion Chiron continued his lecture. "Our first collection of stars may be found in the constellation of Pegasus, to the north." Crossing his arms and gazing into the radiant sky, Chiron stamped his back leg again. Almost immediately a grouping of stars began to grow brighter, revealing a square body with wings above, short legs below, and a long head and neck. "I present to you the Winged Horse." The centaur lifted the palm of his hand to the astral beast. "Let us consult page 249 of *Light at Night* to access the names of the individual stars…"

"Talking about books—did you ever find your copy of *The Science of Light*?" Kaya asked.

"Nope," Iris replied significantly, his ears fidgeting slightly.

"That's it!" she snarled, punching the ground. "I just know The Jerk took it!"

"…in effect, as you look to the left, or West, you will observe that Pegasus' head is formed by the star Enif…" the centaur carried on.

"If he took it then how can we get it back?" breathed Iris. "I need it to prepare for the dissection on Wednesday!"

"I know, I know. Just give me a second and let me think…" Kaya eyes lost focus as she gazed beyond the Winged Horse and deeper into the universe.

"…and Algenib forms the base of the tail…" Chiron said, snapping his own.

"What if it's in the hutch, Iris? We could sneak off, grab it, and be back before class is over. No one would even notice," Kaya suggested.

"What about that angry salamander?" Iris asked nervously.

"He's small—and I bet he's just a bunch of wind, like The Jerk. Yeah, just like a smaller version of The Jerk." Kaya slipped off her backpack and began to crawl south around the slope.

"But I'm small," argued Iris quietly. "A bite from him could rip one of my fingers off!"

"You're fast, so don't worry about it. Just keep an eye on him—I'll kick him if I have to," she whispered in reply.

It was fortunate for Kaya and Iris that the class was facing North, allowing the covert pair to steal away unseen along the lower slopes and down through the kapok gate. Once through, Kaya rose to her full height, drawing near to the prickly roots of the tree to observe the patio area from the shadows in order to ensure that their cover remained intact. Satisfied that the glade was clear, Kaya led the way to the door. She grasped the wicker knob and turned it surreptitiously.

Suddenly a wave of laughter rushed down from the hilltop, prompting one of Iris's ears to shoot into the air. "They're not looking down at us," he said positively. "Chiron must've just said something funny."

"I don't know about you, but I find Astronomy a little dry myself," Kaya stated as she opened the door and stepped through. Though the corners were dark, Kaya quickly noticed the pair of hammocks on either side of the room.

"Is he in there?" breathed Iris anxiously.

"Who? The Jerk?"

"No, the salamander!"

"Oh." Kaya scanned the room, ending with a brief glance down the hallway. "I don't see him, Iris. But there's a sun beetle on a dresser in here." She stepped toward the glowing scarab trapped within the glass jar on her left. "The Jerk must've been the one who caught it when Dosfilos threw it! Can you believe that?"

"It only makes sense. He glows, and sun beetles are attracted to light."

"Well, since he stole your book, we're gonna take his sun beetle," Kaya said defiantly as she snatched up the jar.

Iris contemplated the buzzing insect for a moment. "Kaya, what if Manny's not the one who caught the beetle? What if it actually belongs to Br—"

"Who cares? He deserves to lose it just for putting up with The Jerk!"

"I don't think we should take it," Iris said firmly, crossing his arms and ears. "Dad always says that revenge won't solve a problem—it'll just make it worse."

Kaya took a deep breath, hugging the jar to her side. "Okay then. How 'bout this? If we find your book, we leave the sun beetle. But if the book's not here, we take it until The Jerk gives you the book back."

"So either way, we won't keep the sun beetle?"

"As long as we get the book back," Kaya stipulated.

"Alright, then," nodded Iris. "Let's find mi libro."

With the limited light provided via sun beetle, Kaya began to scour the left half of the room, groping through dresser drawers and below the hammock. Iris, on the other hand, was not so keen on the idea of leaping into the shadows on the opposite side, where the insect's light failed to reach. *After all, that vicious salamander could be staring at me this very moment, just waiting to gobble down one of my toes.* Or so he thought.

"I found The Jerk's backpack!" Kaya exclaimed, crouched in the northeast corner of the room, near the door.

Refusing to tear his eyes from the looming darkness, Iris asked, "I-is it in there?" As he waited for her reply, Iris's heart jolted—he was certain he saw a fluid, slithering movement along the wall, just below the west window. "Kaya—"

"Be patient, Iris," she said sharply. "There are a lot of compartments in this thing. Hey!" she cried, throwing a swift glance at the hare. "Why aren't you searching your side of the hut?"

A chomping sound made Iris's foot jerk nervously. "Kaya, there's something over here, and I think it's bigger than—"

Kaya slammed the backpack on the dirt floor. "Iris, I already told you to run if—"

A crimson blur in the golden light, Iris bolted into the corner behind Kaya; but before she could utter a word of protest a creature with dual rows of snapping fangs and a leafy mane rushed at her from the shadows. Anticipating a full frontal attack, Kaya lifted the straps of the backpack to shield herself, but was quickly surprised when she felt the creature's vine-like arms brush along her back as it hooked left in pursuit of the hare. Just as Iris intended to blast off down the penumbral hall, however, he tripped over the glass jar and screamed.

"It's got my foot, Kaya!" Iris wailed. "¡Sálvame!"

Without a second's thought Kaya slid the pack along the floor, successfully making contact with the ravenous attack plant. As the vegetal predator collided with the west wall, Kaya fired to her feet, snatching up the injured hare in one arm and the jar in the other.

"What was that thing?" Iris squealed as Kaya carried him along the dark hall.

"A flytrap," she muttered, exploding through the front door of the hut and darting left into the fern-filled undergrowth.

"What're we gonna do now?" Iris asked as Kaya set him down next to the jar.

"First, I'll wrap your foot, 'cause you're bleeding," she said, her voice and breath calm.

"I am?!" Iris inquired frantically. Ignoring him, Kaya slid the string of fuchsia beads from her hair, changing them into an ornate box that she flipped open to pull out a white handkerchief embroidered with a pair of pink tulips.

"Just stay calm," Kaya bolstered as she bound the hare's foot, her eyes suddenly gentle, yet set. The hare whimpered. "Don't worry, Iris—I'll take you to my house once class is over. Mamá will heal your foot in no time."

"Alright," sniffed Iris, his violet eyes tracing the path of the insect dancing in its glass prison. "Kaya, what do you mean 'once class is over?' I can't go back up there with my foot like this—if somebody sees me they'll laugh at me!"

"Don't worry—no one will see us." Kaya lifted the hare to his feet. "We'll just sneak back up along the lower part of the hill, back to where we were sitting before. Truthfully," she added, stepping out from the undergrowth, "I doubt anyone's even noticed we're gone."

"What about the sun beetle?" Iris asked, one foot in the ferns and one in the glade.

"We'll have to get that when we leave," Kaya said as she sauntered to the kapok gate. "We don't want to announce we've got it to the whole world, do we?"

"No, I guess not," Iris replied, hopping slowly toward her.

"Your foot feeling alright?"

"Sí, it really doesn't hurt too much with the bandage on, but it's throbbing a little."

"Bueno." Kaya leaned forward and peered though the gate. "Everyone's looking at Chiron again, so we'll just slip in as soon as he turns his back to us."

"Dad would kill me if he knew what we were doing," Iris said ominously.

"Good thing he'll never know," Kaya whispered. "Okay, let's go."

Due to Iris's wound, which only allowed him to hop short distances without pausing, their return was a tedious one, taking nearly ten minutes. Slinking up behind the group of panthers, Kaya set Iris back upon her shoulder, hardly a second before Chiron turned in their direction.

"...as you may have guessed, Pegasus was hard-pressed to help the Princess Andromeda, who was now grief-stricken over the loss of her crown. But as The Winged Horse was a creature of the air, and not the sea, he was forced to enlist the aid of a pair of his aquatic comrades to recover the royal headpiece from the cunning Pisces—which are the fish, of course..." Chiron said, briefly pausing his overview to smile at the familiar hare perched upon the shoulder of a girl certain to be the sister of his student, Keilani. "But who were Pegasus' comrades, you may ask? Let me not spoil all the details of the celestial account! I will now allow each of you to resume your reading of *Pegasus and the Crown Jewels*, which you must finish and be prepared to discuss for our next meeting, two nights from now. You may commence," the centaur directed, the hill full of Lumens squirming and twisting to get comfortable for the task ahead. Chiron, for his part, circulated about the slopes, his dark eyes reflecting the bodies of his students leaning over their glowing texts that told of how Pegasus summoned the aid of Delphinus and Aries, the Dolphin and the Water Goat, respectively.

Iris looked up from his book. "Since when has a goat been able to walk on water?"

"Since the stars were created," answered Chiron from behind the hare. "Recall, Iris, that this is a tale to teach us lessons and values, and is not necessarily true. Be aware, though, that in your studies you may indeed encounter a water goat one day."

"What kind of lesson can I learn from an imaginary princess and her crown, then?" Iris asked skeptically.

"Look deeper into the tale, m'ijo. Why did Andromeda lose her crown?" Chiron asked shrewdly.

"It seems to me she wasn't being careful—she did fall off Pegasus, after all," the hare replied critically.

"Well noted," the centaur said. "From her folly we learn care, not only with ourselves, but for our possessions as well."

"Oh," said Iris, suddenly a little uncomfortable.

"But who is your fair friend, m'ijo? Is she not the same young sister of Keilani whom I met so many years ago?" Chiron asked avidly.

"¡Sí! She is! Her name's Kaya Mireille Bellastrata, and she's my best friend!" Iris exclaimed enthusiastically, the sincerity of the words striking the girl unexpectedly.

"I am?"

"Yeah! Actually, you're my only friend," the hare bluntly confessed.

"Then there is no doubt that the tulip embroidered kerchief on your heel belongs to her," Chiron said wisely. "What happened, m'ijo?"

"He got his foot caught in some spines earlier. But I helped him out and bandaged it, so he's better now," Kaya answered quickly, yet striving to appear nonchalant.

"I could send for Professor Bluebolt if you like, Iris. He's an avid lightboarder—he could be here in a matter of minutes," Chiron offered.

"That's okay, Chiron," Kaya interrupted again. "Mi mamá is a healer—she'll take care of it."

"Are you sure?" he asked Iris. "It's really no trouble."

Both Iris and Kaya nodded in reply. "Thanks anyway, Chiron," Iris said.

With a congenial nod, the centaur resumed his vigilant trek about the hill, conversing quietly with the students here and there while silencing others whose hands seemed to have mysteriously wondered from their books to their Piranha Sweep cards. From above, the stars and galaxies shone down on the enraptured pupils, their minds absorbing the tale of the alliance between The Winged Horse, The Dolphin, and the Water Goat, whose combined efforts

292

helped recover Andromeda's crown, its jewels now lost forever in the bellies of the sparkling Pisces of the night sky.

***

"Okay, Manny, what did you do with my sun beetle?" Brun called loudly.

"Nothing—I haven't touched it," Manny said as he, too, stepped through the back door of the hut.

"Well it's gone, and you're the only one I know of who wanted it," Brun remarked, pointing at his empty dresser.

"In case you haven't noticed, Brun, your underwear's lying on the floor and your books are all over the place!" Manny retorted.

My underwear? "What did you do that for?"

"I didn't!" Manny snapped. "The room wasn't like this when we left for class, and I've been with you the entire time!"

Brun blinked several times. "You're right—sorry."

Glad we could reach an agreement. "Why's Nipper sleeping under my hammock?" Manny asked, his words firing at the plant like a series of missiles. *I bet she was lying in wait for more meat!* "¡Mira! She tore up Lil' Manny's carrier again!"

"She's not sleeping…" Brun said slowly.

"She's not moving, and she's leaning against the wall! What else does she have to do to prove it to you? She has no eyes, Brun!"

"Nipper's arms wriggle when she's sleeping—that's how I know," Brun answered as he crawled up to her, finding Lil' Manny licking a wound on the flytrap's head. Seeing Brun, the salamander squeaked pitifully and continued to clean the oozing cut.

Manny rushed over. "Did she hurt my salamander?"

"No. Somebody—or something—hurt her. Lil' Manny's actually caring for her."

"He is?" Manny blurted in disbelief. He stepped forward to verify the truth. "Who would try to hurt Nipper?" The boy blinked. *Did I really just ask that?*

"I don't know, but I'm guessing they were looking for something." Brun took the flytrap into his arms, then considered his possessions thrown about the floor.

"If they wanted the sun beetle they would've just taken it instead of searching through your stuff," Manny postulated. "What do you think they were really after?"

Brun stood, staring from the scattered books to his mountain of underwear. "You don't think they were after my wand, do you?"

"You mean the monkey? Could be... But why didn't he go through my stuff, then?"

"Nipper probably came in and startled him." Brun's luminescent eyes ran over the flytrap's limp jaws. He lifted her head gently. "Manny, look! There's fur in her teeth!"

"No way! Really?" Manny studied the plant's crooked mouth in amazement. "I can't believe it—the monkey actually followed me here."

Art for Art's Sake

"By Orion's sword, you are a vision, aren't you? Come here! Come here! I must see that radiant skin! That charcoal hair! Those vibrant eyes! Come, star child!" exploded a highly animated female voice.

Manny's heart skidded against his ribs. "Is she talking to me?"

"Well, I'm not glowing," Nate replied baldly.

In an instant a pair of hands grasped Manny's cheeks. "I'm not a star child," he mumbled through squashed lips.

"Of course you're not," the woman replied, her light blue eyes flashing. "But how resplendent you are! What bright color! You are a work of art!"

Manny rolled his eyes. "So are you the Art teacher?" he asked, non-plussed.

"Why yes, I am," she answered, taking the boy by the arm and leading him into the center of the Southeast Garden. "You may call me Caleida. And you?"

"My name's Manny L—"

"Manny! What a beautiful name!" she erupted, spinning around in front of the boy and twirling her magnificent mango robes, the late-morning sun catching her pinned up, golden hair. *She looks like an overgrown flower.*

Nate stepped forward. "Caleida, I'm N—"

"Professor Flores," she cut in, enunciating each vowel clearly.

Nate blinked awkwardly. "I'm sorry, Professor Flores," he said, slightly abashed. "I'm Nate." Flores examined the boy with a severely critical eye.

"He's my friend, Professor," Manny intervened swiftly.

"Caleida," she corrected dryly, giving Manny a slight frown. "Spectacular!" she cried, her demeanor changing completely as she stepped forward to hug Nate. "Any friend of my dear Manny is close to my heart."

Choking, Nate slid from the instructor's embrace. "My dear Manny?" he mouthed, chuckling.

"Oh, shut up!" Manny said, pushing Nate, who burst into laughter.

Flores observed Nate with a perplexed brow. "What an eccentric amigo you have, Manny."

"I'd say eccentric," Nate breathed through the corner of his mouth.

"Allow me to locate an adequate partner for each of you," said Flores, tapping her cheek softly with her forefinger as she scanned the ring of stone tables about her. "¡Perfecto!" she thought aloud, advancing toward a table along the western edge of the garden where a girl with sunny curls stood. "Nate, this young woman will be your partner!"

"Buenos días, Millie," Nate said as he approached the table. "¿Cómo va?"

"Just great, Nate, thanks. It's 'bout time we had a class together!" Millie replied readily.

"Bien," Flores stated in satisfaction as she returned to the center of the garden, where she clasped Manny's hand and patted it gently. *This is so embarrassing.* "Now who would be an excellent partner for you, mi amor?" Manny stared at the flower-strewn lawn at his feet, unable to face his peers. "¡Exacto!" Flores muttered as she led Manny by the hand to the eastern edge of the clearing where an enormous weeping willow grew. "Manny, this is your Art partner for the year—Señorita Bellastrata." Flores gracefully opened her palm toward a girl with chocolate eyes and a pink-beaded strand in her long, black hair.

"Caleida, you've made a mistake—"

"No doubt about that!" the girl said loudly. "Professor Flores, I'm not working with this sour-faced jerk!"

"Kaya Bellastrata, your behavior and words are completely inappropriate!" Flores announced, her eyes flashing an icy blue.

"And I have made no mistake, Manny—Kaya will be your partner for Seventh-Level Art!"

Manny's spirit waned. "All year long?"

"Sí," Flores clipped.

"I refuse," Kaya said stiffly, collecting her backpack from the table and aiming to walk away. Without hesitation Flores shot her hand to the loose bun at the back of her head to withdraw an orange-hued, bamboo paintbrush. She snapped the tool at the girl's feet, creating a thick, dark green hedge to block her exit.

"You will not refuse, nor walk away, Señorita Bellastrata," Flores said acutely. "For I will not tolerate such impertinence in my classroom, and I do not believe that you would risk suspension for a string of shallow pride."

"Suspension?" Manny repeated. "You mean we'll be suspended from the Academy if we disobey our teachers?"

"Yes, Manny," Flores answered, her tone stern.

"But why? Isn't that a little severe?" he continued.

"What is truly severe—even deplorable—is that some students demonstrate such a high level of disrespect that they render themselves unteachable," Flores expounded. "Put simply, if a student refuses to follow my instructions, it is impossible for me to teach that student. Yet it is wise to remember that no student of mine has been suspended for over ten years," Flores added with a sharp look to Kaya.

With a deep breath the girl returned her pack to the table. "Please forgive me, Professor," Kaya said evenly.

"It would be my delight." Flores snapped the mango brush at the hedge to transform it into a shower of colorful orchids, one of which she elegantly caught in the air. The woman gently threaded the flower behind Kaya's ear with a smile. "I'm proud of you," whispered the instructor. Kaya blinked several times as Flores turned and walked away.

Manny stepped awkwardly forward, setting the leather backpack in front of him. *What am I supposed to say now?* He lifted his eyes from the seamless marble surface, then glanced at Kaya, who simply stared soberly toward Flores at the center of the garden

in her incessant designation of additional pairs. *Urgh! Here goes...*
"Friends?" Manny suggested, extending his hand toward Kaya.

After a second or two the girl turned and stared at the boy's glowing hand. Turning back away, she said, "I will never be your friend, Manny López. You are shallow; you mock others and you make judgments based on appearances. And the only reason I'm here now is that I do not want to disrespect any of my professors because of you. In other words, I'm working with you because I have to, not because I want to."

Ouch. Manny lowered his hand, looking away and watching the other groups chatting zealously, particularly the chinchilla and the blue morpho on the right. *I wish Brun were my partner.*

"Listen, Kaya," Manny began. "About what I said on the fruit snake path—"

"Don't talk to me," Kaya cut in dryly.

"But I was being—"

"A jerk? I know! So just don't talk about it," she said with finality.

She-devil. Manny sighed pitifully, and then growled subtly. Highly irritated, he spent the next five minutes drawing cartoons of cackling reptiles assaulting Kaya with rotten tomatoes, among other overly juicy fruits.

"¡Qué emoción!" Flores exclaimed, sparing Kaya a subsequent volley of wet papaya. "How exciting it is to begin our first Art class! But before we dive in, let me ask you a question." She paused, her eyes glittering. "What is art?"

A reluctant silence reigned over the glade as Flores looked from face to face in search of an eager pupil. "Is there no one here with a passion for art?" she asked, completing a full turn. To her delight, a hand shot up. "Manny! Share with us your perspective!"

"As I see it, art is an expression of your feelings. Take drawing, for example. When you're upset you can pour your anger out into the images on paper so that when you're finished, you're calm again. I do it all the time," he added with a cool look of satisfaction toward Kaya, who ignored this gesture completely. "But art isn't just drawing, of course. Back home I really like to work with clay—and I paint, too. When I was young mi abuelito even taught me to do wood carvings."

Kaya coughed, rolling her eyes and raising her hand just as Flores meant to speak. "Um—yes, Kaya?" the woman stuttered.

"Professor, I'd like to share my own views on art," Kaya said affably.

Flores nodded. "Go ahead, then."

"Most of us know that Lumen art involves more than drawing silly cartoons and making bowls with mud—it takes skill in Light Bending and a vivid imagination," Kaya announced, flipping her hair over her shoulder and glancing at Manny with copper eyes. "More than mere representation, the soul of Lumen art is creation—molding tools, designing buildings, and making food from light itself."

"¡Verdad!" Flores cried, clapping happily. "Well said, Señorita Bellastrata. Very well said."

"Gracias, Professor," Kaya replied.

Manny nearly gagged. *Don't make me sick.*

"As Kaya so pointedly mentioned, our goal for the Seventh-Level is to create tools—architecture and the culinary arts must wait for later years. But we must start small, building block upon block as the year progresses to reach our objective. Therefore, this week we will concentrate upon color—tinting the light for artistic use," Flores explained. "Now, ready your wands!"

Manny watched in bitter amazement as Kaya slid the tulip beads from her hair, the wood glowing faintly before merging to form a pink wand. *I knew that's how it worked.*

Under Flores's direction, the students passed the final hour of the morning drawing light down through the air, articulating a distinct range of feelings to alter the frequency of the photons and consequently shift the color of the streams. Manny and Kaya, however, encountered particular difficulty in shifting their light streams from all but two colors—orange and purple.

"Are the pair of you incapable of feeling any emotion besides anger and pride?" Flores asked, gliding up to the table. Neither responded, but Kaya's violet beam changed to orange as she huffed irritably. "Emotional depth is key to developing your artistic abilities," the instructor continued, a gilded eyebrow raised as she tapped the mango brush-wand in her palm. "And from what I can see, your only barrier is the sour disposition you hold for one another. I suggest that you resolve this issue before your quiz on Thursday."

As Flores turned to walk away, Manny's light stream burst in a show of fire. "Why do you treat me like crap, anyway?" he snapped, his words splintering in the air.

"I wonder," Kaya tore back sarcastically, refitting the pink beads in her hair. "Maybe you should learn to keep your thoughts and hands to yourself!"

Hands to myself...? "What are you talking about?" Manny said meanly. Kaya glared back in reply, her hand locked at her hip. A vague suspicion crept into Manny's mind. "Do you mean Iris's book?"

Kaya's eyes flashed. "Why? Do you know where it is?"

Manny reached into his back pocket and grasped the miniature copy of *The Science of Light*. "What would you say if I did?"

"I'd say you're a thief," she replied flatly.

"Well, I'm not." Manny pulled out the hare's text and held it in the air.

"I knew it!" Kaya cried loudly, lunging forward to snatch the tome. Manny, however, performed a well-timed sidestep.

"I'll only give it to you if you promise me something," Manny stipulated.

"No way! Now give it to me!" Kaya ripped, lunging again; Manny simply sauntered around to the other side of the table. "You stole it! Give it back!"

"Kaya, I didn't steal the book," Manny said clearly. "Iris dropped it at Harmony Falls—I picked it up so I could give it back to him."

"I'm sure," Kaya said scornfully.

"I don't care if you believe me," Manny stated frankly. "The only thing I want you to do is promise to return it to Iris for me."

"As soon as you let me have it, I will," she exclaimed.

"Keep your word, then," Manny said, slapping the book down on the table and walking away.

Several moments later, as Kaya walked home for lunch, doubt began to nibble at her heart. *Did The Jerk actually steal the book? Should we really have taken the sun beetle? And what am I supposed to tell Iris now?*

***

"As you have now read, fireflies are the sentinels recognized primarily for their status as light-keepers," called a stout hare from the head of a dell ablaze with a grass the color of burning embers. Behind the hare rose a towering oak tree, the diameter of which measured well over thirty feet.

A dome of darkness engulfed the dell just as the chestnut hare flipped the wooden monocle over one of his silver eyes. The assembled students gasped in amazement as the now missing light merged to form a dense orb that hovered over their heads. Brun jerked his arm from Araceli's grasp as the hare continued. "In absolute darkness a Lumen is at his most vulnerable; therefore, it is essential to create a light-keeper, such as Firefly, to maintain a stable body of light so as not to find yourself defenseless in such places as caves, tunnels, or sealed rooms."

"Let us now direct our attention to the orb that I have clustered," the hare said, signaling the immense globe with the tip of an ear. The orb drew steadily near him. "In its present state it is not self-sufficient. But if I mold the orb into a firefly, I can animate it." With a twist of the monocle, the sphere reformed to the shape of a motionless firefly, its wings, antennae, and tail light bursting to life with a whisper from the hare.

"Now that the sentinel is self-substantial, I can hop about and it will follow me." The hare traversed the dark glade in two surprisingly swift leaps, followed closely by the enormous insect. With a spin the hare landed firmly on his back paws, facing the startled students and flicking his monocle. "We may now observe

301

that although this sentinel harbors light, its photon quantity is limited. Notice that the intensity of the firefly fades as I drain its light into separate streams."

Over one hundred pairs of astounded eyes watched as the firefly's form melted away, its light siphoning into tiny orbs that floated lazily over the children's heads. A hand rose, passing through the orb above it.

"Question, Brun?" the hare asked, his left ear lifting slightly.

"Yes, Professor Firefoot," Brun replied. "I was wondering— when you pull all the light from a sentinel, does it die?"

"In a sense," Firefoot answered.

Araceli let out a small wail.

"Let go of me!" Brun said, jerking his arm away from her a second time.

"Does it hurt the firefly, Professor?" the girl asked, slightly hysterical.

"Not at all, Araceli. Not even for a moment," the hare reassured her, his ears twitching. "We Lumens are incapable of creating living organisms. As such, sentinels cannot feel—they are beings of pure light, having neither nerves nor skin."

"Oh, good," Araceli sighed. Brun rolled his eyes.

"Before we continue with the lesson, I have a gift for you," Firefoot said brightly. The hare raised his brow as the orbs peppering the air shifted into a frozen cloud of fireflies. "A sentinel for each of you!"

"Really? Wow! I've never had my own sentinel before!" called several students, their gaze fixed expectantly on the stationary insects. A minute later, however, the crowd's enthusiasm began to wane. A chinchilla ruffled its hairs impatiently; two tree frogs began to bounce and croak in aggravation.

"Why won't my sentinel do anything?" whined one of the frogs, flipping about like a spring.

Firefoot, his ears half-raised, merely stared at the amphibian humorously. "It appears that none of you has listened to my lecture!"

The tree frog croaked in frustration, teetering back and forth on his webbed paws. A centaur sighed.

"It-it's moving! the centaur exclaimed, his front hooves lifting from the ground for a moment. "My firefly's alive!"

Affronted, the frog crossed his front legs in disbelief. "Is mine defective or something?"

A score of envious eyes directed themselves toward the rejoicing centaur. Brun, however, looked to Manny and Nate, who where prodding their sentinels' wings vainly. **It's not when you touch them, and staring does no good, so...** "Breathe on them," Brun said firmly as he blew on his firefly, then watched as it began to hover about energetically.

Manny, Nate, and Araceli quickly followed suit. "I'm such an airhead," Manny said, aggravated.

"Good eye, Brun!" Nate said, throwing Brun a thumbs up.

"He's a genius," marveled Araceli, her words clinging to Brun's face. Shaking them off, he looked around as the class's sentinels buzzed about, casting broken rays of light across the fiery grass.

"I see that we can proceed with class now," the hare pronounced, his ears reaching high. "Now that we can animate sentinels, we must learn to form them. But forming individual sentinels is a multifaceted process. Tell me—how many parts does Firefly have?"

A lime-tinted quetzal shook her wing. "¿Sí, Evangelina? How many?"

"Thousands, Professor!" Evangelina chirped. "They are very complex creatures!"

"Indeed they are!" Firefoot replied. "But you must recall that we are speaking of the sentinel—not the insect. Think, Evangelina!" The hare's ears danced as he hopped about the dell. "How many parts come together to form the sentinel Firefly above you?"

Evangelina cocked her head to analyze the sentinel floating just over her beak. "Um, it's got wings, Professor!"

"Correct! What else?" Firefoot called back.

"Well, the body and the head—those are obvious," she chirped.

Firefoot nodded. "Just one more part!"

"Hmmm... Oh! The antennae! It has two of them!" the quetzal trilled.

"Precisely! That gives us four distinct parts—wings, body, head, and antennae. In order to form Firefly you must combine both your Light Bending and Art skills. Let us begin with the wings! Wands out and books open to page 17! Notice that your goal is to bend the light in a teardrop shape...

***

"So what are we gonna do about the sun beetle?" Iris breathed, his ears hanging over the side of the canoe.

"What can we do? It's gone," Kaya whispered.

"I still don't get what happened to it. We left the jar in the bushes! How could it disappear? You don't think anyone could see it, do you?" the hare asked apprehensively.

"I don't see how," Kaya sighed. "It was buried beneath the ferns."

Iris frowned, crossing his ears behind his back like a pair of scissors. "We shouldn't have taken it, Kaya."

"He had your book, Iris!" she whispered defensively.

"But he said I dropped it!" the hare cut back.

Kaya was agitated. "He could very well have been lying, you know."

"Or telling the truth!" Iris clicked his tongue. "If he really was out to get me he would've kept the book—or at least torn it up!"

"Well, either way, that doesn't help us find the sun beetle. Now, does it?" snapped Kaya, the canoe suddenly rocking sideways.

Iris toppled out onto the rocky shore as the beaver called, "¡Un sol, por favor!"

Flipping the coin and shouting, "¡Gracias!" Kaya leapt from the boat to pick Iris up by the front paw.

"Y'alright?"

"Sí." Iris shook his head, his propeller ears flying about. "Anyway," he grumbled, "we've got to find that sun beetle and apologize!"

"How do you expect to do that, genius? You might as well try to find a Luna you've dropped in the Plaza!"

"Hey now! I've found a Luna on the ground near the fountain before!" he countered.

"But I bet is wasn't the same one you dropped!" Kaya threw back.

Iris bent his ears. "How do you know?"

Kaya merely frowned in reply. "Get serious, Iris," she said blandly. "We don't even have anywhere to start."

"Oh yes we do."

***

"I told you so," Iris quipped.

"Oh, shut up," bit Kaya.

"What are these? Kinkajou prints? They're too big for a chinchilla," Iris observed, his triangular nose bent down over a patch of dried mud hidden beneath the arms of the ferns.

Kaya groaned. "You're blocking my vision—all I can see is your head."

"Have a look, then," replied Iris positively, chuckling as the girl rolled her eyes and leaned forward begrudgingly.

The chocolate fell from Kaya's eyes, filling the five-fingered print and scanning its depth and size. A moment passed. "I dunno, Iris. This print doesn't have claws—and kinkajous have claws."

"What could it have been, then?" the hare asked. "An overgrown chinchilla? 'Cause Serena's mom is pretty—"

"No way," Kaya interrupted. "Honestly, by the ridges on the fingers, I would say the culprit was a monkey."

"Get out!" Iris slapped Kaya's shoulder with his ear in disbelief. "Monkeys don't live in Isla Verde!"

"That doesn't mean one can't wander in once and a while!" she argued.

"Yes it does! My dad told me that apes aren't allowed within the parameters of the city!"

"That's ridiculous!" Kaya yelled, throwing the words in his face. "Why would that be?"

"What you consider ridiculous, Señorita Bellastrata, the Light Brethren considered a necessary security measure," stated a deep voice, soaring over the foliage.

Kaya's heart stopped in her chest, pincered in the talon's of surprise guilt. Iris melted into the mud.

"I would like an explanation as to why you are hiding in my back patio, alone and concealed, at dusk," the voice called as a hoof stamped and the ferns parted, a pair of midnight eyes staring down at the clueseekers.

"Hola, Chiron," Iris said, waving sheepishly. The centaur blinked in reply. His mind blank, Iris looked to Kaya in desperation.

"Chiron, you see, Iris and I were having a debate," said Kaya, her words falling into the crusty print at her knees.

"This I noted. But why discuss monkeys, of all possible themes, in my yard?" Chiron rejoined coolly.

With a deep breath Kaya confessed, "I think a monkey's been here."

"And you disagree, Iris?" the centaur asked.

"Yes," the hare replied.

"But why do you feel this way?" Chiron asked, looking to the girl.

"There's a print here, below this fern, and I think it's a monkey's," said Kaya, pointing.

"Allow me." Chiron stomped his bracelet clad hoof and pulled down a stream of light to fill the print. With a blink the light transformed into clay, which hardened instantly and rose into the air, suddenly gleaming in the bright light of a firefly that materialized as the centaur caught the clay mold in his hand. The shadow of a frown crossed his star-stained brow.

"What is it, Chiron?" Iris inquired, his words bouncing off the clay above. "Is it really a monkey print?"

"I believe so," the centaur acknowledged darkly. "But I must first verify the matter with Professor Shadowflame—she is the Academy's animal and Lumorphi expert."

In a flash Chiron lifted his back leg and transformed his wand into a simple box, inside of which he placed the clay mold. After sealing the container, he replaced it on his leg as a bracelet.

"May I trust that your investigative exploits in my yard are ended?" the centaur asked firmly.

"Sí, Señor," Kaya and Iris replied, humiliated.

With a nod Chiron turned and trod off down the path, his eyes set.

***

"Are you kidding me?" the woman called vociferously, a lightboard leaning against her side while the last waves of the evening broke weakly at her heels, pleading for attention. "I don't photocache for free, you know!"

"But a monkey stole our sun beetle, Keilani!" Iris cried, slapping the waves with his feet.

"Wait a sec—how did you two catch a sun beetle in the first place? I know for a fact that Shadowflame hasn't taken any classes out yet!" Keilani said accusatorially.

Iris shrugged. "We found it," he said unconvincingly.

Boring into Iris and Kaya with her mocha eyes, Keilani muttered, "Whatever…" But just as she aimed to flip her hair back, she said, "Hold it—did you say a monkey stole your sun beetle?"

"Yes, he did," Kaya said, her foot sinking deeper into the tide-washed sand.

Keilani nearly doubled over in laughter, inflaming Kaya and frustrating Iris. "What a joke! Did he try to steal your wand, too?" Keilani mocked.

"Steal our wands…?" repeated Iris, lost.

Laughing uncontrollably, Keilani dropped her board, which hit the churning sand with a spurt.

"Why can't you just take us seriously?" growled Kaya, her fists balled.

"How can I?" wailed Keilani, slapping her thigh. "You're the perfect match for that kid staying with Chiron!"

Iris winced, for he knew the fury that was to come.

"You're not talking about Manny López, are you?" Kaya's volume increased steadily. "Because if you are—"

"You know his last name?!" Keilani exclaimed incredulously, gasping for air. "You really are perfect for each other!"

Iris attempted to intervene. "Keilani, I think you should st—"

A slap resounded on the beach; the lake waters were now calm and peaceful.

"Shut up, Keilani! Just shut up!" roared Kaya.

"Don't-ever-slap-me," Keilani said dangerously, rising to her full height.

"Don't make fun of Iris and me when we come to you for help, then!" Kaya rebounded.

"Help? You, Iris, and Manny all need help!" said Keilani adamantly. "What can I say to convince you all that monkeys aren't out to get you? They're not after your wands, and they're definitely not stalking you to snatch your sun beetles!"

"We're leaving, Iris," Kaya said quietly, ignoring her sister altogether and turning toward the crepuscular gardens, her back to Keilani as she followed the hare's darting shadow into the darkness. Without warning, however, a tight cord wrapped around Kaya's ankle, dragging her to the wet ground. Rolling around, Kaya's anger rekindled as her eyes ran up the glowing whip connecting her ankle to Keilani's wand.

"Are you insane?" Kaya screeched. "Mom will kill you!"

"Don't turn your back on me, Kaya," Keilani threatened. "I'm older and stronger than you."

"Yeah, but you're not any smarter," Kaya muttered as she reached down to grab the white cord binding her ankle.

"I wouldn't do that if I were you," said Keilani.

Kaya winced as the whip tightened. "I would!" And with a vicious jerk the girl successfully ripped the wand from her sister's hand, the whip disintegrating as the tulip wand soared through the air and into the trees behind.

"Aagh! I can't believe you!" Keilani screamed, bolting at Kaya in a rage. "Just wait 'til I get my wand!"

"Enough already!" Kaya called tiredly as she leapt up and ran for the cover of the trees. "And quit being so dramatic!"

Just as Kaya pulled herself up next to Iris in the thick canopy of a flowering tree, a green band of light appeared, hovering slowly above the upper limbs. The girl and the hare held their breath.

"I'll find you, Kaya—and you'll be in a world of pain when I do," shouted Keilani to the treetops. But as only the wind seemed to be stirring the foliage, the woman soared on, slicing the air with her threats.

"What are you gonna do, Kaya?" Iris asked, fearful for his friend. "I've never seen Keilani that mad before."

"It's normal," Kaya replied offhandedly. "I've just gotta keep away from her until she cools down, or I will be hurting. Keilani can be the nicest person you'll ever meet, but when she gets angry… She broke my leg once when I was eight 'cause I scratched her lightboard. Needless to say, I've learned to hide well."

Iris's mouth was suddenly dry. "She might rip my ears off…"

"No she won't—we'll both be fine. But we should wait here for at least half an hour before we try to move. She'll catch us if we don't," Kaya explained. "Keilani's good at scouting."

Not the least bit comforted, Iris peered through the boughs littered with leaves and flowers to spy the clouded sky above. Minutes passed in silence, peace slowly returning to the creature's tiny heart. "Kaya?"

"¿Sí?"

"How are we gonna catch another sun beetle? We don't know any other First-Level Candidates who can photocache for us," Iris said worriedly.

Kaya breathed in the sweet scent of the flowers, sighing happily. "I guess we'll have to do it, then."

"But we're not allowed!" Iris breathed, his eyes a pair of violet saucers. "And even if we were, it's dangerous!"

"Don't you remember what Keilani said?" Kaya asked unflappably.

"Yeah—she said we all needed some serious help!"

"Not that!" she retorted quietly. "I mean what she said about Professor Shadowflame."

"You mean that she takes some classes out to photocache?" Iris asked. Kaya nodded knowingly. "But she won't take us out 'til after Christmas! That's too long!"

"Why? Manny's not gonna die without his sun beetle. He's got enough light as it is," she mumbled.

"You're real funny." Iris glared sidewise at Kaya, who smiled wryly. "How do you know we'll be the ones to find the photocache, anyway? I mean, the whole class will be hunting for it!"

"Then I guess we'd better practice before that time comes," Kaya whispered resolutely.

"We need to get down from the tree, first," Iris said dryly.

"No we don't!" Reaching into her jade satchel Kaya pulled out Iris's copy of *The Science of Light.* "You need to get ready for the dissection tomorrow—we can start now and practice cutting at my house later."

Iris shivered as his eyes met those of a peregrine falcon. "Alright, then."

Rapa Nui

Throughout the month of September Manny discovered that his academic success hinged on the amount of practice that he was willing to commit. He was grateful that Brun seemed to wield such a strong work ethic, which made studying infinitely easier, as both boys spent their evenings quizzing one another regarding the origins of Lumen society, the seemingly endless facets of the eye, and the cosmic stories that Chiron covered three nights each week. Yet for all this studying, Manny found the most pleasure in the time he spent molding light into whatever shape that crossed his mind, ever steadily competing with Brun to see who could make the most accurate figures.

"How do you always get your shapes to be so perfectly smooth?" Brun asked one afternoon at the end of the month. "Mine are either bumpy or stick out funny at one end or the other."

"I don't know—how do you always remember all those random details about Lumen history and the Light Brethren?" Manny responded.

"Because they're interesting—I like to study society," answered Brun.

"Well, I guess I like making things," Manny concluded.

In spite of his principal misgivings toward Caleida Flores, Manny came to appreciate his experiences in the Southeast Garden, particularly once he was able to forget his anger for Kaya, opening the door for a breakthrough in chromatic articulation. Kaya, for her part, struggled in her attempts to deviate from her original two-color palate, though her contempt for Manny subsided into a silent civility, forced by the necessity to pass this least favorite of all classes.

"Kaya—spectacular!" Flores had exclaimed the day Kaya succeeded in tinting a triangle red. "All Lumens need love to survive!"

Opening her eyes, Kaya stared at the crimson triangle, which flashed orange the moment she noticed Manny staring from across

311

the table. As Manny turned away, chuckling, his own triangle flickered yellow.

"Ten! I've got ten!" Nate cried one evening in early October atop Lookout Point.

Manny blew into the air. "Well, I've got fifteen!"

"I bet you can't beat these two, though!" Brun said confidently. Manny and Nate spun around to find a pair of Fireflies, each the size of a soccer ball, hovering just over Brun's shoulders.

"Show off…" Manny muttered, his own squadron of mite-like Fireflies buzzing about his head.

Midway through October, during a typical noontime session of Light Bending, Nochesol exclaimed the two words that Manny had been hoping to hear since the first week of classes—luminous clusters.

"This is incredible!" Manny whispered effervescently to Brun and Nate.

"Provided that you hone your senses and lend me your entire focus, each of you will leave this deck today with the ability to create mass by means of dense photon grouping," Nochesol said, his gilded-violet eyes sweeping over the balcony of students. Manny sat extra straight on his bench as the instructor continued. "Based on your performance this past month, I can now truthfully attest that each one of you on this platform is capable of molding light into transparent shapes; however, today I wish to teach you how to fold streams of photons over upon themselves, to crowd them into a limited space to such an extent that your desired figure achieves mass. Let us begin by forming orbs."

Manny and his companions obeyed their instructor precipitously, siphoning numerous ribbons of sunlight through the dark clouds above. In spite of the Amazonian downpour, no student found himself wanting for shelter; for prior to class Nochesol had shielded the deck with a canopy of light.

"Good—very good," Nochesol approved. "Now, wrap your mind around the orb and draw down a steady stream of photons, packing them into the sphere until it is opaque." Nochesol strode about the deck, his scarlet cape brushing the dark timbers as his

312

glittering eyes monitored the progress of his students. "Don't allow your orb to grow, Tobias!" the instructor said as he approached the otter. "You must focus your thoughts to limit the orb's size. Compress it!"

"Sí, Señor," Tobias said, squinting his eyes as his sphere began to shrink.

"Much better," Nochesol stated as he proceeded about the deck.

I've almost got it. Manny took a deep breath, stabilizing his orb's size and gazing intently as the sphere became a solid, pale white. "I did it," he gasped.

"Excellent work!" said Nochesol in amazement.

A smile wove across Manny's face. "Gracias, Prof—"

"I've never seen any student cluster three orbs on their first try, much less two! Serena, that's wonderful!" Nochesol shouted.

Three orbs? Manny's sphere burned orange as he caught sight of the tiny chinchilla at the instructor's feet.

"My goal is to be just like Andrés Dosfilos, Professor!" Serena proclaimed, directing the orbs to spin about in the air. "I heard he's a master at Light Bending!"

"I should say that you are very much on your way, sister!" Nochesol said enthusiastically. The chinchilla beamed as she united the three orbs into a single, triangular mass.

Manny glanced at his pitiful, palm-sized orb, which faded to blue and dissolved.

"What did you do that for?" Brun cried, his orb flashing orange. "Yours was perfect!"

"No it wasn't," Manny muttered morosely. "Not compared to Serena's, at least."

"Big deal if she made three orbs on her first try—you could make ten if you actually worked at it, Manny!" Brun said. Manny merely stared at his feet; suddenly a punch tore at his left biceps.

"What was that for?" Manny growled, rubbing his arm.

"I just wanted to bring you back to reality, seeing as you'd left it," Brun said brusquely. "You know just as well as I do that you can cluster as many orbs as you want—all you have to do is keep trying and not give up like you did just now."

Several seconds passed as Manny stared at his companion, whose hazel eyes blazed intensely in those dark sockets framed with white hair. A fist flew at Manny's arm the moment he lowered his eyes, but this time he caught it.

"I'm not gonna let you give up, Manny," Brun said, pushing firmly against Manny's palm.

"Chill out, man—I was just reaching down to pick up my wand," Manny replied coolly. "I dropped it."

"I—you—wow," Nochesol stuttered three minutes later when he finally reached the east side of the deck. The man stood in utter fascination at the dense collection of orbs floating before him—so dense, in fact, that he could not see which student had produced them.

"There are thirty-two clusters Professor," Nate pointed out. "Or at least there were the last time I counted."

"But who—?"

"Brun Dimirtis, Señor," Araceli said dreamily.

"And Manny López," Nate said, sending a crosswise frown to the girl.

Nochesol swallowed hard. "Well, brothers, I should say that the two of you definitely passed your in-class assignment today."

Looking left, Manny smiled to Brun, who winked back knowingly.

"Can you guys teach me to do that?" asked a soft voice that appeared suddenly at their feet. It was Serena.

"No problem," Manny replied, his confident words falling kindly into the chinchilla's ears. "Be at Chiron's Hutch this evening around ten—we can practice 'til Astronomy starts."

"Awesome!" the chinchilla exclaimed, her fur flaring out thickly. "I'll be there!"

Once he had regained his composure, Nochesol asked Manny and Brun to walk around the circle and help their classmates cluster orbs with increasing ease. This they did, and by the end of the session, the entire class held the boys in high esteem.

Manny beamed as he returned to his bench. *Brun was right.*

That was fun. Brun stared contently at the yellow cluster hovering before him.

Nochesol coughed, standing tall and straightening his cloak. "I must say that this has definitely been the most successful meeting of the year—I encourage each of you to continue your hard work," he added, glancing significantly at Brun and Manny. "But before you leave today, Director Rumblefeather has asked me to remind you of the annual Easter Island Lightboarding Competition sponsored by the LIGHT Group, which is to be held on October 21. In order to attend you must bring a permission slip with your parent or guardian's signature on it. We will depart from the subterranean river-way just inside the entrance to Nightcrest Caverns beginning at four o'clock that evening. Bring a few Sols for some food and remember to bring your signed permission slip! Have a good weekend!"

"¡Oye! Brun! Millie and I are planning on going to the competition together—we're gonna meet at four. Would you and Manny like to go with us?" Araceli asked brightly.

"Sorry, Araceli, but we can't. Manny and I aren't leaving until five or later," Brun answered.

"Oh, well maybe we'll see you there," she said sadly.

"Maybe," Brun replied.

Manny opened his mouth to speak, but Nate cut him off. "I guess that shuts down my invitation, then. Serge asked me to go with him and his cousins, and I thought you and Manny might want to go with us. We're taking off at four, too."

Brun glanced at Araceli, her coffee eyes sparkling intently. **Dang.** "Sorry. Like I said, Manny and I can't leave until five."

"That's too bad," Nate replied.

Taking advantage of the silence, Manny elbowed Brun in the ribs. "What in the world are you talking about?" he whispered, irate. "I want to go with Nate and Serge!"

"We'll talk about it later," Brun mumbled through his teeth, nodding significantly toward Araceli on his right.

"Are you two alright?" she asked.

"Sí," Brun responded quickly.

I'm not.

***

"I told you that I don't want to be around Araceli—we have every single class together!" Brun set his backpack down below his hammock. "I don't want to spend the most exciting night of the year sitting next to her! She'll drive me nuts!"

"I still don't see what that has to do with Nate and Serge!" Manny cut back.

"Manny, if I'd told Nate that we could go, it would've hurt Araceli's feelings," Brun said flatly.

Manny opened his eyes wide. "And...?"

Brun glared back. "And I don't like to hurt others, okay?"

"Okay, so why don't we ask Nate if they can leave later," Manny suggested. "Then we won't have to worry about Araceli."

"I'm not going to ask Serge's family to wait on us—that's rude!" Brun argued.

"What you did to me was rude!" Manny shot back.

Brun stared solemnly across the room at Manny before turning and walking out the door. "Nipper, ¡ven!" he called loudly. "Come here!"

Not that stupid flytrap again. Incensed, Manny stomped outside. "I hate it when people ignore me."

"So I've noticed," Brun replied, his back to Manny.

But before Manny could respond, he choked, shocked by the sight that met his eyes. From the ferns emerged Nipper, her jaws chomping customarily, and on her head rode a black salamander littered with yellow spots. *Lil' Manny?* Nipper wound past Brun and stopped in front of the other boy, glancing up with a chomp. The salamander mirrored the flytrap, lifting his snout and biting his jaws with a loud squeak.

"You've turned against me too?" Manny asked, betrayed.

Brun laughed. "Lil' Manny hasn't turned against you, he's just made a friend!"

316

He doesn't have the best taste in friends, then. You'd think he'd have chosen a mudpuppy or something. Nevertheless, Manny could not help but chuckle. "What an odd pair."

***

Manuel,

Yes, your father and I are glad you can make those cluster things—keep up the great work. I'm not so sure, however, about this outing to Easter Island. Isn't that in the middle of the Pacific Ocean? I'm sure it is; in which case, you won't be safe outside the limits of Isla Verde. I don't want you going unless Chiron plans to be there, too.

Have him write me a letter, would you?

Te amo,

Mamá

"Chiron, mi mamá won't let me go to Easter Island unless you come with us. Are you planning on going?" Manny asked, lowering the glowing letter and handing it to Brun.

"Sí, I will be present, but I am a judge," the centaur replied as he glanced up from his plate laden with a substantial strip of carne asada walled in by a mountain of fennel. "If she is concerned about your protection, however, I would be happy to inform her that an identical barrier exists about the sector of the island that we will be occupying, so you will be completely safe."

"¡Gracias, Chiron! That would be great!" Manny rebounded.

"You are welcome," Chiron said, slicing the steak. "Now eat your dinner, both of you."

Manny's soul flashed in contentment as the taste of excitement followed by that of savory steak slid into the depths of his stomach. *Yes!*

"You're a good cook, Chiron," Brun said, swallowing his first bite.

"Thank you," the centaur replied, his eyes not leaving the plate. "I try."

"You're not still mad at me over leaving later, are you?" Brun asked as he and Manny trekked through the forest north of the hut, following a thin tendril of the Lucero.

"Nah—we're good," Manny replied, his eyes wandering through the underbrush and hanging moss on either side of the soundless stream. "I get where you're coming from."

"Good deal," Brun said, relieved.

"Hold up—what are these?" Manny asked, stopping abruptly under a wing of moss that, for some particular reason, glinted blue and red rather than green.

"Oh—those?" Brun said, extending his hand to the reflective curtain. A stream of glassy insects crawled along his fingers from the moss to his palm. "The red ones are Ladybugs and the blue ones are Gentlebugs."

Manny blinked as he digested this answer. "Gentlebugs?" he snorted. "So I guess they're the boys?"

"Of course," Brun replied matter-of-factly, lifting a sapphire specimen to his nose. "Like gentlemen. Do you have Lady and Gentlebugs in the outside world?"

Unable to thwart his war-mongering smile, Manny said, "Oh, we've got ladybugs—but the boys are red."

"That's just weird," Brun concluded, shaking his hand and watching the insects scatter into the air like colorful beads. "The outside world sounds dull sometimes—excluding baseball, that is. And cave exploring. Those sound fun."

"Well, when you come to visit we can do those things," Manny said decisively as they resumed their stream side passage.

"I don't think I can," Brun murmured, his words floating deadly to the ground among the ruby and sapphire bugs.

"Why not? You'd love it!"

Brun's eyes were unwavering. "Mi papá is really protective, remember?"

Manny shrugged. "So's mi mamá, but here I am."

"I'm lucky just to have come this far," Brun confessed.

I guess I am, too.

After a silent minute of hiking the boys came to a shallow pond where a knee-high creature ran about, somewhat frantically.

"Hola, Tobias," Manny greeted the otter. "Is something wrong?"

Tobias spun around, then toppled over backwards into the water, startled by the appearance of his human classmates. Yet he did not immediately reappear, prompting Manny to step forward. "He's surely not drowning, is he?" Manny asked Brun.

"No—otters swim, Manny," Brun said obviously.

Well, duh. Manny furrowed his brow as he knelt down to the water, searching the muddy bottom with his eyes. A moment later the otter's head materialized on the surface of the pond, sending a thin stream from its adequately whiskered mouth and straight into Manny's expectant face.

"I'm sorry," said Tobias in his typically playful voice. "I normally don't have anyone waiting on me at the edge of the water."

Brun laughed. Manny turned and threw back a frown.

"Isn't your name Manny?" Tobias asked, paddling in place.

"Sí," Manny spat.

"That's what I thought." the otter replied, his whiskers fidgeting. "And you're Brun?"

The dark-skinned boy nodded.

"A-okay. Got your names, then. Could both of you help me? I'm in some real trouble." Tobias said, his olive green eyes shining dully.

"What's up?" Brun asked, his hands in his pockets.

"This is really embarrassing, but—I lost my wand," the otter whispered.

Manny swallowed, the taste of mud lingering in between his teeth. "How?"

"Well, my brothers and I decided to swim in this pool 'til 4:30," Tobias began. "That's when we were supposed to head for Nightcrest Caverns. But, you see, as we started off west, I noticed my shell necklace was missing—which is my wand, of course. I told Michael and Ursa to wait for me, but they left anyway. So I've been here hunting for my wand for nearly half-an-hour, and I can't find it."

"You've checked the pond thoroughly?" Brun asked.

"Scoured it," Tobias replied. "It's not here."

"Maybe you left it at your house," Manny proposed.

"No way—I remember it clacking when we were running and swimming along the river north of here," Tobias affirmed.

Brun processed this information. Manny spoke. "Did you take the necklace off before you got in the pool?"

Tobias blinked, his words sinking below the water. "I can't remember."

"I have an idea," Brun said optimistically. "I'll go ahead to the caverns and save us a boat. That'll give you guys a little extra time to search the area without worrying about being left behind. If you're not there by six I'll send out a letter, so bolt straight to the caves if that happens. Sound good?"

The otter nodded. "So Manny will stay and help me?"

"Yes," Brun answered, but Manny stood up and walked over to him.

"Why can't I hold the boat? Manny whispered.

Brun glanced back coolly. "We both know I'm a better people person. And besides, you have experience searching for wands—remember what happened at Tavo's?"

Manny glared back, slightly offended and speechless.

"Good luck, amigo!" Brun said, patting Manny on the shoulder. "I'll see you both at the entrance to Nightcrest Caverns—with your wand, Tobias!"

"Gracias, Brun!" the otter shouted as Brun melted into the mossy foliage in the direction of the Argo Dock. "You're a lifesaver, Manny!" Tobias added passionately.

"You know it," Manny said, his attempt at enthusiasm savoring strongly of impatience. The boy inhaled deeply. *We can do this.* "Okay. This is what I think we should do—just to be sure, you comb the pond again, but this time feel for mud pockets where the necklace might be. I'll rifle through the undergrowth around the pond, and if we still don't find it, we'll head further north along the stream."

"Alright," Tobias agreed, diving obediently into the water as Manny made for the elephantine shrubbery on his left.

An hour later Manny and Tobias stood in the center of the rivulet on a solitary moon lily pad, scanning north and south along the flow of the water. The otter had tears in his eyes. The boy sighed. *Brun's going to be sending that letter any minute.*

"Lo siento, Tobias," Manny said apologetically, "but we've searched up and down the stream, and the wand just isn't here." The otter let out a strangled sob, his pale eyes set on the pink lily floating nearby. *Ugh. I hate this. Why couldn't we find it?* "We're not gonna make it to the caverns if we don't leave now—we came pretty far north."

"I kn-know," Tobias choked, "but you remember what Professor Nochesol said if we lost our wands, don't you?"

Manny's mind was set on the caverns. "Yeah—he said it would be pretty bad," the boy replied distractedly.

"More than bad—horrible! I won't even be able to attend class if I don't find it! I can't be a Lumen without it!" Tobias shook, his desperation building.

"Listen, Tobias—we'll find your wand. I promise." Manny knelt down and set his hand on the otter's damp shoulder. "But we're gonna miss the lightboarding competition if we don't leave now."

"You'll help me?" Tobias asked, looking up.

"Yes—I lost my wand once, and it scared me half to death. I know how you feel," the boy replied, standing tall again.

321

"Gracias, Manny. Let's go, then," the otter said, a shadow of confidence returning. "Can you run fast?"

Manny hopped onto the bank. "Yeah, why?"

"It will probably be faster if I ride on your shoulders," Tobias suggested.

With a half-shrug, Manny said, "Okay."

***

"It's six o'clock, young man," called the coarse voice of an otter captain from across the rapid flowing river, the force of the surging water rebounding off the smooth walls of the rocky tunnel. "If you're riding to the island we need to leave now."

"Just one second, Señor, please," Brun entreated as he pulled a sheet of shining paper from his back pocket. "I'll tell my friends to hurry—I know they'll be here any moment."

"Young 'un, we must depart—stragglers may come, but they ne'er go nowhere," the captain pressed, his voice a shade gruffer now.

"Look! I'm done with the letter," Brun attested as it shot from his hands and around the corner.

Before the otter captain could argue his point any further, a startled yell followed by a sharp yelp resounded in the stone corridor. The next second Brun discerned a dove cry and a heavy thud.

"What in blue sparks is going on out there?" the otter captain roared, more concerned than riled—though Brun could not make this fine distinction, not knowing the captain personally.

"Um, I think my friends were a little closer than I thought," Brun answered as he jogged around the bend and along the tunnel into the waning sunlight. On the grass sat Manny, puffing, the letter in his lap; while behind him Tobias lay flat on his back, staring at the crimson sky.

"Were you trying to kill us?" Manny asked.

"Aren't you hilarious." Brun pulled Manny to his feet. "Hurry up, 'cause this river otter in here doesn't seem to have any patience at all.

Tobias rolled to his feet. "So there's not any time for me to swim over to the Café to grab a snack?" His tiny stomach growled as his gaze ran along the rock face to the lakeside restaurant.

"No," Brun retorted, spinning abruptly and reentering the cavern, Manny at his heels.

However reluctantly, Tobias followed, soon reaching a fork in the tunnel. He turned the corner. "I'd really like some oysters…" Tobias thought aloud as he approached the subterranean river dock.

"Oysters!" the captain half-barked, half-laughed. "I'd like an honest word from you, young pup!" The captain smiled. "You told me that you and your brothers would be riding the river at five. But 'ere y'are, at five past six, w' a pair o' boys I never met, one o' which his skin burns red like he's on fire!" The captain's eyes shone brightly. "So what's your word, tyke?"

Brun and Manny looked wide-eyed at one another before glancing back at Tobias, who dropped to four legs and bolted forward quickly. "Papá, they were helping me—"

"Get yerself lost?" the adult roared with laughter, hopping from the far bank to the wide, wooden ferry. "Ah, Tobias—"

"He did lose something, if that counts for anything," Manny tried to explain, still unaware of the captain's playful tone.

"Hold up, boy," said the father otter, raising a paw. *Ay caramba.* "You lost something, Tobias?" he asked, his eyes falling on his son with concern.

"Yes," Tobias confessed. "And it's not good, Papá."

"No matter what it was, we can replace it," the father encouraged. "T'was just an object, pure an simple, I'm sure. It's not like ya misplaced yer wand!"

Tobias's eyes fell to the floor. He said nothing further.

As the meaning of his son's silence reached his consciousness, the captain straightened, and his emerald eyes turned cold in quiet distress. "Into the ferry—the three of ya," he stated soberly. Tobias sadly obeyed. "What's wrong, gentlemen? Crawfish got yer toes?" the captain inquired, his eyes set firmly on the boys standing awkwardly in front of him.

"Nothing, sir," Brun said, climbing into the boat alongside Manny.

"Yowzers," Manny breathed as he and Brun sat down in the center of the boat. On the back bench, alone and with his head down, sat Tobias.

The father otter hopped to the prow of the vessel, then glanced back at his son. "Hey, tyke, come up by me." Tobias climbed morosely over the center bench and sat down next to his father. "No worries, pup," said the captain as he set a paw on his son's shoulder. "We'll tackle this situation yet." And with a reassuring grip the captain turned and shouted, "Flashbolt! Wetback! Are we ready?" A pair of pink river dolphins emerged from the water, cackling auspiciously. "Vámonos, pues."

"No! Wait!" cried a desperate voice from along the passage. "I'm coming, too!"

The captain turned his steely eyes to meet the small figure of a mahogany hare, its ears folded back and eyes glinting violet. "Get in, then, young leveret," bolstered the otter.

"Thank you, Sr. Greenriver," the hare replied. But just as he prepared to hop into the boat, the hare froze, his eyes locked on Manny's.

"Iris Firefoot, we cannot dawdle any longer. In or out, young 'un. In or out!" Captain Greenriver barked.

"I-I'll just wait for the next ferry," Iris opted with a hop backward.

"This ferry will be the last," Captain Greenriver clarified.

Iris hesitated, glancing at the bench behind Manny and Brun.

"Goodbye, Iris!" Captain Greenriver exclaimed, jerking the dolphins' golden chords with the shake of a wrist. The boat slid swiftly from the dock.

"I'm coming!" Iris shouted, exploding through the air and well over the height of the boys' heads to land on the bench behind them. Captain Greenriver shook his head with an invisible smile.

324

Manny's stomach performed a massive somersault as the vessel plunged into the tunnel, gathering speed as it delved hundreds of feet below the earth, the water occasionally splashing up over the side of the ferry and sprinkling the boy in the face. Yet in spite of the darkness, Brun's skin shone a fiery red, illuminating the walls with a rusty light. No one spoke.

"Whoa!" whooped Iris as the ferry abruptly leveled out, spraying each passenger generously. The walls passed by in a blur as the vessel redoubled its speed.

We've got to be going like a hundred miles an hour. Several minutes passed in this fashion, when Manny felt a nudge on his arm. "What?" he breathed.

Brun leaned in close. "You may not have much time."

Time for what? "Huh?" Manny whispered.

A sigh. "This may be your only chance to apologize, Manny."

Apolo—Oh. Manny threw his eyes over his shoulder, surreptitiously glancing at the hare seated on the bench behind, the creature's ears pinned down and paws locked tensely to the wooden beam. "When?"

"Soon," Brun breathed. "I don't know how long this trip will take."

A knot formed in Manny's throat, a sign of lingering guilt. *How do I do this?*

"And here we are!" Captain Greenriver cried as the ferry emerged from the tunnel like a wooden bullet. *We're there already?*

"No way! Look!" Brun said in awe as he pointed to the left. There, swimming gracefully alongside the ship, was a gargantuan, blue whale, its soft eye blinking subtly at the unexpected submarine guests. Manny's mouth dropped open as he gazed above, his eyes staring up through trillions of gallons of water to spy the bruised sky floating miles above. "Where are we?" Brun asked animatedly as he jumped to the other side of the ship, enthralled by a pack of shimmering squid.

A chuckle erupted from the captain. "Never traveled the EIC, then, I presume?"

"What's the EIC?" Manny asked, finally able to speak.

"That would be the Easter Island Current," elucidated Captain Greenriver.

"So are we under the Pacific Ocean?" Brun asked eagerly.

"Yes, young 'un, we are." The captain's words were gruff, yet happy.

Wow! "Will we get to see any merfolk?" Brun proceeded.

"Merfolk? Those are from fairy tales and movies," Manny stated dismissively.

"Perhaps to the limite' perspective o' the outer world," Captain Greenriver said wisely. "But to answer yer question, red one, I will say yes. There is an undersea colony scattered among the crags below Easter Island."

"You mean like Atlantis?!" Brun said, enthralled.

"That city is massive—and as its name implies, it is located in the Atlantic," the captain corrected.

Electricity pulsed through Brun's veins. "This is too cool, isn't it, Manny?"

"It's almost too much," the other boy replied, glancing down into the shadowy depths of an underwater canyon. *I'll crap my pants if a giant octopus comes flying out of there.*

"What are your names, boys?" Captain Greenriver asked.

"I'm Brun, and this is my roommate, Manny. We're staying with Chiron."

"He's a good centaur—an' a proficient angler, I'll 'ave t'admit," the otter captain said with a perceptive nod. "I guess you've already met my puckish pup, Tobias. I'm his father, Jasper Greenriver. Just call me Jasper, though."

"It's nice to meet you, Jasper." Brun reached forward and shook the otter captain's firm paw. "This trip is fantastic."

"Well, thank you very much, Brun," Jasper rejoined, his cheeks wrought with a smile. "That's wha' I like to hear—and you've got a lot more to go."

"We do?" Manny asked.

"Sure—nearly an hour," Jasper replied.

Over the next ten minutes Brun discovered that the EIC traveled along an oxygen tunnel installed by the stars when lightboarding first became a popular pastime in the mid 16th century. The boy nearly tipped the vessel the moment a pair of blue knights appeared, the massive creatures passing swiftly below the keel before vanishing into the darkness of the canyon below. Puzzled, Manny inquired as to the exact definition of the blue knight, because the only connection that he could make was to the Loch Ness monster. Jasper explained that the blue knights and Nessie were of the same species—that of the plesiosaur, an ancient water lizard. "In fact, Nessie is actually the oldest blue knight in existence," Jasper had asserted. "A real wise lady of the sea." At this Manny cradled his head, boggled by the idea that any exemplars of the Jurassic era still existed. Eventually, however, Brun returned to his seat to watch his first-person aquatic tour in silent serenity.

A tug. *Huh?* Manny's conscience whispered to his heart. He sighed, raising his head and observing over his shoulder as Iris leaned over the side of the craft, the hare's face alight at yet another cloud of colorful squid. The boy took a deep breath. "Iris?"

The words stole the smile from the hare's mouth. His amaranth eyes slid around to glance suspiciously at the boy. Iris said nothing.

"I want to apologize for what I said back in August that night along the snake path—I was mean and cruel, and I understand why you and Kaya have been avoiding me. She was right—I was a real jerk. I hope you can forgive me." At once the ice of Manny's guilt melted in his chest in sweet relief. *I did it.*

Iris turned and stared into the depths of the ocean, his ears hanging over the lip of the bench. *Oh, well.* Lifting his eyes to the roof of the ocean, Manny watched as the sun rays etched an elegant pink design across the waters. *I hope this competition is fun.*

"Do you really mean it?"

Looking back around, Manny found that the hare had turned to face him. "You mean my apology?" Manny asked. Iris nodded. "For sure—I wouldn't lie about that."

"Then I forgive you," Iris said, his honest eyes staring across into Manny's. "How about we be friends?" he asked, extending his arm to the boy.

Manny was speechless for the second time that day. "S-sure," he finally managed to say, offering his hand. Iris smiled and shook it happily, his ears pricking up a little. "But what made you change your mind about me so fast?"

"I've been watching you, Manny, and how you treat other people," Iris answered, "and I've noticed that you help others, like when that unicorn in our healing class accidentally knocked the human eye across the glade and into the bushes, you ran and got it for her. Not to mention the fact that you kept my book safe for me when I dropped it."

Manny's words tumbled out in surprise. "Oh—well, thanks, Iris."

"No problem—it's just the truth. And sorry for running away from you in the Café that day. I bet you were trying to apologize then, weren't you?"

"Sí, I was. But if I were you, I probably would've run, too."

Iris laughed, the last of his inhibitions leaving him. "So, since we're already on the topic of the Café, what's your favorite food, Manny?"

"My favorite food? That's a tough question, 'cause I like to eat." Manny was pleased with the suddenly sanguine tenor of their conversation. "I really like tamales, but I think pupusas would have to be at the top of the list—pupusas stuffed with lots of pork." Memories from the boy's childhood burst into his mind as he considered an infinity of evening meals wrought by his mother's hands.

"Me, too!" Iris stated in accord. "I order pupusas all the time. But not with pork, of course. Just cheese and veggies."

"I'll admit, those are good, too," Manny noted positively. "Maybe you can come with Brun and me to the Café tomorrow for lunch. It'll be Friday, and since we have a three-day weekend, we could go in early!"

"I'd like to, Manny, but on Friday's I have lunch at Kaya's," Iris said, a bit disappointed.

"We could all meet at the Café, but I don't think Kaya would be very keen on the idea. She only talks to me when she has to," Manny explained, his words thudding flatly onto the bottom of the boat.

"No, she really doesn't like you," Iris confessed, the bluntness of which made Manny chuckle. "What?"

"Nothing, it's just funny to hear you say it that way. It's obvious she can't stand me."

"People change their minds, you know."

"Some people. So why didn't she come with you to the competition? Isn't Keilani one of the key players?"

"It's a long and interesting story, but for time's sake, I'll just say that Kaya was grounded for breaking Keilani's board in half," the hare declared wryly.

"Are you serious?!" Manny's words pelted Iris's face in disbelief. "I bet Keilani nearly killed her!"

"If their dad hadn't stepped in, she probably would have. In any case, Kaya's parents made her leave with them at four, and I wasn't allowed to come along. Her mom said Kaya needed to learn to appreciate family time. Boy, was Kaya ticked."

You don't have to tell me twice. "So do you have anyone to sit by?"

"No. I was hoping to find an instructor and sit with them. That's what my dad told me to do."

Manny blinked oddly. "Professor Firefoot? But why didn't he come?"

"He doesn't like lightboarding," Iris answered quietly.

"Huh," Manny mumbled. "Why don't you sit with Brun and me, then?"

The hare's ears fired into the air and curled forward. "Can I really?"

Manny punched Brun on the shoulder. "Yeah. This guy won't mind. Will ya, man?"

329

"Won't mind what?" the other boy asked, peeling his eyes from a wave of manta rays.

"Iris is gonna sit with us tonight during the competition!" Manny asserted.

"Great!" Brun bolstered. Iris beamed.

Throughout the remainder of the trip the boys and the hare chatted animatedly about the countless specimens of submarine life that crossed their path, hoping one day to have the chance to study them in a closer fashion, perhaps one-on-one. Virtually no time seemed to have passed when the shadow of an island cast the subaqueous vessel into sheer darkness; in an instant Iris converted his amaranth ear band into a wand, drawing light from beyond the shadows to form five misty saffron fireflies, one for each passenger. Seconds before the boat surfaced on the northwest side of the island, Brun lurched forward, pointing to a series of ornately carved, shell-clad homes built into the subaquatic cliffs. To his dismay, however, there were no merfolk to be found.

"No worries, briny Brun, ya might spot one enjoying the competition from the waves," Jasper consoled him. "And we're here!" the captain cried as the ship burst from the water, gliding smoothly toward a dock reaching out from the tip of an extensive, crescent-shaped cove. "Welcome to the Bay of Rapa Nui!"

Rays of blood and fire cast their burning light on the white-sanded beaches and up the grassy hill to a rocky peak, now framed by the growing twilight. Thousands of Lumens seemed to have gathered for the competition, covering the upper beaches and the majority of the mountainside like a tide of anxious ants, rushing to and fro in search of food and open space for viewing. "There sure are a lot of people," Manny observed, very nearly overwhelmed, as he, Brun, and Iris leapt from the boat.

"Can I go with them, Papi?" Tobias asked as he looked longingly toward the three friends on the pier.

"No, son," Jasper answered, though his voice was not stern. "I think it's best that you stay here with me tonight. We need to discuss some things."

330

The young otter's heart sank below the breaking waves. "See you later, guys," he called toward the boys and the hare.

"Bye, Tobias!" Manny yelled encouragingly. "I'll keep my promise. Come to Chiron's Hutch when you can."

"Nice meetin' ya, boys!" Jasper barked. "Enjoy yourselves!"

"Okay, thanks for the ride and the guided tour!" Brun called.

"So where are we gonna sit?" Manny asked as they stepped from the pier onto the sand.

"Why not up there?" Iris suggested, signaling with an ear toward the upper slopes of the mountain.

"We really don't have much choice," Brun said dryly. "The hill's packed."

Manny's eyes found the tent for concessions, utterly besieged by hungry Lumens, just a little way up the hill. "Dang—I was hoping for a snack."

"Don't worry, guys," Iris encouraged as he led the way up the mountain, along the northern edge of the crowd. "I packed my satchel full of burritos and taquitos before I left, so we'll have plenty to eat."

Manny glanced down at the khaki shoulder bag at Iris's side. *Resourceful little guy, isn't he?*

Twenty minutes passed before the threesome was able to find an open space, which happened to be a solitary cliff with a panoramic view of the moon sliver bay, with the tide tinged a blazen rose by the sinking sun in the west. Well over a dozen massive stone heads—with long, square jaws, deep eyes, and rounded brows—stretched in a horizontal line along the ledge, gazing endlessly up to the peak looming overhead like a row of stern-faced storm clouds. Brun stepped forward and laid his hand on one of the sentry's massive noses.

"My aunt Liliana told me about these statues once." Brun's fingers ran along the wide pores in the dark stone, neither gray nor fully black. "She told me what they were called, but I forget…"

"Those are the moai," Iris stated congenially, leaning back and scanning the sentry line. "The Rapa Nui carved them out of basalt from the volcano behind us. I like seeing them every year."

Now didn't Jasper say something about that a minute ago? "What's a Rapa Nui?" Manny asked.

"Oh, the Rapa Nui are the natives of Easter Island. Actually, the real name of Easter Island is Rapa Nui—we just call it by the other name because some explorers discovered it a few hundred years ago on Easter; but the natives were here long before that," the hare elucidated.

"So we're on a volcano?" Brun turned to scrutinize the mountain's summit. **I hope it doesn't go off tonight.**

"Yeah, this volcano's called Ukisaru, which is connected to the Terevaka Volcano by the Piku River just on the other side. But we don't have anything to worry about," Iris bolstered as he noted Brun's startled expression. "None of the four volcanoes on the island is active nowadays."

"Do people live here?" Manny gazed past the Ukisaru toward the higher and wider shoulders of the Terevaka beyond. "On the island, I mean."

"Definitely, but not in the Bay of Rapa Nui. This is an exclusively Lumen sector of the island. The outside world isn't even aware that Ukisaru or the bay even exist," Iris said.

"But how can that be? They can see Ukisaru, can't they?" proffered Manny.

"No, they can't," Iris riposted. "An outsider can't set foot or even touch this part of the island. When an outsider stands along the edge of the Piku River, all they see is ocean."

Manny threw frustrated words into the air. "That doesn't make any sense at all."

"How do you think no one from the outside world has ever discovered Isla Verde?" Brun cut in. "Or the castle where I live on the Island of Marajó? It's because they can't see or touch them."

"But why?" Manny persisted.

"Because of the Light Brethren," Iris answered. "When the stars formed the EIC they also made a complex light barrier around Ukisaru and the Bay of Rapa Nui, rendering them invisible and concealing the space within. Dad tried to explain it to me once—he

332

said they wrinkled the air to make two distant points touch. It's got to do with advanced photodynamics and all that good stuff."

"I'll just stick to lightboarding for now." Manny shook his head.

"No, I've got one more thing to show you!" Iris bounced back toward the rock face, which was bounded by a species of grass that reached well beyond the hare's height. "You've gotta see this!"

The weeds scratched against the boys' jeans as they approached a stone wall composed of granite wrought into a myriad of shapes and figures. In the center a tall bird with a curved beak like a toucan reached out his wing toward a glowing man clad in a cloak. A collection of stars shone above a mountain, while large fish and wise-looking turtles populated the water below.

"Did the Rapa Nui carve these, too?" Brun felt the deep lines in the bird's head.

"Sí," Iris acknowledged quickly. "That's the birdman making peace with Aldis, the oldest member of the Brethren. A long time ago the Rapa Nui believed themselves to be part bird and part man. So when they created this memorial, they used a birdman to represent themselves."

"Are these called hieroglyphics, then?" Manny gazed on, highly intrigued.

"No, these are petroglyphs. You see how they pop out at you rather than sink into the stone like hieroglyphs? I think that's the difference," the hare revealed.

"Huh—you learn something new everyday." Brun ran his fingers down along the stone panel to measure the grooves that comprised the petrified water at his ankles.

Manny felt the soft point of one of the stars. "It seems never-ending for me. Learning, I mean. This whole Lumen world if full of unexpe—"

"My, My! What a crowd we have this evening!" erupted a honey sweet voice from the bay below, ergo drawing the boys' attention away from the petroglyphs. "Allow me to welcome you to the Annual Easter Island Lightboarding Competition, courtesy of the LIGHT Group! I'm Melody Nightvine, and I'll be your announcer for this evening, alongside Rush Stickgrip, of course! And now a brief message from our sponsor."

"Need some adventure in your life?" a squeaky voice rang up the mountain. "Are your nights and evenings growing dark and dull? With our wide range of photocaching and lightboard equipment, the LIGHT Group has the solution for you! Looking for explosive lightning bugs? We've got 'em! How about a miniboard for your son or daughter? You'll find those, too! With our virtually limitless directory of photocache challenges, you'll stay focused and your skills will remain sharp. Visit us at our outlet in the Isla Verde Plaza today! Now back to you, Melody."

"Thank you, Rush. Shall we meet our contenders. How many do we have?"

"Nearly two hundred," Rush squeaked.

"'Tis few, I must admit. Yes, few. But let us begin, in no particular order, mind you! First we have Tami Bristletail, an able kinkajou known for her Backside Indy 540's, followed by Keilani Bellastrata, a talented young woman with the habit of executing 50-50 Grinds while riding Fakie…

Manny and Brun leaned against a pair of moai situated near the edge of the cliff, while Iris sat between them, though the hare had scooted slightly back for his fear of heights. All three listened as the announcers enumerated a chain of biographies as the individual surfers waved to the crowd before lying down on their boards to catch the rip tide out into the increasingly turbulent waters.

"You guys ready for a snack?" Iris asked as Melody droned on, occasionally interrupted by Rush.

"Lay a burrito on me," Manny said eagerly.

"Me, too," concurred Brun.

"Phase One of the competition, featuring Board Tricks, has officially begun!" squeaked the tree frog when the final surfer got out among the waves nearly twenty minutes later. "This phase challenges our First-Level Candidates to execute as many tricks as possible while riding a single wave!"

"That's right, Rush! And our panel of judges, ranging from Lumen instructors to veteran lightboarders, will be judging each surfer's progress based upon the following statutes—Originality, Poise, and Style!" the kinkajou shouted.

"Yeah, yeah, get on with it," Iris said dimly.

"A little impatient, are we?" Manny glanced at the hare, a taquito in his paw.

"Kaya takes me to watch this stuff every night, so I think it's boring. She's obsessed with board tricks. What I'm looking forward to is Phase Two," Iris affirmed. "That's when the action starts."

"Action? You mean they do more than wave tricks?" Brun asked, surprised.

"For sure! Phase Two is when they duel—you know, go head to head on their lightboards to see who's the top fighter. They pull out all the best photokinetic attacks and everything. There are explosions, people thrown from their boards… It's incredible," Iris explained.

Manny was completely shocked. "Does anybody die?"

"No, the rules prevent you from going too far. If you get hurt there's a team of healers along the beach—not to mention the fact that Professor Bluebolt's one of the judges. Actually, the winner has to go up against him when it's all over, and if he beats him, he'll receive an enormous prize." Iris continued, his eyes now wide.

"The winner faces Bluebolt? How can a green basilisk even ride a lightboard?" Manny whipped back.

"His is small, to fit his frame," the hare replied simply.

"But he can fight?" Brun asked.

"Oh, can he…" Iris said. "Two years ago, just for fun, Bluebolt and Nochesol dueled, and you wouldn't believe the stunts they pulled. Sparks were flying everywhere…"

"Who won?" Manny asked.

"Nochesol," Iris stated flatly.

"How?" fished Brun.

"Well, in my eyes it was a draw, but Bluebolt forfeited so everyone could head home before morning. They fought for hours," Iris manifested.

Manny shook his head. "Imagine that."

Unlike the custom in Isla Verde, the lightboarders surfed well past sunset, gouging the breakers with all the skill they could muster. At roughly ten o'clock the three finalists were chosen—Dash Stickgrip, Severo Sandtail, and Keilani Bellastrata.

"Stickgrip, Sandtail, and Bellastrata! A most unexpected combination! But is it possible for this otter and young woman to outsurf the most skilled of tree frogs? We'll soon see!" Rush called from his post along the center of the beach.

"My, my, Rush! You sound a bit biased!" Melody came back loudly. "Should a father truly be announcing for his son this far into the competition?"

"Now let's not be bitter because your niece, Bristletail, was shut out by these able surfers! Watch yourself, Melody!" Rush retorted.

"Oh, I am, dear friend! But let's both take that wise piece of advice and proceed with the announcing, shall we? First up we have Stickgrip, catching a rip tide and performing a twirling duck dive to peel through the final wave and slide out just beyond the take off zone," Melody narrated. "From what I've seen tonight Stickgrip is choosy with his waves—"

"You bet his is!" Rush interrupted.

"—which has worked to his advantage," Melody continued, unperturbed. "Now here we are! It appears that Stickgrip has selected a prime swell, and he's well-trimmed, balanced and ready. Notice his excellent stance—very natural—as he builds speed, carving effortlessly along the face of the wave. The crest of the wave has now broken, forming a massive—Oh! What's Stickgrip doing? He seems to be dropping speed, and—he's entered the green room! Was this planned or did he simply begin to stall out?"

"Surely it was planned," Rush contributed, a twinge of doubt invading his tone, nonetheless.

Manny leaned forward. "You don't think he's gonna get caught in the tube, do you?"

"I don't know." Brun's eyes scanned the wave.

"Only inexperienced surfers wipe out in the green room, guys," juxtaposed Iris.

336

"Look! He's exploded from the barrel like a rocket, firing up over the lip of the wave and—what's this?" shouted Melody, hopping onto the announcers table far below. "He's ollied into the air, grabbing the backside of the board with his right paw and spinning backward—180, 360, 540, 720! A Heelgrab Vertical 720! What are our judges thinking now? We'll inform you of the results momentarily!"

"That was insane! How did he not fall off the board?" Manny barked.

"It had to be his momentum," Brun suggested.

"And the fact that he's a tree frog," added Iris.

Oh, yeah. **Well, duh.**

"Stickgrip scores a 2.9!" shrieked Rush. "That's a tenth from perfection!"

"Very nice, I'll admit. The best I've seen tonight," Melody added. "Prime suspense, Stickgrip! That definitely swayed the judges in the Style category."

"Our next surfer is Sandtail, a river otter originally from the area of Iguazú Falls in northern Argentina, an excellent locale for lightboarding," Rush noted.

"Of course," Melody agreed.

"Isn't Iguazú where the Second and Third-Level Academy is located?" Brun asked, turning back to glance at Iris, who nodded.

"I've been there," the hare replied. "And it's amazing. You wouldn't believe how big the waterfalls are there. The Lucero is a pipsqueak—even during flood season—compared to Iguazú."

"We have a flood season in Isla Verde?" Manny queried.

"You didn't know that nearly the whole Amazon River Basin floods during part of the year?" Iris responded dubiously.

"No—I've never even seen a flood, 'cause in Arizona it's pretty dry," Manny answered.

"Really? So do you live in a desert?" Iris continued.

"Actually, yes. It's called the Painted Desert, but it's not just sand. There are a lot of rocks and cliffs, too," Manny explained. "And at sunset, all the rocks and the ground shine different colors. I miss seeing it."

"Well, I'll come visit you at Christmas or next summer so I can see it!" Iris affirmed. "I need to get out of the rainforest for a while. My dad drives me crazy."

"That would be really cool, Iris! I'm sure my cousin Zane would love to meet you. He hopes to start at the Academy next…"

Neither of them noticed, but Brun's head sagged as he turned away, his eyes searching the dark waves south of the island as Sandtail drifted up to the beach at the heart of the bay.

"This is absolutely unbelievable, folks! Sandtail, the underdog, has a 2.93! He's overtaken Stickgrip!" Melody sang. The crowd boomed. "That Rock and Roll Grind followed by the Frontside Kickflip with 360 Varial and Railstand stole the show! Who knew a lightboarder could surf on the rail like that?!"

"Simply riveting," croaked Rush unwillingly.

"…oh, yeah, back to that. The flood season begins a little into November, but it takes months for the whole valley to fill up. When it does, though, you should go check out the Flooded Forest to the south of the island—there are fish swimming between the branches of the trees!" Iris described, his ears raised in excitement.

"No way!" Manny shouted.

"But moving on to our final contestant for Phase One, we look to Bellastrata, native to Isla Verde…" Rush proceeded hastily.

"Oh—it's Keilani," Iris said, breaking the flow of the conversation. "I'd better pay attention or Kaya will kill me, even if she is furious with her sister right now."

Brun stood up and walked around the other side of the moai as Keilani shot along the rip tide into calmer waters.

Manny turned, his eyes meeting his roommate's back. "You okay, Brun?"

"Sí, I just want to stretch my legs for a minute," he replied quietly.

"There'll be a break when Keilani gets done if you wanna wait a minute," Iris said good-naturedly.

"No, está bien," Brun answered as he walked toward the petroglyphs. "That's okay." Rush's voice faded slightly as Brun sat down in the grass, staring up at the weatherworn carvings of the

Rapa Nui. The boy took a deep breath as he felt the cool shell of the sea turtle, forever frozen in front of him. **Manny's good at art—I bet he could carve stone like this someday. Not me, though. I'd rather study animals and people.** He raised his hand to the open mouth of a whale, his fingertips rubbing its bumpy tongue, which shined red in the boy's light. **I know that some turtles are Lumens, but what about whal—**

A trickle of pebbles rolled down from the cliff above, slapping Brun's back and scattering his thoughts. The boy jumped to his feet, stepping back and searching the ledge with sharp eyes. The swirl of his spirit in his chest told him something was up there, watching him, but the grass blocked his view. "Who's there?" Brun asked, his voice gruff. An intake of breath drew Brun's attention to the right, but the person, or creature, had disappeared, leaving only a wave of dancing weeds. A tug at his pants made the boy spin around.

"You like looking at the stars, Brun?" Iris asked.

Manny noticed the startled expression on Brun's face. "Did we scare you?"

"I just thought I heard something on top of the ledge, above the petroglyphs," Brun said quietly. "I felt like it was staring at me."

"Probably a mountain lion, ready to pounce on you," Iris joked.

"They have mountain lions on Easter Island?" Brun rejoined, missing the humor in the hare's voice.

"Not unless they swam here." Iris offered a wide smile.

Oh. "So who won?" Brun asked, forgetting the perceived threat.

"Sandtail," the hare and the boy replied dully.

"What happened to Keilani?" Brun rebounded quickly.

"She got caught in the soup," Manny said bluntly.

In the soup? "What's that mean?"

"It means she wiped out and the waves crashed over her, like boiling soup," Iris clarified. "Her problem was she ollied too high into the air when she executed her shove-it. The board did spin, of course, like it was supposed to, but instead of landing on the deck her toes grazed the rail and the wave swallowed her. It makes me glad I'm sitting up here with you guys instead of down there with her family in the danger zone—Keilani's gonna blow the second she makes it to the beach."

"I do feel bad for her, though…" admitted Brun.

"Don't worry about it—Sandtail may have the trophy for Phase One, but Keilani can still kick some butt in Phase Two," said Iris, his fire renewed. "You won't believe what she can do with her wand! A month ago she made a light whip with it and snagged Kaya by the ankle!"

"Whew! Those two are just crazy. If I had a brother I wouldn't fight with him like that," Manny affirmed.

"You're an only child?" the hare asked.

"Yep. But at least I have Zane. We hardly ever fight." *Except for the week before I left…*

"What about you, Brun?" Iris inquired.

"Same here—no siblings. At home the only person I can hang with is Liliana, mi tía. And Nipper, too. She's my pet flytrap," Brun explained. Iris seemed to wince and shake his foot uncomfortably. **What's he doing…?**

"We all have one thing in common, then!" the hare said swiftly, hoping to forget a most unpleasant memory. "We're only children."

"Huh," Manny mumbled distractedly. "I don't want to change the subject, but do you guys want to walk around a little before the next round starts? I'm gettin' a bit stir-crazy."

Iris and Brun agreed. Before descending the mountain to stretch their legs, they all decided to explore the southern end of the ledge from which they had been viewing the competition. After approximately two hundred steps, however, the ridge came to an all too abrupt halt.

"Now that's a long drop," Manny observed, his eyes bouncing down the belly of the mountain to land on the heads of the spectators below.

Iris refused to come too close. "Why don't we just hop down the other way, then?"

By this time the sky was completely masked in a sheet of star-studded velvet, and the moon had not yet produced itself. Manny was yet again disappointed to see the concessions tent inaccessible, but Iris kindly reminded him that there were still several burritos in his satchel. With a sigh the boy resigned to climb back up the mountain, arriving just minutes before eleven o'clock, when Phase Two was to begin.

Resurrecting the flow of their previous conversation, Manny turned to Iris. "So what's your mom like? I never see her with your dad."

"That's because she's dead," the hare replied frankly.

"I'm sorry," Manny quickly responded. *Me and my big mouth.*

"That's okay. She disappeared when I was five, back in Europe, so I really don't remember her very well. Dad said she was a brilliant biologist, and that her sentinels were even better than his, and that's saying a lot. He also said I have her eyes, and her laugh," Iris explained.

"When did you move to Isla Verde, then?" Brun asked.

"Right after they found Mom's lightboard in a forest near France," Iris stated, his eyes sharp. "There are more details, but Dad still won't tell me about them. I don't think he could stand living in Europe without her, so we came to the island, where we could make a fresh start. You know, we're probably the only two hares in South America—Lumen hares, I mean."

Manny considered his parents, his cousins, his home. *I'm lucky compared to Iris…*

"Mi mamá died when I was small, too," Brun confessed. "Right after I was born, actually. You always wonder what she would've been like, you know?"

Iris nodded. "Yeah, I do."

"And Phase Two has begun, folks!" cried Melody as over two hundred Lumens shot into the air above the bay, eye level with the three friends seated along the moai just below Ukisaru peak. "This looks to be an intense encounter—we all know that these lightboarders completed their final day of classes yesterday, so their

341

skills are polished and acute. But the question is, which one of them will leave on the Argo tomorrow knowing that he, or she, is at the top of the mark?"

"Why are they leaving on the Argo tomorrow, Iris?" Manny inquired, not daring to tear his eyes from the mid-air melee.

"The First-Level Candidates leave—Oh! Did you see Keilani just nail that yellow morpho with a surge? She hit him square in the chest! I mean—they leave to start their final mission, in the northern continent," Iris answered, overwhelmingly engaged in the dueling.

"Melody, it definitely adds a new dimension to the second phase to have the flying beasts enter the fray," Rush commented.

"Sure! It's debatable whether even the most-skilled bipedal rider can outmaneuver a peregrine falcon, quetzal, or morpho," the kinkajou concurred.

"Yet some of them are doing it," observed the tree frog.

"Where's Keilani?" Manny whispered.

"Up there on the left," pointed Brun. "Do you see her? She taking on a quetzal and a chinchilla at the same time!"

"Go Keilani!" Iris shouted as an orb exploded between her opponents, knocking the chinchilla from her board. The quetzal recovered, however, shielded by a perfectly sized dome of light.

"That was a seamless recovery, Tusslefeather—yes, excellent use of Castor's Dome," Melody rang in praise of the quetzal.

"We shouldn't expect anything less from the cousin of the director of our very own Amazon River Academy," Rush declared.

Tusslefeather, an aquamarine quetzal with a purple chest, arced through the air to appear behind Keilani, shaking the polished beads around his neck to command a massive flow of light toward the woman, similar to a stratospheric wave of water. The woman, for her part, faced the swell, flipping her lily-hued hairpiece passively as the tiniest of orbs floated out to meet the wave, imploding in a violent burst of light and absorbing the flow completely. Yet it was not finished. Tusslefeather struggled desperately to fly in the opposite direction, but a set of invisible strings seemed to drag him toward the implosion. In fact, two nearby combatants—a green basilisk and an otter—were ripped from their boards, clinging as though magnetized to the orb's avaricious outreach.

"Can you believe it?! Bellastrata just incorporated a Level 1 Implosion to dispatch not one but three opponents! Nochesol must be proud of her!" the kinkajou exploded.

"There's no doubt about that, Melody! Not every First-Level Candidate can execute an L1 Implosion with that speed. Some barely can at all!" Rush shouted.

Iris bounced on his heels as Manny gazed at Keilani, his mouth agape, as she soared through the sky to confront a tall man pursuing a kinkajou. In his hand the man wielded a massive bow, firing a barrage of light arrows at the evasive kinkajou. Brun shook his head in amazement. "I had no idea you could do this kind of stuff with photokinesis," he said. **We've really got to be responsible.**

"Hey, Iris, will you pass me a taquito?" Manny asked, reaching his open palm out below the moai's right ear.

"Brun ate the last one." Iris cringed as the man turned and shot an arrow at Keilani. "Good dodge," he breathed.

"Pásame un burrito, pues," asked Manny, slightly disappointed.

"Don't get mad at me—they were good," Brun said innocently.

Reaching blindly behind, Iris grabbed a burrito and plopped it into Manny's hand, their eyes glued to Keilani's board as it swerved to miss the glowing projectiles. Manny choked when Keilani converted her wand into a whip handle, snapping the burning chord to ricochet an arrow back at the man, the bolt striking him in the wrist and causing him to let loose the bow. Iris beat Manny on the back as the man plunged through the air after his wand, but Keilani's whip wrapped around his ankle, jerking him from his board and sending him crashing into the water below. As Keilani turned to face the kinkajou, Manny fired his own cheesy potato projectile into the air, sailing down toward the spectators below.

343

"Gracias, Iris," he gasped, the potato now dislodged from his throat. "You saved me."

"Anytime," the hare replied, his ears lying back down tranquilly.

"Unbelievable! Bristletail beats Swallowtail and Stickgrip with a volley of frizorbs! A blue morpho can't fly without his wings, and a tree frog can't surf with cold feet! I guess they'll have to rely on the water to thaw them out!" Melody shouted.

"I suppose so…" added Rush saturninely.

"And that leaves just two contenders—Bristletail and Bellastrata!" Melody rang out amongst the eruption of the crowd in awe of the otter and the woman's feats. "My, my, what a showdown! Who could have suspected? I hardly dared to hope!"

"I bet…" muttered Rush.

"I wonder how they'll do?" stated Brun, engrossed in the one-on-one duel.

"This is it!" Iris exclaimed, exploding into the air.

"What are those?" Manny asked as blue blades of light extended from the woman and the kinkajou's wands. "Are those—"

"Fantastic!" Melody sang. "These Lumen ladies have opted to settle the score in classic fashion—with the Sword of Gaisma!"

"I wanna learn to make that." Brun slid his wand from his ring finger and molded it into a birch hilt. Glancing to his side, he noticed Manny had done the same.

Keilani and Bristletail's blades clashed with a blazing bath of sparks as Manny said, "So, Iris, do you know if we get to make the Sword of Gaisma in the Seventh-Level?"

But no response came.

***

Tight hands. Strangling fingers around the neck.

"I'll kill you if you breathe a word," a dirty voice hissed.

Down below a row of moai stood, staring up as the hare struggled, managing only to kick the rocky ground. Between a pair of the complacent sculptures sat two boys—one glowing red, and one burning white.

The grip loosened as the hare's captor heaved his prey up over another cliff.

"Manny! Help me! I'm up here!"

Esophagus constricting, a low growl. Cranium met rock.

***

"Huh? Iris?" Manny shouted, whipping around.

"Where'd he go?" Brun exclaimed, leaping to his feet. There lay the satchel, limp and lifeless.

Up here...? "Brun, look!" Manny pointed toward the peak. Their brains snapped into crisis mode as their eyes processed the image of Iris's body slamming against the rock and being drug over a precipice. Adrenaline charged through their veins as the boys tore up the north shoulder of the mountain, Manny in the lead as bushes and boulders fell away in a blur. In seconds they had reached another ledge, erratically littered with dark figures of towering moai.

"You filthy little beast," called a hateful voice from behind the sentries. "Why do you all have to make this so difficult?"

"Let him go!" Brun roared as he and Manny appeared from around the statues to find a waist-high figure leaning over the hare's frame. The figure cursed as it struggled to wrench the purple band from his victim's ear with a silver, tong-like tool. A thick, crimson stream ran down the front of the hare's face. Manny noted the attacker's midnight fur, that snake-like tail, those black hands and its snow white beard.

The creature looked up, bearing two rows of glittering fangs and cutting the night with a mind-rending shriek. Manny and Brun shielded their ears as the aggressor resumed his task, nearly twisting Iris's ear off. But Manny's heart pulsed; Brun's core erupted. And a surge of ionized insects dove down into the glade, assaulting the monkey and shocking his every nerve as thousands of bolts struck his savage frame. Smoke rose into the air as the primate dropped the body and bounded up over the rocky overhang above, mercilessly

345

pursued by the cloud of Fireflies. Manny shot forward and lifted the hare into his glowing arms.

"What do we do, Brun?" he asked, his mind suddenly blank.

Brun watched as the monkey melted into a shadowy darkness atop the volcano's summit. "We've got to get him down to the healers."

"But that will take too long," Manny argued, Iris's blood now covering his arm. In an impulse the boy stepped out and around the unpitying moai; he gazed into the sky to find the figure of a woman on a lightboard as she drew up a wall of light to defend herself against the fiery attacks of a jade lizard with a sapphire tail.

"Professor Bluebolt!" Manny shouted, his voice cracking. "Professor Bluebolt, Iris is hurt! Come help us!"

Without a second thought Brun stepped forward and aimed his wand at Manny's neck, a wisp of light curling down Manny's throat. "Okay, shout again. He'll hear you this time," Brun said quietly.

"Professor Bluebolt! Come here!" Manny roared as waves of desperate light shot out from the boy's mouth, striking the green basilisk across the cheek and causing the woman to stumble. The lizard froze, turning as he set his eyes on a pair of radiant figures standing near the top of the mountain.

"Iris Firefoot was attacked! You need to heal him!" Manny continued, almost hoarse.

Confusion gripped the crowd as Bluebolt tore through the air above their heads, disappearing along a moai-lined cliff. "Did I just hear someone was attacked? Is Bluebolt forfeiting? Who's up there?" cried the spectators.

Manny stepped back as Bluebolt leapt from his board, gazing up at the bloody bundle in the boy's arms. "What happened here?" the lizard asked, snapping his tail. "Is that Iris Firefoot?"

"Yes," Manny said tensely. "A monkey came down from the mountain and attacked him. We need you to save him." Just as he finished, Keilani soared over and descended into the glade from behind.

346

"Keilani, this is an emergency," Bluebolt began. "I need you to take Iris down to the other healers. Manny, you lay him flat on Keilani's lightboard. I'll head down and prep the others. But, Keilani, be extremely careful not to allow your board to shake. I fear his spine may be broken."

"Sí, Señor," the woman replied.

Bluebolt disappeared instantly, and a few moments later Keilani had gone as well. However, Manny could not move. The blood on his arms, his shirt, his jeans—was seeping into his mind.

Brun's hand came to rest on Manny's shoulder. "Manny, it's not your fault. We did all we could to save him."

An invisible hand gripped Manny's chest, wrenching his stomach and pulling its contents up through his throat and onto the jagged ground. Brun patted him on the back as Manny heaved and choked. A minute later he had finished, stumbling weakly back onto the ground behind the moai.

"He followed me, Brun," Manny whispered, nearly gagging.

"Who did?" Brun asked, sitting down next to him.

"Th-the monkey," Manny answered.

Brun recalled the creature's fangs. "Are you sure it's the same one?"

"Yes. I remember those black eyes and white teeth." Manny's stomach lurched slightly.

"So he tried to steal your wand in June and now Iris's in October. Did he have that tool thing when he attacked you in Costa Rica?" Brun asked analytically.

Manny considered this for a moment, his mind working slowly. "Yes. He was trying to pick my wand up with it, but I caught him off guard and lunged at him." He grew quiet for a moment. "Then he hissed at me. I hate him."

A scream rose up from the bay below. **Keilani must've just arrived along the beach.** "So he stole my sun beetle, didn't he, Manny?"

The boy nodded. "Sí. I'm sure of it. He knows where we live, and he tried to steal our wands that night, remember? That's when he attacked Nipper."

Brun clenched his wand tightly. "If I ever get my hands on that filthy monkey…"

"Then I'll kill him," Manny finished, standing up. "I want to get down to Iris. He's our friend now, and we should be with him."

"Can you make it?" Brun asked, rising to his feet as well.

Manny nodded. "You up to running?"

"If you are. I think we might need to burn off some of that adrenaline in our veins."

"I don't," Manny said as they reached the shoulder of the mountain. "I think I just spit it all out my mouth, along with the burritos."

Brun laughed as they jogged down the side of the sleeping volcano, each hoping and praying that the healers could help Iris. People of all ages and species turned and stared at the luminescent pair that descended the mountain, liquid bronze and seething fire. Reaching the pier, they swerved, then bolted straight toward a tight group of onlookers.

"Mommy, what happened to him?" asked a tiny kinkajou, pointing at Manny as the boy ran past.

"I don't know, honey, but he looks hurt, doesn't he?" she answered, her eyes curiously following the boy as he stopped at the edge of the amassed crowd.

Brun tapped a centaur's white frame. "We need through."

The centaur turned and glanced at the boy, measuring his stature briefly. Her black hair glistened in the light from the stars above, and she wore a blue tunic that matched her dove-like eyes. "I cannot assume that you are healer," she said finally. "So why do you feel the need to pass?"

Brun opened his mouth to speak, but Manny cut in. "Are you a healer?" he asked condescendingly.

"Yes, I am, actually." She glanced back over the heads of the crowd. "I was watching the competition when I heard someone had been attacked. But by the time I arrived to help I was told my services were no longer needed."

Brun's stomach plummeted. "Do you mean he's dead?"

"No! It's just that a team of healer's were already attending to the individual." Her eyes shone softly like the daytime sky. "Why so interested?"

"Manuel! Why is there blood all over you?" called a familiar, deep voice followed swiftly by the sound of hooves casting wet sand into the waves. "Are you injured?"

"No, Chiron, I'm fine," Manny groaned. *I wish they'd all just get out of our way so we could see Iris.*

"Let me see your arm!" exclaimed the female centaur, dropping down onto her front legs and grabbing Manny's elbow. "All this blood! How did I miss this? Where is the cut?"

"I said I was fine," Manny growled. "This isn't even my blood."

"Then whose is it?" Chiron interrogated.

"It's Iris's, Chiron," Brun stated calmly. "He was attacked a few minutes ago and Manny and I saved him. We want to see him," the boy added, his topazine eyes looking imploringly into Chiron's.

Chiron weighed the truth in Brun's voice, then glanced from him to Manny. "Very well," he acquiesced, taking a deep breath and stepping up to the vacuum-packed crowd. "Make way for these boys," the centaur called sternly. Three panthers, a man, and a woman turned, looking back skeptically. "They saved the hare's life—step aside so they may see him."

However unwillingly, the ring caved just enough for the boys to squeeze through. Manny looked thankfully up at Chiron before cleaving the crowd, Brun just a breath behind. In the center of the hub the boys found five figures—a green basilisk, a woman, a quetzal, a unicorn, and an otter—standing vigil over the hare, who now lay unmoving in a bed of sand. Hope spiked in Manny's chest—the blood was gone.

"I've closed the wound above his right eye, Madison," the woman stated, raising her fuchsia wand from Iris's brow.

"And I his ear," added the purple-breasted quetzal.

"Excellent," replied Bluebolt, his aqua eyes jumping to the patient's legs. "What progress do we have on the gashes on his hind paws, Tavo?"

349

"Repaired, sir," the unicorn replied coolly.

"Tavo?" Manny whispered, verifying the formidable pearl-toned frame, golden mane, and icy eyes. "Brun! That's Tavo!"

Brun sized up the unicorn. "He's got composure. I like him."

"It's time we analyze the status of his skeleton and spinal column," Bluebolt stated. "If you will, Penelope."

"Sí, Señor," the otter responded, lifting her wand high before waving it over the hare. A wide beam of blue light passed from the stars into Iris's frame, illuminating every bone and organ in his body.

"His cranium is damaged, Madison," the quetzal announced. "But the cerebrum is intact and functioning normally."

"Good. Then begin restoring the bone, Alexandria," said Bluebolt. "Ellen, what's the prognosis on his spinal column?"

"Other than a severe subluxation in the neck, everything appears normal," the woman replied, her chocolate eyes focused on the bulging disk in Iris's neck. "But I'll repair that straightaway."

Bluebolt nodded. "Inner organs, Tavo?"

"The hare's liver and stomach membranes have multiple lacerations, sir," the unicorn reported.

"Tavo, address the stomach lining. Penelope, help me tend to the liver—we do not want either to rupture," Bluebolt ordered, snapping his tail. Needle thin streams of light shot down from the sky, entering the hare's body and coming to rest on the damaged organs. Almost immediately new flesh began to grow, filling in the violent cuts. A loud crack wrenched the air. A girl screamed.

"Mamá, did Iris's neck just break?" the girl asked, stepping toward Ellen.

"No, Kaya, I just aligned his vertebrae," Ellen replied steadily. "I still need to reduce the swelling on the disc, so step back or leave—it's possible you may distract me."

The girl melted obediently back into the crowd, her brow enswathed in a deep frown and her face swollen, as though she had been crying.

"Kaya?" Manny said aloud, staring across the circle at his art partner. *That woman is Kaya's mom?*

Hearing her name, Kaya looked up, searching for the person who called her. There, on the other side of the clearing, was Manny, whispering something to Brun and glancing her way. In a breath she was around the circle, face to face with Manny. Unbounded indignation coursed through her veins. A deafening slap slit the air.

"How can you come show your face here?" she whispered, her words lethal.

"What did I do?" Manny shrieked, shielding his face.

"You attacked him!" the girl spit. "You hurt Ir—"

"Kaya Mireille Bellastrata! Did you just slap that boy?" Ellen called, rising to her feet.

"Mamá, he—"

"No more of this," Ellen stated resolutely, her judgment trumping her tolerance as she stepped back and address the pressing crowd. "Everyone! Return to your seats! We have an emergency situation here, and we cannot operate with these incessant distractions." No one moved. "I said go!" the woman affirmed, a formidable look in her eyes, not relenting until the last spectator had left the area. With her palm resting on her daughter's shoulder, Ellen guided Kaya over to where Manny and Brun now stood. "I am unaware of what the situation is between you three, but when I'm done, we will bring the truth to light, and I hope to find this discord utterly dissolved. Now, all three of you, sit down and start talking." The three detainees watched as Ellen returned to the surgical area, disappearing behind Tavo as she knelt beside the hare.

"What prompted such intervention from Ellen Bellastrata?" Chiron inquired, the blue-eyed centaur at his side.

"It's an infinitely long story," Manny mumbled, staring somberly at the blood on his forearm. Kaya glared at the boy.

"We have time now," Chiron observed.

Brun shook his head. "Can we discuss it later, Chiron? I think we all need some time to digest what's happened tonight." Fatigue lined the young man's voice.

Before Chiron could answer the female centaur stepped forward. "A wise suggestion, Brun. Allow the mind to rest and heal itself," she asserted sensibly. **How does she know my name?** "Now,

Manny, permit me to remove the blood from your arms and clothing. Stand up, if you would." The boy so did, watching in fascination as the she-centaur set to work, flicking her thin wooden necklace and causing a glittering white cloth to materialize before his eyes. The cloth swooped down along his arm with a cool, tingling sensation, then began to gently touch Manny's shirt and jeans at various points, absorbing the blood and turning from white, to pink, to red. When the stains were gone the crimson cloth hung lazily in the air, disintegrating entirely with a blink from the centaur.

"What's your name?" Manny asked, captivated.

"Nightwind Arconia," she replied. "But please just call me Nightwind, we centaurs—"

"Don't use last names—I know," Manny finished, smiling up at Chiron.

"So are you and Chiron friends?" Brun asked suddenly.

She glanced toward the other centaur, whose rosy complexion seemed to have deepened slightly. "That would be nice, I think," Nightwind said.

"¡Atención, por favor! ¡Atención!" squeaked a voice over the buzz ringing from the mountain. "Rush Stickgrip here. I must regretfully inform you that the competition has ended due to unforeseen circumstances. However," he continued, drowning out a wave of grumbling, "Keilani Bellastrata remains the victor of this year's competition—let's give her a striking round of applause!" The crowd clapped half-heartedly.

"We do apologize, folks," Melody rang. "Yes, we're very sorry. In any case, we will begin loading in less than five minutes for the return voyages to Isla Verde, Machu Picchu, and Iguazú, so please collect your possessions and your families and head for your respective pier. Thank you."

"Alright," Ellen said as she drew up next to Nightwind. "Have we settled our differences?"

"Is Iris okay, Mamá?" Kaya interposed, in hopes the former question might sink into the oblivion of the sea.

"He is," Ellen answered, nodding understandingly. "Tavo Gilderbrand just finished mending the bones in his feet. He's still

352

unconscious, but he should be fine tomorrow afternoon. He'll be a little sore, though."

"Good," Manny and Brun sighed together. Kaya shot Manny a hateful look.

"I take it that the answer to my introductory question was to the negative," Ellen inferred, her eyes drawn to her daughter's acrid expression.

"Mamá, you don't know what—"

"Peace, Kaya," the woman breathed calmly. "May I have your names, boys?"

Nightwind stepped forward. "Allow me, Señora—?"

"Bellastrata," Ellen finished, slightly surprised at Nightwind's gracious intervention.

"This is Brun Dimirtis and his roommate Manny López. They are staying with Chiron in Isla Verde," the she-centaur elucidated smoothly.

"And you?" Ellen queried.

"I am Nightwind Arconia, a healer from Macchu Picchu."

"So you came down to help us treat Iris?" Ellen guessed, her tone brimming with respect.

Nightwind nodded. "I did. But my help was not needed."

"Thank you, nonetheless," the woman replied sincerely. She turned to face the boys. "Now Brun, Manny, I'm Ellen Bellastrata, Kaya's mother. Could either of you tell me what made my daughter so angry?"

Both boys stared back at the woman blankly. *She's always angry.* **What doesn't?**

"No?" Ellen asked.

"Mamá, Manny's the one who attacked Iris!" Kaya shouted.

"No, he didn't!" Brun roared. "Manny and I saved him!"

"Oh, yeah, from what?" Kaya's words splattered the pair like loose saliva. "Yourselves?"

"Enough," Chiron intervened, his tone unquestionable. "It has already been decided that this matter will not be discussed tonight. Ellen, you are welcome to bring Kaya to my home

353

tomorrow evening after the Argo departs. I will also invite Fidelio Firefoot, and Iris, if he is willing and up to it. Do you agree?"

Ellen took a deep breath, staring into her daughter's eyes, and considered the centaur's proposition. "I believe that is a good idea," the woman said finally. "Kaya and I will be there."

"Excellent," Chiron replied.

"Let's go, Kaya," Ellen directed quietly. The girl rose to her feet, and mother and daughter plodded away through the sand.

"Shall we head home too, now, boys?" Chiron asked, stretching out an arm first to Brun, then to Manny.

"Actually, Chiron, I was hoping that I could visit with Tavo before we left." Manny glanced around Nightwind in search of the unicorn.

Chiron glanced at Manny in surprise. "How exactly do you know Gilderbrand? Isn't he stationed hundreds of miles north of here?"

"Yeah," Manny answered, his energy virtually sapped, despite the prospect of reminiscing with his old friend. "He works in the rainforest in Costa Rica, just southwest of Puerto Limón. I met him there during our eighth grade class trip in June." Manny suddenly caught sight of the unicorn. "There he is!" he exclaimed, pointing down the beach. "Do you mind, Chiron?"

"I suppose we can wait a few more minutes," Chiron said sympathetically. Nightwind smiled. "But prudence demands you hurry because it appears he is about to depart."

"C'mon, Brun!" Manny shouted as they tore off along the beach. "Tavo, wait! It's me, Manny!" the boy yelled as the unicorn's hooves lifted from the sand and came to rest upon water.

Tavo peered around quizzically, turning about to find a pair of glowing figures running straight for him. "Manny López, how are you?!"

Manny leapt out onto the water; but instead of sinking, the waves held his weight—they were solid. This aspect of the water confused the boy, as he was not accustomed to standing on the surface of a liquid. Manny's mind, suddenly disoriented, caused him to lose his balance, and thus he grabbed the unicorn's neck with his hand. *What in the...?*

"Pat twice for friendship," Tavo said gregariously.

"What?" Manny wrapped his arm around the unicorn's neck to remain stable. The boy's eyes sank as he watched the waves churn the sand below.

"It is customary for a human to greet a unicorn by patting him twice on the neck for friendship—using the left hand, mind you," Tavo added. "Or did you perhaps forget?"

Manny blinked several times, still trying to reconcile his newfound aquatic abilities with traditional reasoning. "Oops, sorry, Tavo," he finally stated, patting the unicorn on the neck absentmindedly.

"Twice is quite enough, Manny." Tavo slid from the boy's embrace and stepped further back along the water. "Now who is this young fellow?" The unicorn nodded to Brun. "You didn't tell me you had a brother!"

Manny released a sudden cry as he turned and fell, his hip connecting hard with the surface of the water, which, to his amazement, continued to hold his weight. He stared up at Tavo, who looked down curiously. "That's because I don't," Manny groaned. *Is it possible to break your butt?*

"Tavo, I'm Brun," the other boy said, eschewing the customary greeting as he preferred to keep his feet planted firmly on the sand. "Manny's told me a lot about you."

"He has?" the healer exclaimed. "Like what?"

"Oh, how you healed Julius, stopped that monkey, made a ladder so that Manny could sneak back up into his room before anyone noticed—you know, all the interesting stuff," Brun replied.

"And how do you know Manny?" Tavo inquired.

"We're roommates," Brun said simply.

"Roommates." The unicorn stared from one to the other. "And you're not related at all?"

"Nope." Manny stared helplessly at the unicorn's hooves.

"But you look just alike—you both glow and everything!" Tavo asserted.

"We have different skin colors, actually," Brun clarified.

"And hair, too," Manny noted.

"But maybe you're—"

"Not a chance," Brun cut in. "We were born six months apart."

"On different continents," Manny added.

"To separate families," Brun finished.

His theories snuffed, Tavo searched for an alternative line of discussion. "Why don't you stand up, Manny?" He glanced down at the boy now counting shells below his feet.

"I'd rather sit, thanks," Manny replied dryly. "I evidently don't have very good sea legs—literally."

"How are you two standing—and sitting—on the water, anyway?" asked Brun. "Is that a special power that unicorns have that I don't know about?"

Tavo whinnied humorously. "We have no powers that you or any other Lumens hold, I'll promise you that. In fact, the only thing that separates us from horses is that pretty little spike that grows on our noses," he added with a grin.

"How are my butt and your hooves staying dry, then?" Manny fished, his words striking the unicorn's broad lips.

"Because we're standing on an ATS vessel," Tavo answered obviously.

"I don't see a vessel," Brun stated.

Manny frowned. "What's an ATS?"

"The Atlantic Transport Service. Their vessels are made of a translucent crystal—you can't see it, but it's there." Tavo stomped the floor of the invisible craft with an emphatic thud.

Manny knocked on the thick glass at his feet, observing a trio of fish scatter from the unanticipated sound waves. "How does it work?"

"It's pulled," Tavo replied.

"Over the water?" Brun queried.

"Not this variety—this vessel is specifically for underwater transport, which is faster for long journeys," the healer explained. "Let me introduce you to the muscles behind the operation."

356

Flipping his mane and turning, Tavo shouted, "Hey, Blackfin! Come up for a second!" The water bulged as a massive beast the size of an elephant rose to the surface, its body a glistening black, though its underside and patches around its eyes shone a re-lucent white. Three midnight fins protruded from the creature's corpulent frame—two on either side and one on its back. It had ocean blue eyes and a rounded snout.

"He's big," Brun observed, stunned.

Manny's eyes lit up. "I get it! So this killer whale pulls the ship around like the dolphins do in Isla Verde! That's handy!"

"I am not a dolphin," Blackfin stated with his deep as the ocean voice and enormous, flat-toothed jaws. "And I prefer the term 'orca'—killer whale sounds so, savage."

"Y-you talk," Manny blubbered.

"Of course I do—I'm a Lumen, human child," Blackfin replied. "Is Atlantis not a part of the curriculum at the academies on this continent?"

"He's only in the Seventh-Level, Blackfin," Tavo interjected.

"Oh, then I suppose his ignorance may be forgiven," Blackfin reasoned.

"Blackfin, do you know any merpeople?" Brun inquired suddenly.

"Yes, many," the orca yawned. "What is your name?"

"Brun."

"I will return shortly, Brun." Blackfin disappeared below the water in a massive swell. **That was abrupt.**

"While he's gone let's take a chance to catch up," Tavo proposed, staring down at Manny. "How's your life been?"

"Eventful," Manny sighed.

"Why is that?" the unicorn asked.

"You remember that hare you healed earlier? Brun and I were there when he was attacked, and we saved him."

The air caught in Tavo's throat. "You were? What happened?"

Manny glanced over his shoulder and up the increasingly vacant beach to find Chiron chatting avidly with Nightwind. "It's a long story, Tavo. And Chiron is waiting on us. We really don't have time to tell you now, but—hey! I have an idea! Why don't you come to Isla Verde for the weekend? We're having a meeting tomorrow night at our house about the attack. Then you'd know everything!"

"That was my plan, originally. I'd hoped to visit with you, Julius, and some other friends from the island, but come to find out that rowdy quetzal is out on school business with Andrés Dosfilos for the weekend. So I just decided to visit another time." Tavo sounded rather disappointed.

"You could visit both now and then!" Manny suggested.

"That's not possible, Manny. I haven't asked another healer to cover for me; I need to be back in Costa Rica in case someone gets hurt."

"Alright," Manny relented, his energy now fully deflated. *Dang.*

Suddenly the brine behind Tavo began to churn, giving way to Blackfin's gargantuan frame accompanied by another figure.

"The red one?" the figure asked, its blonde hare wet and clinging to its head.

"Yes," the orca nodded.

The blonde figure propelled itself forward, its crystal grey eyes set on Brun. Reaching the shore, the figure straightened its back, stepping onto the sand with broad, scaly green legs ending in a pair of amply webbed feet. From the waist up the figure's chest was pale and bare, revealing a series of four slits on either side of its ribcage and two on either side of the neck. It looked very much like a man. **But he has fish legs...**

"A pleasure to meet you, Brun." The figure extended its right arm, its fingers webbed. "I am Xanthus."

"Are you a—?"

"A merman? Yes," Xanthus replied. "I live below Rapa Nui. I understand you are fond of my people."

"Y-yes," Brun stumbled. "I've only heard stories about the merpeople; but you're—real. And you can walk."

"Indeed we can," Xanthus said wisely. "We split our tail fins when we reach land so we can maneuver about—but only for a time.

Our legs will dry out and our gills become irritated if we're on land for too long.

Manny's eyes widened. *That's incredible.*

"So, Brun, you're a Seventh-Level, correct?" Xanthus asked. The boy nodded. "What's your favorite subject?"

"I like The Lumen World," Brun said quietly.

"Why is that?" the merman asked.

Brun considered this question for a moment. "I guess because I get to see everything I never could before. I didn't exactly travel a lot as a kid."

Manny nodded. *He's not exaggerating there.*

"That is one benefit to being a Lumen—at least a land dwelling one. You get to see the sky world," Xanthus said sensibly.

"So what's your world like? Underwater, I mean," Brun asked.

"Limitless—there's always more to explore. I often swim south of here to search the Antarctic caves—and fight with the giant squid. Now that's always fun. Not to mention the canyons—you can wrestle some nasty anglers down there, you know," said Xanthus.

"I want to see all that!" Brun ejected.

"Perhaps when you visit Atlantis, you will. But I'd better be going—my throat's getting dry. Maybe I'll see you next year, Brun."

"Really? That would be great!" the boy affirmed as the merman turned toward the ocean. The tide reached Xanthus' chest and his legs fused, enabling him to more quickly slip into deeper water and wet his thirsty gills and throat.

"Tavo!" Brun called urgently. "Is paloma paper waterproof?"

"I suppose so, yes," the healer replied oddly. "Why?"

"Xanthus!" yelled Brun, his hands cupped around his mouth. A second later the merman resurfaced and waved. "Can I write you?"

"Sure!" the merman called back. "Just address the letter to Xanthus del Mar! It'll reach me! See you!"

"Thanks!" Brun yelled.

Blackfin wore a broad smile on his sizable jaws. "Did you enjoy meeting a member of the merfolk?"

Brun nodded gratefully. "Thanks a lot, Blackfin."

"My pleasure." The orca offered a slight bow and the flip of a fin. He then swung his massive tail so that he faced the unicorn. "Are we ready to leave now, Tavo?"

"I think so," the healer replied, noting Manny's vanquished look. "But I'll visit Isla Verde soon enough, m'ijo," Tavo told the boy.

Manny rose shakily to his feet, determined not to fall. "Hasta luego, pues," he said, waving to the unicorn before jumping over the wet gap that separated him from Brun.

"Adiós," Tavo bid as a dome of white light swallowed him, sealing the unicorn inside the glass vessel at his hooves.

"Until next time, sea son!" boomed Blackfin with a farewell glance at Brun. As the orca disappeared below the waves, a pair of silver chains shot up and linked to the vessel, dragging it out a short distance before it, too, followed the orca into the water.

Manny stared at the empty sea. "That was a letdown."

"No it wasn't! That was amazing!" Brun countered. "We met a merman and an orca!"

"But Tavo left." Manny's words faded bleakly as he and Brun turned up the beach toward the chatting centaurs.

"He said he'd visit soon." Brun's positive words fluttering vainly to the ground.

"A lot of good that does me right now."

"That's what hope is for, Manny. That's how I survived those fourteen and a half years on that blasted island—I kept thinking of what it would be like to leave."

"So you're saying I should just sit around and think about when Tavo might come?" Manny sounded annoyed.

"No—I'm telling you to look forward to it, and in the meantime occupy yourself with other things, like monkey hunting," Brun rejoined optimistically.

"What?" Manny wrenched, thrown by the sudden curve in the conversation.

"You know what I'm talking about," Brun cued as they reached the centaurs.

"Oh—you're back." Chiron's tenor was crestfallen.

"I guess I should leave, then," Nightwind blinked quietly. "It was a pleasure meeting you—Chiron, Manny, Brun. Perhaps I will see you in the future."

"I will be in Machu Picchu next month," Chiron suggested.

Nightwind's eyes flashed brightly. "You will?" The other centaur nodded graciously. "Contact me when you arrive and we can get together," she said. "I'll be looking forward to it."

"As will I."

For a brief moment the two centaurs shared a fervent parting glance. Nightwind then turned, her shadowy tresses cascading behind her as she trotted away south along the beach.

"You're going to Machu Picchu next month?" Brun asked, looking up at the centaur's transfixed eyes. "When? During the school week?"

"No, I will only leave during a weekend," Chiron replied.

"Do we get to go?" Manny asked.

"No," Chiron said coyly.

"Who are you staying with?" Brun inquired.

"I have friends in Machu Picchu—it should not present a problem," the centaur answered. Chiron acted as though he intended to ask the boys a serious question, but he must have thought better of it. "Are we ready now?"

"Sí," Manny sighed. "I'm exhausted."

"Me, too," Brun agreed.

"Let's go home, then." Chiron glanced at the fair-skinned centaur on the nearest of the southern docks before turning and following the boys to the far end of the bay.

Reunión

"Mamá, I hate him!" Kaya asserted darkly as she and her mother drew near to Chiron's Hutch.

"Now Kaya, he isn't a bad man," Ellen argued. "And stop saying you hate him—you never said that before tonight, and you definitely shouldn't say it now."

"Oh, yes I did," Kaya retorted. "I just didn't say it in front of you. I hate him now more than ever. You have no idea what he did to Iris, Mamá. He—" She froze. Behind the hut, directly across the glade from Kaya, sat Manny, staring straight at her. "Mind your own business," the girl spat, cutting Manny's face with her eyes as she took the furthest seat from Manny possible and crossed her arms in indignation.

Ellen smiled at the motionless boy across the way. The woman then bent forward to whisper into her daughter's ear. "Kaya, what did I tell you about glaring at people like that? You are now grounded. Your father and I will decide how long when we get home. I suggest you behave during this meeting, or you won't be leaving the house until after Christmas." Standing erect, Ellen turned to face Chiron, who stood next to Manny. "Good evening, Chiron," the woman said politely, stepping forward to shake the centaur's hand. "Thank you for having us."

"Buenas noches, Ellen. It is an honor to have you visit," Chiron welcomed warmly. "Would you like some thundermug tea?"

"Please," she said, turning and smiling again at the boys. Next to Brun sat the keen-eyed Bluebolt. "How are you, Madison?"

"Fantastic," the lizard replied. "I cannot complain."

"Would you or Kaya like some honey?" Chiron inquired from the wooden table stationed behind the woman.

"Sí—Kaya would. But none for me, thanks," Ellen answered as the centaur stirred in a dab of the amber liquid. "Gracias," she said as she reached for the steaming white mugs, accepting Kaya's with her left hand, the wrist of which bore an elegantly adorned rose

362

pink bracelet with various charms. Ellen threw back her long hair as she walked across the glade and passed the mug to Kaya, who received it silently. The woman's soft chocolate eyes met Kaya's.

"Gracias, Mamá," the girl whispered, taking a sip of the infusion. Her mother smiled as she sat down.

"Kaya looks just like her mom, too," Brun breathed into Manny's ear.

"She seems a lot nicer, though," Manny muttered with a frown. "Her mamá, I mean."

"Are you sure you would not like to try the tea, Manuel?" Chiron prodded.

"I like it a lot," Brun attested, taking another sip of his own brew. "But ask him for two spoonfuls of honey—it's better sweet."

"I guess," Manny relented as the centaur stepped forward to pour another cup. "Now what's this stuff made of, Brun?"

"From the roots of some tree, I think," Brun advised.

"Not the roots, Brun, but the fruit," Bluebolt corrected. "Of the rayapa, a tropical tree that grows its fruit when struck by lightning. Lumen farmers then pick the fruit and dry it to prepare the tea blend for consumers."

That seems like a lot of trouble for a cup of tea. "Why don't people just eat the fruit raw?" Manny asked.

"Because it would kill them—dehydration lessens the charge in the fruit, consequently making it safe for consumption. A fraction of the charge remains, thus giving the tea a slight kick," the lizard explained.

"Why aren't you drinking any, Professor?" Manny asked.

"I'm not tired," Bluebolt replied frankly. *Oh.*

"Here you go, Manuel." Chiron handed the warm mug to the boy.

Manny looked down at the yellow liquid trapped in his hand, noting its sweet yet faintly sharp aroma. *Oh well.* As the tea slid down his throat, Manny felt a soothing sensation fill every muscle in his body, and his mind cleared, rendering him suddenly more aware than before. Manny smiled pleasantly. "It is good."

"I told you," Brun said, raising cup to mouth.

"Everyone, we will begin the meeting as soon as Professor Firefoot arrives," Chiron announced to the group. "If you need more tea, please let me know."

"Is Iris coming, Chiron?" Kaya asked, worry lining her voice.

"I know not, Kaya," the centaur replied. The girl frowned deeply.

Twenty minutes and several refills of thundermug tea passed before two tall chestnut ears appeared from around the bamboo hut, escorted by a shorter yet more energetic pair, though of a darker hue.

"Hello, all," Fidelio saluted. His ears sagged heavily as he and Iris entered the glade, the instructor's generally positive nature exchanged for a most uncharacteristic and wearisome visage.

"Iris!" Kaya attempted to leap from her chair. Her mother held her back, however.

"Wait a few days before you hug him, honey," Ellen whispered. "His body needs to finish healing."

"Hi, Kaya!" Iris called enthusiastically, his grin twisting into a wince with each subsequent hop. "Hey, Manny! Hey, Brun!"

"¡Hola!" Manny greeted the hare.

"Still a little sore, Iris?" Brun asked.

"Yeah, but I'm alive," the hare replied fervently.

"Thanks to our excellent healers," Fidelio said as he helped Iris into the chair next to Bluebolt. "I cannot express my appreciation enough, Madison," the father hare nodded, "and Ellen. Without the both of you Iris would have—" He stopped, unable to finish.

"You are most welcome, friend," Bluebolt corresponded.

"Glad to be of service," Ellen replied. "And glad to see Iris up and about already!"

"As am I!" Chiron agreed.

"There seems to be more fire in him than just his feet, that's for sure," Fidelio managed to say, forcing a smile at his bad family joke.

"Don't worry, Dad," Iris bolstered, patting his father on the arm. "I'm fine."

"Shall we begin?" Chiron asked. Everyone nodded. "I assume that we all know one another here, and that introductions are unnecessary. Am I correct?" More nods. "Bien. I would first like to state that Director Rumblefeather regrets his inability to attend tonight's meeting. He is presently indisposed, but I will communicate to him all that we discuss the moment he returns. As is customary during Lumen meetings, allow me to remind everyone that it is a general rule to listen before one speaks—interrupting one's colleagues is strictly prohibited. Are we all of one accord?" The centaur's nebulous eyes passed over the younger members of the group.

"Yes," they all replied.

"Bueno. The purpose of this meeting is to reveal the truth of the circumstances surrounding Iris Firefoot's injury and recovery this night previous," the centaur proceeded. "Reason dictates that we allow the victim to share his account first, from which point questioning and discussion may ensue. Iris, if you will."

"Okay, Chiron," the hare conceded willingly. "Well, Manny, Brun, and I were up near Ukisaru Peak, eating burritos and watching Phase Two of the lightboarding competitions." Kaya coughed noisily; her mother eyed her firmly. "The last thing I remember is that Tami Bristletail was taking on two other Lumens at once, when all of a sudden these steel-like hands wrapped around my neck and mouth, and began dragging me up the mountain. Whoever had me was jumping along cliffs like some oversized hare. When we were pretty far from Manny and Brun, the thing whispered in my ear, telling me to stay quiet or it would kill me. For some reason it let go of my mouth, so I shouted to them for help, and then everything went pitch black. I don't remember anything else; at least not until I woke up in bed this morning with my dad sitting next to me."

Kaya raised her hand, but Chiron spoke. "Did you recognize the voice? Was it familiar to you whatsoever?"

Iris thought for a moment, his left ear rising slightly. "No, Chiron, I didn't. It was raspy and mean, like a wild animal would sound if it could talk. It scared me," he finished quietly.

"Do you recall any other Lumens sitting above you three on the mountain?" the centaur asked, ignoring the girl's hand.

"No. No one was above us," Iris answered quickly. "I'm sure of it. We would have seen them if they climbed up after we did."

"Perhaps they were lying in wait..." Chiron said vaguely. "Are there any questions before we turn to Manny and Brun's account?"

"Yes!" Kaya said breathlessly.

"You may proceed, then, Señorita Bellastrata," Chiron nodded.

"Why were you up on the mountain with Manny and Brun, anyway? I thought we agreed not to talk to them."

Brun frowned. Manny spilt a bit of tea on his shirt. *Are you kidding me?!*

"Manny apologized, Kaya," Iris said, unashamed. "If you haven't noticed he's actually a nice guy—and Brun, too. It's obvious that they saved my life, or I wouldn't be here right now."

Gracias, buddy. Grinning, Manny took another satisfied sip of his new favorite drink.

Brun nodded, his cause vindicated. **You're perceptive.**

"But maybe they're the ones who attacked you!" Kaya contended. "Maybe your memory's a little shaky."

"It's not, Kaya," Iris rebounded, his words unyielding. "Manny and Brun glow at night, like they are right now. That thing drug me up the mountain, but the whole time I saw one red light and one white light between the moai below us. They're my friends, Kaya. I called and they saved me."

Her argument silenced, Kaya now sat back in her chair, not daring to look at either Manny or Brun—nor anyone else for that matter.

"I think it best that we move forward," Chiron stated. "Manuel, Brun, I would like to give the floor to the both of you. Speak freely, but raise your hand if you have something to add before the other proceeds."

Both boys nodded. "You can start," Brun said to Manny.

366

As Manny and Brun related the tale from their vantage point, the dynamics of the group seemed to change—particularly when they alleged that the attacker had been a primate. Iris and Kaya, for their part, glanced at each other knowingly. Chiron took a deep breath, Ellen crossed her arms, Bluebolt snapped his sapphire tail. Fidelio, however, seemed distant, almost passive, as though his thoughts were directed elsewhere, marred in a separate source of pain altogether. Brun ended the account with the arrival of Bluebolt and Keilani on their lightboards.

The adults in the group, with the exclusion of Fidelio, performed an inward sigh, seemingly preparing for a lengthy and wearisome debate. Chiron, naturally, spoke first, but not to the boys.

"Does this account coincide with your recollection of the said events, Madison?" the centaur asked.

Bluebolt cracked his tail against a chair leg. "Yes," he stated preemptively. "But I question as to how Brun executed the photowave enhancement to Manny's voice."

Chiron and Ellen nodded. "A pertinent question," the centaur said practically.

Manny raised his hand to speak. "Why is that such a big deal?"

"Because students do not learn to modify organs until the Third-Level. Brun performed an enhancement that was beyond his abilities, theoretically," Bluebolt replied.

"Could you do it again?" Ellen asked.

"I-I don't know," Brun stammered. "I never really thought about it when I did it. I just knew that we needed to get Professor Bluebolt's attention before it was too late."

"Try, Brun," Chiron urged.

Alright. Brun stood up, his face grave as he transformed his birch ring into a customary wand and pointed it at Manny's neck. Seeing the seriousness in Brun's face, Manny nearly laughed; but he managed to restrain himself. After a moment a stream of light curled down through the branches of the kapok tree behind, touching Manny's neck and dissolving.

"Okay," Brun said doubtfully. "You can speak now."

367

Kaya and Iris plugged their ears. Manny took a deep breath and spoke. "Did it work?"

"No," Chiron said dryly. Brun sat down, slightly embarrassed.

"Very strange," Bluebolt noted.

"But before we turn to the most—prominent—issue at hand," Chiron said, pausing, "perhaps we should pass the baton to Fidelio."

"What now?" Fidelio jerked from his trance. "I have nothing to say about photowave enhancements."

"Most understandably," replied Chiron, "but we are all aware of your mastery of sentinels."

Fidelio failed to make a connection between the two themes. "What do sentinels have to do with photowave enhancements?"

The centaur's jet eyes observed the father hare's tired frame. "I will explain, then," Chiron resumed patiently. "It is irrefutable that Brun implemented an organ modification beyond the scope of his photoregenerative knowledge—a point we must all note. From here we must consider the effect the boys' sentinels had against the alleged—attacker."

Alleged attacker? What's he mean by that?

"Didn't the boys say they scared the attacker off with a swarm of Fireflies?" Fidelio asked impatiently. "How does that have any bearing on the situation? It is obvious that the creature that attacked my son was nocturnal, and that the light startled it, causing it to flee. Debate ended, we can all leave."

"No, we cannot," Chiron asserted sternly. "I understand that you are overwhelmed at the moment, Fidelio, but it is a necessity that you lend great attention to the details of the boys' tale. Manny, remind Professor Firefoot of the behavior of your sentinels."

Manny set his empty tea mug in his lap as he said, "Well, our Fireflies appeared over the monkey's head and started to electrocute him—you know, like little bolts of lightning. That's it. They chased him off and I grabbed Iris. You know the rest."

"Electrocute?" Fidelio repeated disparagingly. "Sentinels cannot conduct electricity, nor can any Lumen produce it, for that

368

matter." The hare's ears shot high into the air. "What really happened up there, Manny López?"

"Exactly what we said, Professor," Brun supported adamantly. "Our Fireflies attacked the monkey, he ran away, and we saved Iris."

"That's a lie!" Firefoot exclaimed.

"No, it isn't!" Brun and Manny rebounded together.

Chiron stepped forward authoritatively. "Peace. We will not yell here. Now I have a theory, but you all need to listen—with an open mind, remembering that I am not attempting to discredit any of you."

The glade grew quiet. **Thanks for that.**

"Bueno. Let us deliberate your hypothesis, Fidelio," Chiron began earnestly. "You mentioned that perhaps Iris's attacker was a nocturnal creature, and that the Fireflies startled him. I believe the latter half of this statement to be true—the light from the sentinels startled the attacker and caused him to flee. Now you may ask why the assailant could not have been a 'wild creature,' in a manner of speaking, but let us wisely remember the barrier surrounding the Ukisaru and the Bay of Rapa Nui. This barrier prevents all non-Lumens from stepping foot on that part of the island, irrevocably and without question. Therefore, we are left to deduce that the attacker was one of our own—a Lumen."

Ellen gasped. "That's a terrible thought, Chiron!"

That's what I've been saying all along.

"Indeed," the centaur answered gravely. "Yet I have not finished. If we are to assume that this—creature—was indeed a Lumen, we must also acknowledge a rift in Manuel and Brun's account."

"A rift? I don't understand," Iris interjected. "What's wrong with their story now?"

"The identity of the attacker," Bluebolt replied with a snap of his tail. Chiron nodded. "It could not have been a monkey," the lizard added.

"Why not?" Kaya asked loudly.

"Lower your voice, Kaya," Ellen warned.

"In this world, Kaya, there are 85 distinct species of Lumens, but not one of them includes primates," Bluebolt answered. "It is simply impossible that the attacker was a monkey."

"What was it then? A kinkajou?" Manny asked scornfully.

"Why, that is exactly what I was about to propose!" Chiron exclaimed. "How insightful, Manuel."

He's a lot more insightful than all of you. "Chiron, we know what a kinkajou looks like," Brun said dully. "And that wasn't a kinkajou on Ukisaru. It was a sharp-fanged, ugly faced, nasty little monkey."

Manny nodded. *I couldn't have said it better myself.*

"That's absolutely ridiculous," Ellen retorted. "Haven't you been listening to what Chiron and Madison have been telling you?"

"But why isn't anyone listening to them?" Iris cut in, nodding toward the boys. "They saw it!"

"They believe they saw it, son," Fidelio said understandingly.

"Just like Iris and I believed we found the monkey print in the ferns over there?" Kaya asked, her voice renting the air as she pointed to the east end of the glade, beyond the hut.

"A monkey print?" Ellen repeated. "¿De qué hablas?"

"I'm talking about the other day, when Iris and I found a monkey print in the mud over there!" Kaya persisted.

"Over a month ago, actually," the centaur muttered.

"Chiron took a mold of the print. He told us that he wanted to verify it with Professor Shadowflame, and he left in a hurry. But we never heard from him—did we, Iris?"

"No, we didn't, Chiron," Iris agreed, looking to the centaur expectantly.

"So was it a monkey?" Kaya asked. All eyes turned to Chiron.

"It was," Chiron replied quietly.

"I knew it!" the girl exclaimed.

"But how can this be, Chiron?" Bluebolt asked, extending his scaled paw in a reach for understanding. "If a monkey set foot in

Isla Verde, then there are dire consequences to consider. Not to mention the fact that the boys' account could be true."

"It is!" Manny and Brun said ardently.

"Let me reassure you—all of you—that there is no cause for concern," Chiron stated, his palms stretched out to the group. "The moment Sable and I verified the authenticity of the print, we swiftly notified Julius, who decided that we should test the longevity of the Brethren's barrier. As such, the three of us hastily left the parameters of the city and detained a handful of monkeys of various species. Not one of them—I am happy to say—was able to enter the city limits. The barrier repelled each one."

"What a relief," sighed Fidelio.

"How exactly did the monkey print get there, then?" Kaya queried.

"That is a good question, Chiron," Ellen coincided.

"One that we asked ourselves, believe me," the centaur answered, his bottomless eyes directed toward the woman. "And the solution is quite rudimentary—the print was a fake."

"But you just told us it was real!" Iris said, his ears jagged.

"Indirectly, it was," Chiron replied.

"How can a print be indirectly authentic?" Fidelio asked. "That's irrational."

That seems to be the theme of the day.

"In reality, it is quite rational," the centaur proceeded diplomatically. "There remain two possibilities—though one of them is slightly morbid. Either the print was made with an authentic molding, or someone used a monkey's actual foot to create a false print. In either case, the print would appear real, though reasoning proves it is not."

"Are you saying someone on Isla Verde is walking around with a dead monkey's leg?" Kaya asked, her disbelieving words barreling the centaur in the chest.

"Possibly—but not openly, of course. They are using the foot as a means to enact practical jokes," Chiron resolved.

"Or they have a mold for the same ends," reasoned Bluebolt logically.

"Or, just maybe, an actual monkey snuck into Isla Verde," Manny postulated, his irate words floating in the air above the glade.

Ellen swatted at Manny's hypothesis. "I'm tired of hearing such nonsensical arguments."

"As am I," Fidelio grumbled, adjusting in his seat.

"Then how do you all explain the fact that Manny's sun beetle was stolen?" Iris said.

"Yeah!" Kaya rallied. "That had to be a monkey!"

"It wasn't my sun beetle that was stolen," Manny said quickly.

"It was mine," Brun stated. Iris shot a glare at Kaya. "But how did you two know about that?"

"We saw it that first night of Astronomy class," Kaya improvised. "You guys keep your windows open all the time, or haven't you noticed?"

"I guess," Brun replied. **I'd never really thought about it.**

"But how did you know it was stolen?" Manny asked suspiciously.

"We haven't seen it since," Iris answered flatly.

"Oh," the boys mumbled. **That would be true.** *I see what they're saying.*

"Am I to understand that someone broke into my home?" Chiron asked, his voice edgy for the first time that evening. Manny and Brun's blank looks confirmed the truth. "Explain."

"When we got back from class that first night, someone had thrown my stuff all over the room and attacked Nipper—they knocked her out," Brun said.

Kaya and Iris exchanged nervous glances.

"Who's Nipper?" Ellen asked.

"His pet flytrap," Manny answered.

"And she survived?" Bluebolt inquired.

"Yes," Chiron said tersely. "Boys, why was I not informed of this?"

"We didn't think you'd believe us," Manny confessed.

372

"And why not?" the centaur rebounded. "Are scattered possessions and a missing sun beetle not substantial evidence to sway my confidence?"

"It's not that, Chiron," Brun began. "We thought you wouldn't listen to us if we told you who the culprit was."

"And who would that be?" Chiron demanded. Kaya's heart twisted in a knot. Iris pinched his ears, expecting the worst. "Do you know who did this?"

"We think it was an animal, Chiron," Manny said, his voice hushed. Iris nearly fainted.

"An animal? What animal?" the centaur asked.

"The same one that attacked Iris," Brun stated.

"How do you figure that?" asked Fidelio.

"Well, remember how we said the attacker had those tongs and was trying to steal Iris's wand? We think the same monkey broke into our room searching for our wands, but before he could get very far Nipper came in and startled him, so he hit her and ran off," Manny divulged.

Kaya swallowed hard.

"That's preposterous!" shot Fidelio. "Beside the fact that there was no monkey, no Lumen tries to steal another's wand!"

"Iris's left ear was nearly severed," Ellen stated pensively. "That was his wand ear…"

"Enough," Chiron said firmly. "We will not entertain irrational hypotheses."

"But Nipper had monkey hair in her teeth, Chiron!" Brun argued. Iris felt his left foot.

"And that was the same monkey that gave me my wand and then tried to steal it back in Costa Rica!" Manny affirmed.

"This discussion is closed," Chiron stated, his solemn gaze weighing on the boys' heads. "Julius informed me of this—ridiculous—notion of yours, Manuel. It will go no further and I will hear of it no more. This is the conclusion of our meeting: a Lumen animal—most likely a kinkajou, if not a panther—attacked Iris. Manny and Brun scared the creature and saved Iris, handing him over to Madison and the other healers. The young hare is now safe,

healed, and in possession of his wand. Are we in agreement?"
Bluebolt and Fidelio nodded. "Ellen?"

"More or less," the woman replied, though in her caramel
eyes Manny discerned a faint shadow of doubt.

"Good. I will thus relay our findings to Julius, who will
notify the Island Guardians to open a formal investigation and
search for this rogue Lumen. As for the matter of the sun beetle,"
Chiron continued, his eyes resolute, "Brun, Manny, you will inform
me immediately if such an event ever occurs again, as you should
have done the first time. It is impossible to determine who stole the
beetle—probably a jealous student—but I am certain a monkey did
not. No monkey has ever stolen a Lumen wand, nor is trying to, nor
ever will."

"Finally, we may be assured that the defensive barriers
instated by our wise founders remain strong and intact." The centaur
heaved a sigh. "Meeting dismissed."

Forging of Wills

After writing a hasty letter of complaint to his cousin, Zane, Manny threw himself into his hammock with a growl. "Can you believe Chiron? He basically just called us a pair of idiots in front of half our teachers!"

Nipper's jaws clamped and Lil' Manny squeaked as Brun fed each of them from a palm full of dead flies. The boy laughed as he tossed the insects into the air, watching as the flytrap and salamander crunched the savory snacks. "He's wrong, Manny. They all are." Another fly arced through the air, followed by a ravenous chomp and a hungry squeak. "Except for Iris and Kaya, of course. They believed us."

"That's a first," Manny said dryly. "At least where Kaya's concerned."

***

"Two Piranhas—I get to steal a card," Iris reveled, relaxing comfortably against the headboard of his pinewood bed.

"Fine." Kaya sighed, then picked up her cards and fanned them out. The tip of the hare's right ear hovered over his opponents cards as he contemplated which to choose.

"This one." Iris reached forward and snatched the second card from the right. "I got one of your Aces!"

"Well, that's just great, now, isn't it?" Kaya replied sarcastically, laying her cards down on the star-patterned quilt and walking to the round window. To the north, through a sky littered with rain droplets, Kaya spotted a kapok tree, its upper branches forming a green umbrella. "I'm tired of playing Piranha Sweep." Deflated, her eyes fell to the roots of the Firefoots' massive oak home. There, at the base of the tree, a handful of mudpuppies scuttled about, gathering lumps of wet earth in their tails and launching the missiles at one another in a chorus of elated squeaks.

"It rains all the time on the island, Iris. Why won't your papá let us go out today?"

"He says I might trip and fall." Kaya turned around, glaring at him skeptically. "What?"

"You're not gonna shatter if you hit the ground, Iris."

"No, but less than three days ago my hind paws were shattered," Iris emphasized.

"You're better now, aren't you?" Kaya eyed his hind paws. "Mamá said you should be good as new."

"Dad's just trying to be careful, Kaya. He'll calm down in a few days."

"I hope," she muttered dejectedly.

A pause. Iris rubbed the tips of his ears together tentatively. "Kaya, when Dad does let me out, I have an idea."

Kaya's eyebrows rose. "Oh, ¿sí? ¿Qué?"

"What if we went—hunting?" the hare asked.

"You mean like photocaching? Didn't you remember Professor Shadowflame said we wouldn't start until after Christmas? I feel just as guilty as you do about Brun's sun beetle, but there's no way we can replace it right now."

"Iris stood up on the bed. "Maybe we don't need to replace it. What if we could find it?"

"How do you expect to do that?"

"Promise not to yell?" the hare stipulated.

"Why would I yell?" she inquired innocently. Iris glanced at her blandly. "Fine," she said begrudgingly. "I won't yell."

"Good!" The hare bobbed lightly on the bed. "Okay, so, let's start with a few questions. Who stole the sun beetle?"

"A monkey, obviously."

"Right. And who attacked me and tried to steal my wand?"

"A monkey," the girl forwarded reluctantly.

"Correct! Just one more." The hare held up a clawed finger and winked. "What boy do we know who almost lost his wand to a monkey?"

Kaya glared across the bed. "Iris, I don't see what that has to do with anything."

"Quit lying, Kaya," Iris chastised. "You know just as well as I do how important that is."

"No, I don't, actually. I'm in the dark on that one," she stated shrewdly.

Iris stomped the bed. "Kaya, Manny and Brun can help us track down that monkey! Stop being so stubborn and let's ask for their help!"

"I'll never ask them for help!"

The hare crossed his arms. "Oh, yes you will."

"You're rotten, Iris," Kaya breathed.

"Only when I have to be," he replied, hopping happily across the grass toward the bamboo hut.

Two bright figures flashed in the corner of Kaya's eye as they passed the window. "You're a manipulative little rat, you know that?"

"Thanks," Iris hummed as they turned around back and approached the dried cane door. Kaya knocked. Not a breath later the door shuddered violently, causing the hare to hop back.

"Just a second!" Brun called. "Get back, Nipper."

Kaya grinned down at Iris. "Still think this is such a good idea?" He did not smile in response.

The door opened wide, as did the hare's eyes. "Kaya?" Brun said. "What are you doing here?"

"Iris and I were wondering if you and Manny would like to come to lunch tomorrow."

"To lunch?" Brun repeated, stunned. "You mean, like, at the Café?"

"No." The word clung to the walls of her throat. "To my..."

"What?" Brun cringed, holding Nipper back with his foot. "I couldn't hear you—you mumbled." Iris punched Kaya in the leg.

"Lay off!" she breathed. "Sorry, Brun. I meant to say 'to my house.'"

"You want Brun and me to come to your house?" Manny gawked, stepping out from behind the door, the yellow-spotted salamander perched on his shoulder. "Why?"

"As a way of saying thanks," Iris answered loudly, "for saving my life."

Recognizing the brown-tufted hare, Lil' Manny began to hiss hatefully. A second later he bolted down Manny's arm, straight for the hare's shocked face.

"Lil' Manny, stop it!" the boy shouted, pinning the salamander to his wrist. "That's Iris—he's a friend!"

The salamander, however, continued to hiss. Iris lost no time in hiding behind Kaya's leg.

"One more hiss out of you and you'll spend tomorrow in your cage," Manny threatened as he lifted the enraged amphibian to eye level. Lil' Manny closed his mouth. Revenge certainly did not outweigh freedom. But then Nipper still had her chance...

Iris screamed in terror, and everyone's eyes snapped to the ground. A pair of deep green tentacles had crept below the door and outside the cabin, winding tightly around the hare's wrists and preparing to pull him toward the space between the wall and the door, just above the bottom hinge.

A swift movement of the wrist and a split-second thought produced a birch mallet that came rapping down on each of the vines. Nipper released a painful growl as she withdrew her tentacles.

"Brun, you just hit Nipper with a hammer," Manny choked in disbelief.

"She needed it," Brun quipped. "I don't want her to start attacking our guests, now do I?"

In a single bound Iris leapt into Kaya's arms. "I don't like flytraps," he remarked, his voice now chary.

"Don't worry, Iris. Nipper'll get used to you," Manny reassured him. "She quit biting me after a while."

A twinge ran through the hare's left foot. "Just as long as she doesn't get used to my taste."

378

"She won't, will she, Nipper?" Brun glared sternly at the flytrap sucking on her tentacles beneath Manny's hammock. Nipper's head sagged.

"Lighten up, Brun," rebuked Manny. "She's just a plant."

"You're one to talk," Brun replied.

"So anyway," Kaya interrupted, switching Iris to her other arm. "How about we all meet at the Northern Docks at around 1:30? Manny, you and I can walk from Art. Brun, Iris told me that you two have The Lumen World right before that, so just take a shortcut to meet us on time."

"I know tons of shortcuts," Iris stated helpfully.

"Me, too," Brun coincided. "Mi tía taught me."

The hare glanced up, his ears perked slightly. "I bet your aunt's pretty smart. But did she teach you how to reach the Northern Docks from the Plaza in just five minutes?"

Brun stood amazed. "No! How d'you find that?"

"He can show you later," Kaya dismissed. "So we'll meet at the docks at 1:30?"

"Fine with me," Brun agreed.

"Waitaminute," Manny contravened. "How is it we're coming to your house for lunch tomorrow if you're grounded?"

A glare of frozen chocolate. "Just mind your own business, like I told you Friday night."

Kachow. Stung by the ice princess.

"Changing the subject," Brun reined prudently, "why don't you two come in for a while? We've still got at least half an hour 'til class starts."

"We could play Piranha Sweep!" Manny suggested.

A violet flash. "I love—"

"That's okay, Iris and I are going to head up to Nahir's Hill a little early to study the Sky Bird constellations," Kaya quickly interposed. "Gotta get ready for that quiz Friday, you know?"

Crap! I didn't look at that stuff all weekend!

"That's true," Brun noted sensibly. "But maybe we can sit by each other tonight. Manny and I like the southwe—"

"No, thanks," Kaya intercepted, effectuately halting all further conversation as she turned and walked off, her hair dancing from side to side. "Not tonight."

Iris slapped Kaya in the neck with the backside of his ear. "What'd you do that for? I love Piranha Sweep!"

Kaya strode gracefully through the kapok gate. "I told you yesterday that I was tired of playing that game."

"Well I'm not!" the hare spat. "Who wants to come up here early to study air fowl, anyway?"

"I'd watch my mouth if I were you," Kaya warned.

"I'll say what I want, Kaya! Let me down! I'm heading back to—"

"Buenas noches," called a fervid voice from behind the hare. "I see that you are out and about, Señor Firefoot. And with your amiga. How fare the two of you?"

"Perfect, Chiron," Kaya rebounded in satisfaction. "We were hoping you could help us with the Sky Birds before class starts."

A violet glare lacerated the girl's left cheek. She did not seem to notice, however.

"Excellent!" the centaur exulted, his eyes to the southern skies. "Why not start with the Phoenix, then? Recall that to locate the Fire Bird, you must first find Achernar, the source of the celestial river, Eridanus…"

"Just for that I oughtta tell Chiron it was us who broke into his house," Iris whispered.

"…and now we glance north and west a few degrees to find Phironis, the brightest star in the Phoenix constellation, which of course forms the tip of the bird's head…" Chiron continued.

"That would be breaking your word," Kaya breathed. "I kept my end of the bargain, now you've gotta keep yours."

***

"Edges trim and sharp—ooh! Definitely. Tapered to eight distinct points? Oh, yes! Sides smooth to the touch? ¡Perfecto! Señorita Bellastrata, you've made a most excellent cube—and it's not even purple or orange! ¡Bien hecho!" the woman in dazzling emerald robes cried, her blonde hair pinned up with an emerald wand. "Yes, very well done!"

"Gracias, Professor Flores." Kaya's euphoric eyes reflected the sunflower glow of the flawless six-sided figure that sat on the stone table before her.

Manny could not help but smile, a smaller version of identical shape to Kaya's figure resting in the palm of his hand. "Great job, Kaya."

"Thanks." She sounded happy, almost smiling as she blinked briefly at the boy, then returned her gaze to admire her work.

Flores noted the empty space on the table. "And Manny, where is your assignment?"

"It's right here, Caleida." Manny stretched out his arm, handing the instructor the figure from across the table. "It's—"

"Exquisitely petite!" Flores shouted, drawing the attention of a number of students in the garden. The boy's cheeks flashed bright white as the cube turned a rose hue.

"Don't be embarrassed, dear Manny!" the woman reared, flying around the stone ring to embrace the boy. "Genius is nothing to be ashamed of!"

I just wanna die.

Kaya gazed on in passive amusement. *Poor dweeb.*

Throwing Manny into the pit of humiliation even further, Flores commenced a trek around the garden, showing the tiny crimson cube to each of his peers.

"Look at the professor's prized albino mudpuppy," a voice jeered from over Manny's shoulder.

Recognizing the overconfident ring in his taunter's voice, Manny swatted the air behind his ear. "Shut up, Treble."

"Shut up?" the red morpho repeated, swooping close to the boy's nose. "Why such a harsh tone, Manny? I just came by to praise your magnificent works."

"How nice of you," Manny stated acidly, cringing as Flores continued her tirade, now kneeling down before a unicorn and a panther across the grove.

381

"Would you happen to have any—advice—for us lowly Lumens?" Treble goaded.

"I'm sure Manny won't have anything constructive to share, but if you're having trouble with the assignment, Brightwing, I'd be happy to show you the underside of mine," Kaya plucked.

The crimson butterfly turned his silver eyes to the girl's cube. "No need for that, Bellastrata. I think I'll just leave you and your novio to play with that oversized building block of yours."

Kaya's cube splashed orange as she grabbed it in both hands and launched it at her fluttering target. Treble narrowly avoided partial dewingification. "He's not my boyfriend, you little snipe!" she yelled.

"Señorita Bellastrata, would you mind explaining to me how I nearly lost my foot to your razor-edged assignment?" Flores demanded a moment later, her face flustered as she carried the fiery cube in her hand. "And why are you away from your designated table, Señor Brightwing?"

"I can tell you I wasn't playing catch," Treble cracked, hovering sporadically.

"Professor, I'm really sorry about that, but this little crow was running his hooked mouth," Kaya defended, a chocolate flame licking out at the butterfly.

"Oh, was he?" Flores set the cube down forcefully.

Here we go.

***

"Why are you guys late?" Iris asked, tossing his purpleheart wand in the air from one ear to the other. "We've been waiting here for, like, twenty minutes!"

"It's true, Manny!" Brun rejoiced. "Iris led me down this path behind the shop buildings that got us here in just five minutes! Araceli had no clue where we went!"

"Well, Kaya decided she'd have an extensive chat with Caleida." Manny approached the pier with the stone silent girl at his side.

"Caleida? Do you mean Professor Flores?" questioned Iris. "She'd skin me if I called her by her first name. She won't even let Dad do that."

"Yeah, well, I think she's in love with me," Manny said unenthusiastically.

"Us, you mean," Brun corrected. "But I think she looks at me as a work in progress."

"Uh, I don't understand why she's so obsessed with—oh." Iris paused. "It's because of your skin, isn't it?"

Manny nodded, then waved his hands dramatically. "We're living works of art."

"Are you three coming?" a gruff voice asked from the Lake.

The boys and the hare turned to find a familiar looking otter seated atop a pink river dolphin. Behind the otter, in the back of a boat, sat Kaya, her expression emotionless.

"Hey, Jasper! It's me, Brun!" The boy quickly trotted along the wooden planks of the dock.

"My clam shells, it is!" the otter cried. "And late as ever! How are you?"

"Great!" Brun stepped down into the ferry to take the front seat. Manny and Iris followed suit, filling in the middle seats. "So I guess you only work along the EIC during the lightboarding competition, then?"

Jasper slapped the dolphin's side. "That would be an accurate assumption." In a pair of seconds the craft shot away from the pier, then glided steadily toward the eastern end of the Café. "Unless o' course you'd like to make a weekend o' it and visit Easter Island with your friends. If that's the case just contact the Lumen Travel Bureau, a few stores down from the LIGHT Group."

"I don't think we'll want to head back that way anytime soon," Brun remarked, turning around to send a knowing glance to Iris, who shrugged in reply.

"Maybe not; we'll just have to talk about it," the hare countered vaguely.

Brun frowned. **Something must be loose in his head.**

"You'll just be seeing me at the Lake, then," Jasper acknowledged.

"How's Tobias?" Manny shouted so that his voice would reach the otter.

"Currently and presently very grounded," Jasper called back. "But otherwise peachy, excluding his depressed mood, of course."

"He never found his wand, then?" continued Manny.

"Heavens, no. That little pup must've dropped it in a bottomless pit, 'cause we can't find it anywhere. His mother's still furious," the otter answered.

"Who's Tobias?" Iris inquired, his ears snapping in the wind.

"He's the captain's son. You should know who he is—he's in our Healing class. His last name's Greenriver," Manny explained.

"Is Ursa his brother?" Iris questioned warily.

"I think that was his name," Manny replied.

"It was," Brun verified as he turned around. "They're triplets—Michael is the third."

"To tell the truth, I can't stand Ursa," Iris confessed. "He's cocky. You know he shut a clam on my ear once?"

"That's mean," Brun said.

Manny leaned forward. "But Tobias isn't like that at all. I think you'd get along with him great, Iris."

"If he lost his wand there's not much chance for that," the hare answered flatly.

"Destination reached!" Jasper called as the ferry swerved sharply, its keel slapping against the rocks. Kaya had already leapt from the boat before the otter could shout, "Watch yer step, now!"

"Gracias, Señor Greenriver," the girl said in her subdued voice as she set a golden Sol in the otter's paw.

"What nice manners!" Jasper exclaimed. "But such a sad face! Can I help you in any way, Señorita?" Kaya shook her head, then turned to walk toward the entrance to Nightcrest Caverns, her back to the Café.

Brun knelt to shake Jasper's free paw. "Hopefully we'll see you soon!"

Manny stepped onto the wet stone next to Brun. "Tell Tobias hi for us, and that we'll keep an eye out for his wand."

"I will," the otter replied distractedly. "I've seen that girl before, lads. Is she a sister to Keilani Bellastrata?"

"Yes!" Iris said. "Her name's Kaya. She's our age."

Jasper's concerned expression remained unchanged. "She seems as down as Tobias today. What happened?"

"It's a long story," Manny replied quickly, "but if we don't hurry and catch up to her she won't be sad much longer."

Jasper gave the boy a confused look.

"He means she'll get mad," Iris clarified.

"Oh," the otter replied knowingly. "I've been there a time or two. Have a g'day, then, and good luck with that one!"

"Thanks!" Brun called, already several steps away.

Manny jogged up next to Kaya. "So I guess you live north of town, then?" No reply came.

"She does," Iris said, hopping along the stone edge just above the glassy water, his bobbing image reflecting shakily. "In a few minutes we'll reach the entrance to the caverns, and from there we hop up the stairs and onto the east end of the Lucero deck. Kaya's house is just a short distance from there," the hare added, smiling up at the girl. She did not look down.

A good ten minutes passed before they stepped—or hopped, in Iris's case—from stair to deck. There, Manny stopped, leaning on the south railing and gazing out along the wooden walkway that spanned the entire breadth of the valley basin, from one stone stair to the other. In the center rose the observation platform above the crown of the Falls, which is of course where Manny and his peers attended Nochesol's Light Bending classes.

"You know, for the past three months I've been wondering why the walkway stretches out over all this naked rock. I don't get it. It would be just as easy to walk along the ledge as waste all this wood on a useless bridge."

"Didn't you listen to anything Iris said at the competition?" Brun asked as he, too, reached the boardwalk.

"How do you figure?" Manny replied.

385

Brun joined Manny at the rail. "Iris said the Lucero grows to cover the entire ledge during flood season."

"That's why the rock's so smooth—the water washes over it for half the year, crashing down into the Lake. At that time you have to walk behind the curtain of the Falls to reach the Café—and the caverns," the hare elucidated, his amethyst eyes peeking through the banister.

Manny suddenly remembered their past conversation. "And you said that all starts around December?"

"Roughly," Iris indicated.

"Let's go, muchachos," Kaya called, her feet planted stiffly on a strip of boardwalk branching northeast into the forest.

"On our way!" Iris's flat paws thumped the stained boards as he and the boys followed. Minutes later the walkway hooked sharply east.

Manny's pupils opened wide. "Whoa."

"Now that's what I'm talking about." Brun's golden gaze ran along the deck that yielded to hundreds of smaller walkways on either side, connecting the main drag to countless buildings hugging the lofty trunks of tropical trees, many of them brazil nut with the occasional kapok or cocobolo. "I didn't know you lived in a tree house, Kaya!"

The girl ignored him, leading the boys and the hare further east to a circular deck pierced by the bough of a magnificent tree, the flower-speckled fingers of its branches stretching up to the distant sun like an upturned octopus whose tentacles were wrapped around scads of gilded fish. From here she turned north, and it was just a short walk before the deck narrowed and forked. Kaya sulked, traversing a sturdy air bridge that met a wrap around deck bursting with floral life, from icy orchids to bromeliads of seemingly endless colors. Moss hung from the branches above as the young Lumens crossed yet another bridge, coming to a stop before a dark-stained octagonal structure with a slanted roof and wide, curtained windows.

Kaya turned around. "This is my house," she said damply.

Brun was in awe. "It's incredible."

386

Blinking wordlessly, Kaya turned around and gripped the polished pecan knob. With a sigh of defeat, she opened the door and stepped inside.

Feet pattered from around a corner to the left. "¡Mamá!" a shrill voice called. "They're here!"

"Remember, Kiki—you don't need to yell for me to hear you," replied Ellen. "Show the boys the house, but be respectful, like we talked about. Kaya—to the kitchen, now."

Manny watched as Kaya ambled lifelessly across the room and through the swinging door to the left. *I wouldn't want to be her right now.*

"Are you The Jerk, or are you Brun?" inquired the high voice at Manny's feet.

"What?" The boy looked down to discover a miniature replica of Kaya, those same chocolate eyes staring up at him from the height of his waist. Unlike Kaya, however, this girl did not wear a string of pink hair beads, but an aquamarine necklace studded with silver animal charms. *Is this a family of clones, or what?*

"Is your name Brun, or are you The Jerk?" the girl repeated.

"Well, I'm Brun," the other boy said, closing the door. "That would leave only one other option." Brun chuckled.

Aren't you funny? Manny glared at his cheeky roommate.

"So you're Manny, then." The girl took the boy's hand and shook it happily. "It's nice to meet you. I'm Kiki."

Brun knelt down. "Kiki, huh? I've never met a little kid before."

"Yeah, I'm the youngest," Kiki replied, jumping forward to hug Brun, an action which caught him by surprise. "But I'll tell you a secret—Papá says I'm the sweetest." She stepped back and smiled.

That wouldn't be hard. "¿Cuántos años tienes?"

"I'm five." Kiki's cheerful eyes glowed up at Manny. "That makes me half your age."

This little chickie knows her division.

"We might as well begin the tour!" she said, glancing down at the hare. "Hey, Iris! Wanna go piggy back?"

"Sure!" the hare exclaimed, hopping behind the girl and leaping into the air, his hind legs slipping through her hooked arms and his paws clinging lightly to her shoulders.

"¿Listo?" Kiki asked.

"Ready," Iris affirmed, nodding his head.

"Okay." She turned to face the half-donut shaped room furnished with white cushioned couches, oaken rocking chairs, and family portraits.

Manny noticed the glass coffee table resting in the center of the room. *That's just like mine back home.*

"As you can see, this is the living room." Kiki maneuvered between table and chairs to reach yet another door on the right. "And this is Kaya's room," she whispered. "I'll let you have a peek, but don't tell her I did."

Brun nodded. "Lumen's honor."

Her eyes wary of the entrance to the kitchen, Kiki stealthily slid the door open, revealing yet another slice of room illuminated by two broad windows. Blossoming flowers painted the walls and bedclothes; on a nightstand sat a vase holding a glass hibiscus. Before the boys could scan any further, the door closed, and Kiki scuttled across the living room to the kitchen.

"Come on," she called, her tone hushed.

Manny tripped over the leg of a rocking chair. "S-shouldn't we wait?"

"Nah—let's just rush through." Kiki pushed the door open, gripping Iris's legs extra-tight as she jogged ahead.

"Whatever," Manny mumbled as he followed Brun into the kitchen. On their right, her back to the boys, stood Ellen Bellastrata, grilling dozens of yellow peppers the size of bullets over an open flame. To the left Manny spied a steel sink, giving way to a pearl-white countertop stretching along to a sliding glass door, through which Kiki had just passed. Brun walked swiftly past the refrigerator beyond the stove, hooking left in pursuit of their young guide.

"Even when arrogant people get under your skin, Kaya, you can't just turn around and attack them. What you did today would be equivalent to rolling a boulder at Kiki. You could have killed Treble," Ellen called, impervious to Manny's presence behind her.

As Manny reached the door and grasped the handle, he noticed Kaya setting silverware around a table for seven, her back to the boy. Curiosity coaxed him to stop and listen.

"Sí, Mamá. But what he said was just so—embarrassing," Kaya answered as she leaned across the table to grab another fork.

The woman peeled the charred skin from a pepper. "Is it really such a bad thing what he said?"

"¡Mamá!" Kaya exclaimed, slamming down a knife. "He's—he's—"

"¿Qué? What is he?" Ellen retorted. "I'll tell you what he is—a young hero. That boy saved your best friend's life."

A spoon slipped through Kaya's fingers; she knelt to pick it up. "I thought none of you believed him."

"I never said that," the mother replied, shaking her tulipwood bracelet to roast another set of peppers over the gas flame. "Do you believe him?"

Kaya evaded the question with one of her own, though menial in comparison. "We need salad plates, don't we?" She then turned around toward the counter, her face flushed. Not a second later she heard the unmistakable *Schwop!* of the sliding door; but no one was there.

"Why are you hiding, Jerk?" Kiki called from halfway along the wooden the bridge extending out from the sliding door. Iris frowned at him.

Manny's eyes avalanched shut as he prayed Kaya had not heard. A violent twang of fear reverberated in his mind as he stood, edging cautiously along the banister toward Kiki.

"We can't play hide-and-seek right now, silly. Mamá doesn't like it when I play at lunch time," the girl explained.

"That's fine," Manny said, relaxing slightly as he glanced up. "So what's in this next part of the house?"

"Ooh—the best part, of course! My bedroom!" Kiki crooned enthusiastically.

"Don't forget your parents' room," Iris said helpfully.

Kiki looked up at Manny. "What did he say?"

Manny stared back oddly. "Didn't you hear him?"

"Yes, but I can't understand him!" the girl said defensively. "I'm not a Lumen yet!" Another strange glance. "What?"

"You acted like you understood him earlier," Manny noted.

"I just guess what he's saying sometimes—all I really hear are squeaks," Kiki replied. "Now what did he say?"

Manny surrendered. "He told you not to forget your parents' room."

"Well, they're not interested in that," Kiki dismissed as she turned and approached the door.

"What was all that about?" Brun whispered, nodding back toward the kitchen.

"Don't worry about it," Manny said quickly.

Brun stared fixedly back. Yet Manny looked past him, pretending to be overwhelmingly interested in what Kiki had apparently begun explaining. "...and Manny can have my jaguar doll—he'll like that. Iris, you can be the elephant, and Brun can—"

"Time for lunch, everyone!" called Ellen from the kitchen.

"But Mamá! We were just going to play zookeeper!" Kiki shouted, one foot indignantly planted in the frame across the way.

"Those boys don't want to play that with you!" her mother shot back. "But maybe you can talk them into a game of cards after lunch!"

"Go Fish?!" Kiki cried, slapping her hands to her face dramatically.

"Maybe," Ellen laughed. "Come on in, boys. It's an honor to have you here." She smiled as Brun and Manny returned through the sliding door. "Sit wherever you like."

"Gracias, Señora Bellastrata," Brun said respectfully as he sat down.

"Please, call me Ellen," she replied graciously.

"¡Papi!" Kiki exclaimed, running across the kitchen to leap into the arms of a rather tall man, his gentle, bronze eyes wielding a sharp intellect, all framed in rectangular, black spectacles. He wore

390

hiking boots, a pair of jeans, and a polo brandishing an iridescent logo that read, "The LIGHT Group."

"¿Cómo estás, Kiki Liki?" the man asked, hugging his youngest daughter with a growl. Kaya shook her head, turning away in shame.

"¡Bien, Papi!" Kiki shouted gleefully.

Ellen stepped to the side. "Manny, Brun, this is my husband, Marcos."

"Nice to meet you, boys." Marcos shook each one's hand firmly. That same nervous twinge suddenly pulled at Manny's stomach again, but he knew not why. "Kaya, the rest of the family, and I all greatly appreciate what you did for Iris five days ago." He smiled genuinely.

"Gracias, Señor," Brun replied, pleased to receive a compliment rather than criticism.

"Well, let's eat, then!" Ellen exclaimed. "Kaya, you'll help me serve the food."

As Ellen and Kaya delivered various platters to the oval table, everyone else took their seats, Iris situated between Manny and Brun, with Marcos and Kiki facing opposite. A moment later Ellen set the bowl of roasted peppers down, taking the seat on the end next to Brun and Kiki, effectively leaving Kaya no other option but to sit at the opposite end of the table between her father and— Manny.

The boy stole a glance at Ellen, who appeared content as she spooned peppers onto Kiki and Brun's plates. *She planned this...*

Kaya filled a small plate with a medley of greens, orange slices, crushed pecans, and edible flowers, then passed the salad bowl to Manny without a second look.

"Manny, right?" The boy looked up, nodding at Marcos. "You'll love this marinated steak pasta. It's one of Ellen's many specialties."

"Looks great," Manny replied nervously, still unable to shake the persistent awkwardness as he watched Marcos hand the platter to Kaya.

391

Just as Kaya placed the pasta next to Manny, her father said, "Why don't you serve it for him, Kaya?" Ice stole over her face. "He is our guest."

Manny clenched his fists below the table. *Just let it alone.*

Without a word, Kaya obeyed, taking the tongs stiffly in her hands and heaping a mountain of noodles on Manny's plate. Manny glanced at Kaya's face—emotionless.

This is so strange.

"Could you pass the pasta, Manny?" Brun asked.

"Uh, yeah." The boy blinked back to reality and quickly complied with his friend's request.

"How's your salad?" Ellen queried, her eyes on Iris.

"The best," the hare replied, chomping a pecan. "Even better than the Café." The woman smiled.

"So, Señor Bellastrata," Brun began as he received the bowl of peppers from Manny, "I see that you work for the LIGHT Group. What's that like?"

"Very enjoyable," Marcos replied after swallowing a mouthful of pasta. "I design obstacles and challenges for photocaching missions."

"Really?" Brun said excitedly.

"¡Sí!" Kiki contributed. "Papi's an archerlect!"

Archerlect?

"I am an architect," the father affirmed, patting Kiki on the back.

"What's an example of an obstacle you've built?" Brun asked.

"Hmm… Sorry, Brun, but I'm actually not allowed to say because the challenges are confidential," Marcos replied.

"Oh, just give them something hypothetical, dear," Ellen said, stabbing an orange.

Marcos contemplated this for a moment, his eyes staring out the wide window behind the boys. "Okay, I've got one. Let's say you finally reach the cache site, and the area is scattered with numerous pillars. Now on top of each pillar sits a glass dome confining a sun beetle. What do you do?"

392

"You mean, like, if there were fifteen pillars with fifteen separate sun beetles?" Brun asked. Marcos nodded. "I'd shout for joy and begin collecting them!"

"Bad move." The man wagged a knife at him.

"Why?" Manny asked, his lips burning from an ají pepper.

"Because there's never more than one photocache," Ellen answered simply.

"Right, dear," Marcos agreed.

"But you just said there were fifteen different sun beetles," Iris argued, pulling a flower aside with his fork.

"Your eyes were deceived," Marcos said, pointing to his own. "Only one of those fifteen domes conceals the photocache. The remaining sun beetles are only an illusion."

"Hold on a minute," Manny interrupted. "So the sun beetle is the photocache?"

"Yes," several voices responded, some more patient than others.

"What's under the other domes, then?" Brun asked attentively.

Marcos wound more cheesy pasta around his fork. "A threat."

"Like what?" Iris fished, discarding his own utensil.

"Who's to say?" answered the man cryptically. Kaya rolled her eyes. "Perhaps an Amazon Horned Frog."

Brun, Iris, and Kiki gasped.

"What's the big deal about some frog?" Manny inquired.

"That frog could swallow my head whole," the hare answered gravely.

"And they don't like to regurgitate their food," Brun added.

"So, hypothetically, Papá, what part of the challenge would you have designed?" Kaya's words were tipped with condescending blades. "The pillars?"

"Yes, sweetheart," Marcos answered clearly. "Not to mention the reflective veils simulating the false photocaches and masking the threats. Does that answer your question?"

"Sí," she whispered, crushing a flower with her spoon. Silence.

"I have ice cream for dessert!" Ellen bolstered, rising from chair to freezer. A moment later each person sat with his or her preferred flavor, from raspberry and orange to vanilla and guava. The tight chords in the air loosened considerably.

Kiki stared at her bowl of ice cream, its vanilla slopes melting slowly. She then looked up and directly at Manny. "Why do you glow?"

Brun raised his eyes, but noticed the girl had not spoken to him. Iris's ears fidgeted. Kaya stared intently at Manny.

"Are you talking to me?" Manny asked, the frozen guava chilling his teeth and lips.

"Kiki, that's rude!" Ellen intervened.

Manny slid his spoon into the bowl. "It's okay. Kiki's one of the few people who has ever asked me that question nicely."

Kiki smiled serenely at her mother.

"The truth is, Kiki, I've glowed like this since I was born," Manny said.

"Was it because your mamá got struck by lightning while you were inside her?" Kiki asked. Kaya let out a chuckle; Ellen shook her head and concealed a smile.

"No," Manny laughed. "At least not from what I've been told. Mi mamá says I just have special skin—nothing weird like that."

Kiki redirected her gaze. "What about your mamá, Brun? What does she say?" Iris flinched at the girl's naïveté.

"I don't know what she would say," Brun answered quietly. "She's dead—died when I was born."

"I'm so sorry," Ellen said, setting her hand on Kiki's shoulder.

"But aren't you boys brothers?" Marcos asked, his tongue orange.

"No," Brun replied, listing the differences between their families.

"I was sure you were twins," Marcos said in disbelief.

394

"Besides everything else I just mentioned, I'm six months older than Manny," Brun added.

"Chiron said we're children of the solstice," Manny contributed.

"Really?" Marcos resumed. "That's fascinating. But I know other Lumens with the same birthdays, and they don't glow."

"What's a soulspiss?" Kiki asked. Ellen explained as the boys and the man continued chatting.

"Oh, well," Manny shrugged. "It doesn't bother me anymore. Becoming a Lumen made me realize that shining can actually be a good thing."

"But don't you ever wonder why you shine?" asked Marcos, his bronze eyes searching Manny's passive face."

"No," the boy replied. "Not really."

"I do," Brun said. "All the time."

Marcos nodded eagerly. "Do you have any theories?"

"Just one, actually," Brun replied. Every eye turned attentively to the boy, even Manny's. "When I met Manny, I began to wonder what might have happened to us at birth to make us this way. All I could figure was that the cells in our bodies were infused with a recessive Lumen gene, causing our skin to have unique reactions to sunlight. Manny's reflects it, but mine seems to absorb and release it later."

"Hold on a sec," Manny interrupted. "My cousin, Zane, and I noticed that my skin can glow in the dark, too. But only when I'm extremely upset."

"And when you're embarrassed," Iris threw in.

Manny looked quizzically at the hare.

"Instead of blushing, your face just gets brighter; I noticed it when Kiki asked you a question a moment ago," explained Iris.

"In other words, emotions can trigger the gene—assuming it is a gene," Marcos said, entertaining Brun's hypothesis. "Is the same true for you, Brun?"

"Not that I've noticed, but then I don't get angry or embarrassed very easily," he replied.

"But that still wouldn't explain why you both look so much alike," Ellen cut in.

"Unless the gene imparts distinct physical features, similar to Down Syndrome," her husband rebounded.

"But they're identical, Marcos," Ellen contended.

"Exactly my point!" he persisted.

"I don't know about Brun, but I look an awful lot like the rest of my family, especially my dad and Zane," Manny said.

"Me, too," Brun added. "I look like mi tía in the face, and my skin matches mi papá's—except for the glowing part, of course."

Ellen appeared content with these explanations. Marcos, however, began to recalculate his thoughts.

"Maybe it's just coincidence," Iris offered. "It could be that the gene's only job is to make them glow."

"I have an idea," Marcos said. "I know how we can disprove or verify the gene theory. Some friends of ours are photobiologists with experience in genetics. You boys could give them a blood sample and they could analyze it. The process wouldn't take long."

"I can't," Manny articulated swiftly. "Mi mamá doesn't want anyone running tests on me. She's said that all my life."

"And I don't know if mi papá would like that, either. He's particular about certain things," Brun said.

"Are you sure?" asked Marcos. "Because the tests wouldn't be—"

"Leave it alone, Marcos," Ellen stated. "We can't go against their parents' wishes." The man's enthusiasm deflated.

"Can we play Go Fish now?" Kiki asked, her legs swinging below the table.

"No," Kaya snapped. Ellen turned staunch eyes on Kaya. "What?"

"You can help me with the dishes," her mother responded.

"But, Mamá, aren't they my guests? It would be rude of me to ignore them," Kaya argued.

This statement seemed to have some persuasive effect over Ellen, as she did not provide an immediate answer. After all, respect was one of the attributes she esteemed most highly.

"We do have several important things to talk about," Iris acknowledged.

"Oh, you do?" Ellen asked. "Like what?"

I was wondering that myself.

"You know, Mamá—everything we're going to do this week," Kaya said, picking up the line for Iris. "This is the first time we've all four been together."

Which nearly took an act of God.

Ellen relented. "Kiki, it sounds like you and I will be doing the dishes."

The young girl's eyes welled up with tears. Manny could see the sob building in her chest.

"We can still play cards before we leave," Brun suggested.

"Really?" Kiki sniffed.

"Sure," Manny said.

Kiki leapt from her chair nearly instantly, running from seat to seat collecting bowls and spoons. "Come on, Mamá! Let's hurry!"

***

Manny turned a tear-shaped candy over in his palm. "What are these things?"

"Jasmine Honeydrops," Kaya replied as she slid into a lounge chair, crossing her ankles and popping a drop in her mouth. "They're my favorite." Sweet, wet gold slowly coated her tongue and throat as she gazed out through the quiet trees, their canopies penetrated by slanted arrows of light. The distant cascades of the Lucero rumbled to the west.

"This is a nice deck," Brun observed, reclining in his chair. "And these seats are really comfortable."

"The candy rocks, Kaya." Manny closed his eyes, enjoying the warmth of the broken sunlight that fell upon the northeast end of the veranda. "It just keeps melting and melting."

"Well, I don't like them very much," Iris said, his feet and ears hanging over the edge of the transparent quartz table at the teenagers' feet. "They make my whiskers sticky."

"Too bad for you." Kaya pulled another drop from the star-shaped tin in her lap. "Brun, Manny, would either of you like more?"

Was that kindness I heard? "Why not?" Brun gladly accepted a second.

"And Keilani really doesn't mind us eating her candy and hanging out on her balcony?" Manny asked tentatively.

"She won't know the difference, especially after being gone for nine months." Kaya nonchalantly unwrapped a third drop. "Besides, mi mamá gave us permission."

"In that case, I'll take two." Manny quickly tagged on a disclaimer. "If that's okay, of course." *I shouldn't push my luck.* But to his surprise, three honeydrops came sailing over Brun's head and straight into Manny's lap. "¡Gracias!"

"Forward Keilani a thank-you letter if you're all that grateful," she replied wryly.

"Talking about letters," Iris began, "how often are you gonna write Keilani, anyway?"

"Nunca," the girl said bluntly. "After getting me grounded for nearly two weeks, I'm not gonna communicate with her, period."

"Grounded from what?" Manny asked.

Iris glanced eagerly at Manny. "Kaya's practi—"

"Hush it, Iris!" she snapped. "And mind your own business, Manny."

Brun's gaze rifled through the tightly wound branches above, searching for a view of the sky. **That seems to be a popular phrase between these two lately.** He glanced from Kaya to Iris. "So do either of you know what the First-Level Mission involves?"

The hare ruffled his ears. "All I've heard is that they start in North America."

"And various other places, I think," Kaya added. "Their professors keep them busy."

Manny's brow furrowed. "Don't they have the same teachers as us?"

"No. The First-Levels work with a special group of instructors who actually leave on the Mission with them," Kaya clarified.

"I never knew that," Manny confessed.

Brun appeared incredulous. "You mean you never noticed Professor Scrumgold hopping past our house on Saturday nights? He and Chiron always climbed the hill together."

Manny sat up. "Are you talking about that old tree-frog? I thought he was just a friend of Chiron's who enjoyed watching him teach."

"Uh, no," Brun said savorlessly. **Pay attention, Manny.**

"How about we discuss our own mission?" Iris suggested.

The muscles in Manny's back stiffened. "You mean the one with the crystal spiders?"

Iris's ear twitched. "No, the one about the monkeys."

"We don't have a mission with monkeys," Brun contradicted smartly.

Kaya stretched. "That's the real reason we invited you here. My family doesn't know that, though."

Manny leaned forward and peered across Brun. "To talk about monkeys?"

"Yes. Unlike the rest of them at the meeting the other night, Kaya and I believe you," Iris replied.

Kaya noted a skeptical light in Manny's eyes. "It's true," she added coolly.

"We appreciate it," Brun spoke.

"So what are you proposing?" the other boy asked, now sitting sidewise in his chair.

The hare's nose twitched. "Could you answer a question first?"

"I guess," Manny answered. "¿Qué pregunta?"

Kaya now spoke. "How did you first meet that monkey? You know, the one that attacked Iris?"

"It's complicated," Manny evaded.

Iris blinked understandingly. "That's okay. We really need to hear it."

"Está bien, pues." Manny relented, recounting again his eighth grade trip to Costa Rica in full detail: the primate poop, Julius' cracked skull, how Tavo hurled the monkey across the path... The boy ended his story several minutes later with his stealthy return to the class compound.

Kaya stared at the mahogany watch on his wrist. "I just can't believe a monkey gave you your wand."

"Well, believe it," Manny said gruffly.

"I do!" she rejoined swiftly. "It's just—do you know what this means?"

Aggravation raked the boy's mind; he was quite exhausted with everyone's level of incredulity to his account. *Oh, please tell us.*

"It means that there's a new Lumen species." Iris spoke quietly, as if in awe.

Manny snapped back in reply. "And why's that so hard for everyone to believe? There are, what, millions of animal species in this world? Why can't a few more become Lumens?"

"Because the stars are dead," Brun stated seriously. "Only the Light Brethren could create new Lumen species."

"Nobody ever told me that!" Manny buttressed.

"In point of fact, Julius did that night he met us up on Lookout Point," Brun retorted. "And besides, don't you listen in Professor Shadowflame's class?"

"I think my eyes glaze over when she starts making us memorize the Brethren's favorite ice cream flavors!" Manny shot back.

"They didn't even have ice cream back then," Brun countered.

"Actually, they did," Kaya interposed. "Tryphena's favorite was strawberry."

"How do you know that?" Brun questioned.

"I read it in a book from the Lumen Resource Center called *Celestial Idiosyncrasies*," she replied.

"We are way off topic, everybody," Iris bridled. "Think about the repercussions of a new species."

"Our world will change," Brun said thoughtfully.

"And for the worse, from what we've seen," Manny added.

Iris hopped up onto the table. "That's the point! Seeing as the monkeys are a new species—and they're mean—it only stands to reason that a new star has come to Earth, and he—"

"Or she," Kaya interposed.

"—must hate us," Iris finished.

"But why?" Manny asked, recalling now that he had indeed defended the same argument against Julius. "What did we ever do to him?"

The deck grew quiet, each individual retreating into the invisible space of his or her own theories and ruminations. A sweet call preluded the flight of a dazzling bird through the foliage above, the westering sun's light illuminating the fowl's multihued, phoenix-like plumes.

Brun sighed. "I don't know, but I see the wisdom in his strategy."

"What wisdom? It's not like they could do anything with our wands, anyway," Manny observed.

"But neither could we," Iris rejoined soberly.

"Our powers would be nonexistent—we'd be completely crippled," Brun said.

"So let's stop the jerk," Kaya said, considering the idea of the rogue star as she reclined unflappably. "We're the only ones who know the truth, and no one else trusts us. We've got to."

"But if he's a star, couldn't he, like, disintegrate us?" asked Manny uneasily.

Kaya tossed her hair back. "Probably. But that's why we've gotta outsmart him."

"To do that you have to find him first; and we have no idea where to start," Manny argued.

Iris sat back down on the table. "As a matter of fact, we do."

"Where, then?" Manny probed.

"The monkey," Brun murmured. "I bet if we trail the monkey, he'll lead us straight to the rebel star."

The hare agreed. "Kaya and I are with you there, Brun."

Manny asserted his point of view. "And how do you expect to do that? We have no idea where the monkey might show up next."

"We do know where he's made his last few appearances," stated Iris.

"Last few? I only count two—Ukisaru Volcano and Chiron's Hutch," Kaya indicated.

"There's one more," the hare clarified. "He stole one of our classmate's wands."

"He did?" Manny exclaimed.

"He did," Brun affirmed, startled by the realization. "He must be the one who took Tobias's shell necklace."

"No w—" Manny paused. "You're right. That little pus sac swiped the wand before he headed for Easter Island."

Iris's brow raised. "And where did that all happen again?"

"In the forest a few minutes east of the stairs we climbed earlier," Manny described. "At a small pond."

"I know that place." Iris slid gingerly from the table. "Vámonos."

"Now just wait a minute," Manny broke in as Kaya and Brun started to rise from their lounge chairs. "Let me see if I've got this right—we're going to the pond to search for clues that Tobias and I never found. But if by some chance we find some, we're going to track the monkey to, where? His secret hideout? Don't you think that's a little out of our league?"

"No." Kaya set the candy tin bluntly on the chair. "If that dumb monkey can sneak around without getting caught, then so can we."

Manny's feet tingled. "It's just that—"

"You're afraid," the girl enounced.

"I'm going one way or another, Kaya," Manny rebounded. "But if we have to leave—"

"Hush!" Kaya breathed, lifting a hand for silence. "Someone just opened the door."

Footsteps sounded from behind. "Kaya, boys, are you still out here?" Ellen called.

"Whoo." Iris sighed, his ears sinking. "It's only your mom; I thought for a second it might have been the monkey." Kaya rolled her eyes.

Ellen appeared from around the corner, her long, white skirt swishing. "Are you aware of the time?"

"No, ¿por qué?" Kaya asked.

"Because it's five 'til four," the woman replied.

"Professor Firefoot's going to kill us, Brun!" Manny nearly shouted.

"If you promise to come back and play cards with Kiki later this evening, I'll send Fidelio a note stating that you're with me and that you're on your way," Ellen offered kindly.

"Deal," Brun said swiftly.

"What about us, Mamá?" Kaya asked.

"Could you write Professor Nochesol?" Iris pleaded.

"I suppose," Ellen conceded. "But don't any of you let this happen again."

I won't.

Monkey Hunt

"A superior review, class. " Fidelio adjusted his eyeglass as he surveyed the students scattered about the ruddy grass. Light danced on the teenagers' content faces, the air flooded with a terrestrial milky way of Fireflies. "Now, siphon the light and dissolve your sentinels." From the peregrine falcons to the green basilisks and all species in between, the students obeyed, lifting their wands to suck photon streams from the steadily dimming insects.

Fidelio nodded his approval from the base of the fire oak at the head of the clearing. "Well done. Now, do I have a wise soul who could attempt a guess at our next sentinel?" An ebullient screech rose from the crowd. "Lakia?"

"May I, Professor?" the falcon asked, her eyes a shining pair of black pearls.

"Please do," Fidelio replied.

Lakia shuffled in place. "Sí, Señor. I've been wondering about this for a while, and I believe I narrowed the sentinel down to one of two possibilities—either Chamaeleon or Reticulum."

"An astute conclusion," the hare noted, a glint in his greystone eyes. "But how did you reach it?"

"I remembered how earlier in the semester you told us we would cover five sentinels this year. We've already mastered Firefly. Since we're not photocaching until after Christmas, Circinus is out. And the Pisces sentinel seems pretty complicated with all those fish," she added sensibly. "That leaves us with the other two."

"Fantastic," the instructor breathed. "So class, which will it be? Shall we learn the art of camouflage, or do we practice trapping adversaries with a photon net? Defense, or offense?"

"If you can't protect yourself you might as well just go home," bawled a kinkajou.

"Good eye!" Fidelio riposted. "The effective Lumen must first know how to defend—or in this case, conceal—himself in order to confront danger. Taking this into account, our next sentinel will

404

be Chamae—" The hare abruptly stopped, staring sternly across the flats at a pair of boys who had just appeared at the entrance.

"I thought Kaya's mom sent him a letter," Manny muttered through the corner of his mouth.

"It's in his right paw," Brun replied, noting the glowing document as he plunged forward through the heavy gaze of his peers.

"I do not tolerate tardiness—Señor López, Señor Dimirtis." Fidelio stuffed the subtle sapphire paper into one of his vest pockets. "No, no, no," he continued as the boys attempted to sit behind the furthermost cluster of students. "You'll sit at the front of the class, right by that tree root. And afterward we'll have a much-needed chat about promptness and truancy."

Ten grueling seconds later the boys sat down at Fidelio's feet, Manny looking a good deal like a walking lighthouse, embarrassment filling his every pore.

Brun, on the other hand, remained calm, even daring to gaze straight into the instructor's stony eyes. **It'll come out alright in the end.**

"I apologize, class, for this rude interruption. I assure you that it will not happen again." The hare's voice was rigid. "Now, as I was saying, the sentinel we will begin covering today is Chamaeleon. I will now demonstrate."

Twisting his monocle, Fidelio assembled the orange figure of a reptile—short, plump, and with a curling tail. "This is a chameleon." He knelt to grab the sentinel with his right paw. "Now, how do I animate it?"

"Breathe!" several students called.

"Precisely." Fidelio whispered silently to the reptile in his hand. A moment later the Chamaeleon opened its jaws, unraveling its tail and gazing at the large hare, who set the creature down on the grass.

"It's staring at me," Manny whispered. The reptile blinked.

"Please notice, class, that once the Chamaeleon is animated, it will follow me wherever I go, as also is the case for Firefly—and most other sentinels." Fidelio hopped to the north side of the dell,

405

the lizard not far behind. A velvet paw rose into the air. "Yes, Orion?"

"How do you activate Chamaeleon's abilities?" the panther asked.

"Good question. First, you must become completely still—do not move whatsoever. Then, glance at the Chamaeleon, and imagine yourself hidden. From there the sentinel will do the rest. Now watch." Fidelio lowered his paw from his monocle. As his muscles relaxed, the hare's eyes fell to the reptile at his feet. In a flash the chamaeleon wrapped its tail around Fidelio's legs, both figures vanishing instantly. A gasp rose from the class—all that could be seen was bare grass and a row of trees.

"That could be useful," Brun murmured.

"Is he still there?" a unicorn asked.

"I bet he's going to scare us," wagered a green basilisk.

"How long does it last, Professor?" called a centaur.

"Until you move." Fidelio's entire figure, beginning with his lips, shimmered and rematerialized. "Or speak, obviously."

"I knew he wasn't going to scare us," a chinchilla told the green basilisk.

"Do you have to hold your breath the whole time, Professor?" Lakia asked.

"Heavens, no!" the hare replied. "It would be virtually useless in that case! You might not want to cough violently, however. And definitely don't sneeze."

"When can we start making Chamaeleon, Professor?" Orion asked eagerly.

The hare perused the class prudently. "That answer depends upon the amount of practice you're willing to dedicate—but we've discussed that already! Open your books to page 184 to discover just how many parts come together to form Chamaeleon. After studying the diagram, drill your partner until you know each part. When you're satisfied with that, read to page 190 on sentinel assembly. Hop to it!" Fidelio shouted, slapping the ground heartily with his foot.

As the boys fumbled to pull their books from their backpacks, Brun heard a familiar female voice from over his shoulder. "Where have you two been?"

Brun opened the book on the grass at his feet. "Extremely busy."

"I looked all over for you this afternoon! I even went to Chiron's Hutch!" the girl asserted.

"Araceli, you'll get Brun in trouble if you keep talking to him," a boy said. "Get your book open before Professor Firefoot comes over here!"

"Oh, shut up, Nate!" Araceli snapped. "He's already in trouble as far as I'm concerned." The girl grew quiet, however, more from fury than concern over further disciplinary intervention by Fidelio. Her book thudded heavily on the ground, none too inconspicuously striking Nate's knee.

"Ow!" the boy exclaimed.

"And where have Manny and Brun gone?" Fidelio inquired some minutes later, finding the boys' class supplies lying abandoned by a fire oak root. Nate looked up from the patch of grass where he and Araceli had been attempting to form a somewhat accurate representation of Chamaeleon's body.

Nate replied distractedly. "Weren't they just here a second ago?"

Araceli's mocha eyes boiled as the bumpy, potato-shaped body of her chamaeleon faded and disintegrated. "If he's left again I'm gonna…"

We'll just see what you're gonna do.

"We're right here, Professor," Manny said cooly, the invisible curtain proffered by his Chamaeleon scintillating before melting away.

Fidelio's monocle fell from his head. "But you—"

"Brun, quit being stupid!" Manny punched the air next to him, prompting Brun's figure to rematerialize.

Brun rubbed his collarbone. "You're lucky that was my shoulder and not my jaw." A book made contact with the boy's elbow. "Ow!"

"How could you do that to me?" Araceli cried. "That's twice in one day!"

"Señorita González, sit down," Fidelio stated tensely. "And change that blasted wooden flyswatter back into a wand. Now— Brun, Manny, please explain to me what just happened." Despite his solid tone, the hare's eyes glinted avidly.

Brun narrowed his eyes at Araceli, ignoring the instructor's question. **That psychotic girl just chucked a paper missile at me.**

"You mean how we made a pair of Chamaeleons, or how we reappeared?" Manny asked wittily. "Because from what I saw earlier in the class, you know the answer to both those questions."

"But, I don't understand…" Fidelio was both flustered and fascinated. "Seventh-Level Lumens don't just enter class and create the designated sentinel on the first day, much less before the end of the period! Has someone been practicing this with you? Chiron, perhaps?"

Brun finally tore his glare from Araceli. "Nope," he replied freely. "We did it ourselves, without ever seeing the sentinel before today."

"That's not possible," the hare murmured.

"I can't even make Chamaeleon's body, much less its tongue and tail!" Nate confessed, staring dispiritedly at the lumpy mass at his feet.

"It really isn't that hard," Manny said matter-of-factly. "You just imagine the body parts, shaped perfectly and all that, then make sure they're interconnected the right way."

"Ooh, interconnection—completely vital," Brun corresponded. "I do, however, have some issues with shaping. But typically Manny's art skills line me out straight away."

"Show me," the hare said breathlessly. "I need to see you do it."

"Sure thing," Manny answered good-naturedly. He lifted his wand and began forming a butter-colored chamaeleon at his feet.

"Easy as pie," Brun said several moments later as he breathed softly on his own reptilian specimen. A blink later and the boys had vanished.

"You guys are incredible!" Nate shouted. Araceli sniffed.

Fidelio stood astounded. "I don't know what to say."

"Can we help you teach the rest of the period?" Manny asked brightly as he flashed back into focus. Brun nodded, reappearing as well.

"I—that would be appropriate," the hare stammered. He bent to recover the eyepiece from the grass. "Just remember to be patient with your peers."

"We will," Brun said as both boys rose to their feet.

"Now, I hope none of you are disappointed," Fidelio pronounced a half hour later from his customary perch, "but Brun, Manny, and I tried to circulate around to help everyone. A number of you even managed to attach the legs to the body! I'm proud! I expect by the end of this week I may just see an empty glade full of invisible students! But let's not rush things, shall we? For Thursday reread pages 184 to 190 and be prepared to demonstrate three of six Chamaeleon parts successfully made! Good luck!"

In an instant the elated Sentinels students began pouring out of Fire Flats; yet none left before first ensuring to thank Manny and Brun for their unexpected instructional aid. There, at the foot of the fire oak, stood the boys, glowing brightly on the eve of the sunset, their classmates now gone.

"Why are you both still here?" Fidelio asked vigorously. "There can't be anything you need to ask me after today's lesson!"

"You told us to stay, Señor," Brun replied.

"We were late," Manny explicated, unable to avoid the pang of shame even after such a lucrative class session.

409

"Oh…" the hare muttered, discovering a crater in his newfound zeal. "Why was that, exactly?"

One boy stared nervously at the other. "Did you read the letter, Professor?" Brun asked.

"The letter? Oh! Now where did I put that?" Fidelio scanned the dell haphazardly before fishing through his blue silk vest pockets to pluck out the glimmering note. His silver eyes hovered over the boys' excuse. "I cannot accept this," he said finally, lowering the note from his spectacled gaze.

"You can't?" Manny spluttered.

"No—Ellen Bellastrata is not an instructor, and it reads that you were at her home, not her office. Academic policy considers this a truant, obliging each of you to serve a detention with me," Fidelio explained.

Brun turned anxious. "A detention! Mi papá will kill me!"

"There is an alternate course of action you could take," the hare suggested.

Manny came with a rebound. "What is it?"

Fidelio was candid. "You could apologize. We'll forget the whole matter."

"Really?" Brun asked, his hope reforming. The hare nodded.

"Lo siento," Manny proceeded swiftly.

Brun concurred. "Me, too. I'm really sorry, Professor Firefoot."

"It won't happen again—I'll make sure of it." Manny began to mentally formulate steps to execute this plan.

Fidelio once again appeared light-hearted. "I'm glad to hear that. Now, you boys have a good evening, and stop by to visit Iris and me sometime. I know he'd love to see you!"

"With pleasure, Professor!" Manny called as he and Brun jogged across the flats.

Brun glanced crosswise at his running-mate. "That worked out better than anticipated."

"That's for sure. Now let's head to the LRC."

"What do we need to go there f—"

410

"H-hi, Araceli." Manny ground to an abrupt halt to avoid slamming into the girl. "What are you standing out here all alone for?"

She looked to Brun worriedly. "I need to talk to you."

"Go ahead," affirmed Brun remotely.

"Alone," Araceli clarified.

Why?

Manny mediated. "I'll just head on up toward the bridge, Brun. Meet me there when you're done."

"Gracias," Araceli answered quietly.

Manny nodded, then turned and jogged away.

After twenty minutes Manny glanced down at his lifeless watch. "What can be taking so long?" Manny stood at the edge of the Isla Verde bridge, watching as a band of otter-clad dolphins raced around the Lake. Five more minutes passed. "That's it," he said stiffly. Manny turned, trotting back down the winding path that lead south and east to Fire Flats. As he rounded the final bend, an image made Manny's feet freeze in mid-lope—there, not ten yards ahead of him, stood Brun, his hand threaded through Araceli's hair as he kissed her passionately.

"I don't need this right now!" Manny grumbled as he jumped back around the bend. He kicked a tree and glowered at the ground. *I've got an idea.* "Hey, Brun!" he called loudly. "Where are you?"

Reverse suction—the sound of lips parting. Manny shivered. *This is so awkward...*

"Go on ahead," he heard Araceli say softly.

"Are you sure?" Brun whispered back.

"Sí—I'll see you tomorrow. I'm sticking to my word," she replied.

"Okay, then." Footsteps drew closer to Manny's niche around the bend.

"Crap!" Manny breathed, hopping to his feet and running further up the path.

"Manny?" Brun called a few seconds later. "Were you looking for me?"

"Uh, yeah," Manny said, spinning around awkwardly.

Brun advanced coolly. "Are we headed to Kaya's, then?"

"N-no—I wanted to head to the LRC first, remember?" Manny walked alongside his roommate, doubting the credibility of his impromptu façade.

Brun did not appear to notice. "Why do we have to go to the library?"

"I don't see what you're complaining about. I had to wait on you for almost half an hour."

"I was busy."

"Exactly how much of that time did you spend kissing, anyway?"

Brun nearly tripped, his pupils nearly eclipsing his irises as he stared at Manny.

"Hah! You get brighter too when you're embarrassed! Mr. I'm Too Cool to Get Upset!" Smack. "Ow! What'd you hit me for?"

"You shouldn't have been watching us." Brun withdrew his fist from Manny's shoulder. "And that was also for nearly busting my jaw earlier. Tell anyone what you saw and next time I'll aim higher."

"Cool your jets, man." Manny segwayed onto the rope bridge. "Your secret's safe with me. We're best friends, right?"

"Right." But Brun's brow immediately crumpled into a blazoned white heap. "What about Zane?"

"A guy can have two best friends, can't he?"

"I wouldn't know—all this is new to me."

Manny smiled. "Especially the kissing, right?" Brun's fist flew through the air; Manny dodged right. "Chill out! It's not like I told anybody!"

"Just watch it, Manny," Brun said, glaring.

"Don't worry—I'll keep my word," he reassured. "About that—so what did Araceli promise to do, anyway?" Brun clenched his fist. "Calm down, already! No one's around! I'm not gonna tell anyone!"

"Fine," Brun growled as they turned and entered a shortcut behind a curtain of moss. "She promised to give me some space."

Manny laughed. "So you won't have to run from her anymore."

"If you don't shut up I'm gonna add teasing to the punch list."

Manny clamped his mouth shut, but continued to chuckle. "Alright," he mumbled, biting his lips.

"We won't sit by each other during class, but we'll have lunch a couple times a week and—" Brun paused tensely, "—and a date on Friday nights."

"Lucky man!" Manny howled.

"You are too loud!"

Manny grinned broadly. "It's a joyous occasion."

"Oh, is it? Then why don't we talk about your girlfriend, shall we?"

Manny stopped cold; Brun kept right on walking, forcing the boy to resume his pace. "I don't have a girlfriend, Brun."

Taunting commenced. "You don't? The way you were staring at Kaya during lunch I would've thought you were in love."

The path grew suddenly whiter. "I—" Manny's tongue suddenly hitched to the back of his throat. "Kaya and I are not going out."

"Yet."

"We won't be, either! If you haven't noticed—"

"Oh, look," Brun interrupted as he stepped from the shortcut to the edge of the Plaza. "It's the LRC, just right up ahead."

Manny did not utter another word as they passed the bank and approached the reception desk of the Lumen Resource Center. Brun found himself to be extremely content, considering the circumstances.

"Buenas noches," the librarian greeted the boys, flitting over the counter with luminescent wings. "How can I help you?"

"Your name's Melinda, right?" Manny asked stiffly. The blue morpho nodded, staring oddly at the boy. "Good. Well, I'm Manny—in case you forgot—and I'm looking for a book about clocks and—"

"Manny López?" Melinda broke in suspiciously.

"Yes," Manny said strangely. "Anyway, I need a manual on how to change your—"

"You're the boy who nearly killed my brother earlier today!" the butterfly bit.

Nearly killed your— "Who on Earth is your brother?"

"As if you don't know!" Melinda spat, dancing in front of Manny's blank eyes. "Treble Brightwing!"

"Oh." *That little twerp.* "I didn't do anything to him—he's the one that came up to me and started treating me like a jerk."

The librarian clicked her antennae reproachfully. "These hooligans never take any responsibility."

"Responsibility? It was Kaya who tossed the cube at your brother, not me!" Manny shot back.

"You, your girlfriend, it doesn't matter which—you're still to blame!" Melinda retorted.

A chuckle emanated from Manny's right. "Shut up, Brun."

"And so rude!" she splurted. "I refuse to help you! You can use the Photon Decimal System and find it yourself!" With that Melinda disappeared in a flash of radiant blue.

"You're so tactful," Brun joked.

"Like you are?!" Manny pushed past his friend. "Where's this picture decibel system, anyway?"

"Photon Decimal System, Manny," Brun corrected. "And it looks like there's an access point on each of the pillars." He approached the nearest marble column, where a blue screen hovered blankly in the air.

"Move," Manny said abruptly.

A female voice spoke. "To access the PDS Database, please touch the screen with the point of your wand."

"Easy enough." Manny transformed his watch and tapped the screen.

"Mahogany, dark. Origin—Costa Rica. Lumen authenticity verified. Welcome, Manuel Luis López." The screen instantly illuminated with various search options and icons. "Touch an access point to begin."

"It knew your name," Brun marveled.

414

"I noticed." Manny relaxed as he manipulated the PDS to narrow down a list of texts regarding clocks and watches. After five minutes Manny tapped the image of a book title.

"You have elected to check out *Lumen Timepieces and Their Functionality*. Enable auto-retrieval?" the system asked. Manny tapped the screen.

"Why didn't you say yes?" Brun squalled.

"Exercise never hurt anyone, Brun. Besides, I know exactly where it is—on the third level, southeast corner."

"Talk about me wasting time," the other boy muttered.

A quarter of an hour later a pair of starfire eyes glittered through the panes of an enclosed balcony of the Lumen bibliotheca. The eyes traced the Carina River below, whose course divided the library's entryway into parallel stone footpaths. A small, aged tome rested in Manny's hand as he gazed up through the glass roof above, while waning puffs of cloud attempted vainly to conceal the coruscation of the stars, their presence begotten by the swiftly fading twilight. *This place is huge.*

Brun approached from behind. "¿Listo?"

"Sí, I'm ready." Manny followed Brun along the terrace to the nearest spiral staircase.

"Next time we're in a hurry you hit auto-retrieval, okay?"

"I guess." He sighed, gripping the book tightly as the pair descended the stairs. Yet Manny's short-lived despondence dissolved the moment his feet hit the marble floor, the boy's ravenous eyes devouring page after page, his focus scarcely shaken from the book as he and Brun traversed the Plaza, meandered along a shortcut parallel to the North Road, and finally reached the docks to ride a ferry for the second time that day.

A very bored Brun peered out over the placid lake. "You know, you're a pretty boring travel companion."

Manny's mind, now engulfed in cogs, springs, shafts and minute hands, scarcely registered Brun's critique. "Okay." Unhampered, Manny continued dissecting the inner workings of wristwatches; Brun thus resigned himself to chatting with the river otter.

Manny's wrist flashed incessantly as he and Brun walked along under the upper ledge of the Lucero Falls. "It should work," Manny whispered as he snapped the lid of his watch shut and nudged the second hand. "All the parts are there—even the Roman numerals and the dial."

"Did you wind it?" Brun asked dully.

"Duh, Manny!" He slapped the butt of his palm against his own forehead. Two breaths later the mahogany watch had begun to tick.

"Are you happy now?" inquired Brun as they mounted the east stairs.

"Yes! We won't be late for class anymore, I'll tell you that!"

***

Kiki squinted at Manny through a thick cloud of feigned scrutiny. "Do you have any Thundermug Tea?"

"Nope—go fish."

"Shucks." She reached for a card at the center of the glass coffee table.

Brun surveyed his cards. "Kiki, do you have any Ants?"

"How'd you know?!" the girl protested, slapping a pair of Sixes down in front of Brun. Each card revealed a collection of six ants—three an icy blue, and three a golden yellow. Brun filed the Ants into his hand.

Manny's turn. "Kaya, do you have a Lightboard?"

A blank stare came in reply as Kaya withdrew a card from her hand and slid it along the table.

"I'm out!" Manny lay his last three cards down triumphantly, his own Sevens now lying next to Kaya's stolen Lightboard.

"And that means it's time for bed, Kiki," Ellen cued from her perch upon the snow-white couch.

Kiki demurred. "But Mamá! I'm not even tired!"

"Tell the boys good night," Ellen directed.

Kiki rushed around the table toward Manny, her bottom lip protruding sadly. "Will I ever see you again?"

Manny laughed. "I bet you will."

"Good!" she cried, hugging the boy then bolting around to pincer Brun. "¡Buenas noches!" she called as she followed her mother through the kitchen door.

"Now that they've gone, how about we decide when to begin tracking tomorrow," Kaya prompted.

Brun noted a discrepancy. "What about Iris? Doesn't he need to be here?"

"Nah, we got the major stuff out of the way this afternoon," she replied casually.

"The only time we could go would be between lunch and Astronomy," Manny indicated. "Will Professor Firefoot even let Iris go out then?"

Kaya glanced vaguely down at her unfinished hand. "I don't know. He still seems to be pretty—domineering—about that issue. He only let Iris come to my house for lunch today because it was between classes."

"Maybe Manny and I can talk the Prof into it," Brun suggested.

***

"Sure, boys!" Fidelio erupted with brio, his voice carrying through the broad dell in the morning light. "Just promise me you'll look after him."

"We will," Manny assured the hare.

"I can only expect the best from the two of you," Fidelio said heartily. "Why don't you come in for a moment while Iris finishes his breakfast? I've got toast with turnip jelly if you like!"

That sounds like a tongue turner.

"I think we'll pass on the toast, Professor," Brun declined. "But we wouldn't mind visiting with Iris for a moment."

"Go right ahead!" Fidelio hopped affably back into the fire oak to reveal a round kitchen with a low roof, miniature appliances, and a smooth, oaken floor with infinite rings radiating from the center. To the left a staircase ran along the inner rim of the tree. "The table's small, but there should be room."

"Hey Brun, Manny," Iris said unexpectedly, setting a ripe smelling slice of toast down on his plate as the boys sat down on either side of the table. "What are you guys doing here?"

"Just came to walk you to class," Manny rejoined coolly. "And to see if you wanted to do something this afternoon," he added with a wink.

"Do something? Like what?" Iris crunched absentmindedly as he took a chunk out of his toast.

"Something constructive, no doubt!" Fidelio exclaimed as he disappeared up the stairs. "While you're out you might show Iris a thing or two about sentinels."

"What's he mean by that?" Iris inquired, his ears going a bit rigid as he swallowed the toast tersely. "I'm pretty good at sentinels already."

Manny pushed the plate toward him. "Don't worry about it."

Iris continued to frown, however.

"It's not a big deal, Iris," Brun contributed. "Manny and I were just able to animate Chamaeleon on our third try yesterday."

"Your third try?" the hare repeated, his voice low. "It took me two. How are you guys suddenly so good with sentinels? Neither of your dads are professionals!"

Manny began to bristle. "Now just wait a minute here…"

"How do you know?" Brun countered. "Mi papá's a—a great Lumen!" he stuttered. **He-he just—** Brun had a sudden realization. **He just doesn't spend any time with me.**

Iris shook his head and took a deep breath. "I'm sorry, hermanos. I didn't mean to say that. It's just that I get touchy when my dad criticizes me."

418

Manny deflated. "We're all good—at least I am. You okay, Brun?"

The other boy nodded dimly.

Ten minutes later, bread and preserved turnips sloshed about in Iris's belly as he hopped from Fire Flats to the path leading to the Isla Verde bridge. "So we'll meet at the Café for lunch at two, then leave for the pond around four?"

"You, Kaya, and Manny go ahead," Brun replied. "I've got—plans. I'll just meet you three at the east stairs around 4:15."

"Plans, huh?" Manny quipped quietly.

Brun glared in reply.

***

Kaya set down her fork. "Who's that girl sitting by Brun over there?" She nodded toward the eastern end of the Café.

Iris hopped around on his chair. "That's the girl he was in such a hurry to run away from yesterday after The Lumen World. What was her name…?"

"They're holding hands!" Kaya breathed in disbelief. "Do you know her, Manny?"

The boy instantly filled his mouth with pizza, mumbling something incoherent.

She kicked him. "That's just gross! Don't talk with your mouth full!"

It worked, now didn't it?

"Ariana, Ariel…" Iris attempted to assemble the pieces of the girl's name from his cluttered memory bank.

"Araceli," Kaya said prudently. "Her name's Araceli. I knew I'd seen her before. She's in my Healing class."

The hare perked his ears. "Does she bug Brun there, too?"

"I wouldn't know—I tend to listen to Professor Bluebolt rather than stare at Brun all period." Kaya took another shrewd sip of maté tea. "But maybe I'll just go over and say hello…"

Manny clamped his hand down on her wrist, nearly choking on the mound of cheese in his throat. "Don't," he gasped.

419

"Don't yourself," she riposted, pulling her hand from beneath Manny's and walking across the Café, her hair swinging.

***

"Dang it, Brun! I've already got a bruise there from yesterday!" Manny barked as he shielded his biceps.

"Then why'd you tell Kaya that Araceli and I were going out?" Brun asked roughly.

"I didn't say anything!" Manny defended. "But it's a little obvious when you hold hands like that in a public place!"

Brun did not respond. Ahead, through the trees, he spied Kaya and Iris leading the way east. Shame pulsed through his veins.

"Don't be embarrassed, Brun. It's a good thing that you have a girlfriend," Manny reassured him.

"Then why was Kaya so smug about it when she walked over to us?"

"When isn't she?"

That's true.

"And besides, maybe she's—jealous," Manny added.

Brun glanced incredulously at Manny. "I'm not touching that. That's your territory."

"Now hold it right there—"

"Is this the place?" Iris asked as Brun and Manny tumbled in through the crowding trees.

Manny pulled a piece of wet moss from his face, flinging it at the pond. "Yeah, this is it," he said, his voice soggy. *I'm gonna get you, Brun.*

Kaya surveyed the area. "So the monkey stole Tobias's wand from here?"

"Or somewhere up the stream," Brun answered, nodding north.

Iris took command. "We'll start here, first. Manny, Brun, you check the west side for prints. Kaya and I will look east. And remember to get really low to the ground, because the last print we found was hidden under a fern."

Easy for you to say. A minute later all Manny could hear was the rustling of leaves and the ticking of his watch. He checked under every fern, between the interlocking roots of all the trees, below every curtain of moss—but still found nothing.

"Get anything yet, Brun?" Manny called some time later.

The other boy's reply skipped over ferns and bounced off boughs. "Not really. Just a few otter prints—and maybe a kinkajou."

"How can you tell?" Manny pushed back a handful of stems to discover a shoeprint. *That must be mine.*

"They have claws—and the otters' are smaller."

Manny advanced like a squat penguin. "What's a monkey print look like, then?"

"Like a human hand, I guess," Brun called back, closer now. "They say they don't really have feet—just four pairs of hands."

"Better to steal with, then," Manny observed darkly.

A light voice tinkled into Manny's ear, startling him and causing him to fall over. "Find anything?"

"Don't do that, Iris!" the boy yelled.

"Sorry. But did you?"

"Just a sneaker print." Manny sighed, enjoying the momentary break for his back. "How 'bout you and Kaya?"

The hare scratched his nose. "Nothin'. I think before we head up the stream we should branch out further—search a wider radius, you know?"

"But I told you guys I already checked out here, remember? What's the point?" Manny sounded slightly exasperated.

"You were looking for a wand, not prints," the hare pointed out. "And besides, four heads work better than one."

The boy leaned forward and got back to his feet. "Whatever."

"Just be patient, Manny," Iris encouraged before disappearing in Brun's direction.

A half hour passed; Manny's back ached, and he was spent. He stood up and stretched, his muscles taut as he ambled through the foliage back to the pond where a pair of young otter pups, not much more than Kiki's age, were splashing and playing. One look at the glowing boy sent them rocketing up the stream.

"How quaint," he muttered, his temperament dry as he lay down beside the water, gazing at the progressively advancing twilight. "If we're out here much longer we're gonna have to use Firefly."

"I already am!" Iris bellowed as he bounded from the eastern edge of the clearing, a trio of burning white fireflies trailing him closely. "We found it, Manny! A little to the northeast of here!"

The boy sat up quickly. "You mean a monkey print?"

"No, a monkey trail! It leads away deeper into the forest!"

"No way—Brun, come on!" Manny shouted, leaping to his feet.

Brun stumbled in from the south. "Did you find something?"

Iris nodded avidly. "Follow me!"

A minute later the hare and the boys were standing over Kaya, who knelt beside a tree. "You guys won't believe this," she whispered.

"What?" Manny replied as all three dropped low to the patch of ground by her hand. Iris's Fireflies revealed multiple prints.

"More than one monkey has been here recently," she said.

Brun touched the prints delicately. "Seriously?"

"Does that mean they're all thieves?" Iris submitted.

"All our evidence points to yes," Manny answered. "And that the problem's bigger than we realized. If there's a whole group of monkeys going at this, then people's wands are gonna start disappearing at a rapid rate."

"That does it—we're tracking them down and getting to the root of the problem," Kaya concluded. "Iris, since you're the shortest, why don't you lead the way. You can see the trail better than any of us."

"Alright," the hare consented, hopping to the front.

"Hold on," Manny interrupted. "We've got a problem. What if the monkeys come along and see us?"

"Good point," Brun noted.

"We just hide at the first sign of one, then," Kaya resolved. "Crouch behind a tree or below the ferns."

"That won't work because they have the vantage point—they can move like lightning and see everything from up above," Manny argued. "We need something faster."

"And what would that be, oh wise guru?" Kaya mocked.

"Chamaeleon," Manny replied officiously. "We'll disappear into the background in less than a second."

"Like any of us can actually produce that sentinel yet!" the girl rounded. "Iris and I just started studying it Monday!"

"Actually, Kaya, according to my dad, Manny and Brun don't have any problems making Chamaeleon at all," Iris replied. "And I don't, either."

"What do you mean, 'you either?'" she snapped. "If you knew how to make it then why didn't you this morning?"

"Because I wanted to help you learn to do it," the hare answered. "I'm sure we'll get that tail down by Friday."

Kaya roared in frustration. "Ugh! Fine! If you can all animate Chamaeleon, then go right on ahead. But don't forget about me, here!"

A few seconds later four Chamaeleons stood at the teenagers' feet. Manny knelt to grab his and handed one to Kaya. "Here," he said. "You have to animate it or it won't follow you."

With a metal-melting frown she breathed onto the lizard sentinel, ignoring its blinking eyes as she returned it none too gently to the forest floor.

Iris glanced up helpfully. "Do you remember how Dad said to activate the camouflage?"

"Yes," she clipped. "I'm not an idiot."

But you do have anger issues. Brun stood frowning at the back of the line. "Are we ready then?"

"Sí." Iris directed the Fireflies to illuminate the imprinted mud, taking a moment to locate the subsequent prints. He then plunged ahead, stopping intermittently to verify the trail.

After fifteen or twenty minutes, Manny began to wonder where they might be. *Chiron's Hutch is probably a mile south of*

423

here and getting further away every second. I bet Kaya lives just to the west; but nobody seems to want to live out this w— Hey, what's that? Between ten and twenty steps ahead a transparent curtain rippled faintly, as though a sheet of the thinnest silk hung down from the treetops. "What's that light, guys?"

Iris lifted his eyes from the prints. "That's just the barrier surrounding Isla Verde."

Manny's feet ground to a halt. "Just the barrier?" he repeated, as though mislead. "We can't pass that!"

"Yes we can. It's easy." The hare hopped carelessly back and forth through the undulating curtain. "You don't feel anything, except maybe a slight tingling."

Kaya stepped forward. "So the trail leads outside the city limits?"

"Yes," Iris nodded.

"Then we've got to follow it," Brun asserted, his words peppering Manny in the back.

"I-I can't," Manny said, his words tumbling out unsewn.

"I told you it's easy, Manny," Iris bolstered.

"What's wrong, López? Scared of what you might find?" Kaya rounded.

"No!" *Not exactly.* "But I made an agreement with my parents in order to come here to school."

"What was the agreement?" Iris fished.

Manny's reply came quietly. "Not to go outside the protective barrier."

"Was the agreement with your parents, or with your mami?" Kaya prodded.

"Why do you care?" Manny fired. "It's not like anything I do matters to you!"

"No, but it shows me who you really are," she cut.

"And what would that be, Kaya?" Brun broke in. "An honest person? You just don't know how to take good people when you see them. So shut up already and let's go on." The boy's eyes blazed. "Manny, you stay here until we get back—we'll only scout a little ways ahead tonight. You and I will come up with a solution to this problem later." With a snap of his wand Brun clustered a band of fireflies, pushing past Kaya and stepping ahead of Iris to resume their trek along the trail. Iris glanced at Manny and let out an inaudible whistle before turning and following Brun. Making no eye contact and saying nothing, Kaya also disappeared through the veil and the trees.

She is like a brick wall. A heaviness descended upon Manny's heart, bringing him swiftly to the ground. He found himself seconds later sitting, his eyes staring vacantly ahead. Several moments passed as Manny sat perched in this daze-like state, when suddenly he noticed a ray of soft blue light shining down on his feet. An odd warble filled the air as the light fused into the essence of a dove. At this Manny blinked, his consciousness returning, and he leaned forward to retrieve the glowing letter, which upon opening boasted a flowing penmanship the boy had not seen in a great while.

Manny,

So this is how I find out the truth about your studies in South America? Through a letter sent behind my back to my son? You do not know how disappointed I am in you right now. I thought we didn't keep secrets in our family. Didn't you think that you could trust your uncle and me?

What am I talking about 'truth'? The content of your letter is ridiculous! For instance, what's all this nonsense about angry centaurs not believing that a rabid monkey attacked a hare? Is this a fairy tale school? I'll tell you this—definitely not! What happened to physical science? Zane tells me you're attending a Lumen Academy. Well, I performed various searches and found nothing of the sort—particularly in the Amazon! And besides, a lumen is a unit of measurement, not an identity. You can rest assured that I'll be speaking to your mother about all this in a matter of moments.

And I don't know what kind of technology this is with letters that fly through the air, but you should know that I'll find your school's address and be down this Christmas to find out what's really going on.

Your aunt (whom you betrayed),

Jane

P.S. If you want to send Zane letters, then fine! Just don't send them late at night when you think I'm asleep—your uncle and I aren't a pair of idiots. We run a newspaper, so we're up late for emergencies, anyway.

P.S.S. It's like you've disappeared from the face of the Earth! I'm tired of secondhand, falsified information from your mother. I expect you to send us letters weekly. You can start now with an apology!

Manny moaned. "This is what I get for following Mamá's instructions—a butt-chewing!" Perturbed, he stuffed the letter in what he thought was an empty pocket, only to withdraw his fist to find a plastic-wrapped, amber tear. "A Jasmine Honeydrop? I must have saved it from yesterday." But just as Manny began to peel away the candy's wrapping, two things happened.

First, another jet of light arced down from above, imploding and dropping a letter on Manny's lap. The same moment the message let out its dismal wail, a cry rushed through the trees beyond the glittering curtain to Manny's right. He leapt to his feet.

"Aaaah!" Kaya screamed. "It's got me! The monkey's got my leg! Get him off me!"

"Where'd you go?" Manny heard Brun shout.

"Well, don't go invisible now, Kaya! It's too late for that!" Iris cried.

426

"He's gonna tear my leg off!" the girl bellowed. "Help me!"

Manny teetered between safety and danger, the thin wall and the dark forest. *But Mamá told me not to…*

Kaya screamed again, her voice lined with pain. "He's pinching me!"

Look where it got me last time. Manny ground his teeth. *So much for that…* And thus the boy dashed through the trees in the direction of Kaya's howling.

"Oh my gosh! Stand back Iris," Brun said cautiously.

"You don't have to tell me twice," the hare replied.

"Beat him off already!" she wailed.

"It's a little more complicated than that," Brun said slowly.

Manny appeared on the scene. "What's going on? Where's the monkey?"

"There isn't one," Brun replied, sizing up the problem.

"What do you mean by that?" Kaya cringed.

"It's an Amazon Horned Frog," Iris said nervously, his ears twisted freakishly.

"It doesn't hurt any less!" the girl shouted, writhing on the ground and kicking her leg. "Aaaah!"

"Don't move—I think it only makes him bite harder." Brun knelt down toward the leaf-toned, amphibious bulge attached to Kaya's calf. The frog's legs dangled limply in the air, its mouth relentlessly gripping muscle and bone. Manny noticed two jagged spikes growing out of the creature's head, one over each of its marble-like, black eyes.

"So can we pull him off?" Manny asked.

"No!" Brun said quickly. "We'd end up tearing her skin."

"It's already torn!" Kaya bawled.

"No, it's not!" Brun retorted. "You're not even bleeding!"

"So do either of you know exactly how to get it off?" Manny asked, searching the boy and the hare's faces.

"Professor Shadowflame hasn't started teaching on Lumorphi yet!" Brun said tensely. "But I remember Tía Liliana saying something about how Amazon Horned Frogs have a favorite snack."

427

"That doesn't help us much if you don't know what it is!" Manny quipped.

"I heard something about them being ticklish," Iris said hesitantly. "But I'm not going near that thing."

"Hurry up!" Kaya roared.

"Ugh! I'll do it. " Brun groaned, leaning forward and putting his hands on either side of the amphibian. The second he touched its sides, the frog curled up, covering its ample belly with its legs.

Kaya shrieked. "It's biting harder!"

"I remember now!" Iris exclaimed. "Its belly is its tender spot!"

"He isn't exactly making it easy to reach, now is he?" Brun shot back.

Manny observed Kaya's face, crumpled in pain. "Brun, I'll grab its legs. As soon as I pull them away, you get him."

Brun nodded. "Okay."

"Sorry about this, Kaya," Manny prefaced as he bent over the girl and reached toward the frog's head. Just before he could grab its legs, however, the creature's eyes turned toward Manny's right fist. In a heartbeat the frog had released Kaya, shot its tongue into the boy's hand, and disappeared with a deep croak.

Iris hopped forward. "What happened?"

"¡Gracias!" Kaya shouted, sitting up and hugging the closest person to her, which happened to be Manny. Realizing this fact, she precipitously let go. "It's great what you did, but let's keep our distance."

Sounds good to me.

Brun stood in a state of perplexity. "What exactly did you do?"

"To tell you the truth, I don't know," Manny said mistily. "It felt like it snatched something out of my ha—" He paused in realization. "I had a Jasmine Honeydrop that I found in my pocket from yesterday! That's what it was!"

"Oh, yeah!" cried Brun in comprehension. "Amazon Horned Frogs eat Jasmine Honeybees all the time! It must've smelled the honey and taken off with it!"

Kaya began to inch away. "You mean you're wearing the same pants as yesterday?"

"Sí—they aren't dirty or anything," Manny defended.

"You're a sick-o!" she bellowed, hopping to her feet.

Frustrated Preparations

Manuel,

Jane just came in, ranting about secretos in la familia and how you were a Lumen. I guess Zane let it slip, or you sent a letter when you shouldn't have. But don't worry about it – I'm not mad. I'll sit her down and explain everything; it's my fault for not telling her, anyway. But you still might want to send her an apology letter in a day or two. You are her favorite nephew!

Te amo,

Mamá

P.S. Whatever you're doing, I hope you're being safe.

"She'll never give me permission, Brun," Manny said, laying the letter on his chest and sinking into the gorge of his hammock. Lil' Manny licked at the boy's fingers.

"Are you sure you can't ask her in just the right way to get her to say yes?" Brun suggested, playing tug of war with Nipper's vines. The flytrap growled happily.

"Yes, Brun, I'm sure."

"Ow! You little snot! Don't bite me!" Brun pulled his hand away from Nipper's football jaw. "Okay, so let me get this straight," he began, looking up at Manny. "You specifically told your mamá that you wouldn't leave the protective barrier, right?"

"Well, I think so." Manny's words were tipped with uncertainty.

"Did you or not?" asked Brun, his voice a bit edgy.

"I don't exactly remember!" Manny answered tensely. "I promised my parents that I—that I would…" His voice trailed off as he thought back to that June night when his parents agreed to allow him to attend the Amazon River Academy. *They read a letter, went outside, then came back in and asked—* "I remember," he said finally. "I promised I would make wise choices."

"Uh huh." Brun nodded knowingly. "But you didn't promise to stay inside the city limits."

Manny chewed on this for a second. "No, but Julius assured my parents that if I did leave, I'd be accompanied by a First-Level Lumen to keep me safe."

"And you will be," Brun stated smartly, "during official outings, that is. But he can't keep tabs on you outside class hours."

"I don't want to make Julius a liar, though!" Manny rebounded. "He's my friend!"

"But if you make wise choices, then you won't get hurt, and your parents and Julius won't have anything to worry about," Brun elaborated.

"I don't know, Brun. Mamá didn't want me going to Easter Island without Chiron when she thought the barrier wasn't there," Manny reasoned.

"A lot of good that barrier did us then! Manny, we're just as vulnerable inside Isla Verde as out!"

"That's true," Manny conceded. "Except for the fact that wild animals aren't running around inside the city."

"Manny! Quit trying to get out of this! We need you out there. You're creative. You come up with solutions that none of us think otherwise."

"If you're talking about the honeydrop, then that was an accident," Manny denoted.

"If it weren't for you Kaya would still have that frog attached to her leg," Brun said swiftly. "If that doesn't convince you, then think about this. I'm not that great at Art, which means it's hard for me to mold sentinels sometimes. But because you and I worked together on Chamaeleon yesterday, I was able to do it after only two tries. Manny, I know that if the four of us pool our talents, we can

431

find those monkeys and stop what they're doing. We've just got to stick together."

Manny sighed. "Just for your information, I didn't get Chamaeleon any quicker than you did. But," he added, sitting up and turning to face Brun directly, "if we're gonna start venturing out beyond the city limits, then all four of us will have to keep my promise to make wise decisions. That means we don't leave again until after we've learned some defensive and even offensive techniques. Chamaeleon is not enough—we have to be observant and careful, taking things one step at a time."

"Sounds smart to me," Brun agreed. "Maybe we can talk Professor Firefoot into teaching us Reticulum early."

"That would be helpful—snagging Amazon Horned Frogs with a net is a much better alternative than enticing them off your leg," Manny acknowledged. "What about offensive moves?"

"That's Professor Nochesol's specialty. I was flipping through *Photokinesis* the other day, and I noticed some pictures of weapons. We could ask him about them," Brun suggested.

"Then that's the plan for Friday. Tomorrow we hit up Iris's dad. Do you think Professor Shadowflame could enlighten us on some Lumen animals?"

"You mean Lumorphi?" said Brun. "Our class is supposed to start on those Thursday. Didn't she tell your class that after the unit test on the Light Brethren?"

"After that essay about the principal differences between Morphus and Eider, my brain was fried."

"Well, that's what she said, anyway."

Manny lay back down on his hammock. "I guess we've got a plan." *And, besides, if I can't protect my friends, then what am I good for, anyway?*

***

"Boys, boys, boys! Such ambition! But if I jump ahead in the curriculum as you suggest then I won't have anything to teach you until after Christmas!" Fidelio stated as he placed a steaming mug on the oak table in front of him, sat down, and began polishing his monocle with the silken lining of his vest.

"That's okay with us!" Manny replied, but an elbow to the ribs quickly silenced him. *That hurt.*

"What Manny means to say, Professor, is that by teaching Reticulum to us now, you'd be giving us the invaluable opportunity to continue tutoring our peers during class," Brun interrupted. "Like we've been doing the past couple days."

Fidelio screwed his monocle back into place, gauging the boys with those sharp, silver eyes. "I just can't accede to that, boys. I agree that these past two sessions have granted numerous benefits to the both of you, but I must allow you time to perfect your Chamaeleon skills—to become flawless in the art of concealment. That will be our task for the month of November, and the Lord knows that Reticulum will take the entire month of December for the class to animate, even for the two of you."

Manny gripped his backpack straps more tightly. "But Professor—"

"There's no discussion to this, boys," the hare broke in. "Your present assignment is to study covert maneuvers using Chamaeleon on pages 191 to 210. Perhaps if you come back later Iris would like to practice with you."

"Dad's right, guys—if we don't practice with Chamaeleon we won't be ready to hide at the first sign of danger." Iris's ears dangled in the air as he leaned over a post at the foot of his bed. "The monkeys would catch us for sure."

"We still need to learn Reticulum," Brun argued from his low seat by the south window. "Otherwise we won't be able to stop anything coming at us."

433

"So we'll learn it," Kaya said to the stars out the north window. "Since the three of you are such professionals with sentinels, it should be a snap."

Manny leaned dispassionately against the door. "And how are we supposed to do that, Kaya, if Professor Firefoot won't show us?"

"You have a book, don't you?" she asked, turning and sitting on the ledge. "There's an explanation of how to make each sentinel for the Seventh-Level, in case you haven't noticed."

"What page?" Manny replied, pulling his copy of *Guardians, Sentinels, and Light-Keepers* from his backpack.

"I don't know," Kaya retorted. "But books generally have an index. Or at least they did the last time I checked."

Iris bounced back on his bed. "Okay, so how about every night we run through evasive moves and research Reticulum together? Surely after a week or two we'll have Chamaeleon down and be able to at least animate Reticulum."

"That sounds like a good plan, but where are we gonna practice?" Brun asked. "Your front yard isn't exactly ideal, Iris—if you're papá sees us we'll probably all get in trouble."

"Page 67!" Manny erupted triumphantly, noticing the image of a web-like net springing from a Lumen's arm. *This looks fun.*

"I know a place," Kaya said, ignoring Manny's exclamation.

"Is it isolated?" Brun asked. "I mean, we don't want other people seeing us use moves that we're not supposed to know yet—especially the instructors."

Kaya remained nonchalant. "Don't worry—it's southwest of the island, just on the edge of the Flooded Forest. I never see anyone there."

Manny lifted his eyes from the book. "Isn't the Flooded Forest where all those dangerous animals are?"

"Sí, but that's why it's the perfect place—we can practice on the real thing!" Kaya said.

"So how do you know about it?" Brun inquired.

"That's my business," she said curtly.

Iris shook his head. "Sheesh," he breathed.

434

***

Dear Student,

The location for The Lumen World has changed. We will no longer be meeting at the Unity Fount, as we have successfully completed our introductory unit of the Light Brethren. From this point forward you will report to the Quay, which of course is the pier mounted on the ridge descending into the Flooded Forest. Do not be late!

Attentively,

Sable Shadowflame

"Nate, do you know anything about the Flooded Forest?" Manny asked as he and his friend trekked southward along a rocky path guarded by towering trees that steadily swallowed the Lake behind.

"Just that you can die there if you're not careful," Nate replied as a falcon cry rent the air. Manny shivered. "Oh, and there's a lot of good photocaching opportunities down there—at least that's what my host-father says."

"Is it really worth risking your life just to find a sun beetle?" Manny asked, his words hanging warily before his eyes.

"But that's what photocaching is all about, isn't it?" Nate rebounded. "Deciphering puzzles, facing the danger, earning the prize—it sounds so, exciting."

"If you're up to it." The rocks shifted uneasily at Manny's feet as the path broadened and the trees thinned, giving way to a semicircular pier looming at the brink of a seemingly endless, tree crusted valley. In the shadows a dense marsh strangled the terrain, only occasionally breached by mounds of mud or rock. *Creepy*...

435

Manny stopped abruptly, tripping on a handful of loose stones and sliding haphazardly along on his posterior toward the pier. He ground to a harrowing halt. There, only a hair from his face, glittered the iridescent photon barrier marking the edge of Isla Verde. Nate, for his part, skidded through, landing with a thump on the Quay, then turned to extend a hand toward his pearl-skinned comrade. "¿Estás bien, Manny? That looked like it might have hurt."

"Sí, I'm fine," Manny answered, though his tone was slovenly as he used Nate's weight as leverage to pull himself through the barrier. Manny eyed the half-moon pier skeptically. "But I thought the Flooded Forest was part of Isla Verde," he said, dusting off his rump.

"It is not, Señor López," replied a voice, its words a river of velvet that brushed past the boy's legs and splashed at his side. Manny again shivered, a reaction that he was still unable to prevent when Shadowflame slunk by, the pistons of her front shoulders rising and falling. "Otherwise we would be at a loss as to how to begin this subsequent unit."

Within moments the Quay filled with Manny's typical assortment of classmates, though few dared approach the edge of the pier, excluding the flying Lumens, of course, as they did not fear the steep drop into the bog below. Shadowflame turned to face her pupils, who marveled at the sudden contrast between her electric blue eyes and the dark verdancy of the trees behind her.

"Young ones," she began, her river of a voice rumbling, "welcome to the verge of the várzea, the Flooded Forest. This Quay," she continued, her silk pads meandering across the sturdy boards, "is your door to the richest collection of Lumen plants and animals in the Southern Continent. Below us, from the very roots of these trees to their knitted canopies, rest what we call the Lumorphi, creatures of the blue world that have been changed—morphed, if you will—by Lumen influence, by starlight. For the next several months we will study individual members of the Lumorph family, from their peculiarities to techniques for handling them. Are there any questions before we start?"

436

Manny raised his hand. "Professor Shadowflame, is it true that in addition to feeding an Amazon Horned Frog a Jasmine Honeybee, you can also tickle its stomach to make it let go of you?"

Shadowflame stared back in utter disbelief, her eyes wide. "It is," she replied breathlessly. "But the second option is quite—"

"Difficult, I know," Manny interrupted wisely.

"How would you know that, Manny?" Shadowflame asked. "You can't have been reading ahead…" Manny merely smiled in reply. "Well," the panther added after a moment, a crinkle in her brow, "I suppose surprises await us in the most unexpected of times—and people." She paused, eyeing the boy with a mixture of prudence and, to Manny's disbelief, subtle fondness. "In any case, allow me to introduce you to our first Lumorph." Then, perching at the edge of the Quay with her back to the students, Shadowflame lifted her haunches and shifted her weight from one hind paw to the other. The next second she exploded from the pier, firing through the air and landing nimbly on the arm of a nearby tree, from which point she disappeared into the forest. Before any of the teenagers could recover from this shock, a series of violent squeals rose up to meet their ears. Seconds later, when Shadowflame reappeared over the ridge with a beast strikingly reminiscent of a furry pig, not one student could be found on the Quay—all stood behind the shield of the light barrier.

"What is that thing, Professor?" a tree frog asked shakily.

A unicorn narrowed its eyes. "Is it a warthog?"

"No, but it's similar," Shadowflame answered casually. "Come closer, everyone. You've no need to fear—she's unconscious."

The students reluctantly returned to the Quay; in fact, a pair of peregrine falcons and one brave quetzal glided down and landed on a trio of posts merely feet from the grey-hued creature. Shadowflame flexed her claws happily.

"Can anyone tell me the name of this Lumorph?" the panther called.

Nate nudged Manny with his shoulder. "Know anything about this one?" he whispered.

"Why would I?" Manny replied, dusting off his arm with a frown.

"No?" Shadowflame continued. "I would have you read the entry in your texts first, but I'm afraid she'll wake up before you're done." This prompted numerous students to take a step, or a hop, back. Shadowflame let out a sharp growl, which Manny recognized as her laugh. "Do not worry—I will keep you safe!" The crowd's shoulders remained tense, however. "Have courage, young ones. We are not to be a people who readily entertain fear. However, I do understand the mind of a novice. But let us proceed," she said, sitting nobly and raising her right paw to the students. "This creature is the renewed form of the peccary, a breed of swine found throughout Central and South America. It's cousin, the javelina, is often hunted in Texas of the United States, as Millie Carroway so excitedly explained yesterday. Now," the panther elaborated, stretching her paw forward and running it along the specimen's spine, "notice the sterling hue of her fur. The average peccary boasts a coat of reddish-brown, but only the Lumorph variety possesses this specific tone, thus yielding the title of the Silverback Peccary, or simply silverback for short. But now I wish to hear from you, young ones. Do you believe her to be aggressive?"

The students swallowed hard. "Is she the one we heard squeal a minute ago? Because if she is, she sounds pretty aggressive to me," a chinchilla replied.

"No, that was her mate," said Shadowflame. "You would be right, however, in assuming aggression in the squeal you heard. Had I been on the ground when I caught her, her mate would have charged me. Lucky for me I am a Lumen, and with my photokinetic skills I transported her here without even flashing a claw." The panther paused for effect. "But let's imagine now for a moment that she and I were down on the floor of the Flooded Forest alone. How would I prevent those fang-like tusks of hers from goading me?"

"Well, if you were a bird or a butterfly, you could easily take to the air and escape," Lakia the falcon propounded from her perch aside Shadowflame. "And as you're a panther, Professor, you could just climb a tree and be done with it. I doubt this silverback could follow you there."

"Well met, Lakia, but let us presume that you are injured or have not the time to escape by foot. What choice do you have now?" the panther posed.

"Pray for mercy," joked the quetzal on the next perch. Several members of the class chuckled.

"She will not hear your prayers, Señor Tusslefeather," Shadowflame growled as she lifted the silverback's head. "And just because your older brother is an accomplished First-Level Candidate does not mean I find your squawking humorous."

Lakia turned her sharp eyes on Tusslefeather; she did not appreciate time-wasters. But the next moment she nearly fell backward from her perch as Shadowflame disappeared, along with the sleeping silverback. Gasps rose from the crowd.

"It worked," Manny breathed in amazement, his honey eyes set on the apparently empty space.

Shadowflame growled humorously again. "An insightful act, Manny." The panther's figure rematerialized as she gently set the silverback's jaw down on the pier. "I see that Professor Firefoot's lessons are not being squandered on you."

Lakia managed to recover with no great loss of grace, her black claws piercing the rough wood as she glanced from Shadowflame to the boy. "You mean Manny just camouflaged you with Chamaeleon?" the falcon asked, her auburn feathers sleek with jealousy.

"Sí." Shadowflame swished her tail contentedly. "Young López successfully discovered the most effective means of curbing a silverback's attack."

Manny grinned for the second time that period, an act that in and of itself was a very rare occurrence for the boy during lessons regarding The Lumen World.

The young peregrine twisted her head sharply. "You mean all we have to do to avoid a silverback is go invisible? Are peccaries really that stupid?"

"No, it's just that the abrupt disappearance of a readily perceived danger confuses the silverback, and so it flees the scene," Shadowflame answered calmly.

A snort rose from the boards below, sending the students back across the barrier. Manny, however, dissolved as a glowing lizard wrapped its tail around the boy's legs. "It appears that my Knockout orb is wearing off. I expect all of you to approach the edge of the Quay as I demonstrate how to evade the silverback's assault using Manny's strategy." Shadowflame shook the wooden bangle dangling from her forepaw, then proceeded to guide the Lumorph through the air with her stern gaze.

When the silverback had reached the ground and rolled to its feet, Shadowflame once again sprang from the pier, ricocheting from tree to tree to reach the entrance to the marshes. A mass of interested eyes gazed down as Shadowflame animated a blue Chamaeleon at her side, then turned to face the wandering silverback. As the panther drew closer, the silverback caught sight of her, squealed in rage, and began to charge with surprising speed across the grass. Many of the students winced; but all kept on watching. Just before the Lumorph met its quarry, however, Shadowflame vanished. The silverback ground to a halt, snorted once, then turned and ran south for the cover of the forest. A cheer descended from the Quay as a shining sapphire orb tore through the air, winding around front of the silverback and impacting her square in the chest. Seconds later the frame of the unconscious peccary floated back to the space below the Quay.

"Would anyone like to have a go?" Shadowflame shouted from below. "You must be able to animate and command Chamaeleon, of course." Manny raised his hand but was not quick enough. "Lakia! Have at it!" The panther stepped into the shadow of the pier as the falcon dove through the air, a keen screech erupting from her beak. No sooner had Lakia landed than she produced her wand, directing it through the air with her beak to quickly carve a pearl-white Chamaeleon.

"Ready?" the panther asked.

440

The falcon nodded in reply, her eyes locked on the sleeping silverback.

Shadowflame created another orb, this time yellow encasing a winding band of silver. This orb hit the silverback's chest and the creature sprang into the air, landing firmly on the ground and wide-awake. A squeal, a charge, and Lakia disappeared. Yet to the falcon's extreme confusion, Lakia felt a sudden pressure on her chest that caused her to stumble backward and rematerialize, dropping her wand. The silverback let out a determined snort and a second squeal as she continued her charge at the fallen falcon.

"Lakia, stay where you are!" Shadowflame cried as another yellow orb zipped through space, connecting with the silverback and sending it in a somersault over the falcon's head. In a flash Lakia was invisible again, despite her missing wand and the absence of additional Chamaeleons.

Shadowflame's eyes pulsated. "Who did that?" she exclaimed.

"Grab your wand, Lakia!" Manny shouted as the confused silverback skirted the peregrine falcon's translucent frame and retreated into the cover of the woods.

"Where is it?" Lakia cried, adopting the desperation in Manny's voice as she searched the ground around her.

"It's there, by the tree to your right!" the boy called back.

Lakia turned and saw her wand lying beneath a thick, wraith-like shadow protruding from the base of the tree. In an instant the falcon flew forward and recovered the instrument, arcing back up to the Quay to safety. She landed on the post beside Manny.

"Did you find it?" Manny shouted to the forest below, ignoring the falcon at his side. The shadow retreated behind the tree. "Lakia! Where are you?"

"I'm right beside you!" the falcon cried loudly. "Quit pretending like you can't see me!"

Manny stumbled backward, bumping awkwardly into a centaur. "But I can't see you!" the boy said to the empty perch.

"Clear the way!" Shadowflame ordered as she leapt toward the pier from an outstretched branch. The teenagers scuttled backward to open space for their instructor. "Where is Lakia?" the panther asked authoritatively.

"I'm right here!" Lakia screeched.

Shadowflame turned her ionized eyes toward the falcon's voice. "Who made you invisible?"

"I don't know!" Lakia said. "I didn't know I was!"

"Stay where you are," Shadowflame directed, her tone now composed, as she approached the falcon and lifted her paw. With a downward sweep the panther pulled away Lakia's invisibility as though it were a curtain or a cloth.

"Can you see me now?" Lakia asked.

"Yes," the entire class replied.

"Now I have a question, and I want a serious answer." Shadowflame turned to face her students. "Did any of you see the person who drew the Veil over Lakia?"

A congregation of blank stares met her in reply. Nate shuffled his feet nervously.

"Señor Perón." The panther's blue eyes met his. "Did you happen to see something?"

"I-I'm not sure," Nate stammered, glancing sidewise at Manny.

"Only a First-Level Lumen could have done this," Shadowflame asserted. "Nate, did you see one or not?"

"No, Señora," he replied quietly.

Shadowflame swished her tail. "Then I must say that our circumstances are very strange. Whoever drew the Veil was acting in Lakia's behalf, concealing her from another charge from the silverback." The panther turned her head and gazed into the dark forest. "I can only conclude that the person was a photocacher who witnessed the incident, formed the Veil, then proceeded on his way."

"But why would he do that?" Lakia asked. "I mean, why wouldn't he show himself?"

"Photocachers are very resolute people, young Lakia," Shadowflame replied. "Most likely he continued his search the moment he saw that you were safe."

"That doesn't make any sense," the falcon quipped.

"We make the best of the evidence we've got," Shadowflame said shrewdly. "Nevertheless, let us now take a break from the action and open our books to page 241 to read the entry highlighting the Silverback Peccary. Then we can practice making the Chamaeleon sentinel and perhaps have another run through with a live specimen."

Anxious glances readily passed throughout the Quay. Not one student, except perhaps Manny, was keen on the idea of confronting a silverback. Even so, as Manny's fingers flipped vaguely through his book, his eyes scoured the tree line for a lingering shadow. But nothing moved—at least nothing that he could see.

***

"Where have you been?" Manny demanded as Brun set foot on the Lucero observation deck. "I've been waiting here for more than five minutes!"

"I came straight here from Art, Manny," Brun replied flatly. "And I immediately caught a ferry to the West Stairs. You had to have run from Healing if you've been here for that long."

"So what if I did?" Manny retorted. "I needed to talk to you!"

"About what?" Brun followed Manny to the south railing. "Light Bending's gonna start in just a few minutes."

"Lakia almost lost her wand during Shadowflame's class this morning."

Brun's eyes widened in disbelief. "Are you serious? What happened?"

In a rush Manny shared the details of Lakia's fall and mysterious rescue.

"So that shadow," said Brun, staring soberly into Manny's eyes, "do you think it was—?"

"A monkey? What else could it have been?" Manny ran the nails of his hand over the grains of the railing. "That's not what's puzzling me, though."

443

Brun glanced over Manny's shoulder. "What is, then?" he fished, his tone growing quiet again.

"Well, I just don't buy what Professor Shadowflame said about Lakia's savior being a photocacher," Manny continued, none too subtly. "I think it's weird that the person wouldn't show himself."

Brun's eyes went out of focus as he stared past Manny.

"What, Brun?" Manny turned around to find Nate standing behind him. "Is something wrong, Nate?"

"I overheard what you and Brun were talking about..." Nate said gravely.

Oh no... Brun clenched his teeth.

"What do you mean?" Manny replied, feigning innocence.

"Manny, I'm not stupid," Nate retorted dryly. "You can stop pretending. I didn't tell Professor Shadowflame about it because I didn't want you to get into trouble."

"For what?" Manny rounded defensively. "I didn't do anything wrong."

Nate leaned in closer. "Then why didn't you tell her that you were the one who saved Lakia?"

Manny blinked foreignly. "Are you crazy? I didn't even have my wand out!"

"I know! But I saw you!" Nate boomeranged. "The moment Lakia fell and the silverback started to charge at her, you reached out your hand in her direction—and you were glowing brighter than I've ever seen you before! The next thing I knew she disappeared again and you were yelling at her to get her wand!"

"So you weren't talking about the monkey?"

"Monkey? There weren't any monkeys below the Quay," Nate said oddly. "Quit trying to change the subject! You were the one who created the Veil!"

"Why the heated discussion, brothers?" called Professor Nochesol as he glided up to the railing from the direction of the island, his cloak flashing crimson as he spun his lightboard around, all the while hovering over the Falls. "I can act as a mediator, if you like."

"That's okay, Professor." Brun threw a wide-eyed glance to Manny. **We don't need anything about monkeys getting out.**

Manny nodded. *I get your drift.* "We're fine, Professor."

"No, we're not," Nate disputed.

"Just drop it, man," whispered Manny through his teeth.

"No!" Nate ejected. "I have a question for the professor!"

"I'm listening." Nochesol unfastened his cloak and threw it over the banister as a crowd began to gather behind the boys. Araceli looked anxiously in Brun's direction. "Stay back everyone," the man directed. "We'll begin class in a minute."

Manny's arms went limp. *Can't we just begin now?*

Please, Professor… Brun's eyes pleaded.

"Gracias, Señor," Nate began. "So, I was wondering, is it possible for a Seventh-Level to create the Veil?"

Nochesol blinked, his amaranthine hazel eyes flashing. "I shouldn't think so, why?"

"Well, there's our answer! Discussion ended!" Manny exclaimed, turning away.

"Because Manny drew the Veil over Lakia during The Lumen World today!" Nate blurted.

Manny spun around. "I told you I didn't even have my wand out!"

"That doesn't matter! You started glowing and then 'Wham!' She was gone!"

"¡Hermanos! Silencio por un momento," Nochesol commanded coolly. "I need one of you to explain to me exactly what happened." Nate gladly obliged, mentioning neither shadows nor monkeys. Brun was distinctly relieved.

"An interesting account," Nochesol said. "I am happy to hear that my dear sister Valwing is safe. But I must admit, Nate, that the probability that Manny formed the Veil is very slim, particularly if he was wearing his wand on his wrist as he is now."

A victorious smirk crossed Manny's face.

Nochesol turned his day and night eyes to Manny. "Heed my words, brother. I did not say impossible—you still may have drawn the Veil."

Manny's smirk vanished. "But how? I'm not a First-Level Lumen!"

"I know this," Nochesol answered, "yet explain to us how you felt when you realized that Lakia was in mortal peril. Were you calm?"

"No! Of course not!" Manny clipped.

"Understandable," said Nochesol wisely. "Then what else did you feel?"

Manny frowned at the instructor. "I-I guess I was confused as to why she fell. Then when I saw her on the ground and knew she was about to get trampled my heart started pounding and I—" He paused.

"You what?" Brun asked.

"I just wanted her to go invisible again," Manny said weakly. "And then she was gone! That's when I noticed her wand was—"

"That proves it, Professor!" Nate interjected.

"No, it doesn't!" Manny maintained.

"Perhaps it does," Nochesol judged. "I still hold to my original ruling. This is far-fetched, of course, but Manny, if you shook your wrist just as you wished Lakia were invisible, it is possible that you unconsciously called the light necessary to form the Veil, making Nate's theory true." The man paused, gathering his thoughts. "I have heard that young and inexperienced Lumens, in times of great stress, have successfully performed photokinetic techniques beyond their competence level. This could have been your case, Manny. After all, look at Brun."

"At me?" Brun crowed, thoroughly thrown. "I wasn't even there!"

"No, but I hear from Professor Bluebolt that you executed a photowave enhancement to Manny's voice box last Thursday during the lightboarding tournament. How else could he have heard you?" Nochesol riposted.

"I—" Brun stammered. He then swallowed his argument. "That's true."

"I knew it!" Nate shouted excitedly. "You two are Lumen prodigies!"

"Settle down, brother," Nochesol told Nate. "One day the same may happen to you. But I must admit," he paused, looking from Brun to Manny, "I for one, greatly anticipate the progress that you boys will make in the coming years! My good friend Andrés Dosfilos should watch out! You both may just surpass him one day!"

Don't set the standard too high or anything.

Gee, you're in for a let down.

"Speaking of friends," Nochesol resumed as he snatched his cloak from the railing, "I hope the three of you will forget your hostilities and leave this matter behind! Do not allow pride to blind you. But enough." Nochesol sliced up through the air toward the north end of the observation deck. "Time for class!"

Nate nudged Manny's shoulder. "No hard feelings, amigo?"

"No." Manny shrugged and shook his friend's hand. *I suppose not.*

"Take your seats along the south periphery of the deck, everyone! Sit one beside another to form a single row!" Waving his hand, Nochesol fragmented the veranda's many plants and benches into a stream of photons, which he just as quickly reformed into four levels of floating targets. "Wands out!" he cried as he leaned his lightboard against the west railing alongside his cloak. Ten seconds later he stood in the center of the deck, his crimson and gold wand at the ready.

"Now, brothers and sisters, I am very pleased to announce that we have successfully completed the Seventh-Level requirements for light clustering and orb formation." Nochesol snapped his wand to form a glowing sphere in his free hand. "For the past few weeks Professor Flores and I have shared the same goal—to stretch your minds by encouraging you to mold light into as many shapes as possible." At this the man transformed the sphere into a series of distinct objects, from a pyramid and a cube to a spiral and even a flower. "But today our paths split. Whereas in Art you will continue to make progressively more complex and detailed figures, in Light Bending we will begin employing our photokinesis for offensive measures."

"¡Sí!" an ecstatic voice cried. Everyone turned to stare at the voice's owner, Serena la chinchilla. "What? I've been waiting for this all semester!"

Nochesol laughed. "So have I. A number of you may ask, however, why we're not covering defensive techniques first. I would then tell you to consider your other classes. What are you learning in Sentinels at present? Chamaeleon? Perhaps Reticulum soon? Those are both defensive tactics, and as you're now finding yourselves face to face with the Lumorphi of our world under Professor Shadowflame's tutelage, it is only fitting that I equip you with the means to combat the dangers you will face. Bear in mind, though, that the weapon I am about to teach you should only be used in extreme need, and never—listen to me here—never aim it at your fellow Lumens. Do you understand?"

A weak 'yes' came in reply.

Nochesol remained still. "I asked 'do you understand?'"

"¡Sí!" the crowd answered.

"That's better. Now follow my example." Nochesol converted the luminescent flower he held into an orb. "Is everyone with me? Good. Okay, now flatten the orb like so to form a disc. Excellent job, Serena! From here we—hold on there, Ryder, that's too big. You don't want a frisbee. Shrink that disc to the size of your palm. Gracias. As I was saying, from here we stretch the disc to form an elongated oval similar to the shape of a large bandage—don't stretch it too far, now! It should be just a tad shorter than the distance from your wrist to your elbow. Cristina, show your oval to your partner—he's still got a disc. Got it, Greystone? Perfect. Last step now, everybody! I'd like you to make a hoop on either end of the oval, leaving just enough room for your pinky—or correspondingly small appendage—to fit through each one. For Andromeda's sake, Pepe—your pinky, not your arm! Serena, show him what I mean! That's better. Your finished strap should look like this, class." By the end of his fingers Nochesol held up a glowing band, which stretched approximately five inches from pinky to pinky. "Notice its elasticity," he noted as he pulled the band an inch or two longer, then loosened his grip as it returned to its original size.

"What are we supposed to do to the monkeys with this, give them welts?" Manny whispered, stretching the strap and releasing the end nearest to his chest with a loud snap.

Brun shot his hand to the back of his calf. "Cripes, Manny, why'd you do that?!" he asked through clenched teeth. "I wouldn't be surprised if my leg is bleeding!"

"Maybe it's more effective then I thought," Manny joked.

"You just wait 'til you fall asleep tonight," Brun replied ominously.

"Professor, this is a really strange weapon," Serena called somewhere from Manny and Brun's left. "How exactly do we use it?"

"You connect it to your wand." Nochesol molded his wand into a y-shape then slid the two prongs of the 'y' through the hoops at either end of the strap. "Done!"

"I have never seen one of those before, Professor Nochesol," Ryder the centaur confessed. "What is its name?"

"It's a slingshot!" Manny exclaimed, pulling the band back and taking aim. "You hold it like this, Ryder! After you place some ammunition in the center of the strap, you just pull it back, aim through the crosshairs, and fire!"

"A precise summation, brother, but the Lumen variety actually bears another name," Nochesol amplified. "The Flareshot—named such for the ammunition it uses. Whereas the slingshot commonly employs stones for arsenal, the Flareshot takes exclusive advantage of orb clusters."

Ryder tested his sling's elasticity. "Do you mean to say that we are to place an orb in this band, stretch it back, and catapult the orb as a projectile?"

"Correct," Nochesol replied.

"That's what I just said, Ryder!" Manny called, his voice breaking on the centaur's name as a pearl rocketed through the air.

The orb in question whizzed just feet from Nochesol's temple, splintering the red-ringed edge of a target hovering above the opposite end of the deck. A gasp rose from the crowd as several students leaned forward to seek out just who had shot the orb such a narrow breadth from their professor's head.

Nochesol's eyes lit like midnight fire. "Manny López, did you not just agree to never direct your Flareshot at another Lumen?"

Manny lowered his weapon, transforming it into a tiny pebble within his palm. His stomach collapsed, forming a gaping chasm that delved much deeper than the dark tunnels of Nightcrest Caverns below. He knew, without a doubt, that his complexion was absolutely scintillating, scattering bright rays of embarrassment across the deck. All were quiet. *I wish I could die.*

"Señor López, I asked you a question." Nochesol's words gripped the boy's chin and lifted his head. The tension in the air brought Serena to bite her bottom lip.

"Yes, sir." Manny's voice was constricted. "I-I broke my word. I wasn't thinking."

Nochesol pointed to his eye. "Do you know you could have blinded me? Much less what might have happened if you had struck my temple."

"I'm sorry, Professor." The boy's repentant words lay flat on the boards at the man's feet. *Why do I have to be such an idiot...*

"So are you telling me you understand the gravity of what you just did?"

A boulder crumbled in Manny's chest, tumbling down the edge of the chasm in his stomach. Guilt choked him.

"Manny, do you understand how dangerous it was to fire that orb past my head like that?" Nochesol's words struck yet another rock in the boy's chest.

"Sí," Manny said, his eyes downcast.

"Then may this be the most valuable lesson that any of you take from class today," Nochesol resolved, his tone now less severe. "The next time I see such a thoughtless act, I will contact the person's parents straightaway, and believe me, detention will be the least of your worries. Do we all understand?"

Affirmation rang around the deck.

"Hold true to your word, everyone, and let wisdom guide your hands," Nochesol admonished as he approached the west end of the deck. "Manny, reform your weapon. It's time for target practice, and your peers need a challenge."

Manny looked up, catching a glint of Nochesol's eyes just before he turned to fire a round and shatter the very same target the boy had nicked only minutes earlier. For a moment Manny stared at the empty space where the bull's-eye had been, surprised by his instructor's sudden change of disposition. But then, as his fingers tightened around the base of his Flareshot and as he restrung the elastic sling, the fissure in Manny's stomach began to shrink. Closing his eye and lifting his weapon, Manny took aim at another target, his gaze fixed and grip sure. He smiled. *Gracias, Professor.*

***

Amaranth eyes watched intently as a shimmering bullet spun across an open field, striking the edge of a crimson target mounted on a bare stump. The target shuddered but held its ground, refusing to fall over or even crack.

"Buen tiro," Kaya noted as Iris lowered his Flareshot.

"Could've been a lot better," the hare mumbled as he grabbed another pearl from the pile of orbs at his side and fit it into the bed of the sling. With steady paws and a sharp aim Iris released the bead, witnessing this time as it struck dead center; but the target slid back only an inch.

"It would be more satisfying if the target would break, Kaya," Iris said as he ruffled his ears and took another orb. "They did during Light Bending."

Kaya stretched out on the ground several feet away. " "I already told you that I don't know how to create wooden materials yet. And besides, if I make the targets too thin then I'll have to make hundreds of them, and we've got more important things to do."

"Yeah, yeah, I'm just giving you a hard time." A third orb impacted the dense photon target. "But anyway, back to what we all were talking about." Iris snatched another orb. "So, Manny, how did you avoid getting a detention? 'Cause Treble did nearly the same thing in my class, and Professor Nochesol nearly pinned him to the banister. He got detention for a week."

"He deserved it," Kaya muttered darkly. "The little red-winged snipe."

Manny leaned back against a log opposite Kaya. "I don't know, Iris. All I can guess is that I apologized."

"Well Treble sure didn't—dang!" Iris shouted as the bullet overshot the target. "He just kept making excuses and Professor Nochesol just kept getting angrier."

"Personally, I think you lucked out," said Brun, seated on the grass in front of the log.

"Whatever the reason, it's a good thing. Mi papá would've been furioso to find out what I did," Manny observed. "Four more shots, Iris, then it's my turn."

"Let's talk some more about Lakia," Kaya suggested.

"What about her?" Brun asked. "We went over the story three times."

"Sí, but think about that shadow Manny saw—how do we know it was a monkey?" the girl reiterated.

"Because it crept toward Lakia's wand, Kaya!" Iris shouted as he released a shot. "Crap."

"Okay, but wasn't it broad daylight?" she persisted. "Why couldn't Manny see the monkey clearly, then?"

"Probably because it was dark under the cover of the trees," Brun said dryly.

"That's true, but Lakia was in the shade and I could still see her clearly," Manny remarked. "Kaya has a good point—it's my turn, Iris."

"Just go." The hare hopped onto the log, fully flustered. "Stupid target."

"So what are you trying to say, Manny?" Brun resumed.

"Well, I guess I'm saying that maybe the monkey used an advanced light bending technique to draw a shadow over himself." Manny let loose a bullet that knocked the target from the stump.

"Idiot stump," Iris grumbled, his ears jagged.

"You mean like the Veil you drew around Lakia?" Kaya called as Manny jogged toward the stump, whereupon he replaced the target, pointing the butt of his Flareshot at the disc to summon several streams of light to widen it.

I bet it won't fall over now. "Yeah, something similar to that—like a dark Veil, you know?"

"That doesn't exist," Brun said abruptly.

"And why can't it?" Kaya clipped. "Just because you've never heard of it doesn't mean it can't be done."

"It's impossible," Brun continued as Manny knelt to collect a subsequent pearl. "Shadows are black, and you can't turn a photon black—light can never do that."

"Because a shadow is the absence of light—another good point." Manny hit the now indomitable target square in the center.

Kaya's mind wandered as she plucked the empty band of her Flareshot. "Maybe they're using dark photons," she proposed.

"That's ludicrous," Brun broke in. "I just told you photons can't be dark."

"Just listen for a second, oh wise one. Stop and consider who the monkeys' leader is—a star, remember? Maybe he, or she, taught them how to make light black." Another orb thumped against the target. Brun opened his mouth to argue, but Kaya cut him off. "Or better yet, what if they're not controlling photons at all? What if they're controlling something like shadow molecules instead? That would explain the dark Veil."

"You're being ridiculous! If there were 'shadow molecules' like you're saying, then we'd be able to see them! It would be like dark light, and when have you ever seen that?" Brun persisted.

"What about at twilight?" Manny proposed, releasing a bullet with a twang, zip, and a thud. Iris rolled his eyes and mumbled something. "That's sort of when light and dark mix, isn't it? And it's the hardest time to see anything because the colors are all off. Maybe that's when shadow molecules, or dark light—or whatever you want to call it—is visible. And hey, maybe you can't see it during the daytime because it's thinner than light!"

"¡Exactamente!" Kaya concurred. "Like the molecules are smaller than photons!"

"You two are full of ape crap," Brun said decisively. "You're welcome to think what you want, but don't expect me to believe this twilight stuff. Manny, if the monkey looked black, it was probably because it was wrapped in dark cloth or something to conceal itself." He paused. "Two more shots, Manny, and it's my turn."

"One more, actually," Iris corrected.

"Thanks a lot, buddy," Manny replied, catching only the corner of the target with his final shot.

"You're welcome," the hare answered brightly as Brun took Manny's place next to the munitions pile.

A silent moment passed as Brun successfully managed to connect shot after shot with the target. "So how long are we staying here tonight?" Manny finally asked.

"I don't know. What do you say, Brun? After all, it is twilight," Kaya said, taking care to emphasize the last word as she gazed about the bare field, from the light barrier on one side heralding the steep drop into the Flooded Forest to the dense tree line on the north. A quetzal sang its rippling melody somewhere to the west, far beyond the stump and the target.

"We only just got here ten minutes ago, guys," Iris complained as he snapped the end of his Flareshot to mold and animate a dozen Fireflies. "You can't be ready to leave—we haven't even started practicing with Chamaeleon yet. And in case you didn't notice, I still need to work on my aim."

"Don't worry, Iris. We'll be here at least two or three more hours before we leave." Brun said, hitting the bull's-eye. "Your turn, Kaya."

"Mamá said she'd have dinner ready at ten if you all wanted to come to my house," Kaya offered as her fist ate a handful of orbs. "We could leave for Chiron's Hutch when we're done to make it in time for Astronomy at eleven."

"Sounds like a plan," Manny agreed, scanning the field as Kaya's orb hammered its mark. "You still haven't told us the name of this place, Kaya. What is it?"

Kaya's neck muscles began to tighten. *Another ignorant question from the living nightlight.* "For our purposes let's just call it the Training Grounds," she replied, attempting to concentrate.

"And you're sure no one knows about this place?" Manny persisted. "It's a pretty wide area."

"No one will bother us here," Kaya said sharply. "So quit nagging me about it."

"Sheesh," Manny whispered as he reached over the log to snatch his copy of *Photokinesis* from his leather pack. "I'm gonna read up on L7 Flareshot maneuvers. I'm sure the weapon's more complex than it seems."

"You just do that, then," she replied roughly.

"Four more, Kaya, and then it's my turn again," Iris said.

Kaya fired off another orb. "Thanks for the reminder, Iris."

Walking Dead

Most Esteemed Student Body:

In remembrance of El Día de los Muertos, I have elected to cancel all classes after 12:00 p.m. on Tuesday, November 2. I am aware that individual students and families choose to recognize this day in distinct ways, but I would like to cordially invite each and every one of you to the Academy's Calavera Festival beginning promptly at 2:00 p.m. in the Plaza. Be sure to visit our activity and food stands—there will be much to see and do! I hope that each of you has a memorable and peaceful holiday.

Ciao,

J. Rumblefeather
Academy Director
Head Counselor

Brun folded up his letter and stepped from the bamboo hut out into the early Sunday sun of the final day of October. Shielding his eyes with his hand, the boy glided forward and slid tiredly into a wicker chair across from his tea-drinking centaur host.

A cup suddenly materialized on the table before the boy. "Buenos días, m'ijo," Chiron said as he filled Brun's mug with steaming, golden liquid. "¿Tienes hambre?"

"No, not really." Brun stretched his legs. "But I might take some eggs later."

"I believe that could be arranged." A thin current of honey dissolved into the whirlpool of the boy's drink. "Is Manny sleeping?"

"I think so," Brun yawned. "He doesn't snore, so I can never really tell."

Chiron took an energizing draft of tea as his deep space eyes stared across the table into Brun's amber ones. The centaur frowned. "What bothers you, m'ijo?"

A sigh. "Well, I don't think I understand Director Rumblefeather's letter he sent out last night." Brun set the paper next to his tea.

"Are you referring to the announcement regarding El Día de los Muertos?"

"Sí. What is it, anyway? I've never heard of Dead Day before."

"In English you would actually call it the Day of the Dead," Chiron corrected. "It is the day both Lumens and non-Lumens of Latin America take time to honor their loved ones who have passed from life to death. I assume that you have never recognized this day with your family?"

Brun did not answer, but instead stared at the dew glinting on a blade of grass at his feet. His mind wandered to a face that he could not remember, to tender eyes he had never seen and soft hands his skin had never felt. "Chiron, who do you think of on the Day of the Dead?"

"My grandfather, Nahir," the centaur answered, looking fondly toward the hill rising up behind the kapok tree to his left. "He taught me his love for astronomy." Chiron paused, considering a distant memory from his younger days. "Whom will you remember?"

"I'm with you, Chiron," Manny said as he stumbled lethargically from the hutch. "I always remember mi abuelo on the Day of the Dead, too."

"What was your grandfather's name, Manny?" Brun asked, intent on diverting all attention from himself.

"Gabriel," Manny replied as he took a seat between his roommate and the centaur. A faint smile touched his face as he realized that talking about his grandfather did not seem to bother him so much anymore. *Maybe because he's the reason I'm a Lumen...*

"And how does your family honor him?" Chiron asked.

"Usually we sit around the table, look at pictures, and eat pupusas, his favorite food. We also tell stories," Manny added, sipping from the mug Chiron had just placed before him. "But I've never been to a Calavera Festival. What's all that about?"

"It is a very lively celebration," Chiron alluded, snapping his charcoal tail. "I am certain you boys will enjoy it greatly."

"Are those demon otters or what?!" Brun shouted as he jumped aside to scarcely dodge a pair of creatures that scuttled by, cackling at the reactions their skull masks seemed to have on unsuspecting Lumens.

Before Manny could give any answer a team of kinkajous blocked his way, staring up at him with tails swishing. The empty sockets of their skull masks revealed four sets of lucent eyes. Each of the kinkajous carried a tiny, bread-like pastry covered in swirls, and one of them held a blood red rose in its paw. None of them spoke.

Are they gonna leap up and suck my blood, or what? They're freaky... "What are you all staring at?" Manny asked after a moment.

"Nothin'," one of the kinkajous answered passively.

"Then why are you standing in our way?" Brun pushed, unable to prevent his skin from crawling as he gazed over the kinkajous heads into the Plaza pulsating with wave after wave of skull-clad faces. **How morbid...**

"Why aren't you two wearing a mask?" another kinkajou asked, ignoring Brun's query. She gripped a sugar skull in her paw.

"Because they just got here, obviously," a third kinkajou replied impatiently. "You guys are a little late, though, you know," he added, glancing back at the boys.

458

"Well, excuse us," Manny said shortly. "And what's the deal with the skeleton faces, anyway?"

"They're called calaveras," the kinkajou with the rose replied. "You know, like skulls? That's why they it's called the Calavera Festival."

Brun's eyes registered comprehension. "I get it—the skull festival."

"But nobody calls it that," the curt kinkajou replied. "Just say Calavera Festival. We all understand that."

Brun raised an eyebrow. **Sorry if I crossed the line, you little reapajou.**

"That still doesn't explain why everyone's wearing the calaveras," Manny pointed out.

"'Cause it's the Day of the Dead," the first kinkajou said lackadaisically.

"Not once in my life has my family recognized El Día de los Muertos by wearing death masks around the house," Manny retorted. "I don't see how the calaveras help you remember your loved ones at all."

"Sure they do," the kinkajou with the rose said, her voice soft. "Seeing all the calaveras around reminds you that death isn't the end, and that part of your loved one keeps on living—their spirit, if you understand me. Now some people believe that their loved one's spirit comes to visit them on the Day of the Dead, but I don't."

"Well, I do!" the impertinent kinkajou interrupted.

"You're free to think as you like, but I say it's all based upon the person's faith while he was alive. He's either on one side or the other, if you get my drift," the kinkajou said as she pointed her rose from Brun to Manny.

"I never thought of it that way," Brun replied slowly. **I think I like that.** "So why the rose?"

"For blood, another symbol of life," she answered, holding the flower's petals up to the eyeholes of her mask.

"And the thorns stand for death," the kinkajou with the sugar skull added helpfully. "It's like from death sprouts life."

"Nice imagery," the other female kinkajou replied as she ran her eyes along the spines on the rose's stem up to the vibrant petals.

The impatient kinkajou snorted. "You two are a pair of mango cakes."

"Maybe they can just see deeper than you can," the first kinkajou proposed quietly.

"Maybe you should go jump in the river!" said the impatient kinkajou, his words pelting the other's mask.

Moving on, then. "How about that bread you're all holding in your hands?" Manny interposed quickly. "Are they supposed to be rats?"

Brun slapped his forehead and rolled his eyes.

"No! They're kinkajous! Like us!" said the kinkajou with the sugar skull as she lifted her mask and pointed to her face. "I don't look like a rat, do I?"

"What was I supposed to think?" Manny said defensively. "They have long, winding tails! And rats and death go together, hand in hand!"

"That's just gross," the first kinkajou said flatly.

"But—"

"Just be quiet, Manny," Brun whispered. "So what are those carbohydrate-packed kinkajous called?" he asked, turning his eyes back to the four creatures at his feet.

"Tanta wawas," the kinkajou with the rose answered. "That's Quechua, the Incan language, for 'bread babies.' There are several stands where you can knead and design them to fit the memory of your loved one. After that you bake it and take it with you for later."

"That's a lot like pottery, and I haven't gotten to do any of that since I left home. Let's go make a couple of those, Brun!" Manny proposed enthusiastically.

Brun sighed as his eyes followed Manny's glowing form into the skull-tossed fray. "Gracias for all your explanations on the Calavera Festival," he told the kinkajou squad. "I better get going before I lose him."

460

"Don't forget to make a sugar skull!" the kinkajou with her mask up cried as she held the sweet mold aloft in her paw. "They're more fun than tanta wawas in my opinion!"

With very little time to think, Brun bolted in through the crowd, following close behind Manny in zigzag fashion as skull-masked figures continued to obstruct his view. Suddenly Manny melted into the mass huddled tightly in front of the shops east of the entrance to the North Road. Brun plunged forward as a rush of skeletal morphos whizzed past his face, causing him to bump into a panther, to whom he promptly apologized before standing erect and discovering that he was now stationed before a wooden table covered in lumps of dough sprinkled generously with flour. Above the doorpost to the bakery behind hung an engraved sign that read, "Pan de luz."

"Buenas tardes, muchacho," a man greeted as he appeared on the other side of the table. "Would you like to make a special tanta wawa to remember your loved one?"

"Sure he would!" Manny bellowed from Brun's left. "He's with me, Señor!"

"Have at it, boy!" the baker exclaimed as he slapped a fist-sized lump on the table in front of Brun. "Just use your wand as a carving tool and it'll be ready for baking in no time! But remember to knead and flatten the dough first, of course!"

"Thanks," said Brun subtly as his fingers dusted the fine powder from the top of the cold, flesh-colored mixture. A laugh ripped up from Brun's chest as he looked over at Manny, who had just converted his wand into a rolling pin. "How did you manage to get flour all over your face? You can't have been working on that for more than a minute!"

"The best artists become one with their work," Manny rejoined as he evened out the dough, dusted his fingers, and began forming the bread into an oval shape.

"You are such a dweeb," Brun chuckled as he pressed his palms into the squishy mass.

"Come on, get into it, man!" Manny bolstered as he slapped Brun's upper arm with a flour-coated hand.

461

Brun slapped the lump down on the table. "You just wait, 'cause when I get done with you this tanta wawa's gonna be in the shape of your face!"

"Funny, mine already looks like yours," Manny said wryly as he etched a pair of long eyes and a squiggly mouth into the wet pastry. Brun only smiled as he produced a birch rolling pin from the ring on his hand and began the process of flattening the dough.

Twenty minutes later the baker handed the boys the completed tanta wawas that each had made. "Careful now, they're still a bit caliente. Make sure not to burn your fingers," the man warned. "But they'll be cool enough for you to eat them later, no doubt about that."

"Do we have to eat them?" Brun asked as he gazed fixedly at the golden brown loaf lying on a thin cloth in his hand. He could feel the warmth from the bread as it bled through to his palm.

"It's tradition!" the man cried eagerly. "I find it disrespectful otherwise—to the one you loved, I mean."

Manny gazed at the bread sculpture in his roommate's palm. "Who is she?"

Brun's eyes ran down along the woman's long, flowing hair to the serene face with dots for eyes and a crescent mouth. A fluid dress stretched down to her bare feet. "It's mi mamá," he breathed, the precious words falling down to add the final confection to his work. **And it's the first time I've ever seen her.**

"She's pretty," Manny said, noticing the delicate curves his friend had used to score every detail. "What was her name?"

"Alzena," Brun said, admiring her face.

"I'm sorry she died, Brun," Manny shared, his voice somber. *It makes me appreciate my own mother, even if she does nag me a lot.*

Brun blinked a few times. "Me, too." A moment passed in peaceful silence. "What about yours? Can I see it?"

"Definitely." Manny held the loaf up and angled it for Brun to see. From the heart of the bread burst the image of a man's long, slender face and short hair. He had lucid eyes that gazed up at a bright star in the corner.

Brun noticed the man's thoughtful eyes. "Your abuelito's name was Gabriel, right?"

"You got it," Manny answered amiably.

"Was he a Lumen?" Brun continued. "An astronomer, maybe?"

"I don't know for sure." Manny scanned his grandfather's ingenuous face. "If he was he never told me. But he sure loved the stars—he taught me my first constellations."

"It sounds like he was a pretty smart hombre."

Manny nodded. "Oh, yeah. He knew about all sorts of topics, because he loved to read. When I was little he always used to tell me about the most bizarre animals and machines. And he loved studying the different cultures of the world and everyone's traditions."

"I hope I'm like him one day," Brun said reverently.

"You are a know-it-all," said Manny with a sportive smile, "which makes you definitely a lot more like him than me."

"No comment there," Brun joked. "So you wanna hit another stand?"

"¡Claro que sí!" Manny shouted. "How about making some sugar calaveras or maybe grabbing a snack?"

Brun glanced at the table. "Aren't you forgetting something?"

Manny followed Brun's gaze to a dark, wooden etching knife. "That's not my wand," he said as he displayed his arm. "Mine's ticking away on my wrist. I know better than to lose it twice."

"Then whose wand is this?"

"Maybe it's not a wand at all—it could be just a normal old etching tool." But as Manny reached out to touch the instrument he felt his hand repelled by a force distinctly similar to that of magnets of identical polarities. Without thinking Manny pushed against the wand's energy, causing the utensil to slide from the table and down onto the cobblestones.

"It's a wand, alright." Manny swiftly ducked under the table to verify the present location of the tool. The instrument rolled into a divide between the cobblestones just as the boy's hands met the cold rock.

Brun popped his head under the table. "What do you expect to do with it?" he asked, annoyed that Manny had made the wand fall. "It's not like you can pick it up."

"Especially considering the fact that it's stuck," Manny grunted as he turned, sat down, and crossed his legs. "I guess I'll just have to guard it until the owner comes back for it."

This is exactly how I'd hoped to spend the afternoon. With a frown Brun said, "And just what am I supposed to do?"

"Pues, if you don't want to sit and talk, I guess you could go hunt for whoever the wand belongs to. But that's up to you, man."

"And how do you propose I find that person? Am I supposed to fly up on top of the kiosk and start screaming? Because we both know that I can't make a photowave enhancement, and I don't think my voice will carry all that far," Brun riposted, uncharacteristically cross.

"Why so edgy, amigo?" Manny lifted his tanta wawa bread up and made the image of his grandfather dance in the air. "It could be a lot worse—at least you're not dead."

Brun did not reply; but the fire in his gaze did subside, however slightly.

"¡Tengo una idea!" Manny said affably. "A really good idea! Why don't you hunt down Julius? He sent us the invitation letter to the Calavera Festival, so he's got to be around here somewhere. Heck, he's probably at some booth sponsored by the Academy in front of the Office of Lumen Studies! That's just right across the Plaza—you'll be back in no time!"

"Fine," Brun said, his voice still slightly constricted. "But don't let that wand out of your sight," he warned as he rose to his full height and took a calming breath. "Nos vemos pronto."

464

"See you in a minute!" Manny agreed as Brun stepped into the skull ocean. Some time passed as the boy stared out from beneath the table at the high-energy antics of his peers, who ran, scurried, and fluttered about as their thrilled voices electrified the atmosphere. There was no time for boredom as colorful morphos flit about in constant attempts to scare their ever-passive panther counterparts, frogs and basilisks rode by, sharing rolls of sweet bread, and otters mounted on centaurs dispensed suckers to match the masks all were wearing. It can be considered no surprise, therefore, that when a quiet, perfectly even yet somehow intense voice spoke from close at Manny's side, the boy very nearly shed his skin.

"Hello, boy," the voice said.

"¡Ay caramba, no me asustes!" Manny exclaimed, catching his tanta wawa bread in midair. "Don't sneak up on me like that!" he reprimanded, turning to discover yet another masked frame with four arms and an elastic tail. The creature stood less than three feet tall and had midnight fur. A frown began to twist itself across the boy's face. *Boneheaded kinkajou.*

"You have no cause to be alarmed," the creature replied, though for some reason—Manny could not distinguish why—the tenor of the unexpected visitor's voice made the boy's skin crawl.

"I just don't like it when people sneak up on me like that—it's creepy," Manny explained. *Not to mention the fact that your calavera isn't particularly the prettiest I've seen all day.*

No reply—the creature merely stared over the cobblestones at Manny's diminishingly bright face.

"Do you need something?" Manny said, glancing toward the crowd in hopes that Brun would appear. But a sudden movement by the visitor drug the boy's attention back instantly.

The creature was now a good deal closer, virtually a hair from the boy's toe. Its eyes were no longer set on Manny, however. The angle of the animal's head was directed at the ground.

"My friend," the visitor began again, his words smooth and black as slate, "my friend lost his wand here. Could this by chance be it?"

465

"I—I don't think so," Manny replied, disliking the creature more every second. "You must be confused." He slid his foot over the wand; blood began to pump more readily through his veins. "I guess you'll just have to look elsewhere."

Nonetheless, the creature sustained its frozen glare at the etching tool partially concealed by the boy's foot.

Manny's mind began to race. *What do I do? What if he reaches out toward the wand? Do I kick him? What if he—*

"What are you doing down there, boy?" called an odd voice from behind Manny. Startled yet again, the boy turned to find the bulging belly of the baker floating ominously before him. But just as his eyes met the full figure of the pastry master, Manny felt a firm grip tighten around his shin followed by a clipping sound.

"Much thanks," whispered a raspy voice. When Manny turned back round, however, the creature had gone.

"Did he vanish?" Manny asked absentmindedly as he stared along the underside of the table, still finding no sign of the visitor.

"If you're talking about your friend who made the tanta wawa in the figure of the lady, then yes," the ignored and now impatient baker answered. "So what's happened, boy? Did ya get so excited you fainted and now ya just woke up?"

What is this dude talking about? "No," Manny replied flatly. "Somebody's wand's on the ground here, stuck between a crack in the stones, and I'm waiting here for mi amigo to get back with Julius."

"Who in white blazes is Julius?" the man retorted.

"Julius Rumblefeather—you know, the Academy Director?" The boy squeezed his gaze between the edge of the table and the baker's ample belly.

"Director Rumblefeather? He's already been by once today—made a beautiful baked specimen of an old quetzal if I do say so myself. I don't think he'll be back—he's a busy bird today, ya know. But—look here—did ya say there's a wand stuck under the table?"

"Sí," Manny sighed, the aggravated word slapping the underside of the table forcefully.

466

"Espera un momento, pues." The man disappeared swiftly through the bakery door.

Manny stared dully at the table leg. "What do you think I've been doing?" But in a very short time the baker reappeared, shoving a pair of metal tongs under the table and nearly gouging out the boy's eye.

"Here, use these to pry out and seize the wand," the baker directed.

Manny wrenched the tool from the man's hand. *I might just pry out your belly button if you keep sticking junk in my face.* Sliding back a bit and repositioning his leg, Manny brought the tongs down close to the cobblestones, upon which point alarm entered his eyes. The boy feverishly scanned the place where he knew the wand had been; but despite his frustrated searching and sliding, the wand was no where to be found. Manny slapped the tongs down on the stones with a clank as his eyes wandered out from below the table in an attempt to rationalize what could have happened. *Where did it go?* Sudden realization hit him. *Idiot kinka—*

The table in front of the baker's belly rocked with a thud. "No need to get overexcited, muchacho. My wand's not going anywhere—I have to work it out of the cobblestones all the time. It just takes a little paciencia when it's stuck down there good and deep."

Manny inhaled sharply as he cradled his head. *You're under the table, dummy. Why'd you try to stand up?* With tears in his eyes Manny grabbed the tongs and gently pulled himself out from under the pastry stand. "You mean that was your wand?" he asked, rising up with a painful heave. The boy's head throbbed.

"'Course it was!" the man cried good-naturedly. "What kind of a pastry-maker would I be if I left my most prized tool locked up in the shop? Best to have it at hand's reach, I say!"

Manny winced in the sunlight. "Did you ever think of wearing it, or at least carrying it in your pocket?"

"Tools to the table is my motto!" the man bellowed. "Personally, I don't like pockets on my aprons—they just get full of flour, if ya get me."

"Not really," Manny mumbled as he lifted a hand from the stand, his palm covered in baking dust.

"Only a Lumen of my profession would understand, I suppose," the baker observed as he grabbed the tongs. "I'll just have to get down and snatch my wand up myself, then."

"You can't do that, Señor."

"Despite my appearance, I am perfectly able." The baker patted his protuberant gut and knelt down. "As I said before, I do it all the time."

Manny rolled his eyes and shook the flour from his palm.

"Sr. López, there had better be an extremely valid reason that your roommate came to drag me away from the Academy booth!" rang a familiar voice from Manny's blindside.

The boy's fists clenched the table edge just before he begrudgingly turned around to face Julius, who landed with a shower of powder. The lower half of Manny's shirt turned from blue to white. *Ugh.* "Didn't Brun tell you what happened, Julius?" he asked, glancing over the quetzal's shoulder toward his friend.

"He most certainly did," Julius clipped, his beaded eyes flashing. "And if I am not mistaken I believe your Astronomy professor clearly told both you and Brun to abandon your incessant arguments regarding missing or misplaced wands."

"No está," the baker grunted as he blundered up from the ground. "Are you sure my wand was down there, boy?"

"Sí, Señor, I promise you the wand was there!" Manny answered, his voice rising defensively. "But right when you came up behind me a kinkajou came along and stole it!"

Julius shot Manny a death glare. "A kinkajou?" the bird reiterated, the words slicing from his beak. "You were so adamant that the wand thieves were monkeys, not kinkajous, am I correct? What brought you to change your conviction?"

From behind Julius Brun drew his finger across his neck, signaling Manny to stay silent. Manny clenched his jaw as he stared into his counselor's sharp eyes, careful not to utter one word.

"It's obvious that the muchacho's confused, Director," the baker said sympathetically. After this the man leaned over the table in an attempt to whisper in the quetzal's ear, but the breadth of his belly only allowed him to stretch so far. "If you ask me," he began, none too softly, "the boy's hit his head one too many times this afternoon. As I see it he passed out and must've dreamed he saw my wand under la mesa. But that's okay—I'll find it later, if ya understand me. I always do."

"That's ridiculous!" Brun blurted, unable to quell his annoyance a second more. "When I left Manny was guarding the wand under the table, and he was wide awake!"

"That will be enough, Señor Dimirtis. You are not to address an adult with such a tone," Julius intervened authoritatively. "I will give you and Manny one final chance to redeem yourselves before I exact punishment for these humorless acts of yours. Apologize to Señor Patino for your cruel joke and I will be much less severe."

Manny and Brun exchanged an amber glance of mulish accord before glaring back at the quetzal. A moment passed as silence strangled the joyous exclamations erupting from the Plaza behind.

Julius' expression suddenly softened. "Juan, I apologize for the deplorable behavior of these two young ones, and I assure you they will bother you no more."

"No need to apologize, Director," Juan Patino replied genially. "They were actually two of the most pleasant festival goers I've seen today, excluding the white-haired fellow's last comment, if ya get me. Brun, was it? Ya might want to work on that temper, I should say. Could get ya in a lot of trouble in the future if ya don't watch it—believe you me."

Brun narrowed his eyes. **And you might try sharpening your thought processing skills.**

Julius spread his wings and took off in an emerald flash. "Vámonos, pues."

"You mean we have to go with you?" Manny set the baked profile of his grandfather on the table impudently.

"One more cross word and I will contact your mother," Julius threatened as he climbed ever higher. "And I doubt she will be as merciful as I."

"That's debatable," Manny muttered as he slid under the table, reaching the other side and grabbing his bread loaf. As he trotted up to Brun he asked, "Where d'you think he's taking us?"

"Probably the Academy stand," Brun purported drearily as Julius wheeled about above their heads. "But before he shuts us up again tell me what happened while I was gone."

As he and Brun darted between their peers, Manny scrupulously recounted the activities of the suspicious creature, not forgetting the eerie inflections if its voice and the ominous, sharp-toothed mask.

"Do you think it really was a kinkajou?" Brun posed as they passed the Unity Kiosk, its vines covered with skull ornamentals.

"It couldn't have been anything else. It had the tail and everything."

"But you said it was wearing a mask," Brun pointed out. "What if it was—a monkey?"

Manny's feet locked, grinding him to an abrupt halt just steps from the Carina River. "¿Un chango?" he repeated, weighing the details. "I—but—how could it have been?"

"Keep walking!" Brun drug Manny along by the arm. "I don't want to see Director Rumblefeather any sooner than we have to. Now, back to our primate pals—we know they can pass through the light barrier whenever they want, so that would mean they can go anywhere in the city that they feel like. The only hitch is we would see their faces; but today that doesn't apply—the calavera masks are the ultimate disguise for them to run around without being noticed."

"So they'd just appear to be kinkajous!" Manny's words exploded from his lips. "Those stinkin' changos are geniuses!"

"Not too loud!" Brun said through his teeth. "We don't want to attract any attention to the issue, especially if one of those apes is nearby—if they find out we know about them they'll probably target us next. And honestly I don't want to fight off any of them sooner than I have to."

Me, either. As he and Brun continued along the Carina toward the bridge, Manny's awareness of all monkey-like creatures drastically rose. Suddenly the profile of every kinkajou within a fifteen-foot radius seemed supercharged with a subliminal suspicion that had not been there moments before. Manny flinched as a pair of ecstatic young kinkajous somersaulted from a bridge.

Brun noticed Manny's reaction. "Chill out, hombre. I doubt the changos are acting as happy as the kinkajous today—most likely they're lying low and scoping out potential victims. And they definitely won't be doing any cartwheels," he added as the kinkajous flipped past.

"Well, aren't you just Mr. Cool again all of a sudden..."

"What's that supposed to mean?" Brun asked, sweeping the area beyond the bridge for dubious-looking creatures. Though he saw none, he groaned as he noticed the Office of Lumen Studies looming ahead.

"I mean how just five minutes ago Julius nearly had to pull you off the baker back there!" Manny retorted, still chary of the ever-energetic kinkajou presence.

"Yeah, well, Sr. Patino was talking nonsense."

"He was confused," Manny said in the baker's defense. "It's not like he was calling us a pair of liars like Julius and Chiron."

Good point. "I guess you're right." Brun sighed as Julius dove down toward a densely packed stand located immediately in front of the office building. He and Manny squeezed through the crowd and into the shade of the blue canopy only to discover a dozen distinctive mountains of skull masks burgeoning from the ground at their feet.

"Your punishment," Julius began smartly, "is to spend the entire afternoon dispensing calavera masks to any and all visitors who approach the Academy stand. And be sure to match the appropriate skull to the Lumen on whom you are waiting—no panthers wearing unicorn calaveras, now."

As if that isn't obvious.

"And from this point forward I will hear neither of you integrate the words 'monkey' and 'wand' in the same sentence. Is that clear?" the quetzal stipulated.

471

"As crystal." Manny's words shattered and tumbled through the eye sockets of the skull army before him.

"And you, Brun?" Julius continued.

"Sí, Señor," the boy answered begrudgingly.

"Get to work then," the quetzal concluded, light glinting from his beaded eyes. "And as the two of you have taken my place, I believe I'll coast around la Plaza for a bit. See you both in an hour or so," he finished with a flutter and a stream of tail feathers.

"My, my! In trouble are we?" a voice rang from the patron-assaulted table. "Now what could you have done to irritate dear Julius so?"

"Wouldn't be a hard thing to do, but you didn't hear me say that!" another voice squeaked as a bolt of light shot past Brun's side to grab several chinchilla masks.

Manny and Brun turned round to find Julius' fellow counselors, Melody Nightvine and Rush Stickgrip, perched on the edge of the table and passing out skull guises like frisbees.

"Hope you're ready for some exercise, boys!" Melody cried as she lassoed ten or so falcon skulls with a band of light.

Brun stared at the kinkajou placidly. **That's precisely why I enlisted.**

"Busy work for Seventh-Levels!" Rush squeaked as his neon blue fingers tossed a trio of basilisk skulls to their giddy recipients. "Considering your inability to transfer objects with light, I mean. It's a pity you're not Sixth-Levels—then this task would be as easy as a fly on the tongue." The frog's blood-red eyes gleamed.

"Move it, Stickgrip!" Melody cried as she hauled another stack of headpieces to the table. "You're setting a bad example for the recruits!"

With a bright wink Rush snapped the minute bamboo rod in his hand, showering the space before him with a mountain of panther masks. "Hop to it, muchachos, before she turns on you next!"

Manny took a deep breath before turning and filling his arms with skulls. As he approached the table his grip went limp at the sight of the thousands still waiting for their masks.

"López, pick those calaveras up!" Melody rang as she set a mask on a quetzal's head. "And make sure not to step on any of them!"

"Did you see how many people are here?" Manny whispered to Brun as he set the last fallen mask on the table.

"Sí," Brun said blandly. "We're gonna be here all night."

Owing to the unending pressure of the crowd and the consequent jaunts back and forth from the table to the mask stockpile and back, Manny and Brun had little time for conversation beyond the phrases, "Get me a centaur, will ya?" or "Don't forget the chinchillas." Nearly an hour had passed before any form of respite came, and even then it came with a request.

"¡Oye! You guys have any calaveras with ear holes?" a positive voice exclaimed from its mid-air perch.

Looking up, Manny and Brun found Iris's small, mahogany frame seated lightly on Kaya's shoulders. He had an ear raised inquisitively.

"I've been wondering what you two were doing today," Manny said as he placed a skull on a baby unicorn's head.

"Like you've had any time to think," Brun added as he tossed two tiny masks into the air. A pair of golden morphos caught them.

"We're actually just getting here," Kaya said, her chocolate eyes solid. "Mi mamá fixed a late lunch, but that's normal para el Día de los Muertos. Eat and talk, talk and eat. I'm sure you know the drill."

"Yep." Manny thought of a dining room of familiar faces discussing his grandfather's unique personality and life.

Brun interrupted Manny's thoughts. "I haven't seen any hare calaveras anywhere, Iris."

"Dang," Iris breathed. "What about you, Manny?"

The boy shook his head. "Nope. But I can check with Melody." Manny jogged away along the table before the hare could reply. Iris had taken a mere breath when the kinkajou precipitously flipped through the air, landing agilely before the girl and the hare.

"Just a tad late, aren't we?" Melody sang as the dark wand in her paw melted, flattening and growing thicker to form a case. As she flipped the clasps she clicked her tongue reproachfully. "My, my, my... Booths close at sundown—that only gives you an hour to enjoy the festivities."

"Sorry, Melody," Iris called back, eager to discover the contents of his light-bringer's case.

"Not to worry—I forgive readily." The kinkajou removed a pearl mask from the box, its ear-studded profile trimmed with the shadows of midnight. Iris's heart leapt.

"Gracias, Melody!" the hare cried, sliding nimbly from Kaya's shoulders, his paws outstretched.

"You're very welcome," the kinkajou replied as she handed the face piece to her student. "It's exclusive, you know—the only one in Isla Verde."

The ends of the hare's digits tingled as he situated the mask on his face. "How do I look?" he asked, his sun-bleached jaw unmoving.

"Terrifying, but that's nothing unusual," Brun joked.

The hare skull skewed slightly to one side as a violet glare penetrated its sockets. "Aren't you hilarious?" riposted Iris, the mask muffling a good deal of the sarcasm in his voice. The boy smiled.

"Here's one for you." Manny held a human mask out for Kaya, who stared passively at the skull in the boy's hand. "¿Qué? Don't you want it?"

"No," the girl answered quietly. "Brings back bad memories. I can participate just fine without one."

Manny retracted the mask. *Okay, then...*

"I'll be off now," Melody exclaimed, cart wheeling along the stand to resume her task as she called toward the boys. "Back to work, muchachos!"

"We've gotta go, anyway," Iris said, noticing Manny and Brun's deflated glances. "Like Melody said, there's not much time left."

Thanks for the reminder.

"But we need to talk to you two about something," Manny whispered significantly.

"It'll have to wait 'til tomorrow," Kaya replied. "Vámonos, Iris."

"Let's head for the tanta wawa stand, first," Iris proposed, hopping back on Kaya's shoulder as she turned into the crowd. "I've been waiting all day for this…"

"How do we get ourselves into these situations?" Brun groaned as he tromped off to collect more masks.

"I know what you mean," Manny corresponded. "You do the right thing and you get shot in the back for it."

"Shot in the back? To what are you referring?" a rich voice beckoned from above. Two swift glances revealed Julius, his jade body perched at the edge of the canopy.

"We're just talking, Director Rumblefeather," Brun replied quickly. "Did you enjoy your flight around la Plaza?"

The quetzal's tails danced. "Most assuredly. And I am sure much more enjoyment awaits us later this evening."

"Us?" Manny crowed.

Midnight Swim

"Why can't we just go back to Nahir's Hill to stargaze with Chiron?" Manny stared churlishly on as he and Brun followed Julius's undulating tails over the planks of the Lucero boardwalk.

"There will be plenty of time for stargazing after the ceremony. For now, you will stay with me, reflecting on the blatant misdeeds you committed toward Sr. Patino."

Manny stomped the deck with extra force. *Misdeeds my foot.*

"What ceremony?" Brun inquired, gazing through the soft air toward the body of the island on his left. The air seemed solemn, yet somehow alive, as though infused with the living memories of Lumens past.

"Did I not tell you both to remain silent a moment ago? The ceremony will be explained when we arrive," the quetzal clipped, his peaceful movements at odds with his voice. But this answer did not bother Brun; he rather enjoyed the latent anticipation in the air. **At least I'm not handing out any more masks.**

Manny's features, on the other hand, glowed in frustration. *This is just like being in Sr. Soriano's class in Arizona—the stupid teacher gets mad at me for nothing, and I have to sit around in detention, or whatever you want to call this ridiculous punishment.* He clenched his fist. *I hope the ceremony's a flop.*

Ten minutes passed before the boys and the bird reached their destination—the Lucero Falls observation deck—which to Manny and Brun's surprise did not lie empty.

"Buenas noches," a cordial voice greeted them, its words lined with a faint sadness.

"Manny! Brun! I didn't know you were going to be here!" shouted another voice, exponentially more ecstatic than the first.

"I thought you were with Kaya," Manny replied to an overjoyed, and apparently relieved, Iris. "Where is she, anyway?"

476

"She and her family rented a boat and are watching the ceremony from beneath the Argo Dock," Iris explained. "And I wasn't invited," he added with a whisper. "You know, family time."

"Gotcha. So you and tu papá watch the ceremony from up here with Julius every year?" Manny nodded toward the melancholy figure of Fidelio, whose argent eyes scanned the rippling lake.

"Yeah, that's our tradition, except Julius hasn't ever come in the past—he's just here to announce."

"Merely here to announce, am I, Sr. Firefoot?" Julius quipped. "It is my honor and duty as Director to open the ceremony, if you please."

Manny and Iris exchanged a pair of knowing shrugs as the quetzal glided past them to perch on the banister on the far side of Fidelio.

"So what all does this ceremony involve?" Brun tore his gaze from the mass of people he had just noticed flooding the northern shore of the island. "Everyone seems to be crowding around the water—why? Does something come out of it?"

"Yes, actually," Iris said, rather astounded. "That was a pretty good guess. You see, once everyone places their candles on the Lake—"

"Come here, m'ijo," Fidelio murmured, interrupting his son's explanation.

"Sorry." Iris sighed as he turned and hopped onto the platform next to his father, in whose paws rested a large, glowing object in the shape of a teardrop.

"I don't mean to be intrusive, Professor," Brun prefaced, his golden eyes set on the transparent globule, "but what are you holding in your hands?"

"This," Fidelio began, raising the specimen a bit higher, "is known as a farolito. Notice its shape, similar to that of a burning drop of frozen fire. It represents the soul of your loved one, and their memory that you carry in your heart."

"That's intense," Manny whispered, watching as Iris reached out and touched the wax drop. Its color suddenly shifted from ivory to creamy lavender.

Iris looked up from the candle. "Did I get it right, Papá?" The father hare nodded, his eyes suddenly glittering with silver wetness. Beyond him Julius stared fixedly into a hovering candle the hue of an earthy purple, almost black.

Though he felt further questioning would probably be intrusive, particularly considering the impromptu pain in Fidelio's gaze, Brun's curiosity won out. "Again, Professor, I don't mean to be rude, but what does the farolito's color represent?"

Hardly able to respond, Fidelio said, "The color of—of Çarai's eyes." A platinum tear dampened his cheek, his paw clasping the farolito tightly.

None too tactfully, or at least so Brun thought, Manny asked, "So do we get a farolito?"

"Hold out your hands," Julius purled, the edge in his voice replaced with the heavy thread of fading memories. Both boys obeyed as two surprisingly dense farolitos materialized in their palms—Brun's a golden hazel, and Manny's aquamarine.

"Abuelito's eyes," Manny breathed, the emotion catching in his throat as a lifetime of memories burst from the sapphire flame in his hand.

"I have her eyes," Brun whispered, a forlorn joy wrinkling the skin on his lips. **I have her eyes...**

"Good evening." Julius's sober voice soared out, flooding the air above the Lake. "It is none other than the Day of the Dead. Tonight, we bring honor to our loved one's memories as we witness the hidden fire of life ignite these humble flames we have constructed. Join me in placing your farolitos on the water."

As the quetzal finished, a wave of innumerable colors spread across the lake, casting the subtle light of frozen memories on the water below. Amazement struck Manny silent for an instant; but then he realized that he and Brun were apparently the only two Lumens still holding their candles. "Julius," Manny whispered, fearing exclusion from the ceremony, "how do Brun and I get our farolitos down there? As Rush explained earlier we're just Seventh-Levels, and we can't transfer objects. Are we supposed to throw them?"

A steel glare tore along the railing as Julius shook the cherry pendant around his neck. "It doesn't matter what level you are—just let go of the farolito and guide it with your mind to the water," he said tersely.

"But we can't," Manny contended. "We don't know how!"

"Believe me—you do. Guiding the farolito doesn't require photokinesis; it requires something—more. But you have it; every being has it. Just think of your loved one and guide the candle down," Julius reassured him. "And don't interrupt me anymore!" Manny and Brun exchanged doubtful glances as Julius shook his pendant and prepared to speak again.

"We really don't have any other choice," Brun muttered.

"Alright, then. On the count of three: uno, dos, tres." Manny reluctantly allowed the candle to roll from his fingers. He winced as the bulb met the open air and stopped, hovering attentively in place and ignoring gravity's unbending hand. "It worked!"

Julius resumed his address. "My fellow Lumens…"

"¡Ándale, Manny! We've gotta get these down there fast!" Brun gazed in earnest as the amber flame floating before his face spun down through the night in a wide arc. Manny's drop did the same, lighting upon the water a mere beat after Brun's.

"…on the Lake, let us now lend our hearts to the past as we don our masks," Julius proceeded.

From their vantage point atop the Lucero Deck, Manny and Brun peered out as each spectator of every species fit his or her respective calavera mask in place. The boys' hearts leapt as a wall of luminous white skulls, like an endless row of moonlit teeth, shone along the dark rim of the island. Even Iris, at their side, had put on his glowing façade.

"For once my face doesn't stand out in the crowd," Manny joked quietly.

"Too bad they're not red; then it'd be me standing in your shoes," Brun articulated with equal subtlety.

But at that instant something red did appear, or something very near red. From the depth of the Lake, beneath folds of undulating water, a figure materialized, its hue that of crimson gold.

At first the figure seemed small, even minute. Seemingly the size of his fist, Manny reasonably mistook the light for a glare reflecting off the bottom of the Lake. As seconds passed and grips tightened on the deck railing, however, the figure grew, eventually encompassing a third of the Lake as it stared expectantly up from beneath the surface, its eyes a purple fire.

"I-is that a bird?" Manny stood agape, gazing from one burning wingtip to the other. Yet before Brun had the chance to respond, the beast's flaming countenance slid from the water, rising hundreds of meters into the air with only two flaps of its great wings. Despite its great altitude, the creature's gold, ruby, and amethyst tail feathers danced evanescently over the cap of the Lake.

Brun exhaled. "Wow."

And then, lifting its beak high and piercing the night with its gaze, the bird released a quivering call that rang to the very marrow of the boys' bones. Before Manny's face appeared a man with chestnut hair, understanding eyes, and a coy smile. Brun, on the other hand, beheld a woman with a glowing countenance, flowing midnight hair, and tender eyes. Though he had not noticed this at first, later, when he described the woman to Manny, Brun recalled that she had held a stone in her left hand. Neither of them understood the meaning of this, however.

As the penetrating cry faded, Manny and Brun were startled to see the air teeming with an army of birds the size of quetzals, all identical in form to the larger that had been present only a moment earlier. In contrast to their predecessor, the new birds each embodied a distinct color and hue as they curved gracefully through the atmosphere, progressively descending to the Lake below. Four birds swept the Lucero Deck in a flash of muddy lavender and golden sapphire, plunging instantly toward the water. Brun leaned forward and witnessed as the golden fowl disappeared and his farolito burst into living flame.

Manny shook his head. "That's the trickiest way of lighting a candle I've ever seen."

The Lake awoke in a river of color as a reverent silence gripped the night. "Now we remember, and reflect," projected

Julius' lugubrious voice. "Blessed be our families, and blessed be our friends. Peace be to—"

A wave of screams rent the air, unceremoniously ending the quetzal's closing address. Sounds of struggling, more screams, and a clap of thick splashes rose up from the northeast corner of the island.

"What is the meaning of this?" Julius careened from his perch in the direction of the Argo Dock. "What sort of irreverent rabble-rou…" Yet in spite of his protest and impending approach, the screams grew louder.

"Let's go!" Manny rocketed from the rail and east along the boardwalk.

"Don't forget about me, hombres!" Iris shouted as he hopped off in pursuit of Brun and Manny.

"Iris Renee Firefoot, come back to this platform, now!" Fidelio ordered. But the three had already gone, and the fires of memories burned bright.

***

"¡Socorro! I can't swim!" cried a girl's voice, her words mixed among the choking splashes of her friends. "Help!"

"Hurry, Papá! They're going to drown!" Kaya cried, leaning out over the prow of the boat and gripping the rim frantically. Her chocolate eyes reflected the flaying of hooves and arms less than one hundred strokes ahead.

"I'm rowing as fast as I can, Kaya, so sit down before we have to rescue you from drowning, too," Marcos replied as he strained against the viscosity of the Lake with all his might.

Kaya obeyed, but then began to fidget nervously. Her sister, Kiki, was crying at the back of the boat, the terror passing from the distressed Lumens' mouths into her own. Her mother tried patiently to console her.

"It's okay, Kiki. I promise you'll be safe. Mami y Papi are here. Nothing's going to happen to you," Ellen assured her.

An idea came. "¡Mamá!" Kaya shouted, her words curving around her father. "Why don't you make another paddle and help Papá row?"

"Marcos, turn toward land!" Ellen bellowed, suddenly realizing what would happen if they continued heading straight toward the wild-eyed centaurs. "They'll flip the boat if you don't!"

This made Kiki wail even louder.

"Aargh!" Marcos grunted as he paddled hard to one side.

"¡Mamá! Make another paddle!" Kaya yelled.

Ellen flipped the tulipwood bracelet on her wrist, calling down an oar-shaped bolt of light from the stars above. Yet before transforming the paddle into wood, she rose to her feet and stared intently at the line of trees ahead. In a swift motion of her hands she converted her bracelet into a thin, flexible bow, stringing it with a cord of light from the floating oar. A second later the oar had condensed into a thin arrow, which Ellen grasped and fired toward the shoreline. As the arrow sunk deep into a tree, Ellen jerked the end of the bow to connect the arrow to her wand with a braid of light. The boat lurched forward as the distance between the Bellastratas and the island grew rapidly smaller.

"Good idea, dear," Marcos sighed as he pulled the dripping paddle in. A moment later the prow collided with the rocky shore.

Kaya leapt from the boat, running west along the rocky outcrop toward the beleaguered centaurs. She knelt down and stretched out her hand over the water when her mother screamed, "Kaya, get back!"

"But they're drowning!" Kaya's voice rang tensely as she reached further toward the frantic gurgling.

A tight grip on the girl's shoulders drug her back. "Kaya, go take care of Kiki, now!" Ellen said unquestionably.

An emerald figure arced down from the sky. "What is going on here?" Julius demanded authoritatively. "Marcos, explain!"

"I don't know, Julius, but we need to get these poor centaurs out of the water before they drown!" the man replied, exasperated.

"Julius, you fly up over them and use Reticulum to start heaving them out of the water from above. Marcos and I will get on either side and do the same from here. Let's move it!" Ellen shouted.

Cradling her younger sister in her lap, Kaya watched intently as her parents and the fiery quetzal reached their positions. The girl marveled as thousands of eerie, silver-blue strings wrapped around her mother's wrist. A second later Ellen extended her arm as if to throw an object into the water; it was then that an icy net exploded from her palm, reaching out and engulfing the body of the nearest centaur. The net mimicked the action of Ellen's fingers, closing around the sinking creature. With a deft pull of her arm Ellen drew the centaur up and out of the water; a breath later the creature landed in a sopping horse mess next to Kaya. Kiki covered her eyes and screamed.

"Kaya, take Kiki and head further that way!" Ellen cried, pointing toward the Argo Dock to the east. Again Kaya did not argue, but as she drug her sister along the shore her eyes never left the newly saved centaur, who after several violent coughs leaned forward and vomited a stream of dark water.

"Oh, God, please let them be okay," Kaya prayed, her legs rigid as she witnessed centaur after centaur land heavily along the shoreline. Kiki hugged her sister's thigh tightly, her fear manifesting itself in chest shaking sobs. Kaya looked down at her sister's quaking frame, rubbing her back understandingly and whispering, "Shhh, Kiki, todo saldrá bien. Everything will be okay… I promise." Looking back up, however, a shard of ice pierced Kaya's heart—two of the centaurs were not moving.

Ellen flew to the side of one such centaur. "Marcos, come here!"

"What do you need me to do?" her husband answered, bolting quickly to her side.

"I need your help resuscitating her." Ellen cradled the centaur's auburn head in her hand. "Place both hands just below the ribcage of her lower body and make ready to compress her chest. But wait for my signal!" Marcos obeyed as Ellen leaned forward and breathed deeply into the centaur's mouth. "Okay, now press! One-two-three…"

Suddenly a figure shot up from the water, turning its dripping head this way and that as it scanned the area. Kaya recognized the creature as one of her mother's coworkers. "Penelope!" the girl called, catching the otter's attention. "There's a centaur over here that's not breathing!"

Without a word of reply Penelope darted to the motionless centaur's side.

Julius hovered in the air. "Is there any way in which I may be of assistance?"

Penelope took a deep breath, exhaling into the centaur's mouth. "You don't weigh enough," she said quickly as she took another breath and exhaled again. "Just tend to the other centaurs," she added as she jogged around her asphyxiated patient's legs, throwing all her girth into the centaur's chest in an effort to revive her. After the third or fourth full-body tackle the centaur shuddered and began to cough.

"That's a good girl." Penelope patted the centaur's horse body. "Just cough it all up."

Nearby a centaur with silver hair rolled to her side, struggling to set her weight back on her hooves. With a weak stomp she asked, "Is Luna going to be okay?"

"She'll be fine," Penelope replied, still patting the coughing centaur at her side.

"I'm not Luna," the centaur choked. "I'm Roanna."

"That's Luna." The silver-haired creature pointed toward the centaur whom the Bellastratas were still trying to resuscitate.

"Good gracious!" the otter cried, ambling around Roanna and running up to Ellen. "Is she not responding?"

Slightly startled, Ellen replied, "No." Tendrils of worry drug her voice deep into the nearby water.

"Dios mío," Penelope prayed aloud as she slid her shell necklace up over her head and transformed it into a wand. "Marcos, stand back. We're going to have to scan her." Just as the man rose to his feet a wide ray of azure light covered the centaur's frame,

484

illuminating her organs from head to hoof. The otter shook her head. "This isn't exactly the ideal place, but we need to pump her second stomach."

"Pump her stomach?" several centaurs who had managed to pull themselves up from the ground repeated from behind.

"Yes," Ellen said, not turning around. "Penelope, keep her abdomen illuminated while I insert the valve."

"Está bien," Penelope consented, concentrating the beam on the point where Luna's two bodies met—her second stomach. Ellen raised her wand in the air, pulling down a nearly invisible strand of light thinner than a hair. Within moments the strand had entered the centaur's body via the abdomen and widened, causing a gush of murky water to pour out onto the ground. The next moment the valve disappeared and Luna's skin appeared just as it was before.

"We must hurry—she has lost a great deal of oxygen." The otter ran over to the centaur's mouth and began to breath for her. "Ellen, compress her chest for me, will you?"

"Sí," the woman replied, waiting a moment for the otter to breath for the centaur again a time or two.

"Oh, Luna, don't die…" whispered a centaur from behind Marcos.

This time, after only two compressions from Ellen's hands, Luna spluttered and coughed as consciousness roused her groggy mind.

"Luna!" the centaurs cried happily.

"Is she going to be okay, Mami?" Kiki asked from Ellen's side.

Ellen turned and saw Kaya holding on tightly to Kiki's hand. "Thank you," Ellen breathed, her eyes filled with pride as she gazed up at Kaya. Then, looking straight into Kiki's red eyes the woman said, "Sí, m'ija. She's safe now."

"Good." Kiki struggled to smile; the lingering fear in her rapidly beating heart began to slowly release the paralysis gripping her tender face.

"Away now, go away!" chirped Julius at a crowd of onlookers congregated between the trees and the shore. "We have a set of injured individuals—stay back while we assess the situation!" An indistinct grumble rose up into the air and shifty eyes met the quetzal; but no one left. "Fine then!" quipped Julius, cutting through the air and shaking his cherry pendant. "Stand there all you like— but there will be nothing to see!" And in a blink a dense wall of light blocked the path, sealing the spectators from the scene.

As Julius curved back around he caught sight of a black-haired centaur falling haphazardly to the ground. One of her friends rushed to her side. "Are you dizzy, Melena?" her companion asked, kneeling and clasping her friend's hand.

"No, not at all," Melena replied, her soft features twisted in confusion. "That's the third time I've tried to stand up, but each time I fall back down."

Julius landed on the grass beside Melena. "Are you hurt in any way? Could you have pulled a muscle while in the water?"

Melena blinked. "Now that you mention it, Director, my back leg is tingling a little. It doesn't hurt, though."

Julius hopped over to evaluate the centaur's leg. As he bent down and cocked his head, what he discovered nearly made him fall over in shock.

"Ellen! Penelope! I need one of you here, now!" the quetzal squawked.

"What's wrong?" Melena's friend asked quickly.

"Relax, Alma, it can't be that bad," Melena said to her friend. "Whatever it is I can't even feel it."

"Un momento, Julius!" the otter called back, racing below a centaur toward the quetzal.

"Look," he said when she arrived, pointing with his emerald wing at Melena's hoof.

"Good heavens!" Penelope exclaimed as her ruby eyes fell on the bloodied appendage, the skin torn and hair missing from around Melena's ankle. "Do you need me to relieve the pain, dear?"

"I don't have any pain," Melena answered somewhat impatiently.

"Then you're in a minor state of shock. Ellen!" Penelope turned about. "I have a tibial-fibular laceration here with possible breakage. We need to perform surgery now!"

"Surgery?" Melena exclaimed incredulously.

"I'm busy at the moment!" Ellen sat in concentration, her wand pointed at another centaur's wrist. "I'm mending a severed artery!"

"I suppose I'll just have to tend to this on my own," the otter reflected, drawing down several strings of thin light toward Melena's ankle.

"Severed arteries and mutilated ankles—just what were you young centaurs doing when you jumped into the water?" Julius asked suspiciously.

"We didn't jump into the water," Alma retorted. "We were pu—"

Suddenly the sound of a heavy splash filled the air, drawing everyone's attention back to the lake.

"Carina!" shouted the silver-haired centaur near Kaya.

"Papi! Save her!" Kiki squealed, noticing her father by the edge of the Lake.

Nearly instantly a platinum net shot out from the man's arm, and Marcos heaved the centaur to safety for the second time that night.

The silver-haired centaur ran over to her unconscious friend. "Her neck is bleeding!" she cried. "And her collar's covered in blood!"

"What is going on here?" Julius exclaimed as he fired into the air with an agitated twirl and landed beside the motionless Carina. "What has happened to her?"

"I don't know!" sobbed the silver-haired centaur. "But I don't want her to die!"

"Julius, we need another healer," Marcos said urgently.

The quetzal trilled, ruffling his feathers as he shot up into the air. "If I had only listened to Mother and become a healer…" As his tiny frame appeared above the trees, Julius' voice shook the island.

487

"Madison Bluebolt, report to the northern base of the Argo Dock now. This is an emergency—your skills are required."

No sooner had Julius turned to descend to the shore than a jade arc appeared, tearing across the sky from the western edges of the city. Seconds later Bluebolt leapt from his lightboard, snapping his tail as he produced his wand and began tending to Carina's neck.

"What is that?" Kaya muttered, breaking her hold on Kiki's hand and slapping the back of her leg. Something had poked her. "Dumb bugs…"

"I'm not a bug," a familiar voice called from behind.

Kiki turned and opened her mouth to scream, but Kaya was too quick for her. "Calm down! It's just Iris," Kaya said, her hand flying to her sister's mouth.

"Hola, Kiki," the hare said with a smile. The young girl lowered her arms and waved, mumbling a greeting through Kaya's fingers.

"What are you doing down here?" Kaya asked. "I thought you were watching the ceremony from the Lucero Deck with your papá."

"We were, until all the commotion started; then we decided to come investigate."

"We?" Kaya repeated.

"Sí—Manny, Brun, and I."

Kaya pulled her hand away from Kiki's mouth. "And where are they, exactly?"

"In the trees," said Iris simply. Turning around, he called, "You guys can come out now."

Before Kaya's eyes appeared a person wearing a glowing mask with frightening fangs. Kaya screamed.

"It's just Manny with a calavera mask," Kiki chastised, slapping her sister on the leg.

"Don't do that!" Kaya said, cuffing Manny even harder on the arm. "Where did you get that ugly thing?"

"There's a bunch of them lying in the woods along the path we took to get here," Brun interposed, stepping out from around Manny, who continued to stare silently at Kaya.

488

"Take that off already, idiota!" Kaya demanded.

With a chuckle Manny slid the mask back. "So did you see what happened here?"

Kaya's face softened. "Not really. All I know is every one of these centaurs almost drowned, and that some of them were injured pretty badly."

"Mamá and the other healers are fixing them, though," Kiki attested helpfully.

"It looks like they might be having a little trouble." Brun noticed Bluebolt, Penelope, and Ellen all leaning over a centaur's body.

Without warning an angry hand reached out and grabbed Manny's shoulder, pushing him back against a tree and knocking the skull guise from his head. "I recognize that nasty mask," blustered a ginger-haired centaur, her grip tightening around the boy's collarbone. "You're one of those that pushed us into the water! You attacked us!"

Brun stepped in between the centaur and Manny. "No, he didn't." Though she was not yet full-grown, the centaur outmeasured Brun by a foot or so.

"Why should I believe you, human? You look just as guilty as he does! The only difference is you discarded your mask and he was too foolish to do the same!"

"There's no way they could have attacked all of you!" Kaya interrupted.

"Oh, is that so?" the centaur said dryly. "So you saw what happened?"

"What's going on over here, Krista?" the golden-haired Roanna asked as she trotted up behind Kaya. Kiki began to grow scared again, sucking her thumb and clutching her sister's hand tightly.

"These boys are two of those who attacked us!" Krista retorted as she held up the mask. "And here's the evidence!"

"How could another Lumen do something so barbaric?" Roanna's eyes flashed as she drew close to Brun's face. "Do you know that I wasn't breathing when they pulled me out?"

Brun blinked awkwardly. "I'm sorry, but—"

"And he tries to apologize!" Krista cried, stamping her hooves furiously. "How can your apology save Carina if she dies? Did you know you slit her neck open?"

"We did not!" Manny shouted.

"Roanna, grab the red one! I'll take this little white snake and we'll throw them in the water! Like treatment for what they did to Carina!" Krista thundered.

"Let go of him!" Kaya yelled as Krista drug Manny away by the wrist. But the centaur's heavy hand hit Kaya in the chest, knocking her to the ground. Kiki hid behind a tree and wailed bitterly.

"Stop it!" Brun kicked Roanna in the leg. A hoof met him in the chest in reply, and he lost his breath.

Manny would have shouted, but Krista covered his mouth with a firm hand. Never in his life had he anticipated centaurs to wield such strength.

With a roar of fury the two centaurs tossed the boys over the edge of the Lake. In midair the boys' skulls collided, their amber eyes going dark as they sank lifelessly into the water...

Twilight. No, suddenly total darkness washes over the pristine lake. A flame, thousands of flames appear on the water. Manny kneels over the shore, staring at an indistinguishable figure in the depths. Not a bird, no… The flames draw near, their fires reaching out and clasping Manny's wrists. He screams, but icy water fills his mouth. The figure, not a bird, draws him nearer. Dark eyes, livid eyes, stare up at him. Not a bird, no…

Floating. Trapped—clenched between the depths and the light. Brun stares up at the surface of the Lake; a figure descends that he cannot touch. Gentle gaze, passionate eyes; a woman… Robe of light, hands of silver, look of gold… Shadow comes. Chilling scream. Darkness dines.

"When will they wake up?"

"Anytime now."

A pause. "But it's been two days."

"I know."

A minute passes. "I thought people woke up from concussions faster than this."

"Generally."

"Then why are they still asleep?"

A wry breath. "Perhaps they are busy."

"Doing what?"

"Sorting, I suppose." A pause. "The mind uses sleep as a means to defragment stress and break down difficult situations."

"Oh. They must be muy stressed, pues."

"Or just exceptionally tired."

***

"Manny."

No response.

"Manny!"

A snort and a grunt. "Yeah?"

"Where are we?"

"I dunno, Brun, I'm tired. Just let me sleep."

Ten seconds pass. "Are we dead?"

"Now why would we be dead?" Manny's voice came hoarsely.

Brun felt his body sway. "Those centaurs threw us into the water, remember? Did we drown?"

Manny's mind was a blur. "If we drowned, how could we be talking?"

"How do you know what happens when we die? Maybe we just float around in the darkness forever."

"Or not." Manny grasped tightly woven chords with his hand. "We're in our hammocks, genius."

"We are?" Brun suddenly discerned the familiar counterweight of the rope bed against his back. "I guess I thought we were trapped in the Lake. I wonder why…?"

"Uh, no." Manny turned and stared through the crimson blackness at Brun's glowing form. "We're in the hutch. Did that centaur kick your eyes loose, or what?"

"One of them kicked me?"

"Sí—square in the chest. You've gotta have a killer bruise."

Brun gently touched his sternum, grimacing and recoiling his hand swiftly. "You're right."

Silence.

"The monkeys attacked those centaurs, didn't they?"

"Yes," Brun breathed, his eyes running along the shadowy grooves in the bamboo ceiling. "The masks along the path prove it—you said they were identical to the calavera of the monkey who stole the baker's's wand, right?"

"No doubt about it." Manny recalled the creature's icy movements and raspy voice. "And that's why that psycho-centaur nearly killed us when she saw me with the calavera."

"Exactly," murmured Brun. "But the centaurs can't have gotten a very good look at los changos… If they had they'd have realized it couldn't have been us."

Manny blinked. "Why's that?"

"Because we're at least twice their height."

Oh. Duh. Silence again entered the hut as Manny's mind tore out the window and back west, descending to the island shore below the glistening moonstone dock. In his memory he saw a band of nearly twenty monkeys with ivory skulls creeping out toward a group of unsuspecting centaurs, the latters' eyes set on seven distinct farolitos floating eerily on the water. Like white lightning the prowlers suddenly strike their targets. "Do you think they got what they came for?"

"You mean the centaur's wands? I'd imagine." Brun checked to ensure his birch ring still clung faithfully to his left hand. "Considering the cut on that one's neck and all. I doubt she was the only one injured like that. I bet the monkey slit her neck while he

494

was trying to wrench the wand off; like Iris's ear back on Easter Island."

"Brun, esos changos have to be one hundred percent evil. They have no remorse."

"You're telling me."

"Do you think we really have a chance to stop them?" Manny asked, his words floating transparently.

"If we keep training," Brun answered after a moment. "But we're not ready now."

From the looks of things I don't even know if that's gonna be enough.

***

"Brun—Dimirtis!" shrieked a livid voice from across the Café. The boy's heart nearly burst from his throat; he steadied his chair and looked over his shoulder to meet a formidable figure with glistening black hair and boiling mocha eyes.

"It's like they're married," Iris chuckled behind his paw to Manny. Kaya, her back to the waterfall, gazed on in quiet amusement.

"What's wrong, Araceli?" Brun choked, his skin suddenly flashing a bright red.

Iris chuckled some more. "So he does get embarrassed!"

"¿Qué está mal?" the girl repeated, tossing her hair back over her shoulder and locking a hand to her hip. "What's wrong is that you lied to me!"

Brun glanced at his knife. "I told you that I was busy for lunch today, but that I'd eat with you tomorr—"

"Where's Chiron, then?" Araceli pursed her lips and stared Brun down. "I don't see him here anywhere. What happened to lunch with him? Could you explain that to me?"

"Araceli," Brun pleaded, "can we discuss this—"

"Afterwards? Uh, huh." Araceli nodded once then ran the fingers of her free hand through her hair. "Well, until then, I'll be sitting at the east end of the Café—alone." And with a glare infused with enough traction to wrench a boulder from a rockface she turned and walked away, leaving Brun's head sagging to the ground.

"And they haven't even been together a month yet," Manny whispered humorously.

After a moment Brun turned languidly to his friends. "I'm sorry about that," he said pathetically.

A waiter unexpectedly appeared at the table. "¿Cómo están todos hoy?"

"Oh, just peachy I think," Iris joked, one ear bent and a broad smile on his face.

"Excellent," the waiter rejoined. "Could I take your meal orders now?"

"Sure!" Manny said eagerly. "I'll have enchiladas—"

"Don't be an idiot," Kaya's voice interrupted. The waiter lifted his pen and an eyebrow, staring peculiarly at the girl.

"But enchiladas are one of my favorite foods," Manny began defensively. "I don't see why—"

"Are you dense or what, López?" Kaya glanced at Manny. "I wasn't even talking to you! Now," she resumed, facing Brun again, "Why are you still sitting here?" The waiter turned an interested eye to the pitiful, white-haired boy.

Brun wilted, setting limp hands on the table and staring at the rose liquid in his perspiring glass. "What else am I supposed to do?"

"Uh, what about getting up and leaving?" Kaya said flatly.

"Is his melon water not to his liking?" the waiter broke in inquisitively. "Because I can bring out another drink—that would be no problem."

Kaya stared incredulously into the man's genuine green eyes, blinked, and coughed. "Just come back in a couple of minutes, will you?" she asked gruffly.

"As you wish, señorita." The man appeared slightly affronted as he stuffed his notepad in his apron pouch and melted away among the tables.

"But I'm ready to order," Iris demurred hungrily.

"You'll survive." Kaya turned back to Brun. "Did you know Araceli spent all her free time over the past two days at Chiron's Hutch waiting for you to wake up?"

Brun did not answer, but blinked uncomfortably.

"Right, then. So, in other words, your girlfriend spends 48 hours worrying while you are in La-La Land and then you go and lie to her to avoid eating lunch with her today? That's worse than something López would do," Kaya signified.

"Hey, now," Manny began.

"Cállate," Kaya said dismissively.

"But the four of us need to discuss what happened on the Day of the Dead," Brun argued.

Kaya lifted an eyebrow. "I think Manny is perfectly capable of catching you up later this evening; that is if his brain isn't any looser than it was before the concussion."

I hope an Amazon Horned Frog jumps out of the Lake and bites you on the lips.

"Whatever." Brun stood up and pulled on his backpack tiredly. "I'll just talk to you all later. Bye." He slunk off to the northeast end of the Café in defeat. **Like a sheep to the slaughter...**

A satisfied smile crossed Kaya's face as she watched Brun approach Araceli's table. "Well, I believe I just saved that relationship."

Manny rolled his eyes. *Don't make me sick.*

"Can we order now?" Iris asked, clutching his stomach.

"Yes," Manny said, perturbed as he jumped to his feet and waved down the waiter.

"Will one of you share a vegetable pizza with me?" Iris asked as the waiter made his way back to the table.

"I will," Manny replied, forgetting his enchiladas as he added spitefully, "Kaya can order something else."

"Fine by me," she said, closing her menu and threading her hair back coolly.

The waiter stood with pen and paper ready. "Ready to order?"

Iris hopped to his feet in his chair. "Sí. We'd like a medium vegetable pizza."

"Better make it large," Manny amended, gauging the rumble in his stomach.

"Muy bien." The waiter flipped the paper in his tablet. "And for la señorita?"

"Enchiladas," Kaya said succinctly. "With lots of cheese."

Manny gritted his teeth but did not turn her way.

"Very well," said the waiter again. "Your orders will be out momentarily."

"Gracias," Kaya replied as the waiter collected the menus, her voice simply angelic.

Manny closed his eyes and flexed his fingers, still refusing to turn back toward Kaya.

"Problem, López?" the girl asked innocently. He did not respond. "Not order what you wanted, perhaps?" Nothing.

"You two can be so stupid sometimes," Iris finally blurted. "Quit aggravating each other so we can talk about the issue at hand."

"Great idea—I'm all for that," Manny corresponded, setting overzealous fists on the table. Kaya simply brushed her hair back serenely, remaining silent.

"He told us the same thing, actually." Iris rose up on the end of his toes and reached for another paw-sized slice of pizza, overladen with broccoli and carrots. "'If I so much as hear one of you use the word 'monkey' and 'wand' in the same twenty-four hour period, I'll suspend you both.' I'm not kidding—that's what he said."

"He's cracked," Manny decided, taking a sweet sip of horchata. "How else does he expect seven centaurs to have lost their wands? It's not like they fell off and sank to the bottom of the Lake."

"No, but that's his theory." Kaya took another bite of her strawberry sopapilla. Dusting some cinnamon from her fingers, she continued, "He's actually sent two otter search parties down looking for them."

"Are you serious?" Manny erupted.

Kaya nodded as she licked vanilla ice cream from her forefinger. "But none of them got very far—I guess it's deeper, colder, and darker down there than anybody thought. One of the otters told mi papá that it's as if an icy force or pressure prevents them from heading below a thousand feet."

A carrot fell onto Iris's lap from his open mouth. "But hasn't anybody ever explored the bottom of the Lake before?"

"Not that I've heard. They probably haven't had a reason to."

"Well, they don't have one now, as far as I'm concerned." Manny stares at the pizza crusts on his empty plate. "First off, wood doesn't sink. So how can Julius honestly believe their wands are down there?"

Iris crunched a broccoli stem. "He's hunting for excuses."

"You're dang right he is," Manny reinforced. "Those monkeys are getting more and more aggressive, and the Lumen authorities are getting dumber and dumber."

Kaya tore more sugary dough from the center of her sopapilla. "That's why we have to stop them before they kill someone."

"Aren't you just slightly worried that 'someone' might be us?"

"I'd be more concerned about those centaurs than the monkeys at the moment, if I were you."

Manny glanced back quizzically. "What?"

"They didn't believe a word of Julius' theory, either," Iris said, sitting back contentedly in his chair.

"So they believed you two when you mentioned the monkeys attacking?"

"No way," Kaya said, her mouth full.

"Nope, they totally blame you and Brun for what happened," Iris yawned lackadaisically.

Manny very nearly choked on his tongue. "How? Didn't you or Julius explain that we were on the Lucero Deck when they were attacked?"

"They don't believe him. They think he's an idiot for believing their wands sank in the Lake," Iris explained.

"They're not too far off then, are they," Kaya mumbled.

"Don't think that, Kaya," Iris said gruffly. "Julius isn't an idiot—he's just stubborn." He paused. "After all, you should know what that's like."

A pair of startled chocolate eyes stared across the table at the hare, who peered back pointedly.

Manny could not prevent the smile from overpowering his face. "Nice one, Iris."

"Very clever," Kaya muttered, nonchalantly covering her mouth as she turned and gazed away over the Lake.

Even she has to admit that was funny.

"In other words, Manny, you and Brun need to watch out for those Sixth-Level centaurs. If I were you I'd walk around with Chamaeleon at my side at all times," Iris advised. "Even though they don't have their wands anymore, I'm sure they'd crack your heads together again if the opportunity presented itself."

"What a pleasant thought," Manny said dryly. "I'll make sure to tell Brun after lunch—assuming Araceli doesn't drag him away. But I'd bet she's already on the look out for them."

"I know she is," Kaya affirmed quietly.

"Are we all on for this evening, then?" Iris asked.

"Training, you mean?" Manny said. "Sure."

"Good, because Dad won't let me stay out after dark unless you and Brun are with me—he really has a lot of confidence in you two, you know," Iris explained.

I hope it's not misplaced.

Chocolate & Darkness

During the month of November, Manny, Brun, Kaya, and Iris passed the majority of their training sessions attempting to master the gamut of unanticipated intricacies of the Seventh-Level Flareshot, primarily the weapon's capacity to allow the Lumen to direct ammo while in mid-flight with the faintest turn of the wrist. Each of them, though Iris in particular, met great difficulty in connecting orb to target when strong winds were present, or simply when the target was moving. Eventually the four friends began spending their evenings designing a complex obstacle course that challenged them to utilize Chamaeleon's evasive techniques, convert Fireflies into Flareshot ammo, and strike moving targets with increased accuracy. Throughout this apparent progress, however, the shadow of a challenge loomed in their minds—the sentinel, Reticulum.

Not mentioning the fact that increased rain in early December made training in the open air virtually impossible, the instructions presented in *Guardians, Sentinels, & Light Keepers* for animating Reticulum were so drawn out and multifaceted that the friends became confused and quickly disheartened. Although Kaya had witnessed her parents produce Reticulum while rescuing the centaurs merely a month earlier, she was able to discern little more than the manner in which the gossamer nets seemed to leap from their hands to enswathe their prey.

When asked one evening to demonstrate how to produce Reticulum, Marcos Bellastrata replied, "Now that's quite a complex sentinel, muchachos, and can be somewhat dangerous in inexperienced hands. I wouldn't want you accidentally dragging your classmates to the ground, now would I? And I rather doubt Professor Firefoot would be pleased to know I showed you before he did—I'd imagine he has a great deal to say about responsibility and the like before you begin on that sentinel. Just be patient, the time to learn it will come soon enough."

Yet, to the teenagers' great frustration, that time did not come, or at least not in December. Fidelio refused to move on to the next sentinel before all students could manipulate the Chamaeleon Chain, a maneuver in which the Lumen may walk several steps while maintaining partial to nearly complete invisibility by activating one sentinel after another. Ironically, it was the last day prior to Christmas Break when Greystone, a chinchilla known for his characteristically erratic attention span, demonstrated just enough focus to consecutively flash in and out of sight three times—the minimum number of disappearances required to pass. "Finally!" Manny had exclaimed, his exasperated voice blending with a chorus of his classmates. When the cheers and sighs faded Manny raised his hand and asked, "Professor Firefoot, will you make Reticulum for us just once so we can study ahead over break?" With a wise twist of his monocle Fidelio replied, "I should think not—it's not my custom to leave a lesson unfinished before Holiday. But if you like I can point you to the section in your textbook." Again deflated, Manny declined.

As Christmas drew near, the sapphire gleam of paloma paper could be seen chasing Manny wherever he went as correspondence from his family honed in on him like a ceaseless barrage of finely thrown darts. With each letter Manny's excitement grew, as his parents, grandmother, aunt, uncle, and cousins eagerly wrote to him regarding his three-week return to Arizona. Not only did the simple thrill of seeing his family course stronger and stronger through his veins as his departure date drew near, but Manny could not resist envisioning the shock on their faces when he introduced his travel guest. Only five days prior to Christmas Break, Fidelio conceded to allow his son to enter the outside world at Manny's side. Iris, for his part, was utterly amazed. "He's never even let me spend the night at Kaya's house," Iris told Manny later. But such was the father hare's confidence in the boy's heart and abilities... and in Manny.

Christmas for Brun, on the other hand, meant a bittersweet journey back to the Island of Marajó, to his residence in Brazil. Despite Manny's incessant invitations to come to Arizona, Brun would not dare ask his father if he could travel to the United States.

"I told you, he's very protective of me," Brun argued two days before Manny's plane was to leave. "Just asking would probably make him angry, because he's so busy all the time. And besides, I haven't seen Tía Liliana since August—we've never spent a Christmas apart since I was born. So don't worry about me—I'm happy I get to go back home." But, truth be told, Brun felt halved. **I wonder if Papá might let me fly to Arizona for the New Year.** "Don't be stupid, Brun," he whispered to himself. "It's a miracle you even got to come to Isla Verde. And it's selfish to leave Tía Liliana…" Yet for all his attempts to persuade himself otherwise, a cold knife touched his heart the day of his departure as he floated away up the Lucero. There, on the observation deck, his three best friends stood, waving goodbye and wishing him a Feliz Navidad. The next breath, they were gone. **Alone… Just like before.** And, in isolation, the river carried him away.

Bristling with the electricity that comes the night before a great journey, Manny and Iris sat out on the terrace off the north end of Keilani's room, chatting animatedly with Kaya about Christmas foods, presents, songs and traditions. They had just entered a staunch debate on whether Santa Claus was actually a human or a hare when a sapphire bolt struck the balcony, leaving a glittering letter to sail down to Manny's lap. "Probably writing to wish us a good trip," Manny said with a smile as he opened the note and began to read. A moment later, as he read the all too familiar farewell, thick, fat tears filled his eyes. Standing up, he gave the letter one last ephemeral glance before turning and walking hurriedly from the room, a tense sob building in his chest. Iris and Kaya exchanged an ominous glance before the hare hopped down from the table and picked up the letter, which now lay askew on the terrace floor. Silently, he read:

Querido Manuel,

Sweetheart, m'ijo, I have some bad news. All flights to and from Iquitos have been cancelled from now until after the New Year, and there's no other airport for you to fly from. I don't know any other way to say this, but you can't come home for la Navidad. I'm sorry, darling, but tu papá and I have done all we can. Your tío Carlos even called independent pilots to request that they come pick you up, but none would.

Somehow, we'll make this up to you. If you're worried about your presents, then don't be. We'll send them using paloma paper—it stretches as far as you need it, you know. M'ijo, we love you and will write you all throughout the break, especially on Christmas Day.

Te amo,

Mamá

The tips of Iris's ears sagged to the floor as he hopped over to Kaya and handed her the letter. A moment later she lifted her eyes from the paper, staring vacantly into the warm darkness, her thoughts strung up in the moss-covered trees.

"Do you think we should go talk to him?" Iris whispered, his words sliding timidly from his mouth.

"Yes," Kaya sighed, retrieving her thoughts from the moss-infused tangle of branches as she stood and folded up the letter. "You lead the way."

Iris's footpads thumped softly along the wooden floor as they journeyed across the room and into the kitchen, half-expecting to find Manny with his face down on the table. But the only figure that met their eyes was that of Kiki, skipping and singing on the other side of the sliding door. The hare and the girl continued across the tiled floor toward the white swinging door, which they pushed open, stepping noiselessly onto the thick carpet of the living room floor. On the couch to their left sat two people, their backs to the kitchen door and facing one another—a woman with midnight hair pulled back in a ponytail, and a glowing boy hugging a pearl pillow. The woman reached out and touched the boy's shoulder.

"Oh, Manny, that's just terrible," Ellen said.

"Tell m—me about it." Manny swallowed a sob. His eyes were puffy and red, and their golden light lay dim.

"I have an idea," Ellen began, the ring in her voice splashing Manny's soul with hope. "Why don't you spend Christmas with us?"

"C—can I?" he choked.

"Sí," she replied readily. "You and Iris could even stay in Keilani's room on Christmas Eve."

"R—really? Your husband won't mind?"

"Marcos? Never! He'll just be happy to actually have some other guys in the house! And let me tell you, I think you'll love the Christmas celebrations here in Isla Verde—I know it won't be like home, but it will be a Christmas you'll never forget."

"Gracias, Señora Bellastrata," Manny expressed, his words whole again.

"I've told you a thousand times, call me Ellen!" She ruffled his charcoal hair. "We're not strangers!"

"So does this mean I don't get to sleep in Keilani's bed?" Kaya suddenly asked.

As if interrupted from a dream, Ellen and Manny turned their heads to find the girl and the hare perched attentively in front of the kitchen door. "Well, I guess not," Ellen replied. "Is that a problem?"

Kaya looked into Manny's eyes and saw a faint sparkle. "No, I guess not." She paused. "Manny, I'm really sorry you can't go home for la Navidad."

"Thanks," he sighed, peace ebbing back into his heart. He felt tired.

"I was really looking forward to meeting Zane, but that can wait, I suppose," Iris said sympathetically. "I'm still excited we get to celebrate Christmas together. Ellen, are you sure my dad will let me stay the night here?"

Her chocolate eyes soft, yet very much alive, she replied, "Why don't you ask him?"

***

A boy walked, alone, uphill along a heavily wooded path, the silent trees giving off a mixed sensation of wariness and vigilance. He looked left, then right, but the columns of the forest refused to reveal their eyes, nor even move. A good time later the sentries thinned, yielding to the dark frame of a mansion, an enshrouded castle resting on a broad, verdant hill. The young man proceeded forward, the gentle trickling of a seasonal stream playing softly in his ears as he lifted his eyes to the myriad of white-curtained windows that gazed down on his somber figure.

A woman stood, her legs shaking over the clouded marble steps as the pearl-haired boy drew near. "Brun," she whispered, clasping her hands together on her chest, her peridot eyes catching him up and carrying him into her heart. At that instant Brun glanced up and saw the fair-skinned, chestnut-crowned woman rooted to the steps. Without a moment's thought he dropped his bags and ran to her, enveloping her thin frame in a much-needed embrace. A tear fell from her eye and struck his mahogany cheek. "How I've missed you..."

When finally they released one another, Brun stared up into the woman's lined face and asked, "Are you sick, Liliana? You look pale."

"No, I'm fine," the woman replied somewhat quickly. "I'm just so happy to see you. Are you hungry?"

"Starving."

"Bueno. Then let's head inside. But don't forget your bags."

As Brun returned with his backpack and clothing bag, he noticed a figure move in the arched window towering high above the steps. "Is Papá here?" he asked hopefully. "Maybe he can eat with us."

Her flat reply seemed to punch Brun in the gut. "He's left."

"But I just saw someone move in his room."

"It must have been one of the servants, then." Liliana turned and weakly climbed the steps. "Never-mind that."

"Where did he go?" Brun demanded, angry that he had traveled the entire distance of the Amazon to discover that his father was not even present to welcome him home.

"Don't worry yourself—"

A fire rose in Brun's veins. "I want to know! What is so important that he couldn't be here to see me—his son?"

Liliana reached the top step and turned. "Brun, calm down now."

"¡No, Tía! Where is he? I want to know, now!"

"I honestly have no idea." She sighed as her worn words melted into the marble.

"Guess!" he shouted. "At least humor me!"

"I don't know, Brun—Europe, maybe." Liliana grabbed the brass handle of a massive oak door.

"Europe?" Brun shouted. "Poland? France? Where?"

Liliana simply stared tiredly in return, her energy faded.

"Fine." He stepped forward and wrenched the other door open with all his might. "I get the point." And with hot tears streaming down his face he returned to his home, to long, empty rooms stocked with loneliness and to an aunt whom he could no longer recognize. The tears he shed, more than for himself, were for her.

***

"Why ever would I mind?" Fidelio said, flicking his grey-rimmed monocle wisely.

Violet eyes peered back across the burnt oak table. "I just thought you might not want to be alone tomorrow morning."

"Iris, I gave you permission to leave the continent, for Heaven's sake. It doesn't bother me in the least that you stay with the Bellastratas tonight." For a moment Iris thought he caught an

507

odd gleam in his father's silver eyes; before the young hare could consider this, however, Fidelio glanced down at his steaming mug of ocher tea, the vestige of a smile hiding on his cheek.

"Professor, thank you," Manny said genuinely.

"For what, my boy?" Fidelio sipped his tea with perked ears. "I've done nothing out of the ordinary, now have I?" Iris caught that same subtle flash in his father's eyes.

"No, I guess not," Manny muttered backwardly. "It's just that, without my family here I…"

"No worries now." Fidelio's eyeglass flashed as a pair of amply-sized mugs met the table followed closely by two curling streams of brown liquid. "Have a nice warm cup of chocolate and forget your anxieties."

"Gracias." Manny reached forward as the heat from the mug surged into his palm.

Iris pulled his mug close. "Aren't you forgetting something, Dad?"

"Well, fire and foxtails, I am!" Fidelio quipped. The next second two bulbous marshmallows floated in the young Lumens' mugs.

"Perfect," Iris whispered, witnessing the marshmallow's sweet promise.

Fidelio raised his mug and nodded kindly. "Feliz Navidad, muchachos."

Manny took the steel ladle from Chiron's hand and dipped it into the barrel-like pot brimming with steaming chocolate magma. The boy stirred the milky concoction leisurely as its sweet fumes intoxicated his brain. "So this is what you call a chocolatada?"

"Not technically. The chocolatada will not formally begin until our young guests arrive, which should be soon."

"And you'd best be ready," Fidelio added with a significant glance. "Because when they start there's no holding them back.

Manny drew up the ladle and allowed a cascade of chocolate to course down. "Am I the one who's serving, then?"

"Sí." Iris leapt nimbly to the seat of a chair next to a table covered in hundreds of pearly mugs. "It's my job to hand the mugs to the server, and this year that's you."

For better or for worse, I guess. "Zane and I spooned punch during my cousin Berta's eighth-grade graduation party a few years back, but we were a little messy." Manny recalled the inalterable pink stain he had acquired on his favorite shirt. "I'll try to keep the chocolate in the mugs tonight, though." The boy wondered how he would accomplish this. "Ladles can be tricky, you know."

"Successful filling hinges on the curvature of your wrist," Chiron instructed. "Twist the ladle as you pour the liquid and the cup will stay dry."

Let's just hope the kids stay dry.

"You mentioned Zane," Fidelio began, his voice curious. "Is he your brother?"

Manny listened to the slush of the cocoa fusion. "No, my cousin."

"Is he a student of the Lumen Academies of North America?" the hare continued.

"Uh-uh," Manny negated. "He's not a Lumen yet. But hopefully he'll be here next year."

"Aha." Fidelio's tone was laced with particular interest. "I look forward to meeting him."

"Soon, I hope." Manny thought ahead to next August and suddenly realized that half the school year had already elapsed. *I can't believe I've been here—*

"Excuse me, Manny, but would you pour me a cup of that delicious smelling beverage you have there," a voice called, its pleasant words lifting the boy's chin and drawing his attention to the angelic figure of a centaur, the black silk of her head and lower body contrasting her creamy skin and dove-like, blue eyes.

"N-Nightwind!" Chiron stuttered, flitting his tail in surprise. "I was somehow under the impression that you—"

"Had holiday plans with friends?" she finished as Manny passed her a chocolate-stained mug. "I do," she verified, flitting the tip of her wooden necklace.

Manny witnessed as a wisp of light wiped the outside of her cup clean. *Dang—I need more practice.*

"With whom?" Chiron inquired.

"With you, of course." Nightwind sipped gingerly from her cup of chocolate, crinkling her sky blue eyes at Chiron's look of incredulity.

"But where are you staying?" he continued, still drowning in his shock.

"The House of the Brethren," she said simply, taking another warm sip. "You performed excellently with this cocoa, Manny."

"I'm just the haphazard server," the boy retorted quickly. "Chiron's the cook."

Nightwind gazed back at Chiron. "Nicely done, Veridai."

A crimson rush filled the centaur's face, leaving him speechless. Lucky for Chiron, however, a pair of young children, no more than six-years-old, appeared from around the corner of the hutch, running and giggling. The girl wore deep blue robes and held a doll in her hands, while the boy ambled forward in brown trappings and clutched a shepherd's crook. They came to a stop just a cane's reach from the vat of vaporous chocolate and stared up at Manny with a pair of candid grins.

"¡Feliz Navidad!" the children exclaimed happily.

"Merry Christmas!" Manny corresponded, gently placing a mug of chocolate in each child's expectant hands. The boy licked the edge of his, wary not to let the flow of mis-poured cocoa escape.

"What do you say?" their mother prompted from behind.

"¡Gracias!" the young Mary and Joseph shouted, their white teeth now flecked with cocoa.

"De nada," the rest replied, including Nightwind, who joined in the chocolatada gregariously.

"Here they come," Iris signaled, readily passing another mug to Manny as a trio of otter pups in shepherd garb rounded the corner followed closely by two holy mother kinkajous.

"You weren't joking, Professor," Manny said, swiftly filling the mug and passing it to Fidelio.

"Certainly not," the father hare replied, leaning forward with a happy greeting to extend the yuletide beverage to the first of the otters.

Manny flexed his hand, which was still sore after three nearly ceaseless hours of chocolate spooning. Tiny mangers flanked the entrances to the rows of tree houses bordering either side of the wooden walkway as Manny and Iris trod forward toward their Christmas Eve destination, their eyes eagerly devouring the brilliance of countless lights, the presence of which made their trip strikingly reminiscent to a stroll through the center of the Milky Way. Crystal streamers descended from every eave, neon wreaths burned from every door, and ribbons of never-ending cascabel orbs of silver, green, and red left the railings virtually unrecognizable. Part of Manny's heart still longed intensely to be with his family; yet the light emanating from all sides penetrated the boy's pores and into his soul, filling him with the excitement only Christmas can bring. Three loud thumps interrupted Manny's musings, and he suddenly became cognizant that he was standing at the Bellastratas' door.

"They're here! I know those foot slaps anywhere!" a voice squealed as the floor shook and the door opened, revealing a very ecstatic Kiki in a red dress with a large, green bow tied around her waist. "¡Feliz Navidad!" Kiki squealed again, embracing Iris tightly. "Hurry in! Papá Noel will be here any second!"

"Santa Claus is coming?" Manny said, closing the door behind him.

"Sí. But don't get your hopes up too high, López," Kaya answered as she strolled forward and leaned close to the boy's ear. "He's not real, you know." This last bit she added in a whisper—for

Kiki's sake—who was now thoroughly describing the intricacies of the family's gold-tinseled tree to Iris.

"I'll try and remember that," Manny said, playing along. "Although," he paused, looking Kaya up and down, "you might make a good elf in that green dress of yours."

"Aren't you an absolute riot," she replied wryly. "But the difference between you and me is that I only dress like one."

"Keep my secret for me, will ya?" Manny proceeded, smiling at Kiki's enthusiasm as he lowered his voice. "So who dresses up as Santa? ¿Tu papá?"

Kaya nodded. "And it's so obvious it's him—I don't know how Kiki falls for it every year."

"It's easier to believe something when you want to, I guess." Manny listened as Kiki relayed Papá Noel's traveling methods to Iris in full detail. "She's lucky he's a good listener."

"I'd say," Kaya mused.

"You're here!" Ellen exclaimed, appearing from the kitchen bearing a tray laden with cups of emerald-colored punch. The flowers of the same hue on her dress danced as she crossed the room and set the tray on the glass coffee table. "My, don't you look handsome, Manny!" she said, noticing his jet slacks and his holly-berry shirt. "Red suits you!"

"Gracias," he replied, glowing slightly.

"Sit down, you two!" Ellen beckoned Manny and Kaya to the couch. "Have a drink while we wait for Papá Noel to arrive."

"Is he here?" Kiki screamed.

"Not yet, honey," Ellen replied on her way back to the kitchen. "Be patient."

"Alright," Kiki said, bouncing eagerly.

"So, López," Kaya began as she took some punch and sat down. "Tell me about Christmas back home. Has it ever snowed?"

"Not at my house," Manny answered, letting the icy liquid slide down his throat. "But I've seen it."

"Really?" Kaya appeared intrigued. "Is it true it's powdery?"

"Sure, but that's not the fun snow," he explained, recalling his last ski trip to Colorado with Zane and the rest of the family. "You want the kind that sticks."

"How's that? Does it stick to your hand?"

"No, it sticks together. You can ball it up and throw it at people—that's what you call a snowball fight," Manny clarified. "The snowballs explode on contact, and it's really cold if you get it down the neck of your shirt."

Kaya stared at Manny, enthralled with the very idea of throwing a ball of powdered ice. After a moment, she spoke. "Well, López, if I ever get the chance, I'll definitely pelt you in the back of the neck with a snowball."

"And I'll return the favor twofold," Manny said, his eyes bright.

At that moment Marcos entered, carrying a wide platter of banana leaf tamales to the coffee table. He then sat down on the couch opposite Manny.

"Feliz Navidad, Señor Bellastrata," Manny predicated.

"Merry Christmas!" Marcos corresponded, leaning forward to shake Manny's hand.

"What are you doing out here, Papá?" Kaya breathed, noticing the man's slacks as opposed to scarlet pants. "You-know-who is waiting for you to come out here dressed up as Santa."

"I don't know what you're talking about," her father replied, a clever glint in his eye.

Before Kaya could argue, Ellen burst from the kitchen, a plump cake in hand. "Kiki! I think I heard someone outside while I was in the kitchen!"

"Really?!" Kiki shrieked.

"Ho, ho, ho!" called a deep voice as loud stomps began to pulsate from the kitchen. Kiki screamed in exultation as a thick shadow obscured the light proceeding from the slit below the portal. She danced with glee as a white glove gripped the door, pushing it open wide to reveal a rather tall man, whose crimson tunic and trousers bulged with uneven stuffing. His beard, far from the natural chestnut color of his eyebrows, dangled loosely from his chin.

513

Grabbing his lumpy belly, this ersatz Santa released another, "Ho, ho, ho," chorus followed by a deep, "¡Feliz Navidad!"

"¡Papá Noel!" Kiki cried, darting forward and attaching herself to the man's leg quicker than life. He sat his protuberant black bag on the floor while patting the girl on the head with his other hand.

"¡Mamá!" Kaya hissed, grabbing her mother by the arm and pulling her near. "Who is that?"

"Papá Noel. Who else?" Ellen said, her feigned innocence striking Kaya against the cheek.

That long face, those high cheekbones and positive, almond eyes—Manny had seen this man somewhere before… *But where?* The answer hid at the back of his mind, tantalizing his memory but staying just far enough from reach to catch. "I know him somehow," Manny said, his distant words trickling crookedly from the side of his mouth and bouncing from his shoulder into Kaya's ear.

Manny's eyes were magnetized, unremittingly locked on the figure of the man who greeted each person by name as he dispensed brightly wrapped gifts around the room. Kaya stared searchingly up at the man as he set a long, metallic pink package in her hands. But her mind remained blank—she could not recall having ever met this individual before in her life, despite her attempts to envision him without the loose-stringed beard.

"And for you, m'ijo," he then said, the sudden sheen of pride in the man's eyes striking Manny's heart with unanticipated emotion. "A very special gift."

"Open it, silly!" Kiki chastised as she pranced about waving her new silver butterfly net.

Manny shook his head and began to tear away the emerald wrapping of the wide, flat box the man had placed in his lap. Pushing aside the tissue paper and discarding the box, Manny held up a blood red shirt, noting the unmistakable, snaky curl of a black letter "D" on the left chest. Refusing to breath, he flipped the garment around; Manny's jaw dropped as his eyes jumped from the number "34" to the black scrawl hovering crookedly above.

514

"What does 'Dos Santos' mean?" Kaya asked, clutching her own box vaguely.

"Not what, but who," Manny replied, his mouth dry. "He's Pedro Dos Santos, my favorite baseball player for the Arizona Diamondbacks—and this is an autographed jersey." The boy blinked, the complexity of the gift rocketing through his mind. "How did you get this?"

The shabby Santa's almond eyes flashed brightly. "I took my nephew to a Diamondback's game in late August," he confessed openly. "It's been waiting for you ever since."

"Papá Noel has a nephew?" Kiki asked curiously. "I wonder if he came too…"

"Dad!" Manny shouted, exploding up from his seat and tackling Santa's lofty frame; luckily the opposite couch caught their fall. "How did you get here?"

"His reindeer, of course!" Kiki cried with childlike candor, her butterfly net buzzing through the air. She suddenly stopped. "Dad?" she repeated. "Mamá, why is Manny calling Papá Noel his dad? Is he Papá Noel's son?"

"Well…" Ellen began, not having foreseen this unexpected boomerang in her plan.

"That's my cue to exit," Carlos said, leaning forward to stand up from the couch. Manny placed his hand against his father's chest, however, preventing his escape.

"You can't leave," Manny whispered, his voice tinged with the shadow of despair. "I—"

"I'll be right back," Carlos muttered into his son's ear. "I've just gotta go change, if you get me."

"Oh." Manny turned aside and allowed his father to stand.

"¡Adiós, Kiki!" Carlos bellowed as he patted the girl's head one last time. "¡Feliz Navidad! I'll see you next year!" And in less than three seconds he returned to the kitchen and was gone.

"He must be in a hurry!" Kiki said, pausing only momentarily to reflect before resuming her carefree dance around the room.

515

Kaya and Iris converged on Manny instantly. "That was your father?" the hare asked, his ears erect.

"I thought the flights were cancelled," Kaya murmured as the kitchen door made its familiar swoosh.

Just as Manny opened his mouth to reply, two warm arms wrapped themselves around his shoulders from behind, an unseen head reclining against his own. "Merry Christmas, Manuel."

Iris watched in shock as Manny flipped around the couch in full cartwheel fashion; Kaya's expression matched that of the hare's as her mind scanned and categorized this second unexpected visitor's slightly plump face, bronze skin, and coffee hair.

"Te amo, Mamá," Manny rumbled, hugging his mother firmly.

"I've missed you, m'ijo," María whispered, sighing in relief with the confirmed safety of her son.

"Are you gonna spend all night like that, or what?" another stranger called sarcastically from behind.

"Who are all these people?" Iris shouted as he leapt into the seat Manny had previously occupied.

"What's a rabbit doing in here, María?" called a fourth visitor, the tenor of her voice a mixture of accusation and slight surprise as her liquid ice eyes scanned Iris's frame. She wore dress slacks and a blue blouse, and her hair flowed obediently down her back, bound tightly in a low ponytail. Beside her stood a boy roughly the same height as Manny, though his skin ranked a shade darker than that of the woman, making for a distinct interplay between his own lightning blue eyes and khaki skin. He was not startled in the least to see Iris perched on the back of the couch; in fact, the sight intrigued him.

"He's not a rabbit, Mamá," the boy told the woman, his almond tufted brow raised in interest. "That's Iris, one of Manny's Lumen friends from school. If you look closely you'll notice he's got long ears and legs, which make him a hare."

Iris turned to Kaya, his ears jagged. "How does that guy know my name? I've never seen him before in my life!"

"How am I supposed to know?" Kaya retorted.

"It's your house! They came out of your kitchen!" Iris threw back.

"And?" Kaya said, pausing for effect. "I've been in my room getting ready for the past hour! My hair doesn't get curly like this just staring at it, you know!"

"So, Zane, that hare is a—a Lumen?" the blonde woman asked, apparently uncomfortable with the use of the word.

"Sí," Zane replied, nodding wisely. "And he can talk."

"All I hear are squeaks," the woman countered.

"That's because you're not a Lumen." Kiki unexpectedly materialized at the woman's side. "All I hear are squeaks, too. But when I grow up, I'll get my wand and I'll be able to understand Iris just like everyone else."

"That's—odd," the woman said slowly.

"Not really," Kiki replied passively. "So what's your name?"

"I'm Jane López, Manny's aunt," the woman answered, kneeling as Kiki introduced herself. "It's nice to meet you."

At that moment María released Manny and stepped to the side. "You're up, Manuel," she said, gently nudging her son between the shoulder blades. "Start the introductions."

With a broad smile and a deep breath, Manny obeyed, and within five minutes everyone was chatting animatedly. Jane even stepped forward bravely to shake Iris's paw, though she could not understand a word of his reply. 'He does have fairly good hand-eye coordination,' she thought. 'For a hare.' Throughout the evening Jane set her crystal eyes on the hare, analyzing his actions and human-like facial expressions, until finally, when he stepped up beside Kiki at midnight to blister a star-shaped piñata, she shed her initial skepticism regarding talking animals and opened her heart to the Lumen world.

Zane, María, and Carlos, on the other hand, needed no convincing whatsoever to admit their credence in Lumen society, all three readily relating to Iris as they chatted back and forth, relying on Manny and Kaya as their interpreters. Iris quickly took to Zane, sensing a kindred spirit in the boy's lively mannerisms and candid wit. Not an hour had passed before they both agreed that, come next

517

August, Zane would be residing with the Firefoots. It would be an understatement to say that Zane was eager to begin his Lumen education—his heart pumped for it, his mind not abandoning the idea of Light Bending for more than five minutes from Christmas Eve to the twilight of his fourteenth birthday.

Eventually, as the food diminished, gifts were exchanged, and everyone's energy level began to wane, Manny inquired as to how his family had reached Isla Verde if the planes to and from Iquitos were grounded; not to mention the obvious fact that they had crossed the city's light barrier. Slightly shamefaced, the boy's parents explained that the airport had not been closed, and that they had in fact flown from Phoenix to Iquitos via Lima. "But don't be angry, son," Carlos said as betrayal stretched its cold fingers toward Manny's heart, threatening to ruin his perfect evening. "We couldn't think of any other way to surprise you like this. For what it's worth, we're sorry, though, for all the pain I'm sure it caused you."

"Don't worry about it," Manny said, accepting the apology and closing the door to negative sentiment. "But I'd still like to know how you got past the light barrier, if non-Lumens aren't truly able to pass through it and all."

Kaya and Iris leaned forward, listening intently as Carlos related the prolonged process of acquiring individual visitor's passes, which came in the form of keys that had to be worn on their persons at all times. "I guess they're like visas," Manny's father explained, pulling out a chain from around his neck to demonstrate his pass, which looked unmistakably like a skeleton key. "They're only valid until January 6, and only one person can issue them—some guy by the name of Dosfilos."

"Andrés Dosfilos?" Kaya inhaled sharply. "He's not just 'some guy'—he's the Chairman to the Lumen Council of South America."

"He would be the equivalent of your president," Marcos said coolly.

"Wow, that's—high up there," Jane commented, stunned.

"The Council takes Lumen security and secrecy quite seriously," Ellen avouched, her chocolate eyes grave.

María shifted in her seat. "I should hope."

***

"Tía, why don't we decorate for Christmas?" Brun's words drifted up from the heart of a poorly tended garden to the shadow-stained east wall of their home, its windows dark and empty. Between the boy and his aunt sat a round, stone table made of a material like black glass, its petrous sheen reflecting the only light in the small courtyard—a slowly spinning orb of the brightest white, reminiscent of a planetary pearl.

"I'll let you ask Renato when he arrives," Liliana answered, not lifting her eyes from the violet-flowered vines reaching across the terra-cotta walkway toward her feet. She blinked; Brun was certain her emerald eyes grew dimmer.

"Can't you just tell me?" Brun pled, his luminous words choking the yuletide darkness. No response. He probed further. "Does Papá not like Navidad?" Still nothing. Brun raised a brow. **Maybe this will get her going.** "Do you?"

The soft crashing of ocean waves rose up from the steep cliffs at the garden's edge, their roiling lullaby a recitation of perpetual loneliness and frustration. "Yes, Brun, I love Christmas," Liliana said tensely, remnants of worry etched in her brow. "When we were much younger, your father and I would decorate madly—our rooms, the house, the yard. We hung lights, painted gourds—one year we even built a life-sized Nativity scene." The hint of a laugh brushed the woman's lips. "The donkey nearly kicked your father."

"Really?" A broad smile gripped Brun's cheeks as he imagined the boy version of his father agitating the donkey. Within moments his smile broke, however. "What happened then, Tía?"

"Your grandmother grabbed him by the ear and drug him off into the house. The next day she made him the server at a ten-hour chocolatada. He could barely lift his arm to open his gifts that night." Her cheeks creased happily now. "After the first gift he gave up, so I had to open the rest for him. I loved it."

519

"That is pretty funny," Brun acknowledged, pausing so as not to be rude. "But what I meant was, what happened that changed everything?"

A green fire suddenly flashed in Liliana's eyes as she turned from her nephew to the house. "Nothing was the same after your mother—died." Her words assaulted the stone mansion. "Your father... I—" Her voice broke.

"What about Papá?" Brun rounded, suddenly upset at the change in his aunt's disposition.

"Nothing," Liliana answered swiftly, wiping away a tear. "Just forget I said anything."

Brun clenched a fist, the same aggravation gripping him as three days earlier. "How can I forget? I haven't seen you happy since before I left, and I'm supposed to pretend like nothing ever happened? That's ludicrous!"

"Brun, you don't—"

The boy's flesh burned scarlet. "I don't what? Understand? How can I when you won't tell me anything and Papá isn't even here? Just because Mamá died doesn't mean you should both stop living!"

Two white hands flew forward, grabbing the boy's wrists. "Brun, you must listen to me now." Liliana's eyes stung his. "You cannot breathe a word of what I've told you to Renato. It—it would upset him."

"Maybe that's what he needs, Tía!" Brun stood as he jerked his wrists away. "Papá needs to get past Mamá's death, to return to the way he was before—"

An abrupt, and mysteriously acute, windstorm suddenly flared up at the edge of the garden, among the shadows creeping over the salty cliffs. Brun's breath caught in his throat as his golden eyes honed in on an inky vortex, which vanished just as quickly as it had appeared.

"And how was I before, Kieran?" an earthy, yet incomparably smooth voice inquired from where the vortex had been. Liliana jumped, receding in her chair as Brun's eyes traced the silhouette of a tall figure stepping steadily from the darkness to the

520

light; the photons emanating from the orb seemed to have miniscule success in illuminating the man's black-cloaked frame, not to mention his formidable face. He could easily have been mistaken for a dark spirit, or perhaps a living shadow, had it not been for the whites of his eyes, which defiantly contrasted his black irises. A half-smile crinkled his murky cheek. It was evident from whom Brun had acquired his skin tone. "Are you surprised to see me, son?"

"Truthfully, yes," Brun confessed, now breathless as Renato stepped into the heart of the garden. "Tía Liliana told me you were out on business."

"My sister should not presume to know my comings and goings," Renato said, his words cutting Liliana's cheek. She did not turn; she did not even flinch.

Brun stepped in to arbitrate. "Don't get mad, Papá. Tía only said where you went, not why or when you'd be back."

"Is that correct?" Renato's silky words and penumbral eyes brushed the gash his words had inflicted earlier. "And where would that be, Liliana?"

"Europe!" Brun answered positively, abandoning all initial resentment toward his father for his now dissolved absence. He had returned, and Brun was simply glad to be with him.

"A wise guess," Renato muttered, his gaze smoldering at the woman. "But enough of that." He fixed his solid eyes on Brun. "Kieran, this is for you." And with the wave of the man's hand a shiny, black package materialized on the table. Liliana pulled away, staring once again at the creeping vines.

"¿Por qué?" Brun asked, his voice a yin-yang of confusion and excitement. "For Christmas?"

"No," Renato replied coldly. "Para tu cumpleaños."

"My birthday?" Brun repeated, his words floating before him.

"I assume your aunt did wish you a Happy Birthday upon your arrival three days ago?" Renato questioned.

"No, I did not," Liliana said, speaking to her brother for the first time since his arrival. Her words were hard, a revenge for the gash his own had made.

"How insensitive," Renato observed superiorly. Liliana glared in reply.

"It's okay, Papá, really," Brun swiftly interrupted. "I'd forgotten all about it myself. I—" He paused, debating within himself for a moment. "I guess I was just so depressed about leaving my friends behind that I didn't think what day it was."

"Friends?" Liliana recovered, her words precipitously hopeful. "Tell me about them! Who are they?"

"Oh, I have lots of friends now, Tía. I wish you and Papá could meet them all." Brun glanced from one to the other affably. "Kaya and Iris are two of my closest friends, but Manny—my roommate—he's my best friend. We do everything together. He even invited me to his house in Arizona for Christmas—"

"That's irrational," Renato interposed dryly. "And dangerous."

"I knew you'd say that, Papá," Brun said thoughtfully. "But that's okay. If I'd gone there I wouldn't have gotten to see you, and I've missed you a lot."

The anger drained from Renato's eyes, leaving him with an emotionless, obsidian stare. He said nothing, probing Brun's joy silently.

"And I bet you two won't guess what species Iris is," Brun said tentatively.

"Could he be a green basilisk?" Liliana asked excitedly.

"Not even close," Brun replied. "Right height, though."

"Then, is he an otter?" Liliana continued.

Brun shook his head and smiled. "Nope."

"A short kinkajou?" she guessed a third time.

"Uh-uh."

"Just state the species, Kieran," Renato said frostily.

Liliana glared at the man. "But that's boring, Papá," Brun argued.

Renato gritted his teeth. Liliana scoffed under her breath.

"Fine," Brun conceded, a bit of edge returning to his voice. "He's a hare."

"A hare?" Liliana said in wonder. "But hares aren't indigenous to Isla Verde—they're a European breed of Lumen. Is he a foreigner? Did he migrate here?"

"Sí, he did," the boy affirmed. "His father, Fidelio Firefoot—who's my Sentinels instructor, by the way—brought him over when he was just a baby. They don't know what happened to his mother—she went missing one day and they think she might have been killed. If you ask me, I think—"

"Enough of this," Renato bit. "The utter nonsense of this hare's life is of no consequence to us."

Shock glistened in Brun's eyes. "But he's my—"

"Acquire your gift from the table, Kieran," Renato said, ending the debate. "Follow me."

Brun quickly complied, scarcely thinking as he lifted the package and sped away after his father's snapping cloak. Darkness enveloped the pair as they traversed the garden path, the crimson light of Brun's skin threatening the overbearing shadows. They had just rounded a diamond shaped fountain when the boy stopped.

"Why do you linger?" Renato asked, his foot freezing on the first step. He did not turn around.

"What about Liliana?" Brun inquired.

"Is she not capable of walking?" the man responded.

"Can't she come with us?"

"No." The word made the air bleed.

"Why are you so cruel to her all of a sudden?" Brun demanded.

Ice crystals escaped the man's nostrils. "That is of no concern to you."

"But she's my aunt!" Brun contended.

"And I am your father," Renato said, clenching a fist before continuing his passage to the door. "You will follow."

A sudden desire to crush the box in his arms surged through Brun's veins, but he thought better of it as he plodded forward, detesting his father for abandoning his sister on this night of all

523

nights, when families should be together, when people should be laughing. Brun paused before passing through the cracked door, glancing sideways to spy the sad light hovering so far away in the garden; his only Christmas decoration. Sighing in defeat he resumed his footsteps that sounded much to him as an elegy, the quiet song of death of his footfalls against black marble as he traversed the all too familiar hall, his face and arms illuminating a magnificent spiral staircase snaking up from the base of the mansion.

A voice from the floor above interrupted his dirge. "You are slow, Kieran."

I shall hurry, master. Brun rolled his eyes. "I'm coming, Dad." His shoes slapped against the broad steps as he jogged up the staircase, allowing his fingers to taste the cool, stone banister on his left. Above him he could hear the faint rustle of his father's cloak as it left the staircase. The boy's feet pounded harder as he passed the second floor, peeling ahead toward the third. His heart thumped oddly in his chest as he again reached level ground—the top floor. To his left and right stretched another hall, swallowed in lightless obscurity. But before him stood a pair of oaken doors, their ominous stature soaring to perhaps fifteen feet or more. As he drew near the portal, voices met Brun's ears. **Who's he talking to?**

"You will leave, now," Renato's voice said lowly. Curiosity pulled Brun forward, his ear nearly touching the door. More murmurs. "Do not argue!" his father's voice vibrated, very nearly shaking the timbers. "Now go, my son is here."

Something made Brun wait to enter, however—whether curiosity or fear, he did not know. His ears strained, his mind hoping the other party would speak just once more that he might determine the identity of the individual. Yet the wind was the only voice he heard—turning, swirling behind the door and then suddenly ceasing. At that moment Brun knocked, thinking it best to announce his presence rather than allow his father to discover him eavesdropping at the threshold.

"Enter, Kieran," Renato pronounced audibly.

Brun pushed the door open, sliding through its thin jaws and scanning the broad room for evidence of a visitor. On either side rose mountains of books framed by the occasional painting or rueful tapestry. A crystal chandelier cast its broken light on the obsidian floor, revealing no one and only faintly tracing the dark mass of a desk spreading before the arched window, its curtains ironically snowy white, somehow alien in this black hole of an office. Renato stood with his back to Brun, his cloak slung over the back of his black leather chair as he stared west, his eyes tracing the thickening swell of the Amazon.

"Set your gift on the desk and stand by me." Renato's voice was even.

Silence preceded Brun as he bypassed the desk and approached the window. Neither spoke. Very few were the boy's memories of this room, for his father rarely welcomed company. As midnight drew near Brun stared at the flawless glass, carefully eyeing his father's solemn expression through the transparent mirror. Minutes passed; but no one spoke. In the end Brun's inquisitiveness got the better of him.

"Papá, who were you talking to?" the boy asked finally.

"When do you mean?" the man replied, his eyes searching the darkness with cold familiarity.

"Before I came in. I heard you talking to someone from the hall."

"I spoke to no one," Renato said gruffly. "You must have imagined it."

"I did not." Brun's tone was defensive. "I heard you clearly. You told them to go away because I was here."

"You are confused—"

"If it was one of the servants then where did he go?" Brun asked, ignoring his father's evasive replies as he searched the room. "There aren't any other doors besides the ones I came through, are there?"

"Kieran, you are being ridiculous," Renato said dismissively.

"But I heard the wind—"

Renato laughed. "I must have closed the window and mumbled to myself, that is all. Quit worrying, son."

Brun glared ahead through the glass, abandoning the argument. **It was more than the wind.**

The veil of silence once again fell between them, the boy frowning through the expertly carved frames and the man peering thoughtfully out over the forest, an eyebrow raised in amusement.

"These friends of yours," Renato said a moment later, his voice peeling back the silence, "are they kind to you?"

"Definitely," the boy replied, a hint of agitation still pricking each syllable. **Although Kaya can be a little impatient sometimes.**

"Is Kaya your—partner?" Renato asked, a dark joke flashing in his eyes.

"No!" Brun rebounded quickly. "She—I mean, I think maybe M—Well I shouldn't say that, he'd kill me—" he babbled to himself. "Papá, no. Kaya is my friend; it's not like that."

"Is there—another?" Renato probed. "A more—suitable—match?"

"If you're asking if I have a girlfriend, then the answer is yes," Brun said, redirecting his typically even keel. "Her name is Araceli."

"Is she beautiful?" the man prompted.

"Yes," Brun said, considering her soft face framed by those sharp mocha eyes and hair.

Renato blinked. "Smart?"

"Sí, Papá."

The man peered through the corner of his eyes. "Faithful?"

"Why wouldn't she be?" Brun asked, offended by the audacity of his father's query.

"Your first mistake," Renato said, his voice foreboding. "You have trusted him—or her—whom you have not truly known."

"I think I can trust Araceli," Brun countered.

"Do you?" Renato asked, a flash of white glinting momentarily through his cracked lips. "And why is this?"

Because she stuck by me for two days when I got knocked out by a band of crazy centaurs. You don't do that if you don't care. But a voice in Brun's mind told him to belie the specifics. "She stood by me when I was down," he abbreviated. **Literally.**

"And exactly what party knocked you down, if I may ask?" Renato asked wisely, as though he had read Brun's thoughts. "Your presumably aggrieved friends? Perhaps Kaya or Manny? Definitely not Iris…" he chuckled. "He lacks in—stature."

"Don't make fun of my friends, Papá." But Renato kept on laughing, reveling in his lark. Brun's skin flashed scarlet. "Shut up, already!"

Brun knew he should have held his tongue the second the words left his lips, possibly sooner. The laughter ceased. A glare strikingly reminiscent of a swirling vortex pierced him, running him through with guilt.

"You will not demonstrate such disrespect to me," the man said dangerously, his features rigid. "You are not a—a heathen."

"I'm sorry, Papá," Brun said wretchedly.

"I should say," Renato replied, his voice relaxing slightly, though his bite not gone. "Your friends may behave in such a way, but I will not permit that here."

"They're not like that," Brun defended staunchly.

"And how are you to know, Kieran?" Renato set a firm hand on the boy's shoulder. "You have known them for only four months—a meaningless slot of time."

"It's not meaningless."

"It is," Renato affirmed, his hand matching the assertiveness in his voice. "Many years, or even an entire lifetime can pass, and those same friends may turn and betray you. Do not trust them."

I trust them with my life. Honey met onyx as the boy stared defiantly back at his father. Brun remained silent, however, for fear his collarbone could not withstand any more pressure. A moment later Renato loosened his grip. **Dang, that hurt.**

"I would like you to open your gift, now," Renato said, turning toward the desk. Brun reassumed his humble obedience, walking to the edge of the dark panel to obtain the box. With a nod from his father the boy began to tear away the midnight wrapping, which fell to the floor and dissolved into mist. Renato smiled as his son held up a tiny, black hoop, no more than two centimeters in diameter.

"A ring?" Brun said, eyeing the band's solemn sheen.

"Yes," Renato answered, the word gliding effortlessly through the air. "A flawless specimen of midnight lace obsidian—frozen magma, a token of the Earth's strength."

The boy ran his finger along the smooth, outer edge of the ring, a halo of liquid darkness.

"Do you like it?" Renato inquired.

"Yeah," the boy murmured vaguely. **I suppose. It looks cool, anyway.**

"Why not put it on?" Renato prompted.

Brun glanced at the birch band on his hand. **But I've already got a ring. Why do I need another?**

"Kieran," Renato prodded.

"Sí, Papá," Brun said, half groaning as the igneous band slid onto his finger, just above his wand.

"How does it feel?" Renato asked eagerly.

Like a ring, what else? Brun measured the anticipation in his father's eyes. He relented. "I guess it's cold, like black ice or something."

"Perfect," the man stated satisfactorily, abruptly adding, "You may go now."

The words struck Brun's jaw with a dry punch. "But it's Christmas; can't I stay with you for a while? Maybe we could talk about Mamá—"

"No. You will leave now," Renato cut. "Go check on your aunt."

And suddenly you're interested in her well-being? But Brun overcame his bitterness, mumbling a forced, "Feliz Navidad," as dejection led him to the doors.

"Happy Birthday," Renato corrected. "Kieran?" he called, just as Brun disappeared into the shadowy hall.

"¿Sí?" Brun replied, not turning around.

"That ring—it will guard you, protect you from danger," Renato said, pausing carefully. "Never cease to wear it. Do you understand?"

"Sí, yo comprendo," Brun said, appeasing his father with his words, yet slipping the obsidian halo from his hand. **Yeah, I understand. You care more about your stupid gifts than you do for me.**

***

"I-love-this-island!" Zane cried, his typically scant attention span fully honed on the hundreds of glowing boards shredding across the crepuscular waters below the rocky outcrop at his feet.

Iris shook his head. "He's hopeless," he muttered, his ears flopping.

"No, he's happy," Manny said, his cousin's enthralled gaze causing him to reminisce about his own first night as a spectator atop Lookout Point. Admittedly, Manny was sorry it had taken nearly the whole of two weeks to bring Zane here, but there had been much to do. Of course, Manny had to give his family a tour of the island, which under normal circumstances would have taken less than a day; under the unremitting barrage of questions released by his aunt and mother, however, a full three-day island safari was all but unavoidable. "I want to see each and every one of these shortcuts you claim you take to class, Manuel," María had said as they returned to Kaya's house at the end of the first day. "I may need to reroute you if you've been taking questionable paths." But whatever misgivings she may have had, María never breathed a condescending word against any of the trails; in fact, the suspense inspired by the snickering fruitsnakes sent her heart pumping with a thrill she had nearly forgotten.

Nightwind, who happened to moonlight alongside Chiron as a fabulous cook, had invited Manny's, Kaya's, and Iris's families to the astronomer's humble hutch for lunch virtually every day of the break; and Jane, whose investigative instinct naturally drew her to the Lumen Resource Center, drug Manny and company along with her for hours of intense cultural study that lasted well into the evening. Unbeknownst to his aunt, Manny took advantage of this time to instruct Zane in the art of Lumen card games, from Piranha

529

Sweep and Mudpuppy Black to Poker played with photon chips. This left very little time for the friends to stroll the Gardens, much less witness the lightboarding at the lakeshore. But even time is not the master of its own design and must relinquish its forceful hold to allot for destiny, or in this circumstance, simple play. And so it was that on the night of January 5, as Jane, reclined on the veranda off Keilani's room, devoured the third volume of a series highlighting Lumen Government, the three humans and the hare were able to sneak away to the edge of the island for some avid board watching.

"Maybe," Zane continued absentmindedly, his eyes never leaving the boards, "I could just register for classes early—you know, get some advance study time in before next fall. Do you think the teachers would mind?"

"He wouldn't even understand what half the teachers would be saying, much less the majority of the students," Iris said shrewdly.

"¿Cómo?" Zane mumbled, reaching his hand out toward the hare's squeaks. "I didn't catch what you said. Kaya, could you translate for me?"

Iris chuckled wryly. "Point made."

"He said you couldn't hack it," Kaya stated, equally engrossed in the lightboarding. "You wouldn't understand anybody."

"Sure I could," Zane said confidently. "And heck, you could translate for me!"

"You are not following me around all day," Kaya clarified, emphasizing the negative. "You'd drive me nuts... You're worse than López..." she mumbled.

"He is a López," Iris muttered through the corner of his mouth.

Kaya raised an eyebrow. "Need I say more?"

Despite the emotional plateau he had been living upon for the past two weeks, Manny could not prevent his eyes from staring down into the canyon of his family's departure, a downhill journey which he would have to make tomorrow. As he tried to reconcile this truth with the excitement of the present evening, a figure floated to his mind—another friend—missing. "So what do you guys think Brun's up to now?" Manny asked, sliding from his stupor.

"Brun... didn't you say he was from Brazil?" Zane said, his eyes still buzzing along the water.

"Yes," Manny and Iris replied together.

"Northeastern Brazil," Manny added. "On an island, actually."

Zane winced as a lightboarder crashed gracelessly into the waves. "That can't be far from the Caribbean—I bet you twenty bucks he's on a cruise," he said phlegmatically.

Kaya snorted. "You're an airhead, then."

"How's that?" Zane retaliated, his eyes momentarily sliding from the wet action to throw a sapphire glare her way.

"Brun's papá is like a recluse—he never leaves the island," Kaya informed him. "So there's no way they'd be on a cruise."

"Actually, Brun's dad goes away on business all the time," Iris said, correcting her account. "At least that's what he told me."

"Which makes him a hypocrite," Kaya readily pointed out, sidestepping any confession of false testimony. "It's hardly fair that he can travel everywhere while Brun and his aunt have to stay locked up in the house."

"He's just being protective," Manny said in Renato's defense.

"Tu mamá is protective," Zane interposed quickly. "But Brun's dad sounds like a Lumen Hitler. At least Tía María let you go to Costa Rica on your own."

"Just barely," Manny whispered. *Even then she still wished she'd gone with me.*

"Are they drunk, or what?" Zane said abruptly, pointing toward the center of the Lake at a pair of men who were riding the same lightboard, rocking dangerously to the left and right as they skimmed the foaming crest of a wave. The board rose with a sudden lurch, throwing both riders into the wave's belly, which roared in satisfaction.

"Idiotas," Kaya mumbled smugly. "I don't know who taught them how to surf, but they stink."

531

A head emerged from the back of the wave with a raucous scream. "Whoohoo! Now that's what I'm talkin' about!"

"Who are they?" Iris asked, his ears perked as he watched the obviously more skilled man slide back onto the board, curving around to collect his partner. "And what's that clumsy guy waving at?" Within seconds the balance-impaired duo meandered pitifully through the air in the vague direction of Lookout Point.

"¡Hola!" the lead boarder shouted now with an jovial wave.

Kaya slid back from her stone seat, concealing herself from the audience below. "I could just die…" she grumbled shamefully.

A broad smile suddenly flashed across Zane's face. "Manny, that's your papá! Tío Carlos is lightboarding!"

"And Kaya's dad is steering," Iris said, his violet eyes glinting humorously.

Kaya contemplated total desertion as Carlos López and Marcos Bellastrata drew haphazardly nearer to the precipice. *He'll probably ground me if I leave, but oh well…*

"Where you headed, honey?" Marcos exclaimed. He wobbled suicidally just a board's length from the edge as his bronze eyes followed Kaya's creeping form in its vain attempt to disappear into the darkness.

"I didn't know you knew how to lightboard, Uncle Carlos!" Zane shouted.

"Me, either," Carlos said as he jumped from the board and shook his hair, spraying the onlookers with cold droplets.

"It was definitely—interesting." Manny eyed his father with a smile. "I think mi papá makes a better anchor than a sail, wouldn't you say, Marcos?"

"I'd say you're right," the spectacled man said with a laugh.

"Hey, now!" Carlos defended.

"Don't you even dare," came Kaya's voice, her tenor threatening yet slightly lined with hilarity as Marcos slopped toward her retreating frame. She screamed as he broke out into a full run, only to find herself locked in a damp embrace. "Aaaah! Let go of me!" she bellowed, slapping her father's wet shoulders and straining to repress any hint of laughter.

Iris seemed to laugh the hardest. "I think he needs to do that more often. It might cool her down a little," he joked.

***

"I—" the voice choked. "I need you to take care of yourself."

Brun's dark forehead surmounted in a heavy pucker as he gazed straight into the fragile emeralds of Liliana's eyes. After three weeks, very little had seemed to change in the woman's countenance; excluding the fact that her cheeks appeared to have regained a touch of their formal color, Brun thought. The boy had discovered the key to defragmenting her impenetrably somber mood, however—or at least until now, when they once again stood on the path before the dark mansion, just seconds from six months of torturous separation. Brun wished he could sit with her in the garden another day, or perhaps cook alongside her in the kitchen one final time, to see healing fill her eyes with one last story of his friends—not of malevolent monkeys but the daily adventures the island provided, of snickering fruitsnakes and Piranha Sweep, of soccer in the Northwest Gardens or stargazing on Nahir's hill. But today her eyes were dim. **And full of fear.**

"Tía, I promise." Brun's hand tightened on her shoulder. "Mis amigos and I are watching out for each other every second of the day."

"Good," Liliana whispered, hugging him for the third time in the last minute, a quantum of strength in the embrace. "And at night, too."

"Of course." Brun stepped back, somewhat wavering. He considered whether it would be easier if he simply turned to walk away, or… **No. I have to ask her.** "Tía, what's really bothering you? What are you so afraid of?"

"Brun—"

He cut off her typically evasive tone. "No! I can't spend this many months away from you without knowing what's really wrong. How do I know you're going to be okay when I get back?"

533

"As long as you take care of yourself, I'll be fine," she said dimly.

"What's wrong?" he reinforced, grinding his teeth. "I'm not leaving until you tell me."

"Just be safe—"

"Liliana!" the boy cried, his fists clenched and voice shrill.

"Brun, you listen to me," his aunt directed, grabbing his cheek with a surprisingly warm hand. "There are some things that I cannot tell you, that you cannot know—"

"Like why Papá hates you?" Brun demanded.

Liliana ran her finger along her nephew's cheek. "Hate is a strong emotion, Brun."

"But that doesn't change the truth that he does! What's changed, Tía? How could you have been so close as children and—and just—ignore each other now?"

Brun was not prepared for the sudden tenderness in Liliana's eyes. "I love your father, Brun," she said, caressing his cheek. "But Renato and I—we are two very different people."

"So what changed things?" No response. "Is it because of how Mamá died?" His voice meandered to a whisper. "Because I—I killed her? Because I'm sorr—"

"Brun!" Liliana gasped, grabbing his bronze chin. "Do not ever for a second believe that her death was your fault!" Pain and anger flashed in the stones of her eyes, her mouth drawing thin. "The blame does not lie on your shoulders…"

"Then Papá…?"

"No," she sighed. "Your father never once hurt Alzena—he only cared for and loved her. She was his—his light…"

This makes no sense at all. "But earlier you said everything changed after she died. Your stories don't match up, Tía."

Liliana placed a golden finger on the boy's lips. "M'ijo, some things aren't for you to understand. Perhaps when you are older, when you're stronger… But not now. Now you cherish your friends, build relationships, and learn. And do not worry about me; as I said, I'll be fine as long as you take care of yourself."

"But, Tía—"

"Bye, Brun," she said. With a kiss and a wave of sandy hair she turned, mounted the steps, and was gone.

The boy sighed, ambling back round to the path, towards woods of solitude. But high above, in the uppermost room of the dark mansion, a figure stirred, a curtain danced, a smile was wrought.

Where can I buy a CPS?

A knock startled Manny. *Who in the world? I'm already late...* Manny set his jaw, annoyed not only by the fact that Brun had left for class without him, but that someone had the audacity to delay him even further. His stomach grumbled as he snatched his leather pack and wrenched the door open. He looked down to find a furry, whiskered figure gazing up at him and tapping its forepaws together tentatively. The boy's eyes softened. "Buenos días, Tobias."

"Good morning, Manny," the otter said precariously, his short tail dragging across the ground lightly. He said nothing further, yet stared somehow expectantly up at the boy, his river green eyes genuine.

A smile fused with a sigh on Manny's lips. "Do you wanna accompany me to class again today?"

"If you really don't mind," Tobias replied, his vain attempt at meekness foiled by the unfettered delight in his eyes and voice.

Manny yielded easily. "It's fine with me. But you're gonna have to ride on my back, because I–am–late," he added distinctly.

Tobias's whiskers bristled. "I've got no problem with that."

"Up you go, then." Manny knelt to allow the otter to scramble onto his back. Seconds later the hutch faded into the scenery as the boy tore off down the heavily trodden footpath, his figure winding away west toward the island.

Manny loved running. Second to baseball, it was his favorite athletic activity; and considering the lack of baseball diamonds in Isla Verde, running just happened to be the sport he enjoyed and practiced the most, a source of clarity and release. Often, when his mind felt cloudy or his thoughts jumbled, Manny would cruise the perimeter of the Lake or sail along the Lucero deck, weighing and diffusing his anxieties with each successive foot pump. As such, Manny took little notice of the otter's additional weight this particular morning, permitting his mind to slide into its usual paradigm of conflict resolution.

First he thought of how very much had changed over the past two months at the Amazon River Academy, and yet somehow had still managed to stay the same. The coming of the New Year had brought on a distinct shift in the island's climate, principally due to the rising waters of the Amazon, which had effectively transformed the normally thin ribbon of Lucero Falls into a thundering curtain covering the entire northern lip of the valley basin. Manny had instantly liked this new version of the Lucero, because he could now walk the pathway below the Falls with the sensation of passing along some aquatic tunnel deep within the Earth, which in turn made him think of Zane. *And he's a whole other matter...* Manny rolled his eyes. *If he doesn't stop sending me letters about everything he's gonna do when he gets here, I'm gonna send him a horned frog wrapped in a box. Maybe if he thinks it's candy it'll bite him on the lips.*

Whatever. Manny sighed, picking up speed. *Where was I? Oh, yeah, flood season...* Now owing to the surplus of water introduced into the Lake, the Lumen authorities had opened the floodgates south of the city so that the island would not become a second Atlantis. *We don't all have gills.* It is to no surprise, then, that the Flooded Forest began to live true to its name, the waters reaching higher with each day as previously unseen fish literally poured into the scene. Every day seemed to bring new species into the forest, affording Shadowflame's students a wide array of Lumorphi specimens with which to interact. Manny had come to appreciate most of these novel creatures, one of which was a tarantula, in fact—a semi-aquatic arachnid known as the Blue Dancer with the twofold ability to walk over and swim through the flood waters in search of prey. *Neat little booger...* But there was one Lumorph in particular that the boy felt a strong aversion toward, and he shivered at the thought as his feet slapped across the east bridge connecting the dirt pathway to the island. *Let's not even go there.*

Changing pace as the Lake glinted peacefully below him, Manny considered his other classes. *Thank God we're done with Anatomy; I don't know what I'd have done if Professor Bluebolt*

537

made us dissect another Lumen liver. He cringed, then ruminated on Art. *Caleida's still a whack-job, no doubt about that, but at least we're about to start creating wooden objects now; I'm so tired of making tools that dissolve the moment you quit thinking of them. That's useless...* His thoughts savored strongly of bitterness as he recalled the two hours he had spent the previous day designing a functional rocking chair, only to watch all his efforts disintegrate just seconds after the end of class. No amount of exaggerated praise from Flores could replace that. *So stupid...*

A sudden shift of environment altered his mood; lime leaves, billowing moss, and an army of ferns filled his vision from all fronts. He smiled, appreciating the beauty of it all, and ran faster. *And Sentinels?* His smile grew wider. *We're finally done with Reticulum—I can't wait to lasso a Silverback Peccary, not to mention one of those idiot monkeys.* His honey eyes darkened as he pondered the habitual thievery that had grown all the more prevalent since the advent of Christmas, despite his friend Julius's staunch denial of the obvious. *Quetzal Land must be a truly surreal place, but here in the real world, Lumens are losing their wands right and left.* Manny's eye's shot up as he suddenly remembered his furry cargo clutching tightly to his backpack straps—Tobias Greenriver, the unfortunate otter whose wand had never been found. *At least not yet.*

Manny ground his teeth as he recalled the otter's devastated face so many months ago when his shell necklace had surreptitiously disappeared while he and his brothers were swimming, and how several days later the boy and his friends had fruitlessly followed a set of monkey tracks beyond the very limits of the city. That night fear tore at Manny's insides. *But not anymore. We're ready, now. We know how to hide, how to attack, and how to pin one of those stupid changos to a tree if we have to.*

Forced to slow his pace as he leapt across the thick moon lily pads of the Carina River, doubt spied an unguarded opportunity to throw a dart into Manny's resolve. What if the monkeys overcame the children? What if they were not merely playing pilfering games, but would murder if necessary? *Oh, but they would.* Manny maintained iron fists as his feet regained solid land. *And that's why we have to stop them; they'll kill if they have to, but even if they don't, they're ruining people's lives. I mean, look at Juan Patino, the baker dude. He had to close shop. What are he and his family supposed to do? Is there Lumen welfare? Good question. And those seven centaurs the monkeys nearly drowned. They can't finish their Sixth-Level without their wands—not that they deserve to, after attacking Brun and me—twice. I still don't know how Iris got us away from them in the woods—he must know every nook and cranny of the island...*

From this point in his cross-country journey Manny began making a mental brainstorm of all the theft victims that he could remember, beginning with the most recent. *That falcon flying through the canopies north of the city last week—dang, that was close to Kaya's!* He frowned. *Those two tree frogs hopping through the Gardens late at night a couple weeks back, that girl who was fishing down in the Flooded Forest last month...* Just before Manny reached the South Docks, his thoughts came full circle. *And then me.* He slowed down to a trot, not only because he could see the pier just ahead, but also for the shock of realizing that he, having been only an eighth-grader on a class trip to a foreign country, was the first victim he knew. *But he never got my wand—not in Costa Rica, and not even when he busted into our room and Nipper got him.* The boy paused, walking now. *I guess the little thief did manage to swipe Brun's sun beetle. I still don't get what good that did him, though. What's a monkey need a beetle for? Oh, well... We'll get it back next week, when we go on our next monkey hunt.*

"Earth to Manny," Tobias drawled, waving a chestnut paw in front of the boy's eyes. "Are you zoning, or what?"

"Oh, sorry!" Manny shook himself from his stupor; he stood five feet from the pier, not moving.

"So are we going to the Quay, or what? I thought you were late."

"I am." Manny realized the truth of this and jumping forward to call for a ferry. Just minutes later the boy was jogging along the gravel trail leading down into the Flooded Forest, rocks flying at his heels as he neared the satin barrier of the city limits. He plunged through blindly, a decision that he swiftly regretted as he tripped over some manner of small creature and landed hard on the planks of the dock, inadvertently sending Tobias flying through the air to crash into a peregrine falcon perched for take off.

"Paws off, water dog!" the falcon screeched as it whirled awkwardly around.

"Sorry! It wasn't my fault!" Tobias exclaimed, pulling himself up off the boards.

The falcon glared at the otter but said nothing further, hopping silently around and spreading its tawny wings before lifting from the dock and soaring elegantly through the thin space between the water and the treetops.

"…I really am sorry," Manny said for the third time, his eyes apologetic as he stared at the retreating figure of a kinkajou, who by all accounts appeared slightly miffed. "I didn't see you there."

"Just forget about it. I have less than a minute to reach the island before I'm late." With that the kinkajou caught a rope from the Quay to the nearest tree then quickly melted into the foliage to the east.

Less than a minute? Manny nearly bit his tongue. "C'mon, Tobias." He grabbed the otter by the torso and leapt into the nearest ferry, fidgeting as the boat traversed the forest alluvion. Just below the turbulent water a Blue Dancer lunged, striving to trap an orange fish in its web net. But Manny paid it no mind, as his eyes were set on the mahogany watch ticking silently on his wrist. He cringed as the hour hand pointed to eight. As he looked up he noticed a tiny, brown figure slide from a vine to land on the island still minutes away. *At least the kinkajou I almost murdered made it on time.* Manny sighed, rolled his eyes, and then stared at his feet the remainder of the trip, fearing Shadowflame's punishment. *I'm probably gonna have to serve a detention… What if she makes me clean out the Silverback pen. I think I'd die.*

A grinding noise signaled to Manny that the ferry had reached its destination; as he and Tobias leapt stealthily from the boat Manny flipped the ferryotter a golden Sol, nodding briefly

540

before turning and slinking uphill toward certain demise. But as they reached level ground Manny was startled to discover a massive crowd of students, much too many for any normal session of The Lumen World. An odd pang struck Manny's stomach as he caught sight of a white-haired boy leaning to see around a centaur's head in front of him. *What the heck...?*

"What are you doing here?" Manny breathed as he bolted silently up to the snowy-haired boy. Tobias ran on all fours to keep up.

"What do you mean what am I doing here?" Brun whispered, one brow raised. "I'm here for class—and on time."

"Your first class is Healing—you don't meet here," Manny contradicted.

"Today we do—everybody does," Brun said, as though reminding him.

A tug pulled at Manny's pant leg. "Hey, can you give me a lift?" Tobias asked quietly.

Manny knelt down and picked up the otter, setting the creature on his shoulder without taking his eyes from Brun. "How's that?" Manny asked, still confused.

"If you'd just gotten up forty-five minutes ago like I told you to then we wouldn't be having—"

"Students, before we continue, I believe it would be best if you all would sit—or lie—down. That way everyone will be able to both see and hear our special presenters today," called a river-like, velvet voice from the other side of the tightly crowded wall.

"I believe," a second voice began, even bolder than the first, "that it would be best if you would space out as well." Manny heard the soft crack of a tail snap.

The pupils obeyed without exception, revealing a wide, open space in the center of a broad circle of students. Manny gawked in amazement to find all his instructors standing there; he blinked, shaking his head once or twice in an effort to somehow clear his head. Upon opening his eyes, however, Manny's thoughts became even more muddled. At his instructors' feet stood a pair of very bright-eyed otters—a male and a female—the second of which was

541

chatting avidly with Flores, who happened to be sporting fluorescent pink robes with matching flowers in the spiraled curls of her hair. The female otter barely came up past the woman's knees, but her mannerisms conveyed such authority and confidence that Manny instantly respected her.

Before Manny could form any additional assumptions as to the character of the female otter, a raucous laugh crashed through the air, tearing the boy's eyes from his present subject. Manny flinched as his senses honed in on the cackling male otter, who stood with one paw on his ample belly while he adjusted his crystal eyewear with the other. Nochesol stood beside the male otter, smiling broadly before asking a question that Manny could not hear.

"Who are they?" Manny asked, his eyes jumping between the otters' frames now. He quickly noticed that the female seemed to have a slightly more russet hue to her fur, while the male boasted a golden coat that appeared to be quickly fading to white.

"I don't know, but if you'll be quiet I bet we'll find out," Brun said edgily.

Manny stared back incredulously. "What's wrong with you?"

Brun flexed his hand, opening his fist as though his joints were cramped, but said nothing.

"Excelente," called Shadowflame's thick voice a second time as she surveyed the ring of students, all of which were eager to discover the identity of the unexpected visitors. "I would like to first thank each of you in advance for the seamless attention and respect that I know you will pay to Mr. and Mrs. Arrowpaw as they introduce you to the most highly esteemed of Lumen sports— photocaching."

"Photocaching?" Manny blurted out in disbelief. In less than a second all eyes zeroed in on Manny, several in curiosity, some skeptical, while still others aggravated. Shadowflame's lightning-yellow eyes fell into the latter category.

"Sí, Señor López." Her voice bordered a growl as she flicked her velvet-black tail dangerously. Manny blushed brightly. A moment later Shadowflame's feline features softened as she turned from Manny and began slinking around the circle. "Before I give the floor to our guests, you should all know that you are very fortunate to receive instruction from the Arrowpaws today. As senior officers of the LIGHT Group in North America, they are very busy; but as a special treat they have come down to speak to all of you. So let's all give a warm, Amazon welcome to the Arrowpaws!"

A gamut of cheers sprang from the circle as students brayed, squawked, and hollered, all ecstatic to embark on their first photocaching experience. Yet after a minute the enthusiasm had not died down. In an attempt to silence the crowd, Bluebolt mounted his lightboard and jetted about the assembly, a sapphire ring of light burning in his wake. In the end, however, it was Chiron's sober glare that finished the job. After all, no one wanted to serve a detention at 2 a.m. mapping stars and constellations on Nahir's Hill.

"I thank y'all very much fer humorin' me wife and me today, pups," the male otter proclaimed in a gruff voice as he waddled forward. In his paws he juggled a large, creamy-blue shell. "I am formally known as Roberto Arrowpaw, but ye can just call me Berto, if ya like. Linda—me wife, o'course—and I are architects for the LIGHT Group, as yer instructor so righ'ly pointed out. We were in the city collaborating with the local challenge designers when we thought, 'Blisterin' conches! Why not see if the Seventh-Levels could use a little brushin' up on their photocachin' skills?' We couldn't have guessed what good timin' we 'ad!"

"I'd say," Linda contributed readily, slapping the ground with her tail as she strolled congenially forward to join her husband. Behind her ear she wore a pink shell with strikingly pronounced ripples. "And if I might venture a guess, I would say you all look mighty capable. I would be willing to bet you've got an excellent team of teachers here on the island. But enough chatter—let's see what you've got." In less than a second she shot her paw up to her ear, transforming the shell she had been wearing into an ivory wand, which she quickly pointed at the surprised students.

"Y'aren't slow, are ye?" Berto shouted. "Wands out!" He shook his head. "Pups these days…"

"Quiet, Berto," Linda mumbled.

543

A mad scramble tore around the circle as the students hurriedly transformed their wands.

"First thing's first!" Berto barked, his wand ready. "Ye can't photocache w'out a CPS! I assume yer Sentinels instructor 'as already covered this subject in complete detail?"

A halo of blank stares met the otter, who snorted loudly. Fidelio, on the other hand, stood behind Berto, unperturbed, perhaps even smug, as he polished his monocle.

"Right, then," Linda said with a slap of her tail, stepping forward to intervene before her husband shared any further sentiments of a negative nature. "We'll have a mini-lesson— Caleida, would you like to assist me?"

Fidelio's ears went rigid as his silver eyes shot to the Art instructor's exorbitantly pink frame.

"I most certainly will, my dear Linda!" Flores called as she swept dramatically forward, her robes very nearly engulfing the otter.

The monocle slipped from Fidelio's eye socket, dangling awkwardly from his blue and gold waistcoat. "This is incredible…" he muttered.

"Circinus is actually one of my specialties," Flores continued, pulling up her sleeves and producing her hot pink, bamboo wand.

Fidelio ground his teeth. "I'm sure," he mouthed.

A chinchilla stepped forward from the ring of students, one paw held high. "Mrs. Arrowpaw," she said. "I have a question."

"By all means," Linda replied attentively.

"Well, my name's Serena, and I'm sure I speak for everyone when I ask, what exactly is a CPS?"

Before Serena had time to blink Fidelio rocketed forward, standing between the chinchilla and the otter. "Great question, Señorita de los Montes," he began swiftly. "You see, CPS is an acronym for—"

"Wait, wait, wait!" bellowed Berto, scuttling up next to Fidelio. "What d'ye mean by interruptin' me wife, hare?"

544

Fidelio stared back in an amalgam of greystone fury and embarrassment. "If you must know, otter friend, I am the Sentinels instructor," he answered brashly.

"'Nough said." Berto placed a firm paw on Fidelio's back, forcing him to reassume his position in the clique of instructors behind. "Consider this yer day off."

Chiron shrugged at Fidelio with sympathetic eyes as the otter waddled back to his wife's side.

Linda turned back to the chinchilla, blinking oddly for a moment before relinquishing a smile and saying, "To answer your query, Serena, CPS is short for the Circinus Positioning System, which is a must-have tool for photocaching. Creating it is as simple as animating the great compass Circinus, the most basic of the Seventh-Level Sentinels." A snort came from behind the otter, but she ignored this. "It is a topographical mapping system that can lead you directly to the photocache, in more or less steps, of course."

"I didn't know a sentinel could be a map," Manny muttered with surprise.

"Me either," Tobias said, shifting his weight on the boy's shoulder.

"There's nothing really amazing about it," Brun spat, his words spraying Manny's arm. "If a sentinel can be a net, then it can just as easily be a map."

Brun's never this moody. "Is something the matter—"

A velvet paw came down on Manny's shoulder, its weight light yet somehow threatening. "One more word out of you, Señor López, and I'll have you serving a double detention tomorrow. ¿Me comprendes?"

There was no need for Manny to turn around to realize just whose presence was effectually raising the hair on the back of his neck. "Sí, Profesora Shadowflame," he mumbled, almost quivering. "I understand."

"Then listen," she said in a low rumble as she bounded back off around the circle, leaping over several students' heads and slinking back to rejoin her colleagues.

Manny shivered, then abruptly became aware that he was the only student whose wand was not angled toward the mossy canopy. He quickly followed his partners' example as the voice of Flores warbled like an insane bell, straight into his ears.

"...I'm sure you all remember that glorious day last November when we created cylindrical paper weights—as I recall the rain had just ended and the clouds departed, the sunlight illuminating the Southeast Garden to meld flawlessly with my saffron robes." Fidelio sat now, a doomed expression on his face. "¡Sí! That most definitely was the day! So let that image of exquisite beauty flood your minds as you call down a wisp of light to form the great Lumen compass, Circinus!"

Manny blinked, ignoring Flores's histrionic behavior as he formed a vibrant yellow cylinder, which he quickly mashed into the shape of a dense pellet no wider in diameter than his palm. *Looks like a compass to me.* Brun was the only other student in Manny's line of vision whose speed at light bending mirrored his own; in stark contrast to Manny's disc, however, Brun's was a deep shade of blood and violet. This startled Manny, but Brun would not look up at him. *There is definitely something wrong.*

"Hurry now!" Flores trilled, clapping her silken hands as she whisked around the circle to hasten her pupils' progress. "One moment more and...done!" She rejoined Linda and Berto in a flurry of pink robes.

Berto voiced his approval. "Never in me life 'ave I seen such quick pups."

"What a very capable teacher you are," Linda agreed.

Chiron knelt on one of his front legs and whispered something in Fidelio's ear. The hare merely grunted.

"¡Paso dos!" Flores rang. "Step two is quite elementary— choose a corner of your compass and mold a needle that signals due north." She paused, taking a long breath as several students began to check left and right, utterly lost as to their cardinal directions. Flores then flicked her wand over her shoulder, painting the north end of the grove with a fluorescent "N." Pink, no less. She cleared her throat as a chorus of, "Ahs," rose from the crowd. "I assume we're ready to proceed? ¡Estupendo! Then the final step…"

***

How do I get myself into these situations?

Of course Caleida Flores had needed a volunteer. *Of course.* Manny swallowed, embarrassment bubbling in his throat as he chanced a sheepish glance at the thousands of eyes now focused on him, surrounding and enclosing him in a great ring of faces. *Yet for some odd reason I thought 'volunteer' somehow inferred a willingness to participate…*

Tobias waited faithfully at the boy's feet, uncomfortably shifting his weight from one paw to the other, his jade eyes trailing Flores's sweeping robes as she all but danced around them in a circle, checking to see that the remaining students had managed to 'boot' the CPS, as she had phrased it. In Tobias's paw now rested the token of Manny's sentinel success—a topaz specimen of the CPS compass—yet the otter took little notice of the photocaching tool, turning it in his paws with absentminded concern. His hunger for the limelight was about as avid as Manny's.

Flores whirled about, her rounds finished, and threw the boy and the otter a blinding smile. Manny and Tobias's shoulders instinctively tensed.

A whisper from behind smacked Manny in the shoulder blade. "No worries, my boy, I know you can do it!"

Unwilling to take his eyes from Flores, whose gaudy approach quickened with each passing second, Manny elected to reply to Fidelio's encouragement with the extent of his sign language—an inert thumbs down from behind the back. Manny thought he caught the sound of muffled laughter escape Chiron's lips. But before the shadow of a smile could reach the boy's eyes, Flores's bouncing curls filled his vision. He blinked slowly, wishing he could teleport to an undisclosed location. *Maybe even Easter*

Island. I bet she couldn't find me there. I'm sure the merfolk could teach me to photocache as easily as Caleida could.

To Manny's surprise, Flores whisked by him. "Good luck!" she chimed as she rejoined her peers, her expression pleased. Manny found himself utterly confused as he turned to stare pleadingly at his instructors, hoping that one might liberate him from inevitable humiliation. None did.

"Eyes a'ead now, ye pups!" called a gruff voice from near Manny's foot. He and Tobias both snapped their heads around to find themselves face to face (or rather, whisker to knee, as was Manny's case) with Berto and Linda Arrowpaw.

Manny blinked, his stomach knotting again. *This could be worse...*

"They are young, Berto, be patient..." Linda commented, patting the ground lightly with her bronze tail on her last word.

"Young," he snorted, eyeing Manny and Tobias carefully. "But still slow. I'll 'ave yer wands out, please!"

"Mine is out!" Manny retorted, gripping the mahogany rod in his fist.

"And 'is?" Berto grumbled, nodding toward Tobias, who now stared at the grass shamefully. "Ye can speak, I 'sume?"

"It was stolen," the young otter muttered quietly.

Linda cradled her chest sympathetically. "My dear... Could you have just lost it, perhaps?"

Tobias shook his head regretfully.

"Then 'owed ye manage to form Circinus, eh?" Berto barked, eyeing the golden compass in the young otter's paw.

"I didn't," Tobias responded, his words disappearing in the grass. "It's Manny's."

"Then give it back to 'im and get to lookin' fer yer wand!" Berto ordered.

"Mercy sakes, Berto!" Linda fired, nearly slapping her husband with her tail.

"Tobias, stay here!" Manny interposed as the otter lay the compass on the grass. "It's not a problem, Mr. Arrowpaw. He can have that one."

548

"Exactly 'ow do ye 'spect to photocache today w'out a CPS, boy? Gonna use yer mind to find the beetle, eh? Feel it out with yer thoughts? Squeeze your eyes tight shut and—oh." Berto froze, staring up at the violet Circinus that now rested in the boy's free palm. The otter blinked. "Yer quick."

"My point exactly," Linda said with clout. "So let's move along and stop harassing the young ones."

"Not harassin' no one…" Berto mumbled.

Linda shot her husband an icy glare. Manny thought he heard her whisper something about a grumpy old water mutt, but he could not be sure.

***

"López looks like such an idiot."

Kaya sat, her chocolate eyes smiling as she watched Manny meander about the heart of the clearing with tentative steps, his eyes yo-yo-ing between the violet compass in his hand and the apparently empty grass. He paused, narrowing his gaze and adjusting his grip on the butterfly net-like contraption extending from his opposite hand. Tobias crept nearer to the boy's position, pointing and nodding to the vacant ground with an expression of certainty. Kaya snorted, her smirk widening.

Just then, his face tense, Manny dropped to his knees and brought the shimmering gold net down on the grass. Tobias's preemptive grin faltered and crumbled as he saw a flash of green zip from the grass and straight into Manny's face, slapping the boy in the forehead and buzzing away across the clearing. Manny sprawled on the ground, rubbing the space between his eyebrows as numerous students chuckled, neighed, and chirped.

Kaya shook her head. "What a joke. He is such a dope."

"I think we should go help him," Iris affirmed, a similar net-like tool clasped firmly in his paw. He stared at Manny with pity in his eyes, quickly glancing down at his own compass to track the flashing green dot that had now reached the southern end of the clearing.

"And spoil the show? Count me out. This is too good to miss." Her eyes followed Manny's now resurrected frame as it torpidly crossed the clearing, Tobias trotting alongside.

"Since when do you take joy in the humiliation of others?"

"Ever since López volunteered to demonstrate his prowess as a photocacher."

Iris clicked his tongue, glaring at a pile of blonde curls mounted atop a pink mountain. "He didn't volunteer."

"Go at it again, Manny! You can do it!" Linda called as Manny passed the eye of the dell. The boy's head sagged slightly.

"Last chance, manpup! Get 'im this time or yerout!" Berto grunted.

"Just remember, Manny—despite its Chamaeleon-like abilities, the viridian beetle shimmers slightly, even on the grass. So take a deep breath, a sharp look, and then snatch him!" Linda bolstered with a hearty tail slap.

"Not to change the subject," Iris resumed, whispering so as only Kaya could hear, "but do you think Mr. and Mrs. Arrowpaw might have brought some radiant beetles of a lighter color?"

"What are you talking about?" Kaya snipped, unwilling to tear her gaze from the object of her ridicule. "Why should I care?"

"Maybe because you managed to lose Brun's sun beetle just days after he got it," Iris countered impatiently.

Highly disgruntled, Kaya peeled her eyes from the hunting scene. "Excuse me, but I lost it? As I recall, you helped me sneak into their room that night," she growled.

"And I nearly got my leg bitten off!" Iris reminded her.

"Too bad you didn't."

Iris glared back momentarily. "Let's just move on to consider the great opportunity staring us straight in the face."

"I don't see any Venus flytraps around…"

"Hilarious, Kaya," the hare said, one ear bent crookedly. "Just think about it—if the Arrowpaws set us loose to photocache, and one of the beetles is gold…"

Realization slapped Kaya in the forehead, and her frown deepened. "If I catch a sun beetle today, it is not going to Brun Dimirtis," she clipped.

Iris's ears went rigid. "It's your fault he lost it!"

"No, it's the monkey's fault."

"The monkey never would have gotten it if you hadn't taken it in the first place," the hare said through his teeth.

Kaya flipped her hair over her shoulder and turned back to watch Manny bend over his invisible prey. "I guess we never can know that, now can we?"

Iris bent the handle to his net as if it were amethyst steel. "You are impossible."

***

"Congratulations, Manny!" Iris called as he hopped hurriedly up to the boy's white figure. On all sides students chattered wildly as they rushed across the dell en route to the southern half of the island. From the hare's right Brun approached, his expression as equally dull as Kaya's as their eyes met the emerald insect struggling fruitlessly to break free of the luminescent net in Manny's hand.

"Gracias, Iris," Manny corresponded as he knelt to the ground, converting his wand into a mahogany briefcase. He placed the beetle inside. The sound of the creature's buzzing ceased as Manny clicked the latch, reforming his wand into the net-like apparatus it had assumed previously.

"I think he's gotten the hang of the Scarab Catcher," Tobias said, nodding his whiskered head at the net in Manny's hand.

"Looks like it to me," Iris agreed, holding his own close to his side in anticipation.

Kaya rolled her eyes, stifling a snort as she mumbled something as to her opinion of Manny's coordination. Brun appeared bored.

"So are we all gonna photocache together?" Tobias asked expectantly, the golden CPS Manny had made for him now attached to his wrist.

"How do you expect to capture the cache without a Scarab Catcher?" Brun said, his words slightly edged as he addressed the otter. Manny glared at his roommate.

"I'm happy just to tag along and read Circinus; I don't need to catch anything," Tobias answered. Brun stared back silently in reply.

Iris took advantage of the momentary lull in the conversation. "Kaya and I don't mean to be loners, but we were planning to photocache alone—we have a little wager going."

Manny and Kaya's brows rose inquisitively. "What kind of wager?" the boy asked.

Tobias shuffled in place. "Is it like a competition or something?" Iris nodded. "Cool!" the otter continued. "Hey, Manny! Maybe you and Brun could compete yourselves!"

Manny blinked awkwardly. "Honestly, I don't mind working as a t—"

"Sounds great," Brun interrupted, his eyes suddenly alight.

"Really, Brun," Manny tried a second time, "there's no problem if you just w—"

"It's already been decided," Brun cut in again, not bothering to look at Manny, who by this time appeared very annoyed.

Iris's eyes darted from Brun's stony expression to the boy's right hand, which he seemed to be flexing absentmindedly. The hare blinked once, disregarding his suspicions, and then quickly said, "We'll see you three later, then." The next breath he shot away south to disappear into the thick stream of students. Kaya teetered in place for a split-second before she, too, turned and jogged away.

"Good luck!" Tobias yelled, excitement plucking at his whiskers. "Ready, guys?"

"I guess," Manny grumbled, his words dissolving in midair.

Brun led the way. "Definitely."

"So what are the details of this contest, exactly?" Kaya asked, the corner of her mouth curled up at the end as she glanced down at the hare.

Iris slowed his pace as he drew near to a huddled mass of students. "Well, seeing as how you're so dead set on not repaying your debts today, I decided that I would do it for you."

Kaya tossed her hair over her shoulder. "How do you figure?"

"I'll catch the sun beetle, and that'll be the end of it," he replied, not looking up. "I just said we were having a contest so we could keep this little endeavor a secret. But," he paused, finally looking her way, "for the sake of sportsmanship, I'll admit that there's a slight chance you could still catch the beetle first, even though you won't."

"Just go on telling yourself that," Kaya said as she stepped up to a star-shaped monolith, each of its five prongs ending in a shallow bowl filled with soft, glowing pearls. Kaya took a moment to read the elegantly carved inscriptions that ran from each bowl to the center of the structure.

The crimson pearls read:

The heart of your desire lies beyond the glare of the fly eater.

The cerulean pearls read:

An amphibious bite awaits he who thirsts for the water scarab.

The sun pearls read:

The eyes of many watchers hold vigil over the golden path.

The fire pearls read:

In a frigid house rests the fire key.

The majestic pearls read:

Not even amethyst pearls are fit for swine

553

"We are not hunting for the crimson beetle," Iris said, emphasizing the negative as he reread the inscription to the red pearls for a third time. "Nipper is the only carnivorous plant in my life, and I want to keep it that way."

"Fine with me. Just don't ask me to photocache the cerulean beetle," Kaya matched. "One bite from an Amazon Horned Frog is enough for anybody."

Iris nodded understandingly. "Agreed. I guess we really don't have a choice, anyway." His eyes roamed back to the bowl of golden pearls. "If we're going to pay Brun pack for his lost goods then we have to catch the sun beetle."

"No, you're going to have to catch it. If I get my hands on it, I'm keeping it."

"Like I said earlier—the chances of that are miniscule."

***

"No way, Brun. No."

Brun stared fixedly across the star-shaped monolith at Manny. "I said I want another sun beetle, so that's what we're going to hunt."

Manny did not waver. "No, we are not."

"Sí, we are," Brun said through his teeth.

"You know I can't stand them, Brun." Manny's voice wavered slightly as an unbidden memory returned to his mind. "Cut me a break—I'll hunt any other one but that."

"I didn't lose a crimson or cerulean beetle, nor any stupid fire or majestic beetle for that matter," the other boy spit.

Tobias scanned the inscriptions quietly. "I'm sure we can come to some sort of compromise," he mumbled abstractly.

"Stay out of this, dog," Brun growled.

"Chill out, man!" Manny barked, his skin flashing a bright white. "Whatever your problem is, don't take it out on us!"

For an instant hatred flashed across Brun's face, twisting his normally calm features into the shape of a stranger. Manny stepped back, startled at the change. A moment later, however, an invisible wave seemed to wash over Brun's countenance, and he blinked as though dazed.

"Sorry, guys," he apologized. "I don't know what's gotten into me."

"Something foul," Tobias whispered inaudibly.

"'S'okay." Manny stepped forward again. "We all get in a funk sometimes."

Brun nodded distantly, flexing his hand. "I just really wanted my sun beetle back for some reason. I'm cool now, though. I understand where you're coming from, Manny. If a Lumorph bothered me that badly I wouldn't want to see it, either. Why don't we just choose another color."

Manny sighed in relief. *Great. Thank you God.*

Tobias coughed loudly, and Brun and Manny both turned to look at him. His whiskers twitched. "So, since I'm the only one of the three of us who has never owned a radiant beetle, would either of you mind if I vote which one we hunt for?" Manny shook his head; Brun shrugged somewhat passively. "Awesome. Then how about we go for the majestic beetle?"

A scoff. "The purple one?"

The frown quickly returned to Manny's face, his eyes snapping back to Brun. "And what's wrong with that?"

"I thought the otter might choose the fire beetle. At least it would put up a fight."

The otter?

Tobias's emerald eyes flared. "For your information, the majestic beetle is the fastest of all seven scarabs; mi papá told me most people aren't even quick enough to catch it."

Words bubbled in Brun's throat, scarcely loud enough for Manny to hear.

"...and your dad's a dog."

I'm done with this. Manny reached forward, swiftly taking a violet pearl between his fingers and laying it on the face of the compass attached to his belt. In less than a second the pearl dissolved. The compass instantly registered a blinking purple dot from some distance behind where Manny's own point showed on the interface.

"Download the first cache site and come on," Manny ordered, turning on his heel as he marched north in the direction of the violet dot. *At least it appears to be on this island.* Manny tapped the CPS with the point of his wand, which he had shrunk to resemble a stylus. The island came into full perspective and the map displayed his own icon heading steadily to the northeast. *Yeah, it is.* His brow furrowed as his eyes met the assortment of silver specs apparently surrounding the violet one. *What are those?*

"Wait up, Manny! We're coming!" Tobias called from nearly twenty strides behind.

Manny rolled his eyes and stopped. *I guess we'll deal with it when we get there.*

***

"I don't see why the heck López has to get all creeped out at the Ojos," Kaya stated as she plunged a paddle into the dark water, the disturbance rippling the already warped reflection of hundreds of spheres floating absently on either side of the canoe.

Iris stared down at the water, watching as an eel darted forward to swallow a flaming fish whole. He shuddered but did not turn away, wary of looking up at the assembly of watchers. "Professor Shadowflame told us last week that several Lumens had been known to go insane because of them."

"That's only if you're neurotic enough to look at them and then keep staring." Kaya alternated her stroke, her gaze set unwaveringly on the point of the canoe. "I guess López would fall into that category."

"Some people probably just can't help it," Iris muttered, his words skittering across the liquid like a water strider. Leaning slightly over the edge of the canoe, Iris caught sight of his reflection. He blinked, trying to look deeper into the water, but he soon found a third eye staring up at him, its obsidian pupil framed in a metallic red—strikingly different than his own. Transfixed, the hare bent further over the boat, when suddenly the alien eye twitched. In less than a second three more spheres appeared, their unblinking, distinctly-hued stares drawing closer to Iris's face. Without another thought the hare's paws snapped up to cover his eyes. He shuddered, imagining the eyes floating less than an ear length from his face.

"I really don't think I favor the Ojos much either, Kaya."

The girl chuckled. "I wondered what was going on; several of the Ojos just lunged for the left side of the boat. I'm actually rowing with my eyes closed at the moment."

An uncomfortable swallow. "How long 'til we can open our eyes?"

"Depends. How many were there?"

"Four," he whispered, his mind drawing up the image of their mysterious pupils fixated upon the back of his paws.

Kaya's voice was relaxed. "A couple of minutes, probably."

After said time, Iris shielded his peripheral vision with his paws, venturing a peek at his CPS and tapping the screen to maximum resolution. "They're still on either side of us, but the ones that were in front of me are gone now."

"You're not looking, are you?" Kaya rounded quickly, her eyes shut tight. "'Cause if you are they'll knock us from the boat!"

"Cool it, Kaya, I'm just relaying what my CPS is showing."

"Oh." She grabbed the oar firmly. "So are we still headed in the right direction, or do I need to adjust our course slightly?"

Iris tapped the interface and the visual retracted, revealing a tiny island to the northwest. "No, we're still good. But it looks like an even thicker cloud of Ojos is waiting for us there." He paused, contemplating the ironic shape of the approaching landmass—a perfect circle. "You know, Kaya, you should be able to see it by now. It's just ahead."

Kaya threw a quick glance past the front of the canoe and then allowed gravity to pull her eyes to the floor. "Nope, all I see is a wall of eyes."

"That can't be ri—" But his voice broke as he realized that the dense mass of green just ahead did not constitute an island at all.

"There is no island, Kaya." His words punctured the floor of the boat, sinking to the flooded depths of the forest floor.

"What do you mean there's no island? There has to be. How else can we find the clue to the next cache site?" She pulled her compass from her satchel. "If there's no island then what do you call all that green ahead with the yellow dot in the center?"

"A cloud of eyes," he said blankly. "And they're guarding the next pearl."

Kaya said nothing, her eyes flitting up and back down again. "They are all green," she commented resignedly with one final stroke of the oar.

"So how does it feel when you touch an Ojo?" Iris asked, bracing himself.

"I don't know. Professor Shadowflame never said."

A brief pause. "Do you think Chamaeleon would help?" No answer. "I mean, would they be able to see us if we're invisible?"

"I doubt it, but they'll definitely see us the moment we reach for the photobead," Kaya replied.

"We don't have any other options, though. It's not like the Flareshot would help."

"No."

"Well, let's make a few extra, then—just in case." Iris tugged at the light he sensed from beyond the foliage to form a collection of five sentinel Chamaeleons. Kaya did the same.

"Are we still on course with the cache?" Kaya asked, animating her final sentinel.

"Dead on." Iris took a deep breath and lifted his head, eyes closed. "Are we ready?"

Kaya nodded. "Sí."

"On three, then. Uno, dos, tres."

Just as Kaya and Iris opened their eyes their figures vanished, leaving the image of an abandoned boat drifting lifelessly through a mist of searching jade eyes. It was all Iris could do not to flinch away and betray his position to the unremitting watchers. Even Kaya's hand lay frozen, gripping the canoe edge tightly. Both strained to stabilize their breathing, but neither was prepared for the sensation the Ojos caused upon direct contact with the skin.

Kaya jerked, gasping as an icy charge of frozen electricity shot through her arm and across her cheek simultaneously. With a cringe Iris twisted his ears together, the nerves numbing as each subsequent sphere brushed his fur. A flicker of reason compelled them to consider their sentinels, and before the Ojos could much more than focus upon the outlines of the girl and the hare, both disappeared once more. Kaya and Iris locked their jaws as a shudder ran through the optical cloud, its verdant pupils searching for the two pairs of now missing eyes. Although the stinging touch of the watchers brought tears to their cheeks, neither Kaya nor Iris moved again.

When the cache finally appeared, Kaya and Iris plunged their fists into the hollow of a stump, retracting a pair of goldenrod pearls in their tightly locked fists. That same subarctic charge shocked their blood as a thousand pupils suddenly fused to their frames, exponentially magnifying the pain. Kaya screamed and the pearl slipped from her grip, splashing into the water.

"Cover your eyes and crouch down!" Iris yelled feverishly as he dropped to the floor of the canoe, his photobead clasped firmly in his paw.

Kaya immediately followed suit; but in her haste she hit the oar, knocking it, too, from the vessel. Yet this mattered little—for the icy pain surmounted any worries beyond those of the present moment.

"They're killing me!" she screeched as the watchers raked her vertebrae, willing her to glance up.

"No! They'll leave! They have to!" Iris screamed, his words digging into the grains of the floor. "We're not doing anything to draw their attention!"

Tremors began to quake throughout Kaya's body, her lungs struggling for breath as she coughed uncontrollably. The chills swiftly dissipated and altogether vanished from Iris's body, lending him the awareness to note that Kaya's condition was worsening. He dared to glance up, and what he found scared him.

Despite the fact that they had successfully left the Ojo nebula behind, a blanket of the astringent orbs had settled over the girl. Iris took quick action. Aiming his wand at the sky, he called down several thick streams of light to improvise a sheet of photons, which he slid between the Ojos and Kaya in an attempt to insulate her entire body. Snapping his wand up again, Iris lifted the Ojos into the air, and with a twirl he sealed the sheet, sending it listlessly away, the imprisoned Lumorphi struggling vainly to escape.

"Kaya?" Iris asked, his words sliding hesitantly up her still trembling back. "Are you—alright?"

The muscles lining Kaya's spine drew taut and her body froze. "You dirty little freak!" she screeched as she whipped her head up. Features livid, Kaya stared pupil to pupil with a lone Ojo. She immediately grabbed the creature in her fist and pitched it through the air until it whirled to a halt several feet in front of of the boat. Kaya wasted little time in exacting justice—in a flurry of wand and wrist movements she produced the Flareshot, hitting her mark with lethal aim. Her chest rose and fell heavily as she watched her tormentor sink into the placid waters, the circle of her retribution complete only when a voracious eel had swallowed the withered Ojo in one swift gulp.

Iris seemed to encounter extreme difficulty in closing his jaw. "So was that thing…?"

"Trapped beneath my face?" Kaya finished, the glacier in her shoulders crumbling. "Sí. It's the reason why the rest of the blasted demons wouldn't leave me alone."

A difficult swallow. "And how did you grab it in your hand like that without flinching?"

Kaya cleared her throat as she called down a stream of photons to craft a replacement oar. "Let's just say I can now sympathize with Manny's hatred for the Ojos." She stabbed the newly formed, pearl-toned oar into the water, then propelled their conversation forward. "How far to our next cache? I need to know what direction to head."

***

"Your nose is bleeding."

Manny shook his head, stunned. "What happened?" he asked, raising a shaky hand to prevent another drop of plasma from staining his shirt. His nose began to throb painfully.

"You got smacked in the face," Tobias answered, throwing a leery gaze at the tightly knit forest looming at his side.

"By what?"

Brun set penetrating eyes on the silent wood rising before them like a host of oversized peppermint sticks. "A bamboo stalk."

"That doesn't make any sense," Manny groaned as he strained to his feet. "I don't remember running into one."

"That would be because it ran into you, in a manner of speaking," Brun said quietly. "But to be exact, it leaned forward and cracked you between the eyes."

"Boy, did it," Tobias mused.

Manny blinked, attempting to reconcile this information with his still-bleeding nose. "I—but that's impossible. Bamboo can't move."

"Battle Bamboo can," Brun amended, his brow raised toward the expectant forest. "It's a common plant Lumorph in tropical regions."

"A Lumorph…" Manny repeated, his brow furrowing. "Then why haven't I heard of it yet?"

"Possibly because you failed to complete the bonus reading Professor Shadowflame assigned last week. She said it might help us with our photocaching today." Brun's words goaded Manny slightly.

I really need to start listening at the end of class.

"So how do we get past them?" Tobias glanced up from his compass to the hollowed trunk of a tree embedded ten or so meters within the bamboo flanks. "My CPS reads the cache is inside that tree there."

Brun swallowed, then continued his discourse as if Tobias had not spoken. "It appears that the cache has been planted in the base of the ant nest just ahead. But Manny, we can't just go waltzing in through the bamboo or we'll both end up with broken jaws."

Tobias crossed his arms; he hated being ignored, and even more so because this treatment was becoming customary from someone who normally addressed him with the respect of an equal. The otter was certain he had done nothing to offend Brun; but in spite of this his one-time friend would not even acknowledge his help. 'I may not have a wand,' Tobias thought, 'but there's no reason he couldn't have let me grab that first cache while he and Manny distracted the peccaries back in the Flooded Forest. But—oh no—he had to do it himself using Manny as bait while I sat behind and watched.' Tobias turned his head thoughtfully. 'He's not totally lost, though. After all, he did grab a pearl for me. I'll keep trying. Maybe he is just having a bad day.'

"…saying there's a thin path we can follow between the bamboo?" Manny continued, gesturing toward the wood.

Brun nodded in reply.

"But one wrong turn and—"

"Professor Bluebolt may have to cure us for cranial fractures," Brun finished.

Manny analyzed the forest, the menace of the bamboo ever present in his mind as he traced invisible paths through the regimented stalks. *For some reason I don't think trial and error would be an effective strategy to the cache. I don't want to act as the guinea pig, at least. Then how…?* "What can we do? I can't see any way through this mess that doesn't necessitate broken bones."

"Professor Shadowflame said that the solution to nearly every photocache challenge can be found in the seeker's surroundings," Brun said, quietly calculating as he scrutinized the area. **We just need to open our eyes a bit wider…**

"You did say that hollowed out tree was an ants' nest, didn't you?" Tobias asked, his question disturbing Brun's musings. The boy flexed his hand but did not respond.

"Sí, it's a light ant nest," Manny answered, eyeing the trunk but spying no such specimen. "¿Por qué?"

"Well, there's a nest up the river from our hovel, and Ursa and I sometimes see a group of ants carrying a load of sugarcane back to their tree. You know, they're pretty strong for such little insects—it only takes three to—"

"How does any of that help us?" Brun interrupted, his words bordering on surly.

Tobias rocked back on his paws, startled that Brun had addressed him directly. "I—I mean, do either of you have anything sweet? You know, like candy?"

Candy?

"I still don't get your point, Tobias, but yes. I packed a few Jasmine Honeydrops in case we came across any Amazon Horned Frogs," Manny corresponded benevolently.

"Those would be perfect!" Tobias slid his CPS into a leather pouch at his waist. "Toss me one!"

"Whatever you say." Manny smiled slightly at the otter's energy as the boy pulled a drop from his pocket and placed it in his friend's paw. Like lightning the otter pierced the drop with a claw then quickly began to drizzle the candy's amber contents over the ground before him. When the drop had been emptied, Tobias laid it in the center of the now gooey grass. He then crossed his arms and fixed his emerald eyes on the lifeless trunk locked away among the bamboo.

The otter had waited no more than five seconds before his efforts were rewarded: from the trunk's hollow shell appeared a three-studded, golden carapace, its antennae twitching momentarily as it tasted the the air's now saccharine scent. With a click of its pincers the insect scurried down the trunk, hastening in its hunt as its six spiny legs met the ground, carrying it deftly and succinctly through the bamboo labyrinth, without so much as disturbing a single stalk.

"Do you see now?" Tobias asked, gazing down at the ant before him. With two satisfied clicks the insect began devouring the spilt honey, working its way in a spiral toward the vacant drop in the center of the bait.

Manny's eyes followed the ravenous ant. "I see that he's hungry."

"Clever," Brun murmured, throwing a glance at the otter. Manny looked puzzled, so Brun turned to explain. "The Honeydrop lured the ant from the nest, correct?" Manny nodded. "So, as we just saw, the ant knows how to maneuver through the bamboo without being smashed. When he has finished eating, he should carry the Honeydrop back to his nest; and then we can trail him to the cache."

"Está bien," Manny said slowly, his eyes wary, "but did you see how fast this little sucker shot through the bamboo? I can't trail him at that speed. One wrong turn and I'm sure to end up with a set of broken ribs."

Brun cocked his head. "True."

"Your nose is bleeding again," Tobias cut in.

Manny mumbled a muffled, "Gracias," as his hand flew up to stave off the flow.

"That's why I'm the one who's going," Tobias affirmed after a pause. "I'm smaller than the two of you; I can turn corners faster and sharper as well. It shouldn't be difficult at all."

Brun inhaled deeply. **This should be interesting.**

"Just don't take a wong tune," Manny half-garbled as he wiped more blood from his face.

"Don't worry." Tobias tightened the leather belt that held his compass pouch to his side just as the ant reached the honeydrop. "I won't." And with that the otter dropped to all fours, shifting his weight in anticipation as the ant lifted the drop onto its back, the golden color of the bug's body and the candy making the tiny creature appear similar to an insectal camel. Tobias had little time to contemplate the ant's aesthetics, however, as the sweet toothed insect suddenly bolted away through the grass. The otter's muscles reacted instinctively, propelling him forward as the ant whipped aside and delved into the bamboo.

Catching up to his prey with a snap of speed, Tobias exerted extreme caution to follow no further behind the creature than three full ant lengths. The otter was admittedly surprised to discover the number of u-turns incorporated into this challenge; at one point, when their course brought them dangerously near the very stalk that had battered Manny's nose, Tobias became worried that perhaps the ant was leading him into a trap. But at the last second the insect performed yet another swiveling turn, dashing straight for its nest. Several seconds later the stitched pattern of bamboo shadows gave way to the strangely cylindrical haven of the light ants.

Tobias ground to a halt at the foot of a towering tree, now only a shell of its former glory, its innards long since devoured. "I wouldn't want to live in there," he muttered, unfastening his pouch and withdrawing his compass as the ant slid lithely down the hole in the tree's hollow heart. "Better have a quick look to see if I was right about the cache site." Tobias tapped the screen of his CPS, zooming in on his present location. Among the whirlwind of bamboo, two alternating dots—one green, the other amethyst—superseded the space where the tree should have been. "Right on the mark."

"What are you standing around for?" Brun carped, his words evading the belligerent stalks. "Our goal is to reach the photocache before the others do—not stand around and sightsee. Move it!"

"Just lay off already," Tobias grumbled as he set down his compass and began searching the base of the tree. A quick peek inside the trunk's crevice revealed little more than ant tracks and wood chips. "Suppose I'll scour the outside." Yet the exterior roots proved fruitless as well.

"¡Án-da-le!" Brun beleaguered, taking care to enunciate each syllable.

Tobias growled, his whiskers rigid. He swept the backside of the trunk with his gaze, his eyes stopping over a peculiar pocket just a hair larger than his paw. "You can't be serious." He stared into the somehow venomous darkness of the hole before him. "They can't expect me to reach my paw in there—what if there's a tarantula? Or a snake?"

"Okay, Tobias—here's the deal. I'll run to the Café and grab us each a coffee. I'll make sure to put extra crema on yours, so please, take your time. We're not in a hurry or anything." The sarcasm in Brun's words made the otter's hackles stand on end.

"¡Cállate!" he barked as he scrambled pointlessly for a stick. "How can there be no sticks—I'm in the center of a forest!" He snarled in frustration, cursing the mystery thief who had stolen his wand. "Enough of this," he rasped, pounding the bark above the hole in hopes of scaring out whatever poisonous creature waited inside. Yet the otter nearly fell forward when the dried skin of the tree crumbled and caved beneath his fist, which by consequence allowed a shaft of light to manifest the pale sheen of lavender pearls.

"Huh," Tobias muttered, his whiskers bristling into a wry smile as he discarded the aftermath of his tantrum. "That worked out better than planned."

"Well, I'm back with—"

"Oh, shut up already!" Tobias roared, his words stripping the nearby bamboo of their bark. "I've got the photobeads and I'm—"

A rock pierced the otter's lower stomach lining, his words escaping in a wisp. "Where is my CPS?" Tobias spun around, dropping the photobeads in shock as he ricocheted forward, his claws desperately outstretched toward the compass now half-submerged in the ant colony's entry hole.

"No you don't!" Tobias bayed, his paws clamping on the golden tool and prying it from the ground's gaping mouth. No fewer than three ants dangled from the opposite end. He shook them off, watching as they splayed through the air, bounding off the inner bowels of the tree and landing back on the ground with a vehement clicking.

"Phoenix and fox tails," the otter yelped, stumbling backward in disbelief. Twenty, now at least thirty ants had come pouring from the ground, their jaws clacking as they advanced on the barbaric creature that had attacked their clan.

As he turned to run Tobias tripped on the pearls, sending him awkwardly to his stomach. Fear, however, combined with ionized adrenaline, have been known to work miracles, as was Tobias's case. In less than a second he managed to scoop up all three photobeads (which he stowed safely in his pouch) and tear halfway along the labyrinth's initial straightaway without so much as blinking.

"What's wrong?" Manny called, his shoulders tensing as he witnessed Tobias hurtling through the maze on three legs, his fourth suspending the compass, which his eyes never left. Tobias executed a life or death u-turn just a meter from the boys' feet, without even

566

flickering a response. But no words of protest escaped Manny's mouth—they could not have if he had tried. The thousands of battle-ready ants now surging from the distant tree had rendered the boy's palate a verbal desert.

Even Brun had nothing to say as, merely three seconds later, Tobias exploded from the foliage.

The otter did not pause as he rocketed out beyond the boys, deftly pocketing his CPS as he continued his marathon across the expansive training field. After a moment the boys caught up to him, the breath ripping through their lungs.

"Close call," Manny managed to mutter after a minute.

"You're—tellin' me," Tobias grunted between gasps, his legs carrying him pell mell across the grass. "If it weren't for that—backtrack feature—I'd have been a goner."

***

"Ooh—nice catch."

Iris cradled the overly soft mango to his chest, nimbly sidestepping a very brown clump of bananas that exploded across the ground at his feet.

"Okay," Kaya grunted as she dodged the squashy splash of a tangerine. "Toss it here and I'll handle the rest."

A ripe chunk of starfruit grazed the hare's leg as he lobbed his prize to Kaya. A chortle floated down from the canopy to their right, and Iris's ears stiffened. "Just hurry it up," he said through his teeth. "I'm not particularly fond of this place, as you may recall."

Kaya evaded a formidable pineapple grenade, launching one of her own back at their attackers. "You can be thankful for one thing, at least—Archer isn't here this time. With any luck he's halfway around the world and never coming back."

"Maybe in the perfect worl—watch out!"

A golden bullet tore through the air, its mark set on the girl's temple. Kaya reacted just in time, catching the tiny sun sphere in her free hand. "Ace in the hole," she chuckled, pulling back her other arm to pitch the mango into the exact clump of leaves from which the photobead had come.

"Or better yet," Kaya continued as she picked up the string of their conversation, "perhaps a yet undiscovered Lumorph will catch him from behind and totally devour him—now that would be a special service to the world." Kaya crouched to avoid a lopsided papaya. "Probably die of indigestion, though."

"My turn!" Iris shouted, exploding from the ground to snatch the second pearl as it zipped over the girl's head. He performed a mid-air somersault before landing several hops ahead of Kaya. In no time he had inserted the cache into the CPS attached to his tawny satchel. "I'm outta here!" he roared, tearing away up the path.

A loose plantain caught Kaya's heel as she turned to follow. "No talent, idiot fruitsnake," she grumbled as the fruit's flesh slid down into her shoe, causing every other stride to feel slimy and unstable. She very nearly fell as she turned the corner to leave the war-zone of the serpents' territory.

"You didn't twist your ankle, did you?" Iris asked as Kaya dropped to the ground with a grimace. She slid off her shoe with a nasty squelch.

"No," she quipped as brown sludge eeked from her shoe. A moment later she pulled her compass from her pocket and pounded the golden pearl into its faceplate. "Where's the next stupid cache?"

Nope--she's fine. Iris lifted his CPS and tapped it with his amaranth wand. "From the looks of it, we should find the third cache just off the Plaza, in the—what building is that? The LRC?"

"Sí. The map shows the Carina running through it, so it has to be that one." Kaya's voice was calmer as she donned her now slime-free footwear. "Vámonos."

The hare and the girl resumed their brisk pace as they followed the path, worried that perhaps the few photocachers whom they had encountered may have overtaken them in some way. After all, who could guess at the skill and speed of their competition? Would the sun beetle remain untouched when they arrived at the photocache site, or would their efforts—particularly those exerted against the Ojos—have been in vain? Only a moment had passed before they left the path, setting determined feet on the West Road. Yet what they encountered brought them to an abrupt halt.

"¡Hola, muchachos!" Manny called, flanked on either side by Tobias and Brun. "¿Cómo va el photocache?"

"Oh, just fine, thanks," Iris replied, slightly guarded. "What about yours? How far along are you?"

"Ours is doing great!" Manny corresponded as he came to a relaxed stop. "We're already heading for our third cache at the Argo D—Ow!"

A sharp elbow from Brun interrupted Manny's candid report. "What do you think you're doing?"

"It's called conversation, Brun," Manny riposted, rubbing his now sore ribs. "Try it sometime."

"But what if they're seeking the same photocache?" Brun growled. "We don't want to tip them off."

Tobias rolled his eyes. "We're hunting the majestic beetle. "¿Y ustedes?"

Iris and Kaya's shoulders relaxed. "Not that one," Kaya said, her anxiety relieved.

"Which, then?" Brun snapped.

Kaya's mood changed instantly. "Listen here, buster," she swelled, her words stabbing Brun in the chest a millisecond before her finger did, "I can't guess at where this sour attitude is coming from, but I'll tell you this—I won't put up with it. López and Greenriver may be pushovers, but I'm not. And one more thing," she continued, pointing her wand at Brun's face, "You are no jerk. So whatever's bugging you, deal with it. It's not our fault your life sucks today." With one final, threatening glare, Kaya turned and stomped away toward the Plaza. "Iris, come on."

Iris shrugged at Tobias and Manny, then turned and hopped away, leaving his three friends behind in an awkward silence. By the time he caught up with Kaya, they were both entering the Plaza.

"You know, Kaya, your subtleties are something we should all learn to emulate," Iris said, his sarcasm slapping her in the leg.

"Oh, shove it," she rattled, a smile tugging at her cheek. They walked quietly for a moment, the Brethren's elaborate mansion sliding by to their right. "You do know I only tell people what they need to hear, right?"

Iris's ears slapped his back. "No doubt about that," he mumbled blandly.

Little more was said as they continued across the Plaza, meandering through the hustle and bustle of Lumens running errands, visiting friends and—to Iris and Kaya's renewed discomfort—holding animated discussions regarding the day's photocaching progress. When they overheard more than one of their peers discussing the sun beetle, their casual hop-steps changed into an increasingly tense jog and weave. As Kaya dashed alongside the Carina through the arched mouth of the library's marble façade, Iris vaulted in one desperate bound to the circulation desk, mounting the dais and the counter in two successive leaps.

"May I help you, young Señor Firefoot?" Melinda Brightwing inquired, her antennae twitching in irritation at the hare's less than discreet appearance into her workspace. Kaya held back, resting her hand nonchalantly against a nearby pillar.

"Mi amiga and I are photocaching, and our latest clue has lead us to the LRC," Iris explained, quickly trying to regain the blue morpho's esteem. "Consequently, I thought it would be best to consult with you as to which direction we should proceed, seeing as how the library is your domain and all."

Melinda shifted her wings pensively as she considered Iris's words. "That was—wise of you," she uttered finally, her wings undulating up and down slowly. "Of the ten or so students who have already entered to search for the cache—"

"Ten?" Iris breathed.

"Sí," she replied, her antennae twitching again. "But, as I was saying, you are the first of your peers with enough sense to stop and ask for directions as opposed to blindly attacking the stacks."

"Are you saying none of them have found the cache yet?"

"Of course not!" she laughed. "But be wary—the advice I am obliged to share is limited." Kaya began thrumming the pillar loudly, her patience waning. Melinda's wings stiffened, freezing in place.

"She would not happen to be the friend you spoke of, would she?" The butterfly threw Kaya an icy glare.

Iris's head snapped around to Kaya's figure. "Sí. ¿Por qué?"

"I will not delve into the particulars, but that young lady nearly smashed my brother, Treble, last fall during their Art class. She's dangerous, Iris. A budding criminal, most likely. In the future you may want to reconsider the company you keep."

"Thanks," he replied, a bit contrite. "I'll keep that in mind." He paused for effect. "Now what was that advice you had for me?"

"Oh! Sorry about that!" Melinda's wings relaxed and budded to life as she shot up from the counter. With the snap of her antennae a tiny notepad appeared, sliding to a stop less that a hair from Iris's feet. "These are Mr. and Mrs. Arrowpaw's instructions: 'Find these books and the location of the next cache will be revealed with pinpoint accuracy.'"

The hare's violet eyes traced over the elegant letters that seemed to carve themselves across the notepad. That's effective. "Am I permitted to use the PDS to find them?"

"I can tell you nothing further," Melinda replied, tearing the sheet from the pad and placing it in the hare's paws with a nod of her antennae. "But if I were you, I would strive to be more discreet in your hunting." Her eyes glinted. "You draw attention to yourself by rushing around and bounding onto counters. Try to appear easygoing, or you'll give yourself away."

"Gracias, Melinda," Iris whispered, flipping lithely from the counter. "You're a real help."

"De nada," she corresponded, hovering in place. "Good luck."

Iris beckoned toward Kaya as he hopped gingerly to a pillar just beyond the counter. Sunlight splashed against his pecan fur as he climbed a short series of steps to reach the wooden platform and screen attached to the pillar.

Kaya laid her hand on the platform and stared at the screen. "What was all that about? Did she talk about me?"

"Let's just say your subtleties have a far-reaching impact," he answered, sliding his wand from his ear. "You are aware that Treble is Melinda's brother, aren't you?"

"Little snipe." Kaya's eyes solidified as she remembered the antagonistic red morpho.

"But enough about that…" Iris mumbled, tapping the screen with his wand.

"Welcome to the Photon Decimal System," a woman's voice coolly greeted. "Please pass your wand through the screen for verifica—Buenas tardes, Iris Renée Firefoot."

"Good afternoon," he replied, tapping the screen a second time.

"Speak voice command," the PDS stated.

Kaya interposed. "Iris, what are you doing? We don't have time for this."

"I'll be finished in un minut—"

The screen flashed. "I could not process your request, please repeat your command."

Iris's eyes dropped to the paper in his paw. "Please retrieve two books. One—*Achernar's Tricks to Successful Lightboarding.* Two—*The Secret Life of a Vagrant Star.*"

"Processing—please wait." A sapphire tentacle emerged from the screen, worming up through the air to snag a velvet volume from the west wall. Seconds later the tentacle snaked back, laying the onyx tome at Iris's feet.

"Shall I place the first book on hold for you?" the PDS asked.

Iris very nearly swallowed his tongue. "On hold? Y-you mean you don't have it?"

"No. It has been checked out."

"Checked out?" Iris croaked.

"Indeed. Please speak your—"

"Hold on," Kaya interposed, grabbing the hare's arm. "Are you telling me we need that book to find the third cache?"

"Yes!" Iris rebounded, his fur frazzled. "Otherwise we might as well return to the Flooded Forest and start over!"

A crimson tone suddenly flushed Kaya's burnt almond cheeks. "I-I know who has the book."

Iris blinked in stunned incredulity. "¿Quién?"

With a look of shame Kaya slid her backpack from her shoulders, unzipped it and withdrew a thick, red-crested book, along the spine of which was written in elegant gold script, *Achernar's Tricks to Successful Lightboarding* by Achernar Westlight. She swallowed ruefully.

"Why in the blue world do you have this?"

"It's none of your business," Kaya murmured, her eyes skipping along the blue and silver tiled floor.

"Whatever," he muttered, stuffing the paper in his satchel and taking the book in both paws. "PDS, dissolve." The blue screen melted away as Iris slapped the heavy volume beside the other at his feet. "What do we do now?"

"How am I supposed to know?" Kaya replied, though not harshly. "What did the snipe's sister tell you?"

Iris racked his brain for a moment. "Uh, she said something to the effect that these books will show us the cache with—uh—pinpoint accuracy."

"How are lightboarding and a tasteless novel about a star supposed to help us?" Kaya frowned at the black volume entitled, *The Secret Life of a Vagrant Star* by Makar del Sur. "I am not about to read that ugly looking soap opera."

"Maybe we don't have to..." Iris said wistfully. "Melinda said we'd only have to find them, not read them."

The two friends ruminated on this point for a moment. Iris glanced up as Kaya drew a sharp breath.

"Pinpoint accuracy?" she asked spiritedly, a spark in her eyes as she lifted the red volume to run her finger along its spine. "That's what she said, word for word?"

"Sí," Iris nodded. "I'm sure of it."

"Then look here," Kaya said excitedly, her finger tracing the byline. "This book's author is Achernar Westlight, a world renowned lightboarding instructor—despite the fact that he's a centaur and never set hoof on a board."

Now came Iris's turn to glare. "And...?"

"And even though he goes by Achernar, his last name is Westlight. Get it? West-light?"

The hare gaped at her. Has she cracked?

He is so dense! "Okay, look here below." Kaya pointed at the reference number under the byline. "It's 75.4357 and his last name is West-light. It's a coordinate!"

"No way!" Iris grabbed the spine and pulled the book close to his face. His eyes skipped back and forth between the byline and reference number. "Pinpoint accuracy... increíble," he whispered. "Then the other book—"

"Must have the southern coordinate!" Kaya finished.

"Iris stood the book up, leaning it against the pillar. "There's no doubt about it! Makar del Sur—'del Sur' means 'from the South'!" His eyes shot to the reference number: 5.7986. "So we can just enter these coordinates in the CPS and, *Bam!*, we go straight to the cache?"

"I think so." Kaya smiled as she slid the pink beads from her glistening hair and transformed them into a stylus. She then pulled the thin compass from her pocket and began scribbling the coordinates on her screen. Seconds laster the CPS flashed, displaying a smaller golden dot next to the large, gilded image of the library.

Iris's eyes snapped up, scanning his peers' rushing forms as they scoured the library in vain. "It's not in here," he breathed, glancing around the pillar and through the South Archway. "It's just outside."

"How clever, hiding the hints to the cache right in front of our faces..." Kaya returned her book to her backpack. "Vamos."

"Waitaminute," Iris breathed. "We don't want to leave half the directions just lying here on the platform." A pause. "PDS, initiate auto-return of *The Secret Life of a Vagrant Star*."

The screen rematerialized as a snaking arm caught the book, then drew it up through the air to the empty slot high upon the west wall.

"Thank you," Iris stated, his ears twitching. "Have a nice day."

"And you," replied the female voice as the screen assumed an empty blue.

"Do you want to ride on my shoulder?" Kaya asked, CPS in hand.

"No. We'll look less conspicuous if we split up and exit separately," he directed, stowing away his CPS. "And you'd better put that away or the others might follow you out the door."

"Good point." The girl slid the compass into her back pocket. "See you outside."

Kaya crossed the Carina to traverse the far side of the resource center, while Iris skimmed the western perimeter, pausing in front of the stacks occasionally to eye the books. Despite his feigned interest, he never allowed Kaya's relaxed form to escape his gaze, seamlessly tracing her steps through the corner of his eyes as she zigzagged across the building. He noted when she lingered beside a coffee table to flip through a magazine, then watched as she tossed her hair and gazed at the westering sun through the crystal ceiling. A few moments later she turned and loped casually through the arch; upon which time Iris executed his own surreptitious exit.

"Took you long enough," she quipped as Iris drew up parallel to her along the opposite side of the river.

The hare ignored her comment, continuing forward at a leisurely hop. He noticed that Kaya was carrying her compass in her hand. "Your side or my side?" he asked, avoiding specifics so as not to pique the curiosity of the readers seated below the nearby palm trees.

Kaya grinned broadly.

Her side. Iris sighed as he scanned the water for the nearest crossing, locating a moon lily path just twenty or so hops ahead. He crossed in less than a minute, plodding on ahead of Kaya as he surveyed the landscape, reflecting upon where the Arrowpaws may have hidden the cache. To his left were various tropical trees, which with each successive hop bent closer and closer to a small pond girded by a latticework path of ferns and flowers. Iris nodded as he continued forward. *That's where it is.*

"Hold up, Firefoot," Kaya chastised. "You know it's rude not to wait."

The hare halted abruptly, turned, and crooked an ear toward her, a smile on his lips. "Please forgive my discourtesy, oh mistress of pleasantries."

She raised an eyebrow, her teeth glinting in a reciprocal gesture as she walked by. "Go jump in a lake."

"What about a pond?" laughed Iris as he rocketed off the ground and up onto her shoulder, grasping a pawful of hair to stabilize himself.

"You little twerp! That hurts!" With a flash of her hand Kaya managed to catch her cargo off guard, snagging his ankle and sweeping him through the air to dangle upside down at arm's length, his ears nearly slapping her knees. She bit back both laughter and tears as she watched Iris hang in midair, several strands of her hair still in his paw.

Iris crossed his arms. "This isn't exactly comfortable."

"Look who's talking, head hunter."

The hare glared at her. "Put me down, Kaya."

"¡Sí, señor!" She released Iris and jumped back to avoid the splash as the hare met the water in a full head butt. She laughed hysterically as Iris struggled to right himself, gasping for air as he snapped his head back, his gummy ears launching a thick string of moss that landed with a dull *plop* halfway across the water.

As the hare wiped algae from his eyes, a pair of lethal violet daggers pierced Kaya's face and chest.

She stopped laughing abruptly, all humor gone, and then dropped to the soggy bank in a tight crouch. "Iris, get out of the water." Her voice was stiff.

"Did it ever occur to you," he began, swinging his satchel through the air and releasing it as it landed with a horrid squelch beside the girl, "that I just may enjoy this?" His fierce scowl and crossed arms betrayed his words.

Kaya's eyes shifted suddenly. "Iris, hop out right now."

The violet daggers sharpened to lances. "Kaya Bellastrata, what makes you think—H-hey! Let go of me!" The hare kicked and scratched to break free from the girl's sudden and uncouth grip on his ears. Kaya let him down roughly over his satchel, cradling her arm and shielding herself from his teeth.

"Dang it, Iris! Why'd you have to go and slit my arm open?!" she hissed, her eyes fixed on the blood now streaming down her wrist.

Iris sat flabbergasted, his wet ears dripping. "I'm sorry, Kaya, but what else was I supposed to do? You threw me in a lake and then nearly ripped my ears off!"

"You're overreacting," she muttered as she slid the tulip beads from her midnight tresses, transforming the tiny spheres into a box from which she extracted her embroidered handkerchief and a large bandage.

I'm overreacting?! "You hypocrite! What gives you the right to go around walking all over everybody and then expect me to shed a tear when you scratch your arm? Your logic's cracked, Kaya!"

You're the one who scratched my arm. And it's a pond, not a lake. Kaya took a calming breath. "Look, Iris, I saved your life."

Iris spread his arms in incredulity. "¿De qué hablas?"

Kaya slapped the bandage on her arm. "I'm talking about the Blue Dancers that were headed straight for you. If I hadn't pulled you out, you'd be sucking dirty water through your lungs at the bottom of the pond this very moment. How would you have liked that?"

The hare's anger faltered as his pupils scoured the surface of the water, a knot forming in his throat as he noted a trail of ripples a meter or so from where he sat. He squirmed uncomfortably as he watched the ripples hook sharply in the direction of a dragonfly hovering only an inch above the water. Just as the ripples drew near to the insect, they stopped. With fantastic speed a sapphire tarantula burst from the water, enshrouding its prey in a pliable fishnet before dragging it beneath the surface. Iris stared, open-jawed, at the place where the dragonfly had been only a second before.

Kaya shut the box with a snap, rethreading her plait through the beads. She turned to Iris and raised her eyebrows. "What?"

"Y-you were telling the truth," he stammered.

"Of course I was!" she snapped. "I'm no liar!" A pause. "But I am sorry for dropping you in the pond. That was foolish of me. You never know what might be lurking in the water around here, especially during flood season."

Iris swallowed hard as he listened to the steady rhythm of water droplets trickling down from the tips of his ears to slap his satchel. His stomach knotted. "I don't suppose the next photobead is in the bottom of this pond, is it?" he asked darkly. Kaya nodded, her head tilted slightly as she considered the hare. He shivered. *Why did I agree to do this in the first place?*

"Don't worry, squirt," she encouraged, rubbing the wet mop between the hare's ears. "There's a solution to every problem, if you look hard enough, that is."

I just hope that solution doesn't involve substantial amounts of pain and suffering.

A calm silence settled along the bank. Kaya took a deep breath, releasing a mournful sigh. "I guess snorkeling's out."

"Well, I should say," Iris chuckled, his mood lightening.

Kaya smiled, then turned her eyes back to the muddy water. *Those little snots aren't keeping my photobead.* "When faced with an enemy with whom you need to make peace, what do you do first?" she asked thoughtfully.

Iris blinked, befuddled. "I don't know. I haven't really had that many enemies."

"You give him a present," she replied, emphasizing the final word. "Say—do you have anything in your backpack a Blue Dancer might want?"

"Like what, live insects?" He paused. "No, Kaya, I left my pet dragonfly in my other satchel." She stared at him blankly. "And I am not about to act as bait."

"That would be ridiculous," she retorted, pulling her own satchel around to her lap. "We need to please our foe, not trick him." Kaya withdrew a cobalt-bound book and began flipping through its

578

ample indices. "You wouldn't happen to remember the Blue Dancer's favorite food, would you?"

"I know it's a fish," he replied helpfully.

That sure narrows things down. Kaya slid her finger down the page to the name of the tarantula then flipped to the section related to Amazonian arachnids. She caught a brief glimpse of the large-bodied crystal spider before prodding the glossy photo of its lesser sapphire brother. *Ah-ha.* "'Although the Blue Dancer maintains a virtually balanced diet of piscivorous and insectivorous means, this aquatic arachnid holds a particular weakness for the Piranha Dorada, a piranha and goldfish hybrid created by both Rei and Eider. Photobiologists attribute this fusing of the species to...'" Kaya's voice trailed away as she softly closed the book. "So where do we find this Piranha Dorada?"

Iris sat in silence as he wrung his ears dry. "I should guess it's nearby, if that fish is truly the key to coercing the pearls from the Dancers."

Kaya stood up absentmindedly. "We're not coercing, Iris—I already told you that we're forming an alliance." She scanned the lay of the land, disregarding the propinquity of the tree line as her eyes jumped over the Carina River and rifled through the lush grass beyond. *That has to be it!* "¡Venga, Iris! Come on!"

"But my satchel's still wet!"

"Just leave it," she called from beneath the trellis. "We'll be back in a moment."

She is giddier than a gopher on Groundhog's Day. "Hold on!" he shouted, chasing her up the river to the lily pad crossing, then rounding back toward a thick wall of grass on the other side. "Whoa." The hare burst through the undergrowth, his eyes reflecting a shimmering pool of the clearest blue, inside of which teamed hundreds of golden fish. *Nice!*

Kaya swiftly slid the tulip beads from her sable hair. As her wand coalesced into rod form, her palm commenced an elegant yet complex dance, propelling thousands of spools of coiling light to twist and weave in the air. Realizing her intention, Iris followed suit, emulating the art of her photokinesis with even more prowess and speed than she. Consequently, both friends ended in the same stroke, staring with pleasure at the intricate webbing floating before them. With a breath from their mouths the nets shuddered, rippling to life as they wound tightly around the young Lumens' wrists.

The corner of Iris's mouth rose in a grin. "You almost beat me that time, you know." He flexed his paw, sensing the dense ball of webbing just waiting to be thrown.

"You may be the Sentinel instructor's son," she began, her eyes darting among the golden medallions slicing through the water at her feet, "but one day I'll out-animate you—then you'll have no choice but to extol my expertise."

We'll see. "I've been working on Reticulum every night for the past two months—if you overtake me, it won't be on this sentinel."

Rather then reply, Kaya thrust her palm forward; Reticulum's compact webbing exploded from her fist, mimicking the curves of her fingers as it pierced the water and enswathed a piranha. Cupping her palm, she raised her prey into the sun-streaked air, satisfaction etched on her cheeks. "Beat that, Firefoot."

It's on. With a flash of his fist Iris sent forth his own sentinel, his eyes focused intently on his prey as the net ebbed across the water. Iris snapped his wrist and Reticulum plunged into the pond, withdrawing in less than a second to display a struggling piranha, its tail tightly vised between the digits of the scintillating net, making the sentinel look very much like a hot air balloon. "How about that, Mireille?"

Iris directed Reticulum through the air, bringing the pisciform's sharp teeth dangerously close to Kaya's nose. The piranha nipped once. "Concede that I won," he taunted. The piranha nipped again, this time grazing her nose. "Come on, say i—"

Fury detonated in Kaya's eyes as she slapped the piranha away from her face. She opened her palm, allowing her piranha to fall back down to the pond as well. Both fish hit the water with a symphonic pair of plops. Before Iris could realize what had transpired, he found himself hovering perilously over the center of the pond, the tips of his ears swaying just inches from the rippling water. His amaranth eyes reflected over the clear pool as the rapacious piranhas zipped along below.

Kaya held her hand high, her grip sure as she maintained the inverted hare like a string-puppet. "You, Iris Renee Firefoot, will neither call me by that name ever again, nor will you flaunt your self-perceived victories in my face," she said, the piranhas at her feet fleeing from the force of her voice. She jerked the hare up another foot. "Understood?"

"S-sí," Iris stuttered, the sunlight piercing his pupils as he stared toward Kaya.

What a fathead! He's acting just like López did on the first day I met him! "You'd better." Suddenly calm, Kaya guided the hare back to the shore, Reticulum unraveling from his ankle as she set him gently on the grass. "Now pick up your wand, straighten you ears, and get ready to move."

Shaken, Iris did as she directed, watching as Kaya netted another pair of Piranha Doradas. He was unsure where his own sentinel had gone. A moment later they bounded back across the Carina, then trudged carefully up to the pond that doubled as the Blue Dancers' hunting grounds.

"I'll just toss your piranha in for you, if you don't mind," Kaya voiced gently.

Iris nodded, saying quietly, "That's fine."

Kaya opened her fist, and the pair of golden fish fell toward the water. But before either could reach the surface, two blue arachnids burst from the water, each of their long, spindly sapphire legs encasing their prey with avarice. Iris jumped, bothered by the rapidity of the Dancers' strike. Kaya sat down next to him and patted his shoulder. "No worries, amigo."

But Iris still felt jittery. He did not like the sensation of being upside down twice in the span of only ten minutes, nor the fact that in both instances he dangled only feet from creatures who would very much have liked to have taken a significant chunk out of his heel. *But it's my fault for being cocky; at least the second time.*

Prior to the advent of any subsequent worries, a single, purposeful arrow cut across the pond, heading directly for the friends' perch and stopping less than a foot away. With an abrupt splash the pond vomited up a small sac, its silken wrapping enclosing a set of sunfire pearls.

"Care to do the honors?" Kaya reached over and set the webbing carefully at Iris's feet.

"Sure," he affirmed, slicing the bulge open with his improvised wand-knife. He handed Kaya her pearl and inserted his own into the CPS that he pulled from his still-soggy satchel.

"Looks like we're headed out toward Harmony Falls," she declared, considering Professor Bluebolt's teaching locale.

"Yep." Iris slid on his satchel, disliking the extra water weight.

Kaya eyed the hare benevolently. "You wouldn't want to ride on my shoulders on the way there, would you?"

Iris looked up, measuring the warmth in her eyes. "Actually, yes, if you wouldn't mind. I feel zapped all of a sudden."

"No problem." So, lifting the hare up onto the nape of her neck, she turned and jogged through the trellis, along the Carina, and away along a path that bordered the library.

Gracias, Kaya.

Mind of Shadow

"I wonder if anyone's ever dived from up here?"

Brun continued forward cautiously, silently mouthing each successive step. He shook his head, trying to both ignore and prevent all further verbal pondering from Manny. **Sixty-three, sixty-four, sixty-five...**

"Good question," commented Tobias, cartwheeling up the next pair of steps. "If someone actually did I'd bet you seven shells it was an otter."

"You never know," Manny replied brightly, gazing over the moonstone railing at the glistening water nearly a mile below. "A human could've done it." He ran his hand along the sheltered flank of the Argo Dock and gazed out over the seemingly diminutive Lake. *Would've hurt a heck of a lot, though.*

"One of the Brethren, maybe," corresponded the otter rather dubiously. "You humans just don't know how to mold your body for minimum water resistance."

Brun stopped short, clenching his fist in agitation. "How can the two of you keep count of the steps while chattering like a pair of fixated macaws?"

"It's easy, man," the other boy replied, slapping a slight hollow in the Argo Dock's balustrade.

"¡Sin duda!" Tobias exclaimed, stamping the step with his foot. "'Orbit thrice then climb the century stair,'" he recited, quoting the message from the scroll they had found concealed at the base of the tower. "It's obvious we've circled the dock three times on our way up. So now, if you've got a wise eye, you'll know I'm on step eighty-seven of the century stair!"

"And I'm on eighty-nine," Manny added casually.

Brun's brain throbbed. "Then I lost count. I thought we were already in the nineties."

"Not 'til we pass this little dip in the parapet." Manny slapped the hollow along the railing a second time.

"How's that?" Brun blinked, massaging his temples.

"You're thinking too hard, man!"

"For sure!" Tobias agreed, swatting the step with his tail. "Didn't you notice that every ten steps there's a square space etched out of the moonstone? That's the ninth one since we stopped a minute ago, and I'm three steps below it. Do the math! It's easier than crackin' scallops!"

One of Brun's hands fell to his side, while the other continued rubbing his temple. "Do you mean to tell me that I've been counting pointlessly like a blundering idiot?"

"Not in those words exactly..." Manny answered warily.

Tobias's sage eyes shone bright. "I look at it like this—some people would rather climb a wall with their fists than use the door. Maybe you're one of those people, Brun."

"Uh, not necessarily," Brun reflected, groggily attempting to debunk the otter's observation. "It's just that today—I mean, I guess I—"

"Have a lot on your mind?" Tobias finished affably. "It happens—no harm done to any party. Besides, friends overlook one another's shortcomings."

"Um, sure," Brun mumbled, still unable to express the pervasive uneasiness and—**Tension?**—that seemed to be corroding his nerves today. **I just can't focus...**

"Just eleven more steps, man," encouraged Manny, his honey eyes flashing. "Maybe this last clue will lead us straight to the photocache."

"Let's go, then," Brun half-grunted, trudging hazily up the stairs.

A moment later the trio reached the hundredth step. Tobias gazed up at the boys' sun and moon faces for a suggestion. "¿Y ahora qué?"

"Look for any flaws in the moonstone at the base of the step in case the photobeads have been hidden in a secret compartment," Manny directed.

Tobias readily obeyed, his paw tracing the adularescent blue stone, which seamlessly reflected the otter's twitching whiskers and sharp, perusing eyes.

"Brun, why don't you check the wall while I scan the railing?" Manny suggested. Brun shrugged, and they both set themselves to their respective tasks.

Within five seconds Manny spoke. "I think I found it." He tapped the dip in the rampart, the center of the rock reverberating in a hollow echo. "Maybe there's a panel or something…" he continued, sliding the tips of his fingers over the flawless moonstone, the rock unwilling to betray any fault. After a moment he gave up and began rapping the stone again.

Brun rubbed his eyes wearily, the obsidian ring on his hand flashing as it caught the sunlight. "Here, try this," he sighed, leaning forward and pressing down on the face of the moonstone. A rectangular panel, hinged at the center, swiveled down to reveal a shallow cavity housing a set of five amethyst pearls. Atop the pearls rested a tiny scroll, wound tightly and girded in the center with a band of lime-colored bamboo.

"¡Bien hecho!" Manny cheered as he reached into the cavity and procured the beads necessary to fuel their compasses. He ignored the scroll, though Brun did not.

Tobias tapped his claws impatiently against the rail wall. "Would either of you enlighten me as to what you found? I can't exactly see anything from down here."

Apologizing, Manny quickly obliged, while Brun scanned the papyrus-scratched message. When Manny had finished, Brun read the scroll aloud:

Much progress you have made — swatted the swine, conquered the carapace, topped the tower — yet one step — or flight, if prefer it you — remains. Should by ground you chose to tread, then insert the bead and trudge ahead. (Though if by land find you contrition, you may slide to your ambition.

"What-the-heck?" Manny ejected, his words piercing the paper.

"It's a riddle," Tobias reflected.

Manny shifted the pearls in his palm, two outer spheres orbiting a center sphere. He blinked and grasped the beads firmly. "It's not like it matters—I mean, we have the photobeads. All we have to do is insert them and then head straight for the photocache. No need to bother with the riddle."

"Maybe there is." Brun contemplated the dregs of the cavity, vacant now save two lone pearls. "I somehow doubt the Arrowpaws placed just five beads in this cache."

"Oh," voiced Tobias in realization. "That would be a problem."

"Are you saying we weren't the first to reach the cache?" Manny asked, annoyed by the idea that one or more of his peers had dared access the pearls before he.

Brun nodded. "And by the lay of the riddle, one would surmise that a path of less traditional means could lead us directly to the photocache." He flexed his fist absently. "Perhaps before our peers have time to overtake us further."

"But the riddle references travel by air, ¿no?" Tobias pointed out. "We're not birds; I doubt the message even pertains to us."

"Sí. Estás correcto, Tobias," Brun precipitated. "However, if you look closely, you'll notice that it mentions sliding." He passed the curl-prone papyrus to the otter. "Honestly, I think we're supposed to rip to the photocache."

"Rip?" Manny repeated, puzzled. *That doesn't sound right.* Yet a hint of understanding crept into his mind. "Did you mean to say zip, like in zip-line?"

Brun shrugged.

"Even if you did," Manny continued, unperturbed, "people don't call it zipping—a zip-line is something you ride. It involves trees connected by metal cables, and you need a special pulley system to jet from one platform to another. Otherwise you'd strip your hands off."

Brun raised an eyebrow.

586

"I know because we used zip-lines to explore various parts of the Monteverde rainforest in Costa Rica last summer," Manny elucidated. "They call it canopy surfing there."

Tobias opened his arms wide, gesturing to the empty space between the base of the tower and the thick rail wall. "Well, there definitely aren't any trees up here."

"Not to mention any pulleys," Manny contributed.

"I'm sure you don't need trees to ride a zip-line," Brun discounted. "And the lack of pulleys is an issue easily resolved."

"You're cracked if you think we're gonna take a zip-line from here," Manny countered. "First off, we don't have a metal cable; I don't see one mounted to the tower. Do you?" Manny jerked his chin up, motioning to the moonstone's girth with open palm. "And second, where would you expect us to slide if we did? Into the Lake?"

Unperturbed, Brun transformed his wand into a thick birch cudgel, rolling it vertically between his hands as he said, "Pues, to begin, I'd imagine that the Arrowpaws concealed the cable with a Veil to prevent people from noticing it." As Brun spoke, the birch wand continued to grow in length yet shrink in breadth, now measuring half the boy's height. "And furthermore, as to our destination, we have to upload the photobeads for that."

By this time Manny had virtually forgotten the beads in his hand; yet even now the thought stole from his mind as he gazed at the birch staff—nearly five feet high—sustained by Brun's confident grip. A pair of half moon dimples appeared at one corner of Brun's mouth as he hoisted the staff into the air, approached the moonstone bulwark, and began fishing apparently empty space. His efforts proved fruitful, as within a pair of seconds a pronounced crack resounded through the air—the sound of wood striking metal. Brun slid the staff along the invisible line above, grinning broadly as his wand skipped along the tightly wound tresses of masked metal, clacking all the while.

Manny leaned back against the bulwark in an attempt to spy any latent hint of the cable. He sighed, his efforts floundering as

Brun's birch staff came to an abrupt stop against the very unadorned wall. "Brun, how do you figure out these things?"

"I guess I'm just analytical," he replied. "And I like puzzles."

"I don't suppose it's irony that the Arrowpaws mounted the cable just above the hundredth step, is it?" Tobias inquired, peering over Manny's head. The boy grunted. "Anyhow, now that we know there's a zip-line, how do we use it? There obviously aren't any invisible pulleys up there, too."

"No, there aren't," Brun swiftly agreed. "So we'll make a pair."

"Out of what? Caleida said we won't learn to create metals until next year—heck, we can't even change light into wood yet," Manny argued. "Don't expect me to risk my life using a pulley made of clustered photons; if I lose my concentration, I'll also lose my life."

"You're wrong—wooden pulleys will work just fine," Brun stated.

Tobias slapped the step sheepishly with his tail. "So you'll be using your wands then," he said, deflated. "I knew we'd come to a point where I couldn't follow you. At least you entertained me up 'til now, even if you didn't really want to…" The otter threw a quick look at Brun before turning to descend the stairs.

"Where are you going?" Manny blurted as he blocked the otter's path for the second time that day. "No one said anything about leaving you behind. You may not have a wand, but you can still ride in my backpack. I'll make sure the straps are tight."

"Don't worry about it," the otter replied, his words tumbling emptily down the steps.

A sudden flash of irritation gripped Brun, the taste of Tobias's apathy bitter in his mouth as he flexed his fist. "Drop the self-pity, otter. It makes me sick." His words were unexpected and sharp, drawing blood from the air. "You didn't come all this way just to forfeit, did you?"

Tobias clenched his paws, a spark of indignation lighting in his stomach. "No," he growled through clenched teeth. 'I thought we were past this…' he ruminated darkly.

"Good." Brun scowled. **Then don't waste any more of my time.**

Manny swiftly attempted to restore the mood. "Okay then! I got a good look at the pulleys in Costa Rica, so I think I can effectively transform my wand into a replica. Why don't we all just sit down and try it out…" he offered, setting upon a detailed explanation of the anatomy of the pulley. Within minutes the boys sat holding the working components of a pair of zip-line trolleys, including two dual-wheeled pulleys with mounted handlebars. "Now all we have to do is position the pulleys on the zip-line and we'll be off." *I do wish we had a set of harnesses or helmets, though.*

"How do you expect to do that when you can't even see it?" Tobias asked stiffly.

"Manny, I think we need to withdraw the Veil," Brun said, his voice level.

Manny racked his mind for a moment. "I remember Professor Shadowflame withdrawing the Veil from Lakia last fall—she just pulled it off as if it were a cloth. But how can we get hold of it from down here?"

After a moment of silence, an idea came to Tobias. "I can sense the photons in the Veil. Maybe you can just draw them away by calling them with your wand."

Manny shrugged. "It's worth a try." Thus Brun and Tobias watched as Manny closed his eyes and pointed the awkward bulk of his mahogany zip-line trolley at the empty air. Manny's expression changed, intensifying slightly, and he pulled his wand toward his chest. A braid of glistening steel materialized overhead, declining at an angle from the tower.

"Nice job," Brun commented.

Tobias twitched his whiskers. "But the cable's only visible up to the ledge, and then it disappears again. Shouldn't you draw off the rest of the Veil?"

"What's the point?" Manny erupted in a skyward stretch. "We know the cable leads to the photocache—no need to waste more time picking at stray photons."

"If I'm going to go soaring through the air I'd prefer to see where I'm going…" the otter grumbled.

Manny reached into his pocket and withdrew the three amethyst pearls that constituted their recently discovered cache. Leaning forward, he placed one such orb in the otter's paw. "There —now you'll know where we're going."

With a look of semi-surliness, Tobias twisted his wrist and implanted the photobead into his compass. The screen zoomed out, presenting a panoramic view of the Argo Dock, the Lake, and a great deal of the forest beyond that comprised the northeastern confines of the Isla Verde city limits. A purple dot materialized on the hologram, its royal hue nearly quashed by thick trees girding a minute pond.

"I can't believe it." The otter tapped the pond with a sharp claw to manipulate the zoom feature. He scanned the pool's perimeter. "The photocache is just south of my hovel, not far from the spot where I lost my wand."

Manny's eyes flicked to the pond on his own CPS. "Weird." He remembered the day that he and his friends had discovered a monkey print in the mud there, following the trail beyond the city's protective curtain. The results had been disastrous, particularly for Kaya. Manny's face suddenly hardened. *But now we're prepared. After we catch this beetle we need to regroup and plan our next hunt. Who knows how many wands have been stolen just today alone, with all the Seventh-Levels running aro—*

"No time to worry, Manny," Brun expressed, interrupting his thoughts. "If we don't leave now, someone else might get the photocache."

The honey in Manny's eyes thickened slightly. "There are issues that supersede a simple beetle, you know," he muttered inkily.

Brun's brow rose unevenly on one side. "And they are…?"

Manny swatted away the question, tabling the discussion for later. "We'll talk about it tonight." Swinging his leather pack from his shoulders, Manny unzipped the central compartment and held it open. "Hop on in, Tobias."

The otter eyed the pack with a skeptical glance. "And the straps—"

"Will be perfectly tight," Manny assured him.

With a sigh of resignation, Tobias slipped into the body of the bag, allowing Manny to slide the zippers up to the otter's armpits. Once satisfied, the boy gingerly lifted the pack, positioned it squarely on his shoulders, and drew the straps so tight that the bag hugged his body.

"Okay back there?" Manny asked.

The otter grunted, attempting to establish his footing. "I think there's a melted candy bar under my leg…"

Crap! "I forgot about that…"

"Vámonos," Brun said restlessly, ushering Manny toward the balustrade.

"You don't want to go first?" Manny inquired, his hand resting tentatively on the ledge where the last cache had lain hidden.

Brun shook his head. "I can get up there easy enough." He knelt and knit his hands together to offer Manny a step on which to climb. "But I don't want you slipping and falling off with all that extra weight on your back."

Tobias growled again. Manny, however, said nothing as he accepted Brun's help. The task proved to be rather awkward for Manny, with the zip-line trolley in one hand and Tobias's shifting presence altering the boy's equilibrium—not to mention the smoothness of the stone. When Manny finally managed to tuck his second knee to his chest—ensuring that the soles of his shoes were grounded firmly on the moonstone—he looked very much like a pigeon squatting in its hollow roost. The boy took a stabilizing breath; his eyes, nevertheless, moved of their own accord.

Brun lurched forward, locking his arms around Manny's waist. "What are you doing?" he accosted, pulling Manny back. "You're gonna kill yourself!"

"Don't look down, Manny!" Tobias barked. "You can't stay balanced if you do!"

Manny shook his head, his cheeks flooding in a crystal hue as he lifted his chin and stared out over the even line of the forest stretching out across the gap before him. *I will never blame Zane for disliking heights again.*

"¿Estás bien?" Brun asked, maintaining his grip in case Manny should teeter forward a second time.

A lump formed in Manny's throat; he swallowed, his voice rasping past it. "Yeah, I'll be alright." He coughed, filling his lungs with air as a zephyr of clarity purged his mind. "You can let go now; I'll take it slow, but I think I'm ready to stand."

Anxiety tore at Tobias's innards as he watched Brun release his grip. "Grab his ankles, Brun, just to help him keep steady." Brun obeyed wordlessly, acknowledging the otter with an oblique nod.

The muscles in Manny's legs, abdomen, and face tensed as he rose into the air, stabilizing his core and consequently his equilibrium. Ten very rigid seconds passed before his free hand closed around the gleaming steel cord above him.

Tobias sighed audibly. "Lo lograste."

Manny's heart pounded with relief as he raised the pulley parallel to the cable; flexing his mind, he wrought a slot in the mechanism's outer casing in order to thread the pulley with the cable. When he had done this, he sealed the slot in the mahogany casing then grabbed the handlebar with the opposite hand.

"Brun, are you sure you can get up here without any help?" Manny felt the trolley slide an inch along the cable. His stomach slid along with it. *I don't want you to die.*

"Completely," Brun murmured. He released his hold on Manny's ankles then flexed his hand, glancing momentarily at the dark ring he wore. **There's no doubt in my mind.** "I'll be right behind you."

Seeing no point in further talk, Manny drew in a deep breath, leaned forward, and kicked off from the edge of the balustrade. Within seconds the trolley was sliding through the naked air, ratcheting the boy and the otter along an invisible vector aimed straight into the heart of the forest. Manny's stomach slipped through his feet and splashed into the Lake below. *I hate it when that happens...* A high-pitched scream registered in Manny's ears, and he very nearly let go of his grip.

"This-is-awesome!" hooted Tobias, his paws in the air as the trolley gained further momentum. By this time the wind had bent his whiskers virtually flat against his round face. He released a sharp bay of ecstasy.

That was unexpected. Manny gazed down as the Lake disappeared behind his toes, yielding to the ever-present jungle, its canopies glistening with the hues of tropical birds and teeming with life. The gargantuan awning of a kapok tree rushed by to the side, the sun's rays filtering through the tall branches and mottling the boy's skin with a fusion of light and shadow for the briefest of moments. Manny smiled, kicking the air as he swung forward, and released a thrilled whoop. *This is just like the cloud forests, only ten times faster and much more dangerous.*

A yelp rent the air as their altitude dropped sharply and they plunged through a subtle rift in the jade ocean, the tide of leaves crashing over their heads. "How are we gonna stop?" squalled Tobias as they descended through a tunnel that pierced the gnarled branches and wove between the boles. Before Manny could halfway formulate a guess, the ground drew up before them, followed instantly by a flash of silver.

Manny screamed, releasing his grip on the trolley to prevent from crashing into the wall of moonlight, but he was too late. In mid-somersault he and the otter crashed into the folds of the wall, which in actuality turned out to be quite soft, cushioning their fall and yielding to their weight. A breath later they tumbled to the forest floor, lying prostrate for five seconds or so before attempting to speak. Manny sat up. His head spun and his vision slid askew as he watched Tobias climb out of the pack and slip back to the ground, the otter's hind paws coated in slimy chocolate.

"¡Eso fue increíble!" stuttered the otter drunkenly, the canopy spinning above him.

"I'd say," Manny agreed, unable to sit straight. The boy chuckled. "You've got chocolate all over your feet."

Tobias flipped his forepaw in the air. "You'd better hope I don't wipe it all over your face."

The sound of wood grating against metal filled the air as Brun flashed into view, his hands confidently clutching the handlebars of his birch-wood trolley. Manny glanced up, eyeing his roommate stupidly as Brun slid to a halt, comfortably suspended from the zip-line.

"How did you do that?" Manny asked, his words fumbling through the air.

"I just decreased the space between the zip-line and the pulley." Brun spun around casually, as if he often spent time dangling from heights of fifty feet or more. He even went so far as to scratch his head. "I assumed that would be the only way to brake while riding." He eyed his companions oddly. "How did you stop?"

Manny thought for a moment, still swaying as though inebriated. "I let go."

"Well, that was intelligent of you," said Brun sardonically. His trolley flashed a bright white, reassuming the shape of a wand as he slid down the silver tarp toward his fellow photocachers. He came to a stop and stood up, dusting off his pants.

Now just how did he keep from rolling down like we did? Manny stared up at Brun accusingly. "What do you mean by that?"

Brun stared back passively. "I mean you're wand-less."

"Of all the idiot things I could have done…" Manny stumbled to his feet, overriding his instability and gazing over Brun's shoulder at the trunk of a broad tree, a living golem from whose twisted boughs flowed the silver tarp. Just above the rim of the fabric hung Manny's mahogany trolley, seemingly attached to the gnarled face. *Freaking heck…*

Tobias stumbled over to the edge of the tarp, bent down, and began picking lazily at the silver fabric, as a pup taunts tadpoles on a sunny day. "It's full of holes," the otter said, lurching forward as the ground shifted in his vision. "Which means it's a net."

Manny grasped the otter's intention, wasting no time in assaulting the tarp. The minuscule perforations in the fabric provided the leverage necessary to propel Manny to the trolley. *No freakin' monkey's getting my wand...* Manny was thankful that the fabric did not yield or cut at his skin like a normal textile might have; conversely, the silver netting maintained a strength reminiscent of steel yet boasted a texture akin to cloth. In under a minute Manny had scaled the net, his arms burning as he reached up to grasp the handlebars of his trolley. He then proceeded to kick the bole of the tree with the balls of his feet, skating backward along the zip-line to dangle roughly 45 feet above his partners. With a deft twist he spun around, the shape of his trolley melting away from the cable as he hit the netting and slid back to his former position on the ground.

"Smooth moves," Tobias complimented as Manny shot onto his feet.

"You seemed determined," Brun noted.

The corner of Manny's cheek hooked up in a faint smile as his wand suddenly lengthened, the shaft yawning at the end and twisting back to form a wide rim. He quickly pointed the butt of the wand at the sky, drawing down a wisp of light that he artfully mended into a pearl-white mesh, which fused to the wand's rim to complete a butterfly net device. He lowered the apparatus, his grip firm on the mahogany shaft as he stared at Brun. "Mold your Scarab Catcher and let's go," Manny affirmed.

"No need," Brun answered, his words sliding idly through the air.

"How do you expect to catch the majestic beetle, then?" the other boy rejoined.

The fingers of Brun's black-ringed hand danced slightly. "I have my ways."

Disregarding Brun's cryptic behavior, Manny withdrew his CPS. By silent consensus Tobias and Brun did the same. Manny's head snapped up and his gaze skipped over his partners' shoulders to a grove robed in thick curtains of ruby and sapphire. *Lady and Gentlebugs...* Nostalgia washed over Manny. *I wonder if those are the same moss curtains Brun and I passed on our way to Nightcrest Caverns...* He shook his head and blinked. "The scarab's in the next clearing there," he said, striding forward as Tobias and Brun drew up beside him. Manny reached out to part the resplendent curtain. "May the best man win, y buena suerte."

Luck? I don't need luck. Brun grunted as he passed into the grove. His eyes leapt to the center of the clearing, where a creature that looked very much like a miniature purple heart lay enswathed in a cone of sunlight. He drew a quick breath. **Mine.**

Manny followed Tobias into the dell, came to a stop, and twirled his Scarab Catcher in anticipation. He fixed his eyes on the fist-sized beetle twenty or so steps ahead, intending to advance but then restraining himself as he eyed Brun's frozen frame. *Why isn't he mov—*

"Manny," Tobias whispered, his voice hushed as he tugged on the boy's heel. "How are you going to catch it?"

"With my Scarab Catcher, how else?" Manny replied. His eyes never left Brun's figure.

"But doesn't the majestic beetle have a special power or something?" the otter asked. Manny shot back a questioning look in reply. "You know, like how the viridian beetle uses camouflage and the cerulean beetle can teleport... Doesn't this type do something, too?"

Manny turned and kneeled, his shoulders facing Brun in case his opponent made the first move. *What a time for last minute details... Why can't I just think ahead...* "Well," he mumbled, reluctantly peeling his eyes from the soles of Brun's shoes, "let me think a minute." *Had that quiz on the radiant beetles last week... Kept getting the moon beetle and the majestic beetle confused... But Professor Shadowflame corrected my test in purple ink...*

"You've got to scare it," Manny asserted. "Otherwise it will never leave the ground, since it doesn't crawl." He paused. "It only flies in straight lines; and it's fast—very fast."

The otter's whiskers twitched as he gazed at the scarab. "Why can't you just walk over there and pick it up? Even I could do that."

"Professor Shadowflame said that lifting the majestic beetle of your own accord would require the energy equivalent to that of

596

displacing a three ton object," he rattled off. "But if you scare it into the air, then it's as light as a feather."

"Can't anything ever just be simple?" Tobias glared at the purple insect. "So how do we scare it?"

"It hates yellow light, the diametric opposite of violet," the boy promptly noted. *It's gonna be a pain trying to direct a stream of light through the air while trying to position the Scarab Catcher...* "Hey! Your CPS is gold! You can help me catch it! All you have to do is get near it and it should zip away, just like that! Then all I have to do is worry about snagging it in my net!"

A mischievous light tinged Tobias's eyes as he glanced from his compass to the beetle. "This will be more fun than I thought…"

Tobias attached the CPS to his wrist and dropped to all fours, advancing on the beetle. Likewise, Manny rose to his full height; but a sudden movement from Brun made his heart jolt.

Brun drew back his hand and produced his wand, which he quickly began maneuvering through the air in a complex series of motions as various tongues of saffron light sifted through the foliage, interlacing across the grove to form a wide mesh, a yawning mouth of gold. Unease wormed its way through Manny's stomach at the sight. *That's rather… substantial.*

Tobias drew up to the scarab as Brun's net wove to completion. "Ready, Manny?" the otter called, a sense of urgency in his voice.

"Uh, yeah!" Manny reset his grip on the Scarab Catcher, sidling in hopes that the beetle might fire in his direction.

Without another word Tobias cartwheeled over the scarab, striking at it with his wrist. "Headed your way!" he bellowed.

Manny raised the Scarab Catcher as a violet blur shot straight at his head. As of its own volition, Brun's gold net slid between Manny and the beetle. A furious buzzing met Manny's ears as the beetle struck Brun's net, ricocheting out and away just before the golden tendrils could lock it in. Tobias yelped and hit the ground as the scarab grazed his head, coming to rest upon the trunk of a tree on the far end of the grove. Brun grinned as he twirled his wand in a simple floret; the golden net spun away from Manny, floating as an idle jellyfish on the west end of the grove.

Manny had scarcely come to terms with what he had witnessed before Tobias leapt up and screamed, "Where is it?"

"Behind you!" Manny exclaimed, bolting past Brun to position himself on the eastern rim of the grove. "Hit it from the left and I'll catch it!"

"¡Está bien!" Tobias assented, tearing across the grass and leaping toward the tree to strike the butt of the beetle. Manny ran to the right, reaching with his Scarab Catcher for the beetle. Brun chuckled as, once again, his saffron net rippled across the clearing to deflect the beetle's course. Anticipating Brun's actions, Tobias had stationed himself at the northeastern point of the clearing, from which the otter slapped the scarab with the back of his wrist, sending it skating along the grass below Brun's net. Brun growled as Manny lowered the Scarab Catcher to trap his prize; but to Manny's disgrace the beetle clipped the rim, rebounding toward the foliage at a right angle. A surge of victory swelled in Brun's chest as his net swept through the air, swallowing the scarab and effectively sealing it inside. The beetle buzzed violently within the confines of its swollen mesh prison, an incandescent pinball of frantic energy.

"Oh no you don't!" shouted Tobias as he dove at Brun's Reticulum sentinel in a last ditch effort to acquire the majestic beetle. Much to his surprise, however, Tobias never reached the net, as an unforeseen force clasped the otter by the tail and ripped him up through the air, leaving him suspended just below the canopy.

"You filthy river mutt!" Brun growled, his voice foreign, serrated and sharp. Brun's hand hung in the air, the obsidian ring flashing upon his tightly clenched fist.

Manny's eyes landed on the soot-colored ring. *Hold the phone—Brun's wand isn't black.* Manny glanced up and espied a dark netting enclosed around the otter's tail. *A—black—Reticulum? What's going on? Wh—* The oxygen suddenly drained from Manny's lungs. *Brun's doing this!*

Brun shook his fist, and Tobias's body rattled. "Why couldn't you just mind your own business, dirt mongrel—leave us alone to photocache in peace? But, no—" Here his voice assumed a patronizing tone. "You had to tag along to aggravate, annoy, and hinder us. You worthless excuse for a Lumen! Whoever heard of a Lumen without a wa—"

At that moment a fist flew threw the air, connecting with Brun's upper jaw and nose. Brun's monologue stopped short as teeth cut flesh and a sickening crunch issued from his nasal cavity. Knocked backward, Brun threw out an arm to brace his fall, consequently causing the golden net encasing the majestic beetle to fracture and tear. In a foray of buzzing the scarab darted out of the disintegrating net and disappeared through the moss curtains beyond. Brun lowered his head, his eyes widening at Manny's multifarious glare of disappointment, rage, and hurt.

Manny stepped forward and grabbed Brun by the collar. "How could you say those things?" He pulled Brun's bleeding countenance toward him. "How could you—ever—insult and degrade a fellow Lumen like that, especially one of another species who is smaller, more defenseless than you and I are?" Manny let go and pounded Brun's shoulder with the butt of his palm. "And how could you ever raise a hand against an innocent person?" Manny stared into Brun's eyes, a wave of electric fury assaulting the strongholds in the latter's mind. Manny's voice assumed an utterly lethal tone. "Let him down." Brun acquiesced, his arm sagging limply to his side as the otter dropped straight to the forest floor.

Manny nosedived to the center of the clearing, catching the creature just in time. "Tobias, ¿estás bien? ¿Estás lastimado? Tenemos que buscar un curan—"

"I'm fine, Manny," the otter interjected. "Just shaken up a bit. I don't think I need a healer. Another second in the air and I might have chucked my shells, though."

Manny smiled tiredly. "Good." The boy's expression then grew solid. "Just know that you're safe now—I will not allow Brun to attack you again. You can re—"

A choking sound came from Manny's side, wrenching his attention away from the otter. Looking back, he found Brun with a tortured expression on his blood and tear-stained face. Brun choked again.

"It's this—this blasted ring," he cursed, wrenching the obsidian band from his hand as he stumbled to his feet. Brun threw the halo on the ground, spit on it, and ground it into the dirt with his heel. "My father gave it to me for m-my birthday; he said it would protect me if I—if I wore it." Brun sighed, and a quantum of strength returned to his voice. "Since we were photocaching for the first time today, I decided to put it on, just in case we ran into any danger. But ever since I touched the rotten thing I've felt edgy, impatient, and... hateful." He ground his heel even harder. "I never want to see it again for as long as I live."

Brun raised his eyes and took a step toward his companions. "Tobias, Manny, you're my friends, and I'm—" His voice caught. "I'm sorry for how I've treated you today. I hope you can find it in your hearts to forgive me. I—" His voice froze. "I need to lie down. I'll be at the hut." And without another word Brun turned and ambled away south, parting the speckled curtains and leaving a trail of blood.

Tobias sat up, his brain slapping against the walls of his cranium. "A ring caused all this?" A note of skepticism lined his voice.

Manny's response was cogent—unmoving rock. "Yes. You and I both know Brun would never act like he did today otherwise."

"Yer right," Tobias grunted, slumping back down to the ground.

In the silence that followed Manny edged over to the flat oval where his roommate had milled the architect of the day's frustration into the dirt. Manny dug his forefinger into the soft clay to extract and examine the beautiful, shadow-bound band. *How can this stone influence a person's feelings? I don't feel any different.* Manny turned the ring in his hand as clumps of soil fell from it. The light reflecting from the band was hollow—dull, seemingly choked. *Well, I'm not going to put it on to find out.*

"Since Brun needs some time to himself, Manny, will you carry me to the Café? I need a milkshake," the otter pleaded, his whiskers limp.

Manny pocketed the ring and rose to his feet. "Sure—I'd be glad to."

An Eight-sided Situation

Kaya stared down at Iris with a dubious glance, her lips pursed and one side of her cheek puckered. "You're incredible, you know that?"

Iris beamed as he hopped along the dirt path, a translucent glass jar clamped tightly between his front paws. His eyes dropped to the golden scarab resting peacefully at the bottom of the jar. The hare grinned as he recalled how just an hour earlier he had managed to apprehend the sun beetle from right below Kaya's nose. *Literally*. Having successfully tempted the scarab into reaching distance using an orb of bright, golden light, Kaya had believed she had unequivocally bested Iris and that she had but to swing her Scarab Catcher to claim the prize. Nevertheless, to her immense vexation, an emerald net filled the space before her eyes, swallowing the sun beetle in its grasp and retracting nearly instantaneously into Iris's paw. Thus the hare had won the day's photocache challenge, leaving Kaya... *scarab-less*.

"You maniacal little twerp," she said, sharing his thoughts with a chuckle. "Had you planned to swipe the sun beetle like that the entire time?"

The hare's eyes flashed brightly. "A wise photocacher never shares his secrets."

Kaya kicked the ground and shook her head. "You're just lucky I didn't catch it, because if I had I sure wouldn't be wasting it on Dimirtis."

"Yes, you would have," he disagreed placidly.

Kaya tossed back her tresses, glancing down vacantly. "How do you figure?"

"Like I said earlier, you owed him. And you're a better Lumen than one who steals from others for her own benefit."

The girl let out an inaudible sigh. *That didn't stop me from taking it in the first place...*

"Don't feel guilty about it, Kaya. The monkeys may have swiped the first sun beetle, but we caught another one, and we're gonna set things right."

The rubber in Kaya's soles seemed to adhere to the ground as they drew increasingly close to a bend in the trail. "Could we at least sneak the sun beetle in through the window? That way Brun won't think ill of us…"

"Buen punto," Iris conceded, stopping dead in his tracks. "That definitely wouldn't make for a positive atmosphere." He paused, his eyes roaming to the hook in the path. "The front door is out. Why don't we creep around the yard from the side?"

"Fine by me," Kaya consented. "But let's not let Chiron find us this time—that was embarrassing."

Iris nodded, watching as Kaya dashed past the crook in the path leading directly to Chiron's Hutch. The hare waited for a moment before he, too, bolted past, then followed the girl into the thick, fern-strewn undergrowth that encircled the centaur's abode. After a minute or so they approached the edge of the yard, parting the ferns' viridian arms to survey the area. The arrowhead leaves tickled their faces as they peered out at the bamboo hut, the door closed, the windows dark.

"Looks like no one's home," Kaya breathed, her shoulders relaxing.

"Guess not," Iris said, his eyes darting around the yard. "But let's wait a couple minutes just to make sure nobody's loitering around the kapok tree out back." And so they waited; but no one appeared.

Enough waiting. "Okay, hand me the jar."

"What are you gonna do with it?" Iris retorted, reaffirming his grip.

"Put-it-in-the-window." Kaya enunciated each word as if addressing a simpleton. "What else am I going to do with it?"

Oh, duh. "Sorry." Iris allowed the jar to roll into Kaya's waiting hands. "Ten cuidado."

"I will," she whispered, shaking her head as she slithered through the ferns and approached the eastern wall of the hutch in a tight crouch. Diving into the afternoon shadow the wall provided, she advanced stealthily, her midnight hair tracing the ground as she moved. Once stationed below the back window, she took a deep breath then rose slowly, the jar fused to her side. She had nearly risen to her full height, holding the jar up over the ledge, when she froze, becoming a rigid tableau. An instant later she dropped into a loose crouch and darted straight for the cover of the ferns from whence she came.

Iris swallowed nervously as he stared at the jar in her hands. "What happened? Did somebody see you?"

"I—I don't now," Kaya gasped, dropping to her knees. "Is anyone in the window?"

Iris parted the ferns, peering subtly at the hut. He shook his head. "No."

Kaya sighed with relief. "He must've been asleep."

"Who? Manny?"

"No—Brun. He was lying on his hammock, but I couldn't tell if his eyes were closed or not."

Iris chanced another glance through the ferns. *Hmmm...* "Kaya," he said after a moment. "Hand me the jar."

"What?" she asked, stunned.

"Brun's asleep, right? So I'll just sneak in through the front door, bob into his room, and set the sun beetle on his dresser. I'll be back in less than a minute."

"My, aren't you gutsy all of a sudden?"

"Just give me the jar."

Kaya relented, watching with wry eyes as Iris wove across the yard, leapt into the air to turn the knob, and melted into the darkness of the hut. *What a goof...* With each passing second Kaya entertained herself by counting the individual leaves of a fern branch dangling lazily before her. Just as she reached her thirty-seventh foil, a slender figure with a tired gait entered her field of vision. *When did he get—*

"Iris?" Manny called, stopping abruptly in front of Chiron's Hutch and staring at the hare hopping out through the door. "What are you doing?"

Iris froze, eyes wide and ears rigid. "I—"

"There you are, Manny!" Kaya lilted, materializing from the undergrowth. "Where've you been?"

Manny's head whirled about. "K-Kaya?" he stuttered, his eyes dancing over the waving ferns. "What in the world?"

"You know, I was just wondering how your photocaching went today," she proceeded, flipping her hair over her shoulder as she drew near. "So…?"

Manny's shoulders tensed. "What are you two doing in my yard?"

"Talking to you, obviously," Kaya replied casually. "Manny, you know it's rude not to answer someone's questions."

Iris slapped a paw to his brow. *Incredible.*

Oh, is it? Manny searched her innocent expression, finding nothing but genuine interest. He sighed, shoulders slumping. "It's a long story, and I don't feel like discussing it at the present moment."

"That's a letdown," Kaya said, her features sagging. *I think he's buying it.*

The back door creaked open; Brun lumbered into view, rubbing his eyes. "Manny?" he croaked. "Is Tobias here?"

"No, he went home," the other boy replied flatly. "But we have some unexpected guests."

"We do?" Brun yawned, dropping his hands from his eyes. "Hello Kaya, Iris. How are you?"

"Just great," Kaya replied equably.

Has he seen it yet? Iris's stomach knotted. "Fine, I suppose."

Another yawn. "So did you two catch a radiant beetle today?"

We're dead.

"None to speak of," Kaya answered genially.

Iris glanced up at her. *Where does she come up with this stuff?*

"That's too bad," Brun consoled them. "If it makes you feel any better, I scared our beetle off with my stupid behavior."

605

"And Millie caught it," Manny added. Brun threw him a lethargic look. "Just after you left, Tobias and I heard a loud 'Whoohoo!' coming from the next clearing. We found her there with Araceli, Nate, and Serge. They all said hi."

Brun nodded and stretched his arms into the air.

A thought struck Manny. "Who fixed your nose?"

"Professor Bluebolt," the boy yowled softly. "He and Chiron were here when I arrived. Said they were leaving, but that they'd be back for a meeting or something."

Iris shifted his weight from one paw to the other. "So what happened to your n—"

"What-is-that?" Manny choked, lifting a quick hand toward the northern horizon. Kaya, Iris, and Brun followed his gesture as a many-legged, jade bulk skirted across the canopy.

"Move!" Iris commanded, propelling across the grass in a blur of feet and ears. His companions obeyed unquestioningly as they plowed through the ferns and concealed themselves behind a cluster of trees. Iris leapt onto Kaya's shoulder to stake a better vantage point, his heart throbbing brutally.

The four friends witnessed the massive entity bounding from the canopy, its complex frame instantly switching from a deep jade to a milky white. Manny and Kaya gasped; Brun gripped the bark with his hand. The color change revealed the creature's true facets— a corpulent body, divided into two distinct sections suspended four feet above the ground by eight arching legs, all of which were covered in a fine, silk hair. A pair of massive fangs, each the length of Manny's arm, protruded from the beast's clicking mouth, and the eyes—*I think I might die*—the eyes glistened like black pearls as the creature scanned the area, its six jet irises blinking in unison.

Manny's legs went limp, but Kaya caught him by the collar. "López, be a man!" she spit threw her teeth."

The boy began to babble. "But it's—it's—"

"A crystal spider," Brun breathed, his lips carving the words.

"The biggest I've ever seen," Iris said, his syllables shattering in the air.

Manny found the creature's movements insidious—the manner in which its legs lifted, one after another, drumming the ground as they spun the arachnid in a quick, rippling circle. The boy shuddered, the hair standing up on the back of his neck.

"You can—you can see its organs," Brun marveled, his eyes piercing the spider's translucent trunk as he identified its beating heart, dog-sized stomach, and miles of intestine-like tissue. **Far out.**

"Incoming," whispered Kaya, her eyes raised to the sky. From around the canopy of the kapok appeared an icy blur, cutting an arc in the air before diving sharply at a patch of empty grass alongside the crystal spider. A tall man clad in blue pants and a pearl tunic leapt from his lightboard, waving his wand mildly as the board compacted in upon itself until it slid effortlessly into a leather pouch at his hip.

I know him from somewhere. Manny gazed at the man's high cheekbones, oval face, and sapphire eyes; a distant nostalgia, as though from a different life, brushed the boy's mind.

Brun leaned forward, also scrutinizing the man's face. **Who is he? That face... so familiar...**

With his cocobolo wand threaded leisurely through his fingers, the man leaned forward and dusted off his trousers. He then rose to his full height, nodded to the arachnid, and bowed slightly. "How fare you, Master Irradius?"

"Neither overly well nor remotely poor, my friend," the spider answered, his voice wise and smooth, similar to melted gold. His fangs clicked once before adding, "And you?"

"A burden rests on my heart, but I am otherwise well."

"I am sorry." Electing to respect the man's privacy, the arachnid changed the subject. "What of your journey?"

"I left Machu Picchu little more than an hour ago," the man replied, sighing. "The wind was at my back; I made good time."

"I should say." With a click, the spider pressed forward. "And what of the centaur? Is he not here? I followed your directions explicitly but found none of hoofed countenance."

The man ruffled his wind-blown, chestnut hair. "He will arrive presently. We are early, I believe."

Brun glanced back over his shoulder. "Who are they?" he mouthed.

Kaya and Manny shrugged, but Iris's ears twitched. "I don't know about the—spider," he gulped. "But the man is—"

"Andrés, you made it!" rang a tenor voice as an emerald and red-crested arrow dropped from the sky, alighting softly on the eaves of the hut.

"Andrés?" Manny repeated, his eyes flitting from Julius Rumblefeather back to the man.

"Sí—Andrés Dosfilos, the Lumen leader of South America," Iris explained.

"He spoke at our orientation, right?" Brun asked. Iris and Kaya nodded. **Then he's the one who gave me the sun beetle the monkeys stole.**

"—Rumblefeather, allow me to present Crion Irradius, Chieftain of the crystal spiders, a good friend to all Lumens," Dosfilos said, gesturing proudly to the arachnid.

"Chieftain?" Kaya whispered. *That's huge.*

"I am most honored, Master Irradius." Julius bowed with an elegant wing extension. "The faculty of the Academy are all eager to work with you."

Irradius glanced about the empty patio pointedly. "As I can see."

The quetzal's feathers ruffled, and he opened his beak to speak, when the figure of a raven-hued centaur strode hurriedly into the glade.

"Pardon my tardiness, friends," Chiron said, his fair skin flushed as he knelt slightly. "But I was addressing a situation." The centaur turned his eyes to the formidable arachnid. "Crion Irradius, I presume? A pleasure." He crossed his chest. "I am Chiron Veridai."

Irradius clipped his fangs. "And your colleagues? I was lead to believe we were to meet today."

"Today was the Seventh-Levels' first day of photocaching," Julius interjected.

"And?" Irradius said mutely, his legs thrumming the ground. "Is photocaching not an independent task? It does not require the supervision of one's instructors."

"Typically, no, but this particular class seems to be rather accident prone." Julius's black eyes turned to face Chiron's. "Has Madison been detained?"

Chiron nodded darkly. "He is mending the wings of three peregrine falcons. Their bones were shattered."

Dosfilos inhaled sharply. "Shattered? How did this happen?"

"I don't suppose it was another monkey attack?" Julius scoffed.

Dosfilos turned a pair of cold eyes at the quetzal.

"They claimed so, yes," Chiron answered gravely. "And their wands were missing."

"Missing?" choked Dosfilos. "Julius, I demand an explanation."

The quetzal blinked stupidly. "It's nothing serious, Andrés. The young ones are simply acting carelessly, throwing themselves into danger and misplacing their wands."

"With what frequency?" Dosfilos asked, his voice low.

"More often than is ideal," Julius said shortly. Dosfilos did not lessen his gaze. "Since last fall we've been averaging roughly fifteen per month."

"Fifteen per month!" Dosfilos repeated, his lungs twisting. "When I instructed here such events happened rarely, if ever."

"Twenty instances have occurred today alone," Chiron said quietly. "Or so I have counted."

All color drained from Dosfilos' face. "That constitutes an emergency, Julius. Following our meeting, I expect you to address this issue appropriately. You will first write a letter to the student body, admonishing them of the dangers. You will then assemble a task force to determine the true cause of these mishaps."

"But is not the true cause not already evident?" interpolated Irradius, his head twisted slightly.

Manny suddenly shivered. *Keep that thing away from me.*

The ferns stirred behind the children's backs. "H-hello," came a shy voice.

Manny, Kaya, Iris, and Brun whirled around instantly, altogether forgetting the meeting. There, only five steps before them, stood an exact replica of Irradius, but half the former's size. Manny's heart stopped; Kaya's eye's widened; Iris's tongue turned to sand; Brun gawked in awe—but not one spoke.

"H-hi," the spider tried again, his six uncertain eyes shifting between humans and hare. "I am called Spencer, but you may call me Spence, should it please you." Silence. Spence clicked his fangs nervously. "Father said it would be safe to accompany him to Chiron's Hutch, that perhaps I would make friends with Manny and Brun, the centaur's host-students." He grew quiet. "But I was scared, so I held back."

A laugh erupted from Manny's chest as he breathed for the first time in over a minute. "You were scared?" he gasped.

The crystal spider rubbed his triangular, velvet lip pads together. "Um, yes," he mumbled genuinely.

"Why?" Brun asked, stepping forward tentatively.

Spence's legs thrummed him backward involuntarily. "Because many of my people say that the non-arachnids despise us and wish us harm; that they do not share Lady Oriana's heart." The spider rubbed his lip pads tensely. "Is this true?"

"No!" Iris blurted. "We don't want to hurt you!"

"Then why do you shun my people?"

Iris's mouth went dry and his intestines knotted. He opened his mouth to speak, but no sound came out.

"I think," Kaya began, blinking back her apprehension, "that most people are afraid that you might eat them."

"Eat another Lumen?" Spence said, his eyes abashed. "That notion is repulsive! That would be akin to cannibalism!"

"But isn't it true that crystal spiders eat Amazonian hares?" Iris accused.

"No more than does the peregrine falcon or the panther," Spence answered matter-of-factly. "And moreover, do not Lumen hares dwell in Europe?"

Brun nodded in agreement. "Typically."

"Just because I live here now doesn't make me anyone's food!" Iris redoubled, though still keeping his voice low for fear of attracting the attention of Spence's father. *I don't want this to become a buffet.*

Manny took an unconscious step forward, extending a hand to the hare. "That's not what Spence is saying, Iris."

Iris glared back, as though betrayed. *So we're on a first-name basis with my primary predator now?*

"Chill out," Kaya said, patting the hare's tense foot. Her shoulders relaxed. "Legs, here—Spence, do you mind if I call you Legs?" The arachnid shook his head calmly. "Good. As I was saying, Legs here has a point; he's no different than any other predatory Lumen. You can hear it in his voice—he's telling the truth. And besides," she paused, her fingers fumbling with her hair, "he's kind of cute."

Cute? Manny gawked at Kaya in disbelief. *He's a spider, a super-charged tarantula for goodness' sakes!*

"Manny," Kaya began, catching the boy's reaction in her peripheral vision, "don't be jealous—I don't date outside my species."

Stupefied embarrassment flooded the boy's cheeks, his skin casting a brilliant, pure light on the moist bromeliads sprouting from the trees. *D-date?*

Spence did not appear to notice the shame in the boy's reaction, however. "Then you are Manny! And you are Brun!"

"Sí," Brun acknowledged, fascinated by the arachnid's vorticose eyes. "And these are our friends Iris and Kaya," he added with a gesture.

"I am honored." The spider nodded his head, bowing slightly with his front legs. "I hope we are long friends."

"Same here," Kaya replied, strolling forward and reaching out her hand to pet the arachnid's glossy neck. Iris performed a desperate back flip off her shoulder, his feet slapping Manny in the forehead and causing the boy to trip over a tree root. "Just ignore them," Kaya muttered as Spence's fangs clicked. "They both tend to overreact."

When Manny had effectively picked himself and Iris up from the ground, he found Brun dialoguing inquisitively with their new guest.

"...on the north side of the river! Really?" Brun blocked Manny and Iris's view of the spider's head. "What is it like? Do you live in houses, caves, plants...?"

"Sort of a mixture, really," Spence adjoined, flexing the joints in his back legs. "Most of our people live in elaborate edifices of multi-colored quartz bent into beautiful designs. My mother, for example, made our home in the shape of a blossomed orchid that changes colors depending on the time of day. She's actually a really talented architect—"

"No way!" Kaya broke in. "Mine, too! Mi papá, I mean—no mi mamá. He works for the LIGHT Group creating photocache challenges."

"Seriously?" Spence rebounded with a trio of excited clicks. "That's the first thing I wanted to do when I came to Isla Verde!"

"Maybe the five of us can go sometime!" Kaya suggested.

Iris grabbed his right ear and began twisting it violently, bringing tears to his eyes. *Oh no, Kaya, please...*

Spence thrummed the ground with his legs. "That would be amazing!"

"So, Spence," Brun proceeded as if uninterrupted, "how does your webbing work? Can you show us?"

The arachnid scuttled back a few steps, whirling to the side to consider a pair of nearby fig trees, their trunks straight and bare. "No problem—just watch." Spence's legs blurred silver as he sped up a tree, completely unaffected by gravity. Suddenly, he paused, bunching his legs slightly and touching his abdomen to the trunk before exploding through the air, a gossamer rope of glittering crystal issuing from his posterior. In less than a second he had landed on the opposite trunk, descended twenty or so feet, and fired back to complete a circle. In this fashion he wove a resplendent curtain of spiraling crystal, treading delicately along the ropes to

612

masterfully weave and tuck the fibers in the appropriate places, his movements tender yet quick and secure. The entire process took less than three minutes.

Descending upon a braid from the heart of his tapestry, Spence said, "So? What do you think?"

"It's the most beautiful thing I've ever seen," Kaya said, wondering at how the olive light reflected off the billions of crystals.

Brun squinted his eyes. "Is it made of real stone?"

"Partially, yes," Spence replied, spinning playfully in the air. "A proper definition for our webbing would be crystal-infused mucus fibers."

"Does that mean it's sticky?" Iris asked, his curiosity superseding his self-preservation instinct.

Spence's eyes glistened. "Very." He then pointed to himself. "But not to us, Iris, not to us."

"So you wrap your prey in this and drink their blood?" Kaya queried benignly.

"Alongside sucking out their innards, yes," Spence rejoined in mild candor. "But let us speak of alternate points of interest. I believe this topic makes Iris uncomfortable."

"Gracias," the hare muttered pallidly.

Rubbing his right arm, Manny said, "How old are you?"

"I will have lived outside the egg sac for fifteen years this next July," the arachnid replied, landing lightly.

Brun raised an eyebrow. **He's our age.**

That means I'm older than him. "Do you go to school, then?"

"Most definitely, Manny. My mother's sister is my personal instructor. All crystal spiders study through an apprenticeship under a greater arachnid as they advance to higher levels with each year. But not for much longer, obviously."

"What do you mean by that? Why would you just quit studying?" Manny asked.

Spence blinked wryly. "Do you not know why my father has come to meet with Chairman Dosfilos and your professors today?"

The three humans and the hare shook their heads. "No idea. I didn't even know mi papá was supposed to be here," Iris stated.

"Of course," Spence nodded as a block of information slid into place. "You are Professor Firefoot's son. Starting next week your father will be my Sentinels teacher."

"Your teacher?" Kaya and Manny reverberated together. *How? No comprendo…*

"Pero mi papá never mentioned anything about traveling to your city and teaching spid-spid—" But Iris could not finish. *That's too dangerous! Even with his best sentinels…*

Spence's eyes brightened, his fangs clicking in amusement. "Do not worry, Iris. Professor Firefoot isn't coming to my home— we will be coming to yours."

The contents of the hare's brain seemed to lighten considerably. "We?"

"My peers and I," Spence clarified.

At that moment Iris rocked and fainted, swallowed by the ferns and moss. Kaya ran to him, picking the hare up and cradling him in her arms.

"Is he going to be okay?" Spence inquired. The crystalline flesh over his eyes wrinkled into a frown.

"Yeah, just give him a minute," she replied, fanning the hare's face with her free hand. *Gutless…*

"So you'll be attending class with us?" Manny asked, his stomach flitting nervously. Spence nodded. "Every one of you?" Another nod. *If I don't get used to this today I think I'll die next week.*

"Manny, Kaya, don't you remember Andrés Dosfilos mentioning this during our orientation?" Brun prompted.

"Vaguely," Kaya answered.

Brun quickly recapped the Chairman's words. "He said the crystal spiders would start school here this spring—that the Lumen community had lived too long divided by the superficial fear of appearances."

"He visited us and shared the same message," Spence recalled. "Many of our people were upset, particularly the elders."

"Now, I remember that part," Manny contributed. "Everyone started mumbling, and I think a kinkajou mother turned and lead her family away."

"I'm not surprised," Spence commented. "Father has suffered a great deal of opposition from our clan for his support of Chairman Dosfilos. But Papá is our chieftain, and in the end our clan will do as he says. They will otherwise face exile."

Kaya voiced her concern. "But are we—I mean, are our societies ready for such a drastic change?"

Manny glanced at the still-sleeping hare. *Iris isn't.*

"Chairman Dosfilos believes so. He says that in order to grow stronger we must confront our fears with pincers ready, and that we cannot become unified by working from separate arenas. I believe him," Spence affirmed. "And though I admit that only this morning I feared our integration, I do so no longer. You four have shown me that we are equals—that your people are good."

Not all of us. Manny's mind relived memories of torture at the hands of Nacho, his childhood rival. *And that Archer guy who made the fruitsnakes attack Iris. He's a jerk, too.*

"Right back at ya," Brun said, stepping between the spider's first and second legs to pat his back. "I believe your people are good."

"I just remembered something Andrés Dosfilos mentioned during the orientation," Kaya said as she switched Iris to the hollow of her free arm. "Is it true the crystal spiders will play a significant part in our Seventh-Level Mission?"

"Yes. Father is arranging for hundreds of my people to participate in the Mission. And, surprisingly, people have been volunteering by the dozens. I had forgotten that; perhaps my clan's apprehension is indeed diminishing," Spence reasoned.

Manny's skin crawled. *By the dozens...*

"So what will we be doing, exactly?" Brun asked, stepping back to stand beside Manny.

"Well, since we Seventh-Level crystal spiders are students, we'll be participating alongside all of you in the challenge. But as for the task itself—Father has woven a web of darkness around that issue."

Brun's shoulders slumped. **Bummer.**

"Why don't we just listen in on their meeting?" Kaya suggested, gesturing back toward Chiron's Hutch. "Didn't you say that's what they're discussing?"

"No, they're actually just supposed to present the faculty to my father and line out the finer details of our integration next Monday," Spence clarified. "They might discuss the Mission at the end, but from Father's words I believe that will have to wait for a later date."

"That sounds boring," Kaya muttered. Spence nodded lightly, and the air grew quiet.

As Manny's mind wandered into the trees, a latent thought awoke in him. "Spence?" The spider's gaze set on the boy. "Um, this may sound stupid, but has your clan encountered any problems with monkeys this past year?"

Dusk drew over the arachnid's eyes, giving him a truly frightening countenance. "Why do you ask?"

Manny swallowed, very nearly choking on his Adam's apple. Then, after reminding himself of the spider's true disposition, the boy proceeded to recount the many histories of wand disappearances, mysterious and ghost-like attacks, as well as his own experiences with the suspect primate group. When he had finished, the spider's frame was no less rigid.

"You actually heard them speak?" Spence asked morbidly.

"Twice," Manny replied. "Like I said, once in Rapa Nui and then again on the Day of the Dead."

Brun nodded. "I heard the one on Easter Island, too. It was the most hateful voice ever to reach my ears."

Spence's eyes dropped to the fern-strewn floor as he ground his fangs in frustration. The sound woke Iris, but the spider took no notice. "Then it is as I feared—they are Lumens."

"That's what we think too!" Kaya rallied.

"And do your elders believe you?" Spence asked, his eyes lifting.

Brun shook his head sadly. "No. They have forbidden us from even mentioning monkeys and wands in the same sentence."

Spence scowled, his lip pads twisting in sickening revulsion. "Mi padre refused to believe as well. He argues that it's impossible, that the Brethren are long dead and no new Lumens can be made. But he is wrong; a new star must have come, and by all appearances he is evil."

"Or she," Kaya added.

"Or she," Spence conceded. "But how are we to know?"

"We seek him out and throttle him," Iris groaned.

Kaya laughed. "That's my kind of attitude."

"Before we talk about that," Manny said, glancing at Brun knowingly, "tell us how the monkeys have harassed your people."

The shadow returned to Spence's brow. "They are tearing out our pincers by the roots."

Kaya blinked in confusion. "What purpose does that serve?"

"Without our fangs we are powerless; we can't even eat without being fed by another spider."

The girl's confusion deepened, but Brun spoke this time. "Their pincers are their wands, Kaya."

"Oh, yeah," she said, recalling this aspect from one of Bluebolt's many anatomy lessons. "So why don't your healers re-grow them?"

"Because our pincers are made of pure crystal, similar to the unicorn's horn and the morpho's antennae, unique to each individual," said Spencer. "Moreover, no Lumen can create stones and ores. We can only reshape them."

A growl emanated from Manny's throat. "We have to stop them."

Iris sat up, his blood flowing properly again. "Let's go this Saturday. If we can find the monkeys' base of operation, maybe we can pilfer back a few wands as evidence to convince Julius of the truth. Then the city guardians could surround the base and crush them."

"May I accompany you?" Spence asked. "The apes incapacitated my cousin. She nearly died."

"Of course," Brun answered. "What ti—"

"Spencer!" called a golden voice suddenly. "Spencer Irradius! ¡Ven aquí! Your instructors wish to know you."

"That's my father," Spence said, glancing through the wall of trees to his side. He thrummed the ground faintly. "Suddenly I am nervous."

Kaya bolstered the arachnid's confidence. "No te preocupes. We'll all come with you. And besides—all the professors are nice, though Professor Flores can get really annoying."

Spence laughed, his lip pads twitching. "Thanks for the info." And with that he proceeded through the underbrush, contorting his substantial frame in twisting shapes to squeeze effortlessly between the trees. A moment later he thrummed onto the back patio of Chiron's Hutch, followed closely by his newly-met comrades. The five young Lumens found themselves face-to-face with the entire Seventh-Level faculty, the three Amazonian counselors, Dosfilos, and Crion. All sets of eyes but one locked on Spence's silver-white frame.

"Ladies and Lumens, this is my son, Spencer Irradius," Crion said with a wave of three of his legs.

"What a simply magnificent specimen!" called Flores, her typical histrionic voice an octave shy of a wail as she strode toward Spence, cerulean robes billowing. The spider flinched as she leaned over him. Something akin to an elated scream erupted from her throat. "Will you look at that design! The astral-cruz, a perfect cross! Exquisite! A living masterpiece!"

"Caleida, give the child some space," said Shadowflame dispassionately, her charged blue eyes glowering.

"Was that Professor Flores?" Spence whispered to Kaya as the golden-haired woman returned to her previous position between Chiron and Rush Stickgrip, who had been peering at Spence with fascinated eyes from the northern wall of the hut. Kaya nodded and rolled her eyes.

During the next ten minutes, Crion presented each of the faculty and staff to his son in turn. All appeared to be fully captivated with the chieftain's son, exchanging polite dialogues

618

fueled by interested questions and answers. Dosfilos, however, took little notice of Spence, nor anyone else for that matter, save two—Manny and Brun. The man's sapphire eyes bored into their frames relentlessly; in fact, he scarcely appeared to breathe.

After a pair of minutes, Manny turned to Brun and whispered, "What is Chairman Dosfilos doing?"

"I do not know," Brun replied uncomfortably from the corner of his mouth. "Did you flip him off or something?"

"Now why would I do that?" Manny riposted viciously.

"Just checking," Brun muttered, his eyes locking with Dosfilos'. After another minute the man had not dropped his gaze, relentlessly probing the depths of the boy's eyes. Brun broke contact. "Let's just try to ignore him. We don't want to risk offending him."

"Too late for that if you ask me," Manny mumbled. Nonetheless, he followed Brun's suggestion, though the eerie sense of alien vigilance did not leave him.

"Well, we should be going," said Crion, following a prolonged discussion between Chiron and his son. "Twilight approaches, and after the theme of our discussion today, I believe it best to have children in shelter by dark."

"Father, must we?" Spence pled. "I would like to continue my visit with the gemini and their friends." Dosfilos' eyes opened wide with shock.

"We aren't brothers," Manny intervened quickly.

"We didn't even meet until last August," Brun contributed. Just as swiftly he added, "And we weren't adopted, if you were wondering." Brun directed this final phrase at Dosfilos, who now appeared stricken.

The crowd jumped as Dosfilos spoke, his eyes breaking in glittering tears. "But your sister…? One of you does have a sister, do you not?"

Manny and Brun glanced at one another, puzzled. "No," said the first boy oddly.

"We are both only-children," stated the second.

The man's resolve faltered, a choked sob erupting from his mouth. In an instant he grabbed his cocobolo wand, waved it through the air, and decompacted his lightboard. "I must go." And with that Dosfilos banked up into the sky, disappearing into the darkness of the southeast horizon.

Cloak & Beard

Manny held three letters in his hand, his eyes roaming the contents of the final message. After a moment he gazed at the ceiling, stretched, and opened his hand, allowing the loose papers to cascade to the dirt floor. His hammock creaked as he grunted. "She's finally off my back."

Brun looked up from his anatomy book as he studied the intricate components of the green basilisk's skin. "And?"

"And I have to follow Julius's curfew," he said, his words striking the dirt bluntly. "How does Julius expect students to attend Astronomy if we can't even leave our homes at night?"

"I doubt you and I will have much difficulty attending, considering Nahir's Hill is in our back yard," Brun answered dryly. Manny turned his head, offering Brun a blank stare. "Cálmate, Manny. It's obvious their parents will escort them to class. After all, they can't teleport."

Manny threaded his fingers through the netting of his hammock, his eyes brushing over Julius's words, now thrown askew. "Do you really believe the Task Force will make any progress?"

Brun turned the page and began a new paragraph. "Not if they keep on denying the truth. And besides, the monkeys are intelligent—they're Lumens. They'll catch wind of the Task Force and change their strategy. You have to know what you're facing to succeed."

"You think we have a chance on Saturday, then?"

"Well, sure. Provided we act smart, of course."

"I suppose we do have the advantage, since they're not expecting us and all," Manny said, his confidence growing. "On top of that, I doubt they know anything about us."

"Other than the fact that we like to photocache," Brun said wryly.

"Yeah, I still don't get that." Manny's eyes snapped to the golden scarab crawling aimlessly in the jar behind Brun's head.

"Why would they return the sun beetle, anyway? Do you think they're trying to intimidate us?"

"No, I honestly think the true culprits are trying to cover themselves." Brun said, rather amused. Manny peered quizzically across the hut. "Didn't you see Iris's face when I asked how their photocaching went today? He looked as if death were imminent."

Manny shook his head. "I was watching Kaya."

Go figure. Talk about staring... "Well, Iris seemed as though he were on the verge of certain death; and Kaya's answer was dodgy, if you ask me. It wasn't hard to put together when the two of them left in such a hurry this afternoon."

Manny gazed at the sun beetle, jaw agape. "So they stole it..."

"And lost it," Brun observed matter-of-factly. "That's why they had to replace it, though ironically on the first day of photocaching."

"We can use this against them," Manny said slowly.

"No harm in a practical joke or two," Brun agreed with a mischievous half-grin.

Manny's mind returned to the manner in which Kaya and Iris had all too abruptly excused themselves after the meeting between the faculty and Crion Irradius. The boy laughed. *This is going to be fun.* "I bet if Kaya had a lightboard she and Iris might've overtaken Andrés Dosfilos." He laughed again, envisioning Kaya on a lightboard. *Yeah, right.*

"Speaking of," Brun said, bringing his book to rest on his lap. "What went down with Dosfilos this afternoon? He acted like he recognized us."

"Possibly—could he have seen us at the orientation?"

"Only as two small figures of light—we could have been statues for all he knew." Brun paused, thrumming the windowsill. "Had you ever met him before?"

"Are you kidding? I didn't even know Lumens existed before last June, and I highly doubt Andrés Dosfilos ever had any business in Siete Arenas, Arizona."

"What about Costa Rica?"

"No, Brun," Manny said dully. "It must've been you. Where did you meet him?"

"Manny, I told you before, I'd never left Marajó from the time I was born until I came here."

"Maybe your papá entertained Dosfilos as a guest sometime in the past few years," Manny postulated. "Tu papá is a businessman, after all."

"It's possible, I guess," Brun admitted reluctantly. "Papá's either always gone or has a meeting with important trade partners in his office…" The memory of voices whispering behind his father's door on Christmas Day flashed into his mind. "He won't always let me meet them, though."

"Problem-solved, then. Dosfilos met you in Marajó and got confused because he couldn't remember you clearly. He travels everywhere—he can't be expected to remember everyone."

"No… But then why did he ask about me having a sister?"

This question delayed Manny's thoughts for a moment. "Maybe," he began steadily, as memories from earlier that day reformulated in his mind, "there's a girl who looks like us." Brun turned and frowned doubtfully. "Don't you remember when Chiron called us children of the solstice?"

Brun nodded, recalling the first night he and Manny had met. "Because you were born on the Summer Solstice and I the Winter Solstice. But how does that apply?"

"It's our only similarity, remember? Maybe, just maybe, when a Lumen child is born on the solstice, when the sun is at its highest, then they share the same physical characteristics."

"Even bone structure?" Brun said, tapping the anatomy book dubiously.

"I don't know, man, but it's the best explanation we've got. How else could Dosfilos have known a girl who looked like us? It's obvious she died, based on his reaction."

"She could have been kidnapped," Brun surmised, his interest renewed. "Didn't Chiron say his sister went missing?"

Manny spun onto his side, a shrewd expression on his face. "Brun, if he was searching for his sister, then why would he ask about ours? You're being thick."

"Am I? Maybe, since we look like his sister, he thought we were the long-lost brothers he never knew he had. Or better yet," he continued swiftly as Manny opened his mouth to contest, "he thought we were her children—how about that paradox?"

"Do you invent impossible realities often?"

Brun ignored this comment. "We do look a lot like him."

"We look like Andrés Dosfilos?" Manny barked incredulously.

"Sure—high cheekbones, long faces, short hair. His nose is a bit bigger than ours, though…"

"He did seem awfully familiar," Manny confessed. "He looks a lot like my dad, especially in the eyes…" He paused. "But it's not the color of their eyes that matches, it's the way they look at you, the way their soul seems to reach out and grab your own." Manny stared into the darkness for a moment, then suddenly shivered.

"I hear you," Brun said, considering his aunt's tender gaze.

A tranquil silence followed as each boy slid into a state of retrospection, their minds flitting peacefully over fond memories of times shared with family—of evenings spent talking, of daytime laughter, of eventual departure and inevitable separation. Manny spent the quiet minutes reliving endless summers of baseball and cave exploration at his cousin Zane's side, while Brun revived the days his aunt had lead him across the vast grounds of their estate, introducing him to the vibrant flora and fauna of the Brazilian jungle.

Even so, the crux of the day's exhaustion outweighed the nostalgia of the night as the boys' lids began to droop, waking dreams coercing their consciousnesses into defenseless submission. Nearly a half hour passed before a disturbance entered their revelries, a muffled warble that wrestled their fluttering eyes awake.

"Brun, it's for you," Manny yawned as he saw the corner of a letter fold lightly onto the boy's chest.

"Oh," Brun mumbled, his fingers struggling to reach and unfold the paloma paper. **No one ever sends me letters.** His eyes danced in and out of focus as he stumbled through the scratchy words. "Manny," he groaned, minutes later, "Spence wants to know if we're on for Saturday at 11 a.m."

"Whatever," he replied, turning onto his left side to breathe the cool night air. "It's not like we can go at night, anyhow."

Brun mumbled his assent as he scribbled a yes on the paper and then faded into the darkness of his subconscious.

***

"Do you jest?" Spence whirled around, his pointed legs effectively anchoring him to the blustering roots of a particularly corpulent tree. Filtered light from the dense canopy struck his skin, camouflaging his crystalline flesh and making him appear very much like a strange, moss-covered growth—a horrific bromeliad—jutting indefinably from the plant life. So consummate was Spence's natural concealment, in fact, that more than once that morning Manny had believed himself to be addressing his eight-legged companion when in all actuality he had been talking to an obtuse cluster of ferns.

Brun glanced quickly at Kaya, then back at Spence. "Why would I?"

The jade-hued spider clicked his fangs together, eye clusters darting between Brun and Manny. "So it actually returned the sun beetle?"

"Apparently," Manny replied, rolling his shoulders faintly.

"But why?" Spence asked, at a loss.

"Probably to intimidate us. Don't you think, Iris?" Brun said, turning to the hare in all sincerity.

The hare, who had apparently been inspecting the tufts of his ears, stopped abruptly. "I suppose so..." he replied uncomfortably.

"They're probably stalking you," Kaya contributed, her words hanging lightly in the misty air as she passed through the center of her companions. "Wouldn't be surprised if they wring your necks some night while you're sleeping."

Manny grinned slightly.

"That is a fairly serious supposition," Spence observed. Manny watched in amazement as the spider's heart beat faster in his pellucid chest. "Perhaps it would be wise to inform Chiron."

"Oh, we're not too worried about it, are we, Manny?" Brun said, throwing his roommate a guarded wink.

"Just hope the monkeys don't start to target our amigos," Manny said, chuckling quietly.

Like they already haven't? Iris rubbed the root of his ear insipidly.

Kaya bent down, parting the ferns at her feet as she inspected a deep, muddy print. "The trail ends here. By the pressure exerted in this footprint I'd say this is where the monkey took to the trees."

Spence spun around, rubbing his lip pads together as he scanned the boles above Kaya's head. His joints flexed with lightning speed as he lifted from the roots, his body spiraling as he briefly lit upon an adjacent tree before bounding over Kaya's head to alight in an inverted pose high on the bole above her. He rubbed his lip pads together again. "I can taste them—their filth hangs in the air," he said darkly.

"Their?" Kaya repeated as Manny, Brun, and Iris drew up behind her. "But there's only one set of prints."

A spitting sound issued from Spence's mouth. "The trees wreak of ape dung. This is a common path for the thieves; they pass by here daily—one this morning, in fact. His are the tracks we have been following. He cannot be far."

Manny turned sharply to Brun. "What if we can capture him? Then we could take him back as evidence for the Task Force."

"That would be much easier than infiltrating their base," Brun agreed. "Iris, where are we exactly?"

Reaching into his satchel, the hare pulled out a pearl-hued compass. "Less than a mile east of the light barrier, roughly level with Chiron's Hutch. Basically, directly east of Isla Verde."

"And from here the scent continues to the north," Spence noted.

"Iris, make sure you're tracking our progress on the CPS; the Task Force will need directions to the base," Brun directed.

"Is it really that simple?" Manny asked.

"If we're lucky," Brun replied.

Kaya rose to her full height. "Everybody's ready? Chamaeleon and Reticulum equipped?" All nodded. "Then whoever gets the first clear shot at the monkey, take it."

"And then I'll bite him and wrap him in webbing. He'll be paralyzed until nightfall," Spence affirmed. "¿De acuerdo?"

"Perfect," Manny said. "Vamos."

And so, in total silence, the three humans and the hare shadowed the arachnid as he bolted along the canopy, his legs drumming expertly among the branches, boles, and leaves, his lip pads tasting, his eyes searching. For their part Manny and company struggled to maintain the spider's pace as they hurdled over roots, stamped across shallow streams, and constantly dodged the lesser dangers of the rainforest. More than once, from his unique perspective, Iris was able to deter the impending threat of an Amazon Horned Frog, enveloping the amphibian's bloated frame with Reticulum then launching the Lumorph through the trees with a deep sense of gratification, a sensation similarly embodied in Kaya's words. Manny and Brun ran with Flareshots ready, occasionally halting the group's progress and releasing an orb or two to deflect a cluster of firespitters, a Lumorph of the poison dart frog genus, which in the presence of a perceived danger would eject a stream of scalding flame from its mouth. At one point Iris became rather upset when a stray firespitter scorched his tail. Despite the boys' profuse apologies, Kaya could not fully stifle her laughter.

After approximately fifteen minutes, Spence halted their progress, spinning around with imperceptible speed. "Stop!" he ordered, the blades from his desperate command peeling the bark from a nearby tree. "Stand on either side of the path we've been following and conceal yourselves! A pair of figures approach in the distance!" The humans and hare obeyed unquestioningly, Manny and Kaya darting behind the spiked roots of a kapok on the north side, while Brun and Iris hid within the knuckled base of a rubber tree. All four melted into transparent oblivion as the curling tails of their sentinel Chamaeleons wrapped around their ankles. Spence, on his account, hugged his perch tightly, his jade-speckled body changing instantly to a rough chartreuse to make him one with the tree's bark. Nearly a minute passed as the five Lumens waited, muscles tensed in anticipation of sight or sound of their prey. Their efforts were rewarded as a low, rasping voice met their ears, its serrated tenor a strict contrast to the pleasant lilt of leaves parting as the owner of the voice walked.

"...Isla Verde alone we have acquired virtually two hundred wands over the past five months, and that is not counting the forty my minions confiscated during the maggots' play day this previous Wednesday." The voice twisted into a coarse laugh. "Lumens are helpless..."

"Yes, they are, General Bloodfang," agreed another voice, its ostentatious cadence seeking to gratify the first individual. "I remember—"

The swishing of the leaves ceased abruptly. "As I conveyed to you earlier, youngling—Mistarcus will suffice. Or even Miscus, if it pleases you," said the rasping voice, its edge sharp.

"Forgive me—Mistarcus," the second voice replied, its pride laced with uncertainty. "But am I not to address my superior with his proper title?"

"You do not fall under my command, youngling," returned the rasping voice wisely. "The Master brought you here to accustom you with our procedures, that I may tutor you briefly in the art of leadership. Or are you not aware that you will soon be my equal?"

"No, of that I was not informed," came the second voice, somewhat estranged. "Am I to lead here?"

"Indeed not—this is my post." A pause. "Though the Master has not been forthright, I believe he deigns to place you where he found you."

"In Europe? But why?"

"He was very pleased with the manner in which you disposed of his—servants—with your most rudimentary skills," the voice rasped murkily. "You slew six with mere photokinesis—imagine the potential you will have upon mastering the Twilight."

"But they lacked form; their ambush was tactless," responded the second voice disdainfully.

"Precisely the reason the Master wills for you to lead them. But let us continue on our way and waste no more time; I have much to show you. Perhaps you will witness my minions in the act of hunting."

"If I am so lucky," the proud voice jeered as the two figures resumed their walk. A moment later the soft rustling sounds of their passage reached the kapok and rubber trees behind which Manny and his companions had hidden. Into the children's motionless view came an ebony-robed figure—a man—his hood lowered to reveal his chestnut hair, fair skin, and pronounced jaw, his eyes haughty, blue. Beside the man bounded a monkey, three-feet in stature, his short fur the hue of midnight velvet, which matched his polluted eyes. The ape's hands and feet were of black leather, and lines of hatred etched his brow. Three steps from the children the man suddenly stopped, glancing down at the ape. The children's lungs froze, their invisible eyes locked on the man's face. Spence prepared to leap down, should the need arise.

"Gen—I mean, Mistarcus," the man ensued, his eyes suddenly filled with respect. "Where will the Master send me next? To Africa, or Australia perhaps?"

Mistarcus turned like lightning and spat on the ground, his brow blistered and his fangs bared beneath his snow white beard. "Do not speak to me of that witch's territory! She can keep her filthy island and witless prey for all I care!"

The man's expression became guarded. "What do you mean?"

"That beast—the austral witch, or so I call her—is the Master's prized harlot," Mistarcus said, spitting again. "No one can compare to the greatness she holds in the Master's eyes—not even I, Chieftain of the emperor tamarins. All my efforts are as nothing to the countless kills she makes each year. By her successes I am constantly measured and deemed a lesser servant. What can the Master expect, when this post just only opened last year and she has been in operation for nigh on a decade? We have yet to establish an infrastructure..."

"He must hold great faith in you if he sent me to study under you," the man bolstered after a moment. "Surely he has noticed your progress."

The monkey—or tamarin, as it were—lifted blazoned eyes, the skin around which crinkled cruelly. "Indeed. I had yet to tell you this, but we have recently enlisted nearly one hundred recruits from among the Lumens' own ranks—a feat I doubt the witch will ever match. We expect over two hundred before this so-called Mission they are feigning in late May. How interesting it will be when—"

A heavy rustling suddenly sounded in the canopy to the west, much like the thunder of a rhino charging through the tree tops. The children glanced up, spying a bulky figure descending through the trees. Realizing they were now visible, humans and hare crouched tightly behind their respective roots, praying not to to be seen. The man whirled around, producing an oak wand from the long sleeves of his cloak. Mistarcus appeared to be clutching a dark sphere in his left palm.

With a shock that shook the earth Crion Irradius crashed to the ground, his front legs slicing through the air as a pair of radiant scythes curved toward the man and the monkey. Mistarcus flicked his wrist, and the dark orb in his hand leapt forth, assuming the shape of a wall of shadow that absorbed Crion's scythes.

"Father!" Spence whispered from his elevated post.

"This is the spider-king I spoke of," Mistarcus growled as he pressed the wall forward, forcing Crion to tread backward several steps. "His death would greatly aid our cause, and you need practice." The emperor tamarin's eyes gleamed deliciously. "Kill him." The man nodded, pulling his hood over his eyes. With that Mistarcus flipped back, clenching his fist as the shadow barrier funneled back into his palm. He then sat idly on a root and stared at the man's back.

"Traitor!" Crion hissed, his fangs clacking once at the hooded man. "You have betrayed our people, training these witless apes to do your bidding." Mistarcus smirked placidly, but remained silent. "Speak, traitor filth! Why have you done this?"

The man betrayed no sign of movement, not even a breath.

"Now you are tongueless?" Crion boomed, his eyes livid. "So quick to rob children of their identity, but saying nothing!" The crystal spider rose from his crouch, extending his legs to raise his body to the level of the man's head. "I will drag you before the Lumen Council, and then you shall speak for your actions."

"I think not," the man uttered flatly, his oak wand pointed at the ground. Mistarcus grinned as a stream of shadows scurried between the ferns at the man's feet.

Crion clicked his pincers calmly. "It is already too late." Before he finished the final word, a glittering, silver mesh descended upon the man and the monkey. Just before the mesh met his hood, however, the man raised his wand, and a rippling cord of shadow burst from the ferns, slicing back through the air and cleaving the net, which clattered lifeless to the ground at the man's side and then dissolved.

Brun's eyes widened. **Incredible.**

"Pathetic," the man murmured as the whip snaked forward, snapping in the air before Crion's pincers. "Now die," he said emotionlessly as he whirled the whip over his head, swinging his arm in a wide arc as the obscure tendril hissed straight for the spider's body. Crion leapt up, the sharp tips of his legs barely clearing the trajectory of the whip as it sliced effortlessly through the base of the kapok tree upon which the spider now sat.

Manny sighed heavily, the whip having passed less than a foot above his head. He turned to his left. "Kaya—are you okay?"

She nodded, her heart beating fast. "I'd say we'd better lie flat on the ground, though."

Crion bounded to an adjacent tree as the whip cracked in the air a second time. A stream of shadow knitted through Mistarcus's fingers as he watched the crystal spider dance among the trees, scarcely evading the man's searing whip that gouged deeply into the sturdy boles. A derisive sneer curled the tamarin's lips as Crion rested beyond the reach of the man's whip.

"Now who is the coward?" asked the man blandly, the whip sinking to the ground, instantaneously devouring the plant matter that it touched.

The spider spit, his fangs clacking as countless streams of light pierced the foliage to converge on his body, his transparent limbs and core growing progressively brighter as he infused his bulk with photons.

"Do it now," whispered Mistarcus as Crion's luminescence began to fill the air with an increasingly blinding light. The man nodded and lifted his wand, the snaking strand of his whip coalescing to form a dark sphere, the obscurity of which grew in tandem with the luminescence of Crion's body.

Brun's hands gripped the entangled rubber roots before him as foreboding suffused his limbs, telling him to flee the scene as quickly as possible. **This is going to be bad.** He intended to turn and grab Iris, when a terrible, air-rending screech sliced his ears. The boy's eyes immediately shot to Mistarcus. The tamarin's paws clutched his right eye as blood gushed between his fingers, staining his white beard scarlet.

"Score," Iris said as he lowered the Flareshot in his paws.

"You did that?" Brun asked, his eyes bouncing between the wailing tamarin and the scowling hare.

Iris nodded curtly. "He nearly took my ear off on Ukisaru Volcano—so I took his eye. Now we're even."

Anger intermingled with pain to compound Mistarcus's wail to a paralyzing octave, driving Brun and Iris to crouch down and cover their ears. Altogether suddenly the tamarin's cry stopped. With ears ringing, the hare and the boy peered over the tangled rubber roots to see the man disappearing through the trees, his ebony robes flaring about the ferns. The monkey was gone.

Crion catapulted through the air at that instant, his legs a seething white that sliced through the underbrush as easily as the man's whip had incised the kapok. His glittering fangs were not five

632

feet from the man's legs when a desperate call from the canopy halted the arachnid's assault.

"Father, no!" shouted Spence, descending from his lofty perch on a crystal thread.

Crion spun halfway around, his eyes hard. "Spencer? What—"

At that moment a terrible wind tore through the air, dragging Crion several feet along the ground and slamming Spence into a tree. Brun and Iris could not move, the gust having pinned them to the roots, while an invisible force seemed to drag Manny and Kaya in the direction the tamarin and the man had fled. Manny locked his forearm with Kaya's, straining against the suction to anchor them to an elbowed tendril of the kapok. After approximately ten seconds had passed the wind disappeared and the mysterious force dissipated.

Kaya pulled herself and Manny up off the ground, brushing back her hair and bolting hurriedly to Crion's side. "What just happened?"

Crion gawked as the humans and hare materialized from the underbrush; he wasted no time with questions, however. "Spencer, get down here immediately," the clan chief said forcefully. Though slightly disoriented, the young arachnid acquiesced. The precise moment his son touched ground, Crion clicked his fangs, the light suffused in his body diffusing to form a thick dome that encased the entire group.

"The five of you will remain absolutely silent," said Crion imperiously. "Follow me and do not stray even a step."

Knotted tension began to build in the children's stomachs as they cautiously progressed through the forest, wondering from which direction the man or monkey might appear to ambush the group. After witnessing the whip slice effortlessly through a tree, Manny seriously doubted the resilience of Crion's dome against a similar strike. The boy swallowed hard as he took another half-step, his eyes testing the thickness of the partially opaque dome. *And I have no means to defend myself against something like that—it's not like my Flareshot's gonna do me any good...*

Crion suddenly stopped, his legs pecking the earth nervously as he drew a deep breath. "Wait here," he commanded, advancing forward and leaving the children within the bubble of light. Manny frowned in his attempt to decipher the confused shapes on the outside of the dome; his efforts were met with only disappointment, however, as he could scarcely discern Crion's bright figure, stationary though it was. A moment later the clan chief spun around and reentered the bubble.

"The traitor and the tamarin are gone," Crion said, his eyes dark and hard. "It is safe for you to walk in the open air again, but let me warn you—I have never witnessed a scene of this state in my eighty years." After pausing to gaze at each child individually, Crion clacked his fangs, causing the dome to disintegrate and the loose photons to scatter in the air.

A collective gasp issued from each mouth as the children struggled to rationalize the sight before them—myriads of tree roots unearthed, twisted and intertwined, their spear-like tips reaching toward a focal point in space as if the trees had purposely uprooted to accuse a common enemy; in fact, as Manny's eyes wandered into the air, he realized that the trees themselves had inclined, the canopies touching hundreds of feet above to form a skeletal teepee.

"The bark has been stripped from the trees," Kaya said, her voice hushed as she tentatively touched one such pale tendril, its naked frame jutting from the ground.

Iris grabbed the hem of Kaya's pant leg, twisting it anxiously. "You're sure they're not in there somewhere?" he asked, his eyes attempting to maneuver between the root storm mounting before him. They could be hiding in the center of it.

"They are not," Crion replied simply.

"How can we be sure?" Manny asked, pushing the point.

"Their scent is gone," Spence answered. "The air no longer tastes of fig dung, or at least not as strongly as before."

In a leap of power and grace, Crion mounted a nearby tree and picked his way along the cock-eyed bole until he rested more or less over the center of the root mess. He then fell through the air, spinning lazily as he approached the apex of the root spears. He tasted the air with his lip pads then rubbed the smooth insides of his crystal fangs together pensively.

A moment passed, and no one spoke. Eager to hear the spider's thoughts, Brun asked, "Master Irradius, what happened here?"

Crion flicked his webbing with a hind leg, pinching the crystallized silk as he spun to face the boy. "Brun, I am just not sure. It is certain that our perpetrators exited from this exact point, but I stumble over the manner of their departure. Their scent is not in the air above, nor does it trail further in any direction." He paused, snapping his fangs at the roots thoughtfully. "It is as if they simply dissolved."

"But that's impossible, right?" Manny queried, his gaze glancing over the razor roots.

The chieftain united the spikes of his front legs. "Until this moment, I would have said yes."

"Could they have teleported somehow? After all, they are both Lumens—perhaps they discovered how to break the cells of their body into light to transfer themselves over long distances," Iris observed.

"If they disintegrated then they would have no means to reconstruct themselves—their cells would merely have fallen lifelessly to the ground," Crion responded. "But allow me to point out—"

"So is that what happened? They killed themselves?" Kaya interrupted.

"No—their scent would be concentrated below the roots in that case," Spence answered. "I personally believe they used some advanced transport mechanism."

"You mean like a dimensional distortion device?" Manny asked, a tinge of excitement entering his voice. All eyes turned to focus on his avid expression. "What?" he contended defensively. "So I like sci-fi; but this fits, doesn't it?" The confused glances of his companions only deepened at the mention of the genre. Just as Manny began to feel quite uncomfortable, Crion spoke.

"Regardless of the manner in which the thieves left, I must clarify a point of obvious ambiguity for the lot of you. Please understand that despite the fact that the emperor tamarins most likely play a significant role in the theft of your peers' wands, the monkeys themselves are not Lumens. That proposition is an utter impossibility; rest assured that the tamarins are simply acting as thieving pets for the man whom I fought just now, who, might I add, is significantly skilled in the art of photokinetic dueling."

Kaya snorted. "He's a blustering idiot."

"I beg your pardon?" Crion replied.

Throwing her hair over her shoulder, she said, "That fool that you fought is Archer Villalobos, my sister's neurotic boyfriend. I'd have recognized that big jaw and exaggerated voice anywhere."

"I knew he looked familiar!" Manny ejected. "It was Archer!"

"But you cannot be certain of that," Crion affirmed, "for his hood lay drawn over his face."

"By the time you got there, sí," Kaya noted. "But we saw him walk up with his hood down—it was Archer alright."

"It is not prudent to rush to such accusations, Señorita Bellastrata," the chieftain advised.

"They speak true, Father," Spence contributed. "We were following the stench of the monkeys through the forest when the human and the tamarin drew near to us while immersed in conversation."

"I will not tolerate foolery and nonsense from my own offspring," Crion warned.

"But we're not lying, Señor!" Iris advocated. "Archer called the monkey Mistarcus, and he even referred to him as a general! They talked about how the emperor tamarins had collected over two hundred wands since last term and how they're going to waylay us during the Mission!"

Crion's fangs rubbed together silently as the arachnid contemplated the sincerity in the hare's amethyst eyes. "My young Firefoot, I understand that the five of you just experienced an extremely traumatic event, and that stress manifests itself in truly

636

unexpected ways after such incidents. Allow me to simply concede that this Archer—if indeed that is the man's true identity—was walking along through the forest maintaining an animated and one way discourse with the tamarin. Though you may be convinced otherwise, I admonish you to rest and consider the matter at a later time—perhaps then you will heed my words. Further arguments to the contrary will only test my patience, and I have none to waste." He paused. "Now, before we return to Isla Verde, I must inquire as to why the four of you and my son blatantly disregarded the boundaries set in Director Rumblefeather's curfew letter?"

Iris, Manny, and Spence shifted uncomfortably under the chieftain's ink-infused gaze. Brun and Kaya, however, remained unfettered.

"We feel an obligation to our peers to hunt down and retrieve their wands, or at least bring a few back as proof that we've discovered the thieves' base of operations," Brun explained, his words sure.

"We're not going to allow these tragedies to continue any further," Kaya added, her hand on her hip.

Crion's brow lifted and his lip pads parted slightly to form a twisted smile the likes of which the children had never seen before—excluding Spence, of course. "Our very own young Lumen task force," he mused. "Please understand, I hold great esteem for your passion, but I cannot allow this behavior to come full circle and conceive itself again."

A watermelon lodged itself in Manny's throat; yet somehow he managed to ask," Master Irradius, does that mean you're going to inform our parents?"

Kaya's resolve faltered. *Oh please, no—I can't handle being grounded for two months…*

Papá would never let me leave the island again… Brun's stomach squirmed at the thought of spending the rest of his life confined to the grounds of his mansion in Marajó.

"Is such recourse necessary, or do I have your solemn word that none of you will leave the city limits without permission again?" Crion blinked, shielding his corpulent eyes briefly.

"I personally don't want to be shipped home tomorrow, so yes, you have my word," Manny answered quickly.

"And I don't want to grade Sentinels tests the rest of the semester, so that's an affirmative from me, too," Iris readily adjoined.

After Brun and Kaya likewise pledged their obedience, Crion turned his gaze on his son. "What say you, young Irradius? Must I inform your mother, or will you follow in your friends' footsteps?"

The young arachnid's eyes widened slightly as a shocked smile entered his countenance. "Aye, Father, I promise."

"Then the matter is settled but for one final detail," Crion said, shifting his weight gently as he began swinging in a pendulum-like motion. "This Archer fellow that you know, Señorita Bellastrata—what was his surname again?"

"Villalobos. His name is Archer Villalobos," Kaya replied, her voice void of emotion as she watched the spider oscillate through the air before her like a ticking clock. *Hope that string doesn't break—I don't want to have to clean up an arachno-kabob.*

"A distinctive name, though Hispanic in origin rather than Lumen. But there's no fault in that." By this time Crion had built his momentum to establish a wide arc, a detail which made Manny's heart lurch with each successive downswing. Crion rubbed the lower shafts of his forelegs together, oblivious to the boy's preoccupation. "Could you tell me his address?"

"He lives southeast of the island, more or less directly south of Fire Flats, but I don't know the road name or anything. I've never been there." *And I never want to—it's probably a rat hole, considering the source.*

At that instant Crion broke loose from the webbing, allowing his inertia to carry him along a sine wave through the air as he performed a somersault to powerfully land beyond the edge of the roots. "No matter," he said, clicking his fangs once for good measure. "I can simply search his name in the database—I'll locate him that way."

"So what now, Father?" Spence asked tentatively. "Will you follow the tamarin trail deeper into the forest?"

"I have already done such," Crion replied coolly.

"You have?" Brun rebounded. "What did you find?"

"Dear Brun, I have found neither trace nor tail of the tamarins' shelter; though I have followed their crisscrossing highways for miles through the stench-filled air and trees. I must assume, therefore, that the true location of the missing wands lies within the mind of the man I fought, be he Archer Villalobos or no. Since our first hatchling alleged that she had been attacked and robbed of her fangs by a white-bearded monkey, I have not allowed a day to pass without relentlessly scouring the canopy for the perpetrator. Yet all of the emperor tamarin packs that I have encountered carried nothing more than figs and fruit."

"I assure you, that man is Archer," Kaya said dryly. *But I doubt you'll find much in that cranium of his.*

"Then allow us to depart," Crion asserted, his legs tensing. "I will leave the five of you at Chiron's Hutch before assembling the Task Force to relate the events of today. With any luck we will apprehend the man and diffuse the problem in rapid fashion. After all, extract the heart, and the beast dies."

Kaya stared at the spider chieftain blandly. *True, but as of yet this beast's anatomy remains unknown.*

Dinner Invitation

Manny needed to find out. He had to.

"I do apologize, Manuel, but I have never heard of such a case," Chiron replied mildly. "That field is not my expertise, however, so there may be a gap in my knowledge. Perhaps you would do better to consult with Professor Shadowflame—she ultimately wields a greater knowledge of Lumen history than I."

Dang it. Manny hated talking to his Lumen World instructor, as she seemed to wield the distinct talent of making him feel the fool.

"Señor López," she began with a low growl, her rhythmic tail snapping a post on the Quay. "Did we not cover that topic in detail during the previous term?"

Manny blinked. "I-I don't remember."

"You don't remember!" she yowled, her ocean eyes opening wide. "Perhaps that's why you very nearly failed your Unit Test over the Brethren!"

"I actually got a C…" he murmured.

"What?" she retorted, her voice dangerous.

"Nothing, Señora," he dodged. "But could you please help me? You see, my cousin—"

Shadowflame's tail snapped again. "Señor López, if this issue is as vital to you as it appears to be, then may I suggest that you refer to page 112, paragraph three of your text? Now I must depart; I have a previous engagement to uphold. Good day."

Oh, yes, so very helpful. Manny snapped the book shut and rolled his eyes. *Like I didn't already know all that…* He blinked. *Maybe he'll know…*

"Definitely not, Manny," Julius said, his feathers ruffling. "I've worked with thousands of new Lumens, if not a million or more, and the rules are always consistent. I am sorry for Zane, but sometimes in life we just have to accept the truth. Disillusionment is bitter, but he will surpass it."

Manny left the Office of Lumen studies with a significantly heavier heart and began to wonder just how he could break this news to his cousin. It had been three weeks since Zane's birthday— March 27, to be exact—and no Wand-Giver, no Light-Bringer, had ever come. According to Julius Rumblefeather, Head Counselor for the entire southern continent, Enlightenment must come by the sunrise following an individual's fourteenth birthday. Manny's cousin was not a Lumen. He never would be.

"That just sucks!" Manny yelled. The Lumens in his vicinity stopped and stared—a unicorn, its brow furrowed; a green basilisk with a paw held to its heart; a kinkajou, its mouth hanging open. Manny's face grew suddenly bright. "Sorry," he muttered, nearly running to escape their accusatory eyes. *Well, it does, though. He's been waiting all year for this. I can't tell him...*

But he did. He sat by the fountain, put his shame to words, and then mailed them. He saw no point in delaying the inevitable; after all, there was no justification for his cousin to hang his hope on a lie. But this was just one more issue on Manny's shoulders that he did not wish to deal with—his classes were getting harder, the Mission was approaching in just over a month, and people's wands were still disappearing, despite the Task Force's best efforts. Not only did Zane need something to look forward to, but so did Manny. And now it appeared that his cousin, his best friend, was to become a casual summer acquaintance. Sure he loved his friends here, but no one could replace family, and Zane was both.

To further intensify Manny's disappointment, his greatest fear appeared to have conceived. Zane did not respond; not within a day, not within two, not even within a week. And Manny began to feel lost—an anchor in his life had been severed; he needed to tell Zane that the attacks were getting worse, that several Lumens were hospitalized, that one had nearly died. He needed to explain just how hard it was to convert photons into organic wood matter, to complain about the mind-bending complexity of creating and controlling a shoal of sentinel fish, to share the thrill of generating an explosion from rushing photons to divert the enemy's attention. Sure he could repair a minor cut on his arm now by using light to stimulate the body's natural restorative properties—those countless hours of anatomy studying had to count for something, after all—but explaining this to Zane would only deepen his cousin's wound, not heal it. And so a quiet wall was built, as bricks of unease and resentment stacked one atop another to drive the boys apart. And another month passed, heralding the end of May and the crux of the Seventh-Level—the Mission.

Late one afternoon, Manny received the following letter:

My Dear Sr. López,

You have been cordially invited to attend a meal in your honor this Wednesday, the 14th of May in the Sapphire Room of the House of the Brethren. Present the enclosed ticket to the Lumen-in-Waiting at the House Door no later than 1:45 p.m. Formal attire is not required. We look forward to speaking with you.

Yours affectionately,

Melody Nightvine

"A meal in my honor? What did I do?" Manny reread the letter with groggy eyes. The unanticipated mail had awakened him from a much-needed nap. "And who is this 'we'?" Upon reading the correspondence a third time, Manny turned his attention to the glimmering sapphire ticket in his hand, and sank slowly back down into his hammock. A faint interest was piqued his heart. *I've never been in the Brethren House before...* The lethargy of the afternoon, however, groped at his consciousness as Manny's hands sank to his chest and his mind began to drift silently through the halls of the mansion.

***

A whisper in Manny's ear made him jerk to the right—another dark room, its masked contents shadowed by a gaping arch, the zenith of which rose nearly thirty feet in the air. Manny clenched his fist, knowing that he had to enter—but a constant unease bit at the edge of his mind. He did not particularly like the idea of turning his back on one darkness to enter another. But he had to—he had to find his friends. So, with a broad, rising staircase twisting up and away to his left and the descending steps disappearing to his right, Manny advanced toward the dark room, a faint light over his shoulder illuminating his steps and lightly brushing the curved frames of a long row of objects before him. He tried to swallow, but his throat had run dry, and a fear—no, a latent terror—suddenly burst to life in his mind as a hushed whisper met his ear. He turned sharply, catching a glimpse of wild hair, bright teeth, and red, malevolent eyes before the light over his shoulder abruptly dissolved and his heart stopped.

***

"Holy cow! Chill, Manny, chill!"

Manny burned—his chest, his legs, his arms, his hair—he felt as though he were wrapped in a steaming blanket, paralyzed and unable to break free. He thrashed and kicked, his wrist striking something hard as he spun and fell, cracking his head as his body hit the dirt floor. He crumpled and gave up the fight, his burning skin finding respite on the cool ground.

"Bad dream, or what?" Brun asked, kneeling as he grabbed Manny's hammock, which was swinging wildly.

Manny opened his eyes, the back of his head pounding. "I guess so," he croaked. "I think I was in the House of the Brethren and this—thing—attacked me."

"The dinner won't be that bad, Manny. They're going to honor us, not eat us."

Manny opened an eye and frowned. "What do you mean?"

"I mean I noticed you'd gotten a ticket for the meal at the Brethren House tomorrow, too. That is before you freaked out and threw it out the window into the rain. Now let me see your wrist."

Manny did not argue as Brun inspected his arm; instead, he closed his eyes and listened to the pounding rain as it penetrated the humid jungle air. *No wonder I was hot—it's like a sauna out there.* Manny sighed as a cool sensation brushed the outside of his wrist. "What are you doing?" he asked, opening his eyes to see Brun pointing his wand at his wrist.

"I'm mending the cut you made and drawing out the bruise. It'll only take another second or two." After a moment Brun released Manny's hand. "Now sit up and face the wall—your head's bleeding."

"It is?" Manny's fist flew to his hair; he pulled his hand back and stared at his fingers, which glistened with blood. *Just great.*

"Sit up already so I can fix it," Brun said, slightly aggravated.

Yes, sir. Manny groaned as he acquiesced, closing his eyes as the pain flared. Brun worked silently as he purged the wound with loose photons, a technique that was much more effective than any disinfectant offered by the outside world, or so affirmed Madison Bluebolt. Having cleansed the wound, Brun set about stimulating the cells within the gash, witnessing as the divided membranes slowly knitted together to make a flawless patch of new skin. He then patted Manny's shoulder and stood up.

"A-okay, bud. Feel alright?"

Manny nodded as he grabbed the windowsill to anchor himself to his feet. "Yeah, thanks. I doubt Professor Bluebolt could have done any better!"

"I don't know about that," Brun replied, threading the birch ring back onto his hand. "Let's just hope you didn't get a concussion—I definitely can't do anything about that."

Manny half nodded, half shrugged, as he noticed a hint of lingering pain on the back of his skull. "Oh, well, whatever. Wait a sec while I run out and get my ticket before it washes away—or Nipper eats it." He disappeared through the doorway then returned, his blue school shirt heavily speckled with raindrops. "Whew! I just saw Nipper and Lil' Manny wrestling in a mud puddle out there—they're crazy!" he said as he dried the slick ticket on his jeans. "So what's this dinner all about?"

***

"¡Sí, señores!" cried a particularly plump chinchilla, the typically gray fur known for his species having long since faded to white. Today happened to be his birthday—fifty-seven years of bliss, or so he had alleged to his wife that morning—which would explain the extra cheer in his voice and perk in his demeanor as he accepted Manny and Brun's tickets before the massive oak doors of the House of the Brethren. Manny smiled to himself as the rodent grinned broadly. The fur of the creature's tail poofed to achieve an even greater flare as he said, "Yes, gentleman, welcome to the House! I see that the pair of you are among the committee's honored guests this fine day! Just one moment—I'll have a tanager right down to show you the way!" The chinchilla clucked his tongue, and from the sky fell a shower of prismatic droplets that, upon reaching a distance of no more that two feet from the boys' heads, transformed into a cloud of shimmering birds, the size of a finch and of a song more pleasing than any music, their notes crystal clear and draining directly into the listener's soul. With a sharp whistle from the chinchilla the song ended, though the tanagers maintained their frenzied flight.

"Piolet, if you please, would you lead these fine gentle Lumens to the Sapphire Room?" the chinchilla asked. An affirmative chirp, like the sound of a drop of water, erupted from the tanager cloud as a bird of brilliant reds and blues dove forward and landed on Brun's shoulder. "Bien. I appreciate that. The rest of you may return to the skies—but not too far, now—if I were a smart rodent—and I daresay I may be—I would say more guests are comin'." With the sound of a melodic splash the cloud of birds shot into the air, reassuming the shape of inverted rain droplets.

645

Manny stared at the bird on Brun's shoulder. *I've never been this close to a crystal tanager before… They're beautiful.*

"Off you go, boys! Piolet, if you please!" the chinchilla squeaked. "And enjoy the meal—my wife's a-cookin'. I daresay she's a fine chef!"

Brun thanked the chinchilla as the boys crossed the threshold of the mansion, their feet meeting a checkered sea of six-foot marble tiles that wrapped around the base of the widest and most elegant staircase they had ever seen. To either side ran a hall large enough to accommodate a train, if not two, and Lumens of all species darted with purposeful grace from the gently curved staircase to the halls to innumerable rooms sprouting in virtually every direction. The boys would have spent several minutes absorbing the scene if not for Piolet, who darted in a shimmering line to the bottom-left post of the grand stair. Shaking their heads, Brun and Manny walked briskly to catch the tanager, who, just as they reached the base of the stairs, shot up along the bowed railing to the banister of the second story, allowing her song to ring sweetly through the air. Taking the steps two at a time, the boys reached Piolet in twenty seconds or so. Again, they had little time to contemplate the velvet carpet the shade of scarlet and the adjacent halls as Piolet mounted the subsequent staircase, effortlessly skirting another two hundred steps. Manny caught a glimpse of what appeared to be a series of circular offices before a wall of verdant tapestries and expressive paintings filled his vision. Though he truly did not mind jogging up the stairs, he hoped that their climb would end on the subsequent floor merely for the sake of exploring the Stars' ancient home. Fortunately, Manny got his wish as Piolet curved gently through the air to his right, her glittering frame disappearing just beneath the zenith of a thirty-foot archway.

A sudden wave of vertigo struck as Manny reached the landing, his mind rapidly processing the similarities between his nightmare the afternoon prior and his present location in the House. Manny caught his breath as certainty flooded his mind. *I was here.*

"What are you doing?" Brun roared, lunging forward to grab Manny by the wrist before he toppled down the stairs. "Are you trying to kill yourself? I'm not going to be able to heal you if you fall down hundreds of steps, Manny!"

"Sorry," Manny said absently as he glanced from the spacious waiting room on one hand to the dining room on the other. *Chairs! Those oval things were chairs!* Manny plunged ahead, entering the dining room with its cerulean carpet, artfully wrought pecan table overhung by a trio of diamond chandeliers, and massive windows that allowed a pure light to flood the football field length room. Something unceremoniously smacked Manny's shoulder blade, and he jumped, recalling the feral figure from his dream.

"Don't ignore me!" Brun said, irritated as he released Manny's shoulder. "I just saved your life!"

Manny winced as he turned around. "Yeah, uh, thanks for that," he said, pausing sheepishly for a moment before his excitement rebounded. "But hey! Let me tell you why—"

A set of four powerful claws suddenly rapped the pecan tabletop as an exasperated voice called, "Sr. López! Enough chit-chat! It's time you found your seat so we can begin—you, too, Sr. Dimirtis!"

Manny glanced over his shoulder to find Professor Shadowflame, her ionic blue eyes extra bright, staring him down. "Sí, Señora," he replied, collecting himself as he swerved and ran down the length of the table to the chair upon which sat Piolet, the sapphire and ruby tanager. Manny reached out to touch the back of the chair; with a rippling chirp the tanager flitted away through the low, bowed frame of a nearby door. "Gracias, I guess…" Manny muttered as he slumped into his seat, slightly put out by the tanager's reluctance to let him pet her.

"Cheer up, hombre," Brun encouraged as he took the adjacent seat.

Grumbling inaudibly, Manny leaned forward over the tabletop, setting his elbow on the wood and resting his head in his hand as he gazed up the length of the table. At the head table sat his six professors and the three counselors, while scores of his peers occupied the remaining seats—or, spaces, as was the case for the unicorns, centaurs, and crystal spiders, who had simply discarded the high-backed chairs and drawn up to the spread. The tight assembly had become a veritable rumor factory as the students swapped hushed hypotheses as to the exact reason why they had been summoned to the House.

"I have it from Caddie Crookbeak that Director Rumblefeather is exempting us from the Mission!" breathed a green basilisk to a tree frog, the lizard's chest puffed out proudly. "Considering our advanced progress and all! S'no need for us to prove our skills through a simple series of tests and tricks! The professors already know we're good enough to enter the Sixth-Level this very moment!"

"Oh, what's Caddie know anyway?" snapped a blonde otter from across the table.

"A lot, I should say!" retorted the green basilisk. "She nests in the brazil nut tree adjacent to the director's imperial oak! Says she talks to him all the time!"

"I bet," the otter barked quietly. "If she's as on the mark as you say the rest of us are then where is she now?"

The lizard placed his forepaws on the cerulean silk tablecloth as he leaned forward and scanned the faces of his peers. "She must be here somewhere. Maybe she's just late…"

The otter rolled her eyes. "That must be it…"

As Manny watched a particularly impassioned kinkajou expound its case to a pair of doubtful centaurs, something about the air seemed to change. The shift was subtle at first, to the extent that Manny simply began to blink more often than usual. But when the shift became more apparent, when the warmth of the room seemed to trade itself for a cool thinness and skin and fur assumed a more melancholy pallor, the rumors hushed, and eyes rose to ascertain the cause of the change. Brun then nudged Manny on the shoulder and pointed at the windows, which, though nothing about the glass had been altered, were now filtering a soft blue radiance. It had not been the air that had changed, in fact, but the light.

"Alumnos," rang Chiron's voice from the head of the table, apparently satisfied with the effect of the altered luminance. "Gracias por aceptar nuestra invitación de honor hoy." A smile.

"Although we know each of you wishes to know the reason for such an honor as this, the faculty and I know that the most fruitful discussions are always preceded by a rich spread. Thus, I bid you all enjoy. ¡Buen provecho!"

The centaur stepped aside as a wave of multi-hued morphos gushed from an archway behind him, the butterflies darting through the air to deliver glasses of variable shapes and sizes to the guests present at the table. The morphos disappeared again through the archway, reappearing seconds afterward trailed by bowls and platters of distinctive foods. Manny marveled at how, in spite of the butterflies' capricious fluttering and sharp turns, none of the dishes spilled or lost a drop of their contents. *Now that's expert service.*

"Wow, this looks good," Brun said, hungrily eyeing the dish that had just landed in the space before him. "But I wonder what it is."

Manny scanned his own plate, turning it to scrutinize the small, grilled thigh resting between a tuber creation of unidentifiable origin and a salad boasting a quintupling of vegetables. "Looks like stubby chicken legs to me."

"It's not chicken," Kaya stated as she walked around the end of the table and took the seat directly across from Manny. "It's pheasant." A second later Professor Madison Bluebolt hooked through the archway, skirting the table on his miniature lightboard and pausing to whisper something in Kaya's ear. He then zipped along behind the row of students to take his seat near the head of the table.

Manny eyed Kaya suspiciously, remembering how Professor Shadowflame had censured him for nearly arriving late. *Why should she be exempt?* "So what was all that about?"

"All what?" she said, leaning back as a pair of morphos delivered her drink and dish.

"You were late," Manny replied laconically.

Kaya threw her hair back and began to unfold her cerulean napkin. "Private lessons," she said passively as she acquired her fork and knife.

"Don't you already have an 'A' in Healing?" Brun asked.

She shrugged as she sliced the pheasant. "Sí."

"Why the lessons, then?" Manny pushed, his annoyance lingering.

"Some of us just aren't satisfied with the basic Seventh-Level instruction." She placed the slice in her mouth and chewed quietly for a moment. "And others of us have talents that need to be developed."

Manny stabbed the baked tuber on his plate. For some reason, his ego had been pierced. *Talents… I'm talented at Art.* But in no way did Manny wish to receive extra lessons from Caleida Flores. He twisted his fork and watched the tuber crumble.

"Don't do that, Manny, you'll ruin the cassava," Kaya scolded him. "Slice it, or you'll lose all the juices."

Manny stabbed the cassava again and did not look up. Kaya simply rolled her eyes and continued eating.

"You mean we're not exempt?"

"No, dear one, you are not," Amaris Nochesol replied as he addressed the particularly abashed green basilisk standing on the center of the table near Manny. The professor twirled his cocobolo wand as he stood at the head of the table, his gentle eyes set on the lizard. "Quite the opposite."

A sharp tap rapped from somewhere near the center of the table's length, on Manny's side. He leaned forward to see a crystal spider with its foreleg raised in the air to call the attention of Nochesol, who, after turning his eyes from the concerned basilisk, nodded gently.

"So, Professor, correct me if I am wrong, but you expect me, and my brethren, to command Lumen troupes of alternate species during this mission?" the crystal spider reiterated, his voice hinting at incredulity.

Nochesol blinked and nodded slightly. "Indeed."

"But that is not feasible," another arachnid affirmed, three spaces down from Fidelio Firefoot. "The islanders still fear us; they will not follow our instructions!"

"That is not true," called a blonde otter to Manny's right as she bounded onto the table. "I am not afraid of you—in fact, one of my closest friends is now an arachnid."

"Then you comprise a singular group," muttered the first spider.

"Peace," affirmed Nochesol, his palm raised in the direction of the first spider and the otter. "We are all brethren," he added, turning to the second spider and giving her a knowing nod. "And this is the very purpose of this Mission—to enable each of you to work seamlessly alongside Lumens of any species."

A peregrine falcon clicked her beak and raised a wing. "But Professor, I cannot lead a troupe of Lumens through the jungle! I wouldn't know where to begin!"

"How you are wrong, sister. For you and every student assembled here today were hand-picked by us, your professors and counselors," Nochesol replied, opening his palms toward his colleagues on either side. "We have seen your abilities—to confront danger, maintain a solid defense, and heal wounds—we have witnessed on a daily basis how you interact with your peers, not criticizing them in their struggles, but instead offering encouragement and guidance. After all, Dominica, did I not see you just yesterday evening atop Lookout Point helping your friend Orion the panther animate the Pisces sentinel? He could not have succeeded without you, now could he?"

She bowed her head slightly, her feathers ruffling in modesty. "I suppose not... He was pretty awful at it." Dominica suddenly caught herself, letting out a short cry. "But oh, Professor, everybody, don't tell him I said that! I don't want his feelings to get hurt!"

"I don't think she needs to worry about that," Kaya muttered across the table to Manny and Brun amid raucous laughter. "He's not exactly the brightest cat in the forest..."

Manny nodded and shrugged, thinking of how Orion still struggled to mold the band for the Flareshot. *Sad but true.*

When the laughter had died down, Nochesol resumed his address. "And please, none of you worry about maneuvering through the forest. These last two weeks prior to the Mission the other instructors and I will focus on review; consequently, each of you will be excused from classes to familiarize yourself with the training area and formulate plans as to completing the Mission successfully."

"Now that's what I'm talking about!" whooped an azure unicorn a few seats up from Kaya. There were several nods and smiles of agreement before Sable Shadowflame placed her forepaws on the table and stood up on her hind legs to verify the identity of the speaker. Fortunately for the unicorn, however, he managed to duck his head down and begin drinking ravenously from his bowl.

When Shadowflame had returned to her previous position, an exceedingly energetic chinchilla with a bow in her hair leapt onto the table and began to dance in place, her paw raised.

"Yes, Serena?" Nochesol called.

"Professor, is it true the Mission will take place in the forest east of Chiron's Hutch?" Serena squeaked.

"Sí, that is the traditional location for all Seventh-Level Missions."

Manny turned in his chair to abruptly face Brun and Kaya. "That's exactly where we saw Mistarcus!" he breathed.

"I know," Brun corroborated.

Kaya glowered up the table at the faculty. "Idiots…" *Didn't Orion Irradius make it perfectly clear to you fools that the forest isn't safe?*

"But that's not safe!" a centaur declared, his palm fixed to the table. "Chiron's Hutch is at the edge of the city limits. That's monkey territory. We could be attacked!"

"In case you hadn't noticed, scores of Lumens are still being attacked every week within the city limits. I don't think it's going to make much difference," said a panther morosely.

The centaur pounded the table. "But we can't be expected to keep our peers safe when—"

"That will be enough, Ronoas," called a firm voice from the center chandelier. The entire assembly looked up to find Julius

Rumblefeather perched among the sapphires, his black eyes intense and bright. "I assure you that no harm will come to any of you and not a wand will be lost during this mission. The Task Force and Island Guardians have been assigned to establish a solid perimeter around the bounds of the training area—no threat will pass through."

"Pardon me, Director," called another unicorn, "but why should we believe you? Hasn't the Task Force been assigned to apprehend the assailants for more than two months now? What makes you believe they can keep us safe from someone they can't even find?"

Kaya snorted and kicked her chair. "Right on, sister," she mumbled. *And they won't even believe you when you see the culprit with your own eyes. If Archer's been in Russia for two months than I'm a pink cow.*

Julius ruffled his feathers yet remained calm. "Do not deceive yourself, Gimelia. Though the success of the Task Force may appear delayed, the culprits will be detained and the wands found. The fact is that the Force has come beak-to-beak with an extremely organized group; but that is all the more reason for us to trump the enemy with sound wisdom and strategy. Where they excel, we shall surpass, and Isla Verde will again be a safe dwelling for all Lumens. Have faith—it is our way."

Silence fell over the assembly as the students digested Julius's message. Gimelia did not argue, and the majority of Lumens seemed appeased by his defense. Nevertheless, after a moment Serena began to dance upon the table again.

"Director Rumblefeather, is it true that the thieves are actually emperor tamarins like some are saying?" the chinchilla queried loudly. All eyes again turned expectantly toward Julius, who threw a brief glance at Shadowflame.

"It is."

Numerous students began whispering to one another when the blonde otter called, "Director, could you verify that we have a new race of Lumens on our paws, then?"

Kaya, Brun, and Manny stared at Julius smugly.

At this Julius's eyes drew very sharp, and he glared at the otter. "No, Carmela, I cannot. And I will add that I do not hold much esteem for such theories, and that you would all do well not to entertain them." The room grew silent once more. "This meeting is adjourned. Rather than report to your traditional classes this coming week, you will meet each day at Nahir's Hill and then be escorted to the training area by a First-Level crystal spider to begin your preparation. You will receive further details and materials on Monday. You are dismissed."

***

"Yeah, mi papá made me sit by him during the meal. Can you believe that!" Iris exclaimed as he, Kaya, Brun and Manny exited the House of the Brethren through the main doors. "It was so boring! I had to sit and listen to Professor Shadowflame go on and on about her curriculum for next year while Flores giggled like a twit."

"Oh joy," Kaya responded as she plunged into the mayhem that is the mid-afternoon Plaza. "Follow me. Let's sit down at the Fount and talk."

No one argued with this notion, so within five minutes the group had reached the edge of the pool, kicking off their shoes and cooling their feet in the water. Iris, for his part, dove in head first, hoping to drown his memories of lunch. He returned from the depths of the pool with three Soles and a Luna in his paw. "Here, guys, have at it. It's not stealing if we throw them back."

So, under the translucent droplets misting down from the towering spray of the fountain at the pool's center, the four friends tossed the coins and made a wish. Brun laughed as his Luna hit the bottom of the pool.

"What?" Manny said, shading his eyes to turn and look at him.

"I just realized that I can't wait for the Mission to be over, yet I hope it never starts," he replied, a tinge of dark humor in his voice.

"Why?" Iris asked, still treading water.

"'Cause he's nervous about leading twelve other Lumens but doesn't want to leave the island when it's over," Kaya answered flatly.

Brun stared across Manny at Kaya. "That's right."

Manny fidgeted, frowning at the water as he remembered his progressively deteriorating friendship with Zane. "You're not alone, hombre. I don't want to go home either."

Paradigm Shift

"And now—to review," called Chiron as he gazed out upon the hundredfold assembly of his pupils seated quietly atop the wide crown of Nahir's Hill. This would be his final lesson of the term, and he could honestly attest, as he had done during his frequent contacts with Nightwind Arconia, that he was distinctly satisfied with the progress of his students, and at times impressed, as was the case with his star astronomers (all of which comprised the body of students now known as the Squadron Leaders). Yes, he was very pleased, and he was certain that this final night would proceed well, if not flawlessly.

"Jóvenes," he said as he wove silently across the hilltop, "please remind me of the title of our final tale."

"*The Warrior's Mission*," replied the assembly in unison.

Chiron nodded. "Verdad. And who can convey the central theme of the story, in a sentence or less?" Raucous squeaking erupted from the southern edge of the hill. "¿Sí, Serena?"

The overzealous chinchilla bounced on her heels as she shouted, "We learn that it is only the evil within us that prevents us from achieving true virtue!"

"Precisely." Chiron stopped, pausing to peer down and grin at a small island of tree frogs perched attentively on the side of a boulder. "And you, my amphibian rock troupe, can you tell me the principal characters of our tale?" And they did, fully meeting his expectations as they recalled Indus, the Warrior, alongside Centaurus, the wise Centaur; as well as the four birds—Tucana, Grus, Pavo, and Apus—denoting the Toucan, Crane, Peacock, and Bird of Paradise, respectively. The frogs also noted the danger of Lupus, the White Wolf, whom they all seemingly loved to hate.

Continuing along his unmarked trajectory, Chiron led the students back through the main events and details of the story, from the Warrior's disoriented predicament in the forest labyrinth to his unexpected meeting with the Centaur, who assigned the Warrior the mission to locate the specimen of great price, the most beautiful of all birds. Upon reaching the specimen, the Warrior confronted his greatest terror, the White Wolf, only too late discovering that the beast had slain the bird. Disheartened, the Warrior returned the bird to the Centaur, who then praised the man's honest humility and led him back through the labyrinth.

"Excellent," Chiron called as the story's analysis drew to a close. Indeed—flawless, just as he had hoped. "Now I will remind each of you to review one last time in preparation for our test on Monday." Several groans floated up from the hill; Chiron knew, however, that not everything in life could be perfect, so he elected to simply overlook this minute blemish in his students' attitudes and proceed on to the astronomical side of the story—the constellations.

"Professor!" a student vociferated as Chiron turned to face the northern sky. "Before we begin identifying stars, I have a question."

Chiron turned to find the blonde otter, Carmela Paddlepaw, facing him from her position on the apex of a rock. "¿Sí, Carmela? What do you wish to know?"

"By asking this I am in no way insinuating that I do not wish to lend my full attention to the rest of this lesson, but I was wondering—do the Squadron Leaders have to take the test this coming Monday? I mean, aren't we spending the last two weeks preparing for the Mission?"

"To your prior query, no. And to the latter, yes," Chiron replied.

"Oh, good," Carmela said, sliding down the back of the rock to sit beside her friend, a crystal spider. "Thanks."

Chiron offered a wise nod in reply and then paused, allowing a moment for a number of the young Lumens to explain his answer to their peers. None argued with his decision, however, as the majority would much rather complete an extra set of examinations and a few auxiliary review days than lead a dozen of their peers during the crux of the Seventh-Level. In the meantime Chiron knelt down to touch his hind leg, from whence he removed a pecan bangle that, glowing brightly, swiftly assumed the shape of a wand. "Are we ready then?" he asked when all had grown quiet. Numerous students nodded, and Chiron once again turned to face the northern sky.

"Let us commence with Lupus, the White Wolf." Chiron flicked his wrist, peering knowingly into the space before him as roughly a dozen stars burned suddenly brighter. He slowly drew his arm back. "I would like a volunteer to ident—"

At that moment a shining silver blade spun through the air, catching Chiron on the cheek as it ripped the pecan wand from his hand and continued in a whirling trajectory across the hill. Chiron instinctively turned his head, watching as the blade carried his wand over the western slope, beyond the ring of students. The blade immediately disappeared, enveloped in living shadow. The centaur's heart jolted as a screech pierced the air—an elated shriek of victory, a cry of triumph. In an instant twenty students were on their feet, whilst the rest remained on the ground, trembling and scared.

"What do you need us to do, Professor?" asked a panther gruffly, his hackles raised.

"Track that shadow!" Chiron asserted as the night phantom melted away behind the curve of the hill. "Tell me where it goes, but do not follow it!"

"What about this one over here, Professor?" cried a falcon, her eyes locked on a similar shadow fleeing along the opposite edge of the hill. Several students darted in pursuit of this second shadow.

"Everyone, stay where you are!" Chiron commanded tensely.

At that moment a net soared through the air, pinning the shadow on the western slope to the ground. "I got him, Chiron!" shouted Kaya. "Hurry!"

"To the side, everybody!" Chiron surged forward through the heart of the crowd. He had not yet reached the center of the hill when a savage hiss erupted from beyond Kaya, the remnants of her Reticulum sentinel splaying wildly into the air.

"Professor, Professor, they're at the kapok!" Serena shouted, pointing to the heart of the towering kapok tree at the base of the hill. Screeches of malicious laughter assaulted the assembly as the thieves passed through the arch and vanished. Numerous students gave chase, but Chiron was swifter, managing to overtake the pursuers and block their passage through the tree gate.

"No!" he shouted, his arms outstretched and hooves planted. "It is too dangerous for any of you to pursue them."

"But Chiron," Manny argued, grinding to a halt just steps from the centaur, "if they get away you'll be powerless!"

"Better powerless than one of you dead!" Silence greeted Chiron in reply; he took that as an affirmative. "Good. Then I want all students to return to the crown of the hill. Squadron Leaders, form a perimeter around your peers and draw a light barrier around us. And somebody please get me a piece of paloma paper! All of mine was stored in my wand!"

The students obeyed, however reluctantly, and as Chiron returned to the now tightly huddled student mass he was greeted with a flourish of glowing blue papers. "Gracias," he said, accepting a sheet from a kinkajou and picking his way carefully among the prostrate masses. "Now would anyone be so kind as to pass me a pen?" Seconds later the pen scratched purposefully across the paper, relaying a message of distress and utmost sobriety. No sooner had Chiron finished scribbling the names of a long list of addressees than the paper leapt from his palm and metamorphosed into a dozen doves that fired off in every direction. The students marveled at this, but were not given much of a chance to ponder it, as Chiron began barking strict orders to the Lumens forming the perimeter.

"More photons, Squadron Leaders! You've only reached an eighth of the density required to establish even a fractionally effective shield. There is no site on this planet closer to the stars' light, so I expect all of you to start pulling it down with greater fervor than you have ever mustered! ¡Ándale! If those despicable thieves return I do not want them to have even a dream of a chance of getting through to us! Hurry!"

The Squadron Leaders set their teeth and fixed their minds as the streams of light siphoning down from the heavens pulsated and increased, pouring trillions of photon particles into the cylindrical shield engulfing Nahir's Hill. Virtually the entire assembly—Chiron, included—stood transfixed by the luminescence of Manny and

Brun, who, burning with such brilliance as to appear light incarnate, were rendered veritable photon wells as particles rushed straight from their bodies into the barrier.

"That should be sufficient," Chiron voiced a moment later, his vocal chords taut. He had never seen a pair of Seventh-Levels command such a quantity of light in so short a time. "Simply incredible," he whispered.

***

"On my back, now."

"Chiron, we can't do that," Brun declared. Manny, Kaya, and Iris nodded. They all new it was extremely uncouth to touch a centaur, much less ride one.

"We don't want to disrespect you," Iris amended.

The centaur stamped a hoof. "You are disrespecting me by disobeying my command."

"Professor, why can't we just wait here until the Task Force returns with your wand?" Kaya waved her hand across the brow of Nahir's Hill, now utterly vacant. The remaining students had been escorted home by the Island Guardians after the Task Force, led by Amaris Nochesol and Madison Bluebolt, had set out in pursuit of the thieves. "I'm sure we'll be fine."

"Without a wand, I cannot be certain of that," Chiron said curtly. "Now, on my back."

So stubborn... "C'mon, Iris," Kaya murmured, catching the hare and cradling him to her chest as she drug her heels toward the centaur's potent frame. "Give me a boost, López," she added brusquely.

Manny rolled his eyes. *Yes, my Queen.* He sighed as he knelt to the ground, his fingers threaded together to offer Kaya a step up. When she had mounted the centaur, Manny turned to aid Brun as well. Brun then pulled Manny up onto Chiron's haunches.

"Kaya, grab my chest. The other three, hold onto one another tightly, for I gallop much swifter than any horse," Chiron said. "Are we ready?"

"Yes," Manny sighed.

"Watch your hands, Dimirtis," Kaya growled dangerously. Brun flushed a deep red and then locked his hands further down along Kaya's abdomen. He knew his grip had not been too high; but nevertheless, Kaya was not one to be tested.

Chiron's muscles flexed as his hooves assaulted the earth with a power and speed neither Manny nor his friends could have predicted. To his grim displeasure, Manny very nearly tumbled off before the party had cleared the kapok. The hutch passed by in a mottled blur, and only a handful of seconds passed before the company was tracing the rocky rim of the Lake bowl. A twinge of vertigo threatened to invade Manny's mind as he glanced down at the shining waters. *One misplaced hoof and I'm a goner...* But a prayer and a minute later they skirted the surging waterfall and soared onto the boardwalk. Manny's unease faded as the treehouses of the Northern Lucero District blended into his vision. Chiron progressively slowed his pace and came to a stop at the end of a landing, whereupon Manny and the others dismounted, stumbling awkwardly along a bridge toward an octagonal treehouse (for the sudden drop in momentum had rendered the youths' balance questionable at best). They knocked torpidly on the door, which was promptly answered by a wide-eyed woman with long, black hair.

"Oh, thank God," the woman exhaled, pulling them all inside, Chiron included. "I was so worried. I would've come myself, but Kiki's asleep, and Marcos left with the rest of the Task Force when the letter arrived."

Kaya rolled her eyes as she sank into the white couch. "Chill out, Mom. We're fine."

"Chiron, I can't thank you enough," Ellen Bellastrata said, crossing her chest with her left arm and bowing in the traditional centaurian greeting. "I know the sacrifice you had to make to get them here so quickly, and I am in your debt."

"No, you are not," the centaur responded, though not severely. "It lays upon my shoulders to keep these children safe, whatever means be necessary." He gazed into her eyes for a brief moment. "Now pardon me, I should be going."

661

Ellen reached out her hand but did not dare touch him. "Chiron, no—please. It isn't safe. I mean, consider your condition. Without your wand—"

"My presence is as useless here as anywhere else," he finished, his fist swallowing the door knob.

"That's not true, Chiron!" Iris intervened. "You're wise—the wisest Lumen I know!"

Chiron hesitated as he opened the door. "I appreciate that, young Firefoot, but as we all witnessed tonight, I am also very ignorant, and perhaps arrogant." He then turned to face Brun and Manny, who stood stiffly beside the couch. "Boys, I never apologized for my misconduct and lack of faith that I demonstrated toward you following Iris's attack on Easter Island, nor when Crion verified that the tamarin's were indeed responsible for the missing wands and the attacks. Tonight I have been humbled and can attest that these thieves are more than mere primates. Their actions are too coordinated, their schemes too precise. Please accept my apology and know that I believe you, on all accounts." Chiron immediately turned and trotted away along the bridge; when he reached the boardwalk he released a burst of speed and did not look back.

Manny and Brun shared a look of disbelief as Ellen strode forward and dead-bolted the door. She did not turn around but instead stood facing the door for several seconds, her head bowed slightly. When she did finally turn, Manny noticed that her eyes were redder than before, and she appeared extremely fatigued. "I—I don't know what to say," she uttered hoarsely. Ellen, in her deepest being, had never believed that the monkeys were anything more than trained pets; but how could she now just disregard Chiron's words and treat him as a foolish child?

"Mamá, just go to bed," Kaya said after no one had spoken for several moments. *Adults are too serious sometimes...*

Ellen nodded as though sedated. "That would probably be for the best," she said, turning toward the kitchen. She had nearly reached the door when she stopped to face the teenagers one last time. "Boys, you can sleep in Keilani's room. Kaya, I don't want all of you staying up too late. It's already past two. And all of you, promise me that you will not leave this house." When they had conceded, she pushed the kitchen door open. "Buenas noches."

"Buenas noches," they all replied.

"Sit down, muchachos," Kaya said, signaling the opposite couch. "We need to talk."

"Why are the four of you still up?"

Kaya, Iris, Manny, and Brun turned dazed eyes upon Marcos Bellastrata, the girl's father, as he closed the front door to the living room. The man's glasses sat slightly askew on his head, and his hair was thoroughly wind-blown. His shirt and pants displayed various nicks and cuts, and dried blood shone faintly from his left elbow. He otherwise appeared healthy, though tired.

"We've been talking about all the emperor tamarins have done," Kaya yawned, strolling over to clean her father's elbow and mend the superficial scratches he had endured. "What'd you do, hit a tree?"

"Yes," he sighed as he took a seat in the wooden rocker next to Iris. "Started to pull a 180 on my lightboard, but I didn't see that limb behind me. Lucky it wasn't my head."

"That's for sure." Kaya kissed him lightly on the cheek and returned to the love seat. "So did you get Chiron's wand back?"

"No," Marcos replied darkly.

Manny clenched his teeth and balled his fists. Iris groaned, and Kaya shook her head. But Brun asked, "Could you even trail them?"

"Oh, yeah," Marcos rasped, his voice dry. "We could, and we did—for several miles. The tamarins split up, so Madison and Amaris took one while Julius and I pursued the other. Eventually Julius and I caught up to ours—a shadow leaping through the trees and whipping along the ground—but every time we thought we had him pinned our photons would just dissolve. After an hour or so he up and disappeared, just like that! Crion showed up with Sable and they both said the trail just ended abruptly, right about where we last saw him. We scoured the area, searching for holes, caves, any manner of cover, but there was nothing—just rivers and flat ground."

"What about Professor Bluebolt and Professor Nochesol's monkey?" Iris asked. "Did it get away, too?"

"Actually, no, it didn't."

"You mean we've got him?" Manny exclaimed, jerking forward. "What'd he say?"

"She said nothing," Marcos replied tiredly. "She'd slit her own neck using a nasty-looking metal tool before they could remove the barrier and restrain her."

"She didn't want us to know the truth, so she killed herself," Brun observed quietly.

"Hardly," Marcos half-scoffed. "Even if we had restrained her we would have gleaned nothing from her—after all, she was just a monkey."

"She slit her own neck, Dad! You said it yourself. Wild animals don't commit suicide," Kaya argued.

"These monkeys are hardly wild animals," Marcos answered. "Emperor tamarins are actually quite intelligent. I believe she knew her owner would punish her in a worse manner if we ever released her, so she simply decided to end it there. There's nothing mysterious or complicated about that."

"But Chiron believes—"

"Manny, I don't care what Chiron believes," Marcos sighed curtly. "He was caught off guard, lost his wand, and cannot reconcile that with the facts. He has had a lapse of reasoning, and none of the rest of the Task Force, including Director Rumblefeather, agrees with him. So anything he told you last night, just forget it. It will only work to distract you from your studies."

"From our studies," Kaya mused, rounding on her father. "I'll tell you what's distracting us from our studies—Archer. Keilani's idiot fiancé is running around with those evil Lumen tamarins as they swipe our wands. I don't care if Keilani has told all of you that they're on mission in Russia or China or blasted Africa

664

right now. She's lying. All four of us saw Archer with our own eyes—he's part of this."

"Kaya," Marcos began, calmly yet dangerously, "Crion and Julius contacted Archer and Keilani's professors; he is where he says he is."

"They're liars too, then!"

"I will not be talked to like this. Go to your room, now."

"No, Father," Kaya growled, gripping her knees tightly.

"Fine. Then you're grounded up through the Mission and for two weeks into the summer. You may only leave the house during school hours when you are to be preparing to lead your squadron, and you may not have any friends over, starting now. Boys, I'll escort you to Fire Flats. You'll be staying there the remainder of the semester. Say goodbye, Kaya."

Instead, Kaya pierced her father with a look of such hatred, that he could only laugh. "Grow up, m'ija," he said, shaking his head as he lead the boys out of the living room and onto the bridgeway.

Brun had just shut the door when Iris said, "Excuse me, Marcos, but why are Manny and Brun staying at my house?"

"Because Chiron's Hutch won't be safe at night. Even though we're posting a pair of Island Guardians to watch over it, Chiron would prefer that they stay with you and your father. After you, boys," Marcos added, stepping to the side as Manny, Brun, and Iris mounted the boardwalk.

Manny's blood boiled as he reflected on the unfair punishment Kaya now had to endure for the next month. He stewed over the whole scene as they traversed the planks of the Northern Lucero District. *And I can't believe he cut me off me like that!* Needless to say, Manny had few positive words to share with Marcos; thus the boy remained quiet throughout the entire walk to the Firefoot abode.

Iris followed suit, ruminating on how he might maintain constant contact with his best friend. *I'll probably just have to resort to paloma paper...*

665

Brun, on the other hand, spoke up again. "Marcos, I don't mean to be rude, but why exactly does the Task Force feel it is safe to hold the Mission in the same area where the monkey you were chasing disappeared?"

"Because we now understand our enemy's tactics; and the area will be secured against all intruders—the Island Guardians have already begun the process. The training area will be safer even than the heart of Isla Verde," Marcos asserted.

I'm sure.

Fat chance of that.

We can only hope.

Jailbreak

To everyone's surprise, particularly that of the Task Force, the next two weeks proceeded seamlessly—not a single wand turned up missing, no Lumen fell victim to attack, and not one Squadron Leader became lost in the training area. All things considered, Julius Rumblefeather was intensely satisfied with the progress of his Task Force. The quetzal beamed when Andrés Dosfilos arrived to inspect the three-meter-thick photon perimeter wall that soared high above the canopies to fully encompass the training area. "I must say, Julius—when I was informed of the situation with Chiron, I believed it best that we cancel the Mission. But now, as I witness the extent of your dedication to the safety of your students, I am confident that only a well-aimed meteor could deter the event," Dosfilos affirmed. "Buen trabajo."

Despite the apparent lull in primatial violence and the fact that Fidelio Firefoot proved to be an exceptional host, Manny quickly found himself to be unhappy. He argued with Chiron to allow him to return to the hutch; but, more than resolute, the centaur sent the boy back to the fire oak, day after day, with the charge to keep safe and prepare diligently for the Mission. And so, slightly off-put, Manny obeyed Chiron's request, coordinating day and night with Brun to establish an effective base of operations where their two squadrons could dwell without fear of detection during the Mission. Iris and Kaya did the same, relaying transmissions via paloma paper sometimes multiple times per minute. Thus, as the two weeks of preparation drew to a close, the four friends were confident that their entire squadrons would complete the task with success.

If only any team were so lucky…

***

"Iris, it's not that difficult."

The hare stared up at Manny, his ears rigid and wand aimed straight at the boy's face. "Manny, I'm telling you that they won't move. I've tried everything to distract them—Pisces, the L7 Explosion, everything short of firing them in the face with an orb."

"Well, the rules state that if you distract them, they'll move." Iris glared back. "Did you not just hear what I said?"

Manny paused; he was growing annoyed. "You must not be doing it right."

"Why don't you just stroll out there and do it then!" the hare countered. "If I'm such an inexperienced fool, then teach me!"

"Cool off, Iris," Brun said, creeping forward along the narrow space toward his friends. "Get too loud and they'll hear you; I don't exactly want Manny and my squadrons to get caught three days before the Mission ends. That would make for one serious headache."

I'll give you a headache... Iris sighed. "Sorry, Brun, it's just that the spiders caught Orion and now I can't free him. They're not responding according to the rules. Besides that, Serge is MIA; I think they got him, too."

Brun turned his head, peering across the dirt tunnel that he and Manny had dug as the back entrance to their base. The scarce light filtering in through the well-placed moss struck Manny's skin, illuminating the tunnel slightly. "I guess you could go help him," Brun suggested.

"Me? Why not Kaya?" Manny retorted.

"Get serious, Manny. Kaya's gotta stay and guard our base, just like Brun's staying to guard yours," Iris said.

Manny growled slightly as he slid the mahogany watch from his wrist. He was tired and hungry. This was the eleventh day of the Mission, and short of grub worms, which he now refused to eat, Manny had not tasted meat in far too long. Sure, tropical fruits were great, brazil nuts and all that jazz, but what Manny really wanted was a steak, or even broiled chicken… "You're gonna owe me big time for this, Firefoot."

"No prob. Just tack it on as another gift for your birthday next week," Iris conceded, his voice noticeably lighter as relief flooded him.

¿Mi cumpleaños? Until this moment, Manny had not realized that his fifteenth birthday would be coming so soon. In fact, he could not believe that a full year had transpired since he became a Lumen, met Julius, saw—*the monkey. Filthy, dung-slinging, wand-stealing tamarin.*

But Manny's thoughts brightened as he took account of the photokinetic progress he had made—in just moments, with barely a perceptible thought, he coaxed the light down from the canopy above and into his moss-covered tunnel to render a perfect specimen of Reticulum, a trio of verdant Chamaeleons, and a shoal of cracker-sized fish that he quickly stowed away in a canvas pouch at his hip.

"Ready, Iris?" Manny asked, his tone abruptly congenial.

The hare raised his brow, throwing a brief glance at Brun. "Uh, yeah." *I wonder what got into him?*

"Buena suerte," Brun whispered, wishing his friends well as he slid back into the base.

"Likewise," Manny corresponded.

Iris peered through the moss to inspect the area beyond. "The coast is clear."

Manny quickly drug himself forward, exiting the tunnel and crouching in the niche provided by a pair of buttress roots. Lifting the jade compass hanging at his opposite hip, he asked, "So where do they have him?"

"Orion's at the northern post, in the hut on the northwest corner," Iris breathed. "Got it?"

His wand now a thin stylus, Manny tapped the screen of his CPS, zooming out to portray an image of the entire training area, the diameter of which spanned three miles. A flashing dot just west and slightly north of the center depicted Manny's current position. A zigzag line with four points—the first of which began in the southeast corner of the screen—delineated the sites where the "enemy" crystal spiders maintained their posts. Each post consisted of five huts, the outer four forming a square around the center edifice. Around each outer hut stood sentry a trio of First-Level crystal spiders; in the inner hut rested a stack of luminescent pearls—the photobeads.

The rules to the Mission were simple: distract the crystal spiders from their posts using whatever means necessary, infiltrate the center hut, and steal a photobead. To complete the Mission each squadron was required to collect one photobead from each post and be in their base with all members present at sundown on the final day. Demerits would be given to squadrons who could not successfully liberate captive teammates or acquire the necessary photobeads; the more demerits, the more summer school the squadron would face. Consequently, each squadron worked together to the best of their ability, and any lost members were quickly rescued from the outer huts.

Hence, Manny drug his stylus down to center his sights on the northern post, tapped the screen, and zoomed in on the area. By drawing a circle around the northwest hut, Manny designated a new target on his CPS. He tapped again to zoom out, and then answered Iris's question with an affirmative. "Who's gonna lead?"

"You can," the hare whispered. "I'll hop behind and take care of the horned frogs with my Flareshot."

"Fair enough. And I'll watch for firespitters."

"Agreed."

Considering the location of the López-Dimirtis base, Manny and Iris did not have to travel far to reach the northern post. In spite of the brief distance, the trek took well over an hour, as "rogue" spiders crisscrossed the land with every turn. There were innumerable traps as well which slowed their trip, from webs disguised as moss to yawning pits rendered to appear as firm ground. But this late in the game Manny and Iris hardly required the use of their compasses to navigate the land, the many traps and typical sentry paths having been burned into the boys' minds from the scores of reconnaissance, rescue, and collection missions completed during the past week and a half. Their journey eventually drew to a close, the tops of the huts materializing through the thinning boles of the forest. Nevertheless, just when Manny began to relax a flash of blonde from a nearby tree caught his attention.

"Alto," Manny hissed.

Iris froze, stationed just behind the boy's heel. "Do we need to go invisible?" the hare breathed.

Manny's eyes narrowed, and then a faint crescent appeared along the corner of his mouth. "No," he replied, glancing down at the hare. "I thought we were about to walk straight into a crystal spider; but it's just Millie."

"Oh, good," Iris sighed. Millie Carroway, the fiery Lumen hailing from Texas, also happened to be a Squadron Leader, and a good one at that. Iris had learned early in the Mission that she had established her base virtually in the heart of the "enemy" territory, somewhere between the southeast and eastern posts, and that none of her members had been captured, a feat that neither he nor Manny could claim. But why is she here now? I thought she finished collecting photobeads days ago.

Snapping his wand forward, then retracting it ever so slightly, Manny sent a faint wisp of light by Millie's face. She turned instantly, brandishing her Flareshot, her eyes a blazing blue below the rim of her customary tan cowboy hat. Her shoulders relaxed, though her expression did not, as she waved Manny over. "Afternoon, gentlemen," she breathed, tipping her hat as she noted Iris's presence. "This is Jet; he's a member of my Squad."

The hare and boy were taken aback as they realized that a unicorn, midnight black from hoof to horn, had been standing beside Millie the entire time. Swallowing his shock, Iris whispered, "Nice to meet you."

"Same here," Manny added.

Jet nodded, his eyes shining. "Un placer."

Before another word could be said, Millie set a firm grip on Manny's shoulder. "Listen, bud, Jet and I here have a problem. D'you and Iris know Caddie Crookbeak?" They nodded in reply. "Well, as you know, she's a falcon, and she's been the eyes of our operation from the beginning. Just yesterday she decided to take a leisurely flight—as we'd already gotten all our photobeads and all—

ut she never made it back. Treble Brightwing—whose base is near nine—swooped by and told me he'd been on a flight of his own when he saw a web fire up from the canopy and suck her in, just like hat."

"But the First-Level spiders aren't allowed to do that, are hey?" Iris rejoined quietly.

Jet blinked, his eyes liquid. "No. They can set traps in the air, but they can't wrap us in webbing like that. Director Rumblefeather old us this the Friday before the Mission."

Manny glowered at the ground, then lifted his wand to point oward the post on the other side of the tree. "Caddie's in there, isn't she?"

"Yep. And the sentries aren't following the rules," Millie declared. "Tried everything."

Iris kicked Manny in the ribs, just for good measure.

"Sí, sí, tenías razón," Manny conceded. "You were right about the spiders."

"Maybe you'll believe me when I tell you something next time," Iris rebounded. Millie and Jet stared at the boys oddly; Iris quickly explained the plight of his squadron member, Orion.

"You've gotta be yankin' my chain," Millie replied. "Caddie's in the northwest hut! Somethin's awfully fishy about this."

"Fishy or not, we're getting Caddie and Orion out of there," Manny said. "If the sentries aren't going to follow the rules, then we'll just push the limits."

"What do you plan to do?" Jet asked.

"I'm gonna get up in their face, that's all."

"But Manny," Iris precipitated, "they'll capture you! Then we'll be in more trouble!"

"Cálmate, Iris." Manny pointed his wand at empty space as a chestnut-sized orb wound itself into existence, the core of which housed a highly-pressured granule of air. His wand then transformed into a Y, which he swiftly fit with a glowing band. Snatching the orb, Manny rose to his feet and silently approached the trees nearest the post. The other three followed, concealing themselves in the

672

underbrush as Manny placed the orb in the sling, drew the band back, and took aim.

Thwop! The orb shot through the air, exploding with such force just inches from the fangs of the nearest spider that it threw the arachnid back against the hut. Manny could not help but jeer as the spider back-trod, its six eyes astonished in their search for the cause of the explosion. *That's what you get for not playing fair.* Manny's grin disappeared, however, as the other pair of crystal spiders rounded the hut, fangs clicking. *They look a bit angrier than usual...* But ignoring this disparaging thought, Manny opened the pouch at his hip as a shoal of emerald fish burst forth, each individual Piscis instantly growing to beyond the size of Manny's head. The Pisces, which apparently numbered well over fifty, swiftly surrounded the pair of charging arachnids, abruptly halting their advance.

"Millie, Jet, get in there and free Caddie and Orion," Manny ordered over his shoulder. "Iris, waylay the first spider with Reticulum and pin him down—we don't want any trouble from him."

The girl and the unicorn launched from the underbrush in a flash of speed. Iris, for his part, pinned the first spider with not one but two Reticulum. The spider spat, fangs clicking as it struggled to break free. A breath later Millie reappeared in the doorway of the hut. "Manny, we have a serious problem."

Adrenaline pumping, Manny kept his palm outstretched as the Pisces continued their relentless cyclone about the spiders. He gazed about the post, ensuring that more arachnids were not already on the way to intercept the rescue team. Once certain, Manny ran ahead and peered through the door. Instantly his mind faltered. Before him lay a stack of Lumen bodies, all wrapped mercilessly in crystal webbing. Jet labored to roll the bodies off of one another so that the paralyzed students could breathe. *This isn't how the rest were captured.*

"There're over twenty of them," Millie said gravely. "We don't have time to get them all out; but if we don't, they might suffocate."

Manny gazed at the wild eyes staring up at him from the floor. "This can't be happening."

"Manny! Get out of there!" Iris's voice was shrill, bordering hysteria. The boy whirled around and realized that he had let down his guard—the Pisces had swum away, and the pair of crystal spiders was now free, eyes locked on the boy's frame as they thrummed toward the entrance to the hut.

"Aw, crap." Manny's stomach plummeted to the ground. Just then a thought flashed in his mind and he raised his wrist as a viridian net splayed from his palm to block the doorway. The spiders hissed to a halt, fangs clacking. *This is just perfect. If we try to go through the window they'll just be waiting for us on the other side.*

"What do we do, Manny?" Millie asked, her voice suddenly tight. "That won't hold them for long."

"Iris!" Manny screamed. "Fire more Reticulum at them so we can get out!"

No response came.

Manny clenched his fist, tears biting at his eyes as his heart began to race, pumping faster, faster. His skin flared, burning white.

"Manny," came Millie's voice, unstable.

Just then the roof of the hut ripped from the walls, lurching forward and landing on the spiders at the entrance. "What the—?" Manny's head jerked up. "Kaya?" The boy's mind could not reconcile what his eyes now saw—ten feet above him, on a pink lightboard, hovered Kaya, Iris beside her. "How—I mean, did you—?"

"Tear the roof off? Yeah," Kaya replied, throwing down a rope. "Now grab on, López. Millie, you too. Blackie, you're gonna have to charge through the wall—I can't tow you. We've gotta book it. Some serious stuff's going down in the forest."

Dumbfounded, Manny obeyed, while Millie knelt down to grab a tiny bundle of white that she cradled to her chest as she latched onto the rope. "Run, Jet!" Millie urged as her feet lifted from the ground.

The ebony unicorn shook his head, then knelt to begin cutting his classmates' bindings with his horn. "I'll free them, then go. Perhaps we still have time to escape."

"Hurry, then!" Millie called as they shot into the air, quickly reaching an altitude of three hundred feet. She reinforced her grip; she had no choice if she wanted to live. "Kaya! We're going too high! You need to let us down so we can climb on!"

"There's isn't time!" Kaya sped up, proceeding forward in a southwesterly trajectory. "Hold on just a couple seconds more! I'll take us down then!"

Manny gritted his teeth, wrapping the rope around his wrist and choking the braid tightly. *C'mon, Kaya, this isn't exactly comfortable.* Had he been atop the lightboard, Manny might actually have tried to enjoy the view—the bright sun piercing the forest mist, the expansive treetops flowing away in every direction before ending abruptly at a glowing wall. But at the moment Manny's primary concern was survival, which was indeed proving a desperate struggle.

As their elevation began to decline, sounds of utter terror reached their ears—screams, cries for help, hideous screeching. Kaya leaned forward, inclining the lightboard to execute the sharpest nosedive she could before leveling out and sinking through the canopy, so as not to hang Manny and Millie up in the branches. A moment later their feet hit the ground, a scene of absolute mayhem unfolding before them. Students bolted in every direction, pursued relentlessly by hundreds of emperor tamarins, who, screaming in delight, leapt onto the students' backs and began pulling out their hair, kicking their ribs, and savagely wrenching their wands from their bodies using a metal apparatus that could be modified and adjusted into several deadly forms, which included a set of glistening pincers and a two-edged dagger. The First-Level crystal spiders were not lacking in presence, either—operating as buffers to corral the terrified students back into the chaos. Manny felt he would be sick.

"In here, hurry!" Kaya asserted, whirling around and giving the foot of an immense tree three sharp taps. The root instantly opened inward and Kaya dove inside, followed closely by her companions as they entered a wide, scythe-shaped room, the inner curve of which bordered the tree's true roots, indistinguishable from the faux set that Kaya and Iris had rendered to conceal their base. Across the now heavily trampled grass and undergrowth stood various tables, above which hovered scores of Fireflies encased in glass bulbs, illuminating the glossy eyes of nearly two dozen Lumens seated in tense anticipation.

"Kaya, Iris, you're safe!" called Nate Perón, his deep sea eyes wide with a mixture of anxiety and relief as he snapped the bark panel back in place. "We thought they'd gotten you for sure!"

A centaur further along the wall stamped a back hoof as she pulled her eyes away from a pair of open slots in the bark. "I just can't believe it! The crystal spiders aren't defending us! They're actually helping the emperor tamarins!"

As though drawn by gravity, each set of eyes within the base slowly turned to face a pair of arachnids perched upon the tree's roots. One spider tried to back away, the bulbous posterior of his carapace scraping the slanted roof and forcing him to scrunch down; the other spider, however, snapped his fangs, his eye clusters flashing. "Don't look at us like that! We're Seventh-Levels, and we're in this just like the rest of you! Those First-Levels out there aren't supposed to be attacking students! Ask Spencer—or better yet, his father, Master Irradius!" He paused and spat, his fangs wide. "Those First-Levels have betrayed our species and the rest of the order to those filthy primates!"

"Then why aren't they attacking their own kind?" rounded the centaur by the spy holes. "The tamarins aren't even approaching the younger spiders!"

The outspoken arachnid appeared stunned. "I-I don't know…"

The first arachnid clacked his fangs weakly as he said, "My sister's out there. She's one of the First-Level sentries."

"And?" growled a panther to Manny's right.

The spider slid forward slightly. "And maybe they just don't want to hurt their own families…"

"So you're condoning their actions?" shouted the centaur.

"No, it's ju—"

"Enough!" barked Kaya, stepping into the center of the room as a panther began to edge forward toward the arachnids. "They're telling the truth!" She threw a stalwart nod toward the spiders. "None of us knows why the First-Levels are doing this, but we're going to stop them."

"Oh, and how do you expect to do that?" shot the centaur.

Kaya snapped her head about, her hair whirling through the air as she pointed at the centaur. "First off, you're going to shut your trap, because Iris and I are the Squadron Leaders of this base, not you." The centaur's eyes smoldered, but she said nothing. "And second, I need someone to send a message to Andrés Dosfilos telling him we're being attacked."

"Andrés Dosfilos?" asked a quetzal. "But why not Director Rumblefeather?"

"Because he probably won't believe us," Iris stepped in. "Nate, you write the letter."

"Yes, sir," the boy replied, producing a sheet of paloma paper and a pen.

Iris twitched his whiskers as he faced the crowd. "Now listen, everybody, we're gonna need to move in formation—"

"Hold it," Kaya broke in.

Iris glanced back, confused. "What? If we don't stop them now—"

Kaya shook her head. "You, Manny and I have something to do first."

"We do?" Manny asked, perplexed and slightly worried.

"Sí. And we need to hurry, or we may never get the chance again," she added in a hushed tone.

"So what do you want us to do, Boss?" the centaur called, though not mockingly, to Kaya.

"Wait for us to get back, then we'll sack 'em all together," Kaya answered. "We shouldn't be long." *Hopefully.* She then turned toward the door and strolled past Millie, who still held an unconscious Caddie Crookbeak in her arms.

"I'm coming with you," Millie said, stretching out an arm to stop Kaya.

"No, you need to stay and get Caddie free," Kaya replied. "We'll be—"

Millie pointed her wand in Kaya's face. "I said I'm coming with you, so don't dare go out that door or I'll lasso ya in two snips of a whip." Kaya merely gazed back open-mouthed as Millie turned to the room and said, "I need a unicorn over here, now! I've got a peregrine falcon wrapped in crystal webbing and I need her cut out. Now hop to it! She'd better be free when we get back!" Turning to Kaya, she finished, "Vámonos."

Seconds later Manny, Iris, and Millie moved alongside Kaya as they darted north, skirting the mayhem to their west. Leaving the base of the tree, they came to the edge of a small space, empty save for a pair of saplings that rose and leaned toward one another, their stunted canopies twisting together a meter or so above the ground. Kaya motioned for everyone to kneel down as she peered into the area, her eyes fixed attentively on the saplings.

A scream rent the air behind Manny and he balled his fists. "Kaya, what are we doing out here? We should be stopping the tamarins!" Kaya forcefully held out her palm to silence him, but after a moment he began again. "And if this is so important, then why don't we go get Brun?"

Kaya reached down and grabbed Manny by the collar, jerking him up and into the space before the saplings as she said, "Because we don't have time, and because I'm sure he's got his hands full already. C'mon Millie, Iris—after us—and be prepared for anything."

Manny stared skeptically at the saplings as Kaya tugged him toward them to face their stunted arch. *Oh, dear.* He rolled his eyes. *If these saplings are akin to Battle Bamboo, then I might not leave here alive.* He scoffed. "Why are you so nervous, Kaya? Afraid the little trees are going to choke us?"

"Shut up, López," she said, transferring her grip from his cuff to his arm. "See you on the other side." And with that she pushed him forward through the archway.

Vile Temple

The space before Manny vanished as a wide valley appeared, draped on all sides by mossy trees akin to a genus of tropical willow. Manny's smirk melted as he stumbled forward, gazing down into the bowl to find a frightening structure, a dilapidated stone temple overgrown with ivy, the expansive entryway gaping toward him in either a broad yawn or a hungry invitation for him to enter. Invisible mites crept across his arms, shoulders, and neck as he considered what might dwell inside the temple—a den of anaconda, a pack of blood-thirsty pumas, a yet undiscovered Amazonian bear measuring twelve-feet in height. *Whatever it is, it's foul.* Manny's nose nearly caved in upon itself as fumes of sour dung rose up from the valley, bathing him in putrid air.

"Adelante, López," Kaya commanded as she pushed him forward.

"Dear Lord in Heaven," Millie prayed as she and Iris appeared through the archway.

"What is this place?" Iris asked, his nose wrinkled as he scanned the bowl. "Smells like a sewage pit."

"It is," Kaya quipped. "It's the tamarins' base."

Manny jerked his head around. "Are you serious?" Kaya nodded back soberly. "But how did you find it?"

"I was just leaning against our base, stretching my legs as I waited for you and Iris to get back with Orion, when I noticed a stream of tamarins just come pouring from the forest to my right. Naturally, I went invisible, scrutinizing the area for the origin of the procession, but I couldn't find it. After several minutes the flow of monkeys tapered off and I crept forward to find them appearing out of midair in front of those saplings." Kaya paused to point back toward the scrawny boles. "That's when I took off on my lightboard to get you guys."

"Since when have you ridden a lightboard?" Iris sounded slightly betrayed.

"Since Professor Bluebolt has been giving me private lessons," she answered. "I wasn't allowed to tell anyone, so don't get huffy about it."

"I thought those lessons were for Healing," Manny observed.

"Oh, Manny, get a clue!" Kaya clipped. "I'm one of the best healers in our level! Why would I need tutoring?"

"I'm not tryin' to be rude, y'all, but shouldn't we get our feet to the ground already?" Millie asked. "I figure those changos could return any moment, and I reckon I don't want 'em finding me standing here admiring their house."

"Point taken." Iris readied his wand and focused on the temple. "Let's move in, get the stolen wands, and move out."

Manny agreed. "Kaya and I will take the front. Millie, Iris— cover the back. If anybody sees a tamarin, pin him with Reticulum and knock him out. We don't want the rest of them knowing we're here."

Kaya smiled briefly, her caramel eyes rich as she peered sidewise at Manny. *Now you're talking, López.*

The four comrades took off down the hill, dodging piles of monkey feces as though they were well-placed land mines capable of potential dismemberment. A pair of minutes later they reached the entrance, the temple looming over them as a dark aura permeated the air. Horrifying sculptures and busts of savage creatures devouring men, women, and children leered down from the frame of the squared portal. All four teenagers shivered, feeling as though the very molecules of the air hovered balefully, waiting for an opportune time to converge on the intruders and swallow them completely. As a matter of fact, the sun seemed to have darkened, though neither cloud nor mist filled the sky above.

"Are we ready?" Manny prompted, his throat threatening to constrict. All nodded in reply as he and Kaya stepped warily forward, wands outstretched while clouds of luminescent Fireflies preceded them into the folds of lurking umbra. They had taken no more than five steps before the light from their sentinels revealed a set of collapsed stones, each the breadth of a great white shark.

"Well, it doesn't look like we'll be heading forward," Manny mumbled.

"Should we go left or right, then?" Millie breathed.

"Left," Iris urged. "I'm getting a really creepy feeling from the tunnel to the right. I've been shining my Fireflies all along it, and when they reach the corner everything turns black—I don't think there's a floor."

"That's settled," Kaya stated, shuffling charily down the opposite passage. They reached the corner, safe yet still unsettled, and turned right, unable to shake the feeling that they were being watched. The feeling grew as they continued along, until Kaya and Manny abruptly stopped. "Caramba."

Before them floated roughly half a dozen, baseball-sized orbs, their pearlescent forms interrupted only by pupils rimmed by irises of iridescent colors. Manny's throat indeed did constrict, and his breathing grew difficult, as he stared into the Ojos floating before them. They terrified him, the bodiless eyes with the unblinking stares; but he could not tear his gaze away.

"Everyone look at the ground," Kaya commanded. Yet Manny could not.

"More are coming from around the corner," Iris warned, their ethereal forms skirting his peripheral vision.

"Eyes down," Kaya riposted. "They shouldn't come near us unless we stare at them."

Manny's stomach twisted and his breathing stopped. He lurched forward, unable to control his legs.

"Manny?" Kaya's startled voice echoed off the shadowed walls as she caught him mid-fall, pulling him up and turning his eyes away from the Ojos. Her heart was now racing, for as she lunged forward she had noticed that where once only six orbs had been, there were now nearly a hundred.

"Whoo, doggy," Millie mused, her voice falling. "Don't those suckers hurt when they touch ya?"

"Yes!" Iris and Kaya replied in unison.

"Manny!" Kaya shouted, grabbing his shoulders. "Snap out of it!" His heart pounded, but his lungs refused to function. Her options exhausted, Kaya slapped him across the face.

Manny drew a sharp intake of breath, then shook his head. "What happened?"

"Everybody duck!" Millie roared. With a bright flash Reticulum leapt from her wrist, swallowing the Ojos in its folds as the net surged around the front of the passage then over the teenagers' heads to envelop the orbs behind. With a snap of her wrist and a sharp "Yeehah!" she sealed the net, twirling it like a lasso. "These are sweet pickin's! Haven't done this in months!"

The group quickly turned their backs on the lassoed Ojos, then paused momentarily to fill in the lapse in Manny's memory due to his brief blackout. "I won't think twice about tackling you if you ever stare at an Ojo again!" Kaya warned Manny.

Hoping that no one had overheard their skirmish, they continued on, the imprisoned Ojos floating along helplessly behind. Moments later they reached a stairwell that rose straight into the heart of the structure. Speculating that the tamarins would most likely hide their treasures in the guts of the temple rather than the peripheral passages, the group turned right and began their ascent. As they rose the darkness pressed down upon them, sticking to their clothes and skin just like the humidity of the jungle. Though terror no longer filled them, a distinct heaviness wore upon their muscles, pulling down their arms and legs to render each subsequent step a struggle. Panting, the teenagers reached a level space—seeing nothing, though glad for the respite.

"That was a doozie," Millie wheezed.

Catching his breath, though finding the air thick in his lungs, Manny strained his arm to raise his wand and illuminate the chamber, which proved to be immense in both height and width. The seemingly pale Fireflies scattered in all directions, revealing the distant corners of the square room. A pair of shadowed frames appeared at 45 degree angles from where he stood—*the exits*—while straight ahead rose a structure of varying striations, poorly illuminated by the thin light of the boy's sentinels.

"What is that?" Iris asked, pointing at the structure.

Kaya intuitively lifted her wand, her cloud of Fireflies now approaching the structure and enveloping it to reveal a pyramid hewn of aged stone. A set of thin stairs proceeded directly to the pyramid's zenith, which ended abruptly to form a flat space less than three meters below the ceiling. The group strained their eyes but were unable to discern what might lay atop the pyramid.

"Let's head up there," Millie said, starting toward the pyramid. "If the wands are here—"

"Wait," Iris said sharply, his eyes fixed intently on a patch of ceiling to their left. "I saw something move." Motioning with the appropriate paw, he sent out a trio of Fireflies that came to rest on an utterly black chord that descended from the ceiling like a tendril of shadow. It spun oddly. "Is that a rope?"

"It could be a vine," Manny noted.

"Growing from the ceiling of a temple?" Kaya voiced. "Not likely."

"Maybe," Millie conceded, "but if you look closely, you'll see that they're hangin' all over the place." Raising her hand, she directed her own Fireflies in a circular track around the room, revealing hundreds of shadowy vines, none of which was moving save the first that Iris saw. "This must be like the tamarins' playground," she observed as her Fireflies returned, hovering faithfully beside her.

"Well, it appears empty, so let's climb the pyramid while it stays that way," Kaya asserted.

"I'm not so sure it is empty," Iris said anxiously. "What made that vine move?"

"Probably just the wind," Kaya dismissed. But as the group started up the pyramid, neither Manny nor Iris felt a breath of air, no matter how hard they tried. Several minutes later, the four teenagers reached the top, their only difficulty having been searing muscles under the intense weight of the atmosphere. Crouched low and lungs heaving, they took a break, caring only for their next gasp of polluted oxygen. Nearly five minutes passed before their postures straightened and they looked down upon the summit of the pyramid.

A broad smile stretched across Manny's face as relief washed over his tired body. "We did it, guys." Before them rested a mound of wands of all kinds, from wooden necklaces, bracelets, headbands, and rings to horns, fangs, shells and antennae.

"I wonder if Chiron's is here?" Iris thought aloud.

"It must be," Kaya declared. "Look how many there are—three hundred or more. I bet that's all of them."

"At least until today," Manny said turbidly as he walked about the mound. "We need to get these out of here and tear down that portal before any more monkeys can return with stolen wands."

Millie knelt down and reached for a horn, but an inch from the ruby-tinted cone her hand met an immovable barrier of antigravity. The muscles in her arms flexed as she strained, but after ten seconds she was no closer to the horn then before. "How are we supposed to transport these if we can't touch 'em?"

"Do like the monkeys," Iris suggested. Millie stared down at the hare blankly. "Watch." Iris displayed his forepaw as a fissure erupted along his wand, effectually halving the rod save for the base, which elegantly united in a wishbone-like joint. He then reached down, clasped the ruby horn between the opposing prongs, and held it up to her. "See? Tweezers."

"I didn't know you could touch someone else's wand using your own," Kaya observed.

"Neither did I," Manny added.

"Those tiny-tike tweezers aren't gonna get us very far very fast, I'm sorry to tell ya," Millie said. "What we need are some extra large bags and a few shovels."

"I've got the shovels," Manny affirmed, pointing his wand at empty air as the light from half his Fireflies siphoned away, merging into a single core that quickly split into three equally-sized shovels. Manny then closed his eyes, concentrating on the complexities of wood, of strong fibers and linked grains. A moment later a clattering sound met his ears. He opened his eyes to find the shovels, now made of solid oak, resting on the mound of wands.

"You're an Ace, Manny," Millie exulted, leaning forward to pick up the spades and pass them out.

"Hey! What about me?" Iris ejected.

"Somebody's gotta catch the wands," Kaya said offhandedly.

The hare's ears went rigid. "¿Y cómo debo hacer eso, eh?"

"How do you think?" Kaya countered sarcastically. "Animate the biggest Reticulum you can and we'll shovel the wands into it. Make sure the netting's tight, though, or else the smaller wands will fall through."

Iris stood unmoving. "But that will drain all my sentinels."

Kaya stabbed her shovel under the mound to acquire her first load. "And?"

"And what if I need them later?"

"For what?"

"To defend myself!"

"You're pathetic." Kaya drew the hair back from her eyes. "Iris, you'll be fine. Manny, Millie and I've got your back."

After several seconds, when Iris had still done nothing, Manny said, "Trust us."

"Fine," Iris grumbled, raising his wand and winding it through the air as his cloud of Fireflies, three Chamaeleons, shoal of Pisces (which he carried in his satchel), and even his CPS drained away to knit a twenty-foot square net, which he quickly breathed upon so that the sentinel would obey his every thought. He arched his paw, and the Reticulum drew close to the peak of the pyramid. The net dipped perfectly to store the forthcoming wands.

"Thank ya much, Iris," Millie said kindly as she began shoveling the wands into the fiery red Reticulum. Kaya and Manny followed suit, and in under five minutes the shovelers had rendered the net a hovering bulge.

"That all of them?" Iris resonated, his tone much calmer now.

Manny drew the last of his Fireflies from the corners of the room to scour the top of the pyramid, kneeling low as he and Kaya tweezed the last few rings and antennae that yet remained. He then rose, huffing. "We got them all."

"Bien." Iris twirled his paw as the corners of the net united and the edges fused to transform the Reticulum into a huge, blazing sphere. "Then let's get outta here." Executing a 90 degree hop, Iris turned and began descending the staircase from whence they came, the wand sack gliding along beside him. Millie followed, while Kaya lingered on the top step, waiting as Manny worked to revert the shovels back into loose photons.

Manny had just finished decomposing the last shovel, when a gust of wind rushed past his face. "Kaya, stop it," he said impatiently.

"Stop wha—"

And then she was gone, a burst of air and shadow striking her and carrying her away to Manny's left.

"Get off me you filthy little pee ant!" called Kaya from the shadows.

Sounds of struggling filled the air as Manny fumbled and nearly dropped his wand in his efforts to redirect his hovering wisp of light to Kaya's position.

"Aaaah!" she screamed with fury. "Don't you bite me!"

Just as Manny managed to locate Kaya and surround her with bands of light, a hideous shriek pierced the air, followed by the sound of hurried scuffling as a dark figure leapt away from Kaya and disappeared into the blackness below her. Kaya hung suspended in the air, clutching her wand with one hand and a black vine with the other. She spit viciously.

"That'll teach you to bite me!" she roared down.

"Kaya!" Manny shouted. "What happened?"

"One of those cursed monkeys body-tackled me and carried me over here on a vine!" she shouted back. "He wouldn't let go of me, so I bit him!"

"You mean there are tamarins in here?" Iris called up worriedly.

"Kaya, just stay there!" Manny ordered. "We'll get below you and then you can slide down."

"I don't think so, López." Kaya threaded her hair through her wand and slid down the vine to gain a bit of slack. She then began to rock back and forth, one arm outstretched as she groped for a vine leading in Iris's direction. "Manny, just keep going. I'll meet you guys at the exit."

Iris's heart began to thunder in his chest as the scant light revealed a shadow hurrying up the stairs below him. "Guys! The tamarin's headed straight for me!"

"Step aside, Firefoot," Millie ordered as she calmly took the lead. In a blink she produced her Flareshot, reaching toward her belt for ammo and squinting as she honed her sights in on the approaching shadow. With a twang she released the bullet, but the shadow leapt into the air to her right and began curving around in a dangerous arc. Millie whirled around. "Manny, he's headed your way! Take him down!"

Manny's legs locked as he anchored himself to the steps above, his eyes searching the darkness as he scattered photons to determine the tamarin's trajectory. In a blind reflex Manny extended his free hand, provoking his sleeping Reticulum to burst forth and swallow the tamarin dead on. But before the tamarin could throw much of a fit Manny jerked his arm toward the ceiling, effectively slamming the monkey's body against the stone and knocking him unconscious. Manny did not release the tamarin, however, but instead maintained a firm clench on his fist in case the monkey reawakened.

"You got him?" Iris asked shakily.

"Yeah," Manny sighed.

"Nice shootin', Tex," Millie said.

"No-you-don't!" shouted Kaya, soaring over her companions' heads as she collided with yet a second shadow. With one swift kick she waylaid her opponent, knocking the tamarin from his vine. The monkey landed, shaking its head and in a daze, not ten steps from Iris, whose voice left him. As the tamarin recovered, it lifted its head and bared its fangs.

"Not this time!" Millie shouted, whirling her hand in lasso fashion as she whipped around her still-imprisoned Ojos and released them over the tamarin's body, electricity illuminating the primate's every nerve. The tamarin screeched pitifully for several moments before he, too, fell unmoving. Careful not to free any of the Ojos, Millie drew Reticulum back, resealing the sentinel and releasing it to float aimlessly about the chamber. She then approached the tamarin, nudging it aside with her boot. Millie turned to the group, which now included Kaya, who had slid from her vine and mounted the stairs. "It's high time we leave."

Without further discussion the four friends bolted down the stairs and back through the outer hall to the temple entrance, grateful that no further tamarins lay in wait in the shadows or upon the feces-strewn lawn. In a matter of minutes the group abandoned the primates' base through the sapling portal. Iris, for his part, had a difficult time molding Reticulum into a form conducive to shuttling the wands through the portal. But in the end he managed, and while he and Kaya stowed the wands in their base, Manny and Millie transformed theirs into saws and set to cutting down the saplings. When Millie sliced through the last sapling (Manny having finished just seconds before her), a brief tremor shook the ground as a curtain of shadow melted and dissolved where the portal had been. Thus, carrying the severed saplings along with them should the tamarins attempt to mend the portal, Manny and Millie darted for the base, tapping thrice upon the buttress root and entering unseen.

Mistarcus Bloodfang

Minutes later Manny, Millie, Iris and Kaya led the latter pair's squadrons through the now silent forest, stopping frequently to care for the numerous victims left after the initial tamarin/spider assault. As they lifted their prostrate peers from the ground and began healing their wounds, the squadrons discovered that the attackers had marched east, advancing on the center of the training area. So Manny and the makeshift militia trekked on, healing and acquiring new recruits (those who by some miracle still possessed their wands, at least), while sounds of feverish shrieking and ravenous clacking grew, causing some in the defense party to second guess their present commitment. The majority proceeded on, rushing toward the screaming mob, which, with each passing step, threatened to be greater and greater. And just as it seemed as though they would fall upon their enemies, Kaya raised her hand and stopped the militia cold. Numerous Lumens sighed with relief.

"We can't pull this off," Kaya said after drawing back from around a tree. "There are hundreds of tamarins and just as many crystal spiders; it would be suicide, plain and simple."

"But what are they all doing?" asked a particularly brave falcon as she tried to peer through the brush. "Just standing around and yelling?"

"That's right," Millie drawled, "standing around the biggest hurricane o' Pisces I ever saw. All mad as hornets 'cause they can't get through, I'd imagine." She paused. "I just hope the rest of the Seventh-Levels are all safely inside."

"But who's strong enough to animate a sentinel that big?" asked a tree frog.

"Do you think it's Andrés Dosfilos?" Iris said hopefully, his eyes meeting Kaya's.

"No way," she refuted. "If Dosfilos were already here the changos and arañas would be long gone; that or just lying around everywhere across the ground, dead."

689

Iris's ears sank. "So we're just gonna wait here for him to arrive?"

Manny jerked his head around, tearing molten gold eyes away from the tamarins' backs. "No." He said it forcefully. "We need to get inside the Pisces barrier to reinforce the others in case the monkeys break through."

"How?" Millie asked zealously.

"Well, as for the quetzals, falcons, and morphos, they can fly in carrying the smaller Lumens like the frogs, basilisks, and chinchillas. Kaya can spot the rest of us," he explained.

"Forgot about that," Millie admitted.

Kaya quickly intervened. "No, I can't. That would take too many trips, not to mention revealing our location."

"True," Iris acknowledged. "We definitely don't want that."

Manny appeared frustrated. "Then what about this—Kaya, you and I can lead the birds in from the back, while Millie and Iris sustain the land-based Lumens out here. That way those inside the barrier will still receive reinforcements, and no one gets caught."

Kaya stared at Manny for a moment, weighing the fire in his eyes. "I'm okay with that," she said finally.

"So what do Millie and I do again?" Iris asked.

"Just make sure nobody gets hurt while you hold out for Dosfilos—there's nothing else to do," Manny concluded.

"A covert-op, then," Millie stated, adjusting her hat. "Can do." She turned and began giving instructions to her newly acquired terrestrial squadron, while Manny beckoned all the airborne Lumens to his side to enumerate the plan. In the meantime, Kaya reached into a small pocket at her waist to withdraw a tiny pink object, strikingly similar to a guitar pick. Lifting her hand out before her at chest level, she released the object, which hovered motionlessly in place as she extended her wand to tap it. The object glowed brightly, growing instantly in length and width to achieve the dimensions of a traditional surfboard. Kaya smiled as she set her free palm on the lightboard—her lightboard—and lowered the vehicle to just above ankle level. She mounted the board gracefully, angling her body ever

690

so slightly to spin the board about, at which point she nudged the back of Manny's leg with the nose.

Manny turned around to find Kaya smiling at him. "What?" he asked, perplexed at her expression.

"Nothing," she said, her grin lingering. "Ready?"

"Yeah." He eyed the board, unsure of how to mount. "Should I sit or stand?"

"If you sit I won't be able to maneuver properly. What I need you to do is step up and position yourself behind me."

Manny's face flushed bright. "Behind?" His voice was nearly an octave higher. "Are you sure?"

"Uh, yeah," she replied, her cheeks reddening. "Like I said, I won't be able to fly it properly if you're sitting on the tail and weighing down the back."

A hard swallow. "O-okay." Manny then climbed onto the board, stepping around Kaya and straining not to touch her. Embarrassed and uncertain of how to anchor himself, he set his hands on Kaya's shoulders.

"Manny, no," she said, lifting his hands away and holding them in hers. "You need to mimic my stance. First, open your footing, pointing your front toe to the nose of the board and keeping your back foot parallel to the tail." Manny obeyed, though a bit clumsily, unable to pull his mind away from his hands. "Bien. Now, extend your right arm out beside you like this and wrap your left arm around my waist so you don't fall off during the flight. Hold on tight and make sure you lean into the turns with me."

Manny coughed, mortified at the stares of the birds and small beasts waiting before them. He closed his eyes, breathing deeply. *Keep your mind clear.* After a moment he opened them and realized that he and Kaya were now floating ten feet above the ground. He relaxed, impressed at Kaya's steadiness. "You're pretty good at this," he whispered.

"Thanks," she matched, bending her knees and angling back as the lightboard carried them higher into the air to the west. A moment later the birds followed, ascending in tandem with Kaya and Manny as they arced south.

A smile touched Manny's lips, and he took another deep breath as the wind rushed past his face. *This is amazing.* Glancing down, he watched as the forest shrank below them and the sun's light grew in intensity above the curling vapor. Trees ran as far as he could see, and to the north, beyond the perimeter wall, Manny could just make out the glint of the Amazon River. His hand relaxed on Kaya's waist and he took another breath, this time for courage. "We should do this more often," he said, leaning close to Kaya's ear.

Her answer did not come immediately. "Perhaps." Another pause, though briefer now. "But under better circumstances."

Manny squinted, remembering the plight of his fellow Seventh-Levels as he set his eyes on the steadily nearing vortex of fish. In the center he thought he descried a red flame, though he was unsure. He quickly became worried. "Is there any way we can fly faster?"

"Not with you on here," Kaya replied. "We'll get there when we get there. Just be prepared for whatever's waiting on us."

The vortex drew closer as they curved northeast, and now Manny could see a large mass huddled tightly behind the flame. A knot formed at the top of Manny's stomach as the hateful jeers and shrieks of the tamarins rose to his ears. *C'mon, Kaya—*

"Okay, Manny, it's time," Kaya said, interrupting his thoughts. "I need you to kneel with me and grab the sides of the board. Hold on for your life—and I mean it—because we're gonna have to take a nearly straight dive into the barrier to avoid any attacks from the monkeys and spiders. Do you understand?"

"Yes," he answered tightly.

"Then follow after me." Kaya carefully lowered her body to the board, grabbing the edges with her hands as she slid her right leg back to anchor her knee on the board's face. Manny mirrored her actions, only releasing her waist when he was low enough to successfully grab the left side of the board. "Here we go."

Manny braced himself, his hands clenching the board in a death grip as Kaya leaned sharply forward, her forehead nearly touching the plank as they shot down at an 80 degree angle, a bullet piercing the air. From a distance they looked very much like a

692

falling star, a heavenly knife descending upon the Earth to exact judgment and right wrongs. But as for appearances, Manny cared not, for his innards had left him somewhere at seven hundred feet and he felt as though one wrong move, or even a cross thought, could lead to certain death. He dared not close his eyes, though, for fear that he might faint; instead, he stared on as gravity pulled them in the direction of the planet's core, toward the vortex, to the burning flame.

Screams erupted as Kaya leaned left and pulled back, whipping around the eye of the vortex as though a bolt of rose-colored lightning had suddenly struck, becoming caught in the pull of the whirling Pisces. The lightboard slowed steadily, however, and in about twenty seconds she and Manny floated wistfully over the grass, dismounting and falling to the ground in a daze as scores of birds rained down above them.

"Kaya! Manny! What are you doing here?" shouted a female voice amid the screams.

The pair lifted still-spinning eyes to a form that appeared much like Kaya's, with coffee skin, long hair, and a thin frame. A name surged into Manny's mind. "Araceli?" he said, nearly vomiting the word as his stomach clenched. He then took a very long breath and lay on his back.

A gentle hand quickly supported his neck. "Sí, soy yo," Araceli replied. "Just lie still for a minute; you'll catch your bearings soon enough."

As the world slowed Manny listened to the avid voices of falcons and quetzals diving about, explaining to the semi-frantic crowd that their arrival had not been an attack and that reinforcements had come. After a pair of minutes Manny felt a sharp kick against his thigh. He opened his eyes to see Kaya staring down at him.

"Get up already, López," she joked.

Supporting his back, Araceli helped Manny to his feet. Though the ground still shifted slightly beneath him, he turned to thank her. "You're more than welcome," Araceli rejoined.

Manny noted, however, that Araceli's eyes were tight with worry. "What's wrong?"

Araceli stepped aside. "It's Brun," she indicated, revealing his glowing figure several yards away; the boy's skin shone a liquid red copper as he stood rooted to the ground, his right hand clenching his wand and his left palm outstretched toward the vortex. The expression on his face appeared strained, as though he were in pain.

"What's happening to him?" asked Kaya, who had never seen Brun's skin achieve such an intensity by day.

Manny's eyes grew wide. "Is he maintaining the barrier all by himself?"

"Yes," Araceli said shakily, "and it's wearing on him. I don't know how much longer he can keep it up before he breaks."

Manny turned his eyes toward the mass of students behind Brun. "Why doesn't everyone just work together to create a second barrier?"

"We tried, but with all the shrieking and the clacking, the others are too frightened to concentrate," Araceli explained.

"Aren't there any other Squadron Leaders in here?" Kaya prompted.

Araceli nodded, though her morbid expression did not change. "Sí, but not enough to make an equitable barrier. They're all standing in a huddle behind Brun, trying to formulate a plan."

Manny and Kaya turned their eyes to the huddle, which consisted of seven students—two centaurs, a human, a panther, a kinkajou, a crystal spider, and a red morpho. Kaya's lip curled as she set eyes on the butterfly. *Ugh. Treble.* Her eyes leapt to the spider. *Is that Spence?*

"Gracias, Araceli," Manny expressed. "We'll see what we can do."

"Please hurry," Araceli responded, biting her lip.

Kaya nodded and then grabbed Manny's shoulder, leading him away several steps and then pulling him close. "Manny, I'll take care of the Squadron Leaders. I think you should go talk to Brun and encourage him or something. He doesn't look good."

694

With wary eyes Manny gazed at Brun, nodding his assent. "Good luck, Kaya."

"You, too," she asserted, turning and jogging toward the huddle of Squadron Leaders.

As Manny walked across the grass, he noticed Brun's wand arm quivering slightly. "Hey, bud!" Manny said, superseding his concern with a heavy dose of encouragement.

Brun did not shift his stance, though his eyes locked on Manny's figure under a rigid frown. Brun blinked in acknowledgment, then turned focused eyes back on the surging fish.

"Well, how's it going?" Manny continued, hoping to distract Brun a bit from his weariness.

"Splendid," Brun answered through his teeth a moment later. He did not look Manny's way this time.

"That's good," Manny said, pretending as though his friend had actually responded happily. "So, uh, guess what Millie, Kaya, Iris and I di—"

"Manny, be quiet." Brun's voice was thin.

Manny stared at Brun, his jaw slightly ajar. "Why? I'm just trying to get your mind off the task at hand for a sec."

"I have to concentrate, Manny, if you don't want the entire barrier to crumble down on us." Brun groaned sickeningly, his brow furrowed as he drew a ragged breath. "It's like—my mind is attached to ten thousand separate bodies, and I'm not exactly used to that, if you know—what I mean."

Manny nodded. *That's one big migra—*

Brun suddenly slumped forward and exhaled sharply, his eyes wide as they focused on a growing bulge in the ring of Pisces. "Manny—something's wrong." He closed his eyes, fighting in his mind against the pressure of an invading force, malignant in nature and brutally strong. But the more he struggled, the greater the pressure grew, and in seconds he could feel a hole forming in the barrier.

The breath caught in Manny's lungs as a sphere of shadow materialized, instantly disintegrating each sentinel fish with which it came in contact. As the sphere grew, so did the number of annihilated Pisces, their orbital course carrying them straight to a black doom. And despite Brun's best efforts to redirect the flow of the Pisces around the sphere, the shadow pulsated, stretching in height and breadth to consume every last passing photon. Brun dropped to his knees, energy spent, and witnessed as an arc of empty air steadily replaced the barrier that he had so painstakingly wrought. In a matter of seconds the students found themselves encircled on all sides by the raging army of tamarins and spiders.

The Seventh-Levels shrank back upon one another, hearts shriveling and limbs failing, while the Squadron Leaders fanned out, bracing for the worst. But just as quickly as the shadow sphere had appeared, its boundaries receded, shrinking to a seemingly miniscule orb hovering over a fifty-foot crater. The orb shot through the air, striking the ground several steps in front of Manny and Brun. A moment later the orb's edges faded to reveal a three foot figure, its chin and mouth framed by a spectacular beard of the purest white. The creature's fur glistened jet over the remainder of its little body, while one beaded eye looked piteously upon the petrified students. His other eye, however, had apparently been gouged out. The tamarin lifted his arm and snapped his fingers, instilling unanimous silence around the ring and halting the army's advance. The students blinked, startled, and all turned to face the army's undisputed leader.

A malevolent grin widened across the one-eyed tamarin's face, a pair of glittering fangs catching the light and piercing what little remained of the students' resolve. Apparently thrilled with his targets' whimpering response, the tamarin twisted his opposite palm in a contorted flourish to produce a steel star, the weapon's sawtoothed points educing yet another wail from the cornered Seventh-Levels. For several seconds the tamarin stood in a motionless jeer. Then, striving to push their fear to the limit, he stepped forward.

A spark lit in Manny's chest, causing him to lift his wand and point it directly at the tamarin's head. "Mistarcus, stop."

The monkey complied, his face now void of relish as his one eye thinned to a tiny slit. "How do you know my name, boy?"

696

Mistarcus' voice was subterranean, his words a coarse gravel tumbling down on the grass before his feet.

Manny gripped his wand more tightly. "I was there the day you lost your eye."

Mistarcus glared, his good eye an obsidian stone. He pointed a rigid finger at the empty socket on the right half of his face. "You did this to me?"

A terse swallow. "No. My friend did."

"Then I shall endeavor to repay him in kind," Mistarcus answered smoothly. "I don't suppose you would mind pointing him out to me?" Manny remained silent. "Reticence—I should expect as much," the tamarin continued dully. "Then I shall tear the answer from you, followed quickly by the wand from your limp hand." Mistarcus made a diminutive wave as a fold of shadow ebbed up from the ground and assumed the shape of an inky fist the size of a small elephant. The tamarin again flicked his wrist as the fist surged forward to strike. And then, for Manny, time froze.

He thought of courage, of how if he failed and allowed Mistarcus to pass, his companions would all be crippled—or worse—killed. He imagined the tamarins discovering the location of all the wands he and his friends had risked their lives to recover. *Unacceptable.* He envisioned Mistarcus leading his army against Isla Verde, conquering the continent, venturing north into Arizona— and Manny's heart burned, the spark in his chest exploded, his eyes flashed. "Never."

Manny's entire body was suddenly engulfed in a blindingly white light. He lifted his wand arm, which now radiated with unbounded brilliance, and pierced the shadow descending to crush him. Executing a wide arc, he severed the tenebrous hand and stepped back as the halves fell to the earth and dissolved. Eyes ablaze, Manny pointed his wand at an alarmed Mistarcus as the very air around the tamarin hovered with photons that latched onto his body and lifted him from the ground. Manny spun his wand and snapped it forward as Mistarcus shot involuntarily into the air then hurtled backward, skirting the tree tops with great speed before slamming into the bough of a mighty kapok a half mile away.

"Manny, watch out!" Kaya screamed.

The boy whirled around and lifted his other hand, energy flowing out from him as a photon wall deflected the body of a charging crystal spider. Spinning the wall through the air to sideswipe a row of tamarins, Manny's mind quickly processed the fact that the entire army would descend upon them in a matter of seconds. He then closed his eyes, aimed his wand at the sky, and discharged the immense well of photon energy coursing within him to seal off a perimeter around the students. Manny instantly collapsed under a veil of white.

Definition of a Hero

Manny awoke to the sound of of a door slamming. He turned his head to see Brun storming across their room to the closet where he grabbed all his shirts and tossed them onto the empty hammock. He then drug out a pair of suitcases and began stuffing them with any and all possessions he could reach, emptying his drawers, pulling down wall ornaments, smashing shoes. Within seconds all signs that Brun had ever lived in Chiron's Hutch began to disappear, and the boy appeared particularly displeased about it.

"Are you leaving?" Manny asked, twisting around to sit in his hammock.

"Yes," Brun snapped, balling up his socks and throwing them into his luggage.

"Why?"

"Because the school year's over and mi papá's waiting for me outside." Brun tore down a photo of Araceli with him laughing at the beach. "I don't know why he has to be such a jerk. Every other kid gets to stay up until the First-Levels return from their mission if they want, but not me. I have to go home the day after ours is over."

Manny leapt to his feet. "Our mission is over? How did it end? What happened with the spiders and the tamarins? Did they steal any more wands?"

"Cálmate. Everybody's fine," Brun said as he zipped up a suitcase. "After you surrounded us with that photon sphere, the spiders and tamarins couldn't get through. They tried for a while, but then Chairman Dosfilos showed up and they all just took off. The Task Force found another pile of wands just off the center of the training area, and when we showed them the ones you recovered they were dumbfounded. They transported all the wands to the House of the Brethren and they plan to begin passing them out to their owners tomorrow." Brun secured his second case and sat down on his hammock with a sigh.

"Did the Task Force believe Kaya and Iris about where we found them?"

"Kaya refused to tell them; she said they wouldn't believe her. So she told Dosfilos instead."

"She did?" Manny exclaimed. "What did he say?"

"He looked worried, but not half as much as when all the students told him they heard Mistarcus talking. The witnesses attested, and he didn't argue. In fact, he didn't say anything. He only asked questions and digested answers. He's not critical like the other adults."

Manny shook his head in amazement. "So did the Task Force or Dosfilos find Mistarcus?"

"Nope. But they found the roots of the kapok where you threw him, all torn up and jutting from the ground like before when Spence—"

"Kieran!"

Brun's ocher eyes assaulted the bamboo door, detesting his father's stern call. The boy did not reply, however.

"Kieran! Outside, now!" Renato's earthy voice redoubled.

"I'm coming!" Brun growled as he leapt to his feet. He kicked a suitcase, his face contorted in frustration. "I'm sorry, Manny." Brun's voice quivered with both anger and melancholy. "I have to go. But I'll see you next year, right? We'll still be roommates?"

"For sure," Manny asserted, gripping Brun's hand and offering him a half hug. Manny stepped back and helped Brun prop up his luggage. "I promise."

Brun nodded. "See you, then," he said, opening the door and heaving his luggage out onto the back lawn.

Manny sank back down into his hammock, staring at the dirt floor as Brun and Renato's voices floated in through the windows.

"You have everything, correct?"

"Yes, Dad."

"Okay, then. Now we—Kieran, where's your birthday present?"

Silence.

700

"Where is your ring? You were to wear it at all times."

"I don't have it."

A pause. "Then you will return to that mangy hut and come back with it."

"But—"

"You will not contradict me."

A second later the door flew open and Brun stepped in, appearing nauseous. "Manny—"

"Don't worry about it, man," Manny answered, retrieving his wand from his bedside table and transforming it into a briefcase.

"But that ring—you know, the one I was wearing the day of our first photocache—"

"Yeah, I remember." Manny withdrew his hand from his briefcase to produce the obsidian ring. "Here, problem solved."

Brun stammered as he reached out for the dark hoop. "H-how did you—?"

Manny shrugged. "I figured you might regret discarding it the way you did, so I stowed it away in my wand. No harm done. Just be careful when you wear it—don't go ballistic and kill anyone."

"I won't," Brun chuckled, disappearing back through the door, the ring clutched tightly in his palm.

"Show it to me," came Renato's voice.

"Satisfied?" Brun riposted.

"Unquestionably. Now put it on."

"I don't want to."

"Kie—"

"Buenas tardes," interrupted a kind voice from around the hut. "Is anybody home?"

Manny peered through the window to see the tall figure of Andrés Dosfilos come into view, stopping opposite Brun and Renato.

"Good afternoon," Dosfilos said, extending his hand to Renato. "I'm Andrés Dosfilos. Would you happen to be Brun's father?"

Renato did not return Dosfilos' gesture but instead glared accusingly at him. "Yes, I am, but what should a murderer like you care of my son and his family."

Dosfilos faltered, his sapphire eyes probing Renato's black ones. "E-excuse me?"

"You heard me, Chairman. I sent my son to this school with the understanding that he would be safe, and what do I discover but that he and his peers were brutally attacked, and on their training mission no less! How can an honest parent reconcile his child's well-being with such administrative disregard?"

"Señor Dimirtis, please allow me to explain the sit—"

"Explain? Exactly what do you intend to explain? How the crystal spiders, who were apparently in league with you, turned and attacked our children? And allowing emperor tamarins to run wild through the forest, clawing and biting? I wouldn't be surprised if a number of Seventh-Levels contract rabies! You, Chairman, are the cause of it all, and I will see that you are removed from your position in short order. The Council won't stand for this, much less the Assembly!"

Dosfilos stood, his palms open to Renato. "Señor Dimirtis, you are blowing this out of proportion…"

"Am I?" Renato growled, lunging forward to glare directly into Dosfilos' eyes . "I will tell you one last thing, Chairman, before we depart." Renato bared his teeth. "If I ever discover that you come into contact with my son again—if you even speak one word to him—then you will answer to me." Renato stepped back and set his hand on Brun's shoulder. "I hope I have made my intentions clear. Let us go, Kieran."

Dosfilos watched with deep concern as Renato and Brun collected the boy's luggage and disappeared around the corner of the hut. Before Brun turned away, he offered Dosfilos a sad glance, a small apology for his father's actions. Then Dosfilos stood alone, and Manny watched as the man shook his head, visibly disturbed by Renato's reaction to the recent events. With a heavy sigh Dosfilos ran his fingers through his hair and turned toward the hut, stopping suddenly as he found Manny staring at him. Dosfilos smiled.

702

"Hello, Manny."

"Hola, Sr. Dosfilos." Manny wanted to apologize for Renato's behavior, but he suddenly felt awkward, talking to the Lumen leader of South America through his bedroom window.

"May I speak with you?"

"Uh, sure, I'll be out in just a sec." Manny slipped from his hammock, quickly changed out of his pajamas into a pair of cargo shorts and a shirt, then donned some shoes and ran out the door. He found Dosfilos sitting in one of two wooden chairs that the man had crafted while waiting for the boy.

"Please, have a seat," said Dosfilos, gesturing toward the sister chair. Manny obliged. "I'd like to ask you a few questions."

"Okay."

"Is it true that you crafted a photon sphere around your peers to shield them?"

"I guess so," Manny surmised, his memory of the act in question not particularly clear. "At least I think I did."

"How do you suppose you accomplished that?"

Manny frowned. "I don't know. I knew that I had to, so I just pushed out all the light from within me so that it would surround us instead."

Dosfilos raised an eyebrow. "From within you?"

"Yeah, I could feel it inside me, in every part. It was much easier to access than funneling it down from the sky. It was just natural."

"So the light was emanating from you, just as it is right now?"

Manny glanced at his arms and legs, which were shining brightly under a ray of sunshine from the foliage above. "No. At the moment I'm just reflecting the light; it's not coming from me. In fact, I can't even feel it inside me—just on my skin, you know. But when I made the sphere—that was different. It felt like my veins were coursing with it, like the light was me."

The man nodded, concentrating intently. "Does this happen often?"

"No, not at all. Just when I'm really stressed, like when someone's in danger."

"For example...?"

"Um, okay, one time I thought my cousin Zane was being attacked by a giant squid, so I just lit up. I was going to tackle the squid myself, but it was a false alarm. He was just overreacting. Then... Let's see... The second time happened when the tamarin attacked Iris on Easter Island, and Brun and I zapped him with a cloud of electric Fireflies. And yesterday was the third. So, yeah, that should sum it up."

"I see," Dosfilos said, the depth of his eyes seeming to fathom far more beyond what Manny was saying. "It appears that you and Brun are a talented pair, capable perhaps of photogenic dermatological absorption, a trait yet unseen in humans. So many similarities... And you're not related whatsoever?"

"No," Manny affirmed. "Our only connection is Isla Verde."

Dosfilos nodded. "Fascinating. I am eager to see what the two of you become; perhaps you will outshine me one day." Dosfilos offered a genuine smile. "I have only a few more questions.

"Shoot."

Dosfilos laughed. "Okay, then. Though I am afraid my joy is about to leave me." He paused, his smile fading. "This Mistarcus— who is he?"

Manny took a deep breath and slid slowly back into his chair. "He's the General over all the emperor tamarins, sir. I guess you could say he's over the crystal spiders now, too. At least the bad ones. My friends and I first saw him walking in the forest with Archer Villalobos one day in March. We heard him mention something about Twilight, about stealing wands, and—" A realization hit Manny. "He mentioned the Seventh-Level Mission! That's why he and Archer tried to kill Crion! He must have been making it hard for Mistarcus to sabotage the Mission!"

"That was as I feared."

"Then you believe me?" Manny asked incredulously.

Dosfilos nodded soberly. "Yes, but I need more information," he added tentatively.

Manny understood, leaning back in his chair and focusing hard. "Like what?"

"Do you ever recall Mistarcus mentioning anything about what he planned to do next?"

"Whoo." Manny bowed his head and pondered for a moment. "No, Crion came before they could get to any specifics. But he did mention something about Archer taking command in Europe and a witch killing people."

"A witch? How strange..." Dosfilos brooded. "As for Archer, I will communicate with him personally." He paused. "I have only one more question. What species of Lumen was your wand-giver?"

Manny swallowed hard, still unsure of what Dosfilos' reaction might be. "An emperor tamarin, sir. He transformed my family camera, ran away, and then came back to steal it."

Dosfilos stared solemnly at the boy. "Manny, I want you to know that I appreciate your honesty and the risks you took yesterday to save your friends and their wands. It pains me to consider what may have occurred had you not displayed such courage and determination. I am in your debt, and I will not forget."

As Dosfilos rose to his feet, Manny asked, "But don't you want to ask me about the tamarins' base and how we got the wands back?"

"I don't need to. Your friends told me, and I believe them." Dosfilos took Manny's hand and shook it heartily. "I'll see you here next year?"

Manny gripped the man's hand firmly. "Yes."

***

Acknowledgments

Above all, I thank Christ for encouraging me (Revelation 3: 7-13 and Ephesians 2:10) and inspiring me during the hard days, when I didn't think we could take Manny any further. But we did it, we pushed on and persevered, and I can't wait to see what He's got next!

Limitless thanks go to Breyanna for the nights spent eating pasta, playing Piranha Sweep and discussing the book endlessly, even when she was tired of hearing about it; to Brenda and Vickie for their much desired and deeply appreciated peer revision of the second draft; to Patrice for critiquing part of the third and for her much valued encouragement; to Gail for helping me line out the details of radiant beetles and the many noontime discussions regarding celestial figures and terrestrial species (Remember the ring-tailed cat and the river otters? That was insane!); to the Cheesmans for encouraging me and helping me print my drafts; to my students for being so eager to read the book and for being incessantly positive about it... I really needed all you guys at the end. Remember that this is for you—I've been dying to share it with you for years and can't wait to hear what you think!

And reader, thank you for investing your time in this book—I hope you've gotten a lot out of it, from laughter to suspense, and that at least one scene or another set you to pondering.

Should you be interested in honing your astronomical skills, I would suggest purchasing *The Night Sky*, a dual-sided planisphere created by David Chandler. It's pretty handy because it allows you to preview just what stars are in the sky on any given night of the year. I use it frequently and enjoy star-gazing with my friends.

Whoever you may be and whatever journey you are experiencing in life, I would like to close with this: Please, please never give up; turn to God, even in the good times, for they come from Him; and always seek Christ—He is a faithful companion and a true, open-hearted friend.

Letters to the Reader

-First Letter–

Most Esteemed Reader:

It has been brought to my attention that the linguistic variation presented in this tale of Lumen history may pique your interest as to the meanings of several words and phrases in the Spanish language. It is my hope that you will reap the benefits of this catalog of definitions that I have compiled in order that you may more fully enjoy the work found in this tome.

Please remember that if you have any questions you may consult me directly at Nahir's Hill during my office hours, which are Tuesdays and Thursday from 1-4 p.m. Or if you find such an avenue to your inconvenience, you may always send me a written inquiry via paloma paper, preferably not too early in the morning.

Best Regards,

Chiron

Chiron Veridai

Professor of Astronomy

Amazon River Academy

Word/Phrase ~ definition

Abuelito/Abuelita ~ Granddad/Grandma
abuelo/abuela ~ grandfather/grandmother
Adelante hay una bifurció y no sé por dónde vaya mi jefe hoy.
　　　¡Vamos! ~ There's a fork in the road ahead and I don't know
　　　which way my boss is going today. Let's go!
agua ~ water
ahora ~ now
almuerzo ~ lunch
amigo ~ friend
¡Basta ya! ~ Enough already!
¡Bestia tú! ~ You beast!
bien ~ well; good
Buenos días ~ Good morning.
Buenas noches ~ Good night
¡Cállate! ~ Shut up!
Cálmate ~ Calm down
Caramba/caray ~ crap
cariño ~ dear
Como sea... ~ Whatever...
¿Cuántos años tiene? ~ How old are you?
¡Déjalo! ~ Leave it alone!
De nada ~ You're welcome
¿De veras? ~ Really?
De verdad ~ I mean it
Dios sabe ~ God only knows
¿Dónde están mis radios? ~ Where are my radios?
Escúchenme ~ Listen to me
Espere ~ Wait
Está bien ~ Okay
Estás loco ~ You're crazy
Es verdad ~ That's true
Hay que... ~ Let's...
hermano/hermana ~ brother/sister
increíble ~ incredible

linterna ~ lantern

Lo siento ~ Sorry

¡Me muero de hambre! ~ I'm dying of hunger!

Me va a matar. ~ She's going to kill me.

Miguel dice que necesitamo' salir ahora. Ya estamo' atrasado'. ~ Miguel says that we need to leave now. We're already behind.

Mira ~ Look

M'ijo ~ child, dear

monstruo ~ monster

muchacho/muchacha ~ boy/girl

¡Muévete! ~ Move it!

necios ~ fools

No hay problema. ~ No problem

no me importa ~ I don't care

no puede ser ~ it can't be

No tengo tiempo para necedades. ~ I don't have time for this.

¡No te preocupes! ~ Don't worry!

¿Oyes eso? ~ Do you hear that?

Perdóname, amigo. ~ Forgive me, friend.

por favor ~ please

pues ~ well

¿Qué? ~ What?

Qué extraño ~ How strange.

¿Qué pasa? ~ What's going on?

¿Qué te pasa? ~ What's wrong with you?

¿Qué tiene, Sr. Soriano? ~ What's wrong, Mr. Soriano?

quizás ~ maybe

Siéntate. ~ Sit down.

Sí, lo puedes ~ Yes, you can

sin duda ~ without a doubt

Sí, sí, ahorita vengo. ~ Yeah, yeah, I'm coming.

¿Sólo una? ~ Only one?

Tavo es tan chévere. ~ Tavo is so cool.

Te dije que no ~ I said no

Tengo hambre ~ I'm hungry

Te lo dije ~ I told you so

tío/tía ~ uncle/aunt

Tienes que levanta'te pa'que no te'lejes del grupo. ¡Ándale! ~ You
  have to get up so that you don't get lost from the group.
  Move it!

tu ~ your

¿Una morena, eh? ~ A copper beauty, eh?

un montón de fotos ~ lots of pictures

ven aquí ~ come here

Verdad. ~ Right.

¿Y tú? ~ And you?

ya ~ enough

*Ya 'stán atrasa'os y si no nos partimos pa'l aeropuerto, perderán su
  vuelo.* ~ You're already late and if we don't leave for the
  airport you're going to miss your flight.

-Second Letter-

Dearest Reader:

I hope you are faring quite well throughout whatever journeys and adventures you are currently pursuing during your free time. As you well know, South America is a continent rich in photobiological culture and diversity, and as such, I have assembled a brief abstract of the thirteen (and debatably fourteen) Lumen species that make the Amazonian continent their home.

Please ensure that you have fully assimilated the information expounded here, as I will be administering a formative assessment upon your return to the Academy for the Sixth-Level, and no one wants to be enrolled in an extra remedial class. Should you have further questions, you may wish to obtain a summer loan of your copy of The Blue Planet from the Lumen Resource Center.

Ciao,

Sable Shadowflame

Sable Shadowflame
Professor of Lumen Studies
Amazon River Academy

Black Panther

Elegant and strong, the black panther actually forms part of the leopard family. With a glistening coat and commonly electric yellow eyes, this species of Lumen is often found to be intimidating and even frightful, though any informed Lumen knows that the panther exerts a great degree of self-control and sleek prowess in interspecific relations. As a quadruped, the black panther stands no more than three feet tall at the head and roughly two and a half at the shoulders. Interestingly, the Lumen panther differs from its sister breed in the outside world in that Bri, the second eldest male of the Brethren, granted flexibility to the panther's fifth claw, rendering it an opposable thumb and effectively capacitating the species to easily grasp and manipulate objects. Black panthers wield wooden wands, as do most species of the Southern continent. This feline prefers wearing the wand either around the neck as a loose collar or on the ankle in bangle form.

(Blue) Morpho

Galatea, the middle Sister, enlightened the morpho species while exploring the mist-covered forests of present day Costa Rica with a declaration that there could be no species in all the Earth to bring more tranquility to the heart. Inspired by the cerulean iridescence of the morphos' wings, Galatea became known for the subtle brilliance of her architectural works, including intricate fountains and river gardens where her cherished species would dwell. She was in fact the sole designer of the Argo Dock in Isla Verde, the warm blue of the structure's moonstone a tribute to her love for the butterfly. The morpho is one of three South American species whose wand forms a part of their anatomy—the antennae. Despite their minute frames—generally not exceeding the breadth of a human head—morphos are quite capable at many tasks and are commonly called upon to move heavy loads, owing to their highly practiced abilities for photokinetic transference. In fact, though the first Lumen morphos indeed boasted wings of purest blue, Galatea soon imbued various exemplars of the species with alternate colors, as she believed that heterogeneity could only enrich the genus further (as well as aid in identification).

Centaur

Uncommonly astute in both stature and wisdom, the centaur's knowledge generally excels that of his peers, particularly in the realm of astronomy. Aldis, the eldest of the Stars, created the first pair of centaurs when he discovered a Spanish conquistador and his indigenous wife at the bottom of a ravine, the man and woman's legs having been crushed under the bodies of their horses, whose necks had broken. Fearing that the humans would die should he not act swiftly, Aldis effectively fused the torsos of the humans with the bodies of the horses, melding their anatomy and granting each centaur two hearts. In order to diversify the gene pool of the species, Lumen volunteers of varying races joined bodies with their equines under the sagacious hand of Aldis. As such, today one may encounter centaurs of numerous body colors and skin tones. The tallest centaur to date measured twelve feet, while the shortest rose to seven. Like the panther, centaurs wear wooden wands around their ankles and necks, though some have been seen sporting wands reminiscent of traditional human jewelry, such as bracelets, belts, and headbands.

Chinchilla

The chinchilla, native to the Andean mountains, is indeed a rodent that arguably possesses the softest fur of any creature found on our blue planet. Lumen chinchillas may range from such fur hues as gray and white to brown, red, and occasionally black (though hot pink and electric blue are becoming progressively popular in the adolescent crowd). While standing on hind paws, chinchillas typically reach a height of one foot. Like Morphus, their creator, chinchillas are known for their intense enthusiasm and avid determination. Though small and often misconceived as scatterbrained, the chinchilla is actually quite analytical and adept in solving the most complex of puzzles, a fact which makes this species a formidable opponent in any photocache challenge. The chinchilla's wand, typically a rust-hued agate, reflects his dwelling among the rocks of the Andes. The majority of chinchillas choose to wear their wands as stone anklets, though some elect earrings instead.

Crystal Spider

This highly controversial Lumen first came into existence when Oriana, one of the Brethren's middle siblings, stumbled upon a nest of tarantulas in the Amazon. Convinced of their beauty and absolutely fascinated with their anatomy, Oriana transformed the entire nest into meter high replicas of their former selves. Seeing that the dark figures of of the spiders scared her siblings, Oriana decided to make her creations transparent, rendering the arachnids' bulbous bodies absolutely clear and capable of both reflecting and absorbing light. In order to complement their glowing forms, Oriana granted the spiders a set of crystal fangs to serve as wands. These changes, though quite extensive, were not sufficient to instill a genuine affection for the species within the hearts of the Brethren and the remaining Lumens, however. It was for this reason that Oriana chose to live in separation from Lumen society, aiding the spiders in the construction of Crystalus, a city rumored of extreme beauty and breathtaking stone formations. To this day few Lumens have ever crossed the river to visit Crystalus, as most such travelers are quickly labeled eccentric and strange.

Green Basilisk (a.k.a. Jesus Christ Lizard)

Distinguished among Lumens for their ability to walk on water, green basilisks spend much of their time racing, swimming, and playing in the aquatic arena. The basilisk ranges in height from a foot to a foot and a half, and its crown is topped with one or more membraneous fans that facilitate underwater maneuverability. Though common basilisks can survive below water no more than half an hour, the Lumen basilisk has been known to swim for hours without need for additional air. Green basilisks sport reed wands, virtually freeing the reptiles from the inconvenience of unwanted buoyancy. In the spirit of their maker, Sophronia, eldest of the Sisters, the basilisk wields stunning discernment, making this Lumen a prime candidate for mediating disputes.

Human

First of all Lumens, men and women have enjoyed the friendship of the Light Brethren longer than all others. Credit for their enlightenment falls not on any specific Star but to all the Brethren. Humans are an endowed species, highly adaptable to virtually all climates and geographies and capable of wielding the widest variety of Lumen tools, offensive and defensive alike. Quite varied in their appearance, grown humans typically range in height from three to eight feet, boast numerous skin tones, and are relatively hairless. Humans are unique in the outside world in that they are the only member of creation capable of complex thought and speech. And though many forget this fact, the Light Brethren themselves formed part of the human number, though strikingly different for the brilliance of their skin and their virtually limitless influence over light.

Kinkajou

Often mistaken for monkeys, kinkajous are in fact not members of the primate family at all. The placement of the kinkajou's ears on the curve of the head rather than the sides is a trait that credits the creature with a strong resemblance to the bear family. Their average height, stretching between two to three feet, mirrors the length of their incredibly elastic tail, which they can use for a myriad of purposes, such as hanging from branches, carrying objects, and even painting. Extremely acrobatic, the kinkajou is the most limber of the species of the Southern Continent. Though the traditional kinkajou maintains a generally nocturnal lifestyle, the Lumen genus spends the majority of its conscious life in daylight hours, despite the fact that a number are given to rising late in the day. Kinkajous frequently don wooden wands with vine-like and floral designs, a characteristic which reflects their particular fancy for flowers and forest fruits. The species complements its originator in this respect, as Juno, the second youngest of the Seven Sisters, was rarely seen without a manner of orchid, bromeliad, or hibiscus in either her hair or raiment.

Otter

Indisputably the most playful species of the Lumen world, the otter possesses a positive disposition that can lift even the most depressed of spirits. With an incomparable cunning for jokes and tricks, the otter makes for an excellent architect for designing advanced photocache challenges—rendering him a prime riddler. Full grown otters stand at a height of two feet; but this small stature does not limit the species, as otters can be found nigh anywhere, from the ocean shores and Amazonian rivulets to the caves of Borneo and the Himalayas. Rei, the youngest of the Brothers, enlightened the otter species, as he found a deep camaraderie in their love of water and ceaseless need to explore. Otters, like a number of Atlantean

Lumens, wield wands of polished limestone that they often wear as shell necklaces, bracelets and bands.

Peregrine Falcon

Lover of birds, Freya, the third eldest Sister, brought light to the falcons, often taking to the skies alongside her prized species as they soared together over the Andean Mountains, spiraled upon the winds, and dove at blistering speeds for prey. The peregrine falcon boasts a curved, ebony beak, a tawny belly, and auburn wings. Their sharp black eyes can see a chinchilla (non-Lumen, of course) scurrying miles below on the rocks, making this bird of prey a fierce predator. Peregrine falcons sit at a height of two feet, theirs wings spreading to nearly four. Before the invention of paloma paper, this species was the primary caretaker of intracontinental mail, aided greatly by their ability to fly over two hundred miles in a single day. Most falcons wear their wand as a band around the leg, though a few can be spotted sporting wooden necklaces while traversing the skies.

Quetzal

Renowned as the most beautiful of Lumens, the quetzal shines emerald in the sun, with the male's red breast and trio of shimmering tails rendering the species a timeless icon, particularly in the outside world. Akin to its stunning brilliance, the quetzal's disposition is often fiery, yet unbounded in its unrelenting fidelity to family, friends, and Lumenhood as a whole. Many quetzals, though no higher than a foot (four if one counts the tails), make unrivaled warriors, fulfilling the function of Guardians in Lumen society. It stands to reason that Eider, the youngest of the Brethren's Gemini, chose to enlighten this species, owing to his fascination with radiant creatures and bioluminescent life. Quetzals, like peregrine falcons, generally sport wooden wands around their ankles or necks, though some are experimenting with a ring adorning the base of the spine known as a tail bud, as revealed recently in the quetzal pop-cultural publications, *Jade* and *Queterra.*

Red-eyed Tree Frog

The smallest species of the Southern Continent, sitting just shy of six inches, is the blood-irised tree frog. With a luminescent yellow belly, blue feet, and a radiant green back, this amphibian is hard to miss whether passing through the Isla Verde plaza or simply exploring the jungle. Though small in size, the tree frog boasts exceptional speed and climbing ability, and is able to outmaneuver nearly any competitor with its explosive jumps and flip-stick skills. Most Lumens of this variety make their homes in ornate gardens, owing to Eudocia's love for horticulture. The second eldest Sister, Eudocia worked alongside her younger sister Galatea to create the intricate gardens found in most Lumen cities, including the renowned Island Gardens in Isla Verde.

Unicorn

Enraptured by the literature and stories of the outside world, Tryphena, the youngest of the Brethren, searched the planet for the legendary unicorn, her mission ending fruitlessly on each continent. Refusing to fall victim to disenchantment, Tryphena sought out the purest and most stately horses that she could find, bringing them to her home in Isla Verde and placing them in a deep sleep. For each horse she crafted a spiraling horn of solid stone, from black pearl and ivory to a mysteriously smooth ruby and diamond; each to match the horse's hue. With great care, Tryphena fused the wand-horns to the horses' skulls and altered their genetic makeup to create the first unicorns. Like Tryphena, unicorns are known for their goodness and profound patience; though, also like their creator, they are recognized for their relentless courage and determination when pushed too far. Unicorns, alongside morphos and crystal spiders, are the last of the three species of the Southern Continent whose wands are anatomically attached.

Emperor Tamarin

Though we know not how, it seems that a fourteenth Lumen has appeared on the Southern Continent, one adverse to our society and determined to undermine our goals. Despite my initial doubt, my incredulity has given way to a foreboding faith under the conviction in Chairman Dosfilos' eyes. I can only imagine how this newest of Lumens came to be... Have these tamarins been living in secret since the arrival of the Brethren so many centuries ago, or could there truly be a new Star among us? How have the tamarins wooed the crystal spiders into such a deep hatred that they would turn and attack our children? Perhaps we were too harsh, excluding the spiders from our society for centuries out of fear... Alienating them...

But enough brooding. Henceforth I will share what I know of the tamarin:

The emperor tamarin, a primate of generally small stature (approximately one foot), dwells in the canopy of the Amazon and dines upon forest fruits, figs in particular. Tamarins possess gray to black fur, dark eyes, and a magnificent white beard that falls to their belly. Numerous students tell me, however, that the tamarins that appeared during the Seventh-Level Mission rose to three feet in height—astounding—and were incredibly strong. (The students, and even

Chiron, attest that these tamarins wield a metal device capable of separating a wand from a Lumen's body via excessive ripping and cutting — a fearful thought. As for the emperor tamarins' wands, I am unsure. Because their metal devices do not transform as normal wands do, but instead twist, fold, and contract to make new shapes and tools, my estimate is that they actually wear their wands on the body, perhaps as a ring on their hands — a hypothesis which would thus explain how this so-called Mistarcus attempted to attack Manny López with a flick of his palm.

I do apologize for the vagueness of my statements, as further information requires close study, of which I have not had the opportunity, nor do I particularly wish to.

May safety slink at your side and readiness ever-steady your paws,

Sable

About the Author

Jonathan Waggoner is a seventh-year Spanish teacher for the Wabash Community School District 348 of Mt. Carmel, IL. Over the past seven years he has divided his time between teaching, writing, and overseas missions. He is working on a variety of projects at present, including the various installments of "The Starlight Chronicles" as well as a handful of other novels. In his free time, Jonathan enjoys playing piano, theorizing and solving puzzles, and getting silly with his two nieces and nephew. Jonathan is an avid lover of both puns and people, and is a dear friend of Jesus. For more information, feel free to contact him via the The LIGHT Group blogs at iamlumen.com.